D0843458

A Russell Hoban Omnibus

A RUSSELL HOBAN OMNIBUS

RUSSELL HOBAN

INDIANA UNIVERSITY PRESS

Bloomington & Indianapolis

This book is a publication of

Indiana University Press
601 North Morton Street
Bloomington, IN 47404–3797 USA

http://www.indiana.edu/~iupress

Telephone orders 800–842–6796
Fax orders 812–855–7931
Orders by e-mail iuorder@indiana.edu

© 1999 by Russell Hoban
The Lion of Boaz-Jachin and Jachin-Boaz, © 1973 by Russell Hoban
Turtle Diary, © 1975 by Russell Hoban
Pilgermann, © 1983 by Russell Hoban
Mr. Rinyo-Clacton's Offer, © 1998 by Russell Hoban
"The Man with the Dagger," "My Night with Léonie," "The Raven," "Dream Woman," "Dark Oliver," "The Ghost Horse of Genghis Khan," " 'I , that was a child, my tongue's use sleeping . . . ,' " and "With a Choked Cry" from *The Moment under the Moment*, © 1992 by Russell Hoban
Poems from *The Last of the Wallendas*, © 1997 by Russell Hoban
"The Marzipan Pig," © 1986 by Russell Hoban

All rights reserved

No part of this book may be reproduced or utilized in any form or by any means, electronic or mechanical, including photocopying and recording, or by any information storage and retrieval system, without permission in writing from the publisher. The Association of American University Presses' Resolution on Permissions constitutes the only exception to this prohibition.

The paper used in this publication meets the minimum requirements of American National Standard for Information Sciences—Permanence of Paper for Printed Library Materials, ANSI Z39.48–1984.

MANUFACTURED IN THE UNITED STATES OF AMERICA

Cataloging information is available from the Library of Congress.
ISBN 0-253-33586-8   1 2 3 4 5 04 03 02 01 00 99

Contents

Preface

Most of my work is out of print in the United States; recent titles have not even been published there. Some of my children's books continue to do well, but there's not a heavy demand for my other writing, so it's brave of Indiana University Press to take a chance with this selection.

The earliest work here is a bit of the unfinished novel *The Return of Manny Rat*, written in 1969; the latest is *Mr Rinyo-Clacton's Offer*, completed in 1997. In my writing I've been flying by the seat of my pants for more than forty years now; I've always worked without a plan or outline: I start with whatever gets me started, and I take it as far as I can. After preliminary notes, the first attempt at a new novel might go thirty pages or so, at which point I find that my understanding of the material is insufficient, so I have to go back to p. 1 and start again. I do a lot of p. 1s, and all the way through a novel or story I go back to rework early pages as I develop a sense of what the thing is trying to be and where it's going. Working this way has resulted in many starts that never got finished, but as I've said elsewhere, and been laughed at for it, the process matters more to me than the product.

The Return of Manny Rat is one of my starts that didn't go all the way. Manny first appeared in *The Mouse and His Child*, and he seemed to have enough in him for another book, but by the time I was eighty pages or so into it, I found that I wanted to leave animals and toys for a while in order to write about men and women and the strangeness of life. I arrived in London in 1969, and by 1971 I was working on *The Lion of Boaz-Jachin and Jachin-Boaz*, my first so-called adult novel. Since then, apart from cruising intervals and occasional theatrical efforts (a stage version of *Riddley Walker* for the Manchester Royal Exchange; *The Carrier Frequency* for the Impact Theatre Co-operative; and *The Second Mrs Kong*, an opera text set to music by sir Harrison Birtwistle for Glyndebourne), I've always had a novel going.

I'm not going to comment on everything in this collection, but I will say that I consider "The Man with the Dagger" and "The Raven" two of my better stories; and of course *The Marzipan Pig* is notable for dealing fearlessly with several kinds of love not usually spoken of by name.

I've said that I wanted to write about men and women and the strangeness of life. My books don't seem strange enough to me, but they're generally considered to be some way off the beaten track. Readers encountering me for the first time might find *Turtle Diary* the most accessible of my novels; I think of it as my haiku book, full of the details of moments specific to particular parts of London and the souls of William and Neaera. The London and Paris scenes in *Mr Rinyo-Clacton's Offer* are also carefully observed, and I think they work pretty well.

Each of the novels has been an interesting trip for me: *Riddley Walker** took five and a half years and revisions past counting; in *Pilgermann* (two years from first notes to final text) the process was one of building a fantastic reality on historical fact: first there were the disjointed notes when I was cruising for a start; then the sighting of Montfort in Upper Galilee that precipitated Pilgermann into a time and place; then a long stretch of research reading, including the Qur'an, the Septuagint, the rereading of the Old and New Testaments in several translations, the buying of many books, and the absorption of such Judaica as enabled me to reinvent myself as an eleventh- and twelfth-century Jew. *Pilgermann* has had nothing like the critical approval received by *Riddley Walker,* but it was a whole lot of fun to write, and it has some of the strangeness and slant reality with which the world shows itself to me and perhaps to some of my readers. It seems to me that the realest reality lives somewhere beyond the edge of human vision; I don't know that it can ever be seen, but I'll keep looking.

R. H. London 1999

---

*New edition by Indiana University Press in 1998.

A Russell Hoban Omnibus

THE LION
OF BOAZ-JACHIN
AND JACHIN-BOAZ

I

There were no lions any more. There had been lions once. Sometimes in
the shimmer of the heat on the plains the motion of their running still
flickered on the dry wind—tawny, great, and quickly gone. Sometimes
the honey-coloured moon shivered to the silence of a ghost-roar on the
rising air.

There were no chariots any more. The chariots, wind-bereft and
roadless in the night, slept with their tall wheels hushed in the tomb of the
last king.

The ruins of the king's palace had been dug out of the ground. There
was a chain-link fence all around the citadel where the palace buildings,
the courtyards, the temples and the tombs had been excavated. There
were a souvenir shop and a refreshment stand near the gates.

The columns and the roof beams, fallen and termite-hollowed, had
been labelled and cleared away. Jackals hunted among them no more.
Where snakes and lizards had sunned themselves the daylight came
through the skylights in the roof of the new building that enclosed the
great hall where the hunting of the king was carved in stone.

The images of horses and men, chariots and lions, were stained by
weather, worn by rain, pocked and pitted by the dust that had stung them

when the dry wind howled. New walls were around them now, a new roof was over them. The temperature was controlled by a thermostat. An air-conditioner made a whirring silence.

Jachin-Boaz had a wife and a son, and he lived in a town far from the sea. Pigeons flew up from the square, circled above it, and came down to perch on clay walls, red roof-tiles. The fountain sent up a slim silver jet among old women in black. The dogs knew where everything was, and went through the alleyways behind the shops like businessmen. The cats looked down from high places, disappeared around corners. Many of the women did their washing in stone sinks near the town pump. Tourists going through the town in buses looked out through the windows at the merchants who sold brass and ivory and rugs drinking coffee in the shade of awnings. The vendors of fruit and vegetables smoked in the street.

Jachin-Boaz traded in maps. He bought and sold maps, and some, of certain kinds for special uses, he made or had others make for him. That had been his father's trade, and the walls of the shop that had been his father's were hung with glazed blue oceans, green swamps and grasslands, brown and orange mountains delicately shaded. Maps of towns and plains he sold, and other maps made to order. He would sell a young man a map that showed where a particular girl might be found at different hours of the day. He sold husband maps and wife maps. He sold maps to poets that showed where thoughts of power and clarity had come to other poets. He sold well-digging maps. He sold vision-and-miracle maps to holy men, sickness-and-accident maps to physicians, money-and-jewel maps to thieves, and thief maps to the police.

Jachin-Boaz was at the age called middle life, but he did not believe that he had as many years ahead of him as he had behind him. He had married very young, and he had now been married for more than a quarter of a century. Often he was impotent with his wife. On Sundays, when the shop was closed and he was alone with her and his son through the long afternoon, he tried to shut out of his mind a lifelong despair. Often he thought of death, of himself gone and the great dark shoulder of the world for ever turning away from the nothingness of him for ever in the blackness. Lying beside his sleeping wife he would twist away from his death-thought, open-eyed and grimacing in the darkness of the bedroom over the shop. Often he dreamed of his dead mother and father while sleeping in their bed, but very seldom could he remember his dreams.

Sometimes Jachin-Boaz sat alone in the shop late at night. The green-shaded lamp on his desk threw his shadow on the maps behind him on the wall. He felt the silent waiting of all the seeking and finding that lived in the maps hung on the walls, stacked in the drawers of the cabinets. He would close his eyes, seeing clear lines in different colours that marked the migratory paths of fish and animals, winds and ocean currents, journeys to hidden sources of wisdom, passes through mountains to lodes of precious metals, secret ways through city streets to secret pleasures.

Behind his closed eyes he saw the map of his town in which the square, the town pump, the stone laundry sinks, the street of the merchants and he himself were fixed and permanent. Then he would rise from his desk and walk up and down in the dark shop, touching maps with his fingers and sighing.

Jachin-Boaz had for a number of years been working on a map for his son. From the many different maps that passed through his hands, from the reports of his information-gatherers and surveyors, from the books and journals that he read, from his own records and observations, he compiled a great body of detailed knowledge, and that knowledge was incorporated in the map for his son. He added to it constantly, revising and making the necessary corrections to keep it always current.

Jachin-Boaz had said nothing about the map to his wife or his son, but he spent most of his spare time on it. He did not think that his son would follow him in the shop, nor did he want him to. He wanted his son to go out into the world, and he wanted him to find more of a world for himself than he, Jachin-Boaz, had found. He had put aside some money for the boy's inheritance, but the map was to be the larger part of his legacy. It was to be nothing less than a master map that would show him where to find whatever he might wish to look for, and so would assure him of a proper start in life as a man.

The son of Jachin-Boaz was named Boaz-Jachin. When he became sixteen years old his father decided that he would show him the master map.

"Everyone in the world is looking for something," said Jachin-Boaz to Boaz-Jachin, "and by means of maps each thing that is found is never lost again. Centuries of finding are on the walls and in the cabinets of this shop."

"If everything that is found is never lost again, there will be an end to finding some day," said Boaz-Jachin. "Some day there will be nothing left to find." He looked more like his mother than like his father. His face was mysterious to his father, who felt that if he tried to guess his son's thoughts he would be wrong more often than not.

"That is the sort of thing that young people like to say to annoy their elders," said Jachin-Boaz. "Obviously there are always new things to find. And as to what has already been found, would you prefer that all knowledge be thrown away so that you might be ignorant and the world new? Is that what they teach you at school?"

"No," said Boaz-Jachin.

"I am glad to hear that," said Jachin-Boaz, "because the past is the father of the present, just as I am your father. And if the past cannot teach the present and the father cannot teach the son, then history need not have bothered to go on, and the world has wasted a great deal of time."

Boaz-Jachin looked at the maps on the walls. "The past is not here," he said. "There is only the present, in which are things left behind by the past."

"And those things are part of the present," said Jachin-Boaz, "and therefore to be used by the present. Look," he said, "this is exactly what I mean." He took the master-map out of a drawer and spread it on the counter for his son to look at. "I have been working on it for years," said Jachin-Boaz, "and it will be yours when you are a man. Everything that you could wish to look for is on this map. I take great pains to keep it up to date, and I add to it all the time."

Boaz-Jachin looked at the map, at the cities and towns, the blue oceans, the green swamps and grasslands, the delicately shaded brown and orange mountains, the clear lines in inks of different colours that showed where all things known to his father might be found by him. He looked away from the map and down at the floor.

"What do you think of it?" said Jachin-Boaz.

Boaz-Jachin said nothing.

"Why won't you say anything?" said his father. "Look at this labour of years, with everything clearly marked upon it. This map represents not only the years of my life spent upon it, but the years of other lives spent in gathering the information that is here. What can you seek that this map will not show you how to find?"

Boaz-Jachin looked at the map, then at his father. He looked all around the shop and down at his feet, but he said nothing.

"Please don't stand there saying nothing," said Jachin-Boaz. "Say something. Name something that this map will not show you how to find."

Boaz-Jachin looked around the shop again. He looked at the iron door-stop. It was in the shape of a crouching lion. He looked at his father with a half-smile. "A lion?" he said.

"A lion," said Jachin-Boaz. "I don't think I understand you. I don't think you're being serious with me. You know very well there are no lions now. The wild ones were hunted to extinction. Those in captivity were killed off by a disease that travelled from one country to another carried by fleas. I don't know what kind of a joke that was meant to be." As he spoke there opened in his mind great mystical amber eyes, luminous and infinite. There blossomed great taloned paws, heavy and powerful. There was a silent roar, round, endless, an orb of reflection imaging a pink rasping tongue, white teeth of death. Jachin-Boaz shook his head. There were no lions any more.

"I wasn't making a joke," said Boaz-Jachin. "I was looking at the door-stop and I thought of lions."

Jachin-Boaz nodded his head, put the map back into its drawer, went to the back of the shop and sat down at his desk.

Boaz-Jachin went to his room on the top floor over the shop. He looked out through the window at the clear twilight, the darkening red-tiled roofs and the tops of the palm trees around the square.

Then he sat down and played his guitar. The room grew dark around him, and for a time he played in the dim light that came from the lamps in the street. Not here, said the guitar to the walls of the room. Beyond here.

Boaz-Jachin put away his guitar and lit the lamp on his desk. From a drawer he took a sheet of paper on which was a roughly sketched map. Many of the lines had been erased and drawn over. The paper was dirty and the map seemed empty compared to the one that his father had shown him. He began to draw a line very lightly from one point to another. Then he erased the line and put the map away. He turned out the light, lay on his bed, looked at the lamplight from the street on the ceiling and listened to the pigeons on the roof.

Jachin-Boaz dreamed every night, and every morning he forgot his dreams. One night he dreamed of the scissorman his mother had told him about when he was a child. The scissorman punished boys who wet their beds by cutting off their noses. Had she said noses? In Jachin-Boaz's dream the scissorman was huge, dressed all in black, with great hunched shoulders, a long red nose, and a beard like that of his father. Jachin-Boaz had done something terribly bad, and he was to have his arms and legs cut off by the dreadful scissors. "It won't hurt very much at all," said the scissorman. "Actually it will be a great relief for you to be rid of those heavy members—they're really too much for you to carry around." When he cut off Jachin-Boaz's left arm the scissors sounded as if they were cutting paper, and there was no pain. But Jachin-Boaz cried "No!" and woke up with his heart pounding. Then he went back to sleep. In the morning he had not forgotten the dream. His wife was in the kitchen making breakfast, and he sat on the edge of the bed trying to remember how many years ago he had stopped waking up with an erection. He could not remember when it had happened last.

A few months later Jachin-Boaz said that he was going on a field trip for several weeks. He packed his map-case, his drawing instruments, his compass and binoculars and the rest of his field gear. He said that he was meeting a surveyor in the next town and that they were going to travel inland. Then he took a train to the seaport.

A month passed, and Jachin-Boaz did not return. Boaz-Jachin opened the drawer where the master-map was kept. It was not there. In the drawer were the deed to the house and a bank-book. The house and the savings account had been transferred to Jachin-Boaz's wife. Half of the savings had been withdrawn. There was a note in the drawer:

I have gone to look for a lion.

"What does he mean by that?" said Jachin-Boaz's wife. "Has he gone mad? There are no lions to be found."

"He's not looking for a lion of *that* shape," said Boaz-Jachin, indicating the door-stop. "He means something else. And he's taken the map that he said he would give me."

"He's taken half of our savings," said his mother.

"If we lived without using the savings before," said Boaz-Jachin, "we can live without the half that he has taken."

Boaz-Jachin and his mother took on the management of the shop, and in the hours when he was not at school Boaz-Jachin sold maps and worked on the special orders with surveyors, information-gatherers and draughtsmen. He, like his father, came to know of the many things that people were looking for and the places where they could be found. Often he thought of the master-map that had been promised him.

I sit in the shop like an old man, selling maps to help other people find things, thought Boaz-Jachin, because my father has taken my map for himself and has run off to find a new life with it. The boy has become an old man and the old man has become a boy.

Boaz-Jachin took his old sketch-map from the drawer of his desk and began to work on it again. He spoke to the information-gatherers and surveyors, and he wrote in a notebook whatever seemed useful. He walked the streets and alleyways of the town late at night and early in the morning. He learned more and more about what people were looking for and where they found it. Boaz-Jachin worked hard on his map, but it still looked empty and confused compared to the one that his father had shown him. His lines were dirty and straggling, and lacked the pattern of intelligent purpose. The routes shown in his father's map had had a clarity and logic that made his own efforts seem poor. He was uncertain of what to seek, and he had little confidence in his ability to find anything. He told one of the surveyors of his difficulties.

"For years I have sighted and measured and located this point and that point on the face of the earth," said the surveyor, "and I have gone back to the same places to find my stakes pulled out as boundaries waver and lose accuracy. I sight and I measure and I plant the stakes again, knowing they will be pulled out again. It is not only stakes and boundaries that are lost—this is what there is to know about maps, and I tell you what I have paid years to learn: everything that is found is always lost again, and nothing that is found is ever lost again. Can you understand that? You're still a boy, so maybe you can't. Can you understand that?"

Boaz-Jachin thought about the surveyor's words. He understood the words, but the meaning of them did not enter him because their meaning was not an answer to any question in him. In his mind he saw an oblong of blue sky edged with dark faces. He felt a roaring in him, and opened and closed his mouth silently. "No," he said.

"You're still a boy. You will learn," said the surveyor.

Boaz-Jachin continued to work on his map, but without real interest. The places he had thought of going to and the routes by which he had thought to reach those places seemed foolish to him now. The more he thought about his father's master-map the more he realized that he had not been capable of judging its worth when Jachin-Boaz had shown it to him. It was not simply a matter of neatness and finish—he saw now that the scope and detail of the conception were far beyond him. That map seemed the answer to everything, and his father had taken it away from him.

Boaz-Jachin decided to find his father and ask him for the master-map. He had no idea where Jachin-Boaz might be, but he did not think that the way to find him was to attempt to trace him from town to town, village to village, and across mountains and plains. He felt that there was a place he must find first, and in that place he would know how to proceed in his search.

He walked up and down the aisles of the shop, passing and repassing the maps in the cabinets, the maps on the walls. He stood looking at the crouching iron lion doorstop. " 'I have gone to look for a lion,' " he said.

There were no lions any more. There were no lion-places. "A place of lions," he said. "A place of lions. A lion-place. A lion-palace." There was a lion-palace in the desert that he had read of. There was a place where the last king lay in his tomb and his lion-hunt was carved in stone on the walls of the great hall. He looked at a map and saw that the palace was near a town that was only three hours away by bus.

That Friday afternoon Boaz-Jachin told his mother that he was going to visit a friend in another town for the weekend. She gave him some money for his travel expenses, and when she was not in the office at the back of the shop he took more money from the cash box. He packed some clothes in a rucksack, took his guitar and his unfinished map, went to the bus depot, and bought a one-way ticket.

There were boys and girls of his own age on the bus, laughing, talking, eating lunches they had brought with them, fondling one another. Boaz-Jachin looked away from them. He had a girl that he had never made love with. He had not said goodbye to her. He sat next to a fat man who smelled of shaving lotion. As the bus left the town he looked out the window at petrol stations and shacks with corrugated metal roofs. Out in the country he watched the dry brown land, the meagre hills, the passing telephone poles. Sometimes people stood waiting with cheap suitcases. Once the bus stopped to let a flock of sheep cross the road. The sky darkened until he saw only his own face in the window.

When the bus reached the town the petrol stations were bright, harshly lit, and closed. Everything else was dark except for a few cafés, yellow-and-red-lit, with a thin wail of music and a smell of stale grease. Dogs trotted through the empty streets.

The man at the ticket window in the bus station said that the palace was three miles outside the town and that the next bus would be at ten o'clock in the morning. Boaz-Jachin weighed himself, bought a chocolate bar, and walked out to the road.

The yellow lamps were far apart, with blackness in between. There was no moon. Few cars passed, and between their passing he heard the chirping of crickets and the distant barking of dogs. Boaz-Jachin did not try to get a lift, and nobody offered him one. His footsteps on the stones of the roadside sounded far away from everything.

It seemed a long time before he came to the chain-link fence around the citadel where the palace had been dug out of the desert. Not far from the locked gates he saw the fluorescent-lit window of a low building where the guards sat drinking coffee.

Boaz-Jachin threw his rucksack over the fence and heard it thump on the other side. He took off his belt, buckled it around the handle of his guitar-case, slung the case from his shoulder, climbed the fence, scraping his fingers and tearing his trousers on the wire-ends at the top, and dropped heavily to the ground on the other side.

He could see well enough in the starlight to find the building that housed the ruins of the great hall and the lion-hunt carvings. The door was unlocked, so he knew that the guards would be coming through it on their rounds. Boaz-Jachin saw skylights above him, but the inside of the building was much darker than the night outside. He carefully felt his way along. He found a cupboard that smelled of floor wax, felt mops and brooms in it. He made a space for himself on the floor so that he could sit leaning against the wall. He fell asleep.

When Boaz-Jachin woke up he looked at his watch. It was a quarter past six. He opened the cupboard door and saw daylight in the building. He walked past the carvings, not looking at them yet. He looked down at the floor until he came to the end of the hall and the corridor where the toilets were. When he had relieved himself he washed his hands and face and looked at himself in the mirror. He said his name three times: "Boaz-Jachin, Boaz-Jachin, Boaz-Jachin." Then he said his father's name once: "Jachin-Boaz."

He walked back through the hall, not looking at the walls on either side, but keeping to the middle by looking up at the skylights. When he was ready, he stopped and looked to his left.

Carved in the brownish stone was a lion with two arrows in his spine, leaping up at the king's chariot from behind, biting the tall chariot wheel, dying on the spears of the king and the king's spearmen. The horses galloped on, the beard of the calm-faced king was carefully curled, the king looked straight out over the back of the chariot, over the lion biting the wheel and dying on his spear. With both front paws the lion clung to the turning wheel that pulled him up on to the spears. His teeth were in the wheel, his muzzle was wrinkled back from his teeth, his brows were drawn together in a frown, his eyes were looking straight out from the shadow of his brows. There was no expression on the king's face. He was looking over the lion and beyond him.

"The king is nothing. Nothing, nothing, nothing," said Boaz-Jachin. He began to cry. He ran to the cupboard, closed the door, sat down on the floor in the dark, and wept. When he had finished crying he left the building by the exit that was not visible from the guards' hut and hid behind a shed until the first bus brought sightseers whose presence allowed him to walk about freely.

Boaz-Jachin went back into the hall. Before going back to the lion he had seen first he looked quickly at the other lion-hunt reliefs. There were many lions being killed by the calm-faced king with arrows, spears, even with a sword. None of the other lions mattered to Boaz-Jachin. For a long time, while voices chattered around him and footsteps shuffled past, Boaz-Jachin looked at the dying lion biting the chariot wheel.

Then he went outside again and walked among the excavated ruins of the several palace buildings, the courtyards, the temples and the tombs. The sky was pale and hot. Everything was lion-coloured, low, tawny, broken, preserved in forgottenness, found so that its lostness might be fixed and made permanent, fenced-in, broken-toothed, stripped naked of time and earth, humbled, refusing to say a word.

At some distance from the palace ruins a sign identified a high mound as the artificial hill on which spectators had stood while the lions, released from cages on the plain below, were hunted by the king.

Boaz-Jachin climbed the hill and sat there, looking out over the lion-coloured plain, dotted now with children and grown-ups photographing one another, eating sandwiches and drinking soft drinks. The grown-ups looked at maps of the citadel and pointed in various directions. The children spilled food and drinks on their clothes, quarrelled among themselves, ran, walked, and jumped violently and at random. Their voices rose in a thin haze like the smell of old cooking in a block of flats. The heat shimmered over the plain, and Boaz-Jachin fancied that he could see in the air the running of the lions, tawny, great, quickly gone. He felt in him the dying lion biting the wheel. By letting go of everything else he could let himself be with the lion.

And being with the lion he tasted in him, raging, the memory of the trap and the fall, the blue oblong of sky above him, the dark faces looking down into the pit, the heavy corded meshes of the net that came down over him and clung and smothered and made impotent his rage. Dark of the pit, blue of the sky, and the peering dark faces of little dark men who were outlanders everywhere, the little dark men who read the wind, who read the earth they walked on. When they hunted they looked from side to side and sniffed the air. In the invisible air that held the spirits of beasts living and dead they felt with quick strong fingers, and they pulled out like a long thread the spirit of the animal they would trap. The lion could kill them with a blow of his paw if they would stand before him, but they were too cunning. The lion was as a child to them.

The memory of the heavy cage-wagons was in Boaz-Jachin, the jolting and the dryness and the thirst. Then the wooden cages on the plain and the other little cages atop them in which the little dark cunning men perched like birds. With poles they opened the cage doors and sent the lions out in the heat of the day to the place of their death.

The lions came out of the cages slowly, snarling and lashing their tails. They crouched, growling while the beaters and their dogs advanced to make them go forward to be hunted by the king. The dry wind offered chaos only. The dry wind sang the hunter hunted, the last kill far behind. The dry wind roared and raged, clashed spears on shields, bayed in the mastiff throats, sang in bowstrings death, death, death.

The lions were out on the plain. Beaters and dogs and spearmen and men with shields made walls they could not break through, could not overleap. The chariots were rolling on their tall wheels and the king was shooting arrows, sending death among the lions.

The lions were brave, but there was no chance for them. If they had had a king he would have led them against the king of the chariots and horses. But they had no time to choose a lion-king. The chariots were among them, with spearmen and bowmen to guard their king and give death to every lion.

The last lion alive was the one whom the others would have made their king if they had been allowed to. He was large, strong, and fierce, and with two arrows deep in his spine he was still alive. The arrows burned like fire in him, his sight was fading, the blood was roaring in his ears with the rumble of the chariot wheels. Before him and above him, racing away, the glittering king was calm in his chariot, his spear poised, his spearmen beside him. The dying lion-king leaped, clung to the tall and turning wheel that brought him up to the spears. Growling and frowning he bit the wheel that lifted him and bore him on to darkness.

The lion was gone. Where the lion had been was a sudden empty giddy blackness, like the sensation produced by straightening up too quickly after bending down for a long time.

Boaz-Jachin was aware of people again, taking photographs, eating sandwiches, drinking soft drinks. He listened for ghost-roars behind the voices, heard only the seethe of absence in the hollow of the silence, as one might hear the sea in a shell.

"There are no lions any more," said Boaz-Jachin.

He thought about his father and the map that he had taken away. What might have been his for the finding if Jachin-Boaz had not taken the beautiful map for himself! He, son of the map-seller, map-maker, map-lover, had no talent for maps, could not make one that was not stupid and ugly and disfigured, and this was his father's way of punishing him—to leave him mapless and alone with his deserted mother, stuck in a dark shop like an old man, waiting for the bell to jingle at the door, waiting to sell the means of finding to other seekers.

Boaz-Jachin had in his rucksack, along with his clothes and his un-finished map, a pencil, some paper, and a small ruler. He went back to the hall of the lion hunt, alone among the people all around him. He measured carefully the dying lion who was leaping up at the king's chariot. He measured the visible parts of the arrows in the lion, measured also the spears of the king and the king's spearmen. In another part of the same relief was an arrow that transfixed a dying lioness. Both ends of the arrow being visible, Boaz-Jachin was able to measure its full length. He wrote down all his measurements, folded the paper carefully and put it in his pocket.

He left the lion-hunt hall and went out to the high mound, the spec-tator's hill. There he sat for a long time. When Boaz-Jachin had taken the money from the cash box in the office he had thought that he would not be coming back to the shop. He had seen himself, a lone wanderer, playing his guitar in the street, the case open on the pavement for passers-by to drop money into. But in the wordless refusal of the ruins about him, in the remembered sound of last night's roadside stones under his feet, he had heard the silence of unreadiness.

He had been with the lion. He had that. That had come to him, and something had made him measure the image of the lion and the images of the spears and arrows. He did not know why he had done it. Something more might come to him. He had come to this place to find what to do next, and at least he had found what not to do next: he would not search for his father now. He would go back to the shop for the present.

At the souvenir stand near the gates Boaz-Jachin bought a photograph of the lion-hunt relief that showed the dying lion leaping up at the king's chariot and biting the turning wheel. Then he bought a sandwich and an orange drink. When the bus came he went back to the town, and from there he took the next bus back to his town.

THE LION OF BOAZ-JACHIN AND JACHIN-BOAZ

3

It was late at night in the city where Jachin-Boaz lived now. He lay awake looking at the pinky-grey night sky framed in his windows. Always in the night sky here was the reflected glow of the great city. He moved his arm to light a cigarette, and the girl who lay with her head on his chest rolled over in her sleep, trailing her hand down his body. Gretel. He said her name in his mind, leaned over to look at her sleeping face, turned back the blankets to admire the graceful length of her, smiled in the dark, covered her again.

Jachin-Boaz watched the smoke drift in the dimness of the room. He thought of stories, fairy tales from his childhood, in which a young man went out to seek his fortune in the wide world. Always the father was dead at the beginning of the story, and the young man went out with his few coins, his crust of bread, his fiddle or his sword. Sometimes he found or won some magic thing along the way. A map, perhaps. Jachin-Boaz bared his teeth in the dark but did not smile.

Now he, Jachin-Boaz, was the old man out in the wide world seeking his fortune, the old man who wanted a new story and would not agree to be dead. The young man was left at home to be a shopkeeper and the companion of his deserted mother. Jachin-Boaz saw in his mind his wife's face, looked away and saw the face of his son Boaz-Jachin outside the shop window, shaded by the awning, looking into the shadows at his father and smiling.

Jachin-Boaz got out of bed. Without turning on any of the lights he walked into the next room. His desk was there, and on it lay the master-map that he had promised to his son Boaz-Jachin. By the light from the window he could see some of the routes and places marked on it.

Jachin-Boaz, naked in the dark, touched the map. "There is only one place," he said, "that place is time, and that time is now. There is no other place." He ran his fingers over the map, then turned away. The sky was lighter than before. Birds were singing.

"I never let him help me with a map," said Jachin-Boaz. "Sometimes he wanted to do a little of the border, but I never let him do it. He showed me little dirty maps that he had made, and he wanted praise. He wanted me to like his music, wanted me to be pleased with him, but I never said what he wanted to hear. And I left him sitting in a shop, waiting for the bell to jingle at the door."

Jachin-Boaz went back to bed and wrapped himself around Gretel. In the mornings now he woke up with an erection.

4

When Boaz-Jachin came back to his town he did not go to his mother's house. This was Saturday. She would not be expecting him until Sunday evening, and he did not want to go home yet.

He called up his girl from the bus station, and went to her house. Waiting for her to come to the door he felt again the being-with-the-lion. It was a flash that came and went, full of strangeness. It made him feel apart from his regular life, apart from all the people in his mind and the girl, Lila, whom he waited for now. He felt guilty and uneasy.

The door opened. Lila looked at Boaz-Jachin's face. "Is everything all right?" she said. "You look strange."

"I feel strange," he said. "But everything's all right."

They walked to the square. The street lamps seemed luminous fruits, bursting with knowledge. Boaz-Jachin tasted their light in his mouth and wondered who he was. He felt strongly the ripe blackness of rooftops against the night sky, the poignancy of roofs and domes of the town fitting into the night sky. The colour and texture of the pavement, the substance of it, were intense with flavour.

He had never been naked with Lila, had never made love with her, had never done it with anyone. His orgasms had been with himself only, rumpled with shame and listening for footsteps in the hallway. He remembered his face in the mirror in the hall of the lion-hunt carvings. Who, he wondered, looked out through the eyeholes in his face?

"What are you going to do?" said Lila.

"I don't know," he said. "I thought I would go and look for my father. But I came back. I sat on a hill and it wasn't time yet. I was waiting for something. I don't know what I'm waiting for. I'm not ready to go yet."

The slim jet of the fountain went up into the starlight, fell back continually. Dogs met and separated, going their separate ways. Boaz-Jachin and Lila sat on a bench. The palm trees rustled. The street lamps had not changed. His throat ached.

"I'm waiting too," she said. "They sit in the living room and watch television. The house feels as if it's crouching over me. On Sundays with them I'm always depressed. I don't know where to go."

When I go, Boaz-Jachin thought, will you go with me? His throat shaped the words but he did not speak them. He thought of his going, and now the sea was in it. He had been on a ship once, on a summer holiday with his parents. "In the middle of the ocean," he said, "it is green and huge and heaving, and you smell the deepness of it and the salt. Grey fog in the morning, wet on the face, cold in the stomach. The big sea-birds are never lost. They can sit down on the ocean, rocking on the waves." When I go, will you go with me? he thought again, but again did not speak the words.

"Yes," she said.

"Where can we go?" he said. "Now, I mean. Where can we go now?"

"I don't know," she said. "Our roof. They were sitting up there after dinner, but maybe they've gone down by now. Maybe they'll be asleep by now."

Lila and Boaz-Jachin took a blanket up to the roof. The air was warm on their naked bodies. The stars were large and brilliant. She had made love before, and she shaped herself to him, put herself where he was, made him welcome in her. He was overwhelmed by the gift. Behind his eyes everything was lion-coloured, sunlit. When the blackness came it was a roaring and an exaltation in him, a losing and a finding of himself. Afterwards he was cool, immensely easy. He was with Lila and with the lion and he was alone. He knew that when he was ready to go he would have to go alone. They slept on the roof until the sky was pale. Then Boaz-Jachin went back to his mother's house.

"It's me," he said, hearing her wake up as he passed her door.

"Come in," she said. "Say hello."

He set down the rucksack and the guitar in the hallway. They leaned against the wall. We were going away for good, they said. We came back. The smell of old cooking seemed overpowering to Boaz-Jachin. What if she gets sick and I have to take care of her? he thought. If I'd left now at least I'd have left her healthy. He went into his mother's room.

Boaz-Jachin's mother looked at her son in the dawn light in the room. "You're home sooner than I expected," she said. "You look strange. What's the matter?"

"Nothing's the matter," he said. "I feel fine. I'm going down to the shop. I left some schoolwork there."

Boaz-Jachin put back the money he had taken from the cash box. He heard his mother's footsteps overhead, felt a wave of hotness pass through him, then a surge of desperation. Stay here, the footsteps said. I have nothing now. Don't leave me. Boaz-Jachin ground his teeth.

When his mother came to his room later to call him for breakfast he was kneeling on a sheet of brown wrapping-paper that he had taken from the roll in the shop. The paper stretched across the full width of the floor, and he had ruled it off into large squares. On it lay the photograph of the relief of the dying lion biting the wheel. On a sheet of transparent acetate over the photograph he had ruled small squares. Now, by making what he drew in each large square on the brown paper correspond to what was in each small square on the photograph, Boaz-Jachin was developing an accurate copy that was the same size as the lion he had measured. He did not include the chariot and the king in his copy: he was drawing only the lion, the two arrows in him and the two spears at his throat that were killing him.

"What are you doing?" said his mother.

"It's for school," said Boaz-Jachin. "I'll be down in a minute."

Boaz-Jachin let the being-with-the-lion come to him. He did not have to remember it—it came when he opened himself to it. He felt the lion-life, the weight and power and the surge of it like a river of violence, calm and huge. He felt the lion-life rush into the death that came on to darken it, and he was at a moving point of balance in between. He drew his lines delicately in pencil at first, then went over them firmly with a felt-tipped pen. His lines were strong and black. The brown paper was clean and unsmudged.

5

Gretel, who worked in a bookshop, had helped Jachin-Boaz find a job as an assistant in another shop. His salary was small and the owner was delighted with him. There was about Jachin-Boaz an aura of seeking and finding that customers responded to. People who for years had not looked for things in books found new appetites for knowledge when they spoke to him. To someone who came in asking for the latest novel he might sell not only the novel but a biological treatise on the life of ants, an ecological study of ancient man, a philosophical work, and a history of small sailing-craft.

With maps he was of course remarkable. He had a way of unfolding a map that was nothing less than erotic, a cartographical seduction. People bought from him stacks of maps and whole atlases of places to which they would never travel, because Jachin-Boaz had made the coloured images of oceans and continents, roads, cities, rivers and ports irresistible to them.

Jachin-Boaz was gay and tireless at his work, and he looked forward eagerly to each evening with Gretel. At that time they needed very little sleep, made love greedily, talked for hours and took long walks late at night. To Jachin-Boaz the street lamps seemed luminous fruits bursting with knowledge. He tasted their light in his mouth and marvelled that this was he, Jachin-Boaz, tasting the night and the love he had found in the great city. He felt strongly the ripe blackness of rooftops against the night sky, the poignancy of roofs and domes of the city fitting into the night sky. The colours and textures of the pavement, the substance of it, were intense with flavour. His and Gretel's footsteps on the bridges over the river sounded miraculous with truth.

Gretel was nearly twenty years younger than Jachin-Boaz, and he had begun to fall in love with her when he heard her talk about the father she had never known.

Jachin-Boaz's father had been a tall handsome man who had built up his map business from nothing, smoked expensive cigars, directed plays in the local dramatic society, had a beautiful mistress, wanted his son to be a scientist, and died when Jachin-Boaz was still a student.

Jachin-Boaz's wife's father had been a grocer in the town who owned a place in the desert that he wanted to make green with trees and orange groves. For years he impoverished his family by sending money to the desert place. It was not yet green when he took his wife and children there and died. They came back to the town.

Gretel had grown up without a father, had never seen him. He had been killed in the war when she was less than a year old. Her mother had never married again.

Jachin-Boaz had met Gretel when buying books at her shop. He was a regular customer, and in time he invited her to lunch. She was a tall fair blue-eyed girl, full of country freshness. She was as rosy, as sweet and pretty as a lady on a cigar-box lid. They spoke of the places they had come from. Gretel's town was only a few miles away from a famous camp where thousands of Jachin-Boaz's people had died in gas chambers and had risen in smoke from the chimneys of crematoria. Gretel told Jachin-Boaz about her dead father who had been a soldier in the medical corps.

She had only a few things to tell. He had been a market gardener, and her mother and her brother continued in that business. He had drawn a little. There was a charcoal drawing of a heath at home that she had looked at and thought about. He had played the violin. She had seen music exercise-books of his. She had spoken to a pianist friend of his who remembered playing sonatas with him. He had been an amateur astrologer, and had himself cast the horoscope that foretold his death in the war.

Jachin-Boaz listened to her speak softly about the dead man whom she had not known. He wondered in what features of hers, in what gestures and movements her father survived, in what thoughts and recognitions. He had never known a woman to hold a man so gently in her mind as Gretel held her unknown father. He had never before known a woman with such a gentle mind. She had never known a man with whom she felt so much herself, felt that her essential self mattered so much, was so valued. They fell in love.

The first time they made love Jachin-Boaz was almost beside himself with the achievement of it. This tall fair girl, the daughter of warriors, naked under him, looking up at him in fear and joy, delight and proud submission! He, the son of scholars, bent-backed men in black, generations of studious fugitives. My seed into your womb, he thought. My seed in the warrior-girl's belly. At the same time it was as if he was taking the most hotly desired girl of his boyhood, unapproachable then and a middle-aged woman now, into the bushes of carnal innocence and joy. He was her strong and cunning old man. Jachin-Boaz was enormously pleased with himself.

He was delighted to find that he did not love Gretel for any reason that he might have thought good in the past. Not for intelligence or accomplishments. Not for anything that she did. He loved her simply because she was. What a thing, thought Jachin-Boaz. Love without purpose.

He hired a small van, triumphantly moved her belongings from her room to his flat. She asserted her domestic status by cleaning it. Cautiously she approached the clutter on his desk that Saturday while he was taking a nap. This could be dangerous, she thought, but I have to do it. I can't hold back.

Jachin-Boaz, unsleeping, heard her move every object and all the papers on the desk as she dusted. I don't care, he thought. Even if she throws everything out of the window I love her.

Gretel had examined the master-map in her cleaning. "I don't think that you made that map for your son," she said when he told her about it. "I think you made it for yourself."

"Do you really think that?" said Jachin-Boaz.

"Yes. And the map brought you to me, so I'm well pleased with it."

Jachin-Boaz touched the smooth skin of her waist, traced with his finger the curve of her hip. "It's astonishing," he said. "For eighteen years

I was alive and you weren't even in the world yet. You were one year old when I got married. You're so young!"

"Make me old," said Gretel. "Use me up. Wear me out."

"I can't make you old," said Jachin-Boaz. "But you think you can make me young, eh?"

"I can't make you anything," said Gretel, "except maybe comfortable sometimes, I think. But I don't think there ever was a young Jachin-Boaz until the old one took his map and ran away. So now there's a Jachin-Boaz that never was before, and I have him."

Sometimes, riding in the underground trains, he would see from the corner of his eye the headlines of newspapers being read by other passengers. JACHIN-BOAZ GUILTY, they said. When he looked again the words changed to the usual affairs of the world.

6

Boaz-Jachin had completed his first drawing. It was an accurate full-size copy of the dying lion and the two arrows and the two spears that were killing him.

Now by transferring the lines of that drawing to another sheet of brown paper he made a second drawing. It was the same as the first except that one of the arrows was no longer in the lion. It lay on the ground under his hind feet as if it had missed him.

As he looked at the photograph from time to time Boaz-Jachin began to pay more attention to the wheel. He remembered the stillness of the original stone under his eyes and under his fingers when he had touched it. Always and always the leaping dying lion never reaching the splendid blank-faced king for ever receding before him, for ever borne away in safety by the tall wheel for ever turning. It made no difference that the king was now as dead as the lion. The king would always escape.

"The wheel," said Boaz-Jachin aloud. Because it *was* the wheel, and the wheel was *the* wheel. The sculptor had known it and now it made itself known to Boaz-Jachin as its turning took away his father and his map and brought the dark shop and the bell and the door and the waiting. Boaz-Jachin was sorry that the wheel had made itself known to him. He wished that he had not recognized the wheel.

Boaz-Jachin shook his head. "Biting the wheel is not enough," he said.

The door of his room was open, and his mother appeared in the doorway. Her hair was disarranged and she seemed unable to compose her face. There was a knife in her hand. "Still the school project?" she said.

"Yes," said Boaz-Jachin. "What are you doing with the knife?"

"Opening letters," she said. She paused, then said, "Don't hate your father. He's sick in his mind, sick in his soul. He's mad. There's something missing in him, there's an emptiness where there should be something."

"I don't hate him," said Boaz-Jachin. "I don't think I feel anything for him."

"We married too young," she said. "My house, the house of my mother and father, seemed to be crouching over me. I wanted to get away. Not to the place in the desert where the money went, not to that place that was a lie, that place that would never be green. They sat in the living room listening to the news on the radio. On Sundays the pattern of the carpet filled me with despair, became a jungle that would swallow me up." She passed her hand across her eyes. "We could have made our own green place. I wanted him to be what he could be. I wanted him to be the most and the best that he could be, wanted him to use what was in him. No. Always the turning away, the failure. Always the desert and the dry wind that dries everything up. I'm not ugly even now. Once I was beautiful. The night that I knew I loved him I locked myself in the bathroom and cried. I knew that he would make me unhappy, give me pain. I knew. Your father is a murderer. He killed me. He took away your future. He's mad, but I don't hate him. He doesn't know what he's done. He's lost, lost, lost." She went out, closing the door behind her. Boaz-Jachin listened to her footsteps going irregularly down the hall, down the stairs to her room.

He finished the second drawing and went down to the shop to get another sheet of brown wrapping-paper. Most of the maps on the walls had been slashed with a knife. Drawers had been pulled out and maps scattered on the floor.

Boaz-Jachin ran up the stairs to his mother's room. The knife lay on the bedside table. Beside it stood an empty sleeping-tablet bottle. His mother was asleep or unconscious. He had no idea how many tablets had been in the bottle.

"Biting the wheel is not enough," said Boaz-Jachin as he called the doctor.

7

Jachin-Boaz dreamed of his father who had died when Jachin-Boaz was in his first year at university. In the dream he was at his father's funeral, but he was younger than university age. He was a little boy, and with his mother he walked up to the coffin among flowers whose fragrance was strong and deathly. His father lay with closed eyes, his face rouged and smoothed-out and blank, his brows unfrowning, his beard pointing out from his chin like a cannon. His hands were crossed on his breast, and the dead left hand held a rolled-up map. The map was rolled with its face outward, and Jachin-Boaz could see a bit of blue ocean, a bit of land, red lines, blue lines, black lines, roads and railways. Lettered neatly on the border were the words *For my son Jachin-Boaz*.

Jachin-Boaz dared not reach for the map, dared not take it from his father's dead hand. He looked at his mother and pointed to the map. She took a pair of scissors from inside her dress, cut off the end of the dead man's beard and showed it to Jachin-Boaz.

"No," said Jachin-Boaz to his mother who had changed into his wife. "I want the map. It was in his left hand, not his right. Left for me."

His wife shook her head. "You're too little to have one," she said. It was dark suddenly, and they were in bed. Jachin-Boaz reached out to touch his wife, found the coffin between them and tried to push it away.

The bedside table fell with a crash, and Jachin-Boaz woke up. "Left, not right," he said in his own language. "Left for me."

"What's the matter?" said Gretel, sitting up in bed. They always spoke English. She could not understand what he was saying.

"It's mine, and I'm big enough to have it," said Jachin-Boaz, still in his own language. "What map is it, what ocean, what time is there?"

"Wake up," said Gretel in English. "Are you all right?"

"What time are we?" said Jachin-Boaz in English.

"Do you mean what time is it?" said Gretel.

"Where is the time?" said Jachin-Boaz.

"Quarter past five," said Gretel.

"That's not where it is," said Jachin-Boaz. His dream had gone out of his mind. He could remember none of it.

8

Boaz-Jachin's mother had her stomach pumped, and she stayed in bed for two days. "I don't know what all the excitement was about," she said at first. "There were only two tablets left in the bottle. I wasn't trying to kill myself—I just hadn't been able to sleep, and one tablet never helped."

"How was I to know?" said Boaz-Jachin. "All I saw was what you'd done in the shop and then the knife and the empty bottle."

Later his mother said, "You saved my life. You and the doctor saved my life."

"I thought you said there were only two tablets left in the bottle," said Boaz-Jachin.

His mother tossed her head, looked sideways at him darkly. What a fool you must be, said the look.

But Boaz-Jachin did not know which to believe—the two-tablet story or the dark look. There's no knowing what she might do now, he thought. She might very well turn into some kind of invalid and I'll have to take care of her. The bell jingling at the door and her voice calling from upstairs. He's run away and left me to clean up after him. Boaz-Jachin stayed home from school for the two days that his mother spent in bed, and Lila came to the house in the evening and cooked for them.

Boaz-Jachin made love with Lila in the dark shop at night, on the floor between the map cabinets. In the darkness he looked at the dim gleam of her body, its places that he knew now.

"This is one map he can't take away from me," he said. They laughed in the dark shop.

Boaz-Jachin made a third drawing: again the dying lion leaping up at the chariot, biting the wheel. But now both arrows were out of him, both arrows were lying on the ground under his feet. The two spears were still at his throat.

He made a fourth drawing: both arrows and one of the spears under the lion's feet.

He made a fifth drawing in which both arrows and both spears lay on the ground under the lion's feet, and he took the evening bus to the town near the ruins of the last king's palace. He carried nothing with him but the rolled-up drawings.

Again he walked from the bus station out to the silent road under the yellow lights. This time the crickets, the distant barking of the dogs, the stones of the roadside under his feet no longer had the sound of being far from everything: they were the sounds of the place where he was.

When he came to the citadel he threw the roll of drawings over the chain-link fence and climbed over it as before. Again the guards were drinking coffee at the fluorescent-lit window. In the moonlight he went to the building where the lion-hunt reliefs were. As before, the door was unlocked.

Boaz-Jachin opened the door, and the lion-hunt hall with the moonlight coming through the skylight was now a place where he had been. It was a place of his time, a home-place. Here he had awakened and come out of a dark cupboard, had wept before the lion-king and the chariot-king. Here he had spoken his name and the name of his father. He knew the place, the place knew him.

Boaz-Jachin walked formally down the middle of the hall in the light of the moon that shone in through the skylights. He stopped in front of the dying lion-king silvered with dim moonlight, leaping up at the chariot that for ever bore the king away.

Boaz-Jachin unrolled his drawings, took stones out of his pocket to hold them flat on the floor.

Boaz-Jachin laid his first drawing on the floor before the lion-king. In his drawing, as in the relief before him, the lion had two arrows in him, two spears at his throat.

"The arrows burn like fire and our strength is fading," said Boaz-Jachin. "The spears are sharp and killing. The turning wheel bears us on to darkness."

He took the second drawing, laid it over the first.

"One of the arrows is drawn," he said. "The flesh that bled is whole, unhurt."

He laid the third drawing over the second.

"The second arrow is drawn," he said. "The darkness is fading. Strength is coming back."

He laid the fourth drawing over the third.

"The first spear lies under our feet. The spearman of the king is empty-handed," he said.

He laid the fifth drawing over the fourth, then stepped back. In the moonlight the lion-king's eyes looked out at him from the shadow of his brows.

"The second spear, the last weapon, the spear of the king, lies under our feet," said Boaz-Jachin. "We rise up on the turning wheel, alive and strong, undying. There is nothing between us and the king."

9

The city was quiet, the birds were singing, and the sky was losing its darkness. The clock said half-past four. Jachin-Boaz could sleep no longer. He got out of bed, dressed, made himself a cup of coffee, and went out.

The street was wet, and on the pavement lay wet blossoms from the trees that overhung the railings. The street gleamed under the blueish light of the street lamps and the blue before-dawn light of the sky. A crow cawed, flapping slowly overhead to settle on a chimney-pot. A taxi hissed softly down the street, passing once, twice, over manhole covers, double-clanging each time. A telephone kiosk, like a large red lantern, lit the drooping blossoms of a chestnut tree.

Jachin-Boaz's footsteps had an early-morning sound. His footsteps, thought Jachin-Boaz, were abroad at all hours. Sometimes he joined them, sometimes not.

Ahead of him were the river and the dark bulk of the bridge under its lamps against the paling sky. Jachin-Boaz heard a manhole cover clang, and found himself waiting for the second clang that would be the sound of the lifted edge dropping back. He had heard no cars passing. There was no second clang.

He looked back over his shoulder and saw, less than a hundred feet away in the blue dawn, a lion. He was large, massive, with a heavy black mane. He had lifted his head as Jachin-Boaz turned, and now he stood motionless with one paw on the manhole cover. His eyes, catching the light of the street lamps, burned like steady pale green fires under the shadow of his brows.

A church clock struck five, and Jachin-Boaz realized that he had heard the lion before he saw him. The hairs on the back of his neck lifted, he felt deathly cold. He had *heard* the lion first. There was no hope that this was like the newspaper headlines, the mind playing a trick on the eyes.

A taxi entered the street, approaching the lion from behind. The lion grunted and turned, the taxi made a U-turn, went back the way it had come. Jachin-Boaz did not move.

The lion turned towards him again, his head thrust forward, his eyes fixed on Jachin-Boaz. He seemed not to move, but only shifted his weight slightly and was closer than before. Again, and closer.

Jachin-Boaz took one step back. The lion stopped, one paw slightly lifted, his eyes always on Jachin-Boaz. The thing is not to run, thought Jachin-Boaz. The lion seemed to be gathering himself. Surely he's too far away to spring, thought Jachin-Boaz. He took another step backwards, trying to move as subtly as the lion had done. This time he saw the rise and fall of the lion's shoulders, the sliding of his heavy paws.

Jachin-Boaz, backing towards the bridge, had reached the corner, his eyes still fixed on the lion. To the right and left behind him lay the road along the embankment. He heard a taxi coming over the bridge, turned his head just enough to see that the FOR HIRE sign was lit. He raised his arm to signal, pointing along the embankment.

The taxi turned right as it came off the bridge and pulled up beside Jachin-Boaz. He was still facing the lion, with his back to the taxi.

The driver slid the window down. "Do you want to go backwards or forwards?" he said.

Jachin-Boaz felt for the door handle behind him, opened the door, got in. He gave the driver the address of the bookshop where he worked.

The taxi pulled away. Through the rear window Jachin-Boaz saw the lion standing motionless, head lifted.

The taxi hummed along smoothly. There was full daylight now, and there were other cars ahead, behind, on both sides. Jachin-Boaz leaned back. Then he leaned forward, lowered the panel in the glass partition between him and the driver.

"Did you see anything back there where you picked me up?" he said.

The driver looked up at Jachin-Boaz's face in the rear-view mirror and nodded his head. "Proper big one, weren't it?"

Jachin-Boaz felt giddy. "Then why didn't you . . . Why didn't you . . . " He didn't know what he wanted the driver to have done.

The driver looked straight ahead as the taxi hummed through the traffic. "It's nothing to me," he said. "I thought it was yours."

IO

After offering his drawings before the lion-king Boaz-Jachin burned them on the plain where the lions had been killed. He took a large metal trash basket from the refreshment stand, put his drawings in it and set them afire.

He expected the guards to see the flames, and stood near the spectator's hill where he would have a chance of dodging out of sight when they came. No one came. The flames leaped up, sparks and flakes of charred paper drifted over the plain, the fire died quickly.

Boaz-Jachin climbed over the chain-link fence again, walked back to the town, and slept in the bus station.

He felt cosy in the bus going home. He felt cool and easy, clean and empty, as he did after making love with Lila. He thought of the road to the citadel of the dead king, how he had felt walking on it each time. Like the lion-hunt hall, it was his place now, printed on the map of his mind. Its daylight and its darkness were in him now, its crickets and its barking dogs and stones. He could travel that road when he liked, wherever he might be.

When Boaz-Jachin got home his mother was out. He was glad to be alone, glad not to have to speak. He went to his room and took out his unfinished map. He put Lila's house on it, the last king's palace, the plain where the lions had been killed, the hill he had sat on, the road he had walked, and the two bus stations.

His mother came home and made dinner. At the table she spoke of the difficulties of managing the shop, of her constant tiredness, of how little she was able to sleep and how much weight she had lost. Sometimes Boaz-Jachin saw her face waiting for a reply but he could not always remember what she had been saying. Her face became strange to him, and he became strange to himself. Again he felt empty, but it was not the easy emptiness that he had had in the bus. It was as if something had gone out of him and now he must follow it into the world. He was restless, and wanted to be moving on.

"Why?" said his mother.

"Why what?" said Boaz-Jachin.

"Why are you looking at me that way, I said," said his mother. "What are you thinking about? You look a thousand miles away from here."

"I don't know," said Boaz-Jachin. "I don't think I was thinking about anything." He was thinking, maybe I'll never see you again.

Late that night he went down to the shop and looked at one of the big wall-maps. He looked at his country on it and the place where his town was. He ran his finger over the smooth surface, felt the lines of seeking that led from his town and other towns, his country and other countries, converging on a great city far away across the sea. His father, he thought, would be there, and with him would be the master-map he had promised to Boaz-Jachin.

He went to the office, opened the cash box. It was empty. His mother, then, had noticed the absence and return of the money that he had taken the other time. Boaz-Jachin shrugged. He had enough money of his own to live on for two weeks or so if he slept rough, and he had his guitar.

He packed his rucksack, put his map in it, took his guitar. He left a note for his mother:

I am going to find my father and get my map.

He went to Lila's house and slipped a note under the door:

I thought that I would ask you to come with me
but I have to go alone.

Boaz-Jachin walked out through the sleeping town, past the palm trees
and the square where the jet of the fountain continually rose and fell, past
dark shops and houses and dogs that went their several ways, past bright
closed petrol stations. He walked out to the road, heard the stones of the
roadside rolling under his feet, felt the night in the road and the morning
that was coming.

II

The taxi driver had winked when Jachin-Boaz paid him. So he didn't see the lion, thought Jachin-Boaz. He saw that I was a foreigner and thought that I was drunk, and he was making fun of me.

The lion was not at the bookshop when Jachin-Boaz got out of the taxi, nor was there any sign of him that day. Jachin-Boaz had been in mortal terror when the lion was stalking him, but there was a strange joy in him afterwards. Lions were extinct. There were no lions any more. But he had a lion. "I thought it was yours," the taxi driver had said, having his joke with the foreigner he thought was drunk.

He *is* mine, thought Jachin-Boaz. There is a lion, and that lion, real or unreal, has the power to accomplish my death. I know it. But he's my lion and I'm glad that he exists, even though I'm in terror of him.

Jachin-Boaz went to a nearby coffee shop and walked back and forth in front of it like a sentry until it opened. Thinking about the lion he felt himself walking differently, set apart from other men, marked out for a danger, possibly a death, that was unique. He carried himself with melancholy pride, like an exiled king.

When the café opened he sat drinking coffee and looking out at the people who passed. He felt new and sharply defined, newly found by himself and fatefully alone among millions, as if he had just stepped from an aeroplane. Everything that is found is lost again, he thought for the first time. And yet nothing that is found is lost again. What is a map? There is only one place, and that place is time. I am in the time where a lion has been found.

All day in the bookshop the lion lived in his mind. He had no doubt that the lion would appear again and he wondered how he, Jachin-Boaz, would comport himself at the next encounter. He did not know whether the lion was real in the sense that he himself and the shop and the street were real. But he knew that the lion could kill him.

At home that evening he was very gay, and made love with Gretel suavely and greedily, feeling like an international traveller, a man of wealth, a connoisseur of wines. He went to sleep with the figure of the lion in his mind as he had seen him last—head uplifted in the first light of day, stem and demanding, like a patriotic duty silently calling.

Again he woke up at half-past four. Gretel was sleeping soundly. Jachin-Boaz bathed, shaved, and dressed. From the back of the shelves under the larder where he had hidden it he took a paper-wrapped package, put it into a carrier bag. Then he went out.

He walked down the street to the road along the embankment, stopped at the corner and looked back. He saw nothing.

Jachin-Boaz crossed to the river side of the road and walked beside the parapet looking at the river and the boats rocking at their moorings. He passed the next bridge, and the sky through its webwork was brightening.

It was this bright when I looked back at him through the taxi window, thought Jachin-Boaz. I wonder if he stops being there when it's broad daylight.

The sky over the river was massed with dark clouds and dramatic lights, like skies in marine paintings. The river ran lapping and gurgling by the wall. The road along the embankment awoke to cars in twos and threes, a cyclist, a running man in a tracksuit, a young couple walking, holding last night's darkness between their close-together faces, their long hair mingled.

Jachin-Boaz was tired, he had had too little sleep, his expectation seemed foolish now. He turned and walked back the way he had come.

The young couple who had passed him were sitting on a bench, embracing sleepily. On the pavement beside them sat the lion, looking at Jachin-Boaz.

Jachin-Boaz had been looking at the river, and was no more than five yards from the lion when he saw him. The lion's head came forward. He crouched, lashing his tail. His eyes were mystical, luminous, infinite. Jachin-Boaz smelled the lion. Hot sun, dry wind and the tawny plains.

Jachin-Boaz dared not move a single step. Never taking his eyes from the lion he reached into the carrier bag for the package that was there, let the bag fall so that both hands would be free. With shaking hands he unwrapped the five pounds of beefsteak he had brought with him. He threw it to the lion, almost falling as he did it. The meat landed with a wet and solid smack.

The lion, still crouching, came forward and ate the meat, growling and staring at Jachin-Boaz. When Jachin-Boaz saw the lion eating the meat all courage left him. He would have fainted if the lion had not moved.

The lion finished the meat and sprang at Jachin-Boaz. Jachin-Boaz, with a scream, flung himself over the parapet and into the river.

He came to the surface choking and retching from the filthy water he had swallowed, and looked up as the current carried him swiftly on. He saw the two pale faces of the young couple above the top of the parapet, bobbing up and down and moving along with him. No lion.

Jachin-Boaz swam close to the wall, letting the current carry him along to the concrete steps that came down to the water. There he dragged himself ashore, staggered up the steps, and stopped at the locked gate that shut the steps off from the pavement. He looked in all directions but did not see the lion.

The young man and the girl were standing before him, faces pale, wild hair wilder than before. They reached forward to help him over the gate but Jachin-Boaz, still trembling violently, was able to climb over it by himself.

"You all right?" said the young man. "What happened?"

"Yes, I'm all right, thank you," said Jachin-Boaz in his own language. "What did you see?"

The young man and the girl shook their heads apologetically, and Jachin-Boaz said again, in English, "Thank you. What did you see?"

"We saw you stop near us, unwrap some meat, and throw it on the pavement," said the girl.

"Then the meat jerked and jumped about," said the young man, "and it tore itself up and disappeared. Then you screamed and jumped into the river. What happened?"

"That's all you saw?" said Jachin-Boaz.

"That's all," said the young man. "Are you sure you're all right? Don't you need help? What happened to the meat? How did you make it do that? Why did you jump into the river?"

"Are you a hypnotist?" said the girl.

Jachin-Boaz, foul-smelling from the river and standing in a spreading puddle, shook his head.

"It's all right," he said. "I don't know. Thank you very much." He turned and walked home slowly and weakly, stopping often to look behind him.

12

Boaz-Jachin stood at the roadside. His rucksack was on his back. His black guitar-case, hot from the sun, stood leaning against him. The road shimmered in the heat. He was no more than fifty miles from home, and he wondered if his mother had sent the police after him. Cars whined past like bullets, followed by long stretches of emptiness and silence.

An old humpbacked-looking open lorry loaded with oranges came puttering up and stopped with a mingled reek of petrol, oranges, and orange-crate wood. The driver leaned out of the window. He wore an old black felt hat from which the brim had been cut. What remained was too big for a skullcap and too small for a fez. His face had too much expression.

"Where are you going?" said the driver.

"To the seaport," said Boaz-Jachin.

"Get in," said the driver.

Boaz-Jachin got in and put his rucksack and guitar on the shelf behind the seat.

"What's in the guitar-case?" said the driver, raising his voice above the roar and rattle of the lorry as they pulled away.

"A guitar," said Boaz-Jachin.

"It doesn't hurt to ask," said the driver. "It could be a machine-gun. You can't tell me that everybody with a guitar-case is carrying a guitar. The laws of probability are against it."

"In the films I think the gangsters use violin cases," said Boaz-Jachin.

"That's in the films," said the driver. "Real life is something else. Real life is full of surprises."

"Yes," said Boaz-Jachin, yawning. He leaned his head against the back of the seat and closed his eyes, smelling the petrol, the oranges, and the orange-crate wood.

"Films," said the driver. "Always the films are full of men with guns. Why do you think that is?"

"I don't know," said Boaz-Jachin. "People like excitement, violence."

"Always in the film posters," said the driver, "the hero is pointing with a gun, shooting with a gun. Because we men feel ourselves to be gunless. You follow me?"

"No," said Boaz-Jachin.

"I've talked to professional men—scholars, lecturers," said the driver. "It's a widespread emotional condition. We men feel ourselves to be weaponless. You know what I mean?"

"No," said Boaz-Jachin.

The driver put his hand between Boaz-Jachin's legs, gripped him firmly, took his hand away before Boaz-Jachin could react.

"That's what I mean," said the driver. "A man's weapon."

Boaz-Jachin took his rucksack from the shelf behind the seat and put it in his lap.

"Why'd you do that?" said the driver.

Boaz-Jachin said nothing.

The driver nodded his head bitterly, looking at the road, both hands on the steering-wheel.

"They should rather make films about the women who take away our guns," he said. "Nobody wants the truth."

"You can drop me off in this town we're coming to," said Boaz-Jachin. "I have an uncle here that I have to see before I go to the port."

"I don't believe you," said the driver. "You didn't say anything about your uncle when I picked you up."

"I forgot," said Boaz-Jachin. "But I have to see him. I have to get out here."

They were almost at the edge of the town. The lorry, roaring and rattling, did not slow down.

"I can stick my head out of the window and yell for help," said Boaz-Jachin.

"Go ahead," said the driver. "You look like a runaway to me. If you make trouble I can always turn you over to the police."

The town flew by on either side: chickens, dogs, children, houses, petrol pumps, awnings, shops, vans, cars, lorries, soft-drink machines, a barber pole, a cinema, petrol pumps, houses, children, dogs, chickens. The lorry roared and rattled. The town grew small in the rear-view mirror.

"You are cruel," said the driver. "You are cruel like all the young. You come out into the world, you want this and that. 'Take me here, take me there,' you say to the world. You don't look at the people who offer friendship along with the ride or the food or whatever you hold out your hand for. You don't see their faces. For them you have no feelings."

"If I'd known you were going to get so worked up over giving me a ride I wouldn't have taken it," said Boaz-Jachin.

"You're going to the seaport," said the driver. "What will you do there?"

"Work my passage on a boat if I can," said Boaz-Jachin, "or earn money so I can pay for it."

"Doing what?" said the driver.

"I don't know. Playing the guitar. Waiting on tables. Working on the docks. Whatever I can do."

"Where are you going with the boat?"

"Why do you have to know everything?"

"Why shouldn't I know everything I can find out? Is it a big secret where you're going with the boat?"

"To look for my father," said Boaz-Jachin.

"Ah-h-h!" said the driver, as if he had finally worked a bit of meat out of the tooth it was stuck in. "To look for the father! The father ran away?"

"Yes."

"Your mother has a new man and you don't like him?"

Boaz-Jachin tried to imagine his mother with someone other than his father. His mind gave him pictures of the two of them together. When he took his father out of the pictures he had nothing else to put there. Would his father have a new woman? He took the mother out of the mind-pictures. The father simply looked alone, subtracted from. He shook his head. "My mother hasn't got anyone," he said.

"What do you want from your father, that you're looking for him?"

Boaz-Jachin thought the word *map*, and it became a no-word, a word that he had never seen or heard, a sound without meaning. Something very big, something very small, seemed present in his mind, but in his mind there seemed no place for him. He squirmed in his seat. The lorry driver in his strange hat with his face that had too much expression suddenly seemed a no-person. Lion, thought Boaz-Jachin, but felt only the emptiness where something had gone out of him. He saw the map of Lila's body spread on the floor in the dark shop. Gone. No map.

"Well?" said the driver.

"He promised me something," said Boaz-Jachin.

"Money, property, an education?"

"Something else," said Boaz-Jachin. "I don't want to talk about it."

"Something else," said the driver. "Something private, noble, sacred even, such as can only be between men. And what will you bring him?"

"Nothing," said Boaz-Jachin. "There's nothing he wants from me."

"You're a real giver," said the driver. He sighed heavily. "Parents are a mystery. Sometimes I think about my father and mother for ten or fifteen miles at a stretch. My father was a prosperous and well-known man, an intellectual. Every morning he read the newspaper from front to back, straight through, and said many profound things. My mother was a whore."

"What was your father?" said Boaz-Jachin.

"A pimp," said the driver, "and a homosexual as well. Classical profession, classical principles. Sometimes he made love with my mother as a special favour, but he never intended to have children. I represent the triumph of whoring over pimping.

"My mother always said that fatherhood broke my father's spirit. He left us when I was five. I grew up among black silk underwear, pink kimonos, the smell of last night's drinks in smeary glasses, ash trays full of dead cigarettes, and antiseptic.

"Be your own father and your own son is what I always say. That way you can have many long talks with yourself, and if you're often disappointed you're no worse off than every other father and son. Black silk underwear is very smooth against the skin when you're alone."

Underwhere, thought Boaz-Jachin. Under our where we wear our underwhere. I have no underwhere. The road to the citadel, the roadside stones, the hill, the lion-coloured plain, the tawny motion, the lion-king, the emptiness where he has gone from. I have underwhere, thought Boaz-Jachin. "I think my father was disappointed in me," he said.

"More likely in himself," said the driver. "You should make love with strangers whenever you can."

"What's that got to do with my father?" said Boaz-Jachin.

"Nothing. Your father isn't the only thing in the world."

"Why with strangers?" said Boaz-Jachin.

"Because that's the only kind of person there is," said the driver. "When you get to know a face or a voice or a smell you think the person isn't a stranger, but that's a lie. With an unknown face and the nakedness of an unknown body the whole thing is purer."

Boaz-Jachin was silent listening to the noise of the lorry and smelling the petrol, the oranges, the orange-crate wood.

"I go back and forth on this road all the time," said the driver. "Always there are new unknown faces on it, new faces coming out into the world, heading for the port. I go to the port, come back again always."

Boaz-Jachin hugged his rucksack to himself in silence.

The lorry slowed down, the roar separated into individual putterings, rattles, and squeaks. The driver pulled into a layby, stopped the lorry, shut off the motor. He put his hand on Boaz-Jachin's knee.

"Don't," said Boaz-Jachin.

"Just for a little while," begged the driver. "On the road between the past and the future. Just for a little while give me your strangerhood, your strangeness and your newness. Give me some of you. Be my father, my son, my brother, my friend. Be something to me for a little while."

"No," said Boaz-Jachin. "I can't. I'm sorry."

The driver began to cry. "I'm sorry I bothered you," he said. "Please leave me now. I need to be alone. Go away, please." He reached past Boaz-Jachin and opened the door.

Boaz-Jachin took his guitar from the shelf behind the seat and got out. The door slammed shut.

Boaz-Jachin wanted to give the lorry driver something. He opened his rucksack, looked for something that could be a gift. "Wait!" he called above the roar of the engine as the lorry started up again.

But the driver had not heard him. Boaz-Jachin saw his face still crying under the old black brimless hat that was not a skullcap and not a fez as the lorry, trailing its aroma of petrol, oranges, and orange-crate wood, pulled out into the road and away.

Boaz-Jachin closed the rucksack, buckled the flap. There was nothing in it that could have been a gift for the lorry driver.

13

Jachin-Boaz continued to wake up very early in the mornings, always with the knowledge that the lion was waiting somewhere in the streets for him. But since he had seen him eat real meat he dared not go out until the rest of the world was awake and moving about. He did not see the lion during business hours or in the evening. He was in a state of excitation most of the time.

"You make love as if you're saying hello for the first time and goodbye for the last," Gretel told him. "Will you be here tomorrow?"

"If there's a tomorrow for me I'll be here if here is where I am," said Jachin-Boaz.

"Who could ask for more?" said Gretel. "You're a reliable man. You're a rock."

Jachin-Boaz thought about the lion constantly—how he had eaten real meat, how the young couple had not seen the lion but had seen the meat being eaten. He dared not encounter the lion again without some kind of professional advice.

He spoke guardedly to the owner of the bookshop. "Modern life," said Jachin-Boaz, "particularly modern life in cities, creates great tensions in people, don't you think?"

"Modern life, ancient life," said the owner. "Where there's life there's tension."

"Yes," said Jachin-Boaz. "Tension and nerves. It's astonishing, really, what nerves can do."

"Well, they have a system, you see," said the owner. "When you suffer an attack of nerves you're being attacked by the nervous system. What chance has a man got against a system?"

"Exactly," said Jachin-Boaz. "He could have delusions, hallucinations."

"Happens every day of the week," said the owner. "Sometimes I, for example, have the delusion that this shop is a business. Then I come back to reality and realize that it's just an expensive hobby."

"But people who have hallucinations," Jachin-Boaz persisted, "powerful hallucinations—what's to be done for them?"

"What kind of powerful hallucinations do you have in mind?" said the owner.

"Well, say a carnivorous one," said Jachin-Boaz. "Just for the sake of argument."

"A carnivorous hallucination," said the owner. "Could you give me an example of such a thing?"

"Yes," said Jachin-Boaz. "Suppose a man saw a dog, let's say, that wasn't really there in the usual way, so to speak. Nobody else but the man can see the dog. The man feeds the dog dog food, and everyone sees the dog food eaten by the dog they can't see."

"Quite an unusual hallucination," said the owner, "to say nothing of the expense of keeping it. What breed of hallucinatory dog is it?"

"Well, I'm not actually thinking of a dog," said Jachin-Boaz. "I was speaking hypothetically, just to give an idea of the sort of thing that's on my mind—the way reality and illusion can sometimes get mixed up and all that. Nothing to do with dogs. What I had in mind was perhaps to consult a professional man about it. Can you recommend someone?"

"I have a friend who's a psychiatrist," said the owner, "if you're talking about something that has to do with the mind. On the other hand, if it eats real dog food, I don't know. And he's expensive."

"Actually it's nothing terribly pressing," said Jachin-Boaz. "I might ring him up or I might not. Sometimes it's good to clear up a thing like that rather than have it on your mind."

"Certainly," said the owner. "If you'd like the afternoon off, you know . . ."

"Not at all," said Jachin-Boaz. "I'm perfectly all right, really." He rang up the psychiatrist and made an appointment for the next day.

The doctor's office was in a block of flats, on the top floor of four floors of cooking smells. Jachin-Boaz climbed the stairs, rang, let himself in, and sat on a studio couch in a big kitchen until the doctor appeared.

The doctor was short, had long red hair and a beard, and was dressed like a man doing odd jobs around the house on a weekend. He turned on an electric kettle, made tea in a little Chinese teapot, put two little Chinese cups on a tray with the pot, and said, "Come in."

They went into the room that was his office and sat on facing chairs. There was a studio couch along one wall. By another stood a big table piled with books and papers, a typewriter, two tape recorders, a briefcase, and several huddles of large brown envelopes and file folders. There were more books and papers on smaller tables, on chairs, on the floor, on the mantelpiece, and on shelves.

"Start wherever you like," said the doctor.

"I'll start with the lion," said Jachin-Boaz. "I can't afford to come more than once, so I'll get to the point immediately." He told the doctor about his two encounters with the lion, particularly stressing the five pounds of beefsteak.

"And always I know that just before dawn he will be waiting for me somewhere in the streets," said Jachin-Boaz. "And of course I know that lions are extinct. There are no lions any more. So he can't be real. *Can* he be real?"

"He eats real meat," said the doctor. "You saw him do it, other people saw him do it."

"That's right," said Jachin-Boaz. "And I'm meat."

"Right," said the doctor. "So let's not split hairs about whether he's real. He can do real damage. He's a real problem that has to be coped with one way or another."

"How?" said Jachin-Boaz, looking at his watch. He was paying for fifty minutes of the doctor's time, and ten of them were gone.

"Try to remember the night before you saw the lion for the first time," said the doctor. "Is there anything at all that comes to mind? Any dreams?"

"Nothing," said Jachin-Boaz.

"The day before the night before?"

"Nothing."

"Anything happen at work? You said on the telephone that you work at the bookshop."

"Nothing happened at the bookshop. There was a lion door-stop at the other shop, my own shop where I sold maps before I came to this country."

"What about the lion door-stop? Anything come to mind?"

"My son said that my map wouldn't show where to find a lion."

"What about your son?"

"Boaz-Jachin," said Jachin-Boaz. "That was my father's name too. He started the business, the map shop. He ran away from his father. I ran away from my son. From my wife and son. My father said that the world was made for seeking and finding. By means of maps everything that is found is never lost again. That's what my father said. But everything that is found is always lost again."

"What have you lost?"

"Years of myself, my manhood," said Jachin-Boaz. "There is only one place, and that place is time. Why do I keep the map that I promised him? I don't need it. I could have left it for him. I could send it to him."

"To your father?"

"My father's dead. To my son."

"Why didn't you give it to him?"

"I kept it for myself, kept it for finding what I'd never found."

"What was that?"

"I want to talk about the lion," said Jachin-Boaz looking at his watch.

The doctor lit a pipe, using up almost a minute, it seemed to Jachin-Boaz.

"All right," said the doctor from behind a big cloud of smoke. "What's the lion? The lion is something that can kill you. What's death?"

"Have we got time to go into that?" said Jachin-Boaz.

"What I mean is, what's death in this context? Is it something you want or something you don't want?"

"Who wants to die?" said Jachin-Boaz.

"You'd be surprised," said the doctor. "Let's try to find out what being killed by the lion would be for you."

"The end," said Jachin-Boaz.

"Would it be, say, a reward for you?"

"Absolutely not."

"Would it be, well, what's the opposite of reward?"

"Punishment?" said Jachin-Boaz. "Yes, I suppose so."

"For what?"

"My wife and son could tell you that at great length," said Jachin-Boaz looking at his watch again. "And meanwhile the lion is waiting out there every morning before dawn."

"Does he come into the flat or follow you to work?" said the doctor.

"No. But he's *there*, and I know he's there."

"Right," said the doctor. "But the choice is yours whether you meet him or not, yes?"

"Yes."

"So what we're talking about is that you're afraid you'll go out to meet the meat-eating lion. You're afraid you'll accept the punishment."

"I hadn't thought of that," said Jachin-Boaz.

"What kind of people get punished?" said the doctor.

"All kinds, I suppose."

"The jury goes out to deliberate," said the doctor. "The jury comes back in. The judge says, 'How do you find the defendant?'"

"Guilty," said Jachin-Boaz. "But where does the lion come from? Explain that."

"All right," said the doctor. "I'll go as far as I can with it. But you have to remember that not only don't I have all the answers but I don't even have most of the questions where you're concerned. Let's forget the technicalities. The lion is something extraordinary, but whether he eats meat or plays the clarinet is academic."

"He wouldn't kill me with a clarinet," said Jachin-Boaz.

"The lion," continued the doctor, "is capable of a real effect on you. But that's not much stranger than television, for instance. Right now coming through the air are pictures of people talking, singing, dancing, maybe even pictures of lions. With a television receiver in this room we could see those images. We could hear voices, music, sound effects. We could in reality be emotionally affected by them even though the images would only be images."

"That's not quite parallel to my lion," said Jachin-Boaz. "Also, everybody with a television receiver can see the programmes you're talking about. But nobody but me can see my lion."

"Suppose," said the doctor, "that you were the only person in the world who had a receiver that could pick up this particular broadcast." He looked at his watch. "A guilt and punishment receiver."

Jachin-Boaz looked at his watch. Less than a minute remained. "But where's the lion coming from?" he said. "Where's the transmitter?"

"From whom are you expecting punishment?"

"Everybody," Jachin-Boaz was surprised to hear himself say as his mother and father unexpectedly rose up in his mind. Love us. Be how we want you to be.

"That's as far as we can get now," said the doctor, standing up. "We'll have to stop there."

"But how can I turn off the programme?" said Jachin-Boaz.

"Do you want to?" said the doctor, opening the door.

"What a question!" said Jachin-Boaz. "Do I want to!" But as the door closed behind him he was adding up the cost of daily beefsteak for the lion.

14

Boaz-Jachin sat down in the layby and marked on his map the place where the lorry driver had left him.

He was still sitting there thinking about the lorry driver when a little red convertible with its top down pulled up, playing music. The number plates were foreign and the driver was a deeply tanned handsome woman of about the same age as his mother.

The woman smiled with very white teeth and opened the door. Boaz-Jachin got in. "Where are you going?" she said in English.

"To the seaport," said Boaz-Jachin speaking English carefully. "Where are you going?"

"Different places," she said. "I'll take you to the port." She swung the little red car smoothly out into the road.

Boaz-Jachin, since his encounter with the lorry driver, felt as if his former peaceful state of not knowing anything about people had been peeled from him like the rind from an orange. He doubted that it could be put back. As he sat beside the blonde woman it seemed to him that people's stories were all written on their faces for anyone to read. Perhaps, he thought, he might now be able to converse also with animals, trees, stones. The lion came back to him briefly, like a memory from earliest childhood, then was gone. He felt guilty because he had made the lorry driver cry.

He looked at the blonde woman. She seemed to carry her womanhood the way men on the docks carried baling hooks on one shoulder—shiny, pointed, sharp.

The wind rushed by, blowing their hair. The music was being played by a tape machine. When one side was finished the woman turned over the cassette and there was new music. The music was smooth and full, and it sounded like the marvellous cocktail bars in films where unattainable-looking women and suave violent men understood each other immediately by a look.

Boaz-Jachin knew the blonde woman's story as if she had told him everything. She had been married several times, and was now a wealthy divorcée. She, like the lorry driver, was looking for new faces coming out into the world. She too would want him to be something to her for a little while on the road between the past and the future.

There would be a hotel or a motel on the road, the little red car would pull up and stop, and she would look at him as the film stars looked, with her delicate eyebrows raised, without a word.

The room would be cool and dark, with slitted sunlight coming through the blinds. Ice would tinkle in glasses. She would speak low and huskily, with her lips against his ear. There would be room service, hushed, respectful, and envious—some young man a year or two older than he.

She would be artful and tigerish, would please him in ways unknown to him before, and he would give to her because it was unfair always to take without giving. He would be her stranger, and she his. He would appease the hungry ghost of the lorry driver by his generosity to this woman. It would cost him a few days—she would not want to part with him quickly—but they would both be enriched by it.

Boaz-Jachin thought of the parts of her body that might not be tanned by the sun, how the scent of her flesh would be and the taste of her. He was getting an erection, and crossed his legs discreetly.

Afterwards she would offer him money. He would not accept it of course, although he needed money very badly. On the other hand, he asked himself, was there any difference morally between that and taking money for playing the guitar and singing?

The wind lessened, the music was louder, the car stopped. Boaz-

Jachin looked all around for a hotel or motel but saw none. There was a road going off to the right.

"I just remembered," said the woman, "I have to turn off here. I'd better drop you now."

Boaz-Jachin picked up his guitar and his rucksack and got out. The woman closed the door, locked it.

"When a boy your age looks at me the way I think you were looking at me," she said, "then one of us is in bad shape. Either I shouldn't think that way or you shouldn't look that way."

The little red car pulled away, playing music, going straight ahead towards the seaport.

15

The analogy of the television broadcast stayed in Jachin-Boaz's mind. He was receiving a lion. The lion was a punishment. His wife and son would of course wish to punish him. Did he want to be punished? Was the lion simply a punishment? He could not arrive at a simple yes or no to either of those questions.

The lion ate real meat. What had it eaten since the five pounds of beefsteak three days ago? Would it be thin now, hungry, its ribs sticking out? If it was a lion that appeared exclusively to him, surely he was responsible for feeding it?

A customer came into the shop and asked for a book on ancient Near-Eastern art. Jachin-Boaz showed him the two paperbacks and the one hardback that were on the shelves and went back to unwrapping the shipment that had come in that morning.

The customer was one of the shop's regulars, and inclined to be chatty over his purchases. "The lions are quite remarkable," he said.

Jachin-Boaz stood up from the books, the brown paper and the string, bolt upright and alert.

"What lions?" he said.

"Here," said the customer, "in the reliefs in the north palace." He laid the open book on the counter in front of Jachin-Boaz. "I suppose the sculptor was bound by convention in his handling of the king and the other human figures, but the lions have immense distinction—each one's an individual tragic portrait. Have you seen the originals?"

"No," said Jachin-Boaz, "although I used to live not very far from the ruins."

"That's how it is," said the customer. "Here's one of the artistic wonders of the world, absolutely the high point of the art of its period, and when you live next door to it you don't bother to look at it."

"Yes," said Jachin-Boaz, no longer paying attention to the man's words. He was turning the pages, looking at the photographs of the lion-hunt reliefs. He came to the dying lion biting the chariot wheel.

"Easy enough to see where the sculptor's sympathies lay," said the customer. "His commission may have been from the king but his heart was with the lion. The king, for all the detail and all the curls in his beard, is little more than an ideograph, a symbol referring to the splendour of kings. But the lion!"

Jachin-Boaz stared fixedly at the lion. He recognized him.

"The king is almost secondary," said the customer. "The mortal stretch of the lion's body meets the length of the spears he hurls himself upon, becomes one long diagonal thrust of forces eternally opposed. That thrust is balanced on the turning wheel and the lion's frowning dying face is at the centre, biting the wheel. Masterfully composed, the whole thing. The king *is* secondary, really—a dynamic counterweight. He's only there to hold the spear, and nothing less than a king would be of suitable rank for the death of that lion."

Yes, thought Jachin-Boaz, there was no mistaking that frown. That was his frown, and the mane grew from the forehead in the same way. The set of shadowy eyes was the same. He had been thinner when he had seen him last, he thought, than he appeared here. And he had given him nothing to eat for days! Was the lion only able to eat food that came from him, Jachin-Boaz? No one else saw him. Did he see anyone else?

Jachin-Boaz seemed with his eyes to be possessing the lion in the picture beyond the possibility of its belonging to anyone else. The customer felt that his cultivated appreciation was being made unimportant. He began to feel protective towards the book he was buying, and made little patting motions on the counter with his hands. "I'll have the book," he said, and took out his chequebook.

"But it's the wheel," said Jachin-Boaz, his eyes fixed on the implacable eight-spoked studded chariot wheel in the photograph, part of it lost in erosion and the weathering of the stone. "It's the wheel. He should understand that. It isn't the king. Maybe the king doesn't even want the lion to die. He knows that the lion too is a king, perhaps one greater than himself. It's the wheel, the wheel. That's the whole thing. The sculptor knew it was the wheel and not the king. Biting it doesn't help, but one has to. That's all there is."

"That's one way of looking at it, of course," said the customer. "Really," he said, looking at his watch, "I must be moving on."

"Yes," said Jachin-Boaz. Mechanically he rang up the sale and wrapped the book, wondering how many pounds of meat were required to keep a lion in good flesh. And of course there must be something cheaper than beefsteak. Horsemeat? Perhaps if he called the zoo they would be able to advise him—he could say tiger instead of lion. Was it possible that the lion didn't know that it was the wheel? But he must know—there was such knowledge in his face.

"Please," said the customer, "may I have the book?"

"Yes," said Jachin-Boaz, putting it at last into the customer's hands and thinking how strange it was that anyone else should carry a photograph of the animal so intimately and oddly connected with him.

He was nervous and jumpy for the rest of the day, putting books in wrong places and forgetting where he'd put them. He moved quickly and suddenly from one part of the shop to another without remembering why he went where he did. His mind darted from one thought to another.

He dreaded the lion, trembled and went cold at the thought of him, but at the same time craved the sight of him. The feeding of the lion now seemed his responsibility, his peculiar obligation, and he worried about the expense of it.

Jachin-Boaz rang up the zoo, said that he was doing research for a magazine article, and asked how much meat a full-grown tiger would require daily. He waited while the young lady at the zoo made inquiries. When she returned to the telephone he was told that the tigers each received a twelve-pound joint six days a week and were starved for one day.

"Twelve pounds," said Jachin-Boaz.

Well, actually that included the bones, she said. The meat in such a joint might be six or seven pounds.

How long could a lion . . . tiger, he meant to say, go without food?

Another absence from the phone. Five to seven days, she said on her return. Tigers in a wild state might consume forty to sixty pounds at one time, then go hungry for a week. Certainly one could say that they were able to go without eating for five to seven days.

Where did they buy the meat for the tigers?

They bought condemned meat, he was told, and was given the name of the butchers who sold it.

Condemned meat! thought Jachin-Boaz after he had rung off. The thought made him uncomfortable. Condemned meat, no. He would economize somewhere else.

Then he became preoccupied with the wheel again. He saw his life as the wheel's track printed on the desert, left behind by that inexorable and monstrous onward rolling. He wanted to make the lion understand that the wheel that forever bore the unscathed king away from him bore the king away from himself as well. However many wheels there were, there was in reality only one wheel. The wheel on the cage-wagon that brought the lion to the place of his death was the chariot wheel that hurried the king to his own death farther on its track. There was only one wheel, and nothing and no one had power against it.

Jachin-Boaz took another copy of the art book from the stockroom and looked at it several times during the afternoon. Often he was on the verge of weeping. He wanted to buy the book, but thought of the cost of beefsteak and borrowed it instead. When the shop closed he hurried home with the book, stopping on the way to buy meat.

At the butcher's he looked at the carcases hanging on hooks, stared at their nakedness.

All evening he sat at his desk, silent with the book before him, looking at the picture of the lion biting the wheel. Gretel had come to know his moods by now and was accustomed to them. She did not ask Jachin-Boaz why he had particular expressions on his face at certain times.

He knew that he would go out to meet the lion before dawn. He felt like a condemned man, and was surprised to find that he wanted to make love. There were times when it seemed to him that the different parts of him were not all under the same management.

Afterwards he lay looking at the glow in the night sky over the city. He fell asleep, dreamed that he was running on an enormous master-map with the bronze-studded tyre of the chariot wheel rolling behind him, scraping his back, tearing flesh from his back as it pursued him.

At half-past four he woke up remembering nothing of his dream, bathed, shaved, dressed, and went out carrying the meat for the lion.

Jachin-Boaz saw the lion as soon as he came out of the building. He was lying on the pavement across the street, the light from the overhead lamp making harsh black shadows under the frowning brows.

He knows now that I know who he is, thought Jachin-Boaz. We are countrymen. Jachin-Boaz's legs became weak, and there was coldness in the pit of his stomach. He wanted and did not want to go towards the lion, and he felt his body advancing while his mind sat like a passenger inside his head, looking out through his eyes and seeing the lion grow larger as the distance between them lessened.

The lighted red telephone kiosk was only a few yards to his left, and he moved in that direction as he walked diagonally towards the lion. When the telephone kiosk was ten feet away and the lion was twenty feet in front of him Jachin-Boaz stopped. Again he smelled the hot sun, the dry wind, the lion-smell.

The lion got slowly to his feet, stood watching him. He *was* thin, Jachin-Boaz saw.

Jachin-Boaz moved forward a little farther, threw the meat to the lion. The lion pounced, tore at the meat as he held it between his paws, ate it quickly, growling. He licked his chops, looked at Jachin-Boaz, his eyes like steady green fires.

"Lion," Jachin-Boaz heard himself say, "we are countrymen, you and I." His voice seemed loud in the empty street. He looked up at the dark windows of the flats behind the lion. "Lion," he said, "you have come out of the darkness into which the wheel took you. What do you want?"

For answer his mind showed him lion-coloured desert, singing silence in the heat of the sun, taloned sunlight opening endlessly in the eyes of his mind, lion-sunlight, golden rage, blackness.

"Lion," said Jachin-Boaz. He was humbled by the lion-feeling his mind had given him, he was dominated by the lion's commanding presence, found it difficult to go on. "Lion," he said, "who am I that I should speak to you? You are a king among lions, I see that plainly. I am not a king among men. I am not your equal." While he spoke he watched the lion's face, his feet, his tail. He kept his eyes on the lighted telephone kiosk and edged a little closer to it.

"But it is you, lion, who have sought me out," he continued. "I did not seek you." He paused as he heard himself say that. The lion had come out of the wheel's turning darkness. Had not he, Jachin-Boaz, entered that darkness, seeking with his map?

The sky was paling quickly. As on the first morning, a crow flapped slowly overhead, settled on a chimney pot. Perhaps the same crow. Jachin-Boaz, thinking of the turning darkness from which the lion had come, wanted to close his eyes and enter it, but was afraid to.

Then words imprinted themselves on his mind, large, powerful, compelling belief and respect like the saying of a god in capital letters:

TO CLOSE ONE'S EYES IN THE PRESENCE OF A LION

He felt, as in a dream, the layered meanings of the words that stood upright in his mind as if carved in the stone of a temple.

Jachin-Boaz closed his eyes, felt the darkness slowly rise up in him, felt its turning endlessly revolving through him, rested on its constant motion. He saw sunlight in his mind again, rich patterns of colour mottled with falling gold, sunlight as on oriental carpets.

He remembered the darkness with a smile. Yes, he thought comfortably in the sunlight, turning always. One way. No way back. The blackness surged up through the sunlight, bright with terror, snaky, brilliant. One way. No way back. I shall cease to exist at any moment, he thought. No more world. No more me.

He dropped through blackness, sank through time to green-lit ooze and primal salt, to green light through the reeds. Being, he sensed, is. Goes on. Trust in being. He rested there, prostrate in his mind, awaiting his ascent.

From the green light and the salt he rose, opened his eyes. The lion had not moved.

"My lord Lion," said Jachin-Boaz. "I trust in being. I trust in you. I fear you and I am glad that you exist. Respectfully I speak to you, and who am I that I should speak?

"I am Jachin-Boaz, trader in maps, maker of maps. I am the son of Boaz-Jachin, trader in maps before me. I am the father of Boaz-Jachin, who now sits in the shop where I have left him. He has no love for maps, I think, and none perhaps for me.

"Who am I? My father in his coffin lay with his beard pointing like a cannon from his chin. While he lived he praised me and expected much of me. From my early childhood I drew maps of clarity and beauty, much admired. My father and my mother wanted great things from me. For me. Wanted great things for me. Which of course I wanted also." Jachin-Boaz felt a tightening in his throat—a sound, formed and ready and aching for utterance, a high-pitched single note, a wordless plea. "Aaaaaaaaaaa-aaaaaaaaa," he sounded it, a naked, wanting sound. The lion's ears went back.

"They wanted," said Jachin-Boaz. "I wanted. Two wantings. Not the same. No. Not the same."

The lion crouched quietly, the green-fire eyes fixed always on Jachin-Boaz's face.

"What is the sound of not wanting, my lord Lion?"

The lion rose to his feet and roared. The sound filled the street like a river in flood, a great river of lion-coloured sound. From his time, from the tawny running on the plains, from the pit and the fall and the oblong of blue sky overhead, from his death on the spears in the dry wind forward into all the darknesses and lights revolving to the morning light above the city and the river with its bridges the lion sent his roar.

Jachin-Boaz swam in the river of the sound, walked in the valley of it, walked towards the lion and the eyes now amber in the morning.

"Lion," he said, "Brother Lion! Boaz-Jachin's lion, blessed anger of my son and golden rage! But you are more than that. You are of me and my lost son both, and of my father and me lost to each other for ever. You are of all of us, Lion." He moved closer, a heavy taloned paw flashed out and knocked him off his feet. He rolled upright, fell towards the telephone kiosk and was inside it closing the door, waiting for the shattering of glass, the heavy paw and its talons and the open jaws of death. He fainted.

When consciousness returned to Jachin-Boaz the sun was shining. His left arm hurt terribly. He saw that his sleeve hung in blood-soaked shreds, his arm was bloody, there was blood on the floor of the telephone kiosk. Blood still ran from the long deep cuts of the lion's claws. His watch was smashed, stopped at half-past five.

He opened the door. The lion was gone. There was very little movement in the street, nobody waiting at the bus stop. It must still be early morning, he thought as he staggered back to the flat leaving a trail of blood behind him.

He had wanted to tell the lion about the wheel, and he realized now that he had forgotten it completely.

16

It was evening, and Boaz-Jachin was still on the road. In the last town he had stopped at he had earned a little money playing his guitar and singing, had bought some bread and cheese, and had slept in the square. I can always get through every night into the morning, he had thought while sitting on a bench looking at the stars.

Now he was tired, and the twilight seemed a lonelier time than night. Always the road, said the twilight. Always the fading of the day. The look of moving headlights on the evening road under a sky still light made Boaz-Jachin's throat ache. He remembered how there used to be a house he slept in every night, and a father and mother.

An old dented van, puttering unevenly, petrol-and-farm smelling, slowed down and stopped beside him. The driver was a young man with a rough unshaven face, squinting.

He leaned out of the window, looked at the guitar-case, looked at Boaz-Jachin, cleared his throat.

"You know any of the old songs?" he said.

"Which ones?" said Boaz-Jachin.

"*The Well?*" said the farmer. He hummed the tune off-key. "The girl is at the well waiting for her lover and he doesn't come. How many times will she fill her jug? say the old women in the square. And the girl laughs and says the vessel will not be filled until there comes to her that young man with his smiling face . . . "

"I know it," said Boaz-Jachin. He sang the refrain:

> Black is the olive, black are his eyes,
> Sweet are his kisses, sweeter his lies,
> Dark is the water, deep is the well,
> Who will give tomorrow's kisses none can tell.

"That's it," said the farmer. "Also *The Orange Grove?*"

"Yes," said Boaz-Jachin. "I know that one too."

"Where are you going?" said the farmer.

"The port."

"Take you another day at least. You want to earn some money? I'll drive you to the port afterwards."

"How do I earn the money?" said Boaz-Jachin.

"Making music for my father," said the farmer. "Singing songs. He's dying." He opened the door, Boaz-Jachin got in, the van started up.

"Tractor went over him, smashed him all up," said the farmer. "He'd stopped on a slope, forgot to put the handbrake on, got down to fix the harrow hitch. Tractor rolled back on him. He's all smashed up. Wheel went right over him, broke half his ribs and he's got a punctured lung. He was haemorrhaging inside for a long time before anybody went out to look for him.

"It's his own goddam fault. He never had his mind on what he was doing any more. All right. So that's how it is. He'll hear the songs Benjamin used to sing and he'll die and that'll be that.

"By now he can't talk, you understand. He's lying there having a big struggle just to breathe. Can't move his right arm at all. With his left arm, with a finger of his left hand, he makes on the table the name *Benjamin*. Benjamin I can't give him. I figure I'll give him at least the songs. Maybe he won't know the difference. Son of a bitch." He began to cry.

My second crying driver, thought Boaz-Jachin. "Who's Benjamin?" he said.

"My brother," said the farmer. "He went away ten years ago, when he was sixteen. We never heard from him again."

He turned off into a bumpy dirt road. The headlights looked at stones and dirt, the sound of crickets came in through the open windows. There was cow dung on the road, pastures on either side, the smell of cows. The sparse grass, pale in the headlights, seemed to have been dragged unwilling from the earth blade by blade.

The van bumped and jolted until there were lighted windows ahead, went in through a gate, pulled up by a shed with a corrugated metal roof. There was a barn behind it, a house to one side. The house was squarish and ugly, made of cement blocks with a tiled roof. In the doorway, silhouetted against the light, stood a woman, a bulky dark figure.

"Is he still alive?" said the farmer.

"Certainly he's still alive," she said. "He's been dying already for quite a few years. Why should he rush the job now just because a tractor ran over him? Who's this? You decided this is a good time to bring company home for dinner, or you're opening a youth hostel?"

"I thought, let him hear some music," said the farmer.

"Wonderful," said the mother. "That'll cheer everybody up. We'll have a nervous breakdown together while your father dies. With ideas like this you should work in a resort, a hotel. You should be a social director."

"Would you feel better if we stood out here all night or may we come in?" said the farmer.

"Come in, welcome, have a good time, enjoy yourselves," said the mother. She left the doorway and went into the kitchen.

"Probably our guest wouldn't say no to something to eat," the farmer called after his mother.

"Anything you want," she said. "Twenty-four hours a day. Serving you is my supreme joy."

The farmer and Boaz-Jachin sat down in a parlour with ugly pictures on the walls, a bowl of fruit on a sideboard, a short-wave radio, some books, some ugly vases. The spaces between things in the room separated them rather than connected them.

"Maybe we better have a look, see what kind of shape he's in," said the farmer. "If he's dead it's no use singing for him." He got up, led the way upstairs. Boaz-Jachin followed with his guitar, looking at his back, the frayed shirt with the sweat dried into it, the heavy dragging trousers with a rusty bolt sticking out of one pocket, a coil of wire in another.

"Even if he's dead it might be nice for him to have a song," said Boaz-Jachin. "If nobody would mind."

Upstairs the father lay in a strong dark bed while the room stood up around him. The chairs stood up, the wallpaper stood up, the windows stood up in the wall, the night stood up outside the windows.

A chromium-plated pole with a crossbar stood up beside the bed, a plastic bottle hung on a hook from the bar, a plastic tube fed the big vein in the father's arm.

There were white bandages across his chest and over his right shoulder. The skin of his neck and chest that was usually exposed by his collar opening was creased and dark and weathered. Elsewhere the skin was white and inexperienced-looking. His eyes were closed, his head lay back on the pillow, his beard pointed like a cannon from his chin. His breath whistled in and out, fluttered, broke, went on unevenly.

His wrist, coloured like his neck, came out of his thin white arm, presented itself as the wrist of a boy. Forget the years, said the wrist. This is how I used to lie on the coverlet when someone else was the man and I was the boy. I had nothing in my hand then, I have nothing in my hand now.

The doctor sat in a chair by the bed. He wore a dark suit, open sandals over dark socks, looked at his watch, looked at the father's face.

"The hospital's twenty miles away," said the farmer to Boaz-Jachin. "The ambulance was out, couldn't get here for hours. The doctor came, did what he could right here, said not to move him now."

The farmer looked at the doctor, pointed to Boaz-Jachin's guitar.

The doctor looked at the father's face, nodded.

The mother came in with coffee, fruit and cheese, while Boaz-Jachin tuned his guitar. She poured coffee for the doctor, for her son and Boaz-Jachin, then sat in a straight-backed chair, her hands in her lap.

Boaz-Jachin played and sang *The Well*:

> By the well in the square
> See her waiting daily there . . .

The sound of the guitar, round and expanding, moved out from him to the standing-up walls, came back into the centre of the room, said to the walls, Not you. Beyond you.

The father's breath whistled in and out unevenly the same as before. When Boaz-Jachin sang the refrain the mother walked to the window and stood before her reflection on the night:

> Dark is the water, deep is the well,
> Who will give tomorrow's kisses none can tell.

Boaz-Jachin sang *The Orange Grove*:

> Where the morning sees the shadows
> Of the orange grove, there was nothing,
>   twenty years ago.
> Where the dry wind sowed the desert
> We brought water, planted seedlings, now
>   the oranges grow.

"Did you bring in the tractor?" said the mother to the son.

"It's in the shed," he said. "His eyes are open."

The father's eyes, large and black, looked straight up at the ceiling. His left hand was moving on the bedside table.

The son stood over his father's moving hand, watched the finger spelling on the dark wood of the night table.

"F-O-R . . ." he read. The finger kept moving. "'Forgive,'" said the son.

"Always the humorist," said the mother.

"Benjamin he forgives," said the son. "Always."

"Maybe he meant you," said the doctor.

"Maybe he's asking," said Boaz-Jachin. "For himself."

Everyone turned to look at him while the father died. When they looked back at the father there was no sound of breathing, the eyes were closed, the hand on the table was still.

Boaz-Jachin spent the night in the room that had been Benjamin's. In the morning the mother made the funeral arrangements and the son drove Boaz-Jachin to the port.

They travelled all day, stopping halfway for lunch in a café. The son had shaved and was wearing a suit and a sports shirt. It was evening when they came to the port. The sky showed that they were at the sea.

They went down steep cobbled streets towards the water, came to the open cobbled quayside of the harbour, and cafés with red and yellow light-bulbs strung outside. Lights of ships and boats tied up at piers and lights of quayside buildings were reflected in the water.

The farmer took folded money from his pocket.

"No, please," said Boaz-Jachin. "There shouldn't be money between us. You gave me something, I gave you something."

They shook hands, the van pulled away, climbed the cobbled streets back to the road away from the port.

Later, when Boaz-Jachin marked his map, he found that he had only the name *Benjamin* to give to that family.

17

Jachin-Boaz had fainted again when he got to the flat. Gretel called an ambulance, and he was carried to it on a stretcher.

At the hospital admitting office Jachin-Boaz said that he had fallen against a spiked fence while drunk. He told the same thing to the nurse who cleaned his wounds when she questioned him. When the doctor came to sew up the worst cuts he too asked how Jachin-Boaz had got them.

"Spiked fence," said Jachin-Boaz.

"Yes," said the doctor. "It seems to have lashed out at you with tremendous speed and force. Dragged its spikes right down your arm too. One wants to be careful about provoking fences like that."

"Yes," said Jachin-Boaz. He was afraid that he would be locked up as a lunatic if the truth were found out.

"It didn't happen to be a spiked fence near the tiger cages at the zoo, did it?" said the doctor.

"I didn't see any tiger cages when it happened," said Jachin-Boaz. For all he knew there could be heavy fines involved, revocation of his work permit, even his passport. But certainly no one could prove that he had been interfering with the tigers.

"I suppose in your country they have a certain number of strange cults, strange rites," said the doctor.

"I am an atheist," said Jachin-Boaz. "I have no rites."

While the doctor stitched up Jachin-Boaz's wounds an orderly called the zoo to enquire whether there had been any disturbances having to do with tigers, leopards, or other large felines. The zoo had nothing to report.

"I shouldn't be surprised if he was wearing an amulet of some kind," said the doctor after Jachin-Boaz had gone, "but I didn't think to look. They come into this country and they take advantage of the National Health Service, but they cling to the old ways among their own."

The orderly said to his wife that evening at dinner, "There are things going on at the zoo that the ordinary citizen knows nothing of."

"Among the animals?" said his wife.

"Animals and people—how much difference is there if it comes to that?" said the orderly. "Cults, sex orgies, the lot. Our immigration policy wants a good overhauling, and that's the long and short of it. Our way of life can't stand up to this foreign influx indefinitely."

"But foreign animals, you know," said his wife. "What's a zoo without them? Think how the children would miss them."

Gretel and Jachin-Boaz both stayed home from work that day. Jachin-Boaz rested in bed, his arm wrapped in white bandages. Gretel looked after him with soup, peppermint tea, brandy, custards, strudel. She cooked and baked all day, thumping and banging in the kitchen and singing in her own language.

When Jachin-Boaz had come home all bloody that morning he had fainted without an explanation, and in the ambulance had begged to be excused from going into the matter just then. Gretel had become aware of his early-morning departures from the flat, but she had said nothing. If he needed to go out at quarter to five every morning she would not question it. She had been terrified by his bloody return this morning, had listened, unquestioning, to his spiked-fence story at the hospital, and continued to ask no questions. Her no-question-asking stalked through the flat like a tall silent creature that stared at Jachin-Boaz all day.

For most of the day Jachin-Boaz could do nothing but concentrate all his energies on holding himself together. The snaky black and brilliant panic that had surged up in him when he had closed his eyes in the presence of the lion had tom away the sodden rotting cover from a well of terror in him, and into that well his mind dropped like an echoing stone.

He cowered under the covers, hugging himself and shivering with a chill that soup and brandy and peppermint tea could not take away. When he look around the room his eyes could not take in sufficient light. The day, however it varied from sunny to grey, had less than normal light in it. The twilight was appalling. The lamps when lit seemed feeble, unavailing. His terror stood up strong in him while he lay down. What brought him back to here-and-now was worrying about more beefsteak for the lion.

"Will you be doing any shopping later?" he asked Gretel casually.

"I did quite a bit of shopping yesterday," she said. "There's nothing we need unless you want me to get something for you."

"No," said Jachin-Boaz. "I'm fine. Thank you anyway." He began mentally to rehearse different ways of mentioning seven pounds of beefsteak. He couldn't say, You might pick up seven pounds of beef at the butcher's. He couldn't send her out three times for two pounds of beef and once more for one pound. He couldn't go out and come back with it inconspicuously or in defiant silence.

While he deliberated Gretel was in and out of the bedroom, the living room, the kitchen, filling the flat with domestic sounds, singing incomprehensibly, bringing him coffee, chocolate bars, cleaning, dusting. His silence rose up in him like a pillar of stone while her no-question-asking stalked in and out with her, looking over her shoulder and staring.

After a time Jachin-Boaz said in a strained voice, "We're good together, you and I. These months have been good ones."

"Yes," said Gretel, thinking, Now it comes: bad news.

"We can be together, but we can also be alone with each other," said Jachin-Boaz, "each with privacy, one's own thoughts."

"Yes," said Gretel. Who could be after him? she thought. Brothers of his wife? With knives? What kind of cuts were those on his arm? Not knives.

"We can tell each other everything, every kind of thing," said Jachin-Boaz. "And also we can allow each other to have things that are not told."

"Yes," said Gretel. Not his wife's brothers perhaps, she thought. The brothers of some other woman? Some other woman herself? I'm eighteen years younger than he is. Is she younger than I am? Prettier?

"If I asked you to go out and buy seven pounds of beefsteak and not ask me why, would you do it?" said Jachin-Boaz.

"Yes," said Gretel.

"Thank you," said Jachin-Boaz. "Take money from my wallet. It's on the desk." He sighed, feeling relaxed and sleepy. Would he, wouldn't he, go out to meet the lion tomorrow morning? He would think about it later when he woke up before dawn.

Jachin-Boaz took a nap. He dreamed of a lion-coloured plain and himself walking slowly across it with nothing in sight. From the silence behind him he heard a whispering rolling that grew louder, brazen and heavy.

He knew without turning to look that it was the wheel, and the urge to escape became gigantic in him, too big for his body. He could not convert the urge to action because the vastness of the space made running impossible. There was no place to escape to. There was only empty time-less space all around him under a flat blue sky, and he continued to walk slowly while the escape-urge leaped up in him as if it would burst his throat.

The wheel was closer, the sound greater, filling all the emptiness of the plain. Jachin-Boaz felt the studded bronze tyre on his back, crushing him, printing its track upon him, passing over him but not going on, not going away. Again it approached from behind, clamorous with voices, and on its rim now, turning with it, were the coffins of his father and his mother.

The wheel went over him again, splintering the coffins, pressing the bodies into his own body—his father's maleness, his mother's belly and breasts that now became those of his wife, and it was her body on the wheel crushing him. He turned and clung to her, face to face and front to naked front as the wheel crushed him. It's all right, he thought. This is the way back, the wheel will take me back. The world won't go away now. There'll be world and me again.

He looked up as the wheel passed over him, saw it pass beyond him, saw spears fly over his head into his son Boaz-Jachin who already had two arrows in him and was leaping up at the wheel.

"No more other," said Jachin-Boaz. No more great dark shoulder-world-wheel turning away. He laughed and felt his naked mother warm above him. "It's all right now," he said as she opened her scissor-legs and brought her weight down on him. The blades enclosed his penis as he thrust, safe and cosy, deep into his wife. "World again, me again," he said. "No more other."

He woke up with Gretel lying partly on him, her head on his chest. Her tears were wet on his skin. How am I here? Who is she? he thought as he kissed her wet face. What am I doing with her? He remembered nothing of his dream. In his mind was a memory of Sunday drives when he sat between his father and his mother, watching the waning sunlight with dread. He always got carsick on those drives.

Gretel cooked dinner and brought it in on a tray. Jachin-Boaz sat up in bed, eating and wondering how he had got to this place and this girl. Gretel sat on the edge of the bed with her plate on her lap and ate in silence.

That night Jachin-Boaz slept well, and he awoke at the usual time. In the dimness of the morning he walked into the living room, to his desk and the master-map spread on it.

Jachin-Boaz ran his finger over the smooth paper. If he poked sharply his finger would make a hole in the map, go through it and come out on the other side without having penetrated anything but the thickness of the paper. So his life seemed now: he could poke himself through the flat paper of the map-city he walked on and he would come out on the other side, having only made a hole in non-reality.

Jachin-Boaz spoke to the map. "The man says to the place, 'What will you give me?'

"The place says, 'Take whatever you want.'

"The man says, 'What do I want?'

"The place has no answer for him.

"The place asks a question in its turn, 'Why are you here?'

"The man looks away and cannot speak." Jachin-Boaz touched the map again, then turned away.

He was out in the street with the beefsteak in his carrier-bag before five o'clock. It was dark and rainy, and only when he saw the glistening street was he aware that he seemed to have decided to meet the lion again. Will the lion be wet too? he wondered.

The lion too was wet and glistening. The lion-smell was stronger in the rain. Jachin-Boaz threw him the meat immediately, and the lion ate it, growling. With his bandaged arm Jachin-Boaz felt a little easier than before with the lion, felt comradely with him, as if they had both fought on the same side in a war.

"Comrade Lion," he said. He liked the sound of that. "Comrade Lion, you will kill me or you will not kill me. Your frown is the frown I have seen on the face of my son and on the face of my father. Perhaps it is also the one I see in the mirror. Come, let's walk a little."

Jachin-Boaz turned his back on the lion and walked towards the river. He went along the embankment, looking back to see if the lion was following. He was. What does he see? Jachin-Boaz wondered. Does he see only me? Is everything else not there?

He walked past the first bridge to the second with the lion following, walked up the steps and on to the bridge, looking up at the cables and the dark sky, feeling the rain on his face. At the middle he stopped, leaned his back against the parapet. The lion stopped ten feet away and stood with his head lifted, watching him.

"Doctor Lion," said Jachin-Boaz, "my father used to look at the maps I drew and say that I would be a man of science. But he was wrong. I never became a man of science. The money that he spent on my education was wasted." He laughed, and the lion crouched. "I am alive and he is dead, and the money was wasted.

"He used to say, 'I can tell by the way he writes, the way he draws, his exactitude, his sense of order, the questions he asks, that this boy will be a scientist. He will not sit in a shop waiting for customers to jingle the bell.'

"One day when I was still a little boy, still playing with toy guns, he brought home for me two presents to choose between. One was a western cowboy suit, like those worn in the films, splendid in black and silver, with a sombrero, with a leather waistcoat, with great flapping leather trousers with silver bosses, with a cartridge belt and two shining pistols in black and silver holsters.

"The other was a microscope and a box of scientific equipment and materials—slides, test tubes, beakers, retorts, graduates, chemicals, a book of experiments. 'Choose,' he told me.

"I wanted the black-and-saver leather, the sombrero, the shining pistols. I chose the microscope and the test tubes. Are you looking at your watch, Doctor Lion? The sky is dark, but it is almost daytime now."

Jachin-Boaz walked towards the lion. The lion backed away, growling. Jachin-Boaz shouted, "I TOLD YOU OF SOMETHING THAT I WANTED ONCE. ARE YOU BORED, LION? ONCE I CLEARLY WANTED SOMETHING, NOT A VERY BIG THING. IS YOUR TIME TOO VALUABLE FOR YOU TO LISTEN ANY LONGER?"

The lion had turned his back on Jachin-Boaz, and now walked off the bridge, down the steps, and was out of sight behind the parapet of the embankment.

Jachin-Boaz followed. When he got to the embankment there was no lion. Only the rain, the pavement and the street wet and glistening, the hiss of tyres on the road.

"YOU WEREN'T LISTENING!" shouted Jachin-Boaz to the empty air, the rain. "THERE WAS A TIME WHEN I WANTED SOMETHING AND I KNEW WHAT IT WAS. I WANTED A BLACK-AND-SILVER COWBOY SUIT WITH TWO PISTOLS."

"Cheer up, mate," said the police constable with whom Jachin-Boaz collided while going down the steps. "Perhaps Father Christmas'll bring you one. You've plenty of time till December."

18

Boaz-Jachin walked on the quayside in the darkness beyond the lights of the cafés. Above the harbour were the honeycombed lights of the big new hotel, and behind it the coloured lights and smoky flames of the oil refinery. Sometimes the wind brought dance music down from the hotel. The jukebox music from the cafés had darkness all around it, like the red and yellow bulbs strung outside. Boaz-Jachin did not want to go into the cafés. He did not want to play his guitar again for money just yet.

He walked out on to a pier between boats tied up on either side, creaking at their mooring lines while the water of the harbour slapped at their sides. Some showed lights, some were dark. Across the water at the harbour mouth the light on the mole turned and flashed. Boaz-Jachin smelled fish and sour wine, the salt-wood smell of boats, the harbour-water quietly slapping piles and planking.

He smelled petrol, oranges, and orange-crate wood, and thought of the lorry driver. The smell was coming from a boat with lights in the wheelhouse and cabin skylight. The boat was broad-beamed and big-bellied and painted blue, with a stumpy mast forward, the sail loosely furled on a short boom. Automobile tyres hung along its sides. The high bow curved back on itself with certain classical pretensions, was ornamented with two blind bulging wooden eyes, and sported an archaic anchor. A blue dinghy was tied up astern.

I'm the real thing, said the backward-curving bow, the wooden eyes, the archaic anchor: brown-faced men squinting into the morning fog, women in black waiting. Maybe the sea and I will kill you.

Boaz-Jachin walked along the pier the length of the boat, read the name on the stern: *Swallow*. The home port, where the oranges were going, was where he wanted to go. There he could find another boat to take him farther or he could travel overland in the direction of the city where he expected to find his father.

He sat down on the string-piece, took out his guitar, and played *The Orange Grove* without singing the words, thinking of the desert in the song that was far from the sea, the sparse green of the grass at the farm of the Benjamin family.

A man came out of the *Swallow*'s wheelhouse and leaned against it, his face mostly in shadow. He wore a wrinkled dark suit, a wrinkled white shirt with no tie, and pointed dark shoes. He looked like a rumpled waiter.

"Nice," said the man. "A nice song. Sounds good, music like that coming over the water."

"Thank you," said Boaz-Jachin.

"I see you looking at the boat," said the man. "She's a sweet one, this one, eh? Catches the eye. *Swallow*, her name is. Over the waves like a bird. Comes from the other side. Here they don't build them like this."

Boaz-Jachin nodded. He knew nothing about boats, but this one looked slow, burdensome, heavy. "Do you sail her or has she got an engine?" he said.

"Engine," said the man. "The sail is just to keep her steady. She used to be rigged for sail when my father was alive. Not now. Too much fucking trouble. This way I get there, I get back, I have a good time ashore, no trouble. I come over with wine and cheese, I go back with oranges, melons, whatever. You're on your way somewhere, right? You're going somewhere. Where are you going?"

"Where you're taking the oranges," said Boaz-Jachin.

"You're hanging around looking for a boat. You're hoping maybe you can work your way across," said the trader. When the light at the harbour mouth flashed and turned one side of his face was lit up. He had a big smile, large teeth, looked desperate.

"I had a feeling when I saw you," said the trader. "Sometimes it's like that—you see a person, get a feeling. I'll make a bet with you: I'll bet you've never been on a boat before, you don't know how to steer, you can't cook, and if I told you to cast off the mooring lines you wouldn't know which rope to put your hand to."

"That's right," said Boaz-Jachin.

"That's what I thought," said the trader. Again a big smile. "It's all right. You're in luck anyhow, because my cousin isn't coming back with me this trip. You can help me take her over. I'll show you how to steer, and all you have to do is keep awake."

"All right," said Boaz-Jachin. "Thank you."

"We'll go out in the morning," said the trader. "You can sleep on board."

The bunks were below, next to the galley, and smelled of petrol, salt wood, tobacco smoke, and old frying. Boaz-Jachin took a blanket and lay down on deck, watching the stars, large and bright, rocking above him. Between him and the stars the beam of the harbour light swept as it turned. He fell asleep thinking of Lila and the night they had slept on the roof of her house.

In the morning he was awakened by the sun on his face. There was a professional-looking seagull perching on the mast. It looked down at Boaz-Jachin with a contemptuous yellow eye that said, I'm ready for business and you're still asleep. Other gulls were flying over the harbour with creaking cries, screaming over the garbage behind the cafés, perching on masts and piles.

The trader treated Boaz-Jachin to coffee and rolls at one of the cafés. Then he took on fuel, cleared his cargo at the harbourmaster's shack, hoisted the steadying sail and started the engine. Towing her dinghy astern the *Swallow* puttered past freighters and tankers from whose galleys came the clink of cups and the smell of coffee. Here and there men in shorts or pyjamas leaned on railings looking down, standing in the morning shadows that moved slowly in the sunlight on the metal decks. This is life, thought Boaz-Jachin. This is being out in the world.

They cleared the harbour mouth, passed the old stone mole with its lighthouse now standing sleepy like an owl in strong sunlight, and went out past the channel markers, heading into a fresh wind from the west and a slight chop outside. The sunlight danced in glints and sparkles on the green water. The gull, still on the masthead, expressed with his eye that it was a late start but never mind.

The trader was still wearing his pointed shoes, his dark suit trousers, and his wrinkled white shirt, now more wrinkled and less white, but no jacket. The boat pitched slowly as she went, her big-bellied hull pounding in the chop. The sunlight glinted on the little brass wheel as the trader handled the spokes.

"She pounds, eh?" he said. "She's not built for an engine, the old bitch. Built for sail. With an engine it's like driving a big heavy pancake over a bumpy road. Wears you out."

"Why don't you sail her?" said Boaz-Jachin.

"Because she's motorized now," said the trader. He seemed almost angry. "She's not rigged for sail any more. This is not the old days. My old man used to keep me hopping. One of these things rigged for sail, you've got two masts, big long yards. Every time you go about you have to dip the yard, bring it around the other side of the mast, set everything up again on the weather side. Big sailing deal. 'Move, boy! Hop!' I can still hear him. Big deal sailor, my old man. Fuck that. This is modern times, eh? He was a wonderful man." The trader spat to leeward from the wheelhouse window. "Sail like the devil, afraid of nothing. Great pilot. You never saw anything like it. Knew where he was anytime. Middle of the darkest night, no land, no nothing, knew where he was."

"How do you know where you are when you're out of sight of land?" said Boaz-Jachin. He saw nothing scientific-looking in the wheelhouse but the compass and the fuel and engine gauges. No instruments that looked like navigation.

The trader showed him a wooden board in which were drilled many little holes in the thirty-two-spoked wheel of a compass rose. Below that were short vertical lines of holes. Pegs, attached to the board by strings, were in some of the holes.

"When I need to I use this," he said. "Every point of the compass is divided into half-hours. I mark with a peg how long I've been on any heading. Down below I mark the speed. I add on or take off for wind and current with me or against me, and that's how I know where I am. That's how my father did it, and I do it the same."

"I thought you had to have instruments, charts, maps, take sights and all that," said Boaz-Jachin.

"That's a lot of crap for playboys with yachts," said the trader. "I know the winds, the currents, the bottom, I know where I am. What do I need all that machinery for? My father was the best sailor, the best pilot out of our port. Fifteen, twenty other men masters of their own boats in our village, but if you came there a stranger and asked for 'the Captain' they knew you meant him, nobody else. From him I learned the sea."

"You had a good father," said Boaz-Jachin.

The trader nodded, spat again through the wheelhouse window. "Nobody like him," he said, and sighed. " 'Keep the boat and follow the sea,' he told me. Left it to me in his will. So here I am. This trip oranges, next one wine, cheese, olives, whatever. It's not a bad life, eh? I mean it's a proper thing for a man to do—not like running a restaurant or some shore thing like that. Dressed up like a gentleman all the time, greeting your clientele, making them feel big by remembering their names. White tablecloths, flowers, snapping your fingers for the wine waiter. A mural on the wall with the bay and the grottoes. All the same, for some people that too is a way of life. Takes all kinds, eh?"

"Yes," said Boaz-Jachin, "I guess it does."

"That's how it is," said the trader. "For me, as for my father, it's the sea. Always the other thing looks good, you know—the thing you don't have, the road you didn't take." He put his arm out through the window, slapped the side of the wheelhouse. "*Swallow*'s all right," he said. "She's all right."

The coast slid by—stretches of brown, stretches of green, old red rocks, lion-coloured cliffs, ruined forts, oil tanks, water tanks, pipelines. Blocks and planes and facets of houses, roofs, walls, angles scattering down hillsides, each casting a morning shadow. White walls, red tile roofs, black-cut windows and doorways. Clusters of boats painted blue, painted white. Boats in twos and threes, single boats passing. Sometimes a tanker, sometimes a big white cruise ship. The gull flew off the masthead as the *Swallow* left the coast astern and headed out to sea. The salt wind had a deep-water smell.

"Where are we on the chart?" said Boaz-Jachin towards the afternoon. There was no land in sight.

"I don't have a chart," said the trader. "A chart's a picture. Why bother with a picture of the ocean when you've got the ocean to read? We're half a day out from the port we left and we're two days away from the port we're bound for. Keep her on this heading while I make some lunch."

Boaz-Jachin, alone in the wheelhouse for the first time, suddenly felt the weight of the sea that *Swallow* pounded through, the depth and the weight of it heaving against the boat's old bottom. The engine chugged steadily, driving her on. She answered the wheel easily as he gave or took a spoke, his eye on the quivering compass card. Ahead of him the sunlight on the water danced, and dancing light reflected from the water rippled on the wheelhouse ceiling like flashes of mystic writing, like word-flashes in an unknown language. The blue dinghy followed astern like a child of the boat, its bows slapping the water in the wake of the *Swallow*, its own smaller wake spreading briefly behind it. Up forward the smoke from the galley stovepipe heat-shimmered against the sky and water, wavered the near and distant images of other boats and ships.

Sometimes Boaz-Jachin saw his face reflected in the wheelhouse windows, recalled the blank face of the king, the frowning face of the lion-king. The being-with-the-lion came back for a moment and was gone again. Again the emptiness, the urge ahead towards something gone out from him.

The chariot wheel, the wheel in his hand . . . He felt himself on the verge of understanding something, but could go no farther. He held fast to being where he was.

The trader came on deck with a napkin over his arm, carrying a tray on which was a covered dish, a bottle of wine, a basket of bread, a wine glass, silverware, a clean folded napkin. He set the tray down on the hatch cover, took the napkin from his arm, spread it out, arranged a place setting on it, put the covered dish, the wine bottle, the bread basket in their proper positions, stepped back, looked at everything critically, then came aft to the wheelhouse window.

"The gentleman's table is ready on the terrace now," he said. "I will take the wheel. I ate below before I brought your lunch up."

There was an omelette under the dish cover, very light and delicate, flavoured with herbs. Boaz-Jachin sat on the hatch cover and ate and drank while the trader watched him from the wheelhouse, smiling his desperate smile and showing his large teeth.

Late in the afternoon the trader took a nap while Boaz-Jachin steered.

[85]

When he took the helm again he said, "Tonight we'll stand regular four-hour watches." In the evening he told Boaz-Jachin to heat a tinned stew and brew a pot of coffee, and he had his dinner in the wheelhouse. "I'll stay here for a while yet," he said to Boaz-Jachin. "You might as well get some sleep."

When the trader woke Boaz-Jachin it was two o'clock in the morning. Boaz-Jachin looked out through the windows of the dark wheelhouse, saw nothing ahead but the phosphorescence of the bow wave in the blackness of the night. "Aren't you afraid to leave me alone at the wheel for four hours?" he said. "What'll I do if something goes wrong?"

"What could go wrong?" said the trader. "All you have to do is stay awake and keep out of the way of big ships. Our running lights are lit. Here's the switch for the masthead light if you think somebody doesn't see you. Here's the button for the horn. I've showed you how to steer and how to reverse the engine. If you have to relieve yourself you use these two eye-spliced lines on either side to tie down the wheel."

"How do I stop the boat if I have to?" said Boaz-Jachin.

"For what?"

"I don't know. But if I have to?"

"It's not like an automobile where you can put on the brakes," said the trader. "And it's too deep to drop the anchor out here. You have to steer around things or put her in reverse if something shows up in front of you. And if you shut off the engine and let go of the wheel the sail will bring the boat up into the wind and she'll lose way, stop going forward gradually. Right?"

"Right," said Boaz-Jachin.

The trader looked at his watch, moved some of the pegs in his navigating board, gave Boaz-Jachin a new compass heading. "In a couple of hours we'll pass a light on the horizon on the starboard side," he said. After that there's nothing until I come on watch again. All you do is stay on the heading I gave you. Right?"

"Right," said Boaz-Jachin. The trader went below, and he was alone in the dark wheelhouse with the lighted circle of the compass card and the dim green eyes of the gauges before him. Forward in the blackness the phosphorescent bow wave parted always while the *Swallow*'s wooden eyes looked blindly into the night.

After a time the aloneness became comfortable, the darkness was simply where he was. He remembered the road to the citadel and the ruined palace, how it had seemed nowhere the first time, but the second time it had become the place where he was. The wheel felt good in his hands. When he found his father he would simply say, May I have my map, please? Nothing more than that.

There was a light, a light that turned and flashed from a lighthouse, but it was much closer than the horizon, much sooner than a couple of hours, and it was on the port side.

He said starboard side, thought Boaz-Jachin, and he said it would be on the horizon in a couple of hours. Him and his fucking pegboard. He shut off the engine, let go the wheel, and went below to wake the trader.

"What time is it?" said the trader. "What happened to the engine?"

"I shut it off," said Boaz-Jachin. "It's quarter past three and there's a light on the port side and it's pretty close."

"Shit," said the trader, and started for the deck. As he got out of the bunk there was a horrible grating sound along the keel. The boat lifted sharply as they reached the deck, they heard the splintering of planks. The boat lifted again, grated again, with more splintering.

"Get into the dinghy and pull clear," said the trader in a calm voice to Boaz-Jachin as they half-fell down the slanting deck towards the stern.

Boaz-Jachin, pulling away from the *Swallow* into the darkness, heard the engine start up as the masthead light went on. The *Swallow* leaped glaringly out of the night, the sea lifted her again, she came off the rocks in reverse and started to settle by the bow as the trader jumped clear with a great splash.

My guitar and my map, thought Boaz-Jachin. Gone. By the time the trader had got himself into the dinghy, half swamping it, the masthead light had gone under and they were in darkness again, across which the beam from the lighthouse regularly swept.

"Son of a bitch," said the trader. "Son of a bitch." The sea slapped and gurgled quietly against the dinghy as Boaz-Jachin pulled farther away from the rocks that had sunk the *Swallow*. He could see the trader's hunched shape leaning forward, darker than the sky behind him. Whenever the light swept over them Boaz-Jachin saw his wet white shirt and dark trousers, his face open-mouthed and wet. Suddenly the being-with-the-lion feeling came to Boaz-Jachin. He almost roared. Then it was gone. Emptiness.

"How did I do this to myself?" said the trader quietly. "How did I find you? What demon possessed me to put my boat in your hands? Mother of God, who sent you to me?"

"You and your fucking pegboard," said Boaz-Jachin. "How did that lighthouse get on the wrong side at the wrong time?"

"That's for you to tell me," said the trader. "I was sure at least that you could hold a wheel in your hands and look at the compass. When I went below at midnight you were on a safe course. Tell me, you fateful one, imp of the devil, bringer of ill fortune, what did you do then?"

"It wasn't midnight when you went below," said Boaz-Jachin.

"All right," said the trader. "So it was ten past twelve. Not exactly midnight. We're not quite so precise here as in the navy. My humble apologies."

"It wasn't ten past twelve either," said Boaz-Jachin. "I looked at my watch."

"Don't play games with me, imp," said the trader. The light swept over them, and Boaz-Jachin saw doubt in his face.

"It was two o'clock in the morning," said Boaz-Jachin. "The little hand was at the two and the big hand was at the twelve. If you want to call that ten past twelve, go ahead, do as you like."

"Ten past twelve is the other way around," said the trader. "The little hand, the big hand."

"Wonderful," said Boaz-Jachin. "You're learning fast."

"Two o'clock in the morning, not ten past twelve," said the trader. "We were two hours past where I thought we were when I put you on the new heading."

"Right," said Boaz-Jachin. "Which I stayed on as you told me to, and here we are."

"Son of a bitch," said the trader. "The big hand and the little hand."

" 'Keep the boat and follow the sea,' " said Boaz-Jachin, and he began to laugh.

"I'll tell you something," said the trader. "Fuck the sea. I'll never be able to collect the insurance on *Swallow* because of the way we sank her, but I have a piece of land I can sell, and I'm going to open a restaurant."

"One thing about a restaurant," said Boaz-Jachin—"when you wake up it'll be exactly where it was when you went to sleep."

"Right," said the trader. "So that's that. It's out of my hands. The sea made the decision."

"Tell me," said Boaz-Jachin. "What's the name of the rocks that sank us?"

"The rocks I don't know. The light is Rising Sun Light."

"s-u-n or s-o-n?" said Boaz-Jachin.

"s-u-n," said the trader. "It faces east."

"Where the son sank," said Boaz-Jachin. "Well, on my new map the rocks will be called Rising Son Rocks, spelled s-o-n. I'm naming them after you."

"Thank you," said the trader. "I'm deeply honoured."

The sky was pale now, and in the water they saw oranges floating. The trader leaned over and picked up two.

"If the gentleman would like breakfast," he said, "his table is now ready."

19

Jachin-Boaz's wife, with her husband and son both gone, now considered the situation in which she found herself. In the first months after Jachin-Boaz's departure she had gone through torments thinking of him in the arms of young and beautiful women. Wherever she looked she seemed to see only girls and young women, all of them so pretty that she wondered how men could choose among them. But she had talked to other women since, and the consensus was that men of her husband's age often did what he had done, that after a few months or a year they yearned for the comforts and habits they had left, and, if allowed to, returned. She was determined to encounter such a possibility from a position of strength. She did not expect her son to come back, and made no effort to trace him. Nor did she attempt to locate his father. She concentrated her energies on the shop. She had long had her own ideas about how to run the business, and now she put them into practice.

She hired a girl to help her. She stocked paperback books, and made lively displays of them in the window. She worked up a line of fortune-telling maps for each sign of the zodiac. She took good-luck charms and cheap jewellery of an occult character on consignment from local craftsmen. She installed a palmist in the parlour above the shop—an elderly lady with jet-black hair and piercing eyes who was clothed entirely in black and turned over to Jachin-Boaz's wife a percentage of whatever she took in. To create an atmosphere around her a coffee machine, tables and chairs were added, and regular coffee-drinkers appeared. A small ensemble of young musicians, playing folk songs and paid by the passing of a basket among the coffee-drinkers, attracted a larger clientele. Soon Jachin-Boaz's wife took in more money in a week than her husband had done in a month.

During business hours she was comfortable, even gay. Sundays were bad. Sundays with Jachin-Boaz had often been depressing. Without him they were frightening. Alone at night she found her thoughts difficult to control. She washed her hair often and took many baths, luxurious with scented soaps and essences, but she avoided looking at her body. She looked at her face often in the mirror and felt unsure of how to compose it, what to do with her mouth. After not having worn her wedding ring for months she put it on, then took it off again. She began to read more than she had for years, and every night took sleeping tablets. Often she dreamed of Jachin-Boaz, and in her waking hours, however she occupied herself, there were thoughts of him most of the time.

Boaz-Jachin was in her mind less often. Sometimes he had seemed a stranger to her. They had not thought alike, had never been as close as she had expected a mother and son to be. Now he seemed less an absent son than an emptiness, an end of something. Sometimes she would be surprised not to hear his footsteps, his guitar, would catch herself thinking of what to cook for him. Sometimes she wondered what he might be doing at a particular moment. His father is in him, she thought. He is lost and wandering, seeking chaos. Sometimes the two of them blurred together in her mind.

She looked at books of poems that Jachin-Boaz had given her when they were young. The inscriptions were full of love and passion. He had found her beautiful and desirable once. She had thought him beautiful, exciting, the young man with whom she would make a green place, a place of strength and achievement. She had sensed greatness in him as a desert-dweller senses water, and she had thirsted for it. She had fallen in love with him, and she had locked herself in the bathroom and cried because she knew that he would give her pain.

Jachin-Boaz and she had met at university. She was in the arts course, he was reading natural sciences, a brilliant scholar. Then unaccountably he had failed his examinations, had left university to work in his father's shop. Soon after that the father had died. Then she too had left university, and they had married, living with Jachin-Boaz's mother above the shop for what seemed long years while the mother throve in chronic ill health until struck down by a bus. If not for that bus she would still be here, thought Jachin-Boaz's wife, surrounded by her medicines, telling me how to take care of her son, telling me what a wonderful life they had when the father was alive, telling me what a wonderful husband the father had been, not telling me about the mistress that everybody knew about but her. Did she know? The wonderful husband. Another one like my father with his green place in the desert. The good place is never here, the man's heart is never here.

When Jachin-Boaz's mother had died his wife had expected him to emerge into a new life. She had never abandoned the conviction she had when she had fallen in love with him that he would be a famous scientist. She had always felt the seeking-and-finding drive in him, his talent for associating seemingly unrelated data. She knew that she could nurture his gifts and help him to develop them.

With his education incomplete, his start in life delayed, she did not expect him to rise fast and smoothly to eminence, but she was confident that he could find a gentlemanly scientific speciality—beetles it might be, or ancient artifacts—and on it build a reputation. She imagined letters from fellow scientists all over the world, papers by her husband read at symposia, printed in journals, international visitors drinking coffee, listening to music, talking late into the night, the lamplight warm on a life of culture, of achievement and significance. Jachin-Boaz went on with his work at the shop and found no scientific speciality.

She tried to encourage him to expand and develop the business. He was content with it as it was.

She tried to interest him in a house in the country. He had no interest.

Gone. Nothing. Dry wind in the desert. The pattern of the carpet of her childhood came into her mind, and she shuddered. Here she was. A different carpet. In the square the palm trees rustled in the light of the street lamps. The globes of the lamps were like great blind eyes, the street was empty below the window, a dog trotted past with a black trotting shadow. Here she was and he was gone, the middle-aged man who had turned away from her in bed or made love feebly, made her feel less than a woman, incapable of giving or taking pleasure. And she had seen how he looked at girls. In the shop, in the street, wherever he was. All that he had not been with her when naked he would try to be with someone new. New and young. But false. False to his abandoned talents. False to the best in him that would be for ever lost now, for ever lost. How strange that he should have left it all so soon, so young, so long ago. How strange that all these years he had been busy with maps, with paper ghosts of finding, with finding-masturbation, and all the finding in him dead! There was nothing left for him to do but die now, really. Poor fool, poor mad failed son and husband. She took her wedding ring out of the drawer, threw it on the floor, stamped it out of shape, put it back in the drawer.

Jachin-Boaz's wife no longer cared where Jachin-Boaz was, but she felt a strong need to write a letter to him. She reasoned that he would certainly be working at a map shop or a book and map shop wherever he might be. From the information-gatherers who worked on the special-order maps she obtained the names and addresses of the principal journals of the book trade in five foreign capitals. In each of the journals she placed an advertisement notifying Jachin-Boaz that there was a letter for him to be had at the box number given. To each journal she sent a copy of her letter to him:

> Jachin-Boaz,
>   What are you looking for with your master map that you stole from your son, with your savings that you stole from your wife and child? What will your map show you? Where is your lion? You can find nothing now. For you there never were, never could be lions, failed man. Once you had talent, power of mind and clarity of thought, but they are gone. You have taken yourself away from all order, you have hurled yourself into chaos. What was fresh and sweet in you has gone stale and sour. You are the garbage of yourself.
>   You will wake up one morning and realize, whoever is beside you, what you have thrown away, what you have done. You have destroyed me as a woman and you have destroyed your-

self, your life. You have been committing slow suicide ever since you failed your examinations, and soon you will come to the end of it.

Your father with his cigars, his theatrics, his mistress that you never knew about until I told you—your father, the great man, died at fifty-two. His heart was bad, and he died of it. You are now forty-seven, and you too have a bad heart.

You will wake in the night—whoever lies with you cannot hold back death—and you will hear the beating of your heart that moves always towards the last beat, the last moment. Wherever you are, whomever you are with; you have only a few years left to you, and suddenly they will all be gone. The last moment will be *now*, and you will know what you have lost, and that despairing thought will be your last.

You will want to come back to me, but you cannot come back. You can go only one way now—to the end you have chosen.

These are the last words you will ever have from

the woman who was

once your wife.

When Jachin-Boaz's wife had posted off the five copies of the letter she felt fresh and clear and clean. As she walked back from the post office (she could have trusted no one else with that errand, had felt that she must see with her own eyes the letters disappear into the slot) it seemed to her that she saw the sky, felt the sunlight and the air on her face for the first time in months. A burst of pigeons upward from the square was like the winging up of her spirit in her. Her step was youthful, her eyes bright. A man younger than she turned to look at her in the street. She smiled, he smiled back. I will live long, she thought. I have strong life in me.

At the shop she hummed songs that she had not remembered for years. An old man came in, stains on his clothes, flecks of tobacco and dandruff. *He* won't live to be as old as this one, she thought.

"Stroller's map?" the old man said. "New one out yet?"

"Voyeur's map, you mean?" said Jachin-Boaz's wife with a bright smile.

"I don't speak French," said the old man, and winked.

She went to a cabinet, opened a file drawer, took out cards. "Two alleys crossed off," she said. "The servant girl at the bedroom window has gone, and the new one draws the curtains. The house where the two girls always kept the lights on is up for sale and empty now. The revised map isn't ready yet."

The old man nodded as if it were nothing to him one way or the other, and pretended to be interested in paperbacks.

"Let me show you a pasture map," said Jachin-Boaz's wife. "You can watch sheep and cows. You've no idea what goes on at farms." She was laughing. The old man became red in the face, turned and left the shop, stumbling against the lion door-stop at the open door. Through the shop window Jachin-Boaz's wife watched him going down the street. Dogs trotted past without looking at him.

Later that day the surveyor who had told Boaz-Jachin what he knew about maps came in. He was tall, with a weathered face and an aura of distance, desert wind in open spaces. He gave Jachin-Boaz's wife the special-order maps he had been working on.

"Some people," he said when they had finished their business, "don't need maps. They make places for themselves, and they always know where they are. To me you seem such a person."

"I don't need maps," said Jachin-Boaz's wife. "Maps are nothing to me. A map pretends to show you what's there, but that's a lie. Nothing's there unless you make it be there."

"Ah," said the surveyor. "But how many people know that? That you can't learn—either you know it or you don't."

"I know it," she said.

"Ah," said the surveyor. "You! I'll tell you something—with a woman like you my whole life might have been different."

"You talk as if your whole life's behind you," she said. "You're not that old." She leaned forward over the counter. He leaned towards her. Music drifted down from the coffee shop upstairs. The assistant rang up a sale and rattled money in the till. The lion at the door seemed to smile as customers came in, went out. She kept the door open most of the time now. "A man like you," said Jachin-Boaz's wife, "could be of great value to oil companies, foreign investors. A monthly newsletter, for instance, with the latest information on property and development trends. Who knows what you might do if you cared to? A man who knows what's what, who sees what can be done and puts his hand to it . . . " She saw bright offices, large windows overlooking the sea, charts on the wars, teletypes clicking, conferences, telephones with many pushbuttons, international visitors, articles in business magazines. She picked up the maps he had brought in, laid them down again. "Boundaries," she said. "Wells. Water wells. Did you ever hear of a water millionaire? How are water shares doing on the stock exchange?" They both laughed.

"You see what I mean?" said the surveyor. "I think little thoughts, you think big ones. Ah!" They leaned towards each other across the counter, both humming the tune that was drifting down from the coffee shop. "Perhaps we could have dinner this evening?" he said.

"I'd like that," said Jachin-Boaz's wife. That afternoon she left the assistant to close the shop, and went upstairs early. She lay in the bathtub for a long time, steeping in the silky heat of the steaming water, smelling the scented bubbles, feeling back to the youth still somewhere in her, the excitement of an evening out. She remembered painting quiet landscapes when she was at university, afternoons of sunshine and her hair blowing in the wind. She would get her paintbox out of the cupboard. She would paint again, sit in quiet places in the sun, feel the wind. Green places.

She dressed, made up her face carefully, practised relaxing her mouth in front of the steamy mirror. In the twilight she went up to the roof, looked at the palms in the square darkening in the fading light. She remembered a song that her father used to sing, sang it softly to herself while the evening breeze stirred her hair:

> Where the morning sees the shadows
> Of the orange grove, there was nothing twenty
> years ago.
> Where the dry wind sowed the desert
> We brought water, planted seedlings, now the
> oranges grow.

She had bent her wedding ring back into a circle and put it on, and she touched it now. She remembered Boaz-Jachin as a baby laughing in his bath in the sink, remembered herself singing in the kitchen and Jachin-Boaz young. She shut the memories out of her mind. She thought of the five copies of the letter she had posted, and smiled. Pigeons circled the square, and she cried.

THE LION OF BOAZ-JACHIN AND JACHIN-BOAZ

20

A mighty fortress is our God, sang Gretel in her mind, hearing the voices of the choir in the church of the town where she had been born as she stood behind the counter in the bookshop. Painted on the wooden gallery-front were Bible pictures, pink faces, blue and scarlet robes, too much colour, leaving a taste of marzipan in the eye. The three crosses on Golgotha, black sky, grey clouds. The Resurrection with many golden beams of light, Jesus in white gooseflesh. Potiphar's wife, lusty, opulent, clutching at Joseph.

From deep despair I cry to thee, sang the choir in her mind. The dead nobles in the crypt beneath the altar were only acoustics now. Sound-absorbers, however gauntleted and sworded, fierce in battle and the chase, dead wives virtuous beside them. Silent they were below the altar, but clamorous in stone monuments in the sanctuary, praying in stone effigy, noisy with stone silence in the hymn. From deep despair I cry to thee, Lord God hear thou my call. The street outside the shop moved slowly in its daily march of buses, cars, pedestrians. "Do you sell ball-point pens?" a lady asked.

"No," said Gretel. "Try the newsagent at the corner."

"Greeting cards?"

"No," said Gretel. "Sorry, books only." Apple cores came into her mind. Why apple cores, what apple cores? Brown apple cores in the autumn in a neighbour's garden. Yellow leaves and she scuffling among them, squatting to eat the apple cores dropped there by someone else. Baskets of apples at home. Why had she wanted someone else's brown cores? How old had she been? Five, perhaps, or six. Her earliest memory. What did Jachin-Boaz dream of? What waited for him in his sleep? What waited for him outside in the early morning? How could he go out into the street and come back with claw-marks on his arm? What was the meat for? Something that he was afraid of. Something that could kill him. Something that he wanted to be killed by? A man could not be completely a liar in his lovemaking. Jachin-Boaz made love like a man who wanted to live, a man who wanted her. How could he be so full of life and so full of despair? His face above her in bed was easy and loving, the morning face before the dawn was haggard, haunted.

"Perhaps we could have lunch one day soon?" That was what he had said to her that first time, after buying a book on string quartets. She had had another man at that time. Wednesdays and weekends. It isn't that I don't want to marry you, he said. It would kill my mother if I married a girl who wasn't Jewish. Right. Here's another one. Perhaps we could have lunch one day soon. Yes, let's have lunch. My people killed six million of you. He had brought her a single rose. A yellow one that day, red ones later. She had talked about her dead father. No one else had asked about her father, invited him from the silence. He had kissed her hand when he said goodbye outside the shop. This was not, she had felt, going to be Wednesdays and weekends. She wanted to belong wholly to a man, and this man's quiet face was claiming her and she was afraid.

Now his haunted face awoke beside her every morning. A mighty fortress, sang Gretel in her mind, imposing her will on the choir. The sound surged into a lion-coloured roar, a strong river of violent . . . what? Not joy. Life. Violent life. I knew that I'd be happy with him, unhappy with him—everything, and more of everything than ever before in my life. Something there is that won't die. A mighty fortress is our something.

21

The night sky, pinky-grey, leaned close to chimneys, rooftops, hesitantly touched black bridges and the winding river. I am beautiful only if you look at me, the sky said.

I can't be everybody, said Jachin-Boaz, wise with the mind of sleep and knowing his dream for a dream. His words were an answer to which the question was a sensation of something very big, something very small. Which part of it am I?

Ha ha, laughed the answer, strutting in the mind that would forget it on awakening. See how simple it is? Male or female? Choose.

Something very big, something very small, thought Jachin-Boaz. There is a sob I don't let out, there is a curse I don't speak, there is a turning away from whom, there is a black shoulder of what?

Well, said the answer, this is the place you tried to avoid, but it is not to be avoided.

I can cover it with a map, said Jachin-Boaz. Then there will be world.

He spread out the map, so thin! Like tissue paper. The black shoulder heaved up through it, tore it. As from a heaving mountain Jachin-Boaz fell away.

I can cover it with a map, he said again, spreading vast miles-wide tissue paper over the black abyss. He ran lightly across its surface that billowed in a dreadful rising black wind. See! he cried as he fell through the tearing tissue paper, I'm not falling!

Right, said the answer. See how simple? Betrayed or betrayer? Choose. Either way you win the loss of everything.

I cry in the throat, said Jachin-Boaz.

Yes, said the answer.

I curse in the dark, said Jachin-Boaz.

Yes, said the answer.

From me all turns away, said Jachin-Boaz.

Loss unending, said the answer.

She will save, said Jachin-Boaz.

Whom you betray, the answer said.

He will save, said Jachin-Boaz.

Who turns away, the answer said.

World is there if I hold fast to it, said Jachin-Boaz.

What is there if you let go? the answer said. Dare to find out?

I'll let go if I can hold on while I'm doing it, said Jachin-Boaz. Lion-skins make stronger maps than tissue paper, he thought. He stood on the window ledge looking down. Far below him the firemen held taut the lion-skin.

No use telling me to jump, said Jachin-Boaz. Not even in a dream.

We all know what a no is shaped like, said the answer.

Right, said Jachin-Boaz. We know and the noes know.

Had your noes cut off lately? said the answer.

Come closer, said Jachin-Boaz darkly to the answer. It was very big, and he was very small and frightened. He woke up with his heart beating fast, remembering nothing.

Half-past four, said the clock on the night table. The lion would be waiting. Let him starve, thought Jachin-Boaz, and went back to sleep.

22

"I can't find it," said Boaz-Jachin in his own language, talking in his sleep.

"What?" said the girl beside him in the narrow upper berth in the pre-dawn dimness of the stateroom. She spoke English.

"Where to go," said Boaz-Jachin, still asleep, still speaking in his own language.

"What are you saying?" said the girl.

"Ugly maps. Can't make nice maps. Only where I've been," said Boaz-Jachin. "Lost," he said in English as he woke up.

"What's lost? Are you lost?"

"What time is it?" said Boaz-Jachin. "I have to get back to the crew's quarters before breakfast." He looked at his wristwatch. Half-past four.

"Are you always lost?" said the girl. They were nested like two spoons, her nakedness warm and insistent against his back, her mouth close to his ear. Through the porthole the darkness was greying. Boaz-Jachin tried to remember his dream.

"Are you always lost?" said the girl.

Boaz-Jachin wished that she would be quiet, tried to call back the vanished dream. "Everything that is found is always lost again," he said.

"Yes," said the girl. "That's good. That's true. Is it yours or did you read it?"

"Hush," said Boaz-Jachin, trying to fit into a silence with her. The porthole was like a blind eye in the dim stateroom. On that round blind eye, whitening with the morning fog behind it, he seemed to see his map, the one he had newly drawn from memory after he and the trader had been picked up by the big white cruise ship: his town, his house, Lila's house, the bus depot and the other bus depot, the road to the citadel, the hall of the lion-hunt reliefs, the hill where he had sat, the road to the seaport, the place where the lorry driver had dropped him, the brief distance with the woman in the red car, the farm where the dying father had written FORGIVE with his finger, the *Swallow*'s track to Rising Son Rocks. The city where he thought his father was now with the other better map, the map of his future.

The map faded, only the round blind stare of the fog was left. In that stare Boaz-Jachin doubted that his father's map would be of any use to him. He had remembered it as large and beautiful. Now he thought of it as small and cramped, too neat, too calculated, too little cognizant of unknown places, of the night places waiting beyond the day places, of the somewheres dropping from the open wombs of nowheres. He felt lost as he had not done since being with the lion.

"Maps," he said softly. "A map is the dead body of where you've been. A map is the unborn baby of where you're going. There are no maps. Maps are pictures of what isn't. I don't want it."

"That's beautiful," said the girl. " 'There are no maps.' What don't you want?"

"My father's map," said Boaz-Jachin.

"That's good," said the girl. "Is it yours? Do you write? It sounds like the beginning of a poem: 'My father's map is . . .' What is it?"

"His," said Boaz-Jachin. "And he can keep it." He threw back the sheets, rolled the girl over on her stomach, bit her buttocks, got out of bed and put his clothes on.

"I'll show you my poems tonight," she said.

"All right," said Boaz-Jachin, as the girl's room-mate, yawning, came back from where she had spent the night. He went back to the crew's quarters and got ready to serve breakfast to the first sitting.

The trader had been dropped off at the last port. Boaz-Jachin, signed on to replace a waiter who had left earlier in the cruise, would stay with the ship until it reached its home port. From there he could travel over-land most of the way to the city where he expected to find his father. Boaz-Jachin no longer wanted the map, but he wanted to find his father and tell him so. While serving breakfast that morning he thought about what he would say to his father.

Keep it, he would say. I don't need it. I don't need maps. At first he imagined himself only, saw and heard himself saying the words without seeing his father in his mind. Then he tried to imagine Jachin-Boaz. Per-haps he would be lying in a dirty bed, unshaven, ill, maybe dying. Or dim and pale, lost in some shop of dust and shadows in the great city, or stand-ing alone on a bridge in the rain, looking down at the water, defeated. What have you found with your map? he would say to Jachin-Boaz his father. Has the future you drew so beautifully for me come to you? Has it made you happy?

The dishes clattered, the music played anonymously its tunes that were the same in airports, cocktail bars and lifts, the children quarrelled and left their eggs uneaten. The parents sat with the faces and necks of every day coming out of their holiday clothes, spongy backs and flabby arms of women in sun-back dresses, festive trousers on men with office feet. Girls displayed in the shops of their summer dresses the stock that had not moved all year, their mouths open with surrender, their eyes blurred with hope or sharp with arithmetic.

Boaz-Jachin walked behind his smile, served from behind his eyes, looked down on bald heads, bosoms, brushed ardent shoulders with his thighs, said thank you, nodded, smiled, cleared away, walked back and forth through swinging doors and galley smells. Every person here had had a father and a mother. Every person here had been a child. The thought was staggering. The feet of the men in the festive trousers made him want to cry.

Boaz-Jachin served the table of the girl he had slept with last night. She shaped the word *hello* with her mouth, touched his leg with her hand. He looked down her dress at her breasts, thought of last night and the night that was coming. He looked up and saw her father looking at him.

The father's face was busy with horn-rimmed glasses and a beard. The father's eyes were sad. The father's eyes spoke suddenly to Boaz-Jachin. You can and I can't, said the father's eyes.

Boaz-Jachin looked at the mother looking at the father. Her face was saying something that his mother's face had often said. But he had never paid attention to what it was. Forget this, remember that, said her face. What was the *this* to be forgotten? What was the *that* to be remembered? Boaz-Jachin thought of the road to the port and of the time after the lorry driver when it seemed to him that he could speak with animals, trees, stones.

Beyond the windows of the dining room the sea sparkled in the sunlight. Part of an island passed, a straggle of ruins, a broken citadel, the pillars of a temple, two figures on a hill. Gulls rose and fell on the air currents beside the ship. This, said the sea. Only this. What? thought Boaz-Jachin. Who? Who is looking out through the eyeholes in my face? No one, said the sea. Only this.

"Thank you," said Boaz-Jachin serving the mother, averting his eyes from her bosom.

That night again he went to the girl's stateroom.

"Wait," she said as he began to take his clothes off. "I want to read you some poems."

"I just want to be comfortable," said Boaz-Jachin. "I can listen with my clothes off."

"All right," she said. She took a thick folder from a drawer. The sea and the sky outside were dark, the ship thrust cleaving its phosphorescent bow wave, the engines hummed, the air-conditioning whirred, the lamp by the berth made a cosy glow. "They mostly don't have titles," she said, and began to read:

> Black rock rising to a neverness of sky,
> Black alone, no sky above the
> Far-down lost and winding
> Blood-red river and my
> Frail black boat, dead
> God my freight, too heavy for my
> Craft, blind broken eyes.
> Blind father-stone between my thighs . . .

"Shit," said Boaz-Jachin. "Another father."

> . . . Deflower my death, seed
> My defeat, get NOW from nothing,
> Fierce upon your daughter.

Lot was made drunk, salt
Wife behind him in the
Desert. Stone is my lot, dead
God my steersman.
Blind,
Find
Star.

"What do you think?" said the girl when she had finished reading.

"I don't want to think," said Boaz-Jachin. "Can't we not-think for a while?" He pulled her T-shirt over her head, kissed her breasts. She twisted away from him.

"Is that all I am?" she said. "Something to grab, something to fuck?"

Boaz-Jachin bit her flank hopefully but with lessening conviction. She sat motionless, looking thoughtful.

"You're beautiful," she said, ruffling his hair. "Am I beautiful to you?"

"Yes," said Boaz-Jachin, unbuttoning her jeans. She rolled away with her jeans still on.

"No, I'm not," she said. She lay on her stomach, leafing through the poems in the folder. "You're saying I am because you want to fuck. Not even make love, just fuck. I'm not beautiful to you."

"All right," said Boaz-Jachin. "You're not beautiful to me." He sat up, got off the bed, put on his trousers.

"Come back," she said. "You don't mean that either."

Boaz-Jachin took off his trousers, climbed back into the berth. When they were both naked he looked down at her face. "Now you're beautiful," he said.

"Shit," she said, and turned away. She lay with her face averted, inert while Boaz-Jachin tried to make love. "Oh," she whimpered.

"What's the matter?"

"You're hurting me."

Boaz-Jachin lost his erection, withdrew. "The hell with it," he said.

"Daughters are supposed to attract their fathers sexually," said the girl as he lay beside her, sulking, "but I don't. I'm not beautiful to him either. He once told me that boys would love me for my mind. In some ways he's rotten."

"My God!" said Boaz-Jachin. "I am so sick and tired of fathers!" He sat up, swung his legs over the edge of the berth.

"Don't go away," she said. "Goddam it, have I got to plead for every lousy minute of human companionship? Have I got to pay for every minute of attention with my pussy? Can't you talk to me, just one person to another? Can't you give anything but your prick? And even that isn't given—you're only taking."

Boaz-Jachin felt his childhood vanish as if he had been launched from it in a rocket. As if with ancient knowledge he recognized the departure of innocence and simplicity from his life. He groaned, and lay back on the pillow staring at the ceiling. Lila seemed long ago, never to be found again.

"What do you want me to do?" he said.

"Talk to me. *Be* with me. Be with *me*, not just parts of me."

"Oh God," said Boaz-Jachin. She was right. He was wrong. He hadn't wanted to be with *her*. He had sensed that she would be willing and he wanted a girl to cuddle with, a no one. But everybody was a someone. He cursed his new knowledge. He had known this girl for a few days only, and it seemed a lifetime of mistakes. He felt roped together with her on the sheer face of a bleak mountain. He felt immensely weary.

"What?" she said, looking at his face. "What's the matter?"

Boaz-Jachin stared at the ceiling, remembering Lila and the first night on the roof, remembering the brightness of the stars and how it was to feel good and know nothing. The lion came into his mind and was gone, leaving emptiness that urged him forward.

"What do you want to do?" the girl said. "I don't mean now, this minute. In life, I mean."

What *do* I want to do? thought Boaz-Jachin. I want to find my father so I can tell him I don't want his map. That's not a lifetime career. "Shit," he said.

"You're a real intellectual," said the girl. "You're a real deep thinker. Try to say something in words, just for the novelty of it."

"I don't know what I want to do," said Boaz-Jachin.

"You're a very interesting person," said the girl. "I don't meet people as interesting as you every day in the week. Tell me more about yourself. Now that we've been to bed, let's get acquainted. Have you ever done anything? Have you ever written a poem, for instance, or painted a picture? Do you play a musical instrument? I'm trying to remember why I *did* go to bed with you. You were beautiful and you said something good. You said that you were looking for your father who was looking for a lion, and

I said there were no lions any more, and you said there was one lion and one wheel, and I said that was beautiful, and then all you wanted to do was fuck."

Boaz-Jachin was out of the berth and putting his clothes on. "I play the guitar," he said. "I drew an ugly map that I lost, and then I drew another map. I copied a photograph of a lion once. I've never written a poem. I've never painted a picture." He was angry, but as he spoke he became unaccountably elated, proud. There was something in him not drained off by poems or pictures, something unknown, unavailable but undiminished, intact, waiting to be found. He tried to find it, found only emptiness, was ashamed then, humbled, felt mistaken in his temporary pride, shook his head, opened the door and stepped out into the corridor.

As he closed the stateroom door behind him he saw the girl's father coming towards him. The father's face became very red. He stopped before Boaz-Jachin, his face working behind the horn-rimmed glasses and the beard.

"Good evening, sir," said Boaz-Jachin, although it was the middle of the night. He attempted to walk around the father, but the father stepped in front of him, blocking his way. He was a small man, no taller than Boaz-Jachin, but Boaz-Jachin felt in the wrong and looked it.

" 'Good evening, sir!' " mimicked the father with a dreadful grimace. "Good evening, father number such-and-such of girl number such-and-such. Just like that. Smooth and easy."

Boaz-Jachin saw in his mind a map of the sea, its islands and ports. If he were put off at the next port because of a passenger complaint he would have another sea voyage to make, another boat or ship to find, other people with their lives and histories to drag him down with hard and heavy knowledge. It was as if his shirt and all his pockets were filled with great lumpy potatoes of unwanted knowledge. He wished that he could be at the end of his journey and not have to talk to anyone for a while.

"Excuse me, please, sir," he said. Still the father blocked his way.

"What are you?" said the father. "For you life must be one girl after another, and sometimes an older woman who pays you a little something for your services, I suppose. Now you're a waiter on a cruise ship, now a beach boy at a resort. You get the daughters that fathers have stayed up with when they were sick, have listened to the troubles of, have wanted the best for. You with your smooth face and clear eyes and long hair."

Boaz-Jachin sat down on the floor, his arms resting on his drawn-up knees. He shook his head. He was almost on the point of crying, but he began to laugh.

"And that's funny to you?" said the father.

"You don't know what I'm laughing at," said Boaz-Jachin. "Nothing is smooth and easy for me, and my life isn't one girl after another—it seems to be one father after another. And how would it help you if I had a wrinkled face and clouded eyes and short hair? Would your daughter then become a nun?"

The father's face relaxed behind the beard and the glasses. "It's hard to let go," he said.

"And it's hard to hold on," said Boaz-Jachin.

"To what?" said the father.

"The wheel," said Boaz-Jachin.

"Ah," said the father. "I know that wheel." He smiled and sat down beside Boaz-Jachin. They sat together on the floor, smiling while the ship hummed, the air-conditioning whirred, and the dark sea slipped by on either side.

23

Darkness roared with the lion, the night stalked with the silence of him. The lion was. Ignorant of non-existence he existed. Ignorant of self he was a sunlit violence with calm joy at the centre of it, he was the violence of being-as-hunter constantly renewed in the devouring of non-being. The wheel had been when he ran tawny on the plain, printing his motion on the grateful air. He had died biting the wheel that went on and left him dead. The wheel continued, the lion continued. He was intact, diminished by nothing, increased by nothing, absolute. He ate meat or he did not eat meat, was seen or unseen, known when there was knowledge of him, unknown when there was not. But always he was.

For him there were no maps, no places, no time. Beneath his tread the round earth rolled, the wheel turned, bearing him to death and life again. Through his lion-being drifted stars and blackness, morning sang, night soothed, dawn burst its daylight from the womb of vital terror. Oceans heaved, frail bridges spanned the winding track of days, the rising air sang lion-flight in wings of birds. In clocks ticked lion-time. It pulsed in heartbeats, footsteps walking all unknowing, souls of guilt and sorrow, souls of love and pain. He had been called, he had come. He was.

24

After his last encounter with the lion Jachin-Boaz felt childish, stupid, shaken. That the lion had turned his back on him now frightened him more than the previous attack. He felt as if the present had vomited him out like a Jonah. He lay gasping on dry land under the eye of an exacting God. "There is no God," he said, "but the exactions exist, so there might just as well be a God. Perhaps there is one after all."

"People always assume that God is with people," said Gretel. "But maybe God is in the furniture, or with stones."

Go and preach, thought Jachin-Boaz, his mind still on Jonah. The king sleeps with his chariots, the lions are dead. I have not marked the lion-palace on my master-map. Boaz-Jachin's master-map. I have a lion, and I have told him about a cowboy suit.

He tried to remember why his old life had seemed intolerable. Admittedly he had not felt himself to be a whole man, but at least he had been a reasonably comfortable failed man, lacking nothing but his testicles. If only he could have the comfort of his mife, his wife rather, without his wife! Whother, whether he could get along without her he doubted. Despite his new-found maleness it seemed that he had nothing, was nothing.

He marvelled that he went on making love with Gretel. Something in me lives its own life, full of appetite, he thought. Where am I while this is going on? On what map?

Why am I afraid now? he thought. When I was impotent I was secure. It isn't safe to have balls. Now I ramp like a stallion while my soul is sick with terror. Stallions surely aren't afraid, lions aren't afraid. I have a lion. I don't have a lion—a lion has me. A lion hallucinates me. To a lion appears Jachin-Boaz in the early morning. When I was impotent I was safe. What was all that nonsense about wanting my manhood, idiot that I am? Let him starve, that lion. I don't want to see him. They can go on transmitting but I won't receive.

For several days Jachin-Boaz, awaking at the usual time, went back to sleep, sulking, while in his imagination the lion grew thinner daily. Beside him every morning at half-past four Gretel woke up, waiting with closed eyes for him to go out while Jachin-Boaz went back to sleep, dreaming dreams he would not remember.

Jachin-Boaz was dreaming. With a microscope he was looking at an illuminated drop of water. In the water swam a green and spherical form of many-celled animal-algae. Thousands of tiny moving whips on its surface made it revolve its green-jewelled globe like a little world.

Jachin-Boaz increased the magnification, looked deep into one of the hundreds of cells. Closer, closer through the luminous green. Oh yes, he said. The naked figures of his father and mother copulated in the brilliant field of the lens with darkness all around them. So big and he so small. A shoulder turning away within the luminous green world in the drop of water.

The cell withdrew, grew small, receded into the green and turning world that closed up again, its whips propelling it in sparkling revolutions.

Unlike the infinitely ongoing asexual amoeba, said the lecturer, this organism has differentiated within itself male and female cells. Sexual reproduction occurs, followed by another phenomenon unknown to the amoeba: death. In the words of one naturalist, "It must die because it has had children and is no longer needed." That is why this wheel dies. The invention of the wheel is nothing compared to the invention of death, and this wheel invented death.

Jachin-Boaz increased the magnification again, again looked into the same cell. Darkness in the brilliance. His mother cried out. The lecturer, nodding in a chalk-dusted grey suit, came between him and what was happening in the darkness. *This is the wheel that invented death,* he said.

Jachin-Boaz hurled himself into the dark and shining tube of the microscope, saw the green wheel bright before him, leaped upon it, holding it to him, trying to stop its turning.

The wheel won't die, he said, biting it, tasting its wet greenness. This wheel has had children but he doesn't die. The lions die.

It seems a kind of intellectual suicide, said the lecturer, looking down on Jachin-Boaz who lay in a paper coffin, his beard aimed up at the lecturer whose beard was aiming down at him.

Now you are dead, said Jachin-Boaz to the lecturer. But the paper coffin lid came down on Jachin-Boaz. No, he said. You, not me. Turn it around. Let the little green cells die instead. It's always I who die. It was I then and it's I now. When is it my turn, when the others die?

It keeps turning but it's not your turn, said the lecturer. *Never your turn.*

My turn, said Jachin-Boaz. He was walking away from the coffin, looking back at it and noticing that it was much shorter than before. There was no father's beard sticking up. The hand that held the map was smaller, younger. My turn, my turn, he wept, smelled the lion, wept and whimpered in his sleep.

Gretel woke up, leaned on her elbow, looked at Jachin-Boaz in the dim light, looked at his bandaged arm that he flung over his face. She looked at her watch. Four o'clock. She turned on her side away from Jachin-Boaz and lay there, awake.

At half-past four Jachin-Boaz awoke, feeling tired. He did not remember his dream. He bathed, shaved, dressed, took meat for the lion, and went out.

The lion was standing across the street. Jachin-Boaz crossed to him, threw him the meat, watched him eat. With the lion-smell in his nostrils he turned and walked towards the embankment, not looking back.

When Jachin-Boaz and the lion had gone some distance down the street towards the river a police constable stepped out from behind a corner of the building where Jachin-Boaz lived. He stepped back as Gretel came out, fully dressed, with a carrier-bag in one hand.

THE LION OF BOAZ-JACHIN AND JACHIN-BOAZ

Gretel looked towards the river, then followed Jachin-Boaz and the lion. The police constable waited a few moments, then followed Gretel.

Jachin-Boaz walked along the embankment on the side away from the river. He stopped at a garden above which rose a statue of a man who had been beheaded after a theological dispute with a king. There was a bench on the pavement. Near it was a telephone kiosk. The sky was cloudy, the before-dawn light was grey, the bridges were black over the quiet river.

Jachin-Boaz turned and faced the lion. Down the street a girl with a carrier-bag stepped into a doorway. Beyond her a man's dark figure turned into a side street. There was no one else in sight.

Jachin-Boaz sat down on the bench. The lion lay down on the pavement five yards away, his eyes on Jachin-Boaz's face.

"Always the frown, like my father," said Jachin-Boaz. "How was I to be a scientist, father Lion? Science is knowing. What could I have known? Others always did the knowing, knew what was in me, what should come out of me, what was best for me. I didn't know who I was, what I wanted. I know less now, and I am afraid."

The sound of his own voice and the words he was saying became boring to Jachin-Boaz. He felt a wave of irritation flooding through him. He didn't want to say what he was saying. What did the lion want? The lion was real, could kill him, might very well do it at any moment. Jachin-Boaz felt himself disappearing into terror, felt himself coming back, went on.

"My thoughts are useless to me, and I cannot remember my dreams. I have forgotten more of my life than I remember, and with my forgetting I have lost my being. You expect something of me, father Lion. Maybe only my death. Maybe you are too late for that. Maybe I have beaten you to it. Not that my death belongs to me.

"One of my teachers said it was an intellectual suicide when I failed my examinations. But science is knowing, and how could I know anything, how make a profession of knowing? Little things, yes. Places on a map.

"When you kill yourself you kill the world, but it doesn't die. He'd had a bad heart for some time, so it couldn't have been my fault altogether. Why did he never talk to *me*? Why did he seem always to be talking to a space that I hadn't moved into? Why was he always holding up an empty suit of clothes for me to jump into? He talked to clothes I never did put on. A sleeve with no arm in it struck him down. An empty shoulder turned away from him. He closed his mouth and lay down, but he is more alive in me than I am.

"I am a coward, and you are patient with me. You are a sporting lion. You want my death to stand up like a man in me before you spring. You have contempt for anything that turns away.

"But if you kill me I shall then be more alive than ever, strong as the brazen tyre on the wheel. My son will feel me heavy and unfinished on his back, big in his mind."

Jachin-Boaz was silent for a time, then stood up. "Perhaps I too have never spoken to my son," he said, "but to an empty place where he was not. Now I talk to you, his anger. I will stand before you, look at you. If I did not look at him at least I will look at you, his rage. My rage. Can I roar like you? Can I make a big sound of whole anger?" Jachin-Boaz tried to roar, broke off in coughing.

The lion crouched, gathering himself, lashing his tail. The lion roared, and the river of lion-sound rolled beside the other river, thunderous under the broken sky.

"No!" cried Gretel, running towards the lion from behind. "No!" She had thrown away the carrier-bag, and held the carving knife she had concealed in it. She held the knife in the manner of knife-fighters, with the blade extending the line of her wrist, ready to thrust in and up.

"Get back!" shouted Jachin-Boaz. But the lion had turned at the sound of Gretel's voice. Jachin-Boaz saw the muscles bunching for the leap, threw himself on the lion's back as it sprang, his fingers locked in its mane, his face buried in the coarse rank hair.

The lion, turning his head to seize Jachin-Boaz's right arm in his jaws, landed short as Gretel jumped aside.

"Here!" shouted the constable, striking the pavement with his truncheon. "This won't do! Stop it at once!"

"Into the telephone box!" yelled Jachin-Boaz to the constable. "Get her into the telephone box!"

But Gretel flung herself at the lion, drove her knife at his throat. The blade was partly deflected by the thick mane, but it went in, and the lion let go of Jachin-Boaz's arm and swung his head around towards Gretel.

"Here!" shouted the constable. He pulled Jachin-Boaz from the lion and thrust Gretel back.

Jachin-Boaz, strong as a madman, hurled himself with arms flung wide at Gretel and the constable, slamming them against the telephone kiosk. Gretel and he together shoved the constable out of the way for long enough to open the door, then pulled him savagely inside.

"No, you don't," said the constable, his face red. He had been in family situations many times before, and more than once had had the combatants turn on him like this. Simultaneously he gripped the wrist of Gretel's knife hand and brought his knee up into Jachin-Boaz's groin.

"Imbecile!" gasped Jachin-Boaz, sinking to the floor with the pain. In a red and golden haze with black and shooting lights he felt a rage too big for his body, too strong for his voice, immense, unlimited by time, amber-eyed and taloned.

"Good God!" said the constable, staring through the glass door. "There's a lion out there!"

"Aha!" said Jachin-Boaz, exulting. "You can see him now! How do you like him! He's big, he's angry. He can say no to anybody, eh?"

The constable, jammed between Gretel and the side of the telephone box, was writhing desperately while Gretel, bloody knife in hand, glared at him wildly. "I beg your pardon, madame," he said. "I am trying to get to the telephone." He looked away from the lion, dialled his station number, looked back again.

The constable identified himself, reported his location. "What I think we need here," he said, "is the fire brigade with a pumper. Big net too. Stout one. No. Not a fire. Animal situation, actually. Yes, I should say so. With a strong cage, you know, as fast as they can. Ambulance too. Well, let's say a large carnivore. No, I'm not. All right, a tiger, if you like. How should I know? Yes, I'll be here. Goodbye."

As the constable rang off there was a screech of brakes, followed by a crash. Looking past Jachin-Boaz the constable saw two cars stopped on the road, the front of one and the rear of the other crumpled together. Both drivers remained in their cars. Jachin-Boaz and Gretel were looking beyond the cars at the pavement and the parapet along the river.

"Where is it then?" said the constable.

"Where is what?" said Jachin-Boaz.

"The lion," said the constable.

"Lions are extinct," said Jachin-Boaz.

"Don't try that on with me, mate," said the constable. "Look at your bleeding arm."

"Spiked fence," said Jachin-Boaz. "Stumbled. Fell. Drunk again."

"What about you, madame?" said the constable.

"I walk in my sleep," said Gretel. "I don't know how I got here. This is very embarrassing for me."

"You two stay here," said the constable. He opened the door of the telephone kiosk, looked all around, and stepped out. The motorists were still there, sitting in their cars with their windows rolled up. The constable went to the first car, motioned to the driver to lower the window.

"Why'd you stop?" said the constable.

"Quite extraordinary," said the driver. "Somehow my foot slipped off the accelerator and came down on the brake. I don't know how it happened."

"What did you see in front of you when you stopped?" said the constable.

"Nothing at all," said the driver.

The constable walked back to the second car. "What did you see?" he said.

"I saw the car in front of me stop so suddenly that I hadn't time to stop myself," said the driver.

"Nothing else?" said the constable.

"No, indeed," said the driver.

The constable took the names, addresses and registration numbers of both drivers, and they drove slowly away.

A polyphonic blaring was heard as a fire brigade pumper, an ambulance, a fire brigade car and a police car, all with flashing lights, arrived at high speed and slammed on their brakes. Armed men came out of the police car.

"Where's the tiger?" said the firemen and the police together.

"What tiger?" said the constable.

"I take a dim view of practical jokers, Phillips," said the police superintendent. "You called for a pumper and a stout net and an ambulance and some people from the zoo with a cage. Here they are now," he said as a van pulled up. "Now where's this large carnivore or tiger or whatever?"

"That call must have been made by this chap here impersonating me while I was unconscious," said the constable. "I was trying to break up a fight between this couple, and in the struggle my head struck the corner of the telephone box with such force that I was rendered totally unconscious for a short time."

"Did you ring up for all this then, while impersonating a police constable?" the superintendent asked Jachin-Boaz.

"I don't know," said Jachin-Boaz. "I feel confused." He was feeling faint. He had taken off his jacket and wrapped it around his arm, and it was now thoroughly soaked with blood.

"What happened to his arm?" the superintendent asked the constable.

"Spiked fence," said Jachin-Boaz.

"She had a knife," said the constable. "Best give it me now, madame," he said.

Gretel gave him the knife. There was no longer any blood on it.

"Are you putting them on a charge?" said the superintendent.

"I believe," said the constable, "that these people are in a mental state that makes them a danger to themselves and to others, and I think that we had better have them committed for observation under the Mental Health Act."

One of the men from the zoo came over to Jachin-Boaz. He was small and dark, looked from side to side constantly and seemed to be sniffing the air. "I don't suppose I could have a look at this gentleman's arm?" he said.

The police constable unwrapped the bloody jacket from Jachin-Boaz's arm, peeled away the blood-soaked torn shirt sleeve.

"Yes, indeed," said the man from the zoo to Jachin-Boaz. "Very mental. How did you come by these particular teeth-marks?"

"Spiked fence," said Jachin-Boaz.

"Knife," said the constable. "Also, she may have bitten him during the struggle."

"Regular tigress," said the zoo man smiling, showing his teeth, sniffing the air.

It was full morning now. The sky had got as light as it was going to be that day. The clouds over the river promised rain, the water ran dark and heavy under the bridges. Cars, cyclists and pedestrians were active on the embankment. The pumper, with horn blaring and light flashing, went back to the fire station. The ambulance, also flashing and blaring, followed with Jachin-Boaz, Gretel and the constable in it. The police car followed the ambulance.

The zoo van stayed where it was for a time while the little dark man walked all around the telephone kiosk, back and forth before the statue of the man who had lost his head for some notion of truth, and up and down the pavement along the embankment. He found nothing.

25

The world seemed to be owned by a freemasonry of petrol stations, monster tanks and towers and abstract structures of no human agency or purpose. Wires hummed aloft, giant steel legs stalked motionless on frightened landscapes past haystacks, mute blind barns, wagons rotting by dung-hills on tracks to isolation where brown dwellings shrugged up from the earth. We knew it long ago, said huts with grass on the roofs. Hills went up and down, cows grazed on silence, goats stared with eyes like oracle stones. Cryptic names and symbols in strong raw colours flashed signals one to the other across the roofs and haystacks, across the stone and lumber of towns and cities. Flesh and blood spoke ineffectually in little voices of breath, feet hurried, plodded, pedalled. Faces passed on the road asked unanswerable questions. You! exclaimed the faces. Us!

The petrol stations, owning the world, called to their brother monsters. Distant towers flashed lights. The petrol stations kept up their pretence, fuelled cars and lorries, maintained the fiction of roads for humans. Vast pipes slid effortlessly over miles of world. Huge valves regulated flow. Lights flashed at sea. Music played in aeroplanes. Never did the music name the pipes and petrol stations, the great steel stalking that laughed with striding legs. God is with us, said the valves and towers. With us, said the stones. Cars moved on roads.

Boaz-Jachin felt the miles spinning out behind him. Mina's leg was warm against his. Her leg was named Mina like all the rest of her now. Her someoneness had established itself in him since the nights in her stateroom.

Words came to his mind unbidden, unresisted. They were there like a smell that carries memory or like a change in the temperature of the air: the father must live so that the father can die. Boaz-Jachin groaned inwardly. Tiresome reversals somersaulting in his brain. Found and lost, always and never, everything and nothing. Where had these new words come from? What was wanted of him? What had he to do with such things?

No longer subtle as air, but now like sudden men in armour, implacable, cold with the night wind of a road hard ridden, barbarous with savage unknown meaning useless to resist: the father must live so that the father can die. Quickly! What quickly? Hot waves of irritation leaped in Boaz-Jachin like flames. He sweated, ignorant and anxious.

"Petrol stations own the world," said Mina. "Tanks and towers signal one to the other in strong raw colours. Goats have eyes like oracle stones."

"That's very well observed," said her father. "They do. Urim and Thummim."

Stop telling me everything, thought Boaz-Jachin. Stop presenting the world. I'll see the goats and the petrol stations or I won't. Let them be whatever they'll be to me.

"Isn't anybody but me hungry?" said Mina's mother.

"There's a book you have to read," said Mina to Boaz-Jachin. "It's a poet's notebook."

No, I don't have to read it, he thought. Quickly. What quickly? A breathless sense of hurry rose in him like a whirlwind.

"That part about the uncle's death or the grandfather's death, how it was so strong in him and took so long," said the father. "Unforgettable."

"I know," said Mina. "And the man who walked funny that he followed in the street."

"I'm *starving*," said the mother.

"Take a look at the guide," said the father. "Where are we on the map?"

"You know how I am with maps," said the mother. "It takes me a long time." She unfolded the map clumsily.

"Look," said the father, pointing with his finger on the map. "We're over here somewhere, heading north."

"Keep your eyes on the road," said the mother. "And I wish you'd stop driving so fast. We passed a place about five miles back that looked good, and it was gone before I could tell you to slow down."

"There," said Mina.

"What?" said the father.

"It had an orange tree in a red clay courtyard," said Mina. "There were white doves."

"I can turn round," said the father.

"Never mind," said Mina. "I'm not even sure it was a restaurant."

"Where are we?" said the father. "Have you found us on the map yet?"

"You make me so nervous when I have to look at a map that my hands shake," said the mother.

The rented car hummed to itself. Whatever happens is not my fault, said the car. From ahead the miles surged towards them in numberless sharp-focused grains of road that rolled beneath the wheels and spun out behind. Boaz-Jachin felt stifled in the car with Mina and her parents. He drew deep breaths, expelled them slowly. He wished that he had not accepted their offer of a lift. He wished that he had a guitar again and were travelling alone and more slowly. But he felt compelled to hurry. Emptiness leaped forward in him, rushing towards something.

"*That* road!" said the mother. "There! About five miles down there's an old inn, five forks and spoons in the guide. We've passed it now. You simply *refuse* to slow down."

The father swung the car around in a U-turn, sideswiped a van just then overtaking him, slewed off the road, up a bank, and crashed into a tree. Broken headlights tinkled. Steam drifted from the smashed radiator. All was silent for a moment. Not *my* fault, said the car.

It's her fault, thought the father.

It's his fault, thought the mother.

It's both their faults, thought Mina.

It's the kind of thing that can be expected from this family, thought Boaz-Jachin. I'll be lucky if I get away from them with my life.

The petrol stations, the valves and towers, the giant steel legs that strode across the landscape said nothing.

Everyone looked at everyone else. No one seemed injured.

"My God," said the mother.

"Right," said the father. "Very good. We can walk to the goddam famous old five-fork-and-spoon inn."

"My God," said the mother. "My neck."

"What's the matter with your neck?" said the father.

"I don't know," said the mother. "It feels all right now, but sometimes you don't get the full effects of backlash until months later."

"But it feels all right now," said the father.

"I don't know," said the mother.

"You could have killed us all, the two of you," said Mina.

The father got out of the car to talk to the driver of the van. The van had a dent in the side and several long scrapes. "I'm sorry," he said. "That was my fault. I didn't see you coming."

The van driver shook his head. He was a large man with a gentle face and a drooping moustache. "These things happen," he said in his own language. "You're from another country, not used to these roads."

"The fault is mine," said the father in the same language. "I do not look, I do not see. I regret."

"Now we have to fill in forms with details of the accident," said the van driver. He and the father exchanged licences, insurance cards, made notes.

"I knew something was going to happen," said Mina to Boaz-Jachin. "I could *feel* it. If my mother and father were sitting in a perfectly stationary box with no wheels and no motor they could make it crash by psychokinesis."

The car could no longer be driven. The van driver took them and their luggage to a petrol station. Arrangements were made for towing away the car and renting a new one.

"We might as well go to the five-fork-and-spoon place now," said the father. The van driver offered to take them there, and everybody got into the van but Boaz-Jachin.

"You're invited, you know," said the father. "And we'll be going on to the channel port as soon as we get another car." Please, said the father's eyes, don't leave us yet. Love my daughter for a while. Let her be beautiful for you.

"Thank you very much," said Boaz-Jachin. "You've been very generous, but now I want to travel alone again for a while."

Stay, said the mother's eyes. She can't have her father but she can have you.

Boaz-Jachin kissed Mina goodbye, shook hands with her father and mother while looking away from their eyes. Mina wrote her home address on a piece of paper, tucked it into Boaz-Jachin's pocket. He walked down the road away from the petrol station.

"How do you manage to do it?" he heard Mina ask her parents just before the van started up. "How do the two of you make everything not be there all of a sudden?"

26

Jachin-Boaz was taken to the same hospital where his wounds had been dressed before. The same doctor saw him and led him away from the nurse at the admissions desk, beckoning to the police constable to follow. Gretel stayed in the waiting room with another constable.

"This is no surprise to me at all," said the doctor. "I knew it would be a matter for the police sooner or later. I suppose that spiked fence has been after you again, has it?"

"Yes," said Jachin-Boaz.

"Very well, then," said the doctor. "I'm going to be blunt with you, my good man. If you expect to stay in this country you'll jolly well have to learn our ways. This mucking about with large carnivores won't do. Those animals at the zoo are laid on for the enjoyment of the general public, and not for the deviant religious practices of the foreign element." He turned to the police constable. "This is the second time he's come in this way, you know."

The police constable did not want to be drawn into a discussion of large carnivores. "There's a young lady with him," he said.

"Of course," said the doctor. " 'Look for the woman,' eh? Not to put too fine a point on it, there'll be sex at the bottom of this sort of thing nine times out of ten." He snipped off the remnants of Jachin-Boaz's shirt sleeve and swabbed the wounds with antiseptic. "Burns a bit, eh?" he said as Jachin-Boaz went pale. "You've got some jolly deep bites in you this time, mate. I don't mind telling you I consider this a shameful abuse of the National Health Service. I hope there's going to be an inquiry," he said to the police constable as he medicated and bandaged the wounds.

"Well, we're having him committed for observation of course," said the constable.

"Use up a little more of the state's money, eh?" said the doctor. "Everything laid on. Here's this fellow with his cult and his women and his practices . . . " He paused, unbuttoned Jachin-Boaz's shirt, looked for an amulet, found none, and went on, "And you fetch him in, with a motorcycle escort I shouldn't doubt, and I patch him up, and now he'll have a free holiday in the loony bin. Probably make a few converts there, too. Where'd you find him, and what was going on at the time?"

"On the embankment," said the constable. "The lady had a knife." He met the doctor's eye for a fraction of a second, looked away, encountered Jachin-Boaz's face, looked away again.

"You're not having me on now, are you, old boy?" said the doctor. "You're not trying to tell me that the lady's knife produces large-carnivore teeth-marks, upper and lower jaws?"

"As you say, this whole thing's got to be looked into," said the constable. "If you've finished with him now we'd better be going."

"Quite," said the doctor. "You don't mind giving me your name and number, do you? I'd like to ring up some time just to find out what develops."

"Not at all," said the constable. He wrote down his name and number, gave them to the doctor, and took Jachin-Boaz and Gretel to the police station.

At the police station another doctor appeared with a folder in his hand. Gretel waited with the constable while he took Jachin-Boaz into a little office. "Well, old man," said the doctor, looking at Jachin-Boaz's bandages, "been having a little domestic trouble?"

"No," said Jachin-Boaz.

"What about foreign trouble then?" said the doctor. "Who's Comrade Lyon?"

"Comrade Lion?" said Jachin-Boaz.

"That's right," said the doctor. "A lady who lives on your street reported that she was awakened quite early one morning by your shouting. You were having an argument with Comrade Lyon. He was gone by the time she got to the window, but she's described you accurately. What about that?"

"I don't know," said Jachin-Boaz.

"Perhaps it was someone else having the argument?"

"I don't know."

"Hadn't you made a suicide attempt not long before that?"

"Suicide attempt," Jachin-Boaz repeated. His wounds were very painful, he was very tired, and he wanted more than anything else to lie down and go to sleep.

"The young couple who saw it described to the police a man very like you," said the doctor. "They were quite concerned. Actually we ought to have had a talk with you then. Did Comrade Lyon have anything to do with that?"

"There's no Comrade Lion," said Jachin-Boaz.

"Then whom were you shouting at?"

"I don't know."

"And what did this unknown person or persons say to you?"

"I don't know," said Jachin-Boaz. By now the situation felt familiar. The doctor, like the father long ago, was holding up an empty suit of clothes for him to jump into. Jachin-Boaz was too tired not to jump. "This is what he said," he told the doctor, and tried to roar. It was not the sound of real anger because he felt no real anger, only a sad and defeated fretfulness, defeated in the foreknowledge that his anger was of no consequence. His feeble roar ended in a fit of coughing. He wiped his eyes, found that he was crying.

"Right," said the doctor. "Very good." He signed the commitment order. Then Jachin-Boaz was taken outside to wait with the constable while Gretel went into the office with the doctor.

"What is your relationship to this man?" said the doctor.

"Close."

"And your status is what exactly?"

"Working-class. I'm an assistant in a bookshop."

"Marital status, I mean."

"I haven't any. I'm a spinster."

"Do you and this man live together?"

"Yes."

"Cohabitant," said the doctor, writing the word as he spoke. "And what precisely were you doing with the knife?"

"I was co-walking with it."

"Did you in fact attack this man with the knife?"

"No."

"Please describe what took place."

"I can't."

"Had he been running around with some other woman?"

Gretel stared at him levelly. Her manner of looking at the doctor was like the way she had held the knife that morning. She belonged to a man who had fought with a lion and she carried herself accordingly. The doctor reminded himself that he was the doctor, but felt himself to be less impressive than he would like to be.

"You see two foreigners and immediately the picture is simple for you," said Gretel. "Women instead of ladies. Sex, passion, fighting in the street. Hot-blooded foreigners. Bloody cheek!"

The doctor coughed, fleetingly imagined himself involved with Gretel in sex, passion, and fighting in the street. "Then perhaps you'll tell me what the situation is," he said with a red face.

"I'm not going to tell you anything at all," said Gretel, "and I've no idea what you want with me."

The doctor reminded himself again that he was the doctor. "You will allow, madame," he said stiffly, "that going about with a knife is rather a dodgy business: one never knows who's going to be injured. I think it might be just as well for you to have some peace and quiet for a few days and think this whole thing over calmly." He signed the commitment order.

While they waited for the van that would take them to the hospital Jachin-Boaz and Gretel sat down on a bench, and the police constable tactfully walked a few steps away.

Jachin-Boaz sat with tears running down his face. He looked at Gretel, looked away again. His head began to ache. This was somehow her fault. If she hadn't attacked the lion . . . No. Before that even. Would the lion have appeared to him if he had not . . . No. And of course the lion was in any case his . . . what?

The map. Not here. At home, on the desk. In another desk, in the shop where he had once been Jachin-Boaz the map-seller, was a notebook. Were there recent notes in it that were not incorporated in the master-map? The map was on the desk. Were the windows closed? The desk was near the window, and if it rained . . . And who would feed the lion?

His mind raced on but he was too tired to pay attention to it any longer. He sat on the bench with both arms bandaged and tears running down his face. Gretel leaned against him, saying nothing.

The police constable indicated that the van was at the door, and they got into it. Another constable joined them, and the two constables sat across from Jachin-Boaz and Gretel as the van moved away through the daytime streets. Around them flowed the traffic of the ordinary day. Cars and lorries, vans and buses herded together. People on motorcycles and bicycles threaded the narrow spaces between. People walked the pavements, passed in and out of shops, ascended and descended the stairs of underground stations. Aeroplanes flew calmly overhead. Jachin-Boaz sat up straight, craned his neck once to look through the small rear window. A greengrocer in overalls stood under an awning filling a brown paper bag with oranges.

The van stopped, the doors opened. Green shrubbery and lawns appeared around a handsome old red brick building with a white cupola and a gilt weathercock.

Jachin-Boaz and Gretel came out of the van, blinked in the sunlight, walked into the hospital, and were in turn admitted, undressed, examined, drugged, and taken to a men's ward and a women's ward that had the names of trees. In the corridors a smell of cooking wandered like a minstrel of defeat.

Jachin-Boaz, wearing pyjamas and a robe, lay down on his bed. The walls were cream-coloured, the curtains were dark red with yellow-and-blue flowers. There was a long line of beds down each side of the room and french windows that opened on the lawn. The sunlight slanted gently down the walls, not with the harshness of the streets outside. Sunday sunlight. Give up and I'll go easy with you, said the sunlight. Jachin-Boaz fell asleep.

27

Boats sink under me, thought Boaz-Jachin. Cars get smashed. At a farm he leaned against a fence and looked into the eyes of a goat. "What?" he asked the goat. "Give Urim or give Thummim." The goat turned away. Goats turn away, thought Boaz-Jachin. The father must live so that the father can die. It became a tune that his mind sang, hurrying him on.

Why am I hurrying? he thought. I've got nothing to do with his living or dying. But hurry was in him. He had no rucksack, no guitar, nothing to carry now. His passport had been in his pocket when the *Swallow* sank. That and the money he had earned on the cruise ship, the new map he had drawn, a toothbrush and the clothes he wore were all he had now. He walked down the road with long strides, going fast, signalling for a ride as he went. Who now? he wondered. Cars, vans, lorries, motorcycles whined, roared, hummed and puttered past.

The van that had taken Mina and her parents to the inn pulled up beside him. The large gentle face of the driver looked out of the window, spoke as a question the name of a channel port. Boaz-Jachin repeated the name, said, "Yes." The driver opened the door and he got in.

In his own language the driver said, "I don't suppose you speak my language."

Boaz-Jachin smiled, lifted his shoulders, shook his head. "I don't speak your language," he said in English.

"That's what I thought," said the driver, understanding the gesture rather than the words. He nodded, sighed, and settled down to his driving. Ahead of them the numberless grains of the road flowed into sharp focus, rolled beneath the wheels, spun out behind.

"All the same," said the driver, "I feel like talking."

"I know what you mean," said Boaz-Jachin, understanding the voice but not the words. Now he spoke not English but his own language, and his voice was more subtly inflected. "I feel like talking too."

"You too," said the driver. "So we'll talk. It'll be just as good as many of the conversations I've had with people who spoke the same language. After all, when you come right down to it, how many people speak the same language even when they speak the same language?"

"After all," said Boaz-Jachin, "it won't be the first time I've spoken to someone who couldn't understand what I was saying. And when you come right down to it, how many people speak the same language even when they speak the same language?"

They looked at each other, shrugged, raised their eyebrows.

"That's how it is," said the driver.

"That's how it is," said Boaz-Jachin.

"Empty space," said the driver. "There's a funny thing to think about. The back of the van is full of empty space. I brought it from my town. But I've opened the doors several times since I left. So is it still empty space from my town or is it now several different new empty spaces? This is the sort of thing one thinks about sometimes. If the back of the van were full of chairs the question wouldn't arise. One assumes that the space between the chairs remains the same all through the trip. Empty space, however, is something else."

Boaz-Jachin nodded, understanding not a word. But the driver's voice, large and gentle like the rest of him, was agreeable to him. He felt very conversational with him.

"I offered the drawings," he said, surprised to hear himself saying it but pleased with what he was saying. "I offered the drawings. I burned the drawings. Something went out of me, leaving an empty space in me. Sometimes I feel myself hurrying towards something up ahead. What? I'm a rushing empty space. The father must live so that the father can die. Are

THE LION OF BOAZ-JACHIN AND JACHIN-BOAZ

you a father? Certainly you're a son. Every man who is alive is a son. Dead men as well are sons. Dead fathers too are sons. No end to it."

"You're young," said the driver. "Your whole life is ahead of you. Probably you don't think about such things. Did I when I was your age? I can't remember. Yet I suppose there must be empty space in you. What will you put into it?"

"The space wasn't always empty," said Boaz-Jachin. "Only after the offering of the drawings. Now I'm hurrying. To what? Why? I don't know. Lion. I haven't said that aloud very often, that word, that name. Lion. Lion, lion, lion. What? Where?" He leaned forward, leaning into the forward speed of the van. "That he took the master-map he'd promised to me, what's that to me? I don't need it. Maps." From his pocket he took the new one he'd sketched on the cruise ship, opened the window, started to throw it away, put it back in his pocket, closed the window. "I'll keep it the way people keep diaries, but I don't need maps for finding anything." He ground his teeth, wanted to roar, wanted to do violence to something.

"Years and years," said Boaz-Jachin. "My eyes only as high as the edge of the table. 'Let me help,' I said. 'Let me work on a little corner.' No. Nothing. He wouldn't let me. I couldn't make clean beautiful lines. Always he had to do the whole thing. He looked at me but he spoke to a place where I wasn't. 'You will not follow me into the shop,' he said. 'For you there is the whole world outside.' Fine. Good. Go into the wide world. Go away. I wasn't good enough to work with him. So now *he* goes into the wide world. The shop for him and the world for him. For me nothing." He ground his teeth again. "I have to . . . What? What do I have to do? I have to tell him . . . What? What do I have to tell him? Benjamin's father wrote *forgive*. Forgive whom what? What is it to forgive? Who has forgiveness to give? He held up a suit of clothes for me to jump into: the wanderer. Here's your map. Then he ran away with the map. I jumped into the wandering clothes. Is he happy now?" Tears streamed down Boaz-Jachin's cheeks.

"Name of God," said the driver. "What an outburst! After all that surely there must be empty space inside you. My word. There's something about a road. One thinks, one talks. The van eats up the miles, the soul eats up the miles. At the port I'm picking up some wooden crates. In the crates is the machinery for a new press for the local newspaper. The editor's wife ran off with a salesman. So he needs new machinery. That's reasonable. With his new machinery he will print the news. This one is born, that one died, so-and-so is opening a bakery. Maybe even the news that he is married again. All of this comes out of what is now an empty space. There are depths in this. It's a lot to think about. From an empty space the future. If there's no empty space where can one put the future? It all figures if you take the time to think it out. It's a pleasure talking with you. It's doing me a lot of good."

Boaz-Jachin wiped his eyes, blew his nose. "It's a pleasure talking with you," he said. "It's doing me a lot of good."

28

The man in the bed next to Jachin-Boaz was sitting up crosslegged, writing on a foolscap pad a letter to the editor of the city's leading newspaper. *"With our Sanitation Department on the job regularly cleaning the streets,"* he wrote, *"is it not astonishing that so far no measures have been taken towards resolving the problem of image accumulation? The private citizen, however diligently he may divest his home of mirrors and however carefully he may cover windows and polished tables, has daily to encounter public mirrors, shop windows, and innumerable reflecting surfaces from which decades and scores of years of faces, his own and those of strangers, peer out impertinently to mock him.*

"As a law-abidding citizen and ratepayer . . . " He stopped writing. He had been aware of figures moving past his bed towards the french windows, and now he looked up. Three patients were standing at the windows looking out at the lawn. Two male nurses who had been sitting in chairs stood up, looked out, and sat down again.

The letter writer got out of bed and walked over to the group at the window, sensing at once that they shared a secret from which the nurses were excluded. He too looked out for a time at the lawn that was green and golden in the afternoon sunlight. Then he came back and sat down on the edge of his bed, looking at the sleeping Jachin-Boaz. He stared at him fixedly, and after half an hour Jachin-Boaz opened his eyes.

"Is it yours?" said the letter writer. "It must be—you're the only new arrival." He had a small aristocratic moustache and goatee. His eyes were pale blue and very sharp. "What do you feed it?"

Jachin-Boaz smiled and lifted his eyebrows interrogatively. The powerful tranquillizing-drug dose had left him sluggish, and the question did not immediately make itself clear to him.

"The lion," said the letter writer, and saw Jachin-Boaz look somewhat more alert. "It *is* your lion, isn't it? It seems to have arrived with you."

"It's here?" said Jachin-Boaz.

"Walking about on the lawn," said the letter writer.

"Everybody sees it?" said Jachin-Boaz.

"Only a few of us. Those who did and were on the lawn when it appeared came inside directly. Some of the staff and a number of pseudonuts are still outside with it, quite blind to its existence. I must say it seems a well-behaved animal. It isn't bothering anyone."

"I don't think it takes notice of everybody," said Jachin-Boaz.

"Naturally not. Who does?" said the letter writer. "As I was saying, what do you feed it?"

Jachin-Boaz became wary and sly. Hold on to everything you have, said the sunlight slanting down the wall. He didn't want anyone else to know what or how much his lion ate. "How do you know it eats?" he said.

The letter writer's face flushed. He looked as if he had been struck. "I'm so sorry," he said. "I beg your pardon."

In a flash Jachin-Boaz understood that it was as if one duke who owned a rare and expensive motorcar had been rude to another duke who happened not to own such a car. He blushed. "Forgive me," he said. "He should have six or seven pounds of meat a day, six days a week. I've been feeding him beefsteak, but not regularly."

"Something of a supply problem," said the letter writer cosily. "I don't suppose that he could accustom himself to shepherd's pie and toad-in-the-hole? Meat is a bit thin on the ground here."

"I don't know," said Jachin-Boaz. "Actually, it may even be possible that he can do without food altogether. He's real enough, but not in the ordinary way."

"Quite," said the letter writer stiffly, as between dukes to whom such things need not be explained.

Jachin-Boaz fell silent. He did not want to see the lion just now, and he began to think about the other people who could see it. Already this other man wanted to feed it. Jachin-Boaz began to get a headache. "Why can they see it, the others?" he said, speaking to himself but saying the words aloud.

"Sorry about that, old man," said the letter writer. "But you've got to expect that sort of thing here. After all, why have they put us in the fun house? The straight people agree that some things are not allowed to be possible, and they govern their perceptions accordingly. Very strong, the straight people. We're not so strong as they. Things not allowed to be possible jump on us, beasts and demons, because we don't know how to keep them out.

"Others here can see my faces and they can see your lion, even though you may want to hug it to yourself like a teddy bear. If your lion weren't possible you'd be happy to share the impossibility. But people get very possessive about possibilities, even dangerous ones. Victims become proprietors. You may have to grow up a little. Perhaps you'll even have to let go of your lion one day."

"And your faces?" said Jachin-Boaz.

"They accumulate faster than they can be taken away," said the letter writer smugly. "There'll always be more."

"Lovely," said the man who had just returned to the bed on the other side. Empty-handed and in bathrobe and pyjamas, he appeared to be fully and impeccably dressed and carrying a tightly furled umbrella and a respectable newspaper. "Lovely," he continued. "Lovely wife, children, home, weather, central heating, career, garden, shoelaces, buttons and dentistry. All modern conveniences, or nearest offer. Lovely bank lessons, music account, lovely miles to the gallon. Lovely "O" Levels, "A" Levels, eye levels, level eyes. Lovely level eyes she has and sees through everything but."

"But what?" said Jachin-Boaz.

"That's what I mean," said the tightly furled man. "The butness of everything. I don't go home any more. Goodbye, little yellow bird. That's the cracks of it, sweetheart."

"Crux," said Jachin-Boaz.

"Show me a crux and I'll show you the cracks," said the tightly furled man. "You're not talking to squares now, darling. Don't try to slide by on crossword puzzles and ninety-nine-year leases. The blank spaces are bigger than ziggurats here, and it's a long, long climb. Deeper than a well."

"Rounder than a wheel?" said Jachin-Boaz.

"You're forcing it, poppet," said the tightly furled man. "Just let it happen."

"Don't be a snob," said Jachin-Boaz.

"Look who's talking," said the tightly furled man. "Him with his lions and his traveller's cheques and his cameras. Obesity is the mother of distension. A bitch in time shaved mine. Take the bleeding castles apart and ship them home stone by stone for all I care. Piss off, you and your lion both. Tourists."

"There's no need to take that tone," said Jachin-Boaz.

The tightly furled man began to cry. Kneeling on the bed, he bent forward, burying his head in his arms, thrusting out his bottom. "I didn't mean it," he said. "Let me pet the lion. He can eat my dinner every day."

Jachin-Boaz turned away, lay back on his bed with his arms behind his head and stared straight up at the ceiling, attempting to find silence and privacy in the space over him that was presumably as wide as his bed, as high as the room, and his personal domain. The sunlight said, Once you begin to doubt you will lose everything. Begin now. "No," said Jachin-Boaz to the curtains. You will perish, said the red, said the yellow-and-blue flowers. We abide. Many have come and gone here, said the smell of cooking. All have been defeated.

Jachin-Boaz became aware that someone with mental-hospital-doctor feet had arrived at his bed. He had sometimes heard clocks whose tick-tocks became words. When the doctor spoke, his words became tick-tocks unless Jachin-Boaz listened very hard.

"How are we tick-tock today?" said the doctor. "Tick-tock?"

"Very tock, thank you," said Jachin-Boaz.

"Tick," said the doctor. "Ticks will tock themselves out, I have no doubt."

"I tick so," said Jachin-Boaz.

"Tick all right last tock?"

"Very tock," said Jachin-Boaz. "No dreams that I can remember forgetting."

"That's the ticket," said the doctor. "Tock it tick."

"Cheers," said Jachin-Boaz, making an upward gesture with two fingers.

"You do it the other way for victory," said the doctor.

"When I see a victory I'll do it that way," said Jachin-Boaz.

The doctor's feet went away, and the doctor went with them. Civilian feet appeared. Familiar shoes.

"How are you feeling?" said the owner of the bookshop. "Are you all right?"

"Not so bad, thank you," said Jachin-Boaz. "It's kind of you to come."

"How come you're here?" said the bookshop owner. "You seem the same as you've always been. Was it the dog-food-eating hallucination?"

"Something like that," said Jachin-Boaz. "Unfortunately a police constable saw it too."

"Ah," said the bookshop owner. "It's always best to keep that sort of thing to yourself, you know."

"I should like to have kept it to myself," said Jachin-Boaz.

"Things'll sort themselves out," said the bookshop owner. "The rest will do you good and you'll come back to work refreshed."

"You don't have any reservations about taking me back?" said Jachin-Boaz.

"Why should I? You sell more books than any other assistant I've ever had. Anybody can come unstuck once in a while."

"Thank you."

"Not at all. Oh, there was an advert in the trade weekly. Letter for you at a box number. Here it is."

"A letter for me," said Jachin-Boaz. He opened the envelope. In it was another envelope, postmarked at his town, his town where he had been Jachin-Boaz the map-seller. "Thank you," he said, and put the letter on his bedside table.

"And here's some fruit," said the bookshop owner, "and a couple of paperbacks."

"Thank you," said Jachin-Boaz. He took an orange from the bag, held it in his hand. The paperbacks were two collections of supernatural and horror stories.

"Escape literature," said the bookshop owner.

"Escape," said Jachin-Boaz.

"I'll stop in again," said the bookshop owner. "Get well soon."

"Yes," said Jachin-Boaz. "Thank you."

29

Only you, said the black water rushing past the ferry in the night.

"Only I what, for God's sake!" said Boaz-Jachin. He saw no one near him, and spoke aloud. He leaned over the rail, smelled the blackness of the sea and cursed the water. "Every fucking thing talks to me," he said. "Leave me alone for a while. I'll talk to you some other time. I can't be rushed all the time." He walked aft to the stern, saw flights of white gulls rising and falling in eerie silence above the wake. Out of the darkness into the light. Out of the light into the darkness. Boaz-Jachin shook his fist at the gulls. "I don't even know if he's there!" he said. "I don't even know if I'm looking for him in the right place."

You know, said the white wings silently rising and falling. Don't tell us you don't know.

"That's what I'm telling you," said Boaz-Jachin leaning out over the rail. "I *don't* know." He saw no one on the afterdeck, and he began to talk more loudly, to shout into the darkness and the wake. "I don't know! I don't know!" Two gulls slanted towards each other like eyebrows, became for a moment a pale frown following the boat. Boaz-Jachin put one foot on the bottom rail and leaned farther out, staring at the darkness where the white wings had crossed and separated.

He felt a hand gripping his belt from behind. He turned, and was face to face with a woman. His turning had brought her arm halfway around him and their faces close together. She did not let go of his belt.

"What's the matter?" said Boaz-Jachin.

"Come away from the rail," she said, still holding his belt. Her voice was one that he had heard before. They moved towards the lighted windows of the lounge, and he saw her face clearly.

"You!" he said.

"You know me?"

"You gave me a ride. Months ago it was, on the other side, on the road to the port. You had a red car with a tape machine playing music. You didn't like the way I looked at you."

She let go of his belt. Under his shirt his flesh burned where her arm had been around him.

"I didn't recognize you," she said.

"Why did you grab me by the belt?"

"It made me nervous to see you leaning out over the rail that way and shouting into the dark."

"You thought I was going to jump overboard?"

"It made me nervous, that's all. You look older."

"You look kinder."

She smiled, took his arm, walked with him along the deck past the lighted windows. Her breast against his arm made it feel hot.

"*Did* you think I was going to jump overboard?" said Boaz-Jachin.

"I have a son about your age," she said.

"Where is he?"

"I don't know. I never hear from him."

"Where's your husband?"

"With a new wife."

They walked the deck all the way around the boat, then around again. Hearing her say that her husband was with a new wife was not the same to Boaz-Jachin as the word *divorcée* that had been in his mind that day on the road.

"You've changed," she said. "You're less of a boy."

"More of a man?"

"More of a person. More of a man."

They drank cognac in the bar. In a corridor a group of students with back packs sang while one of them played a guitar. Honey, let me be your salty dog, went the song.

When the boat docked they drove off in the little red car. "Purpose of your visit?" said the customs officer as he looked at Boaz-Jachin's passport.

"Holiday," said Boaz-Jachin. The customs officer looked at his face and his black hair, then at the blonde woman. He stamped the passport, handed it back.

It was raining, drumming on the canvas top. Numberless splashes leaped up from the road to meet the rain coming down. Red tail-lights blurred ahead of them. Yes, no, yes, no, said the windscreen wipers. The woman put a cassette in the machine. Where the morning sees the shadows of the orange grove there was nothing twenty years ago, sang the tape in the language of Boaz-Jachin's country. Where the dry wind sowed the desert we brought water, planted seedlings, now the oranges grow. A woman's voice, harsh and full of glaring sunlight.

Benjamin, thought Boaz-Jachin. Forgive. "You can buy that on a cassette?" he said.

"Sure," she said.

Boaz-Jachin shook his head. Why not thought cassettes too? Any kind. What an invention. A slot in the head and you just put in the cassette for the mood you wanted. Lion. Yes, I know, thought Boaz-Jachin. You're in my mind. I'm in your mind.

"Oranges," said the woman. "Oranges in the desert." She looked straight ahead into the darkness and the red taillights and drove on through the rain. For an hour they said nothing.

She turned off the main road, drove two or three miles to a half-timbered cottage with a thatched roof. Boaz-Jachin looked at her.

"Yes," she said. "Houses. Houses I have. Three of them in different countries." She looked at his face. "Last time in the car you were thinking of a hotel, weren't you?"

Boaz-Jachin blushed.

She lit lamps, took covers off the furniture in the living room, went into the kitchen to make coffee. Boaz-Jachin took kindling from a basket, coal from a scuttle, started a fire in the fireplace. The books on the shelves came and went in the firelight, red, brown, orange, all their pages quiet. Thin gleams of gold showed in the insets of picture frames. Boaz-Jachin smelled coffee, looked at the couch, looked away, looked at the fire, sat in a chair, sighed.

They drank coffee. She smoked cigarettes. The silence sat down with them like an invisible creature with its finger to its lips. They looked at the fire. The silence looked at the fire. The fire seethed and whispered. They were both sitting on the floor, on an oriental carpet. Boaz-Jachin looked at the pattern, the asymmetry of the endings of rows and the border. He covered the asymmetry between them by moving close to her. He kissed her, feeling as if he might be struck dead by lightning. She unbuttoned his shirt.

When they were both naked her body was surprising. It was as if not being allowed to be a wife had kept her flesh firm and young. Boaz-Jachin was staggered by the unbelievable reality of what was happening. Again, said the backs of the books, the golden gleams in the picture frames.

My God, thought Boaz-Jachin, and led her to the couch. She turned and hit him in the jaw. She was strong, and it was not a woman's blow. She pivoted athletically, like a boxer, and hit him with her feet planted solidly and all of her weight behind her fist. Boaz-Jachin saw shooting coloured lights, then everything went black for a moment as he flew across the room and fetched up in an armchair. He was speechless.

He stood up shakily. Naked she came towards him and hit him in the stomach. All the breath went out of him as she brought up her knee. Blackness and coloured lights again, pain and nausea. Boaz-Jachin, rolling on the floor, caught her ankle as she tried to heel-kick him. He pulled, and she came down hard with a thump and a little scream. He crawled over to her on his hands and knees, struck her hard across the face with a backhanded blow. She rolled over on to her side, drew up her knees and lay there crying while her nose bled.

Boaz-Jachin lay beside her until the pain and nausea went away. Then he got up, stirred her with his foot, helped her up, led her to the couch, mounted her as one who had arrived with chariots and spears, and took his pleasure.

"You," she said into his ear. "Oranges in the desert."

In the morning there was sunlight. He felt deathless, invincible, the initiate of mysteries, blessed.

30

It would be better for me not to open this letter, thought Jachin-Boaz as he opened the letter. Fading, fading, said the afternoon sunlight slanting down the wall, slanting on the red curtains, on the yellow, on the blue of the flowers. See how tactfully I die! said the sunlight. Twilight follows. Fade with me.

Jachin-Boaz began to read. In the next bed the letter writer was hard at work. *Violet's face, for instance,* he wrote. *Is there, in all justice, any necessity for that? She married the young lieutenant to whom I'd introduced her. Everyone said the baby looked exactly like him. Yet only this morning there was Violet's face in a spoon. Not a silver spoon either. Not even a clean spoon, mind you.*

On the other side the tightly furled man was looking at a magazine in which girls in black suspender belts and stockings achieved difficult juxtapositions. He was quietly singing *Oft in the Stilly Night* in a high falsetto.

The letter writer looked up. The tightly furled man put down his magazine, left off singing. Jachin-Boaz had put the letter in the drawer of his bedside table, flung himself back on his bed, and lay looking up at the ceiling in a silence that filled the air with waves of terror. The two men on either side felt as if they had been fused with the sounding metal of some monstrous bell that was rhythmically annihilating them.

"Stop clanging, can't you?" said the tightly furled man. "It's driving the very marrow out of my bones." He doubled up in his bed and covered his ears.

"Really," said the letter writer to Jachin-Boaz, "I think you might have the civility not to indulge in effects like that. I can hear mirrors shattering for miles around. Do make an effort, won't you?"

"I'm sorry," said Jachin-Boaz. "I didn't know that I was doing anything." Bad heart, she said. His father had died of a bad heart and he had a bad heart too. He *had* had twinges now and then, and his doctor had pointed out that he was a cardiac type and would do well to be careful. Suddenly he felt his heart clearly defined in his body, totally vulnerable and waiting for the inevitable. Angina pectoris. Had the doctor said anything about that? He'd looked it up once. Something associated with apprehension or fear of impending death, said the dictionary. He must remember not to be apprehensive or fearful of impending death. He closed his eyes, and in his mind he saw the map of his body with the organs, nerves and circulatory system illuminated in vivid colour. The heart pumped, drove the blood through the branching veins and arteries. Around went the blood on the animated map, and around again. It seemed miraculous that the heart kept pumping. How had it continued twenty-four hours a day for forty-seven years? It could never stop for a rest. When it stopped that was the end of everything. No more world. Only a few years left, suddenly they will all be gone, the last moment will be now. Intolerable! Father died at fifty-two. I'm forty-seven. Five more years? Less, perhaps.

You will want to come back to me.

Yes, I do want to come back. Why did I want to go away? What was so bad? Certainly I never felt *this* bad before.

The letter writer and the tightly furled man got up and went to the lounge. Jachin-Boaz went to one of the nurses, asked for something to calm him down. He was given a tranquillizer, went back to his bed and reasoned with himself.

She can't actually make my heart stop, he thought. That kind of magic doesn't work unless you believe that the other person has the power. Do I believe she has the power? Yes. But she doesn't really have any special power. She didn't have the power to keep me, did she? No. Then could she have the power to kill me? Of course not. Do I believe that? No.

Jachin-Boaz lay with his ear to the pillow, listening to the beating of his heart. The map, he thought. The map of Boaz-Jachin's future that I stole, the future that I cannot have. I'll stop smoking.

He lit a cigarette, got out of bed, stood against the wall. As soon as I feel a little better, he thought, I'll stop smoking. My father with his cigars. Why did she have to tell me about the mistress? She found out from her aunt in the dramatic society, but why did she have to tell me?

He thought of Sunday afternoons in childhood, smelled the car upholstery, looked out through the windscreen at the waning sunlight, felt his father on one side, his mother on the other, himself between them, sick. I haven't been committing suicide, he thought. Suicide has been committing me.

All of his unremembered dreams seemed to walk silently behind him, passing one by one between him and the wall, smirking over his shoulder at invisible phantoms in front of him. If I turn very quickly, he thought, and turned. Something very big, something very small, whisked around the corner of his mind. Either way, said the answer in the wall that faced him: betrayed or betrayer. Betrayed *and* betrayer.

"Be reasonable," said Jachin-Boaz quietly to the wall. "I can't be everybody."

Loss unending, said the wall. Dare to let go?

"I don't know," said Jachin-Boaz.

Suppose, the wall said, sometimes he laughed away from home. What then? You owe her nothing. He wants to rest. If you stand up they lie down. Follow your noes.

"Lion," said Jachin-Boaz silently, only shaping the word.

Oh yes, the wall said. Play with yourself.

Jachin-Boaz turned away. Everyone else was going to dinner. The thought of food sickened him, the smell from the dining area was offensive. The lion was still outside, no doubt. He would be waiting all the time now until the end. Everybody would want to feed him, look at him, share him. No, no, no.

The tightly furled man had taken his plate to the door near the french windows. "Pss, pss," he called, making the sound one makes for a cat. Three others came and stood near, looking over his shoulder. One of them, a man with a round white face, looked back at Jachin-Boaz and said something to the others. Everyone laughed.

Jachin-Boaz felt immensities of rage in him, infinities of NO. Crying, he burst into the group by the door, flung them in all directions, and rushed out on to the lawn.

31

Boaz-Jachin had arrived in the city and was staying with friends of the blonde woman. When he told them that his father was likely to be selling maps they advised him to advertise for Jachin-Boaz in the book trade weekly, which he did.

Boaz-Jachin bought such clothes as he needed and a cheap guitar, and every day he went into the underground stations and sang and played. The money he had earned on the cruise ship would keep him for several months, but he wanted to be able to support himself for as long as he needed to remain in the city.

His advertisement would not appear until the next week, and while he waited he played his guitar and sang in two different stations every day. He timed his arrival so that he would be at one when people went to work and at the other when they went home. Each day he went to new stations in the hope of seeing Jachin-Boaz. Each station had its own sound and its own feel. Some felt as if Jachin-Boaz was not to be found in them, others seemed full of probability. Boaz-Jachin made a list of the latter. If there was no answer to the advertisement he would keep only those stations on his guitar route as time went on.

The advertisement appeared, but there were no telephone calls or letters for Boaz-Jachin at the house where he was staying. He went on with his guitar route, trying new stations daily. He made enough money to live on cheaply, found a room for himself, and settled down to stay until he found his father. He no longer asked himself whether he knew or how he knew that Jachin-Boaz was in this city. He felt it as a certainty. Every day he inquired for letters or telephone calls, and every day there was nothing.

Boaz-Jachin's ear became attuned to the roar of trains arriving and departing, the constant numberless footfalls approaching, receding, voices and echoes. He sang the songs of his country, sang of the well, of olives, of sheep in the hills, of the desert, of orange groves, his voice and his guitar echoing in the corridors and stairways under the ground in the great city.

Boaz-Jachin inserted another advertisement, subscribed to the trade weekly, and went on to new underground stations with his guitar. He became known to his regular clientele. At each station the same faces smiled at him day after day as coins dropped into the guitar case. He smiled back, said thank you, but said nothing else to anyone. In the morning he saw the daylight and in the evenings he saw the fading of it. Above him the city was immense with all that the lines on the master-map led to. Bridges crossed the river, birds flew up circling over squares, and Boaz-Jachin lived underground, singing in corridors and stairways. He had not spoken aloud the word *lion* since the ride to the channel port with the van driver.

Boaz-Jachin found that he was thinking less in words than he used to. His mind simply was, and in it were the people he had been with, the times he had lived. Sounds, voices, faces, bodies, places, light and darkness came and went.

He had no sexual appetite, wanted no one to talk to, read nothing. Often in the evenings he sat quietly in his room doing nothing. Sometimes he played the guitar quietly, improvising tunes, but more often he had no wish to let out anything that was in him, nor did he look for anything new to take in. Whatever thoughts and questions were in his mind carried on their own dialogues to which he paid little attention. The feeling of emptiness rushing towards something became a waiting stillness.

Sometimes at night he walked in the streets. The leaves of the trees rustled in the squares. Lights shone on statues. Often he seemed to be without thought. It ceased to matter to him who was looking out through the eyeholes in his face and it ceased to matter who was looking in. He had no amulet to wear around his neck, no magic stone to hold in his hand. He held nothing. He was. Time passed through him unimpeded.

One day Boaz-Jachin took his guitar to an underground station, put the open case on the floor beside him, and tuned the instrument. But he did not begin to play immediately.

Faces passed him. Footsteps echoed, pattering like rain. Trains came and went. Boaz-Jachin listened past the footsteps, past the trains and echoes to the silence. He began to play music of his own, improvising on themes that he had composed in his room. He was unwilling to let the music out of him but unable to make himself stop.

He played the shimmer of the heat on the plains and the motion of the running flickering on the dry wind, tawny, great, and quickly gone. He played the silence of a ghost roar on the rising air beneath a shivering honey-coloured moon.

He played lion-music, and he sang. He sang without words, sang only with the modulations of his voice rising and falling, light and dark in the dry wind, in the sunlit desert under the ground in the great city.

Beyond the footsteps, beyond the trains and echoes he heard a roar that flooded the corridors like a great river of lion-coloured sound. He heard the lion.

32

No lion. Nothing. A faint smell of hot sun, dry wind. The green lawn darkening, empty in the twilight. Ha ha, said the twilight. Fading, fading.

Jachin-Boaz stood on the empty lawn with his fists clenched. I might have known, he thought. I was there, I was ready, high on a great cresting wave. Gone. The chance missed. He's gone. I won't see him again.

He went slowly back inside. The men who had laughed by the door looked at him warily from a distance.

"How're we feeling?" said one of the male nurses, laying a heavy hand on his shoulder. "We're not going to be acting up any more this evening, are we? We don't want to be plugged into the wall, do we? Because a little E.C.T. time is just the ticket for smoothing out the wrinkles in our brow and settling us down nicely."

"Feeling fine," said Jachin-Boaz. "No more acting up. All settled down. Don't know why I made such a fuss."

"Lovely," said the nurse, squeezing the back of Jachin-Boaz's neck. "Good boy."

Jachin-Boaz walked slowly back to his bed, sat down. "What's E.C.T.?" he asked the letter writer.

"Electro-convulsion therapy. Shock treatment. It's lovely. From time to time when the faces get too many for me I act up and they let me have it. Ever so soothing."

"You like it?" said Jachin-Boaz.

"Can't really afford any other kind of a holiday, you know," said the letter writer. "It scrambles the brain nicely. One forgets a good deal. Sometimes it takes months for everything to come back. Everyone ought to have a portable E.C.T. box, like a transistor radio. It isn't fair to leave a chap all alone and unprotected at the mercy of a brain. Brains don't care about you, you know. They do just as they like, and there you are."

"Transistor, transbrothers, transfathers, transmothers," said the tightly furled man. "Real rock. Groovy. 'No motion has she now, no force; She neither hears nor sees; Roll'd round in earth's diurnal course, With rocks, and stones, and trees.' Sometimes there's nothing but Sundays for weeks on end. Why can't they move Sunday to the middle of the week so you could put it in the OUT tray on your desk? No. Bloody bastards. Let the shadow cabinet work on *that* for a while, and the substance cabinet too. Man is a product of his Sundays. Don't talk to me about heredity. Darwin went to the Galapagos to get away from the Sunday drive with his parents. Mendel pea'd. Everybody tells a boy about sex but nobody tells him the facts of Sunday. Home is where the heart is, that's why pubs stay in business. Forgive us our Sundays as we forgive those who Sunday against us. Parent or child, no difference. Lend me a Monday, for Christ's sake." He began to cry.

"Today isn't Sunday," said Jachin-Boaz.

"Yes it is," said the tightly furled man. "It's always Sunday. That's why business was invented—to give people offices to hide in five days a week. Give us a seven-day week, I say. It's getting worse all the time. Inhuman bastards. Where'd your lion go?"

"Away," said Jachin-Boaz. "He won't come back. He only shows up on weekdays, and it's always Sunday here." He smiled cruelly, and the tightly furled man cried harder and burrowed into the blankets and covered up his head.

There would be no more lion for him here, Jachin-Boaz knew. The great cresting wave of rage had not been honestly earned, had been artificially forced up in him by the sly teasing of those who had no lion of their own. He would have to be good, be quiet, muffle his terror and wait for his rage until he was out of here. He would have to hide the clanging in him when it came again, would have to wear his terror like quiet grey prison garb, let everything flow through him indifferently.

From that time on his walk became like that of many other patients. Even when wearing shoes he seemed to go barefoot, ungirded, disarmed. The smell of cooking sang defeat. He nodded, humbled.

"How's it ticking?" said the doctor when his feet brought him around to Jachin-Boaz again.

"Very well, thank you," said Jachin-Boaz. From now on he would remember to answer as if the doctor were speaking real words.

"Tockly," said the doctor. "I told you ticks would tock themselves out, didn't I?"

"Indeed you did," said Jachin-Boaz. "And you were right."

"Someticks all it tocks is a little tick," said the doctor. "My tockness, ticks get to be too tock for all of us someticks."

"They do," said Jachin-Boaz.

"Tick," said the doctor. "That's when a good tock and some tick and tocket will tick tockers, and then a fellow can tick himtock toticker."

"Right," said Jachin-Boaz. "Peace and quiet *will* work wonders, and I *am* pulling myself together."

"That's the ticket," said the doctor. "Well tick you out of tock in no tick."

"The sooner the better," said Jachin-Boaz.

"What's all this about lions then?" said the doctor with every word clear and distinct.

"Who said anything about lions?" said Jachin-Boaz.

"It's difficult to have any secrets in a place like this," said the doctor. "Word gets around pretty quickly."

"I may very well have said something about a lion at one time or another," said Jachin-Boaz. "But if I did I was speaking metaphorically. It's very easy to be misunderstood, you know. Especially in a place like this."

"Quite," said the doctor. "Nothing easier. But what about the bites and the claw-marks?"

"Well," said Jachin-Boaz, "everyone's entitled to his own sex life, I think. Some people fancy black rubber clothes. Consenting adults and all that is how I feel about it."

"Quite," said the doctor. "The thing is to keep it in the privacy of one's own home, you know. I'm as modern as anyone else, but it's got to be kept off the streets."

"You're right of course," said Jachin-Boaz. "Things get out of hand sometimes."

"But the claw-marks and the bites," said the doctor. "They certainly weren't made by any human partner."

"Animal skins," said Jachin-Boaz, "can be got with claws and teeth, you know. It's been disposed of since. Really, I'm terribly ashamed of the whole thing. I just want to get back to my job and settle down to a normal life again."

"Good," said the doctor. "That's the way to talk. It won't be long now."

Gretel came to visit Jachin-Boaz. He had scarcely thought of her since being admitted to the hospital and would have preferred not to have to think about her just now. He was amazed at how young and pretty she was. My woman, he thought. How did it happen? It's dangerous to have balls but there's something nice about it.

"They're letting me out tomorrow," she said.

"What did you tell them?" said Jachin-Boaz.

"I said that it was all sex. You know how it is with us hot-blooded foreigners. I said that I thought you were running around with other women and that my jealousy had driven me wild and that somehow I found myself in the street with a knife in my hand."

"And they're willing to let you go?"

"Well, I said that I mightn't have been so upset ordinarily, but being pregnant as I was it was all too much for me. And the doctor said oh well, of course, poor dear and unwed mother and all that. And the doctor said what about the father, and I said not to worry, that everything was all right but we couldn't get married until you had a divorce. And he patted my hand and wished me all the best and said he hoped I'd not be going about with knives any more and I said certainly not and they're letting me out tomorrow."

"That was a very good touch, the pregnancy," said Jachin-Boaz.

"Yes," said Gretel. "It was. I am."

"Am what?"

"Pregnant."

"Pregnant," said Jachin-Boaz.

"That's right. I was two weeks overdue and had a test just before coming to the loony bin. I never found an opportune moment to tell you about it the day they brought us in. Are you happy about it?"

"Good God," said Jachin-Boaz. "Another son."

"It could also be a girl."

"I doubt it. With me it'll always be fathers and sons, I think."

"What I said about getting married, you know, was just for the doctor. I don't care about that."

"It's something we have to think about, I guess," said Jachin-Boaz.

"We don't have to think about it right now, anyhow," said Gretel. "How do you feel about being a father again?"

"I'm happy about the baby," said Jachin-Boaz. "I don't know how I feel about being a father again. I don't know how I feel about being a father even once, let alone twice."

"It'll be all right, whatever happens," said Gretel. "A mighty fortress is our something."

"What do you mean, whatever happens?"

"If you leave me. Or if the lion . . ."

"Do you think I'll leave you?"

"I never know. But it doesn't matter. I'll love you anyhow, and so will the baby. I'll tell him about his father, and he'll love you too."

"Do you think the lion will kill me?"

"Do you want the lion to kill you?"

Jachin-Boaz looked at Gretel without answering.

"What is there to say about a lion?" she said. "There are no lions any more, but my man has a lion. The father of my child has a lion."

Jachin-Boaz nodded his head.

"Maybe," said Gretel, "if you go out to meet it again . . ."

"I'll tell you," said Jachin-Boaz.

"All right," said Gretel. "When I get home I'll do some house-cleaning so the flat can welcome you properly. You'll be out soon, I should think. I shan't come to visit unless you ring me up. You have a lot to think about."

"I do," said Jachin-Boaz. He kissed her. My woman, he thought. The mother of my child. I'm an unwed father, and my heart may stop beating at any moment.

The owner of the bookshop came to visit Jachin-Boaz again. "You're getting to be quite popular," he said, and showed him an advertisement in the book trade weekly:

Jachin-Boaz, please contact Boaz-Jachin.

A telephone number and box number were given. Jachin-Boaz wrote them down.

"Jachin-Boaz, please contact yourself turned around," said the bookshop owner. "An odd message."

"What do you mean, myself turned around?" said Jachin-Boaz.

"The names," said the bookshop owner. "Jachin-Boaz, Boaz-Jachin."

"My son," said Jachin-Boaz. "He's not me turned around. I don't know who he is. I don't know him very well."

"Who can know anybody?" said the bookshop owner. "Every person is like thousands of books. New, reprinting, in stock, out of stock, fiction, non-fiction, poetry, rubbish. The lot. Different every day. One's lucky to be able to put his hand on the one that's wanted, let alone know it."

Jachin-Boaz watched the bookshop owner walk out of the hospital looking modestly carefree and comfortable, tried to remember when he had last felt easy in his mind. Soon I'll be out of stock, he thought. All the books that I am. And out of print too, for good. Leaving a new son behind. No way back. A wave of terror flooded his being. No, no, no. Yes. No way back. Goddam her. Goddam both of them—the one he had left and the one who now stood between him and the one he had left. No going back. He didn't want to be a father again. He wasn't yet finished with being a son, and here was the last moment coming closer with every beat of his heart, that beating that he was aware of most of the time now. His heart and all the other organs in his tired body, no rest for forty-seven years. And the imminent final rest intolerable to think of. The last moment will be *now*, she had written.

He tried to find hiding places from the terror in his mind so that the letter writer and the tightly furled man would not complain of his clanging, and he avoided anyone else's company. He availed himself of as many tranquillizers as the nurses would give him, slept as much as possible, entertained himself with sex fantasies, sang songs mentally. The song that became habitual had only one word: *lion*. Lion, lion, lion, sang his mind to dance rhythms, battle tunes, lullabies.

He did not write to Boaz-Jachin or call him on the telephone. When the doctor made his rounds Jachin-Boaz spoke reasonably and cheerfully, said that the rest had done him good and that he was eager to get on with his life.

"Tockly," said the doctor. "There's a world of tickerence between the way you tock now and the way you ticked before, eh?"

"Yes, indeed," said Jachin-Boaz.

"New ticksponsibilities coming up now, eh?" said the doctor. "Tock-spectant father, I hear. Best of tock, you know. Smashing young tickly you've got there. Saw her before she left."

"Thank you," said Jachin-Boaz.

"No more tockolence, I hope," said the doctor. "Won't do, you know, in her tickition."

"Good heavens, no," said Jachin-Boaz.

"Good boy," said the doctor, gripping Jachin-Boaz's shoulder hard. "That's the ticket."

At the end of his third week in the hospital Jachin-Boaz was discharged. He watched his feet as he walked through the corridors to the front door, careful to walk like a man wearing shoes.

As he was going out he met the doctor who had treated his wounds coming in with a police constable, a social worker and a male nurse all gripping him firmly.

"Bloody wogs defiling our women," said the doctor. "Atheists, cultists, sexual deviants, radicals, intellectuals."

"Cheerio," said the nurse when he saw Jachin-Boaz. "All the best, and don't come back too soon."

"What's wrong with the doctor?" said Jachin-Boaz.

"Went for his wife with a poker," said the nurse. "She said it was the first time he'd touched her with anything stiff for a long time."

"Whore," said the doctor. "She's a whore." He stared at Jachin-Boaz. "He's got a lion," he said, "and nobody does anything about it. The authorities turn a blind eye. See him smile. He's got a lion."

33

When Boaz-Jachin heard the roar it came to him that there was in the world only one place. That place was time. The lion was in it and he was in it. He knew now that he must have known it when he shouted into the darkness and the ferry's white wake spreading astern. He must have known it always, from the time he had first seen the frowning face of the dying lion biting the wheel. He had made his feeble attempt at maintaining the fiction of ordinary reality, had placed the advertisement in the trade weekly. But it was towards the lion that he had been moving the emptiness in him these many miles. And it was the lion's call that he had waited for here in this city.

He put his guitar in the case, picked it up, and walked in the direction of the sound, listening past the footsteps, voices, trains and echoes. Again the roar. It came from a particular direction and seemed to be in him at the same time. No one else seemed to hear it, no one paused to listen or to look at him as if the sound were emanating from him. Listening and seeing nothing he followed through the corridors, up the stairway and the escalator to the street, smelling hot sun, dry wind and the tawny plains.

Past the traffic, past the buses, lorries, cars, footsteps, voices, aeroplanes overhead, boats on the river he listened, walking slowly. Everything that is lost is found again, he thought. The father must live so that the father can die. In him were all the faces, all the voices since he had first looked at the motionless stone in which the dying lion bit the wheel, all the skies and days, the ocean that had brought him to the time in which the lion was and he was. He walked, and in his mind he sang his wordless song.

West he followed the roar, seeing nothing, and south towards the river and its bridges. Found again, lost again, he thought. The father must live. Time flowed through him. Being was. Balanced he flowed with time and being, following the lion, his face cleaving the air, his mind singing wordlessly.

Alone among those he walked with on the streets he listened to the roar that led him on, came to the embankment. Spanned by its bridges the river flowed beneath the sky. Boaz-Jachin did not hear the roaring again. He sat down on a bench facing the river, took out his guitar and played lion-music softly.

The day faded, the moon appeared in the sky and in the river. Boaz-Jachin played his guitar, waiting.

34

On the morning after his first night at home Jachin-Boaz awoke without an erection. Hello, infinity, he thought. He remembered now that most of the time for the last few weeks he had not had an erection on waking. He sighed, thought of yellow leaves falling, quiet bells in monasteries, cool tombstones, poets and composers who had died young, pyramids, broken colossal statues, dry wind in the desert, grains of sand blowing, stinging, time.

Last night they had made love, and as always it had been good. Someone had felt good—he, she, it, they. Jachin-Boaz wished them all the best of luck in their new venture. The earth had to be populated with people for the aloneness to wear. Congratulations.

Gretel was still asleep. He put his hand on her belly under the blankets. One more brain to hold the world in. One more world-carrier. Like a disease the world was passed from one to the other, each to suffer alone. And yet—tiny sunrise, catch it before it's gone—the aloneness was in fact no worse than it had ever been. Even now with death coursing through him with every beat of his heart it was no worse. Secure in the womb he had been alone. The terror that was now was then as well. The terror inseparable from the primal salt, the green light through the reeds. The terror and the energy of life inseparable. Secure with his wife and son he had been alone, pulling the blankets of every day over his head to shut the terror out.

Here, anchorless and lost in this time with Gretel he was alone with the terror but no more alone than the person-to-be in her womb. Sunrise, caught. Night again. Hello, night. No darker than ever. No darker than before I was. No darker than for you in her belly before your beginning. It takes a million noes to make one yes. Who said that? I said it.

He got out of bed, stood up naked, stretched, looked at the not-yet-morning light in the window, listened to birds singing. I said I'd tell her, he thought.

He said he'd tell me, thought Gretel with her eyes closed.

He gently uncovered her, kissed her belly. I've told her, he thought.

He's told me, thought Gretel. What? She kept her eyes closed, heard Jachin-Boaz in the bathroom, heard him dressing, making coffee, going out. I don't think he bought meat, she thought. I don't think he took meat with him.

Summer, thought Jachin-Boaz. Seasons pass, the air on my face is mild, the day that is coming will be a summer day. This is better than my selfish rage in the hospital. There is no magic, nothing and no one to help me. Cool before the dawn I must do it alone, up from nothing, out of nothing. In his hand was the rolled-up master-map. Across the street stood the lion. Jachin-Boaz took from his pocket an envelope addressed to Gretel, a cheque in it payable to her for all the money in his account. He posted it in the letterbox near the telephone kiosk. The telephone kiosk was still lit. The chestnut tree, wet with morning, was in full leaf. The lion-smell hung stilly in the air.

"No meat," said Jachin-Boaz to the lion. He turned and walked towards the river. The lion followed. As on the first day, a crow flew overhead. Jachin-Boaz came to the bridge, turned right, walked down the steps to the part of the embankment below street level. On his left were the parapet and the river, on his right the retaining wall. Behind him the steps to the bridge, ahead of him a railing at the edge of the stonework and the water stairs. The lion followed. Jachin-Boaz turned and faced him.

No magic. Reality unbearable, inescapable. Violent death. Violent life.

Being beyond all reasonable bounds. Being unbounded, terrifying, violent medium of death and life, indifferent to both, contemptuous of mortal distinctions. Frowning brows. Amber eyes luminous and infinite. Open jaws, hot breath, pink rasping tongue and white teeth of the end of the world. Jachin-Boaz smelled the lion, saw him breathe, saw the breeze stir his mane, saw the muscles taut beneath the tawny skin. Immense, the lion, dominating space and time. Distinct, forward of the air around him. Immediate. Now. Nothing else.

"Lion," said Jachin-Boaz. "You have waited for me before the dawns. You have walked with me, have eaten my meat. You have been attentive and indifferent. You have attacked me and you have turned away. You have been seen and unseen. Here we are. Now is the only time there is.

"Life," said Jachin-Boaz. He took one step to the left. "Death," he said. He stepped back to the right. "Life," he said, looked calmly at the lion, shrugged.

"There are no maps," said Jachin-Boaz. He unrolled the map in his hand, rolled it the other way to flatten it, lit a match, set it afire. Flames danced up. He dropped the map as the flames consumed it, oceans and continents darkened, writhing in the fire.

"No maps," said Jachin-Boaz.

He remembered Boaz-Jachin as a baby, laughing in his bath in the sink. He remembered his wife singing. He remembered the feel of Gretel's belly against his mouth, remembered Boaz-Jachin as a boy standing outside the shop and looking in through the window, his small mysterious face shaded by the awning. He remembered the palm trees and the fountain in the square.

"No way back," said Jachin-Boaz.

As long before, words appeared in his mind, large, powerful, compelling belief and respect like the saying of a god in capital letters:

TO SING IN THE PRESENCE OF A LION

Jachin-Boaz looked into the eyes of the lion. Someone was coming down the steps from the bridge with a guitar, was playing the guitar, was playing lion-music.

Jachin-Boaz was not trembling. His voice was firm. He was surprised at how strong his voice was, how pleasing. He sang:

Lion, lion, ten thousand years,
Ten thousand more and still
The motion of your running,
Tawny, great, the motion of your running
Printed on the air.
The earth upon your amber eyes, lion,
Ten thousand years, ten thousand more.
Dead the kings are, lion,
Fleshed with earth their bones,
The earth upon your amber eyes,
Like a window you looked through it, lion.
The wheel you died on turns, you rise.
The river and the bridges, lion,
Crossings always, birds of morning,
The motion of your running,
Tawny, great upon the air.

The air was dense and shimmering, thick with time. The taste of salt was in the mouth of Jachin-Boaz, Boaz-Jachin. Ocean behind him, the father saw the lion through the green light in the reeds, ceased to be himself, and only was. A channel through which life surged up, returned again to earth, to ocean. Immense in him a million rising noes to make one yes. No words. No *no* great enough. Jachin-Boaz opened his mouth, Boaz-Jachin opened his mouth.

The sound filled all space like a river in flood, a great river of lion-coloured sound. From his time, from the tawny running on the plains, from the pit and the fall and the oblong of blue sky overhead, from his death on the spears in the dry wind forward into all the darknesses and lights revolving to the morning light above the city and the river with its bridges the lion, father, son sent his roar.

"Right," said the police constable on the bridge, speaking into the little two-way radio he held. "Right. I am standing at the north end of the bridge. I am facing west, looking down the steps. There are two men there with a lion. Right. I know. The lion is loose. I am dead sober. I am in my right mind. What I think we need here is the fire brigade with a pumper. Big net too, stout one. Chaps from the zoo with a strong cage. Ambulance too. Yes, I know this is the second time. As quick as you can." The constable looked up and down the bridge, chose a position from which he could climb a lamp-post or jump into the river, and waited.

More, thought Jachin-Boaz. This is not yet all. I have not yet gone all the way. I have not yet become unaware of the beating of my heart, have not yet eaten up my terror, not yet been angry enough. Let it come, let it happen. Words in his mind again:

TO RAGE WITH A LION

Nothing else was enough. No more thought. His mouth opened. Again the roar. He or the lion? He smelled the lion. Life, death. He hurled himself at the immensity of lion.

Boaz-Jachin leaped from the other side on to the lion's back, his face against the coarse mane and hot tawny skin, his arms embracing, fingers clutching raging death.

Jachin-Boaz, Boaz-Jachin screamed in blinding fires of pain, raw nerves and ripped flesh flaming, muscles torn, ribs cracking, lion-entered, lion-killed, lion-born, howling in millennia of pain, impossibly absorbing infinities of lion. Blackness. Light. Silence.

Their arms were around each other. They were whole, unhurt. There was no great beast between them. The day was bright on the river, the air was warm. They nodded to each other, shook their heads, kissed, laughed, cried, cursed.

"You're taller," said Jachin-Boaz.

"You're looking well," said Boaz-Jachin. He picked up his guitar, put it in the case. They walked up the steps, turned down the street towards Jachin-Boaz's flat. The fire brigade pumper and a red car passed them flashing and blaring. The ambulance, a police car, a police van, a van from the zoo, all flashing and blaring.

"You'll have breakfast with us," said Jachin-Boaz. "I don't mind being a little late for work today."

The police constable came forward as the pumper, the ambulance, the cars and vans screeched to a stop. In a moment he was the centre of a circle of policemen, firemen, ambulance and zoo people, and his superintendent. The little dark man from the zoo sniffed the air, looked from side to side, bent to study the pavement.

The superintendent looked at the constable, shook his head. "Not twice, Phillips," he said.

"I know how it looks, sir," said the constable.

"You've got a good record, Phillips," said the superintendent. "Good prospects for promotion, a fine career ahead of you. Sometimes things get to be too much for all of us. Marital problems, economic pressures, nervous strain, all kinds of worries. I want you to talk to a doctor."

"No," said the constable. He put the two-way radio carefully on the bridge parapet.

"No," he said again. He took off his helmet, set it down beside the radio.

"No," he said once more, took off his tunic, folded it neatly, laid it on the parapet beside the helmet and radio.

"There *was* a lion," he said. "There is a lion. Lion is."

He nodded to the superintendent, passed through the circle as it parted on either side of him, and walked away down the street in his shirt-sleeves.

TURTLE DIARY

I

William G.

I don't want to go to the Zoo any more.

The other night I dreamt of an octopus. He was dark green, almost black, dark tentacles undulating in brown water. Not sure what colour an octopus is really. Found colour photos in two of the books at the shop. One octopus was brown and white, the other was grey, pinky, brown. They change colour it seems. Their eyes are dreadful to look at. I shouldn't like to be looked at by an octopus no matter how small and harmless it might be. To be stared at by those eyes would be altogether too much for me, would leave me nothing whatever to be. There was a black-and-white photo of octopuses hung up to dry on a pole at Thasos on the Aegean Sea, black against the sky, black bags hanging, black tentacles drooping and drying, behind them the brightness over the sea. They're related to the chambered nautilus which I'd always thought of only as a shell with nothing in it. But there it was in the book full of tentacles and swimming inscrutably.

Then I wanted to see an octopus. On Friday, my half-day at the shop, I went to the Zoo. Grey day, raining a little. Went in by the North Gate past the owls. *Bubo* this and *Bubo* that, each one sitting on its bar with wet feathers and implacable eyes. Over the bridge past the Aviary towering high against the sky, a huge pointy steel-mesh thing of gables and angles full of strange cries and dark flappings. There were little shrill children eating things. There was steam coming up in the rain from three square plates in the paving at the end of the bridge. Two girls and a boy bathed their bare legs in it. The tunnel on the other side of the bridge was echoing with children. Copies of cave-paintings on the walls of the tunnel. They didn't belong there, looked heavy-handed, false. One wanted to see SPURS, ARSENAL.

Very dark in the Aquarium. Green windows, things swimming. People black against the windows murmuring, explaining to children, holding them up, putting them down, urging them on, calling them back. Echoing footsteps of children running in the dark. Very shabby in the Aquarium, very small. Too many little green windows in the dark. Crabs, lobsters, two thornback rays, a little poor civil-servant-looking leopard shark. Tropical fish, eels, toads, frogs and newts. There was no octopus.

Sea turtles. Two or three hundred pounds the big ones must have weighed. Looping and swinging, flying in golden-green silty water in a grotty little tank no bigger than my room. Soaring, dipping and curving with flippers like wings in a glass box of second-hand ocean. Their eyes said nothing, the thousands of miles of ocean couldn't be said.

I thought: when I was a child I used to like the Zoo. The rain had stopped. I went to the Reptile House. No. Didn't want to see the snakes on hot sand under bright lights behind glass. Left the Reptile House, approached the apes. The gorilla lay on his stomach in his cell, his chin resting on his folded arms. No. I couldn't think which was worse: if he could remember or if he couldn't.

I went out of the Zoo to the 74 bus stop at the North Gate. There was a young woman with a little boy and girl. Maybe the boy was eight or nine. He had a little black rubber gorilla on a bit of elastic tied to a string and he danced the little black gorilla up and down in a little puddle, spat spat spat, not splashing. It was only a bit of wet on the pavement.

"Stop that," said his mother. "I told you to stop that."

2

Neaera H.

I fancied a china castle for the aquarium but they had none at the shop, so I contented myself with a smart plastic shipwreck. Snugg & Sharpe are expecting a new Gillian Vole story from me but I have not got another furry-animal picnic or birthday party in me. I am tired of meek and cuddly creatures, my next book will be about a predator. I've posted my cheque for 31p to Gerrard & Haig in Surrey for a Great Water-beetle, *Dysticus marginalis*, and I should have it by tomorrow. I've asked for a male.

On my way home wheeling the tank and all the other aquarium gear in the push-chair I stopped at the radio and TV shop because there was an oyster-catcher on all the TV screens in the window, a B.B.C. nature film it must have been. It was like encountering someone from childhood now famous. I used to see oyster-catchers sometimes on the mussel beds near Breydon Bridge when the tide was out. They were nothing like the gulls and terns, their black-and-white had a special air, they went a little beyond being birds. They walked with their heads down, looking as if they had hands clasped behind their backs like little European philosophers in yachting gear. But it was a less rhythmical walk than a philosopher's because the oyster-catchers were busy making a living with the mussels. In childhood at Breydon Water the day was wide and quiet, there was time enough to think of everything with no hurry whatever, to look at everything many times over.

The oyster-catcher on the TV screens was gone, there was a shot of mudflats and sea. The oyster-catcher had been very elegant in colour: creamy white, velvety black, orange bill and eye-rings, pink legs. On the black-and-white screens it had been more existential, a working bird alone in the world. Here I am, I thought, forty-three years old, waiting for a water-beetle. My married friends wear Laura Ashley dresses and in their houses are grainy photographs of them barefoot on continental beaches with their naked children. I live alone, wear odds and ends, I have resisted vegetarianism and I don't keep cats.

I passed the place where they're tearing up the street and the three workmen in the hole said "Good morning" for the first time. Before this we've nodded.

As I was going into my flat Webster de Vere, the unemployed actor next door, was coming out of his. "Fascinating hobby," he said when he saw the tank. "I've been keeping fish for years. Black Mollies, you know. Nothing flash, just neat little black fish. What will you have in your aquarium?"

"A water-beetle," I said.

"A water-beetle," he said. "Fascinating pet. If you ever need any snails do let me know, I've masses of them. Keep the tank clean, you know."

"Thank you," I said. "It's all new to me, I must see how it goes."

He went down the hall swinging his cane. As far as I know he's been out of work the whole five or six years he's been my neighbour. He keeps so fit that it's hard to tell how old he is but by the brightness of his eye I'd say he's at least fifty-five. Most of the voices I hear through the wall belong to young men of the antique-shop type but I think he lives off old ladies. I've no reason to think it except his looks. His eyes look as if he's pawned his real ones and is wearing paste.

After I'd set up the aquarium I looked in my book of Bewick engravings for an oyster-catcher but couldn't find one. Bewick has drawn the dotterel, the spotted redshank, the godwit and the little stint but there's no oyster-catcher in my book. He would have drawn it very well, it's his sort of bird. The best bird drawings I've done were for *Delia Swallow's Housewarming*, one of my early books. The story was rubbish but the swallow was well observed, she was a distinct Laura Ashley type.

3

William G.

It must have been soft plastic, that gorilla the little boy had. I don't think they make those things out of rubber any more.

There are green turtles whose feeding grounds are along the coast of Brazil, and they swim 1,400 miles to breed and lay their eggs on Ascension Island in the South Atlantic, half way to Africa. Ascension Island is only five miles long. Nobody knows how they find it. Two of the turtles at the Aquarium are green turtles, a large one and a small one. The sign said: "The Green Turtle, *Chelonia mydas*, is the source of turtle soup . . . " I am the source of William G. soup if it comes to that. Everyone is the source of his or her kind of soup. In a town as big as London that's a lot of soup walking about.

How do the turtles find Ascension Island? There are sharks in the water too. Some of the turtles get eaten by sharks. Do the turtles know about sharks? How do they not think about the sharks when they're swimming that 1,400 miles? Green turtles must have the kind of mind that doesn't think about sharks unless a shark is there. That must be how it is with them. I can't believe they'd swim 1,400 miles thinking about sharks. Sea turtles can't shut themselves up in their shells as land turtles do. Their shells are like tight bone vests and their flippers are always sticking out.

Nothing they can do if a shark comes along. Pray. Ridiculous to think of a turtle praying with all those teeth coming up from below.

Mr. Meager, manager of the shop and the source of Meager soup, stood in front of me for a while. When I noticed him he asked me if I'd got something on my mind. Green turtles, I said. Was that something we'd subscribed, he wanted to know. No, I said, it was the source of turtle soup. He went away with a hard smile.

It's hard to believe they do it by observing the angle of the sun like a yachtsman with a sextant. Carr doubts it and he's about the biggest turtle authority there is. But that's what penguins do on overland journeys. They're big navigators too. I think of the turtles swimming steadily against the current all the way to Ascension. I think of them swimming through all that golden-green water over the dark, over the chill of the deeps and the jaws of the dark. And I think of the sun over the water, the sun through the water, the eye holding the sun, being held by it with no thought and only the rhythm of the going, the steady wing-strokes of the flippers in the water. Then it doesn't seem hard to believe. It seems the only way to do it, the only way in fact to be: swimming, swimming, the eye held by the sun, no sharks in the mind, nothing in the mind. And when they can't see the sun, what then? Their vision isn't good enough for star sights. Do they go by smell, taste, faith?

In the evening I went downstairs for a cup of tea with Mrs. Inchcliff, my landlady. She wasn't in the kitchen, I found her in the lumber-room. Her boy-friend Charlie when he lived here used to spend a lot of time in that room. There's a workbench there and she was sitting on it under a green-shaded light with her feet on a sawhorse. She's sixty years old, still a good-looking woman, must have been beautiful when she was younger. Goes about in jeans and shirts and sandals mostly, wears her hair long. From the back she looks like a girl except that her hair is grey.

"With just a little more capital Charlie and I could have made a go of the antique shop," she said. "If we could have hung on for another year we'd have been all right. Charlie loved it."

Charlie had indeed been very good at finding things, stripping off paint and varnish, rebuilding and restoring. He was twenty-five when they broke up a couple of years ago. He went off with a woman of fifty who had a stall on the Portobello Road.

When he and Mrs. Inchcliff had been in business a good many of their antiques had cost them nothing at all. They used to go out scavenging in her old estate-car almost every day. They'd had a regular route of rubbish tips and she still kept her hand in. When a building was due to be condemned she usually beat everyone else to the knocker on the front door and she seemed to find the most profitable skips on both sides of the river. She was always shifting odd doors and dressers and various scraps of timber and ironmongery, more out of habit than anything else though I daresay she made a few pounds a week selling things to dealers.

"If you ever want to do any woodworking," she said, "shelves or anything, you can use the tools and everything here whenever you like." She's said that to me several times.

"Thanks," I said. "There's nothing I need to make right now." When I had a house I used to make things. When I had a family. When the girls sat on my lap and I read to them.

I sat down on a chest. There was a sack trolley leaning in the corner, left over from the antique-shop days. I saw myself walking down a dark street in the middle of the night wheeling a turtle on the sack trolley. Just a flash and it was gone. There was a pebble in the pocket of my cardigan, left there from the last time I stopped smoking. From the beach at Antibes. Look, Dad, here's a good one. It was cool and smooth between my fingers.

"I wonder what Charlie's doing now," said Mrs. Inchcliff.

There must be a lot of people in the world being wondered about by people who don't see them any more.

4

Neaera H.

I don't think I've ever seen anyone pick up a box of matches without shaking it. Curious. It takes more time to shake the box than it would to open it straight away but it's less effort. It's pleasant to hear a lot of marches rattling in the box, one has a feeling of plenty. No one wants to open a matchbox and find it empty.

I lit a cigarette and looked at the water-beetle parcel. A nice little brown-paper parcel, short and cylindrical with airholes in the top. When I undid the brown paper there was a nice little tin with airholes in the lid. Inside the tin was the beetle on damp moss. It was a female, I could tell by the ridges on the wing covers. No males available, said the invoice taped to the tin. That's life.

With a pencil I prodded her into the little net I'd bought, then lifted the aquarium cover and put her into the water. She swam right down to the plastic shipwreck and scuttled out of sight inside it.

One of my books quoted a naturalist who'd kept a water-beetle on raw meat for three and a half years. I dropped some raw meat through the feeding hole. The beetle rushed over to it, flung it about a bit, then left it and moored herself to a water plant.

Something will come to me, I thought. *Delia Beetle's Sunken Trea-*

sure. No, I used that name for the swallow. Cynthia Beetle, Sally Beetle, Victoria Beetle. *Victoria Beetle, Secret Agent.* A woman of action. I went out and sat in the square.

There is no statue in our square. When I look at statues I find later that I have usually not paid close attention but I have paid close attention to the statue that is not in our square. I've come to think of it as a fountain really. There's a large stone basin and a little thin bronze girl with her skirt tucked up, paddling in the water. She's not in the centre of the basin but near the rim. In the centre there's a little jet of water that shoots up taller than the girl. Sometimes the wind blows drops of water spattering on the girl. When it rains, the water in the basin is spangled with splashes that leap up to meet the rain. The bronze girl gleams in the rain. When the sun shines her shadow moves over the water, over the stone rim, over the paving round the fountain. The bronze girl is always at the centre of the circle of her revolving shadow that marks the time.

In Sloane Square there really is a fountain. With two basins and a proper fountain lady in the upper basin pouring water from a shell, a kneeling bronze physical-education sort of lady, naked but unapproachable. I think of her name as being Daphne. Sometimes an empty Coca-Cola tin, bright and shining, circles her basin like part of a water clock. But that bronze lady and her fountain are cold and heavy compared to the statue and the fountain that are not in our square. There would be beach pebbles in the basin of the bronze-girl fountain.

Having reviewed my customary fountain thoughts I find all at once that I really don't care about it at all. Let the square be however it is, it doesn't matter to me any more.

I have only one beach pebble from my childhood, from Caister. I don't suppose it makes any difference, the others are always there in a way. The books call them pebbles but I always think of them as stones. I have many stones from beaches I've visited as a grown-up, one bit of sea-china with a voluptuous fairy with little butterfly wings on it, and several bits of sea-glass. The stones from each place are in separate baskets: St David's head, Folkestone, Staunton Sands etc. At Folkestone I gave a talk to teachers and librarians one evening, and in the afternoon of that day I went to the sea front and down steep steps to the narrow pebble beach and the sea.

There was a long row of little beach-huts side by side like garages. It was a rainy day in early spring. A man had his hut opened up, the whole front open like a dolls' house. He was doing the sort of things men do when they smoke pipes and repair their boats in early spring. Mending something I suppose. There was no boat, his hut was his boat. All the little beach-hut fronts pushed me towards the sea and I jumped down from the wall on to the pebbles that rolled and clicked under me as I walked. I thought: what if there were a stone with my name on it? Then I thought, what if my name were on every stone? Then: the name of every stone is in me. I can't say the name of every stone but it is in me. There were no birds that I remember that day. The hotels along the front were as high as in childhood and as remote, even when seen close to.

This afternoon I bought a marked-down bird book with plates by John Gould (1804–1881). There's a handsome picture of two oyster-catchers. "At running, diving, and swimming they are unrivalled, while their vigilance is greatly appreciated by the other birds of the shore," says the book. The newer bird books have hundreds of posh pictures, the proficiency of the artists is dazzling. But the birds all look as if they'd been done from photographs. Certainly there were no such bird pictures before the camera came into use. Gould's birds are beautiful but modestly done and he seems to have looked at each one carefully and long. His eagle owl, *Bubo bubo*, is all ferocity but without malice. Dangling from his beak is a dead rabbit who looks exactly like Peter Rabbit without the blue jacket. *Bubo bubo*'s dreadful amber eyes say simply, "It has fallen to me to do this. It is my lot." His fierce woolly owl-babies huddle before him waiting for their dinner.

5

William G.

I went to the Zoo again.

Cold day. Windy. Walking down Parkway from the Camden Town tube station I passed a girl with her anorak zipped up pushing a baby in a push-chair, looking cold. Autumn? No, spring. Summer next. Four seasons to a year. I can easily imagine getting up one morning and deciding not to bother with any more seasons. I went in by the South Gate and passed the Waders Aviary on my way to the sea turtles.

Lots of noise from the reeds and marsh plants inside the cage. More than one voice, some sort of a controversy: kleep kleep kleep. Kleep kleep. Two black-and-white birds with orange-ringed eyes set neatly in their heads, long orange bills and the sort of chilblained but durable-looking purplish legs one sees on some lady birdwatchers. But these birds were both men I think. Maybe it was one bird and a doppel-ganger. They were walking side by side shouting at each other. They passed out of view behind the reeds. I went round to the other side of the cage where I could see them as they came out on to the concrete beach round their wading-pool. They were walking with their heads down and if they'd had hands they would have had them clasped behind their backs. Each one's bill was pointed down and away from the other and they looked stubbornly sideways at each other as they conversed.

"Kleep it and have klept with it for God's sake," said one.

"I don't have to kleep it just because you klawp I should," said the other.

"Then don't kleep it," said the first one. "It's no klank off my klonk."

"Oh aye," said the second one. "You klawp that now but that's not what you klawped a little klink ago."

"I klick very klenk what I klawped a little klink ago," said the first one. "I klawped either kleep it or don't kleep it but stop klawping about it. That's what I klawped."

"It's all very klenk for you to klawp 'Kleep it,'" said the second one. "You're not the one that has to kleggy back the kwonk."

I didn't want to hear any more. There was a sign inside the cage with pictures of the inmates. Those two were oyster-catchers. That's a laugh. I'd like to know when the last time they caught an oyster was. At one end of their pool, which was nothing more than a depression in the concrete with some standing water in it, some very old mussels were lying about. There were other birds with their pictures on the sign but I didn't want to know.

Have the gibbons been corrupted by captivity? How can they possibly be happy in a cage, but they seem not to care about it especially. Debonair is the only word for them. Maybe aerial acrobatics are to them what jazz is to musicians who do it wherever they are and whether they get paid or not, just for the thing itself.

They have quite a large sort of flight cage with transverse bars at regular intervals for them to swing on. They saunter through the air in great long easy arcs, long arms revolving alternately: catch, let go, catch, let go, and all the time not particularly paying attention and as if with their hands in their pockets. Their manner is cool but lively, not withdrawn. Their small black faces are full of Zen. Jazz acrobats is what they are and they seem philosophically beyond such trifles as a cage. They're above me, I admit it. And they don't seem to be snobs about it either.

I had sort of a bursting feeling as if my self were a wall round me that I couldn't knock down or climb over. I have no talent, no Zen like that of the gibbons. Once, twice, long ago. Out of it, away and in the clear. What's the use of remembering. Out of it was at the same time into it. There's a wall inside the self as well. Can't get through any more. Can't live is what it amounts to. No place to live. Get through the days, the seasons, oh yes. But no place to be. No way to hold the sun in the eye, be held by it swimming, swimming.

The wax people downstairs at Madame Tussaud's contemplating in wax their crimes get through the days, the nights, the seasons. The thought escapes me, there was more to it. Prisons are all we know how to make, even in wax. No wax sea turtles, thank God for that.

There they were in the golden-green murk of their little box of sea, their little bedsitter of ocean. One almost expected a meter in the corner of it where they had to put in 5p to keep the water circulating. Thousands of miles in their speechless eyes, submarine skies in their flipper-wings. No beach of course, no hot sand for the gravid females to crawl up on to, to lay their eggs.

A little boy pointed to the big loggerhead turtle. "Could he get rid of me?" he said to his mother. She was ever so well-groomed.

"Oh no," she said, laughing upper-class and mumsily. "They're quite harmless."

The male loggerhead bit the female on the neck and tried to mount her. Not on. She wasn't having any. Maybe the females in the Aquarium don't get gravid, have no eggs to lay. The lady walked away with her knickers full of gentility, her son followed, still not got rid of.

Thousands of miles of navigation, I couldn't get it out of my mind. There was a girl standing next to me, a burstly sort of girl, bursting out of her tight trousers and blouse, bursting with health and burstly genes. *She'd* have no trouble getting gravid whenever she liked. I was still thinking of the thousands of miles. "Nobody knows how they do it," I said.

"You just have to be here at the right time and you can see them do it," she said. Burst burst.

The air seemed full of noise, I sat down on a bench and closed my eyes, saw golden-green water, thousands of miles.

6

Neaera H.

Madame Beetle seems not to fancy raw meat. All of what I'd given her lay about in the plants and on the shipwreck and went white and sodden. On the other hand, maybe she *has* eaten it. In the larval stage the water-beetle doesn't eat in the ordinary way, it injects digestive fluid into its prey and sucks out the liquefied tissues. Maybe Madame Beetle's never grown up. The meat certainly looks as if there's no nutrition left in it. I tried her with a bit of braised beef and I think she ate some of it.

She spends a good deal of her time hanging head-down with her bottom just breaking the surface of the water. That's the end she breathes through, where her spiracles are. Might she have a periscope? *Victoria Beetle, Submariner.* When she dives she takes a shining bubble of air with her under her wing-covers. If I took the lid off the tank and opened the window she might fly away but it would be a long trip to the nearest pond. I sometimes think of her as waiting patiently but I doubt that she really experiences what people call waiting and if she doesn't then she has no need of patience.

Victoria Beetle's Summer Holiday. Bugger that. *Sunken Treasure* is better. What would a beetle treasure be? I'll try catching some flies for her.

Maybe a moth will turn up, she'd like that. But the treasure in the story should be jewels or money.

> It was a lazy summer afternoon,
> and Victoria Beetle was enjoying a quiet cup of tea
> when she heard a knock at the door.
> She looked out of the window
> and saw Big Sam Bumblebee the gang boss.
> "If he thinks he can try on that
> protection lark with me he'd better think again,"
> said Victoria, and she picked up the poker.

Victoria Beetle or Victoria Water-Beetle? The hyphenated name sounds better. How would Snugg & Sharpe feel about gangsters? After all they're part of modern life even at schools nowadays, according to the newspapers. Big Sam knows where the lolly is but he needs Victoria's help because it's at the bottom of the pond. Dropped there by Jimson Crow perhaps, whilst making a getaway. He's always stealing things. He was flying over the pond with Detective Owl hot on his trail.

I wanted to see an oyster-catcher so I went to the Zoo, not feeling at all good about it. The Zoo is a prison for animals who have been sentenced without trial and I feel guilty because I do nothing about it. But there it was, I wanted to see an oyster-catcher and I was no better than the people who'd caged oyster-catchers for me to see. And I myself have caged a water-beetle. On the other hand perhaps some of the birds and animals don't feel the Zoo to be a prison. Maybe they've been corrupted by it.

At the Waders Aviary a little sandpiper who would never have allowed me to come that close in real life perched on a sign a foot away from me and stared. He knew that he was safe because the wire mesh of the cage was between us. He has lost his innocence. He appeared to have lost a leg as well, and for a long time stood steadfastly on the one very slender remaining member whilst looking at me through half-closed eyes. Having kept me there for nearly half an hour he revealed a second leg that matched the other perfectly, then flew down to the sand and entertained a lady sandpiper with an elegant little dance that seemed done less for the lady than for the thing itself. He made his legs even longer and thinner than they were, drew himself up quite tall in his small way, spread his wings, wound himself up and produced a noise like a tiny paddle-wheel boat whilst flapping his wings stiffly and with formal regularity. At the same time he executed some very subtle steps almost absent-mindedly, with the air of one who could be blindingly nimble if he let himself go. The lady watched attentively. At a certain point, as if by mutual agreement that the proprieties had been observed, he stopped dancing, she stopped watching. They went their separate ways like two people at a cktail party.

Oyster-catchers were what I'd come to see and there were two or three of them mooching about but there was something wrong that made the seeing of them flat and uneventful. I'd never been that close to them before, part of their character had been that they were always seen from a distance on the open mudflats with a wide and low horizon far away. These oyster-catchers were so accessible as to be unobservable. One of them wound himself up as the sandpiper had done and released quite an urgent kleep kleep kleep. The sound independently hurried off round the pool and the bird hurried after it like a cat or a child working up interest in a toy. When the sound stopped the oyster-catcher abandoned it and began to potter about with some rather old-looking mussels.

There were all sorts of waders in the Waders Aviary, not all of whom would ordinarily have been seen in the same place I think. The sign showed pictures of a redshank, guillemot, razorbill, eider duck, oyster-catcher, ruff, kittiwake, white-breasted waterhen, rufous laughing thrush, curlew, laysan duck and hooded merganser. They had their concrete pool to wade in, they had reeds and bushes and a strip of sand. The Zoological Society had pieced together a habitat that was like the little naif towns one sometimes sees in model railway layouts. The elements of it were thing for thing a rough approximation of reality but the scale wasn't right and the parts of it didn't fit together in a realistic way.

The birds were all quite good-natured and reasonable about it, they seemed more grown-up than the Zoo management, as if they'd been caught and caged not because they weren't clever enough to avoid it but because they simply didn't think in terms of nets and cages, those were things for cunning children. So here they all were, interned for none of them knew how long. They made the best of it better than people would have done I think, and all of them appeared to get on rather neatly together. The sandpipers, the curlews and the redshanks, all pure Bewick, seemed to draw serenity from the sheer detail of their markings. A ruff was bathing with its ruff spread out as large as possible. It looked of the film world and as if it might call everyone "Darling."

I felt dissatisfied, as one does when morally strong preconceptions have to be questioned. The birds were not silent prisoners wasting away like Dr Manette in the Bastille nor were they beating pitiful wings against the wire mesh of their captivity. Their understanding of the whole thing seemed deeper and simpler than mine. Of course it may be that they're going decadent. I've seen a film in which Dr Lorenz pointed out the differences between two colonies of cattle egrets, one free and one caged. The free ones, who had to provide for themselves, were monogamous and energetic and kept their numbers within ecologically reasonable limits. The captive egrets were promiscuous, idle, overbreeding and presumably going to hell fast.

I passed the gibbons who seemed at the same time active and reflective, of more mature understanding than the party of French girls who stood before the cage shouting, "Allez, allez!" at their aerial artistry. I avoided the lions, the rhinoceroses and the elephants, walked along with my head down, not wanting to see anything and not wanting to go home. I fetched up at the Aquarium as it began to rain, and went inside.

Aquaria have always been interesting to me as sources of illumination, the fish are secondary. Madame Beetle's tank with its sunken wreck, water plants, pebbles and one bit of sea-china is very pretty when lit in the evening. Madame Beetle is more active than she was at first, submarining elegantly, her red fringed hind legs going like perfectly co-ordinated oars. I like the sound of the pump and filter too, it's better than the ticking of a clock.

When I was a child I had a fishless aquarium. My father set it up for me with gravel and plants and pebbles before he'd got the fish and I asked him to leave it as it was for a while. The pump kept up a charming burble, the green-gold light was wondrous when the room was dark. I put in a china mermaid and a tin horseman who maintained a relationship like that of the figures on Keats's Grecian urn except that the horseman grew rusty. Eventually fish were pressed upon me and they seemed an intrusion; I gave them to a friend. All that aquarium wanted was the sound of the pump, the gently waving plants, the mysterious pebbles and the silent horseman forever galloping to the mermaid smiling in the green-gold light. I used to sit and look at them for hours. The mermaid and the horseman were from my father. I have them in a box somewhere, I'm not yet ready to take them out and look at them again.

Here in the dark of the Aquarium were many green-and-gold-lit windows, huge compared to mine but not magical. The fish all look bored to death but of course fish aren't meant to be looked at closely, will not bear close examination. The lobsters scarcely looked more alive than those I've seen waiting to be selected by diners at sea-food restaurants. I don't think the Aquarium ought to do a shark at all if they're not going to lay on a big one. The leopard shark they have is so small that his vacant stare and receding chin make him seem nothing more than a marine form of twit rather than a representative of a mortally dangerous species. Rays I think ought not to be seen at all outside their natural habitat, too many questions arise.

I'd been aware of the turtles for some time before I went to look at them. I knew I'd have to do it but I kept putting it off. When I did go to see them I didn't know how to cope with it. Untenable propositions assembled themselves in my mind. If these were what they were then why were buildings, buses, streets? The sign said that green turtles were the source of turtle soup and hawksbills provided the tortoise-shell of commerce. But why soup, why spectacles?

Relative to her size my beetle has more than twice as much swimming-room as the turtles. And in that little tank the turtles were flying, flying in the water, submarine albatrosses. I've read about them, they navigate hundreds of miles of ocean. I imagined a sledge-hammer smashing the thick glass, letting out the turtles and their little bit of ocean, but then they'd only be flopping about on the wet floor.

I'm always afraid of being lost, the secret navigational art of the turtles seems a sacred thing to me. I thought of the little port of Polperro in Cornwall where they sell sea-urchin lamps, then I felt very sad and went home.

7

William G.

What a weird thing smoking is and I can't stop it. I feel cosy, have a sense of well-being when I'm smoking, poisoning myself, killing myself slowly. Not so slowly maybe. I have all kinds of pains I don't want to know about and I know that's what they're from. But when I don't smoke I scarcely feel as if I'm living. I don't feel as if I'm living unless I'm killing myself. Very good. Wonderful.

One time I grew a beard. I didn't want to see my face in the mirror any more while shaving so I stopped shaving, I'd already stopped looking at myself when brushing my teeth and washing my face and I used to comb my hair without a mirror, feeling the parting with my fingers. It was a relief at first but when the beard reached a state of full growth I was constantly aware of walking around behind it so I got rid of it. Since then I've had to see my face almost every morning. I don't shave on my Saturdays off nor on Sundays unless I'm going out in the evening.

I used to think when I shaved and looked at my face that that bit of time didn't count, was just the time in between things. Now I think it's the time that counts most. It's those times that all the other times are in between. It's the time when nothing helps and the great heavy boot of the past is planted squarely in your back and shoving you forward. Sometimes my mind gives me a flash of road I'll never see again, sometimes a face that's gone, gone. Moments like grains of sand but the beach is empty. Millions of moments in forty-five years. Letters in boxes, photos in drawers.

So breakfast is a useful thing, a rallying point for all the members of me. We all sit together at the table by the window to start the day off. My face comes along as well. Breakfast is always the same, perfectly reliable, no decisions, no conflicts: orange juice, muesli, a three-minute boiled egg, a slice of buttered toast, coffee that I grind myself.

There's a tiny kitchen on the landing just outside my door, a cooker and a little fridge and a sink. Mr. Sandor uses it before me in the morning, Miss Neap comes after me. Mr. Sandor always leaves the cooker sticky and smelling heavily organic. I don't know what he has for breakfast. Squid maybe. Kelp. Nasty-looking little parcels in the fridge. I always leave the cooker clean for Miss Neap. I could have a word with Sandor about it but cleaning the cooker seems less tiresome. The problem only arises in the mornings. Even on weekends he always has lunch and supper out. Once I attempted a conversation with the man and he waved a foreign newspaper about and grunted something through his heavy moustache about scoundrels in government. He seems violent and heavily burdened with thoughts of whatever country the newspaper is from. He carries a briefcase, the kind that looks as if it might be full of sausages. I've no idea what he does for a living. Miss Neap works at a theatre-ticket agency and visits her mother in Leeds some weekends. Her hair is that kind of blonde that only happens after fifty, she wears a pince-nez and a tightly-belted leopardskin coat and has blue eyes like ice. If Sandor breakfasted after me and before her I think he'd leave the cooker clean.

The sea turtles are on my mind all the time. I can feel something building up in me, feel myself becoming strange and unsafe. Today one of those women who never know titles came into the shop. They are the source of Knightsbridge lady soup and they ask for a good book for a nephew or something new on roses for a gardening husband. This one wanted a novel, "something for a good read at the cottage." I offered her *Procurer to the King* by Fallopia Bothways. Going like a bomb with the menopausal set. She gasped, and I realized I'd actually spoken the thought aloud: "Going like a bomb with the menopausal set."

She went quite red. "What did you say?" she said.

"Going like a bomb, it's the best she's written yet," I said, and looked very dim.

She let it pass, settled on *Lances of Glory* by Taura Strong and did not complain to Mr. Meager about me, which was really quite decent of her. But I have to be careful.

Every evening a lady and her husband and their greyhound bitch go slowly past the house. The husband and wife must be in their early sixties and the greyhound isn't young. The husband drags one leg and when the windows are open I can always hear them coming and know who it is even if I don't look out. They walk on opposite sides of the street, wife and greyhound on one side, husband on the other. The husband works for London Transport I think. Why a greyhound? Perhaps it's a retired racer. The street is very narrow and so are the pavements, which may explain why they walk on opposite sides although I've seen other couples walk side by side. Perhaps he needs more space around him because of his bad leg. The greyhound of course walks very slowly too, as if she's forgotten any other way of going. When I see them in the evening slowly passing by they look larger than life and allegorical.

The Underground trains are above ground where the District Line passes the common. On the right the tracks disappear behind a wall, on the left they converge towards Parsons Green and Putney Bridge. I watch the trains a lot. There are six lights on the front of each train, two vertical rows of three, and the pattern in which some are lit and some are dark tells the destination. For Special trains all six are lit. Three on the left and the bottom one on the right say Upminster, and so forth. There's a little sign as well that says where they're going. By watching with binoculars I've learnt most of the light code, I still don't know all of the signals. I rather like seeing the lights pass in the dark and thinking: Tower Hill or whatever. Sometimes I look at the empty tracks with my binoculars. The solid grey iron is peculiarly pleasing to the eye, the coloured lights almost taste red and green in the mouth. I used to go birdwatching with the binoculars. Sometimes I hear an owl on the common.

Weekends are dicey. Saturdays aren't too bad, there's the shop to go to or errands to do and lots of people on the street, football crowds in the afternoon. Sundays are dangerous, the quiet waits in ambush. Close the museums and there's no telling what might happen.

Saturday afternoon I did not go to the Zoo, I went to the National Maritime Museum at Greenwich to look at Port Liberty.

8

Neaera H.

There is a connection between my turtle thoughts and Polperro thoughts but I'm not sure I can find it. Polperro is mentioned in the guide-books as one of the prettiest fishing villages on the Cornish coast. I'd never seen it until last spring when I was visiting friends in Devon. We drove along many narrow roads winding between hedgerows, crossed the Tamar Bridge into Cornwall, passed through Looe and arrived at a car-park. Near it was a whitewashed inn on which was mounted a millwheel smartly painted black and slowly revolving. I don't remember seeing any stream to turn the wheel, I have the impression that a little gush of water had been piped in for that purpose.

One of the principal industries in Polperro is parking cars. We parked, then joined many people walking slowly through the narrow streets eating ice-cream, leading, pushing and carrying infants and scowling at such cars as had not parked. There were many postcards, many sea-urchins, many pottery things and shiny coppery things for sale, many Cream Teas. There was a model village, the entrance to which was through an orange-lit souvenir shop with music. We passed through the souvenirs, the orange light and the music as under a waterfall, paid 10p and came out into what must have been the garden once and was now the model village.

There was organ music, very reduced and scant-sounding, playing *Abide with Me*. I guessed it was coming from the model church and I was right. The model village was Polperro itself, as could be observed by looking over a low wall towards the real street. There one saw a full-size sign that said GARNER and next to it the Claremont Hotel, then looking down saw the miniature GARNER and the Claremont Hotel, lumpish and simplified in the model.

The model houses and shops, thick and awry, had an air of stolid outrage. It was as if the anima of each place, private and indwelling, had been nagged into standing naked in the little streets before the deformed buildings. As if someone had said, "We need the money, you must help." The very boats in the model harbour, oafish and out of scale in the still water, cursed almost aloud, denied any connection whatever with real boats, fishing and the sea, tried by dissociating themselves to make amends to the poor household gods of the port.

A large orange tiger cat settled comfortably on one of the model roofs and a black-and-white cat picked its way through the streets as if looking out for model sinners on a model Day of Judgment. There were pence and halfpence on the bottom of the model harbour. People do that everywhere in fountains I know. Is it possible that they made wishes here when they threw in their coins?

We emerged, went on past Cream Teas and sea-urchins to the full-size harbour, a small one sheltered by a breakwater. The fishing boats were few, there was one called *Ocean Gift*. A young woman with a Polaroid camera repeatedly photographed her bald baby who had the face of a mature publican, showing him the picture each time. Gulls with cruel yellow eyes paced the quay. A jackdaw perched on the sea wall, neat, detached, seeming full of critical comment but saying nothing. There was a sign at the harbour which I copied:

POLPERRO HARBOUR
Polperro is the best example
of the
small Cornish fishing ports
and the Harbour Trustees
are anxious to retain
its character without resorting
to commercialization

The cost of maintenance
far exceeds the income
WILL YOU PLEASE HELP?

There was a box with a slot. A few feet away were a souvenir stand and a shop full of pottery things and coppery things and sea-urchin lamps with light bulbs in them shining through the sea-urchins. I put no money in the box. Polperro seemed to me like a street-walker asking for money to maintain her virginity.

The tide hadn't come all the way in and there was a patch of dry stony beach on the seaward side of the wall. I went down the steps and walked there. The beach offered little more than broken glass and contraceptives. At least there was some vitality left here I thought. I contented myself with two stones and three lumps of glass and a bit of china worn smooth. As we left the harbour I saw a boat lying on the mud. It was full of loose planks and had a hole in its side. Someone had lettered SHIT on it with a paint brush.

Would it be just as well for Polperro to break up its boats and pave its harbour for a car-park? But of course without the harbour and the token boats no one would come to park there. If the turtles were set free, where is there for them to go really? To what can they navigate? They swim hundreds of miles to the beaches of their breeding grounds. The hundred eggs the females lays each time are just barely enough to ensure the race against wild dogs and predatory birds on the beaches, sharks in the water. I've read in Carr that wild dogs from far away travel to the beaches to wait for the arrival of the turtles. Still the hundred eggs would be enough, but nothing ensures the turtles against the manufacturers of turtle soup. Three-hundred-pound turtles navigate the ocean and come ashore to be slaughtered for the five pounds of cartilage that gets sold to the soup-makers. They're torn open and mutilated, left belly-up and dead or dying on the beach.

Is my wanting to set the Zoo turtles free a kind of Polperrization, a trying to pretend that something is when it isn't? Would they have to swim with signs and slotted boxes begging for protection and support? There's rubbish in the oceans now far from any land, Coca-Cola tins perhaps circling among the icebergs. If turtles have memories the beaches the old ones remember are not what they would find now. Perhaps the only decent thing would be a monster Turtlearium charging a proper admission, with turtle rides 10p and YOUR PHOTO WITH A SEA TURTLE 50p. Something has got to be whole in some way but my mind isn't strong enough to work it out. Carr's turtle station at Tortuguero in Costa Rica sounds a lovely place in his book. It sounds the sort of place where at night if you looked through the palm trees there'd always be lights on and coffee and people with clip-boards. Tortuguero. The name sounds like hot sun, blue water, white surf.

Often in the evenings Madame Beetle hangs head-down in the water cleaning her legs with great diligence like a woman really looking after herself. She seems to have settled in quite nicely, has a good appetite. She attacks the raw meat vigorously when I drop it in, then hangs head-down holding it in her front legs while her mandibles are busy with it. I don't know whether any of the meat actually disappears, there's always a good deal of it about that goes white and filmy after a while, but she must get something out of it because she's still alive. I remove the old bits from the tank with a skewer. When I first took the cover off to do that I thought Madame Beetle might fly away but she simply retired inside the shipwreck until I'd finished.

I've bought a little china figure, a bathing beauty in a 1900s mauve bathing-suit and cap, red bathing-slippers. She's sitting on a rock leaning back on her elbows, her right knee raised and her right ankle resting on her left knee. Her pretty rosy-cheeked face is turned to the side and as she sits before the aquarium on my desk she looks as if she's been watching Madame Beetle and has just turned away towards me. Possibly there's a story in her as well. Possibly there's no story either in her or Madame Beetle. It may happen to me at any time that everything will be just what it is, with no stories in anything.

9

William G.

Briefcases. Businessmen, barristers carry briefs. When I was in advertising we always talked about what our brief was. *Brief* means letter in German. Brief is short. Life is a brief case. Brief candle, out, out. In the tube there was a very small, very poor-looking man in a threadbare suit and a not very clean shirt, spectacles. He made a roll-up, lit it, then took from his briefcase a great glossy brochure with glorious colour photographs of motorcycles. Many unshaven men carry briefcases. I've seen briefcases carried by men who looked as if they slept rough. Women tramps usually have carrier bags, plastic ones often. I carry one of those expanding files with a flap. Paper in it for taking notes, a book sometimes, sandwich and an apple for lunch. The apple bulges, can't be helped.

I took the tube to Surrey Docks, the 70 bus from there. There were some children on the bus singing *Oranges and Lemons* and they seemed to spin it out very slowly. I found myself waiting, waiting for "Here comes a chopper to chop off your head, chop, chop, chop!" which arrived in due course and very loudly.

At Greenwich I went straight to the Port Liberty model after the guards at the door had looked into my envelope and found no bombs.

They have to take precautions, that's understandable. A place like Greenwich is a temptation. The greenness and the stillness, the augustness of the buildings and the observatory dome almost make one want to set off a bomb just out of respect.

There seem to be more children than there used to be. Always lots of them about even on school days. Children seem to be the permanent population while adults drift in and out and fall away. Each year the schoolgirls in their white knee-socks seem more erotic, more secretly knowing, one thinks probably nothing would surprise them. There are always children at the Port Liberty windows. I looked over the shoulder of a girl who must have been about twelve, the scent of her hair was in my nostrils. I don't know where my daughters are now. I don't know if Dora's remarried. Someone pressed the button and the three-minute sequence began. The model sky grew slowly dark. Such a perfect world, so small and yet so full of distance. A long time ago I copied the signs that tell about Port Liberty:

APPROACHING PORT LIBERTY BY NIGHT

When night falls the navigator has to rely on the navigation lights shown by other vessels to avoid colliding with them and the lights shown by buoys, beacons and lighthouses to keep him in safe waters.

A confusion of fixed and flashing lights confronts him when he approaches a port but trained to interpret the various light colours and sequences in conjunction with his chart he can safely identify and follow the correct channel into port.

What you can see

The lighthouse on Patrol Point, whose white light is visible 20 miles out at sea, occults once every 30 seconds, while dead ahead can be seen the white light of the Landfall buoy, flashing every second.

A steady red light over a steady white light near the Landfall buoy identifies the pilot launch waiting for our arrival with a pilot ready to board and assist us through the channel to the anchorage.

The white masthead lights and green starboard navigating lights of a large vessel can be seen moving down the main channel, while the navigation lights of a smaller ship are visible coming out through the secondary channel.

Three white lights in a vertical triangle indicate a dredger working at the inner end of Crushers Bank and that it is safe to pass on either side of her.

The masthead light and port and starboard lights of a small craft off our starboard bow indicate that she is heading towards us.

The edges of the main channel are marked by the flashing lights of buoys, and further up the river the lights of fixed beacons can be discerned which assist the navigator to keep in the deeper water.

Model made to the requirements of the Department of Navigation by Thorp Modelmakers Ltd.

There were the lights fixed and flashing, each in its proper place in that perfect night miniature and vast. Then the night faded, there was sunlight on the distant hills of the port, sunlight on the water before me and on the vessels coming and going, and I was:

APPROACHING PORT LIBERTY BY DAY

When a ship approaches port the navigator has various aids to help him.

He has a chart of the area, which he keeps up to date by Admiralty Notices to Mariners, issued weekly.

He has leading marks and the international system of buoys and beacons which mark the channel which he will have to follow and which he has to look out for as he approaches.

In most ships he usually has an echo sounder to indicate to him the depth of water and a radar set to supplement his eyes if visibility is poor because of fog or rain or falling snow.

What you can see

Imagine you are standing on the navigating bridge of a ship approaching the estuary of the River Line and Port Liberty.

The Landfall buoy marking the entrance to the channel is right ahead of you and close by you can see the pilot launch displaying its distinguishing code flag waiting to put a pilot on board.

Steaming out through the main channel is a 12,000 ton cargo vessel and astern of her a coaster is about to pass through the secondary channel used by smaller craft.

There is a fishing boat heading out to sea off Plushers Point and at the inner end of Crusher's Bank a dredger is working.

Port Liberty can just be seen around the bend in the river and the buoys marking the main and secondary channels into the River Line and up to the quay are clearly visible.

Model made to the requirements of the Department of Navigation by Thorp Modelmakers Ltd.

So clear and sharp, Port Liberty. So precise and real. Realer than anything else I know. Of course it doesn't exist. There's no such place. There is no River Line, no Crusher's Bank, no Plushers Point, no Port Liberty. The chart and the soundings, the channel markers and the buoys have no counterparts in the full-size world. Port Liberty is a fiction invented by the Admiralty as Fig. 67 in the *Admiralty Manual of Navigation Volume I*, and the National Maritime Museum conmissioned a model of it.

There's more to the model than meets the eye. I once got in touch with Thorp Modelmakers Ltd and was astonished to find that the tiny fixed and flashing lights are not actually on the tiny vessels, the lighthouse, the buoys. I couldn't believe it. The scale was too small for that, I was told. The lights are underneath the model and there is a system of mirrors derived from an old theatrical illusion called "Pepper's Ghost." The night window is a mirror and the lights fixed and flashing so perfectly, each in its proper place, are not in fact where one sees them. I think about it often.

Neaera H.

I think there is less merit in Gerard Manley Hopkins's poem "The Wind-hover" than there would have been in not writing it. I think that Basho's frog that jumped into the old pond has more falcon in it than Hopkins's bird, simply because it has more of things-as-they-are, which includes falcons and everything else. "The Windhover" seems to me a wet poem and twittish. But my judgment has become so subjective that there are many things I must avoid. For some time I've been avoiding poetry when possible but in an unthinking moment I opened *The Faber Book of Modern Verse* and there was Hopkins. Windhover is the old name for the bird that is now called a kestrel. I've seen them hovering over hedgerows, they don't want mannered words but only the simplest and fewest, certainly nothing longer than haiku and preferably no words at all. I'm less reasonable than I was when young.

There was a kestrel a long time ago, perhaps that's why I was so annoyed by the poem. We were lying in a field, we looked up and opened our mouths and said nothing.

The range of human types and actions is not terribly wide. I have seen the same face on a titled lady and a barmaid. And there seem to be only a few things to do with life, in various combinations. I could not have accepted the idea of myself as a stereotype when I was young but I can now. I'm a more or less arty-intellectual-looking lady of forty-three who is unmarried, dresses more for style than for fashion, looks the sort of spinster who doesn't keep cats and is not a vegetarian. Looks, I think, like a man's woman and hasn't got a man. When I was a child grown-ups often told me to smile, which I found presumptuous of them. People still tell me that sometimes, mostly idiots at parties.

Sometimes I wonder if I ought to give up the push-chair that I use instead of a shopping basket on wheels. It has red and white stripes like the little tents one sees over holes in the street. It may well be that the same company makes both, I'd like it if they did. It was lent me by a friend whose children have outgrown it on the occasion of her giving me an orange tree and I've never returned it. One sees a certain kind of poor old person wheeling battered prams loaded with rubbish or shabby push-chairs full of scavengings. My push-chair is still smart however and I am not yet poor and old.

Somehow I keep up with my work, always in arrears, often uncertain whether I'm sleeping or waking. My files decline gently from order to chaos, all kinds of things are accumulating dust in the spare room. I can't always find what I'm looking for. Easy is the slope of Hell. I sit at the typewriter, I sit at the drawing-table, proof copies appear from time to time, then bound copies, so I seem to go on doing what I do. Royalty cheques twice a year. *"Gillian Vole's Jumble Sale* was absolutely the hit of the sales conference," writes my editor, "and we expect it to do even better than *Gillian Vole's Christmas.* Whatever Gillian is up to now, we and all of her other fans look forward to her next appearance."

Well, Gillian Vole may jolly well have packed it in. I couldn't think of another Gillian Vole story right now to save my life. I've become quite fond of Madame Beetle but simply as a flatmate. Suddenly I don't know, haven't the faintest idea how people make up stories about anything. Anything is whatever it happens to be, why on earth make up stories.

At three o'clock in the morning I sat in the dark looking out of the window down at the square where the fountain is not and I thought about the turtles. The essence of it is that they can find something and they are not being allowed to do it. What more can you do to a creature, short of killing it, than prevent it from finding what it can find? How must they feel? Is there a sense in them of green ocean, white surf and hot sand? Probably not. But there *is* a drive in them to find it as they swoop in their golden-green light with their flippers clicking against the glass as they turn. Is there anything to be done about it? My mind is not an organizational one.

What is there to find? Thomas Bewick diligently followed the patterns of light from feather to feather, John Clare looked carefully at hedgerows, Emily Dickinson cauterized her lopped-off words with dashes. Ella Wheeler Wilcox implacably persisted. Shackleton came back against all odds, Scott didn't. There was a round-the-world singlehanded sailing race in which one of the yachtsmen stopped in one part of the ocean and broadcast false positions.

There is no place for me to find. No beach, no breeding grounds. Do I owe the turtles more or less because of that? Is everyone obliged to help those who have it in them to find something? I bought a second-hand mathematical book, I don't know why, on self-replicating automata. Not robots but mathematical models. The book said that random search could not account for evolution. Something evidently wants there to be finding. Time's arrow points one way only. Even the moment just past cannot be returned to.

I went into the kitchen, had some tea and toast, came back and sat in my reading chair with my eyes closed. When I opened them it was time for lunch. I had some cheese and apples, went out. I had no intention of going to the Zoo but I went there. The penguins were yawping and honking in a way that had unmistakably to do with procreation. An Australian crane was performing a remarkable dance for his mate. It was as if place and time were internalized in them and not in their surroundings, like Englishmen who dress for dinner on plantations in Borneo. The lions and tigers have no such faculty, must pace madly or lie still and doze.

I stood in the darkness by the turtle tank for some time, not so much looking at the turtles as just being near them and waiting. A man in shirtsleeves came out of a door marked PRIVATE and stood in front of one of the fish tanks as if checking something. He was obviously one of the keepers and he had an air of decency about him, as if he paid attention to the things that really need attention paid to them.

I rehearsed the question several times in my mind, then spoke to him. "Were any of the turtles full-grown when they were brought here?" I said.

"No," he said. "They were only little when they came here, no more than a pound or two. The big ones have been here twenty or thirty years."

"Full-grown turtles," I said, "how are they transported?"

II

William G.

A lady came into the shop one afternoon, arty-intellectual type about my age or a little younger. She was wearing a long orange Indian-print skirt, an old purple velvet jacket, a denim shirt and expensive boots. Not at all bad-looking. Rather troubled face, circles under her eyes. All at once I felt a strong urge to talk to her for hours and hours about everything. And at the same time I felt an urge not to talk to her at all.

She drifted about the Natural History shelves for a time in a sleep-walking sort of way, picking up books and turning the pages without always looking at them. Then she picked up a book on sea turtles by Robert Bustard and read about a quarter of it where she stood. Eerie, the way she read, as if she'd simply forgotten to put the book down. And eerie that she was reading about sea turtles. Obviously I can't be the only one thinking about them but I had the shocking feeling that here was another one of me locked up alone in a brain with the same thoughts. Me, what's that after all? An arbitrary limitation of being bounded by the people before and after and on either side. Where they leave off I begin, and vice versa. I once saw a cartoon sequence of a painter painting a very long landscape. When he'd finished he cut it up into four landscapes of the usual proportions. Mostly one doesn't meet others from the same picture. When it happens it can be unsettling.

Had we anything new on sea turtles other than the Bustard, she asked. Her voice was as I expected, low and husky. She spoke as if she'd come a long way from wherever she'd been in her mind and couldn't stop long.

No, I said. Nothing else new. Had she read Carr?

Yes, she had. She looked directly at me when I mentioned Carr as if registering the fact that I knew of him. Then it seemed her mind went elsewhere, she thanked me and left the shop.

Pity, in a way. If she'd been young and pretty would I have tried to extend the conversation? Maybe. Maybe not. I don't really want to talk to a woman who's accumulated the sort of things in her head that I have in mine. And I haven't had much interest in women at all for a while, not in a realistic way. Fantasies, yes. But not actualities, not practicalities. For a time after the break-up I went to bed with as many girls as I could but nothing lasted and I didn't want it to. They wanted attention paid to them, attention paid to a present they were part of and a future that belonged to them, and my mind was elsewhere.

I used to want to find someone to listen to Chopin with. Now I don't even like to hear Chopin. Nor Scarlatti. Nor the Haydn, Mozart, and Beethoven quartets. Not even Bach. I haven't listened to the B Minor Mass for more than a year. The idea of music has seemed totally foreign to me for some time now. I can't think any more why anyone would want to bother with sounds in that way. I can stand on the platform in the Underground and listen to the wincing of the rails as the train comes in, listen to the rumble as it goes. I can listen abstractly to the football players on the common, trains going by, aeroplanes overhead. Raw sound I don't mind but music has nothing to do with me any more. And it's not as if I can meditate or anything like that. It's just that plain sounds and silence are all I want to hear.

On my Friday half-day I went to the Zoo again. One of the keepers in the Aquarium came out of a PRIVATE door and I asked him about the turtles. The big ones have been there twenty or thirty years, he said. I asked him if it was possible to look at the tank from the other side. Yes, he said, and took me into PRIVATE.

One had to go up a few steps and climb through a hole in the wall, then there were planks across the back of the tank. It was brightly lit, had a backstage feeling. The turtles looked different seen from above.

"That's not the colour they'd be in natural light," the keeper said. "Their colour fades here."

"Would it be a big job moving them out of here?" I said.

"We do it sometimes when we clean the tank," he said. "Put them in the filters. Bit awkward getting them through the hole, you have to mind their jaws. But it's not too difficult."

"Suppose," I said, "some sort of turtle freak decided to steal the turtles and put them back in the ocean. What would he need for the job?"

"You're talking about me," he said. "That's what I've wanted to do. I've told them we ought to let the big ones go, replace them with little ones. We go fishing off Southampton for specimens two or three times a year, and I've said why don't we take the big turtles along and put them into the Channel. Apart from wanting them to go free I'm tired of cleaning up after them. But they don't want to know, they're not interested in the turtles here."

"Wouldn't transport be a problem?" I said. "Don't they have to be kept from drying out? And isn't the Channel too cold for them?"

"Funny," he said. "You're the second this week that's asked me about turtle transport. A lady was chatting to me about the turtles the other day. Sometimes no one asks about them for six months at a stretch. Drying out's no problem on a trip as short as from here to Southampton. Put them on wet sacks, they'd even be all right without anything for that distance. I don't think the water'd bother them. Cold water makes them a little sluggish but I think they'd backtrack up the North Atlantic Current till they hit the Canary Current or the Gulf Stream. I bet they'd be in home waters in three months."

"The lady," I said, "was she rather arty-intellectual looking? Husky voice?"

"That's the one," he said. "Friend of yours?"

"No," I said. "Then there isn't all that much to it, is there? Just a matter of hiring a van and taking along a trolley or something. But the place must be guarded at night?" I wondered when he'd start looking at me hard and ask me about the questions I was asking.

"Securicor," he said. "But they make their rounds on a regular schedule. That's no problem."

Was he inviting me to have a go at it? I liked the look of him, he seemed a right sort of man. Suddenly it all seemed hugely possible, I began to go trembly. "It's been nice talking to you," I said, and got his name and telephone number. George Fairbairn. He's the Head Keeper. It seemed almost too much to think about at the moment, almost as if it were thrusting itself upon me. And what had *she* in mind for the turtles? Probably the same sort of lark or at least the same sort of fantasy. Funny, two minds full of turtle thoughts.

12

Neaera H.

Children in the sunlight and the green shade of the square. They seem shaped of light, of silver air or green shade, changing substance as they move from one to the other. Their little shouts and cries are like coloured dots that make a picture of noise but looked at closely the dots are coloured silence. High-legged and quick the children wade in twos and threes through light and shade like shore birds.

What I do is not as good as what an oyster-catcher does. Writing and illustrating books for children is not as good as walking orange-eyed, orange-billed in the distance on the river, on the beaches of the ocean, finding shellfish. And of course they fly as well which must be worth a good deal. Oyster-catchers fit into the world, their time fits. I don't know how long they live. Herring gulls can live as long as twenty-eight years. The eyes of herring gulls are utterly pitiless, have no pity even for the bird they're part of. They seem not to be bird eyes but ocean eyes, yellow eyes of the ocean looking out of the bodies of birds.

The man in the bookshop who knew about Carr, his eyes too seemed other than of himself, seemed not to be seeing things on his behalf. It was as if he found himself always in strange houses looking out of the windows of rooms in which nothing was his. A tall hopeless-looking man with an attentive face and an air of fragile precision like a folding rule made of ivory. There was something in my memory: *The Man in the Zoo*, the David Garnett novella about the man who had himself locked up in a cage and exhibited as *Homo sapiens*. Not that he seems part of such a story but the idea of him has something of hapless patience in it.

George Fairbairn, the Head Keeper at the Aquarium, seemed quite willing to tell me anything I wanted to know about the turtles. I have the feeling that if I told him what's in my mind he might even help me do it and of course that frightens me.

I can't possibly do it alone. I'd need someone to handle the turtles and drive the van, I can't do any part of it really except pay the expenses. There'd be the long drive to Cornwall, it would be night-time. I'd put them into the ocean at Polperro. The mystery of the turtles and their secret navigation is a magical reality, juice of life in a world gone dry. When I think of the turtles going into the ocean I think of it happening in that place that so badly needs new reality.

The ends of things are always present in their beginnings. T. S. Eliot has of course noted that. But it seems to me that the ends are actually *visible* in the faces of the people with whom one begins something. There is always an early face that will be forgotten and will be seen again. Sometimes one simply sees the death that will come too soon, as I did with Geoffrey long before the afternoon with the kestrel. But there's something else, some aspect of the person that is always seen early and will inevitably be seen again no matter how the seeing changes in between. The man who looks a rotter at first and then is seen to be charming will look a rotter again, that can be depended on. The scared person will look scared again, the lost one lost. That man at the bookshop has been seen as hopeless-looking long ago by someone, by himself as well, and his face has returned to that look. My face does not look back at me now when I look into the mirror. That too is a return.

More and more I'm aware that the permutations are not unlimited. Only a certain number of things can happen and whatever can happen *will* happen. The differences in scale and costume do not alter the event. Oedipus went to Thebes, Peter Rabbit into Mr. McGregor's garden, but the story is essentially the same: life points only towards the terror. Beatrix Potter left it to John Gould to show us Peter dangling from the beak of *Bubo bubo*.

The turtle in Lear's *Yonghy-Bonghy-Bò* looks like a hawksbill in the drawing. The man at the bookshop has not got a tiny body nor does his head grow too large but there is a good deal of Yonghy-Bonghy-Bò in him.

> Through the silent-roaring ocean
> Did the turtle swiftly go;
> Holding fast upon his shell
> Rode the Yonghy-Bonghy-Bò.
> With a sad primeval motion
> Towards the sunset isles of Boshen . . .

Madame Beetle is shaped somewhat like a sea turtle, especially in profile. Seen from above she's more elongated, less shield-shaped. Her motion is primeval but not sad. Today I cleaned the tank and the filter and she's been patrolling her domain with renewed interest, repeatedly going up and down one side that was green with algae and is now clear. I wonder if she's looking at her reflection. "Domain," I said as if she were free and not the prisoner of my flagging invention. The shipwreck looks quite good now, a little furry and spotty, its foretop lost in green curling fronds. All of the plants are putting out new growth.

Very naval Madame Beetle looks, as neat and boaty as a model at the Science Museum. Her underside is tan with regular transverse black lines as neat as the planking one sees in models. A Victorian one-man submarine perhaps, or a little armoured galley. Up and down the sides she goes then once round the tank rowing her smooth and undulating course. Beyond her little ocean I see rooftops and the sky.

I was on the South Bank one day by the Royal Festival Hall. It was a sunny day with a bright blue sky. I was looking up at a train crossing the Hungerford Bridge. Through the train I could see the sky successively framed by each window as the carriages passed. Each window moving quickly forward and away held briefly a rectangle of blue. The windows passing, the blue remained.

13

William G.

Now suddenly the weather is hot, the days are heavy and humid. There are more and more strong-voiced people in the shop with sunglasses and cameras and American Express Travellers' Cheques. Many American couples as they age seem to make a sexual exchange: the man looks feminine, the woman masculine. Or perhaps the woman takes over both sexes and the man vacates his altogether. One big strong leathery lady was in yesterday buying guidebooks and maps. She seemed to be carrying her husband under her arm as some ladies carry little dogs on buses. "You'd better go buy some antiques, John," she said to him. "I'm going to be here for a while." "Right," said John when she'd set him on his feet. He went out with his telephoto lens thrusting before him like a three-foot optical erection. If the authorities ever twig what cameras are about they'll make old men stop flashing their telephotos.

The ocean is striking back. In this morning's *Times* there was an item about a Japanese seaweed called *Sargassum muticum* that's spreading everywhere. It fouls propellers and traps boats, said the report. That was to be expected.

Saturday afternoon I went to the Zoo again. The sunlight was brilliant in Regent's Park, the air was sticky with ice-cream and soft drinks, people were rowing boats, there were girls in bikinis everywhere in the green grass and young men walking with their shirts off. Inside the Aquarium it seemed darker than ever. I scarcely looked at the turtles, saw them out of the comer of my eye swooping like bad dreams in the golden-green.

I found George Fairbairn and we went into the room behind the turtle tank. There was another room off that one with a lot of small tanks in it, and he showed me a little turtle somebody'd given the Aquarium when they found out how big it would grow. It was some kind of Ridley he thought but he wasn't sure which kind. I held it in my hand. One wouldn't expect a little black sea turtle to be cuddly but it was. It was about nine inches long, heavy and solid, and waggled its flippers in a very docile way. It felt such a jolly nice little piece of life.

After we'd been chatting for a while I came right out with it, standing there between two rows of tanks with the little turtle in my hand. There were big cockroaches hopping about on the floor. "What if the turtle freak were to propose a turtle theft to the Head Keeper?" I said.

"Head Keeper wouldn't be all that shocked by it," he said.

"How would we go about it?" I said.

"Best time would be when we're cleaning and painting the tank," he said. "We take the turtles out and put them in the filters and they stay there for a week maybe while the maintaining gets done. So they're not on view and maybe for the whole week the Society wouldn't even know they're gone."

"But if you help me do it there's really no way of hiding your part in it, is there?" I said.

"No," he said, "I guess there isn't."

"Would they bring charges against you?" I said. "Would you get sacked?"

"They wouldn't bring charges," he said, "and I don't think I'd be sacked either. I'm Head Keeper and I've been here twenty-seven years, that counts for something. They'd take it up at a Council meeting and consider my reasons but they'd be batting on a sticky wicket actually. The R.S.P.C.A.'s always interested in anything that might be considered cruelty to animals and if I said that keeping the turtles here was cruel the Zoological Society mightn't want to push it too far."

What about me? I wondered. Would I be had up for it? Not unless George Fairbairn grassed on me, and he wasn't the sort to do that. "Are you willing to do it?" I said.

"Yes," he said. "It's one of those things that's pretty well got to be done. I'll let you know a couple of days in advance when we're going to clean the tank. It won't be for a month or two yet. Where're you thinking of launching them?"

"Brighton?" I said. Brighton was close, and I was beginning to want it over and done with as quickly as possible.

"Brighton's as good as any place I suppose. Although they might have a better chance starting out farther west."

"Where'd they come from?" I said.

"Madeira."

Madeira. The name sounded like boats and sunlight. I gave him my telephone numbers at the shop and at home. We shook hands and I left without looking at the turtles. They'd become an obligation now, and heavy.

On my way to the South Gate I saw the woman who'd been in the shop asking about turtle books. She was coming towards me, heading for the Aquarium I had no doubt. Damn you, I thought, surprised at the violence of my feelings. Damn her for what? I might as well damn myself as well, for not being young, for being middle-aged and nowhere and unhappy, for having turtle fantasies instead of living life. She had turtle business in mind, I was certain of it. And I knew she was going to ask me some kind of direct question and I was going to answer it and then we'd both be in it, it wouldn't be just mine any more. It was the sort of situation that would be ever so charming and warmly human in a film with Peter Ustinov and Maggie Smith but that sort of film is only charming because they leave out so many details, and real life is all the details they leave out.

She was looking at me and I couldn't look away or pretend not to recognize her. Damn her, damn her I thought. We both stopped and I could see her turning the whole thing over in her mind. She has the kind of face that doesn't hide anything, you can read it right off. Vulnerable, I suppose. Why hasn't she learned not to be vulnerable, she's old enough. She was certainly going to speak, was bound to speak, couldn't help but speak but it was difficult for her, she felt shy. Suddenly I felt sorry for her. Maybe she'd been thinking about the turtles longer than I had, maybe I and not she was the one who was intruding. All right, I thought, I'm sorry. Go ahead, speak.

"Hello," she said, and went on past me.

"Hello," I said.

Why didn't she speak?

14

Neaera H.

Alas! What boots it with uncessant care
To tend the homely slighted Shepherds trade,
And strictly meditate the thankles Muse,
Were it not better don as others use
To sport with Amaryllis in the shade,
Or with the tangles of Neaera's hair?

Fathers are prone to name first daughters elaborately. I don't mind so much being named after a nymph but I really don't care to be associated with the pastoral tradition. An idyll based on illusion has no charm for me, but then of course idylls are almost by definition illusion. Even the lovely music of *Acis and Galataea* does not incline me favourably towards nymphs and swains. I think a shepherd ought to tend sheep and a poet ought to write poems. If I owned sheep I don't think I'd send them out with a poetic shepherd. Although if one forgets the shepherds of Theocritus and thinks of David herding sheep while armed with a sling that's quite different. David, yes indeed. A poet-shepherd with a strong right arm. I wonder why I never thought of him in that light before.

My hair is often tangled and no one withes it now. There are fashions in emotion as in other things. If I were twenty now and my fiancé died in a car crash I think I should soon find another man. My generation was somewhat in between things, neither free nor much supported by whatever held us in. More of us were capable of being brought to a halt by something of that sort than young people now would be. Our songs were different, our dances and our choices. Rubbish. Even in the privacy of my own mind I can't be entirely honest with myself.

The man from the bookshop, when I saw him at the Zoo I thought he was going to say something to me. I had the feeling that he was coming from the Aquarium, that he had turtles on his mind. All he said was "Hello," and we went our separate ways. It's curious how the mind works. I see the world through turtle-coloured glasses now. Because of the turtles I expect a stranger to speak significantly, am prepared for signs and wonders, my terrors freshen, I feel a gathering-up in me as if I'm going to die soon, I await a Day of Judgment. Whose judgment? Mine, less merciful than God's. It is not always a comfort to find a like-minded person, another fraction of being who shares one's incompleteness. The bookshop man has many thoughts and feelings that I have, I sense that.

I went into the Aquarium but I didn't see George Fairbairn and I was glad not to have the chance to talk further about the turtles. The Aquarium was intensely dark after the violent sunlight outside, I could scarcely see the benches down the middle of it. Young couples were black against the green-lit windows of the tanks. I sat on the bench nearest the turtles but I didn't look directly at them. At one particular moment that part of the Aquarium was empy except for the turtles and the fish and me. Then a young man and a girl came out of the darkness and stood in front of the turtles. He murmured something that I couldn't quite make out, and she said in a voice that was like a clear mirror, "No, it's too late, it's too late."

I was surprised at the effect of her words on me. I didn't burst into tears. I didn't know what she was referring to—it might have been love or theatre tickets but it struck me at once that her observation was probably accurate. Very likely it *was* too late for whatever they were talking about. She sounded the sort of girl who sees things clearly, and young as she was there was something for which it was too late.

Too-lateness, I realized, has nothing to do with age. It's a relation of self to the moment. Too-lateness is potentially every moment. Or not, depending on the person and the moment. Perhaps there even comes a time when it's no longer too late for anything. Perhaps, even, most times are too early for most things, and most of life has to go by before it's time for almost anything and too late for almost nothing. Nothing to lose, the present moment to gain, the integration with long-delayed Now. Headlights staring out on sleeping streets. Sea-smelling turtles and the smell of wet hessian from the sacking. The tide in or out drawn by a moon seen or unseen.

The man from the bookshop, would he be willing to drive the van? I think he's perhaps already thought of it, without me of course. Possibly it isn't something he'd like to share with anyone, I might be intruding. But the turtles are after all public, so to speak. Perhaps they no longer want the ocean and I'm wrong to impose my feelings on them. But I believe they do want the ocean, that must be in them. No, it's not always a comfort to find a like-minded person. If the bookshop man and I both have designs on the turtles we have got to muddle through it as decently as possible but there's little to be said between us beyond that. We've too much in common for us to be comfortable in each other's presence for very long.

15

William G.

They won't stop killing the whales. They make dog- and cat-food out of them, face creams, lipstick. They kill the whales to feed the dogs so the dogs can shit on the pavement and the people can walk in it. A kind of natural cycle. Whales can navigate, echo-locate, sing, talk to one another but they can't get away from the harpoon guns. The International Whaling Commission is meeting here in London right now but they won't stop the killing of whales.

The drinking fountain on the common is gone. It was there for years and years, probably ever since the foot-paths and the playground and the paddling pool and the football pitch were made. The people next door have been here for twenty years and it was there when they moved in. Vandals pushed it over the other night, broke the pipes. Now it's been taken away. There's a little square hole full of water with a Coca-Cola tin in it and that's all.

There's something about the common at night, something about the dark open space facing the lighted houses that provokes savagery and terrorism. Youths on the common at night yell horribly as they pass the houses. They feel themselves to be part of the night outside and they want the people inside to be afraid. They get into the playground and scream and shout and hurl the swings about with a savage clashing of the chains as if they could destroy the world by pulling down the playground. In the morning the chains are all wound round the crossbar and the maintenance man has to come with a ladder to disentangle the swings.

The drinking fountain and the whales are all part of the same thing in my mind. I feel as if the life is being torn out of the world.

Fear. Some days I have to go to the loo three times before I leave the house in the morning. I can feel the fear thrilling in me the same way the rails feel the trains coming. Fear of everything. I wasn't sorry to give Dora the car when we parted, I hated to drive it, always felt as if something dreadful might happen at any moment. I never felt as manly and powerful as other male drivers. When I stopped at traffic lights I never pulled up nose to nose with other cars, always stopped a little way back so as not to challenge anyone. If I take the turtles to Brighton I'll have to drive the van but that'll be all right. The turtles are depending on me. *Something*'s depending on me.

I was looking at a book on shamanism at the shop, by Mircea Eliade. In Siberia and South America, whereever they have shamans, they're always the unstable, the epileptics, the weird ones of the group, people prone to terrors and depression as I am. But unlike me they get initiated into power and a place of importance, they become seers and healers. There's something between them and animals, a bond, a connection, channels of power. Speech with animals, magical transformations. Could I be a turtle? Could I through an act of ecstasy swim unafraid and never lost, finding, finding? Swimming with Pangaea printed on my brain and bones, the ancient continent that was before the land masses drifted apart. That's part of it too: there were no seas between, the land was one, there was one thing, unbroken. Now there are thousands of miles of open water and the strong ones, the swimmers, the unlost, are driven to trace the paths between, maintain the ancient connection. I don't know whether I can keep going. A turtle doesn't have to decide every morning whether to keep on bothering, it just carries on. Maybe that's why man kills everything: envy.

A confusion of fixed and flashing lights confronts the navigator, that's what the sign on the Port Liberty model says. That's how life seems to me sometimes. At other times it's a confusion of fixed and flashing darknesses. More darknesses than lights I think. Port Liberty doesn't exist and Pangaea having separated will never again come together. Unless he is already doomed, Fortune favours the man who keeps his nerve. *Beowulf.* Of course it's easy to keep your nerve when you've got a grip that can tear the arm right off a sea monster. Am I doomed? Flashing darkness is pretty much the same as flashing light really. Fear isn't at all the same as courage but after a certain point perhaps being afraid of everything is the same as being afraid of nothing. It doesn't feel that way now but then I haven't reached that point yet. If the fool would persist in his folly he would become wise, said Blake. If the coward persists in his cowardice does he become brave?

Maybe I could stop smoking, that would give me more years to get brave in. It's getting to my legs, they seize up on me now whenever I climb stairs. When I stopped smoking for nine days not long ago I could run right up the stairs in the Underground like other people.

I've met several other men who were divorced and didn't see their children any more because their wives had left the country. It didn't seem to bother them all that much. I feel as if it'll kill me but then when I was with the children I felt that being married to Dora was taking my life away. Maybe I'm just one of those people so accustomed to being miserable that they use the material of any situation to fuel their misery.

Sometimes I think it must help to have a conviction in one's birth-place, to feel a significance in having been born in one place rather than another. Perhaps if more of my childhood had been spent in Polperro I'd feel stronger about it. My father retired there to paint, met my mother in the teashop where she worked, married her and died two years later. I was one year old when Mother and I came to London and I still can't see the point of my having been born in Polperro. I've never been back there.

For some time now on bad days I've been falling back on a news item I read last month. An important witness in the current American government scandal was said to be desperately afraid of going to prison because he's so good-looking that all the homosexuals will be after him. I have many problems but not that one.

16

Neaera H.

The one beach pebble I have from my childhood is the one I call my Caister two-stone. It's an amalgam of two different kinds of material, half grey and half brown.

My father took me to the Caister Lifeboat Station once. There was no boathouse like the one that's there now, the boat, the *Charles Burton*, was on skeets on the sand. It had saved seven lives that year. One of the vessels the Caister men had helped was the *Corn Rig* of Buckie. "Rendered assistance" was the expression used. "We rendered assistance to the *Corn Rig* of Buckie," said the brown-faced man my father was talking to. It had a gallant sound like a line in a narrative poem. My father said to me afterwards that Caister men never turn back. "They may die, they may drown, but they never turn back," he said wonderingly and shook his head. His words and the words of the other man have stayed together in my mind:

> We rendered assistance to the *Corn Rig* of Buckie,
> We may die, we may drown, but we never turn back.

As if to reprove the Caister men for their obstinate courage the Royal National Lifeboat Institution took away their boat and shut down the station several years ago, economizing the service. The Caister men of course got themselves another boat and carry on unofficially. The stone is on my desk and I handle it often.

This preoccupation with the turtles, this project that insists on forming itself in my mind, wants to be seen in its proper light. I have got to try to understand it a little better. Not perhaps entirely, I'm not given to examining too closely the actions that really matter. I can deliberate long over a dinner-party invitation, considering carefully every aspect of the occasion and what it will cost me in time and equilibrium but when the venture is crucial I simply trust to luck and plunge into the dark. And even now at the age of forty-three I still can't say whether I've been lucky or unlucky. Sometimes it looks one way and sometimes the other.

On reflection I really don't want to understand it better. It may be silly and wrong and useless, it may be anything at all but it seems to be a thing that I have to do before I can do whatever comes after it. That it seems to involve other people is inevitable, everything does in one way or another.

I went to the bookshop. The man and I said hello to each other and I went to the Natural History section where I turned the pages of books without looking at them. My heart was pounding somewhat and I found myself mentally rehearsing what I would say. I always do that, I can't help it. Even when I go to the Post Office I say in my mind before I reach the window, "Twenty stamps at 3p, please." Then I say it aloud at the window. "I wonder if you too are thinking about the turtles?" I would say. Or "Perhaps we had better discuss the turtles?" I cursed him for not being man enough to speak up and broach the subject when it loomed so large and visible between us.

I became aware that he was standing near me emanating silence and in my mind I cursed him again.

"The turtles . . ." I blurted out.

"The turtles . . ." he mumbled at the same time. We both laughed.

"It's almost lunch-time," he said. "Perhaps we could talk about it then. Can you wait a few minutes?"

I nodded and went to the Poetry section, opened A. E. Housman at random and read:

> The world is round, so travellers tell,
> And straight though reach the track,

Trudge on, trudge on, 'twill all be well,
The way will guide one back.

But ere the circle homeward hies
Far, far must it remove:
White in the moon the long road lies
That leads me from my love.

It was James Haylett of Caister who first said that Caister men never turn back. He was a lifeboatman for fifty-nine years, and at the age of seventy-eight he went into the surf and pulled out his son-in-law and one of his grandsons from under the lifeboat *Beauchamp* the night it capsized in November, 1901. At the inquiry it was suggested that the *Beauchamp*, which had gone to the rescue of a Lowestoft fishing-smack on the Barber Sands, might have turned back because of the force of the gale and the heavy seas. That was when James Haylett said, "Caister men never turn back." Nine of the lifeboat crew were lost including two sons and a grandson of James Haylett. The fishing-smack had got herself off the sands, anchored safely in deep water, and knew nothing of the disaster until later. Rescuers and those to be rescued don't always come back together.

Lunch-time came. We went to a little place nearby where the take-away queue waited partly in the street and partly at the counter. There were no empty booths so we shared one with two fresh-faced young executives eating eggs and sausages and grease.

"The brief is really quite clear," said the one next to me.

"We've put in the think time," said the one next to the bookshop man. "We're ready to move on it."

"And we'd jolly well better do it soon," said mine.

"Those chaps in the City can't be kept dangling indefinitely. Once we've separated the sheep from the goats we've got to make our bid."

"Precisely what I said in my report," said the other as he wiped up some grease with a bit of Mother's Pride sliced bread. "When they get back from Stuttgart I want to see some action."

Their faces were pink, their eyes were clear and bright, their shirts and ties what the adverts call coordinated I believe. Mine had dirty finger-nails and his handkerchief was tucked into his jacket sleeve. The other had clean fingernails. Their voices were loud, they were eager to impart the dash and colour of their lives to the drabness about them.

I had a salad. If I were to say that today's tomatoes are an index of the decline of Western man I should be thought a crank but nations do not, I think, ascend on such tomatoes. The bookshop man had fried eggs with sausages, chips, grease and Mother's Pride sliced bread and butter. He put ketchup on the chips. No wonder he looks hopeless I thought.

"I always bring a sandwich for lunch," he said. "But I can have it for tea."

"If the bananas aren't unloaded soon they'll spoil," I said. I felt like talking like a spy.

"I'm waiting to hear from our friend at the docks," said the bookshop man, rising in my estimation. "I can't arrange the haulage until he gives me a date."

The two young executives raised their eyebrows at each other.

"Have you booked them right the way through?" I said. The waitress reached across us with sweets for the executives. Mine had trifle, the other fruit salad with cream.

"Only tentatively," said the bookshop man. "Brighton's close."

"I was thinking of Polperro," I said.

The bookshop man went very red in the face. "Polperro!" he said. "Why in God's name Polperro?"

I indicated the two executives with my eyes and busied myself with my salad. They were both having white coffee with a lot of sugar. Life mayn't always be that sweet for you I thought.

There was a long silence during which the executives smoked a king-size filter-tip cigarette and a little thin cheap cigar without asking me if I minded. The bookshop man took something from his pocket and began to play with it. It was a round beach pebble, a grey one.

"Where's it from?" I said.

"Antibes," he said. "I haven't smoked all morning."

The executives excused themselves. We had coffee, no sweets. On the wall two booths away from us was a circular blue fluorescent tube in a rectangular wire cage. It was probably some kind of air purifier but it looked like a Tantric moon or some other contemplation object. I contemplated it. The bookshop man looked into his coffee as if viewing the abyss.

"Did I say anything wrong?" I said. "About Polperro?"

"No," he said. "It just took me by surprise. Why Polperro?"

"If I said that Polperro and the turtles together add up to something, would that mean anything to you?" I said.

He looked at me strangely. "Yes," he said.

On the way out I went over to the Tantric moon and read the name-plate on it. INSECT-O-CUTOR, it said.

"I'll ring you up when I hear from George Fairbairn," said the book-shop man.

I gave him my name and telephone number.

"Neaera," he read. "Eldest daughter?"

I nodded.

"My name's William G.," he said.

We shook hands and parted. Going home on the tube I was astonished at the number of paint- and ink-stains on the skirt I was wearing.

17

William G.

Neaera H. The penny didn't drop until a few minutes after we'd parted, then I remembered the Gillian Vole books, Delia Swallow, Geoffrey Mouse and all the others I used to read to the girls. *Delia Swallow's Housewarming* was Cyndie's favourite for a long time, she never tired of it. This must be the same Neaera H., she looked too much like a writer-illustrator not to be one.

Back at the shop I went to Picture Books in the Juvenile section and looked at a copy of *Delia Swallow's Housewarming*. No photograph or biographical details on the back flap. All it said was that Delia Swallow, though the stories were written for children, had long been a favourite with readers of all ages, as had Gillian Vole etc. I looked at the first page:

"Just any eaves won't do," said Delia Swallow to her husband John when they were looking for a nest.
"I'd like eaves on the sunny side and with a view."
"Field or forest?" said John.
"Field with forest at the edge I think," said Delia.
"Riverside or hill?" said John.
"Riverside with a hill behind," said Delia.

"Right," said John, and went to sleep.
He always kipped after lunch.

Ariadne and Cyndie always liked it that John Swallow kipped after lunch. In the evenings he usually dropped in for a pint or two and a game of darts at the *Birds of a Feather*, after which:

He sometimes flew a little wobbly going home.

Strange. While I was married to Dora and living in Hampstead and working at the agency Neaera H. was writing those books. Now here we are, both of us alone and thinking turtle thoughts. At least I assume she's alone. She looks as if she's always been alone. Of course I'm seeing her out of alone eyes, I could well be wrong.

The turtles share a tank at the Zoo. I share a bath at Mrs. Inchcliff's. Hairy Mr. Sandor. I taped a little sign to the bathroom wall:

PLEASE CLEAN BATH AFTER USING

Not that it'll do much good. It's not too bad really, he only baths a couple of times a week. Miss Neap baths daily and when she's been before me the bathroom smells very blonde and militantly fragrant, as if mortality could be kept at bay by lavender in the same way that garlic repels vampires. If Dracula and Miss Neap were to have a go I think he'd be the one to come away with teeth marks in his throat.

When I had a bathroom of my own. I think about that sometimes. When I was an account executive. When I owned a house. When my daughters sat on my lap and I read to them. When they collected pebbles with me on the beach. Ariadne's twenty now, Cyndie's eighteen. I haven't seen them for three years. I don't know where they are.

The past isn't connected to the future any more. When I lived with Dora and the girls the time I lived in, the time of me was still the same piece of time that had unrolled like a forward road under my feet from the day of my birth. That road and all the scenes along it belonged to me, my mind moved freely up and down it. Walking on it I was still connected to my youth and strength, the time of me was of one piece with that time.

TURTLE DIARY

Not now. I can't walk on my own time past. It doesn't belong to me any more.

There's no road here. Every step away from Dora and the girls leads only to old age and death whatever I do. No one I sleep with now has known me young with long long time and all the world before me. Rubbish. I remember how it was lying beside Dora in the night. O God, I used to think, this is it and this is all there is and nothing up ahead but death. The girls will grow up and move out and we'll be left alone together. I remember that very well. It's the thisness and thisonlyness of it all that drives middle-aged men crazy.

Why turtles for God's sake? Helping them find what they're looking for won't bloody help me. And now I'm lumbered with it. I'll have to find out what it costs to hire a van. I wonder if the two of us can get the turtles on to the trolley. She doesn't look that strong. We'll need a board or something for a ramp. Maybe I should build crates for them, they'd be easier to handle that way. I hate details. And now it's got to be Polperro just to make life more difficult. I know there'll be some kind of physical problem like having to climb a million steps or lower ourselves by ropes or the tide will be out and we'll have to drag the turtles across a mile of mud in the dark. What on earth can Polperro mean to her?

I saw a film years ago, *The Swimmer*, with Burt Lancaster. In it he was an American advertising man whose mind had slipped out of the present. He thought he still had a wife and children and a house but it was all gone. The film began with a golden late-summer afternoon. He turned up at the swimming pool of some friends who hadn't seen him for a long time. They looked at him strangely, he wasn't part of their present time any more. While he was there it occurred to him that there were so many swimming pools in that part of Connecticut that he could almost swim all the way home. So he went from pool to pool, public and private, swimming across Fairfield County meeting people from different bits of his life whilst swimming home as he thought. And wherever he went people became angry and disturbed, he didn't belong in their present time, they didn't want him in it. At the end of the film he was huddled in the doorway of the empty locked house that had been his while rain came down and he heard the ball going back and forth on the empty tennis court and the voices of his daughters who were gone. Dora and I saw the film together.

No swimming pools for me. Just a bath that I have to clean Mr. Sandor's pubic hair out of while Miss Neap's lavender scent marches up and down the walls like a skeleton in armour. The water is not relaxing. Or indeed it may be relaxing, may be totally relaxed but I'm not. I don't want to be naked with anybody now, especially myself.

Haven't smoked for three days. Busy night and day not smoking. Already I can climb stairs better but that's not much of a life. With smoking one has a life while dying. How did the Greeks ever run a whole culture without it? Maybe that's why there was so much homosexuality. The turtles are no substitute for smoking. I'm tired of playing with pebbles and sucking wine gums. Breathing straight air seems an empty exercise. I may kill somebody if I don't smoke. Mr. Sandor's life is hanging by a thread if he only knew it.

Shamans in a state of ecstasy fly, travel long distances or think they do, say they do. When I was between twelve and thirteen I was lying in bed one night not asleep, not awake, and all at once I was looking down at myself from the ceiling. It wasn't a dream, I don't know what it was. I don't know anything about ecstasy. It happened another time that year too. I was standing by the window looking at myself lying in bed. Twice in my life I've been out of myself in that way. I don't think I've been into myself yet. *In* myself like a prisoner. But not into my self.

Ocean. When I think that word I want to be immersed in it and at the same time contain it all. Great green deeps of ocean. A medium of motion and being. And of course the sharks. Walking on the ground is not comparable to that underwater flying, green water touching every part.

I walk a lot at night now, sit on benches in squares feeling the dark on my face, looking at the street lamps. Most of the other people on the street are young. I don't want to sit in my room. I don't want to do anything particularly.

Actually we're all swimmers, we've all come from the ocean. Some of us are trying to find it again.

Eliade says in his book on shamanism:

> In the beginning, that is, in mythical times, man lived at peace with the animals and understood their speech. It was not until after a primordial catastrophe, comparable to the "Fall" of Biblical tradition, that man became what he is today—mortal, sexed, obliged to work to feed him-

self, and at enmity with the animals. While preparing for his ecstasy and during it, the shaman abolishes the present human condition and, for the time being, recovers the situation as it was in the beginning. Friendship with animals, knowledge of their language, transformation into an animal are so many signs that the shaman has re-established the "paradisal" situation lost at the dawn of time.

That's the crux of it: abolishing the present human condition. Shamans wear bird costumes and they fly. Somehow they experience flying. They're gone and they come back with answers. Could I abolish the human condition? Could I swim, experience swimming, finding, navigating, fearlessness, unlostness? Could I come back with an answer? The unlostness itself would be the answer, I shouldn't need to come back.

18

Neaera H.

More and more I feel that I ought not to have forced myself into that man's turtle thoughts. Perhaps he wasn't even going to do anything about them, perhaps I've precipitated a harmless fantasy into an active crisis. None of us can be sufficiently sensitive. We feel our own pain wonderfully well but seldom attribute agony to others. When we were talking there were moments when his face made me think of the John Clare poem about the badger hunted out of his den by men and dogs and taken to the town and made to fight until he was dead. There's a line in which he "cackles, groans, and dies." William G. looked as if he might be going to cackle.

I wonder about myself. Why didn't I simply write a turtle letter to *The Times* and let it go at that? Certainly I've felt like taking some kind of action but I'm not sure I'll feel that way when the time comes. And now I've committed myself with this stranger. I have breached my own privacy as well as his and almost I wish I hadn't. How on earth are we going to get through all those hours together driving to and from Polperro? I don't think either speech or silence will be comfortable. I feel terribly uneasy about the whole thing. I haven't even considered any of the physical problems of getting the turtles into the ocean. I haven't been practical about it at all.

I'm *not* committed actually. At any rate I needn't be. For years now I've had only myself and I must be economical with that self. I can simply say that I hadn't quite understood what we were talking about when he rings me up. Or I can be up to my neck in work which is always true. I'm rather a cheerful person as long as the minutes of my days buzz at home like well-domesticated bees. When I come and go too much I'm afraid that they may fly away to swarm elsewhere. I think there still are people in Norfolk who tell the bees when the owner of the hive has died, even pin a bit of crape to the hive so the bees can mourn. When they've done their mourning they get on with making honey. One only owns the hive I suppose, never really the bees. Not like cattle.

Sometimes I think that the biggest difference between men and women is that more men need to seek out some terrible lurking thing in existence and hurl themselves upon it like Ahab with the White Whale. Women know where it lives but they can let it alone. Even in matriarchal societies I doubt that there were ever female Beowulfs. Women lie with gods and demons but they don't go looking for monsters to fight with. Ariadne gave Theseus a clew but the Minotaur was his business. There are of course many men who walk in safe paths all their lives but they often seem a little apologetic, as if they think themselves not quite honourable. And there are others, quiet men, obscure, ungifted, who yet require satisfaction of some grim thing that ultimately kills them. William G. has found some monster and . . . What? Almost I think he's swallowed it. It's alive and eating inside him, much worse than if it had swallowed him.

There, I'm worrying about him. I've breached my privacy badly. There's not enough of me for that, I have no self to spare. I must keep my bees.

19

William G.

Sometimes I think that this whole thing, this whole business of a world that keeps waking itself up and bothering to go on every day, is necessary only as a manifestation of the intolerable. The intolerable is like H. G. Wells's invisible man, it has to put on clothes in order to be seen. So it dresses itself up in a world. Possibly it looks in a mirror but my imagination doesn't go that far.

It's been at least twenty-five years since I read *Crime and Punishment*. Now I'm reading it again. I'd forgotten that when Raskolnikov murdered the old lady pawnbroker, Alyona Ivanovna, he also killed her half-sister Lizaveta. Lizaveta was "a soft gentle creature, ready to put up with anything, always willing, willing to do anything." When she came back to the flat just after Raskolnikov had killed the old woman he had to kill her as well.

Alyona Ivanovna and Lizaveta always *do* live together, always die together. You try to kill some aspect of the intolerable and you kill the gentle and the good as well. Over and over. And whoever kills some form of the intolerable becomes himself a manifestation of it, to be killed with *his* good and gentle by someone else. Two by two up the gangway to the ark. But the waters will never recede.

I'm intolerable. It's got into me, when I feed me I feed it. There's only one way to kill it.

The idea of ringing up a van place and hiring a van and driving all those miles is so heavy I can hardly lift my head up. Bloody details. Too heavy. Too much.

20

Neaera H.

It was past three in the morning and I was staring into the green murk of Madame Beetle's tank. The plants are all shrouded in long green webs of algae, there are white and ghostly bits of old meat hanging about blooming with mould, the sides of the tank are very dim. It's like the setting for a tiny horror film but Madame Beetle doesn't seem to mind. I can't think now how it could have occurred to me that I might write a story about her. Who am I to use the mystery of her that way? Her swimming is better than my writing and she doesn't expect to get paid for it. If someone were to buy me, have me shipped in a tin with airholes, what would I be a specimen of?

I went to the bookshelves, got *The Duchess of Malfi*, sat down in my reading chair, turned to the scene where the executioners enter *"with a coffin, cords, and a bell."* I read the Duchess's speech:

> I know death hath ten thousand several doors
> For men to take their exits; and 'tis found
> They go on such strange geometrical hinges,
> You may open them both ways . . .

While I sat there looking at the lines I drifted out of wakefulness but I wasn't asleep. I was seeing Breydon Water at low tide, the oyster-catchers on the mussel beds and the water silver in the sunlight. Then it wasn't low tide any more but high water, green ocean, deep. I was in it swimming, flying, green ocean over me, under me, touching every part of me. And a glimmering white shadow coming up from below. Ah yes, my mind said, the shark's mouth too is after all a place of rest, they call them *requin*.

This is not mine, I thought, coming awake again. This is someone else's ocean, someone else's shark. I hadn't asked William G. for his telephone number when I gave him mine. I looked in the directory, not expecting to find it. He probably lived in a bedsitter and the telephone would be in someone else's name. There were seven William G.s.

It was a quarter to four. I looked at the calendar. Saturday morning. I looked at the telephone. Sometimes when I look at the telephone at that time in the morning it looks as if it just happens to be that shape at that time. I simply didn't have it in me to make possibly seven calls on the chance of finding him when I felt certain that he wasn't in the directory.

I don't know how I'd got it into my head that he lived in a bedsitter and not a flat of his own but when I thought of him at home that's where I saw him. With a very tall brown Victorian wardrobe, a sort of Palaeozoic brown upholstered chair, an indeterminate bed that metamorphosed into an indeterminate couch during the day and wallpaper that baffled the eye. Still he *might* be one of the seven William G.s in the directory. I believed it to be a matter of life or death but I couldn't make myself ring up any of the William G.s. The bookshop is open on Saturday mornings and I should have to wait until 9.30 to find out if he was there or at home.

I sat in my reading chair waiting but nothing came to me. I am not after all a telepath or a clairvoyant. I left the flat and sat in the square resting my mind on the fountain that wasn't there. The air was heavy and still, the bronze girl would be dim in the bluish light of the street lamps, her bronze would be cool and damp, the fountain jet would be shut off, the pebbles would be glistening with dew. A police constable's footsteps approached, then the glimmer of his shirt, then the constable, one of the ones I know. They're used to seeing me about at all hours.

"Very close, isn't it," he said.

"Yes," I said, "it's very close." The constable passed on, the shirt became a glimmer again, the footsteps receded.

I could scarcely sit still. I had one of those thoughts that sometimes come in dreams and put themselves into words that stay in the mind: the backs of things are always connected to the fronts of them. This is the back of the turtle thing, I thought. What? What is it? I had a feeling of dread. The back of the turtle thing was despair. Mine? His? Not mine. My despair has long since been ground up fine and is no more than the daily salt and pepper of my life. Not mine.

The square was moving towards morning. Railings that had gleamed under the street lamps were black against the first light of day. But it was a dark dawn. Weekend weather. I went back to the flat. It was much closer inside. I felt as if I were being smothered in wet sheets. I opened all the windows. The window frames were sooty and my hands got dirty. The air outside joined the air inside, all of it was like wet sheets.

I looked down at where I had been sitting in the square. The bench was empty, the square was green and vacant in the early light like one long uninflected vowel. It seemed to have lost all particularity. The trees, the bushes, the benches had no reference to anything, were altogether incomprehensible. The fountain that wasn't there was doubly not there, was incapable of being associated with the square.

It was half-past five. I was drowsy but I didn't want to go to sleep, I didn't want to dream. I lay down and of course I did fall asleep. I dreamt that nothing had a front any more. The whole world was nothing but the back of the world, and blank. No shape to it, no colour, just utter blankness. How could even the buses have lost their shape and colour, I thought. Even from the back they're red and bus-shaped. Some part of all this blankness must be a bus. But there was no bus, no anything. Just blank terror.

Then another of those dream thoughts came to me: every action has a mother and a father and is itself the mother or the father of the action that comes out of it. An endless genealogy branching back into the past, forward into the future. There is no unattached action. I woke up and it was half-past seven.

I looked at the telephone again. Don't be ridiculous, the shape of it said. The daylight in the windows threatened rain. I had breakfast and a cigarette and then another cigarette. I walked about the flat picking things up and putting them down, shuffling through unanswered letters and unpaid bills and dire things in brown envelopes On Her Majesty's Service. In the spare room are cartons of books demoted from the active shelves. 16 Giant ARIEL, said one. OUTSPAN Lemons, said another, and in my lettering: SITTING ROOM BOTTOM. That cardboard box is twenty years old, I labelled it when we emptied the shelves at home and packed the books to move to London. The longevity of impermanent things! I sat down in the chair again, dozed off, woke up at a quarter to nine, left the flat quickly and went down to the bus stop.

The bus came sooner than I expected, they always do when I'm early. I sat next to a man with a newspaper in which I read about a "vice girl" who'd entertained various businessmen for a pop singer. She'd been instructed to sleep with a Mr. X for a fee of £5, said the girl. She'd been requested to dress and act like an eleven-year-old schoolgirl and to refer frequently in her conversation to certain breakfast cereals and other products by their brand names. Mr. X was in advertising it seemed. He proved incapable, said the girl. Incapable of sleeping, I thought, smiling at the ambiguities of polite speech. I shouldn't be surprised if Mr. X *did* have difficulty in sleeping what with all those brand names dancing in his head.

It occurred to me then to imagine lives packaged and labelled and ranged on shelves waiting to be bought. I couldn't think of any likely brand names right off except Brief Candle. And what if the ingredients were listed on the box? Many lives would go unsold, they'd have to discontinue some of the range. Sorry, we don't stock that life any more, there was no demand for it really. Hard Slog for example or Dreary Muddle, how many would they sell a year? On the other hand Wealth and Fame would move briskly even with a Government Health Warning on the packet.

It was only five past nine when I got to the bookshop, and I spent the next twenty minutes looking at the books in the window. I observed that Taura Strong continues to be productive, ecology was enjoying a rising market, sex was holding its own but a little more quietly than formerly: there were glossy books with photographs of naked people kneading each other thoughtfully. Gangsterism in government was under examination in America and government in gangsterism was being looked at as well. The backs of things are getting into print more and more these days and heterosexuality is increasingly thin on the ground in biographies. Fallopia

Bothways, smiling a virile smile on the showcard for her new novel, has changed her haircut. Through the glass doors I could see the books on tables and shelves resting quietly and holding themselves in reserve until opening time. I found myself mentally turning away from the too-much-ness of them.

At 9.25 a girl who seemed to have bought Hard Slog arrived with keys and unlocked one of the glass doors top and bottom. She smiled briefly, went in and locked the door behind her. I waited while she picked up the morning post, turned on the lights, went to the office at the rear of the shop, came back with brown paper bags and put money into the till. Then she looked up, seemed gratified by my patience, smiled and opened the door.

"Good morning," I said.

"Good morning," she said. "Can help you?"

"Will Mr. G. be here today?" I said.

She shook her head. "It's his Saturday off."

"Can you tell me where to reach him, his phone number?" I said. "It's rather urgent."

She looked at me carefully. Did I look like an old girl friend who rings up and breathes into the telephone, I wondered. I didn't think so. She shook her head with some reluctance I thought but still she shook it.

"Our manager, Mr. Meager, is quite firm about that," she said. "Best thing is to come in again on Monday, Mr. G.'ll be here then."

"I think he might not be," I said. I watched a bus go past the door, first the front then the back. "I think he may be quite ill. Would you mind ringing him up yourself just to make sure he's all right? I think it really is urgent." By then I was quite possessed by my fixed idea and feeling a little demented about it.

"He looked perfectly well yesterday," she said. "He's probably not up yet. It's early for a Saturday off."

I didn't say anything. I must have looked a fright.

"All right," she said. "I'll ring him. It's a little odd, you know. After all if you're a friend of his you'd have his number, wouldn't you."

I couldn't think of anything to say, just looked at her dumbly.

"All right," she said again. "Who shall I say it is?"

"Neaera H.," I said.

Her face changed, her manner as well. Little softenings and flutters. "The one who does the Gillian Vole books?" she said.

"Yes," I said.

"Well," she said with a fleeting smile, "I'll see if I can raise him." She went back to the office and closed the door. Through the little office window I saw her look up the number on a list she took from a drawer. She dialled, waited, spoke while watching me through the window. I couldn't hear what she said.

"I've rung the house where he lives," she said when she came out. "They say he doesn't answer his door. He doesn't seem to be at home."

"This isn't anything personal," I said. "It's nothing personal at all really." I could feel my face not knowing what to do with itself.

An American lady came in. "Have you anything on Staffordshire figures?" she said.

The girl went to the shelves, took out three books.

"I have all of those," said the American lady. "Is there anything else?"

"That's all there is just now," said the girl.

"Oh, dear," said the American lady. "Thank you." She left.

An intense-looking young man with long hair, a beard, an immense mackintosh and a large shoulder-bag came in and headed for the Occult section.

"Would you leave your bag at the counter, please," said the girl. The young man flashed her a dark look, left the shoulder-bag with her, went to the shelves and appeared to be deeply interested in alchemy.

"Keep your eye on him for a moment," said the girl. "He pinches books." She went back to the office, returned quickly and handed me a slip of paper with William G.'s address and telephone number on it.

"Here," she said. "You look as if it's important."

"Thank you," I said, and hurried away.

Someone got out of a taxi and I got in. Just like a film, I thought. People never have to wait for taxis in films. Old films, that is. They never used to get change when they paid for anything either, they just left notes or coins and walked away. Now they get change. Perhaps they sometimes have to wait for taxis too. I gave the driver the address, it was in S.W.6.

"Do you know the street?" he said.

"No," I said. "Don't you?"

"I'm a suburban driver," he said as he turned down the Brompton Road. "I don't know London all that well. Most of the lads graduate to London after a while, go about on a moped getting the knowledge but I haven't bothered. I'm a Jehovah's Witness and we think God's going to step in and put things to rights in a couple of years. There won't be any taxis then."

"What will there be?" I said looking in my *A to Z*. "I think it's off the Fulham Road."

"The Lord will take care of the righteous," he said as we came to the Brompton Oratory and turned left into the Fulham Road. "We've been interested in the year 1975 for some time."

"You go to Fulham Broadway and turn left into Harwood Road," I said. "What'll you do if nothing happens in 1975?"

"A lot of people ask that question," said the driver. "We'll . . . " We'd come to a place where they were tearing up the street and I couldn't hear what he said.

"Sorry," I said leaning close to the opening in the glass partition. "I couldn't hear you."

"We'll . . . " he said as a plane screamed low overhead.

I sank back in the seat, didn't ask again.

The house was on a crescent opposite a football pitch, a paddling pool and a playground. The far end of the crescent looked more posh, the houses a little grander and overlooking the common. William G.'s end was Georgian terraced houses, three storeys, quite plain. I paid the driver and as he drove off I wished I'd asked him about 1975 again. I really did want to know what he'd do if it came and went without the Lord's taking a stand either way. Too late, the chance was gone.

There were no nameplates, only one bell. I rang it. A fiery-looking foreign-looking man with a violent moustache answered the door. He was wearing a Middle-Eastern sort of dressing-gown that had more colour and pattern than one really cared to see in a single garment. Red velvet slippers, very white feet and ankles with very black hair. He looked as if he had strong political convictions.

"I've come to see Mr. G.," I said.

"Top," said the man and stood aside.

I went up, stood outside William G.'s door waiting for my heart to stop pounding. Too many cigarettes. The violent-moustached man had come upstairs too and was producing violent smells in a tiny kitchen on the landing. I could ask him to force the door if necessary. I tried not to think of what we might find. I knocked.

William G. opened the door, looked startled. "Good morning," he said. "Come in."

I gasped, found nothing to say. The room was not as I had imagined it, had white walls, an orange Japanese paper lamp. Modern furniture, mail-order Danish.

"You look quite done up," he said. "I'll get you some coffee."

21

William G.

It was absolutely uncanny, gave me the creeps. That woman actually thought I'd been thinking of suicide.

I *had* been thinking of it right enough, I often do, always have the idea of it huddled like a sick ape in a corner of my mind. But I'd never do it. At least I don't think I'd do it, can't imagine a state of mind in which I'd do it. Well, that's not true either. I *can* imagine the state of mind, I've been in it often enough. No place for the self to sit down and catch its breath. Just being hurried, hurried out of existence. When I feel like that even such a thing as posting a letter or going to the launderette wears me out. The mind moves ahead of every action making me tired in advance of whatever I do. Even a thing as simple as changing trains in the Underground becomes terribly heavy. I think ahead to the sign on the platform at the next station, think of getting out of the train, going through the corridor, up the escalator, waiting on the platform. I think of how many trains will come before mine, think of getting on when it comes, think of the signs that will appear, think of getting out, going up the steps, out into the street. As the mind moves forward the self is pushed back, everything multiplies itself like mirrors receding laboriously to infinity, repeating endlessly even the earwax in the ears, the silence in the eyes.

When I was a child there was a mirror in the hallway and at some point I became aware that the mirror saw more than what was simply right in front of it. It privately reflected a good deal of hallway on both sides out of the corner of its eye so to speak. By putting my nose right up against the glass I could almost see round those corners, could almost see what the mirror was keeping to itself, the whole hallway perhaps. All of it, everything, things I couldn't see. Spiders in webs in the shadows, the other side of the light through the coloured leaded glass of the door. The shadow of the postman today, tomorrow, the day after tomorrow.

My father did, I think. Commit suicide. Although they called it an accident. His car went over a cliff into the sea. On to some rocks that you can see at low tide but not high water. No collision, no skid marks or any-thing. My mother kept the newspaper cutting, I still have it somewhere. Who knows what might have appeared in the road coming towards him. The rest of his life maybe. At Paddington I've seen pigeons on the tube platform walk into a train and out again while the doors were still open, knowing where they didn't want to go.

Neaera H. can't be in very good shape either if her mind is running on that sort of thing. She was deathly pale when she turned up at my door. It took her a while to come out with it, then she said in a half-whisper looking down at her coffee cup that she'd had all this green water in her mind and a white shark coming up from below. Well of course they're al-ways in me I suppose, coming up from the darkness and the deep-water chill. But I wouldn't say I'm *broadcasting* sharks, and if she's pulling them in out of the air she must be pretty well round the bend.

She told me a little about herself, and her kind of life isn't much better than mine. At least in the shop I'm out in the world, get out of myself a little. She goes for days sometimes without seeing anyone, staying up till all hours. No wonder she gets morbid. And now it seems she's on my wavelength. That's all I need. My mind isn't much of a comfort to me but at least I thought it was private. She's going to wear herself out if she keeps tuning in like that. The inside of my head is a pretty tiresome place for someone whose own head isn't all that jolly.

I must find out about a van. It's well over two hundred miles to Pol-perro, closer to three hundred I should think. Night driving. I'd rather drive at night than during the day but either way the thought of it fills me with dread. And I'm scared of the turtles. That big male loggerhead could take your hand off with one bite. I could ask George Fairbairn to come with us and he might do it but that's no good. Whatever this awful thing is that I've got myself into it's my thing and I've got to do it alone with that weird lady.

I can't imagine that it'll come off without some sort of disaster. If we drive all night we'll have to sleep part of the next day before starting back. I'll be away from the shop one whole day, maybe more. I can always say I'm sick. Things are pretty slow now, Mr. Meager and Harriet can get along without me for a day or two. I won't say I'm sick but I won't say turtles either. I need the time off for personal reasons.

Good God, is she going to become some sort of responsibility now? Have I got to keep happy thoughts singing and dancing in my mind so as not to plunge her into a suicidal depression. How much do I know about her actually when it comes right down to it. She lives alone, writes and illustrates children's books, doesn't seem very happy. She's not interested in me romantically, I'd have felt it if she were. But we've fallen into something together whatever it might be. I don't think I want to know any more about it just now.

22

Neaera H.

Oh, dear. What have I done now? Where are my bees? Suddenly I feel a stranger in my own flat. The clutter on the drawing table, the books and papers on the desk, the typewriter, Madame Beetle in her tank and the plants in the window have all gone blank and baffling.

Caister men never turn back. But I'm not a Caister man. My Caister two-stone confers no magic, it's only a touchstone for the terrors that I try to cover up with books and papers and plants in the window. My mind feels as if it's gone into hiding from me and is reflecting privately on matters of its own. Identity is a shaky thing. This is my place, my work, my water-beetle. Silly. Water-beetles can't be owned any more than bees can. Nothing can be owned for that matter. A typewriter? Not really. You pay for the machine, keep it in your flat, use it. But I might go out one day and never come back and the typewriter would remain, belonging only to itself. When a ewe licks a new-born lamb all over I believe that's called owning it but the ewe never really owns the lamb. That awful gathering-up feeling is in me again. My life can't be drawing to a close yet. I'm not greedy but it can't be ending so soon. Who will tell my bees and will they make honey for their next mistress. Same bees, different people, over and over.

If I could see an oyster-catcher . . . No, it isn't just the bird, it's the distance, the wideness. I am so *unquiet*. What have I done. Making a fool of myself is the least of it. What's happening to my mind? The green water, the white glimmer and the open jaws: my ocean and shark, not his? Mine as well as his, that certainly. I wish I'd never seen those turtles, never seen Polperro. Could someone tell the turtles, give them a bit of crape to stream behind them in the water? If it hadn't been the turtles I suppose it would have been something else.

I can't get it out of my mind, how I must have looked sitting there with the cup clattering in the saucer. "Are you all right?" he said. "Is anything the matter? You don't look well."

"I'm sorry," I said. "You must think I'm insane, I've never done anything like this before, I had such a dreadful feeling, I thought you might be . . . They gave me your address at the shop, I said it was urgent, possibly a matter of . . . There was all that green water and a shark coming up from below, terrible, terrible." I actually went on like that, blurted out all those things.

He lit a cigarette and kept shaking the match but it wouldn't go out. He blew it out. "Why did you think I . . . Why did you think it had anything to do with me?" he said, and certainly his voice was shaking.

"Well, it wasn't mine," I said lamely, hearing how idiotic I sounded.

"How could it not be yours?" he said. He looked cruel when he said it. "You had a dreadful feeling, a terrible dream or thought or something and you say it wasn't yours but mine. That's rather curious, isn't it?" His voice seemed to be coming from a dark and tiny place, he seemed clearer and smaller and sharper and farther away as he spoke. I felt as if I might faint.

"Stop it," I said. "You're not being honest."

"Perhaps you're not either," he said. "Some people won't look at what's in them, they sweep everything under the carpet. Everything's quite all right with them, they're never depressed. When the shark comes up out of the dark and the chill that's somebody else's shark not theirs. *They're* all right, Jack."

I almost hated him for that. Any situation imposes rules of some kind and a gentleman abides by them. By coming to his door in a half-crazed state I'd created a situation in which a gentleman would have been equally open even if it made him look as crazy as I was. William G. was not wholly a gentleman and I was sorry for us both.

"You're being careful," I said.

"*I'm* being careful!" he said. "What about you? You've had green water and a shark and now you're trying to put it on me so it won't be you that's falling apart."

We were both frightened and angry, a long silence followed. Then we began to speak calmly and politely, avoiding the shark. We exchanged humdrums, presentable bits of ourselves: what I did, what he did, how this was and that. We became slightly acquainted in the dreariest conventional way. I wanted to be shot of the whole turtle affair and I knew he did too but there it was like a massive chain welded to leg irons on both of us and clanking maddeningly.

We couldn't get to a better place in our conversation. It simply became a matter of sitting there until we could move away from our common discomfort and go back to our separate individual ones. We repeated things that needed no repetition: I said of course we must share the cost of the van, he said he'd let me know as soon as George Fairbairn got in touch with him. We both mumbled about the possible inconvenience of having to act on short notice, both agreed that that's how it was with this sort of thing.

I went home by bus.

23

William G.

"Did Miss H. ever reach you?" Harriet said when I came into the shop on Monday.

"Yes," I said, "she did."

"I hope it was all right," she said, "giving her your address and telephone number."

"Perfectly all right," I said. "Silly of me not to have given it to her before."

"I had no idea she was a friend of yours," said Harriet.

"Haven't known her long actually," I said busying myself unwrapping a shipment.

"Funny when you meet authors," said Harriet. "Mostly they don't look as you'd imagine them."

"How would you have imagined her?" I said.

"Short rather than tall," said Harriet, "plump rather than thin. Married rather than not. She isn't married, is she?"

"No," I said. "She isn't." I made a lot of noise with the wrapping paper and the conversation lapsed.

Harriet is next in line to Mr. Meager and senior to me at the shop. She's about thirty and I can remember when she did her hair in the style of the Ladies-in-Waiting at the Coronation. She's a tall thin girl from quite a good family, her father is an M.P. and her face is a constant reproach even though she's not at all bad-looking. She used to dress very conservatively, lived at home, walked as if the streets were full of rapists and wore shoes that looked as if they were designed for self-defence.

I don't recall just when it happened but all of a sudden she came in one day wearing sandals, the kind you get at shops where they sell Arab dresses and incense. There were her white naked startled feet at the bottom of the still conservatively dressed pleated-skirt Harriet and I guessed she'd lost her virginity but little else. Her nervous-looking naked feet still hadn't left home. Thank God my feet are in shoes most of the time. They don't look as if they will ever walk in happy ways and I'm pleased not to see them.

Harriet's feet walked easier after a time. She took to wearing long full skirts and cheesecloth blouses, her hair came down. She got herself a room, stopped wearing a bra every day and bought *Time Out* every week.

So there was her copy of *Time Out* in the kitchen at the shop and I had a look at the Classified adverts. CLAIRVOYANT and HYPNOTISM were available. ANOREXIA NERVOSA, CONSULTATIONS IN CONFIDENCE. Also NUDIST CLUB (Females free), MASSAGE TUITION, RUBBER ENTHUSIASTS, TAROT DIVINATION, NATURAL FOODS, CANDLE-MAKING, ATTRACTIVE ORIENTAL CHICK (Why was she in *Miscellaneous* instead of *Lonely Hearts*?), HOMOSEXUAL MEN AND WOMEN. PICNIC—Bring just one ingredient to share, ENCOUNTER, GROWTH CENTRE, QUAESITOR, KALEIDOSCOPE—Bio-Energetic Workshop. I glanced only briefly at *Lonely Hearts* in which Sensitive sensual male, 23, Handsome Aquarius, 37, and UP TO SIX DATES from only £1 offered themselves.

There are times when I do something and then I say: It's come to that. *That* is of course different things at different times. It's come to a lot of *thats* in my life and I suppose they'll keep happening right up to the last and final one when perhaps my last words will be: It's come to that.

BIO-FEEDBACK, said one advert. Alpha-Wave Machine. I'd read something about that in a magazine. People who can do proper meditation get into a state of quiet alertness in which their brain waves change, and there are now machines for monitoring the brain waves so you can hear yourself getting into or out of the state that produces alpha waves. I didn't think I could make even one alpha wave, I didn't think there was one quiet place in my brain. I just wished the turtles and Neaera H. would go away although sometimes I didn't. I wished that I could turn off my head, stop thinking. My dreams are usually busy with Dora and the girls so I don't even have any spare mental time when I'm asleep and I mostly wake up feeling worn out. Sexual fantasies offer a little distraction but aren't really restful. Reading is all right but not always, Dostoyevsky overstimulates my mind. Cinemas are cosy until you have to go home, TV feels like self-abuse.

Lately my fantasies have been of a place that doesn't exist. Not Port Liberty. Port Liberty is for the clear-eyed, the competent, the strong. My fantasy is of a give-up place. At County Hall maybe, in a grotty corridor, a door with frosted glass: DEPARTMENT OF CAPITULATION AND UNCONDITIONAL SURRENDER. The usual stand-up desks along the wall with dried-up biros on chains. Forms to fill in: Campaigns in which served, Terms if sought, Next of kin. A kindly Indian civil servant to give procedural advice. One capitulates or surrenders unconditionally, signs things over and is sent to some kind of refuge for noncontenders. I never imagine the refuge, just the giving up. Whether they have TV or books or brothels I don't know but it's out of the struggle. Sleep after toil, port after stormy seas, ease after war and all that. At least there's a model of Port Liberty but the Department of Capitulation and Unconditional Surrender doesn't exist anywhere in any form. The loony-bin isn't the same thing. I'm not crazy but then maybe nobody is. So I rang up Mr. Bio-Feedback.

The place was in St. John's Wood. Big bright spacious flat, high ceilings. The kind of flat that so many young Americans seem to have found or inherited from expatriate uncles before rents went up and unfurnished flats became impossible to find. Mattresses on the floor with Indian spreads, many colourful cushions, some modern things, some rattan. Home-made abstractions and blown-up photos on the walls. Lots of shelves, lots of books. Expensive sound-equipment, speakers about four feet high.

The young man with the Bio-Feedback machine was a sleek and healthy beard-and-sandals American with a wonderful head of hair that looked as if it might charge him like a battery pack. Very peaceful and serene-looking, looked as if there were *mostly* alpha waves in his head. Cheques from home, I thought. Very likely never worked a day in his life. Family man too, the bathroom was full of toys and infant gear.

The alpha-wave detector was quite a modest little plastic-box affair that didn't look as if it had more than £5 worth of parts and labour in it. He'd set it up on an impressive scaffolding of planks and pipes but it still didn't look like more than £5.

"What do you do for a living?" I said.

"This," he said peacefully. "And I'm the company's representative for the machines so I'll be selling them too."

I sank into one of those big plastic hassocks that look like overripe tomatoes that have hit the ground and somehow not burst.

"You?" he said while he dabbed electrolytic jelly on the side and back of my head and fitted the electrodes. I felt ashamed of my dandruff.

"Assistant in a bookshop," I said.

"I thought it might be something literary in one way or another," he said. He turned on the machine, set the volume. "It's a wave frequency filter and amplifier," he said. "You'll hear the alpha waves."

I listened. Dead silence.

"Close your eyes," he said.

"I don't think I've got any alpha waves," I said. "I don't think I've got anything but noise and static in my head."

"You'd be surprised," he said. "Everybody has alpha waves. Are you into meditation at all?"

"No," I said. I closed my eyes. Silence from the machine. I thought of a grey heron I'd seen once flying over a marsh flapping very slowly. A nice serene thought. Silence from the machine. I let go of the heron, let myself sink back into whatever there might be to sink back into in my mind.

Cluck cluck cluck, said the machine quietly.

"That's alpha waves," said the young man.

I drifted into it again. Cluck cluck cluck cluck, said the machine in another little burst of chicken talk.

I went on with it for a while, I'd paid £2 for the hour. Sometimes I got bursts of ten or fifteen clucks together and was quite pleased with myself. That accounts for my not having gone mad, I thought. There must be quiet places in my head where I get a little rest now and then without knowing about it. A cheering thought.

I took off the electrodes. "What about *your* alpha waves?" I said. "Are you good at it?"

"Don't you want to keep going?" he said. "You still have more time."

"I don't think I have the patience for a whole hour of it," I said. "I'd like to hear you do it."

He wired himself up with the electrodes, closed his eyes and looked even more serene than before. Cluck cluck cluck cluck cluck cluck, went the machine steadily and smoothly like a Geiger counter next to a piece of uranium. It clucked almost continuously, with only the briefest of pauses.

I shook my head. What was there to say? He wiped the jelly off my dandruff.

"Thank you," I said, and got up to leave.

"Do you think you'd like to do it again?" he said.

"I don't think so," I said. "But it's nice to know the alpha waves are there sometimes."

As I was going out he said, "I didn't give you quite a straight answer when you asked me what I did for a living."

"Please," I said, "there's no need to, I only asked out of curiosity."

"Actually I've been living on money from the States," he said. "But I hope to get going with this."

I went home with my alpha waves. You never know what you've got going for you. Who knows what other kinds of waves are clucking along inside me, maybe homing me in on something good somewhere, some-time.

I didn't go straight home. When I changed from the Bakerloo Line at Paddington I went up into the Main Line Station. I felt like being with a lot of people in a big open place. Ordinarily I don't like pigeons but I like them under the glass roof of Paddington Station. Mingling with the rush of people the pigeons are quite different from the way they are when plodding about in squares and being fed by people who have nothing better to feed. Intolerant of me to think that. Pigeons, turtles, what's the odds.

So much purposeful movement at Paddington, so many individual directions crossing one another, so many different lines of action! I always think that everyone else has good places to go to, they all seem so eager to get there. I sat on the low flat wooden railing by the Track One buffers and watched the figures passing in front of the light from the news-stand and under the grey glass sky of the roof. So many pretty girls! They were never so pretty when I was twenty. Two men were talking and one of them taking some change from his pocket dropped a 1/2p. While looking to see what he'd dropped he kicked it without seeing it. I watched it roll along the floor to be kicked in the opposite direction by another man who didn't see it. By then the man who'd dropped it had moved on and when the 1/2p stopped rolling I went over and picked it up, put it in my pocket and went home.

24

Neaera H.

In this morning's *Times* I read that the astronauts on *Skylab-2* have got two spiders with them. One of the spiders, named Arabella, has spun something like a normal web. "Weightlessness disoriented her at the start," says the news item from Houston, "and her first attempts produced only a few wisps, mainly in the corners of her cage. But today, on the thirteenth day of the *Skylab-2* flight, Dr. Owen Garriott was quite pleased with the work done by the spider. 'This time the web is essentially, at first glance, like one you would find on the ground,' Dr. Garriott said."

That Arabella should have spun any sort of web, should have made the effort at all, overwhelms me. In her place I should have sulked or been sick I am sure. She didn't even know which way was up let alone where she was or why and yet she spun a reasonably workable web out there in space. I hope they had the decency to bring along some flies for her to catch, I can't think they'd make her eat tiny frozen dinners squeezed out of tubes or whatever astronauts subsist on. And if they did bring flies those flies must appear somewhere on *Skylab-2*'s manifest: *Flies, 12 doz.* If there are flies up there no mention is made of them or how they adapted to weightlessness. Perhaps they'd use dead flies just as they use dead mice to feed the owls at the Zoo. In any case Arabella deserves a plaque on *Skylab*-2. But of course she doesn't need one, hasn't got the sort of mind that thinks about plaques. She needs no recognition, can recognize herself and spin a web wherever she may be. What good things instincts are!

Last night I had a dream thought that I held on to carefully until this morning. It was: Those who know it have forgotten every part of it, those who don't know it remember it completely. Aggravating. Those who know or don't know what? I haven't a clue and what's most annoying is that something in me knows what was meant.

There was a week of nature films on the South Bank and I went to see one about sharks. The film was made by a man of apparently unlimited wealth who fitted himself out with a large ship and any amount of special underwater gear for shark photography. He and his companions all agreed that diving among sharks was for them the ultimate challenge. They were particularly keen to encounter a great white shark, a rare species and the one most feared as a man-eater. They went from ocean to ocean looking for the great white shark and I couldn't help wondering all the time how much it was costing. I think the money spent on even one of the special diving cages would keep me in high style for half a year at least.

For a large part of the time they followed whaling ships, photographing sharks feeding on whale carcasses. Sometimes they took their pictures from inside a cage but often they swam fearlessly among the sharks. They swam among blue sharks, dusky sharks, oceanic white-tipped sharks and several other kinds but they were continually frustrated by the absence of great white sharks.

Eventually they found a great white shark which they attracted with whale oil, blood and horsemeat. It was a truly terrifying creature and they very wisely stayed in their cage while the shark took the bars in his teeth and shook it about. The wealthy man said that it had been fantastic, incredible, beyond his expectations. His friends congratulated him on the success of the expedition and the film came to an end.

I found myself resenting that man, however unreasonable it might be of me. All the money in the world does not give him the right to muck about with a direful secret creature and shame the mystery of it with words like "fantastic" and "incredible." The divers were not the ultimate challenge for the shark, I'm certain of that. Socially they were out of their class, the shark would not have swum from ocean to ocean seeking *them*. It would have gone its mute and deadly way mindlessly being its awful self, innocent and murderous. It was the people who lusted for the fierce attention of the shark, like monkeys they had to make him notice them.

Money can do many things, even the great white shark can be played with by wealthy *frotteurs* in posh diving gear. But they have not really seen him or touched him because what he is to man is what is he to naked man alone-swimming. They have not found the great white shark, they have acted out some brothel fantasy with black rubber clothing and steel bars. Aluminium they were actually.

When I came out of the Queen Elizabeth Hall with the crowd there was a threadbare man playing a mouth organ. The lamps were lit along the promenade and on the bridges, trains rattled across the Hungerford Bridge, boats apparently powered by music went past with people dancing, lights glittered on the river and in the buildings across the river, there was a full moon, the night was balmy. The mouth organ buzzed its little music fiercely, the man's eyes looked out fiercely over the mouth organ. I gave him 10p, he thanked me, sent his music after me like bees.

At a party I drank more than I should have done and found myself going on and on about Oedipus and Peter Rabbit, Thebes and Mr. McGregor's garden to Harry Rush of Pryntward Rush & Hope. Two days later there was a letter affirming his strong interest in my forthcoming *From Oedipus to Peter Rabbit: The Tragic Heritage in Children's Literature* and offering me a £1,000 advance on signing.

On the morning when the letter came I was thinking that possibly the biggest tragedy in children's literature is that people won't stop writing it. It was one of those mornings when there suddenly seemed nothing whatever that could be taken for granted. I felt a stranger in my own head, as if the consciousness looking out through my eyes were some monstrous changeling. Here was the implacable morning light on all the books and litter that were always there but nothing was recognizable as having significance. What in the world was it all about, I found myself wondering.

People write books for children and other people write about the books written for children but I don't think it's for the children at all. I think that all the people who worry so much about the children are really worrying about themselves, about keeping their world together and getting the children to help them do it, getting the children to agree that it is indeed a world. Each new generation of children has to be told: "This is a world, this is what one does, one lives like this." Maybe our constant fear is that a generation of children will come along and say: "This is not a world, this is nothing, there's no way to live at all."

25

William G.

Somebody'd told Harriet about a free demonstration of something called Original Therapy and she asked me if I'd like to go with her. Neither of us had any idea of what it might be and I couldn't care less but I went. Anything to keep my mind off the turtles.

The place was in Maida Vale, the people had long hair and wore sandals which they mostly took off. There were a lot of good-looking feet in the crowd. The bearded men looked like Great Men of History from the neck up: Darwin, Pasteur, Mendeleyev, Faraday. From the neck down they looked like layabouts. The girls looked better to me but then girls usually do, there seems to me to be more human solidity in women than in men. Odd how one says *girls* and men. More than half the men were boys and more than half the girls were women who looked as if they'd seen a good deal of a certain kind of life and had cooked many hundredweights of brown rice. Oriental pillows on the floor, Buddhist and Zen books on the shelves, the *I Ching*, Laing, Castaneda, Hermann Hesse, *The Whole Earth Catalog*. Smell of old incense in the air.

The Original Therapy lady was a rampant-looking woman of about forty. Shiny red hair in the style of old musical films, tight white trousers, gold sandals, silver toenails, bursting purple silk blouse. Swarthy boy-friend with a St Christopher medal and a racing-driver watch strap.

Her name was Ruby and she sounded as if she lived in a caravan, her voice and her way of talking. She began to tell us about her therapy while some of the people in the room sat in the lotus position with very straight backs and others held their heads. One girl wailed a little now and then, another muttered the whole time.

She was American, this Ruby. Told us how she'd knocked about, been a rodeo rider, done roller derbies, wrestled, had three husbands and all kinds of troubles. Discovered her Original Therapy whilst wrestling one night. Another lady had a scissors grip on her and was squeezing very hard, got a bit over-enthusiastic and wouldn't let go. Under the pressure Ruby experienced a strange alteration of consciousness.

"I was seeing all kinds of coloured lights and shooting sparks," she said, "and the sound of the crowd was beginning to come and go like the roar of surf far away. Something began to happen to me. I could feel my-self going way way down and way way back, like thousands of years, mil-lions of years, glaciers coming and going and the dinosaurs sinking into the swamps and the primitive trees being crushed into coal. Farther back than that even, crawling out of a warm ocean and gasping on the beach and beyond that back to the sea and smaller and smaller, all the way back to a single cell. And back beyond that to nothing, just the warm sea, what they call the primordial soup."

Ruby went farther than the soup even, she got to a point where there was nothing, no time, no her, no anything. Then there came something like the idea of a question, a kind of original YES or NO? It put itself to-gether as YES. There was a mystical green pattern with no sound, then a red explosion in Ruby's mind and the people in the ringside seats were picking the other lady wrestler out of their laps. That was the turning point in Ruby's life, going back to the origin of life and finding the big YES, and she was going to show us slides and then demonstrate her therapy.

A lot of the people in the room were shifting about and trying to find space on the floor to lie down. Some were smoking hash. There was one chap who looked as if he'd been thrown together by dustmen from odd bits of upholstery and discarded clothing, he asked Ruby whether when the spirit goes out of the body another spirit could come into it. He had a high choked voice, fat unshaven face.

Ruby said that nothing like that had ever happened in her experience. There were no other questions, it was quiet in the room, one or two people were asleep. The last light of the day came through the windows, smoke drifted. Then the window curtains were drawn and Ruby showed us slides.

We saw many slides of Ruby in a bikini scissors-gripping people who also wore swimsuits or shorts. "The skin contact makes a difference," she said. "Smells are important too." We saw people bursting free as they reached YES, saw their happy faces afterwards. Ruby told us that people were revitalized in a variety of ways by returning to the origins of life via her scissors-grip. Illnesses disappeared and one man who'd been losing his hair stopped losing it.

The curtains were pulled back. It was evening now, the dim light of the street lamps came a little way into the room, ended in darkness. Candles were lit. Ruby withdrew briefly, bounced back in her bikini. A powerful presence. I felt depressed and anxious, Harriet seemed nervous, hugged herself forlornly. The wailing girl said, "Oh Jesus." The dustbin chap went red in the face. Several of the thinner people got up and left.

"What's the lady going to do?" a little girl asked her mother.

"Therapy," said her mother.

"Like Daddy?" said the little girl.

"A different kind," said her mother. "Watch."

Ruby put on a record. For atmosphere, she said. "There was this wonderful Disney film, *Fantasia*, years ago," she said. "There was a part with the beginning of the world, the red sky and the steaming oceans, and then later came the dinosaurs and all. I've always loved the music."

It was Stravinsky's *Le Sacre du Printemps*. In all the photographs I've seen of him Stravinsky looks to me like a man who was potty-trained too early and that music proves it as far as I'm concerned.

A mat was brought in and one of the bearded fellows took his shirt off and lay down on it. Ruby lay down at right angles to him and wrapped her legs round his waist. "Let your mind go completely blank if you can," she said. "Breathe out when I squeeze, breathe in when I ease up. Keep looking at me."

The muscles leaped up in Ruby's thighs, the bearded fellow gasped as the air went out of him and they were away. In about five minutes he reached YES, burst free, was happy like the people in the slides and Ruby went on to the next applicant. Nobody'd been told to bring a swimsuit, most of the men took their shirts off, some of the girls had a go in bras and knickers, others kept everything on. Ruby made a real effort with everyone, squeezing hard until they reached YES or said they had. One chap cried "Pax!" but he was the only one. After a time I stopped paying close attention. We were all crowded round very close, Harriet's bottom was partly resting on my right hand and a bare foot belonging to one of the better-looking girls was touching my left. I felt cosy and relaxed with the candlelight, the smell of hash and sweat, the breathing and the grunting as one person after another returned to the origins of life between Ruby's muscular thighs. Even the Stravinsky became soothing with repetition.

It went on and on. I must say I rather fancied being squeezed by Ruby but I wasn't sure I felt like doing it in front of everybody. Harriet was not tempted but we were both beginning to enjoy the evening in a quiet way.

Ruby was scissors-gripping a very good-looking young man named David when he began to groan but not in the ordinary way. His eyes were closed and he seemed to be in a sort of trance. He braced his hands on Ruby's thighs and pushed as if trying to squeeze out from between her legs, worked a few inches of himself out of her grip. "Can't breathe," he murmured as if talking in his sleep. "Round my neck, strangling me."

"It's the cord," said a blonde woman with frizzy hair and a wrinkled face. She was American too.

"What cord?" said Ruby.

"The umbilical cord," said the blonde woman. "I'm a therapist too. He's doing a natal, he's re-experiencing his birth. Quick, turn him, get him untangled. Loosen your grip so I can turn him."

Ruby loosened her grip, the blonde woman rolled David round between Ruby's legs. "There," she said. "That's all right now. Let him squeeze himself out the way he was doing."

"I don't know," said Ruby. "This never happens back in Los Angeles. They just go back to that big YES and Zonk! They're out again."

Murmurs and crowd noises. This wasn't Los Angeles, said several other Americans. Small stirrings of solidarity between the expatriates and those of us who were English, feelings of pride that things in London might perhaps be not quite so simple as in Los Angeles. There was renewed interest all round. David was wiggling and shimmying, parting Ruby's legs with his hands and uttering rending groans.

"Whatever it is it feels good," said Ruby. "It feels like something big happening. You have to stay open to whatever comes up in this kind of work."

"He needs help," said the blonde woman. "I'll push from behind. Somebody else take his head and shoulders and ease him along when he tries to get himself out."

"What are they doing now?" said the little girl to her mother.

"David's being born," said her mother.

Willing hands were laid on at both ends of David, Ruby, and the blonde lady. More and more people joined in the delivery. By this time David, still with his eyes closed, was half way out of his trousers with all the wiggling. He was wearing black knickers. There was more pushing and pulling, much encouragement and advice, and finally with one big hoarse cry David was all the way out. Of Ruby's legs and his trousers both.

There was a general happy clamour and some of the girls had tears in their eyes. I looked at Harriet and saw that she did too. I squeezed her hand and she squeezed back. Ruby hugged David. "Give Mommy a big kiss," she said.

David still had his eyes closed, and as he moved into Ruby's embrace he fumbled one big bouncy breast out of her bikini top and applied himself to it like a veteran infant.

"Jesus!" said Ruby and pressed his head to her bosom. There was a spontaneous ovation from everybody except Ruby's boyfriend, who said something violent in Italian, rolled his eyes up and made a gesture. David opened his eyes and smiled a happy smile, Ruby put her breast back, somebody brought her a cup of tea. People lit cigarettes and joints, settled back cosily.

There were many earnest questions put to David by girls with glistening eyes and men in whose faces there now shone an awful lust for infancy. How had it felt, where had he been, how did he feel now? David said it had been a deep experience, it had taken him back to the darkness of the womb, his pre-natal anxieties, his ambivalence about his mother, his resentment of his father, his fears about coming out into the world. He told of his joy at the first light of emergence and Ruby's boob. He felt good, renewed, serene. There was less tension in his neck. That was as much as he could say now, it was something he'd have to reflect on, it had been a very deep experience.

Now there was a rush to be next for Ruby's Original Therapy but the primordial soup wasn't in it any more, being born was what everybody wanted to have a go at. Harriet put her name down on the list, I didn't. Not my time for rebirth just yet. Ruby promised to take on all comers, to go right through the night if necessary, and after a short break the therapy resumed.

Some wept as they were reborn, others raged. Some both raged and wept. The wailing girl went dead silent when she did it, the one who'd muttered to herself shouted the whole time. Stravinsky was abandoned, no one needed music any more. Additional mats were brought in to afford as it were a longer birth canal. Some thrashed about in Ruby's grip while being pulled and pushed the length of the room and others shimmied smoothly through her legs like fish. Ruby was red and blotched and chafed all over from being scraped along and struggled with up and down the room but she said that she was so energized by the atmosphere that she wasn't tired at all.

Even though many of the girls did their writhing in bras and knickers the whole thing was not sexually stimulating, everyone was in such terrible need of something harder to find than sex. I particularly noticed one impressively handsome bearded young man who had sat in a lotus position with a very straight back and a very aloof face earlier in the evening. Now he actually grovelled and whimpered waiting for his turn.

I could never have imagined Harriet squirming on a mat in the grip of a lady wrestler's legs but when her turn came there she was. She was fully clothed of course but her face was naked and I'd never seen her look like that before. I thought of films in which strange harsh voices spoke through women who were mediums. Harriet groaned and sobbed in her own voice but her body arched and twisted as if some terrible thing in her wanted to shed her like an old skin and get out. I couldn't help noticing, what with the disarray of her clothing and her skirt sliding up, that she had much more of a figure than I'd given her credit for.

By then I wasn't feeling cosy any more. One moment I was safe and a little detached and the next I looked at the candle flames and moving shadows and was sick with terror. It was as if the evening had reversed a giant devil-mirror with its picture of a world and I was silvered at the back of things, lost atoms speeding to infinity. Terror was all there was, nothing else. It might reflect the images of aeroplanes or cathedrals or Ruby in a bikini and the faces in the room but there was no reality but the terror, all that it reflected was illusion.

When Harriet had finished we left. The night outside was quiet and peaceful but the silver terror was all about us. We got a taxi and Harriet cuddled tiredly against me. Well, I thought, here we are, and took her in my arms and kissed her. When we got to her place I paid the driver, she opened the front door and we went up to her room without a word.

We took our clothes off with the terror in the room. The terror was the energy that moved us, our naked bodies moved together like the sound waves of a scream. Most animals don't make love face to face, I thought as I fell asleep. Male and female face the same way, seeing what's about them. Whales and humans show two backs to it.

26

Neaera H.

"Death of the oyster-catchers" was the heading of an article in the *Observer*:

> A programme to kill 11,000 sea birds has been under way for the past
> month on the sands of the Burry estuary on the Gower peninsula in
> South Wales.
> Men with shotguns have been shooting oyster-catchers on the morning
> and afternoon tides and, so far, several hundred have been killed. The
> marksmen are being paid a bounty of 25p a bird.
> The South Wales Sea Fisheries Committee, which is running the cull-
> ing programme, believes it is necessary to kill the birds in order to save
> the world-famous cockle beds of Penclawdd. The birds, they say, are
> eating five to six million baby cockles each winter and they can eat more
> in a month than the cocklers can gather in a year.

Cockling in Penclawdd, the article went on to say, was one of Britain's first
forms of social security in that it offered a livelihood to women who had
lost their men in mining accidents. The article ended with the words of a
cockler from Crofty. "We're having a struggle to even reach our daily
quota of cockles nowadays," he said. "Quite simply, it is either us or the
birds."

Uncanny, I thought. Is there something keeping its eye on my mind, waiting to strike down whatever I think about? I'd never in my life seen a word about oyster-catchers in the news before. Now they're killing them. "Us or the birds," said the cockler.

Harry Rush's letter still lay on my desk unanswered, heavy with the burden that would be on me if I accepted. Of course I needed the £1,000, when would there ever be a time when I shouldn't? The letter nagged at me like a paper devil, I knew I'd never finish such a book if I were fool enough to start it, I'd sicken at the very first page. I had feelings of doom and damnation, utter lostness, and now the dead and dying oyster-catchers seemed to put the seal on it. Everything seemed too much for me, I was overwhelmed.

I was getting hot flashes of desperation and running about the flat picking things up and putting them down aimlessly. I wanted a rest, wanted peace, wanted the world to let me alone for a bit. *King Kong* was playing at the Chelsea Odeon, so I went.

Wonderful inside the Odeon, cool and quiet and sheltered from the world. The place had been redone, the seating was spacious and comfortable. The lights had not yet dimmed, the screen was still playing music to itself the way they always do before a film starts. I like that music whatever it is, it sounds the same in all cinemas, light and gay and full of safe expectation.

The film was first released in the United States in 1933 during the Great Depression. That sounds strange: the Great Depression. One thinks of millions of people sitting with their heads in their hands and groaning all at the same time. Many did of course but there was no atom bomb then, the world was still like a child too little to know about death. Whatever was happening beyond the camera's field of vision, innocence was still possible and one felt it in the opening of the picture: the dark and foggy harbour, the film entrepreneur with his ship bound for a secret destination, the beautiful hungry girl he recruits when he finds her stealing apples. He holds her at arm's length looking intently at her face, she returns the look almost fainting, full of surrender that is transcendentally sexual and innocent. She knows she is beautiful, knows that her beauty has been recognized, that good things will happen if she surrenders.

On the ship he rehearses her in front of the camera, has her look up ("Higher, higher!") and scream. He doesn't tell her what she'll be screaming at later but he knows he's going to bring her to some giant terror. It's a reversal of the *Schöne Mullerin* theme of the unattainable beauty: the voyeur, the picture-maker, must put his attainable beauty within easy reach of the colossal beast. I watched her scream at the unknown horror she was heading for. That was a good touch, it was absolutely right. She screamed with complete acceptance of her place in life.

When Skull Island appeared it was mostly a painted backdrop but that didn't matter; even if the studios and camera crew and all the behind-the-scenes equipment had been visible in the film it wouldn't have mattered. Even showing the animator moving his little articulated models and photographing them frame by frame wouldn't have made any difference in the effect: Kong with his teddy-bear fur is a fifty-foot-tall idea even if the reality was only eighteen inches high. Kong lives. There *was* a giant arm for close-ups of Fay Wray screaming in Kong's grasp and that seems right too. Possibly somewhere in Hollywood that giant arm lies in a warehouse, empty-handed now. Kong had no visible male member even when presumably excited but then he was *all* male member in a manner of speaking so that doesn't matter either. On the other hand maybe that's why he only wanted tiny women to play with instead of looking for a fifty-foot-tall she-ape with whom to have sexual kongress. The psychological ripples are ever-widening. Now that I think of it why *weren't* there any other fifty-foot high gorillas about? What had happened to Kong's mother and father? That too must be part of the pathos of the thing: Kong is an orphan and alone of his kind. Not just an orphan but a giant orphan, a monstrous Tom o'Bedlam.

Carl Denham, the film man, comes ashore with Anne Darrow (Fay Wray) and his crew to look for the legendary beast-god of Skull Island. They see the natives making ready to offer a bride to Kong. The massive wooden gates at the edge of the village suggested the size of the beast they were meant to keep out, his colossalness preceded him. There were the black men dancing in gorilla skins and chanting for Kong to come and claim his bride: "Something something KONG! KONG! Something something KONG! KONG!" flinging up their furry arms at each KONG. The music by Max Steiner was just right. Then they saw Fay Wray and that night they went out to the ship in their boats and captured her and offered her instead of the local girl.

There she was in the light of the torches, wearing a white silk frock I think, all blonde and helpless with her head drooping and her arms outstretched, hands tied to two posts. Then she looked up, higher, higher, and screamed and screamed when Kong's luminous face rose above the trees like a giant ape-moon. It was at the same time laughable and ineffably real. Yes that's a big fake ape, ha ha. But the fake ape is only the cipher for the real thing before which we stand with outstretched arms, hands tied, head drooping, and we scream or are silent.

By the end of the film Kong too is a victim, tragic in his greatness and the height (the Empire State Building) from which he falls. When he's brought a captive to New York to be exhibited on the stage it is he who stands with arms outstretched, crucified by midgets and manacled with great thick chains.

"He was a king and a god in the world he knew," says Denham, "but now he comes to civilization merely a captive, a show to gratify your curiosity. Ladies and gentlemen, Kong, the Eighth Wonder of the World!"

Fay Wray is on the stage as well. When the photographers' flashbulbs go off near her Kong thinks she's in danger, he growls and strains at his chains. Then comes one of the very best lines in the film or indeed anywhere: "Don't be alarmed, ladies and gentlemen, those chains are made of chrome steel," says Denham. Then of course Kong breaks loose, kills some people, derails and smashes an overhead train and climbs up the Empire State Building with Fay Wray, there to be shot down by aeroplanes.

"Don't be alarmed, ladies and gentlemen, those chains are made of chrome steel." Wonderful line. Marvellous how one's afraid of the thing that's going to break its chains and then so quickly one *is* the thing that's broken its chains and climbed the heavenward spire to be shot down.

"Oh no, it wasn't the aeroplanes," says Denham standing by the fallen Kong (there must be a giant head in the warehouse too), "it was Beauty that killed the Beast."

What a sad life. On his island Kong had plenty of other monsters to fight with, he was very good against the tyrannosaurus I thought. But he had no one to be friends with. Poor thing. At the end when he's dying from the aeroplanes' machine-gun bullets he reaches towards Fay Wray who's lying on a ledge where he'd put her. Weak and swaying, his grip on the spire loosening, he touches her gently, then lets go and falls. The year 1933 was full of many things. Showing with *King Kong* was a documentary film on Hitler's rise to power. In 1933 there was Goebbels officiating at a book burning. "You do well at this midnight hour," he said, "to exorcise the past in these flames." Exorcise the past. Surely that thought alone was sufficient evidence of madness. But more and more I think that madness is the world's natural condition and to expect anything else is madness compounded. In the train derailment scene in *King Kong* the engine-driver could not believe his eyes when he saw Kong's face rising through the gap where he'd torn away the tracks but that was just another day in 1933. That trains mostly stay on rails, that the streets are mostly peaceful, that the square continues green and quiet below my window is more than I have any right to expect, and it happens every day.

Madame Beetle swims in her green world expecting neither continuation nor sanity, I don't think expectation is a part of her. While there is water she will swim. Arabella spins her weightless web on *Skylab-2* and the white shark goes its way without rest. There is no buoyancy in sharks, they cannot rest, they must keep swimming till they die.

27

William G.

Sermons in stones. The other day coming home from work I noticed for the first time a manhole cover near my corner. Square plate in the pavement, K257 on it. All right, I thought as I stepped on it, go ahead, play Mozart. It didn't. When I got home I looked up K257 in the Köchel listing in my *Mozart Companion*. It was the Credo Mass in C. *Credo*. I believe. What does the manhole cover believe, or what's being believed down in the hole? I don't like getting too many messages from the things around me, it confuses me. Now whenever I walk on that manhole cover it'll say "I believe." When Mozart was my age he'd already been dead for eight years. I don't think I've ever heard the music.

Having slept together Harriet and I woke up together. I woke up first actually. Dora had always looked angry in her sleep. Harriet was calm and beautiful, better-looking than when awake. Lineaments of satisfied desire. I was impressed, pleased with myself as well. Maybe not a bad chap after all. Harriet kept looking beautiful when she woke up. She has quite an elegant figure too, long and graceful. Breakfast was cosy, we didn't talk much, mostly looked at each other.

That evening we had dinner together, went to my place and Harriet spent the night there. Sandor stuck his head out of his door and opened his eyes wide as she passed on her way to the bathroom. "I believe," said K257 as we walked over it together the next morning.

All right, I thought, I'll get through this turtle business and that'll be out of the way. I'd been giving some thought to turtle-shifting and I'd decided they could best be handled in crates. I rang up George Fairbairn and he gave me the measurements I needed. The big day would probably be in a fortnight or so, he thought. A fortnight. Right. If I'd drop off the crates first he'd have the turtles boxed and ready for pick-up. Wonderful.

Harriet was emanating weekend availability and I was more than willing but I wanted to make the turtle crates on Saturday and I wanted to keep her and the turtles separate. I told her I had things to do at home all day and evening and couldn't get over to her place until late Saturday night.

On Saturday afternoon when I finished at the shop I bought the wood for the three crates and I bought six ringbolts and a hundred feet of half-inch rope. The ringbolts and the rope are for lowering the crates or dragging them up steps or whatever. Should I have got one-inch rope I wondered. I also bought a five-gallon container for extra petrol.

Mrs. Inchcliff was very pleased to see me active in the lumber-room. As soon as she heard me sawing she brought me a cup of tea. "What're you making?" she said.

"Turtle crates," I said. "I'm going to steal three sea turtles from the London Zoo and put them into the sea."

"Good," she said. "That's a good thing to do."

I'd started with a hand-saw but she went to the cupboard and got out Charlie's Black & Decker power drill with a circular-saw attachment. Marvellous, the things men leave behind. Of course she'd paid for it.

"I don't know why he didn't take it with him," she said.

"Yes you do," I said.

"I expect I do at that," she said. "But he'd have been welcome to it."

I've always been afraid of power tools. Castration complex. Castration complexes are reasonable though. More and more chances these days to have one's members lopped off by labour-saving devices as civilization progresses. All right, I thought, be a man, be powerful with a saw. So I used Charlie's Black & Decker and I didn't cut anything off after all. I was quite proud of myself. An afternoon and evening's work and there they were, three turtle crates with two ringbolts each. They were just plain open boxes, no lids, four feet long, twenty-eight inches wide, one foot deep. The turtles would lie on their backs with their flippers pressed to their sides.

"Tools," I said. "With tools you can do anything."

"With tools and a man," said Mrs. Inchcliff. "It takes both." She'd kept me company the whole time I was working, couldn't stay away. Gave me supper too. Odd how young she looks. As far as I know she's never done anything special to keep herself young except not smoke. Maybe it's because she's never been able to get through all the stages of her life. Her youth is still in her, not lived out.

Miss Neap, back from an evening out, came down to look in on us. "What goes in those?" she said when she saw the crates.

"Turtles," I said. "I'm going to put some sea turtles into the sea."

She was standing outside the circle of the green-shaded light, her pince-nez glittered in the shadows. She had a theatre programme in her hand, fresh air and perfume had come in with her. Her blonde hair and leopardskin coat looked as if they'd go out even if she stayed at home. "The sea," she said. "It always seems so far away even though the Thames goes to it." She smiled and went upstairs.

I hadn't expected to create a sensation but I was a little surprised that Mrs. Inchcliff and Miss Neap were so incurious about the turtle project. Speaking of turtles and the sea seemed to make their thoughts turn inwards.

Mr. Sandor came home while Mrs. Inchcliff and I were still sitting in the lumber-room admiring the crates and drinking tea. He had several foreign newspapers under his arm, was carrying his briefcase as always and smelt of his regular restaurant. "Not strong joints," he said looking at the corners of the crates. "Dovetail joints better."

"They're as strong as they need to be," I said. I didn't say anything about turtles.

I must try to remember my first impression of Harriet, how she looked to me when I first started at the shop. Reproachful, that's what I thought. I'd said to myself quite recently that her face was a constant reproach. I mustn't forget that, however cuddly she seems now. The reproach is waiting to appear again I'm sure. I think it's always like that. Dora looked angry when I first met her and the angry look was what her face came back to in the end. And I'm sure whatever look gave Harriet her first impression of me is waiting to return to my face.

I ought to give some thought to what I'm getting into. Casual affairs with people one works with are probably best avoided. And if this isn't a casual affair what is it? I'm not in love with Harriet. I feel good being with her, like sleeping with her, don't want to think beyond that.

It was cosy going to her place on Saturday night, walking under the street lamps looking up at lighted windows and knowing that I too had a lighted window waiting where I shouldn't be alone.

In bed we lay looking up at the patterns of light, the shapes of the windows thrown on the ceiling by the street lamps.

"What were you so busy with all afternoon and evening?" Harriet said.

"Odd jobs I'd been putting off," I said. I thought of the first time we'd made love in this room with the terror in it, wondered if the room would slide away, the light patterns on the ceiling and the clothes on the chair, and leave only the terror. It didn't. The room stayed. Harriet was there, warm and smooth along the whole length of me. Tomorrow we'd wake up together but I couldn't tell her about the turtles.

"A penny for your thoughts," said Harriet.

I hate it when people ask me what I'm thinking.

28

Neaera H.

I was reading about colliery horses in this morning's paper. Pit ponies, they're called. They live underground and work with the miners. They've saved lives, the article said, by stopping in their tracks and refusing to go ahead seconds before a roof-fall. They've led miners with broken lamps through black tunnels to safety, and it was said that a horse once pressed its body against a collapsing wall to give the men time to escape.

I like thinking about the horses and the men working together underground. A large strong animal and a man together add up to more than a man and an animal. They aren't afraid of the same things, and where the senses of one leave off, those of the other go on. I wish I had a horse to work with. Either I think the roof's going to fall in all the time or I think it'll never fall. I'm sure a horse would give it no thought at all except when the actuality impended. One can't have a horse to help with writing or drawing. Mice perhaps. Madame Beetle is not a help in any practical way but I feel that her attitude is exemplary. Swimming, diving, coming to the surface for air or sitting quietly in her shipwreck she is in harmony with her small world, has a good style.

How very patronizing of me, now that I consider it, to think that of Madame Beetle. If she's in harmony with her "small world" then she's in harmony with as much of the world as she has contact with. If I enjoyed comparable harmony I'd speak of it as being with *the* world, not my "small world." And if I find her exemplary how can I say she's of no practical value? If I were paying a Zen master for instruction I'd consider him an exemplar whose example had practical value. Madame Beetle cost only 31p and her tiny daily fee is not even paid in money so I discount her value.

I wrote a letter to Harry Rush thanking him for his offer but saying that I simply did not have a book on The Tragic Heritage in Children's Literature in me. I wasn't sure I'd post the letter but I took it with me when I went out. I didn't feel like cooking or eating in the flat. I took Tolstoy's *The Cossacks* with me and went to an Italian restaurant in Knightsbridge near William G.'s bookshop.

It was early and the place was almost empty. I settled into a booth, ordered *escalope milanese* and a half-carafe of red and began *The Cossacks*, which I'd last read twenty-five years ago. At the end of the first short chapter I came to:

> . . . the three shaggy post-horses dragged themselves out of one dark street into another, past houses he had never seen before. It seemed to Olenin that only travellers bound on a long journey ever went through such streets as these.

Perfectly true, I thought as I drank my wine. The same streets do not exist for everybody. Only travellers bound on a long journey go through such streets as those. Only solitary sojourners go through other streets, sit at tables such as this.

My seat shook a little as someone sat down in the booth behind me. I was facing away from the door and hadn't seen them come in. I went on with my Tolstoy until I heard William G.'s voice say, "I'm having *escalope milanese*."

"Where's that on the menu?" said a female voice, one I'd heard before. The girl at the bookshop who'd given me his address and telephone number. Her voice came from beside him rather than opposite.

"Here," said William. Odd how people do that with menus. One person reads aloud the name of a dish and the other person requires to see it in print as if the word were a picture.

"I'll have the scampi," she said. I didn't want to overhear their conversation but my *escalope* hadn't come yet.

"Jannequin, Costely, Passereau, Bouzignac," said William. "Renaissance madrigals with soprano solo."

"Couperin, Lully, Rameau, Baroque songs for soprano," she said. "I know those three but I've never heard of the others." Probably they were on their way to the South Bank and looking at the programme.

The booth creaked as the voices became murmurous, there were silences. I concentrated on Tolstoy until my *escalope* arrived, ate as quickly as possible, finished my wine, didn't bother with a sweet or coffee. I had to pass their booth to get to the door. If they noticed me I'd say hello, if not I'd just not see them.

I passed the booth, they both looked up at me. It wasn't William G. and the girl from the bookshop. It was two people I'd never seen before.

29

William G.

I rang up a van-hire place. £2.75 per day, 2 1/2p per mile, £10 deposit. God, how I hate the thought of driving the thing. In films people like Paul Newman and Burt Lancaster leap into vehicles they've never seen before, cars, lorries, buses, locomotives, anything at all, and away they go at speed. Sometimes they have to fight with someone first, knock him out before they can drive away. Well of course that's how it is in films. How can reality be so different?

I still haven't said anything about the turtles to Harriet and I still don't want to. She's begun saying "We." So-and-so wondered if we could come to a party. There was a series of early music recitals and ought we to subscribe. We went to the party, we subscribed to the series.

I keep waiting for the phone to ring from that other world where the turtles are. It's not another world really, it's this one. Everything happens in the same world, that's why life is so difficult. I'll pick up the van right after work, deliver the crates, come back later, meet Neaera at the Zoo and drive to Polperro. Maybe I ought to pick her up earlier, maybe we ought to have dinner first.

Yesterday evening I looked out of my window and saw the greyhound lady go past alone. No husband. The Greyhound Widow, like a figure on a tarot card. A train went past on the far side of the common. One vertical row of three lights: Tower Hill. I knew the husband was dead, it was in the way she walked with the greyhound. I asked Mrs. Inchcliff about it, she knows everything that goes on in the neighbourhood. Yes, she said, the husband had died a week ago. If he'd lived two weeks longer his widow would have got two years' salary but as it was she wouldn't.

There's an owl in the Charing Cross tube station. *Bubo tubo*. Not really an owl. The sound comes from an escalator but it's as real as the owl I hear on the common and never see. There's only one world, and animal voices must cry out from machines sometimes.

There it was: the telephone call from George Fairbairn. Thursday would be the day. This was Monday. If I could drop the crates off about half past six he'd have the turtles ready for me in half an hour or so. He was talking to me in a matter-of-fact way as if I really existed and was a real grown-up person who could drive vans, be at a certain place at a certain time and do what I'd undertaken to do. Incredible. I said I mightn't be able to get there till after seven. Right, he said, he'd see me then.

Maybe there wouldn't be a van available, maybe all the arrangements would break down. I rang up the van-hire place. Yes, I could have a van on Thursday.

Maybe I'd not be able to get away from the shop. Late summer, still lots of tourists. I asked Mr. Meager if I could have Friday off. Personal matter. He said yes of course.

I thought of ringing up the Zoo and warning them that a turtle snatch was planned for Thursday. I didn't do it. All right, I thought. Let it happen.

30

Neaera H.

I hadn't posted the letter to Harry Rush, it was still in my bag. I wasn't going to do the book but nothing else was happening. Madame Beetle's good for companionship and philosophy lessons but nothing in the way of commercial profit, and Gillian Vole and that lot seem to be a thing of the past. So I wasn't completely ready to let go of the £1,000. Wasn't ready to let go of the *idea* of the £1,000. I could no more write the book than swim the Channel. Actually, with training I might in time swim the Channel but no amount of training will get that book out of me.

William G. rang up. Thursday would be the day. He spoke as if it was all really real and we were real people who were simply going to go ahead and do what we'd said we'd do. Had I in fact said it? That first day at lunch I'd talked in code, talked about hauling bananas. Had I ever said *turtles*? Yes, my very first words to him in the shop before we went to lunch. And then that awful Saturday morning when I went to his flat we talked about the turtles before I left. Perhaps I could still back out of it. But there was his voice coming out of the telephone and I said yes, Thursday would be all right. He asked if he could pick me up on his way to the Zoo with the crates and we'd have dinner before setting out. I said that would be lovely, yes of course and I'd be ready at half past six.

I looked at the telephone after I'd put it down. Sly thing, getting words out of me I'd no intention of saying. This was Monday. Tuesday, Wednesday, Thursday. Oh God, more than two hundred miles each way. I'll pack sandwiches and a flask of coffee but how much time will eating sandwiches and drinking coffee get us through. The whole thing is quite likely to end in disaster with the van and the turtles and us overturned in a ditch somewhere in the middle of the night, all blood and splintered glass, groans and whimpers. Maybe we'll be killed outright, and all for some stupid notion long since gone out of my head. Oh shit.

Blankets. We'll want a bit of a rest before the drive back. Pillows. Surely he won't book hotel rooms, it isn't that kind of thing. No, no, just let it be done and out of the way as quickly as possible. Towel and soap, toothbrush, toothpaste. Have a wash in the public lavatory before starting back. Wear jeans and a shirt, take a cardigan. Cigarettes, mustn't run out. Has he got maps? He looks the sort to have maps, torches, compasses. He's the anxious type and I know we'll get lost.

The tide. Will it be in or out. What's the use of bothering to find out. However it is is the way it'll be. I wonder if they're still killing oyster-catchers at Penclawdd. They must be.

I asked Webster de Vere to feed Madame Beetle, left him a key and the remains of the lamb chop she's been living on for the last week. I still haven't posted the letter to Harry Rush.

And here's Thursday.

31

William G.

Thursday. Grey and rainy. That was a help, sunny blue-sky days always look like bad luck to me. Harriet wanted to know where I was going but all I said was that I had things to do.

"There's no need to make a mystery of it," she said.

"And there's no need to ask me either," I said.

"Look," said Harriet, "you're perfectly free to do whatever you like . . . "

"Thanks very much," I said.

"Oh, you know what I mean," said Harriet. "You don't have to treat me like a stranger just because you're going to be with someone else."

"Everything isn't sex," I said. "There are other things that are private." I hadn't minded telling Mrs. Inchcliff and Miss Neap but I just wasn't willing for Harriet to know everything about me. She walked away looking reproachful, had very little to say to me for the rest of the day.

After work I went to pick up the van. It was a Ford Transit 90, 18 Cwt, huge, smooth, bulgy and white, not a dent or scratch on it. I couldn't believe I'd get it there and back intact. They gave it to me with no hesitation whatever. *VANS 4-U Van Hire* in big black letters on both sides.

The man at VANS 4-U said the petrol tank held thirteen gallons and the van would do from fifteen to twenty miles to the gallon. I thought fifteen more likely than twenty although the engine certainly sounded economical, I wondered if it would go up hills with two people and three turtles. I filled the tank, later I'd fill my five-gallon container as well. On the map our route looked like about two hundred and fifty miles, and at night I couldn't count on petrol stations being open. If the van did fifteen miles to the gallon that was one hundred and ninety-five miles on a full tank and seventy-five miles more on the extra five gallons in the container, so we ought to be all right even if there were no stations open.

It felt strange sitting up so high with all that van around me. The gearbox was at least an ordinary four-speed one. The width of the thing was appalling. I was behind a bus when I first pulled out into the street and I was only about six inches narrower than it. I kept going up on the kerb with my left front wheel when I thought I was a foot away from it.

The rain was still coming down gently and steadily. I drove to my place, loaded on the crates, the trolley, the petrol container, the rope, torch, map, road atlas, an eiderdown to lie down on, an old blanket to put under it, a couple of blankets to cover us. Us? I didn't think either of us had any hanky-panky in mind and we'd have our clothes on. Couple of pillows. Thermos flask, we could probably fill it and get some sandwiches at one of the services on the M4. I felt very jumpy the whole time. Cigarettes. I took four packets. I couldn't think of anything else. I went to the loo twice, got into the van and drove off, mounting the kerb from time to time when I made left turns and getting angry looks from pedestrians. I stopped to fill the petrol container, then headed for Neaera's place.

She was waiting by the front steps when I drove up. She looked doubtful. Her basic look, I realized. Dora had looked angry, Harriet reproachful, Neaera doubtful. Not that it mattered in a permanent way, there was nothing between us except the turtles and there wasn't likely to be anything. Why not? I don't know, I think we have too much in common. We're not complementary, she doesn't fill in the blanks in me nor I in her. Both afraid of the same things maybe. We don't fit together. What if we did? There's a cheap little toy one sees at various shops, a little flat wooden clown hanging from strings between two sticks. You squeeze the sticks and the clown somersaults. His body and face are in profile and he's made so economically that one cut shapes the back of him and the front of the next clown to come from the same piece of wood. There he is with the back of his head indented by a nose-and-chin-shaped space. Looking at him one wants to fit the one behind into him and him into the one ahead. And if one fitted fifty flat wooden clowns together in a line the one at each end would still be out in the cold, one with his back and the other with his front. Fitting them together in a circle solves the problem I suppose. Then they'd just keep going round in circles.

Neaera had sandwiches and a flask of coffee in a carrier bag, pillows and blankets as well. She seemed about as nervous as I was.

"I'm not used to the width of this thing," I said. "It would be a help if you'd tell me when we're too close to the parked cars or the kerb." We started off for the Zoo.

"Too close," she said about every two minutes. I nodded and swung away, trying to think of anything I might have forgotten. There were meant to be a spare tyre, tools and a jack somewhere in the van but I hadn't thought to ask where they were. Never mind. The rain was a nice little bonus, just enough of it to make the windscreen wipers work smoothly. I liked that, it was cosy.

George Fairbairn was on the lookout for us at the works gate, we left the crates with him and drove to a kebab house on the Finchley Road. They always play Greek music there but not too loud, just a pleasant background sound that gives privacy. I hate those places where there's a shouting kind of silence in which people make display conversation for the people listening at the other tables.

It was still light outside, the rain was coming down nicely and it was shadowy enough in the restaurant for the candle at our table to have some effect. I felt all right. Atoms speeding to infinity aren't necessarily lost, are they. They're just going where they're going. There's a thing that happens in my mind, a foreshadow of a waiting thought. Sometimes I know it's a thought that'll fill me with dread and then the dread comes before the thought. Sometimes I sense round the corner an easy thought and the ease comes. What was it, I wanted to hold on to it. Going where they're going, that was it. Things and people are as they are, where they are. Dora and Ariadne and Cyndie are where they are, Neaera and I and the turtles. That's all, nothing to be afraid of. One needn't even hold on to that, no holding on. Just let go of the terror, don't hold on to the terror. Simple if only I could remember that.

"Where is it on the menu?" said Neaera, and she laughed. I'd said I was going to have the doner kebab.

"What's funny about doner kebab?" I said.

"I was laughing because I asked you where it was on the menu," she said. "It's one of those odd things people always do."

I showed it to her on the menu. We ordered a carafe of red and we both had doner kebab. Did the waiter think we were married, I wondered. I was feeling all right, smoking a cigarette and craving another cigarette at the same time but holding on to nothing else. Comfortable in a way. I'll never cease to be amazed by the fact that people uncomfortable in themselves can give comfort to other people. Even I have given comfort, Ariadne and Cyndie used to feel cosy with me. Neaera was an uncomfortable person, I could feel that. But I felt comfortable with her.

"Do you know anything?" I said.

"Not a bloody thing," she said.

"Don't know what's best for anybody?"

"Not even for myself. Especially not for myself."

"Wonderful," I said. I raised my glass. "Here's to not knowing anything."

"I'll drink to that," she said, and raised her glass. We both laughed, it just came out.

"Except the turtles," I said. "We know what's best for the turtles, eh?"

"Oh shit," she said. No laughter. "It seemed to want to happen, didn't it."

"Yes," I said. "It seemed to want to happen." Her face was sad. I felt at home with her face. Maybe it was a beautiful face, I don't know. It looked as tired as my own, dark circles under her eyes. Very black eyebrows, no grey in her long black hair. Harriet. Well, yes. We'd subscribed to a series of recitals but that wasn't a lifetime contract. I'd never seen Neaera's flat but I could image books, drawing-table, typewriter. I could imagine being there with her in the evening reading, writing maybe.

"You haven't got a cat, have you?" I said.

"No," she said. "Do I look as if I've got a cat?"

"No," I said.

"I have a water-beetle," she said.

"Why not," I said. "Nothing wrong with water-beetles."

"It started as insect exploitation," she said. "I thought there might be a story in her."

"Don't reproach yourself," I said. "If I had anything to exploit I'd exploit it. Why should insects have special privileges, they're no better than the rest of us. We can take the beetle to Polperro as well if you like."

"No," she said, "she's a fresh-water beetle and she's stuck with me, we're in it together."

"How do you know it's a she?" I said.

"Ridged wing covers instead of smooth," she said, "and she doesn't have the same kind of front legs as the male. No suction pads for holding on whilst mating."

"Male turtles have an extra claw for that," I said.

"Nature provides," said Neaera.

It was dark and still raining when we came out of the restaurant. We got back to the Zoo a little after eight. George Fairbairn wheeled out the crated turtles on the trolley. The turtles lay on their backs with their flippers pressed against their sides, their mouths open. I could hear them sighing, they knew they had fallen among fools. They had a fresh ocean smell.

"Got the champagne?" he said.

"Champagne," I said.

"For the launching," he said.

"I'll get some on the way," I said. I hadn't thought of such a thing as gaiety and celebration in connection with the turtles. If I can possibly miss the fun in life I'll do it.

Neaera was standing behind me and she kicked me. At the same time I realized I'd said the wrong thing. I hadn't even thought of including him. What a stupid lout I am, it's marvellous.

"I took the liberty of laying on a bottle," he said. "Give you and the lady a little send-off. And it's not every day I send my turtles out into the world, you know. Something of an occasion."

Why do I always end up feeling like a child. I'm the big turtle humanitarian but he thinks of people as well. We left the turtles sighing in the van and went into the Aquarium, through the green-lit hall to the STAFF ONLY room near the entrance. We sat down at the table and he brought out the champagne. Moët-Chandon it was too. He popped the cork, it hit a photo of a lady with great big boobs that was pinned up by the duty-roster. He'd brought stemmed glasses as well and as the champagne foamed into them it did feel something of an occasion.

George Fairbairn raised his glass. We stood up with him, raised ours. "Here's to launching," he said. "Anything, anywhere, any time."

And I'd scarcely given him a thought! I felt like crying. "Here's to you," I said. "Here's to the man who made this launch possible."

"Here's to the man who pays attention to what needs to have attention paid to it," said Neaera.

There wasn't a great deal said after that, we got through the champagne quickly, shook hands all round, promised to let him know how it had gone as soon as we got back.

How does that part in *Moby Dick* go:

> Ship and boat diverged; the cold, damp night breeze blew between; a screaming gull flew overhead; the two hulls wildly rolled; we gave three heavy-hearted cheers, and blindly plunged like fate into the lone Atlantic.

Blindly plunged like fate into the lone M4.

32

Neaera H.

On our way to the M4 William stopped at an off-licence and bought a bottle of champagne. "We owe it to the turtles," he said. Before we started off again he showed me our route on the map. "We stay on the M4 until after Swindon," he said, "then we go through Chippenham, Trowbridge, Frome, Shepton Mallet, Glastonbury, Taunton, Exeter, Plymouth, cross the Tamar, go through Looe and there's Polperro." The rain was running down the windscreen, our heads were close together as we bent over the map, the light of the torch playing on the red and blue and green roads made me feel young again, daring and illicit after bedtime. But it was difficult to make out the place names without my reading-glasses, the map was only a beautiful abstraction.

We drove off, the windscreen wipers took up their steady beat. We were still missing kerbs and cars by scant inches on my side. "Too close," I kept saying as I leant away from anticipated scrapes, always expecting to hear the rending of metal. William's head was held in such a way that I knew his neck would ache before he'd been driving an hour. I don't drive, couldn't relieve him, he'd have to do it all himself.

I was determined to be alert, to take in everything and not miss anything. I continued alert on the Hammersmith Fly-over and past the Chiswick Roundabout but soon it was like concerts where I vowed to listen carefully but drifted off and dozed. I didn't actually doze in the van but fell into a sort of travel trance that alternated with an intense uneasiness about the too-closeness of everything on my side. Whatever William used to drive must have been about two feet narrower than this van. If he was still sitting in a car that wasn't there any more, was he still in his mind sitting with whoever had been in it with him? There was a long stretch of yellow lights, utterly placeless. The road seemed to come from nowhere and lead to nowhere, it seemed wholly outside of time. I listened to the hum of the engine, the hiss of the tyres, the swish of the windscreen wipers. William had said that he'd worked in advertising but he hadn't told me much else about himself.

"Were you ever married?" I said.

"Yes," he said. He opened his mouth and I thought he was going to say more but he closed it again. Then he said, "Were you?"

"No," I said. I too opened my mouth, closed it again.

"Turtles," I said, and shook my head.

"Yes," said William. "Turtles."

Suddenly it seemed to me quite incomprehensible that for the last fifteen years I'd been writing and illustrating Gillian Vole, Delia Swallow and that lot. Drawing birds was what got me into it. I was working at an art studio and I'd done a little advertising campaign with cartoon birds. Somebody said I ought to try children's books and I sold my first one to Bill Sharpe. *Delia Swallow's Wedding*, that was.

A little after ten o'clock we stopped somewhere near Swindon and topped up the petrol tank. We'd done about sixty-five miles, William said, and the tank took something over three gallons. That seemed to please him, getting twenty miles to the gallon. When the van was stopped and the engine switched off we could hear the turtles breathing.

When we turned off the M4 and drove through Chippenham and the other towns William was still shaving things too close on my side. I kept saying "Too close" and being irritated at the sound of my voice and his having to be told. This *wasn't* whatever he used to drive and this wasn't the time when he used to drive it, it was here and now and us and the turtles, damn it. There was something insulting about it, like having a man continually call you by the name of the woman he used to be with.

"Here," I said. "Now. Tonight. This week, this month, this year. Turtles. Us. Ford Transit 90, 18 Cwt."

"Yes," said William. "Yes, yes, yes." He knew what I meant. He changed the poise of his head, brought his neck up out of his shoulders. "It's not too bad actually, this," he said. "In-between," is really where I feel best. Neither here nor there."

"There isn't any in-between," I said. "Any place you pass through is this moment's *here*. In-between is an illusion."

"Thanks very much," he said. "You've just invalidated most of my life."

"Mine as well," I said. There were reflecting studs in the road shaped like crabs without legs, each with two little eyes like crabs, continually advancing out of the darkness. Each one stared at me as the van swallowed it up. I stared back.

By 11.30 we'd done a little over a hundred miles and we stopped outside of Frome for sandwiches and coffee. The turtles breathed patiently. Crated and lying on their backs as they were they couldn't even look up at the ceiling of the van. Their ocean smell seemed fainter now, mixed with the petrol fumes from the five-gallon container. The three plastrons were pale in the light of the torch, looked heraldic: three plastrons supine on a field Ford Transit. *"Navigare necesse est. Vivere non est necesse."*

I've seen films of newly-hatched turtles racing to the sea, whole fleets of them almost flying over the sand in their rush to the water. These three lay on their backs ponderous with the finding in them, passively waiting. Looking at them I couldn't think there was any expectation in them. When they felt themselves once more in ocean they would simply do what turtles do in ocean, their readiness was whole and undiminished in them. If permitted to live they would navigate by the sun, by chemical traces in the water, by the imprint in their genes of an ancient continent now sundered. They were compacted of finding, finding was embodied in them. There were the five gallons of petrol. I thought of the turtles burning in silence.

I got out of the van. The rain had stopped. I stood by the van, leant my forehead against the cool wet metal. The crab reflectors in the road looked at me or not as cars went past or didn't. In the pocket of my mac was the Caister two-stone. It must have been there from the last time I wore the mac, I hadn't put it there today.

33

William G.

The sky was clearing, a full moon appeared in a ragged opening in the clouds. There'd be a spring tide then, would it be in or out? I felt as if I knew about tides, felt as if I remembered them.

"I've never told you that Polperro is the place where I was born," I said to Neaera.

"Good God," she said. "But when you were a child surely it wasn't how it is now?"

"I don't know," I said. "We left when I was a year old and I've never been back since. My mother never talked about it much. Why'd you choose it?"

"It was real once but it isn't any more," said Neaera. "It's souvenirs and cream teas and a box with a slot for money to preserve the character of the old Cornish fishing village. The turtles may be headed for extinction but they're real, they work. When we put them in the sea they'll do real turtle work."

"We can't magic the whole world with three turtles," I said.

"We'd need more?" said Neaera. "Would a dozen do it?" We both laughed.

My mother never had said much about Polperro. She had no stories of the pilchard fishery, the huers signalling from the shore to the seine boats and that sort of thing. She was born in Calstock where her father worked at an arsenic factory until he died of it. In those days the only protection they had was lint to cover the nostrils and a handkerchief over that. My mother remembered the trees all grey and blighted near the works and the way it smelled on foggy days. She was living at home and teaching in a school but when her father died she left Calstock. Her two younger brothers were working by then, her mother had died earlier. She came to Polperro because she liked the sound of the name and she wanted to be near the sea. She used to remember the jackdaws walking on the quay among the gulls and the fishermen, how they looked as if they might speak.

She became a waitress at a tea-shop. She used to say that was the year she gave up school-teaching, Methodism and arsenic all at once. She met my father soon after and in two years she was a widow living in London with a year-old son. She bought a tobacconist-newsagent business in Fulham and then she used to get books out of the library and read about Cornwall. She liked legends and folklore. I remember her telling me about the spirit of Tregeagle who howled when the hounds of the Devil were after him and was finally sent away to weave ropes of sand by the edge of the sea. I remember how she used to say that part: "Forever weaving ropes of sand that crumbled in his hands and the wind blew them away."

When I think of her seeing the jackdaws walking on the quay I seem to see them with her eyes and I can see the rest of the scene as well, the grey sky over the sea and the headlands, the white-and-black-and-grey gulls with yellow beaks and yellow staring eyes, the fishermen solid and heavy in the grey light with scales and barrows, the boats rocking at their moorings or standing on their legs. I never see it sunny, always grey. I've never told anyone about my mother's jackdaws. My three uncles are dead, I have cousins in Cornwall I've never looked up. The house in Fulham where we lived over the shop until my mother died was close to where I live now but it's been pulled down, there's a block of flats there now. The road where my father went over the cliff was on the other side of Polperro, we'd not be seeing it this trip.

Near Glastonbury there was a self-service petrol station open. I put a pound note into the machine and the tank took 96p worth. 4p worth of petrol left for whoever might come along next.

The van hummed along swallowing up the little crab-shaped reflectors with their little crab eyes. The moon disappeared, reappeared as broken clouds hurried past. Oh yes, I thought, feeling something good just round the corner of my mind: just be all the way in it and you're all right. Just let go of everything like a falling star. The far-away ones, when you see their light it's already happened millions of years ago. This too, my brief light, maybe it had flashed across the darkness long long ago. Not *my* light, just a light. Now I was the one to be it, to flash across the darkness with it. Somebody else's turn next. Nothing to be selfish about, be it while it's you and then let go. The van rushed ahead but I let my mind be where it was.

34

Neaera H.

At two o'clock in the morning near Exeter William topped up the tank again. I was glad there weren't more petrol stations open. He seemed to want to arrive at Polperro with a full tank, as if he had information that all the petrol stations on the road back would disappear by morning.

At a quarter to three we had more sandwiches and coffee about twenty miles from Plymouth. We'd done two hundred miles by then, only about fifty to go. I wondered if he'd stop for petrol between here and Polperro. The road was quiet, there were long intervals between cars, I listened to the turtles breathing. Ahead of us in the lay-by a big articulated lorry was resting like a tired monster. The crabs in the road marched on inscrutably towards London. What would they say when they got there?

We went on through Plymouth, wakeful through the sleeping streets. We crossed the Tamar Bridge at half past three under bluish lights that seemed quite outside of time, like the yellow ones earlier. Lear's words about the silent-roaring ocean had got into my head and I felt myself filled with silent roaring. It may in fact have been snoring although if it was, William was too tactful to say so. I dozed off and woke up as we came down the hill into Polperro. The sky had cleared completely and there was bright moonlight over everything.

BEYOND THIS POINT ONLY EXEMPTED VEHICLES PERMITTED 9 A.M.–6 P.M., said the sign. We went beyond this point down the main street, past the model village in its model sleep, past the dark and silent cream-teas and souvenirs, turned into the street that led to Jonathan Couch's house and parked on the little bridge in front of it. We could have turned into the very narrow street that went the remaining two hundred yards or so to the outer harbour but William drew the line at that, he didn't want to risk scratching the van or waking anybody up with the noise of our manoeuvres. As it was we kept expecting lights to go on, windows to fly up and policemen to appear.

We'd neither of us bothered to find out about the tide in advance. Whether it was in or out we'd launch the turtles. But I think we both felt the same: if the tide was in the ocean was with us and our venture would prosper, if it was out it meant that things were no different from the way they always were, just a lot of damned bother and aggravation. Then I stopped caring about signs and omens and whether it would go well or badly. Our part in the rhythm of things was to put the turtles in the sea and however it went would be the way it went. Getting stuck in the mud or drowning or breaking a leg or being had up by the police might or might not be part of it. I stopped caring about people waking up, I felt relaxed and invulnerable.

We rounded the corner, went down the street. The boats in the inner harbour were all afloat. "It's in," we both said at the same time. The wind hit us in the face, we heard the crashing of the waves as we half ran round the next corner and up the incline to the outer harbour. The low-tide beach was gone, under the full moon the tide was surging wildly against the breakwater, spray was flying and the sea was breaking half way up the steps. And the wind, the wind, the full-moon spring-tide turtle wind.

Back to the van we went without a word. William dragged out the first crate, tipped it on to the trolley and wheeled it away with an amount of noise that would have waked the dead. I followed with the rope. I thought it would take both of us to get the trolley up the incline but William did it by himself. At the break-water we wrestled the crate off the trolley, laid it on the steps as on a slipway and lowered it with the rope through the ring-bolts. "Don't be alarmed, ladies and gentlemen," I said, "those chains are made of chrome steel." William must have seen the film, he was laughing whilst standing on the steps with the tide breaking over his feet.

I gave him slack as he up-ended the crate on the edge of a step, he tilted it forward and with a great splash the turtle hit the water and dived. We hugged and kissed each other, ran back for the next turtle, launched it, then the next. Each one dived under the wild water and was gone. It was done, it had actually happened. Three empty crates and the turtles safely off.

"The champagne!" said William. He rushed off, came back with the bottle and the two cups from the Thermos flask. He popped the cork into the wind, the champagne foamed up in the moonlight. "Here's wishing them luck," we said, and drank to the turtles. The waves were silver under the moon, the spray flew up from the rocks on either side of the harbour entrance, there was a beacon on the headland. The champagne tasted like clear and bubbling bright new mornings without end. We gulped it greedily and threw the empty bottle into the ocean. The ocean was rough and real, always real, only real. It wasn't Polperro's fault that the place had to go begging with souvenirs and money-boxes and a model village. I forgave Polperro, loved it for what it had been and what it now was, for its happiness and sorrow by the sea. I forgave myself for not loving it before, loved myself for loving it now. I forgave everybody everything, felt the Caister two-stone in the pocket of my mac, flung it out into the moonlit ocean.

35

William G.

When I felt the wind on my face and saw that the tide was in it seemed all at once that I didn't need any answers to anything. The tide and the moon, the beacon on the headland and the wind were so *here*, so *this*, so *now* that nothing else was required. I felt free of myself, unlumbered. Where the moon ended and I began and which was which was of no consequence. Everything was what it was and the awareness of it was part of it.

The crates came out of the van and on to the trolley easily, went up the incline smoothly, there was no separation between crate and trolley and me and motion. It happened, turtles happened into the ocean, champagne happened in the moonlight.

On the way back to the big car-park we stopped at the public lavatory. *Adamant*, said the urinal. There was a device like the Order of the Garter but with a lion on top. Something that looked like an owl's face in the middle. Here, now. Coming out I listened to the stream that runs through the village, heard an owl quavering in the dark. Not adamant, nothing adamant.

We pulled into the car-park, I switched off the engine. We got into the back of the van with the eiderdown and the blankets and the pillows. We lay down with our clothes on, side by side with a little space between us. First we lay on our backs then we rolled over on our sides. The space rolled over with us, stayed quietly between us all night, shaped of the front of me and the back of her.

36

Neaera H.

I woke up in the van. Ah yes, I thought, this is where I went to sleep. There was wood near my face smelling salty, oceany. Empty turtle crate. I put my ear to it, listened: silent-roaring ocean. There was rope, I touched it, licked my fingers: salt. I touched the trolley, salty as well. I rolled over, there was William still asleep. It seemed like spying to look at his sleeping face so I got out of the van.

It was afternoon. Vans with curtains in the windows were parked on either side of us and people inside them were being domestic. Refreshment and souvenir stands were open at the car-park entrance. A man with a horse and a bedizened yellow wagon half full of passengers beckoned to me like the coachman who took Pinocchio to the Land of Boobies.

Stupid really, to feel as I did just then: low-spirited and dissatisfied. There was no reason for it. We had come to Polperro to put turtles into the sea and we'd done it.

The sunlight was hot, the sky was blue. I felt all astray. At home the day and I always approached each other by slow degrees: brushing my teeth, washing my face, the first cup of coffee, the first cigarette, opening the post. Here I had nothing, just suddenly some rough beast of a day with vans and curtains and people feeding children.

Scale is a funny thing. Sometimes on hot days everything seems too big and spread out. Not to be grasped by the mind, not to be held in the eye. I thought of winter. Winter grey skies, winter early evenings make London small like a model town. Lighted windows in shops are like model shop windows, tobacconist, launderette, bakery. I saw the little model streets in my mind, the shops. In the model bakery a three-tiered wedding-cake, great in its tinyness. Pictures of other wedding-cakes: the "*Windsor*," the "*Paradise*," the "*Wedgwood*." Small, small, astonishing detail in the model memory, all there to be found. The model Polperro here at Polperro was still in my mind, I compared it to the model London. The Polperro one was much bigger, huge and thick, not to be held in the mind or in the eye.

37

William G.

When I woke up and saw the bright sunlight the night before seemed far away and small. I was stiff and sore all over. Neaera wasn't there. I opened the doors and saw her leaning against the concrete wall of the car-park. I thought about the turtles and I couldn't believe they'd got out to sea against that heavy tide. Surely they'd been beaten back against the break-water or swept into the harbour through the gap where the boats go in and out. They were probably in the harbour now, they'd probably been picked up by fishermen.

We slowly made our way through tourists and their children to the public lavatory. I hadn't brought a toothbrush or shaving things or any-thing. I brushed my teeth with my finger, washed and let it go at that. Slowly and blinking in the sunlight we went to a tea-shop where we had sausages and eggs. It was while we were eating that I most felt the awk-wardness of this morning after. Afternoon actually, worse than a morning. Sometimes I've felt that way after sleeping with the wrong person, and the intimacy of sex is nothing compared to the intimacy of driving two hun-dred and fifty miles at night and putting turtles into the sea. But it wasn't that, it wasn't that she was the wrong person for the turtles. I didn't know what it was. There seemed to be little for us to say to each other. Nothing in fact.

We walked to the harbour. The tide was out when we got there, the boats were standing on their legs or sitting on the mud. The little beach beyond the break-water displayed broken glass and contraceptives. There were some fishermen sitting on the quay and I asked them when high water had been. Seven in the morning, they said. No one said anything about turtles and there were none in sight. They must have got out to sea all right. We walked back to the car-park, got into the van and drove back to London.

38

Neaera H.

Well, then. This was the back of the turtle thing. Not quite despair as I had thought before. Just a kind of blankness, as blank and foolish as a pelmet lying face-down on the floor with all the staples showing. That's all right, a pelmet can have a front and a back, it's only a thing. A dress can have an inside and an outside. A drawing is only on one side of the paper, even a drawing by Rembrandt.

But an action, no. An action with a front and back is no good.

We drove back to London. We scarcely spoke a word. We had lunch and supper at road-side places full of motion and absence where there was ketchup in red tomato-shaped plastic bottles. The people who sat in the booths seemed to be played on a tape that erased itself. Only the motion remained, the absence. Outside on the road, inside with the ketchup. Red, heavy.

Night came but there was no rain. William only stopped for petrol once. I'd forgotten to look at the mill wheel on the inn near the car-park in Polperro. I still don't know whether or not it was turned by water that came out of a pipe.

39

William G.

Sometimes I can't believe that some mechanical happenings are only chance and nothing more. K257 in the pavement, the escalator owl at Charing Cross. At the place where we had supper on the way home I went to the lavatory. No sooner had I opened the door than there was a metallic belch and three 10p pieces leapt out of the contraceptive machine and clanged on the floor. Why, for God's sake? Why did it do it when *I* walked in? I was fully ten feet away when it happened. There was something insulting about it, contemptuous. Here, it seemed to be saying, here's a refund. Bloody cheek.

The miles rushed towards us, shot under the van. I felt absurd, couldn't find a place to put myself in relation to the three turtles now in the sea. What in the world did it all mean? Why was I in this van with this woman? Would it keep on for ever, going round and round like chewing gum on a tyre? Could it be made to stop and if it were stopped would there be anything else to do?

I had a lot of trouble with my eyes after it got dark. The road kept going abstract. Confusion, fixed and flashing. Flat shadows assumed bulk, distances lost depth, the red tail-lights of cars half a mile ahead appeared to be up in the air.

In time the Chiswick Roundabout appeared, the Hammersmith Fly-over. It was after eleven when we got to Neaera's place. I switched off the engine and we sat there ticking over in silence for a few moments.

"Have you kept track of the expenses?" she said.

"I haven't got all the figures yet," I said. "I'll add it up after I take back the van tomorrow."

"I'll ring you up," she said, and sat there, not quite knowing how to leave. I knew she didn't want to ask me up to her flat for coffee or any-thing.

"There isn't any exit line for this sort of thing," I said. "About all you can do is shake your head and walk away kicking a stone if you have a stone to kick."

"I've thrown my stone away," she said. She gathered up her blankets and pillows and got out of the van. She looked in through the window. "I shan't say anything now," she said. She walked away without shaking her head.

I drove home, parked the van, unloaded it. Not a dent or a scratch on the great bulgy thing, I couldn't believe it. It took me a long time to get to sleep that night. I lay in bed listening to cars going down our street. I don't know why they have to go so fast, the sound of those roaring engines al-ways fills me with rage. I kept expecting to hear one of them scrape the van. It's quite a narrow street.

40

Neaera H.

When I opened the door to my flat it was like opening a box of stale time. Old time, dead time. The windows were all closed, the place was quite airless. I opened the windows, looked out over the square. I think I've read that grains of wheat taken from Egyptian tombs have grown when planted. Wheat yes, time no. There's a mummy at the British Museum, a woman if I remember rightly, I haven't been to the Egyptian Antiquities collection for a long time. Strange, to be dead and collected. She's lying on her side in a sleeping position and as I see her in my mind she looks more alone than if she were lying formally on her back with folded hands. Her skin is old parchment, there's nothing personal about it, her bones are just bones. But her sleeping attitude is naked and private, the privacy of her sleep remains even though there's no longer a person inside it.

When I turned on the lights the night outside looked so black that I switched them off again. Shutting out the night makes it blacker. I remembered being a child out of doors in the dark of summer evenings, winter evenings, late dark and early. One saw perfectly well, it never seemed really dark until I came into the house. Then the night outside the windows would be very black.

I didn't know what to do really, didn't know how to pick up where I left off. There no longer seemed to be continuity in my life. The road went up to the turtle-launching and ended there at a chasm where the bridge was out.

I turned on the light in Madame Beetle's tank. There were snails in the tank, red ones, six or seven of them. They were cleaning up the algae, there were little clear meanders on the glass where they'd been working. Yesterday's and today's meat lay pale and wan on the bottom. The snails were working on that as well. Madame Beetle was in the corner of the tank under the filter sponge. There was a note under the china bathing beauty, I read it by the light of the tank:

> Took the liberty of dropping in
> a clean-up squad. Can take them
> back if you don't want them.
> Best wishes,
> WEBSTER DE VERE

Cheek, I thought. If I wanted to run a dirty aquarium that was my business. Come to think of it Madame Beetle was a predator, why hadn't she had a go at the snails? Tired maybe.

I looked in my bag for cigarettes and there was the letter to Harry Rush still unposted. I lit a cigarette, went out of the flat and down to the corner. There are two telephone kiosks and a pillar box there. The telephone kiosks aren't the same size, one of them's larger and more heavily built than the other. I always think of them as bull and cow. They stood there, red in the dark, dark in the light of the street lamp, the bull telephone and the cow telephone and the pillar box. None of them said a word as I pushed the letter through the slot and it dived into the dark. Goodbye £1,000. It was never really there.

41

William G.

I woke up. There you are, I thought: life goes on. There was an old German film I saw at the National Film Theatre, Harry Bauer was in it. Massive man, head like a bald granite statue. In the film he was in prison for a long stretch, twelve years I think. He marked off the days on the wall of his cell with a bit of charcoal. When he got to the half-way mark he threw back his head and let out a hoarse cry. I thought of trying a hoarse cry, decided not to. Anyhow I was past the half-way point.

Saturday it was. Nine o'clock. I looked out of the window. The day was grey and wet. Harriet would be on her way to the shop. My mind turned away from everything all at once. I realized at that moment that the end of all things need not be difficult. No effort of any kind, just a turning away by whatever means might come to hand.

I went to the bathroom. Sandor hadn't cleaned the bath. A ring of Sandor dirt round it, Sandor pubic hair. Rage coursed through my veins. I'd had a whole life, a house and a family! And it had come to this: Sandor's pubic hair in a rented bath.

I cleaned the bath, had a bath, shaved even though it was Saturday. Dressed, went to make my breakfast. Sandor'd left the cooker filthy and evil-smelling as usual.

I went down the hall, knocked on his door. I was shaking all over. Sandor opened the door. He was in his dressing-gown, some lurid Persian-looking thing. He was wearing red velvet slippers that made his feet look very white, the hair on his ankles very black. His feet turned out as if there were no limit to the amount of space they could take up.

"Too much!" I heard myself saying. "Too much!" I said it again.

"What you mean?" said Sandor, filling up the doorway and growing larger. His breath smelt the same as the cooker. Squid? Kelp? Goat hair?

"Too much!" I said again like some clockwork idiot.

"What?" said Sandor with a very red face and a very black moustache. "What the devil you mean?"

"You clean that cooker," I said.

"What clean cooker? Who say?" said Sandor. More breath.

"*You* clean cooker, *I* say." I poked him in the chest with my finger. Springy chest, great deal of hair.

"Mind," he said. "Go slow, I caution you. Piss off. All best."

"No," I said. "Not all best. All bleeding worst. Clean that cooker right now." I grabbed him by the lapels of his dressing-gown. I was quite surprised to see my hands shoot out and do it. Thin wrists.

"Aha!" said Sandor. "You better don't make trouble, you." *His* hands shot out. *Thick* wrists. All of a sudden I was turned round with my left arm twisted up behind my back. I flung my right arm back as hard as I could and caught him in the face, then we were both on the floor and he had me in, yes, a scissors grip. I started to laugh but lost valuable breath doing it. What a terrible pong he had. His personal smell, no amount of bathing would have helped. He tightened his legs and I felt all my ribs crack. I might have known that a man with a moustache and an accent like that would be an accomplished wrestler. I wished I'd waited till he'd got his trousers on, he was only wearing underpants and I hated having his bare legs round me.

We'd fallen out of his doorway into the hall. My face was on the musty threadbare carpet, one ear pressed to the silence of the carpet, the other listening to Sandor's heavy breathing as he squeezed harder. A train went by on the far side of the common and in my mind I saw it under the wet grey sky, under the trailing edges of grey cloud drifting, the single clatter of the train as lonely, as only as a trawler out at sea, the only diesel putter on the wide grey sea with silence all round as far as the eye could see.

In my mind I saw the wet iron rails receding Putney-wards, cold wet iron in the rain, red lights, green lights shining on the iron, shining red, shining green, fixed and flashing, no confusion. The rails led very likely to Port Liberty. That was my mistake, I'd always thought a sea approach and never thought how very iron and wet the rails were. Tower Hill, the lights would say that passed beyond the trees along the common, Upminster or Edgware. I could see in my mind the grey and rainy air over the trains, over the common, in between the branches of the trees. I stretched out my hands, thought of holding the grey air cool and wet in my hands.

I'd been wrong to feel my past no longer mine. I was joined umbilically to all pasts but why labour it. Squeezing was all very well, the question was: did one in fact want to come out. Was one willing. To be. For whom was the effort being made? Not the untold jackdaws walking on the quay, I wasn't going to believe that. I'd asked a straight question and I wanted a straight answer. Was it for her? Was it for him? I didn't think it was for me. Go ahead and squeeze, I thought. I'm not coming out just because you want me out. It bloody isn't for me.

Not for me at all. On the other hand what was. For anybody. Nothing really. Not for her when she came out and not for him. Nor would my coming-out be for anyone whatever they might think. In that case why hold on to me. A futile gesture. Life went on, one couldn't stop half way. I was getting angry. There was a redness silently exploding in my mind. Violence. Lovely. Bumpitty bump.

I was on the landing feeling quite wrenched and pulled about. Mr. Sandor was one flight down, rubbing himself in various places and looking up at me with great concentration. Now he's *really* going to be angry, I thought. I didn't mind. I didn't care if we killed each other.

Mrs. Inchcliff came racing up the stairs. She'd never smoked, stairs were nothing to her even at sixty. "What's happening?" she said. "Why is everyone lying on the floor? Are you both all right?"

"We have collision," said Sandor. "Down we tumble." He was still staring at me and I saw in his face that he saw in my face that I wasn't afraid of him any more.

Later I drove the van back to VANS 4-U. Five hundred and fifteen miles without a dent or a scratch! I was tremendously impressed by that. The shape of the van was so different from the shape of me and my life, how had we managed to stick together without hitting anything for all those miles!

42

Neaera H.

Something very slowly, very dimly has been working in my mind and now is clear to me: there are no incidences, there are only coincidences. When a photograph in a newspaper is looked at closely one can see the single half-tone dots it's made of. There one sees the incidence of a single dot, there another and another. Thousands of them coinciding make the face, the house, the tree, the whole picture. Every picture is a pattern of coincidence unrecognizable in the single dot. Each incidence of anything in life is just a single dot and my face is so close to that dot that I can't see what it's part of. I shall never be able to stand back far enough to see the whole picture. I shall die in blind ignorance and rage.

The men who used to work in the hole in the street are gone, the hole is closed up. I don't know if the street is different or not. In the shop where I'd seen the oyster-catcher on TV all the screens showed two men in sombreros shooting at each other with revolvers from behind rocks.

I passed an antique shop. There was a brown and varnished sea-turtle shell in the window. A black man—was he from the Caribbean?—was looking at it. He wore a white mac, it was a wet grey day. Next door was a fruiterer, there were oranges. The rain stopped, the sun came out into a gunmetal sky. "Well, yes," I said aloud. "Of course."

The black man turned and looked at me. "Tortuguero," he said. He said it like a password but made no secret sign. He said it because he needed to say the name aloud just there and then to me. I nodded, felt dizzy with my face against the dot. How did he know that I knew where Tortuguero was? I shall never see the picture. I could grind my teeth and weep.

On my desk in the middle of the night does some tiny figure look at Madame Beetle and dream of setting her free? Is there any limit to small-ness and largeness? Is it possible actually to hold an orange in the hand? Iron and wind are both grey. Would there be oyster-catchers in armour on the rooftops if I looked up?

The sea was wherever it was, and the turtles. It couldn't be done again. Of those who did the launching there were no survivors. I passed an empty playground. The rocking horse was rocking, all its five seats empty.

I went to the Zoo, to the Aquarium. The turtle tank was empty, still being cleaned. I opened one of the PRIVATE doors, found George Fairbairn on the duckboards behind the fish tanks. There was a clean ocean smell, the illuminated water seemed like clear green time, the wood of the duck-boards was like the wood in boats.

"Well," he said, "they get off all right?"

"Yes," I said, "they must have done, unless you've heard any reports of turtles being picked up off the Cornish coast."

"Not so far," he said.

I had nothing to say but I felt safe on the boat-feeling wood in the green light of salt-water time.

"All right?" he said. "You look a little peaky. Fancy a cup of tea?"

"I'd just like to stay here a while and look at the water," I said.

"I'll bring it here," he said.

Below me the leopard shark swam his aimless urgent round like an office boy. Twit, I thought.

George Fairbairn came back with the tea-tray, set it down on a plank. I'd never really looked at him closely, he didn't compel attention. He was a very medium-looking man, neither tall nor short, neither dark nor fair, about my age. His face was just a plain face, cheerful and undemanding.

"How do you stay cheerful?" I said.

"I don't mind being alive," he said. He poured the tea, took a tin of tobacco out of his pocket, rolled a cigarette, lit it. "There's nothing you can do about this, you know," he said. "Nothing to be done really about animals. Anything you do looks foolish. The answer isn't in us. It's almost as if we're put here on earth to show how silly they aren't. I don't mind. I just like being around them."

I began to cry. I leant against him and sobbed.

"It's all right," he said, stroking my hair. "You needn't hold back, these are all salt-water tanks."

43

William G.

There's nothing like a little physical violence to make a man feel young again. I was half crippled from it. Sandor must have trodden heavily on my left foot, the next morning it was so tender and swollen that I could hardly put my weight on it. My ribs felt as if I'd been run over by a lorry, my left arm and shoulder weren't working right, my neck was stiff and sore and the left side of my head felt soft.

The cooker was clean when I got to it to make breakfast but I was sure that was only because it was Sunday and Sandor was sleeping in. I doubted very much that I'd find it clean on Monday morning. I spent a quiet day with the newspapers, went to a Japanese film at the National Film Theatre in the evening, took a late walk. Harriet rang up while I was out but I didn't phone her when I got home. I had Monday morning, the bath and the cooker on my mind. In bed I lay awake for a long time with fantasies of beating Sandor into a state of abject obedience but the fact was that I couldn't do it. He was younger and bigger and stronger than I and he handled himself very well indeed. I thought of getting up earlier so as to be first at the bath and the cooker which would leave Miss Neap to follow him. She'd see to him. But that would be cheating.

Monday morning I woke up early. A grey and dreary morning with no hope in it. Things would always be the way they were, it said. Why struggle. I thought of the dawn wind over the ocean. "Out at sea the dawn wind/Wrinkles and slides," said Eliot. I took *Four Quartets* off the shelf and looked at *East Coker*. It begins with "In the beginning is my end." The line I'd remembered was at the end of Part I:

> Dawn points, and another day
> Prepares for heat and silence. Out at sea the dawn
>   wind
> Wrinkles and slides. I am here
> Or there, or elsewhere. In my beginning.

Towards the end of the poem I read:

> There is only the fight to recover what has been lost
> And found and lost again and again: and now,
>   under conditions
> That seem unpropitious. But perhaps neither gain
>   nor loss.
> For us, there is only the trying. The rest is not our
>   business.

The last words were:

> In my end is my beginning.

All this for Sandor's ring round the bath and his muck on the cooker. Ridiculous. But so is everything. So was Thermopylae. The things that matter don't necessarily make sense. My end seemed immanent in every breath and my beginning seemed never to have happened.

The turtles would be well on their way now, following whatever track they followed. Just doing it. Not thinking about it, just doing it.

No sound from the bathroom. Sandor didn't have a bath every morning. I heard his door open, heard him padding to the kitchen, heard and smelled his cooking, heard him go back to his room.

I dressed, went to the kitchen. Muck all over the cooker again. I got the cloth that I always cleaned it with, held it under the cold tap, got it good and wet, knocked on Sandor's door.

"Who is it?" said his voice from inside.

"Me," I said.

He opened the door. Persian dressing-gown, red slippers, hairy ankles. I held up the wet cloth. "Clean the cooker," I said.

"I clean your cooker right enough," he said. "I break your bones, you don't go away."

I shoved the cloth into his face, brought my knee up hard into his crutch. When he doubled over I got both hands on his head, forced it down as I brought my knee up again into his face. What am I doing, I thought. He'll kill me for sure this time.

He was on the floor with blood all over his face and I thought it might be wise to beat him unconscious if I could but before I could get in another blow his feet shot out and I went flying. Slammed into the wall and that was the last I knew for a while.

When I came to I was on my bed and Mrs. Inchcliff was sitting by me. "Where's Sandor?" I said.

"He's gone off to the doctor to get his nose seen to," she said.

"How'd I get here?" I said.

"We carried you," she said. "Mr. Sandor and I. What *is* all this between you two?"

"It's nothing," I said. "Thermopylae. In my end is my beginning."

So I came limping into the shop rather late and there were all those books and Mr. Meager and Harriet selling books and customers buying books and I thought, What in the world am I doing here, what's all this nonsense with books and who are these people? As I came in through the door the books and people seemed to get farther away instead of closer, receding from me as the shore recedes from a boat that sails away.

"Got everything sorted out all right?" said Mr. Meager.

"Yes," I said, "thank you. Sorry I'm late, it couldn't be helped."

"Feeling all right?" he said. "You look a bit off this morning."

"No more than usual," I said. "It's just that you haven't seen me for a few days. You probably don't notice how I look ordinarily." My mind seemed clear but my head felt a funny shape. I turned to look at him from the hard side of it. He looked back at me with his whole head nice and hard. He has very bright blue eyes like Paul Newman but nobody would ever buy a poster of Mr. Meager.

Harriet brought me a mug of coffee with a manner that seemed unnecessarily domestic. She looked heavily understanding, which irritated me. I felt there wasn't anything to be understood. And my head really did hurt where I'd hit the wall with it.

"I rang you up last night," she said, "but you were out." There was the reproachful look again, the same look I'd seen when I first met her.

"I got home too late to ring you back," I said.

"How are you?" she said very seriously as if I'd just come back from the hospital.

"I'm fine," I said, and she looked hurt. You can tell *me*, her eyes said. No, I couldn't tell her. What was there to tell? You can't do it with turtles, that's all. You have to fight Mr. Sandor and everything else. Every day, every inch of the way.

"You can't do it with turtles," I said.

"You can do it with me," she said, and gave me a quick grope behind the counter. The singlemindedness of the woman!

"That's not the only it there is," I said.

"*Sorry,*" said Harriet, and removed herself to the Occult section.

I rang up Neaera when I had a moment. She wasn't home.

At lunch-time I went to Hyde Park and ate my sandwich and apple under a tree and did not give up smoking. Soon maybe but not yet. I looked at the yellow leaves on the grass and the boats on the Serpentine and the people around me as if I'd come back from the Lakes and the Torrible Zone and the hills of the Chankly Bore. But nobody said how tall I'd grown. All the yellow leaves were too much for me, I didn't know if I could go back to the shop and last the day out.

I did last the day out. Just. In the afternoon Harriet said, "Will you be over this evening?"

"Harriet . . . " I said.

"God," she said, "you sound so *weary.*"

"I'm pretty thin on the ground right now," I said. "There's not all that much of me. I need to be by myself."

"Well, good luck to you and all the best," she said, and quickly sold a Knightsbridge lady *Rising Sap*, by Taura Strong.

44

Neaera H.

Things appear from unexpected quarters. The single dot before the face becomes another dot of different shape and density.

George Fairbairn had been a background person until now. Now he was the dot before my face, the face before my face. Knowing that I should never see the whole picture I didn't bother to ask myself what it was.

He had seemed so medium, so unspecially placed between the top and bottom of life that I hadn't really given him full human recognition until that evening when he brought out the champagne. I'd assumed that he was married, part of a closed circle, no lines moving on his map.

He wasn't married. He had a flat off Haverstock Hill and that's where I woke up on Tuesday, the morning after I'd gone to see him at the Aquarium. There was very little in the place, mostly it was furnished with light and quiet. It was on the top floor and looked out over rooftops. There was a Chinese teapot in the kitchen, there was a copy of Lilly's *The Mind of the Dolphin* on the table by the bed. In the sitting room were R. H. Blyth's four volumes on haiku and some natural history. "I don't buy books much any more," he said. There was a radio but no gramophone.

A curious man, somewhat off to one side of things. As he said, he didn't mind being alive but I don't think it meant a great deal to him. I asked him nothing about himself and he offered no information, that was how it was. He had a clean look and a clean clear feel, nothing muddy. That was enough. There was about him the smell or maybe just the idea of dry grass warm in the sun.

He made breakfast for us. Looking out of the window and across a lawn I saw other people having breakfast in their windows.

"Do you think you'll go on doing children's books?" he said.

"I don't know," I said.

We left the flat. In the lift at the Belsize Park tube station there was a Dale Carnegie poster. MAXIMISE YOUR POTENTIAL, it said, and showed a drawing of a thick-faced man in simplified light and shade. He had a pencil poised in his hand and stood looking down at a graph on his desk. Whether you read the graph from his side of the desk or mine the line on it went down.

At Camden Town George kissed me and got out of the train. I went home to Madame Beetle and the snails.

45

William G.

Tuesday morning. I woke up and groaned. I ached all over, and when I got out of bed I could scarcely walk. If Sandor was going to fling down the gauntlet again I didn't know whether I had the strength to pick it up.

The bath was clean. The cooker was clean. What had happened to Sandor? He was as regular as clock-work, never overslept. Had I done him a serious injury? For a moment I hoped so, then I hoped not. I knocked on his door. No answer. I knocked again, looked at the threadbare musty carpet where my face had been the other day, heard a train go past beyond the common.

"Who is it?" said Sandor's voice from inside, a little more distant than last time.

"Me," I said. "Are you all right?"

"Come in," he said. He was in bed wearing some sort of wild Islamic pyjamas. He had a sticking-plaster across his nose, his face was flushed, his moustache looked dismayed. There were stacks of foreign newspapers, a chessboard with the pieces standing on it in the middle of a game, flow-ers in an *art nouveau* vase that incorporated a naked lady. There were framed photographs of men with moustaches, sad-faced women, young

Sandor in shorts and a jersey with some school team, a river with a bridge. The wallpaper was old and dark, the furniture was dark, the room had a dark and foreign smell. There was a thermometer in a glass on the bedside table.

"Are you all right?" I said. He looked as if he might be wearing a nightcap but wasn't.

"I am grotty a little," he said. "I have 39 degrees temperature, maybe a touch of influenza."

"Have you had breakfast?" I said.

"I have slightly vertigo," he said. "I stand up, room goes round, floor is slanty. Not hungry."

"I'll make you some tea and toast," I said.

"Not to bother," said Sandor. "I get up later."

"It's no bother," I said.

"Very kind of you," he said. "You are pacific this morning. You don't make aggression."

"I don't usually make aggression," I said. I made the tea and toast, brought it to him.

"What do you usually have for breakfast?" I said.

"Half grapefruit," he said. "Seaweed, squid, coffee. Very healthy. Top protein."

I nodded. Cookers simply have to take what comes to them, that's life.

"You don't like foreigners, yes?" he said. "England for the English. You don't like foreign breakfast on cooker. Not nice, yes?"

"I don't dislike foreigners," I said. "You've got the wrong idea completely."

"Cobblers," said Sandor. "You make effort, put fake smile on face, make politeness. You nod hello but you don't look at foreigner like regular human person. You look at me as if you think I carry in my briefcase nothing but sausages."

"What *do* you carry in your briefcase?" I said.

"Sausages and newspapers," he said. "I read and speak Hungarian, Russian, German, French, English. How many languages do you have?"

"Only English," I said.

"Wonderful," said Sandor. "Let the rest of the world learn to talk to you. You don't waste your time with such foolishness."

"Maybe not," I said, "but I leave the bath and the cooker clean for the next chap, the next human person. I'd better be going now or I'll be late for work."

Sandor lay back on his pillow, closed his eyes. "Thank you for your visit," he said.

46

Neaera H.

When I got back to my flat after leaving George Fairbairn the sky went hard and blue, the sun came out in real postcard style. I didn't like it. Sunny days have always been more difficult for me than grey ones.

The snails grazed slowly on the sides of Madame Beetle's tank, the little china bathing beauty turned her back on them, Madame Beetle stayed under the filter sponge. Everything seemed stupid. I walked about from room to room, took books from shelves and put them back, dug up old letters and read lines here and there.

The place seemed suddenly intolerably full of things. The cupboards were bursting with clothes and shoes I'd never wear again, the drawers were full of rubbish, the files choked with defunct correspondence.

I began to thin out my belongings, tied up clothes in bundles, stacked old newspapers, filled carrier bags with what had filled the drawers. Then I felt exhausted, had some lunch, drank coffee, smoked.

I didn't want to be in my flat for the rest of the day. I put some paper in a file envelope and went to the British Museum. I sat on a wooden bench on the porch. Pigeons and tourists were active all round, the sunlight seemed tolerable there. I held the envelope on my lap, feeling the weight and thickness of the blank paper inside. I closed my eyes, thought of all the years of Gillian Vole, Delia Swallow and the other animals and birds I'd written about and drawn. They led such cosy cheerful lives, that lot. I'd written them but there no longer seemed a place in their world for me.

With my eyes closed I could still see the sunlight. For a moment I saw ocean, sharp and real, the heaving of the open sea, the sunlight dancing in a million dazzling points. The turtles would be swimming, swimming. It *had* been a good thing to do and not a foolish one. Thinking about the turtles I could feel the action of their swimming, the muscle contractions that drove the flippers through the green water. All they had was themselves but they would keep going until they found what was in them to find. In them was the place they were swimming to, and at the end of their swimming it would loom up out of the sea, real, solid, no illusion. They could be stopped of course, they might be killed by sharks or fishermen but they would die on the way to where they wanted to be. I'd never know if they'd got there or not, for me they would always be swimming.

I was in my ocean, this was the only ocean there was for me, the dry streets of London and my square without a fountain. No one could make me freer by putting me somewhere else. I had as much as the turtles: myself. At least I too could die on the way to where I wanted to be. Gillian Vole! Not enough, not nearly enough.

I took paper out of the envelope, took a pen out of my bag. What was there to write? Anything, everything:

> Madame Water-Beetle lived in a plastic shipwreck in a tank by the window. In the same tank lived seven red snails. The snails did the snail work and she did the beetle work.

The perversity of the human mind! I folded the sheet in half, put a fresh one on top of the stack, sat there with it blank for a long time. I wished I had somewhere to go besides my flat. Somewhere bright and empty with uncluttered shadows, somewhere not crusted with years of me. Like George's place.

47

William G.

Sandor stopped in bed Tuesday, Wednesday and Thursday, and for those three days I found the bath and cooker clean every morning. If he used the cooker at odd times when I was out there was no evidence of it. Maybe Mrs. Inchcliff was looking after him. And of course he wasn't buying fresh supplies of squid and seaweed while he was laid up. Maybe he was cooking things that left no trace. I wasn't quite interested enough to visit him again.

Friday he was up and about again. The bath was almost clean, only a hair or two. The cooker was just that tiny bit mucky but without the usual smell. Well, I couldn't make a career of it really. The two fights had been sufficient satisfaction, or almost. I could fight Sandor every day and maybe even win now and again by foul means if not fair but I had no way of forcing him to clean the bath and the cooker.

At the shop Harriet and I were polite to each other. It had come to that. Instead of brushing against each other and touching as often as possible we now avoided contact like thieves wary of a burglar alarm. With no prospect of getting her clothes off again I found the thought of her naked charms vivid in my mind from time to time but I didn't want to be half of the "We" who did this and that and were invited here and there. I didn't want to be expected anywhere as a regular thing. I didn't fancy any more early music either, and there were still two recitals left in the series we'd subscribed to. I'd give her the tickets, she could find someone else to go with easily enough.

On Tuesday I'd rung Neaera up to tell her what our expenses had been. The van and the petrol had come to £26.56, which made her share £13.28. The crates and the rope were on me. "We promised George Fairbairn a report of the expedition," I said. "Maybe we ought to drop in at the Aquarium one day soon."

"I have done," she said. "But I'm sure he'd like a visit from you as well."

I went to see him on Saturday. The two small remaining turtles were back in the tank now, they looked like orphans. Well, I thought, take care of yourselves and grow big and maybe one day somebody will take you to Polperro.

"Anybody say anything yet?" I asked George.

"Nobody's been," he said, "except the blokes who work with me. Nobody from the Society."

"Maybe nothing'll happen at all," I said. "is that possible?"

"It's what I expect," he said.

Well, I hadn't done it to make the headlines. Still I would have thought *some* notice would be taken in this part of the world at least.

He gave me a cup of tea in STAFF ONLY. The lady with the big boobs smiled from her photo by the duty-roster. No champagne today. It occurred to me just then that I could have brought him a thank-you bottle of something but of course I hadn't. I never miss.

"How're you feeling now that you've done it?" he said.

I shrugged. "I think the turtles are better off," I said, "which was after all the object of the exercise."

"But?" he said.

"You know how it is," I said. "Launching the turtles didn't launch me. You can't do it with turtles." Why was I talking to him like a son to a father. He wasn't older than I or wiser. Just calmer.

"You can't do it with turtles," he said. "But with people you never know straightaway what does what. Maybe launching them *did* launch you but you don't know it yet."

"How's Neaera?" I said. "She said she'd been to see you. I haven't seen her since we got back."

"She's all right," he said, and rolled a cigarette. He did it very deftly, it was a nice smooth cigarette.

"You think it's launched her?" I said.

"Hard to say," he said.

We finished our tea and I left. There were friendly feelings on both sides but neither of us urged the other to stay in touch.

48

Neaera H.

I came home from the museum on Tuesday having written nothing but that Madame Beetle paragraph. I looked at the telephone and said, "Ring." It rang but it wasn't George, it was William phoning to tell me what our expenses had been. Then in a few minutes it rang again and it was George. He invited me out to dinner and I asked him to my place for drinks first.

The flat looked different with that to look forward to. Everything in it, all the clutter on the desk and the drawing-table, all the books and objects took on new character with the prospect of being seen by him.

I bought whisky and gin and flowers. I had a long bubble-bath, washed my hair, put on the Arab dress I look best in and my posh boots. Patchouli too. I'd bought it for the first time only the other day at Forbidden Fruit but it seemed as if it'd always been my scent.

There was a knock on the door about an hour before George was due.

"Good evening," said Webster de Vere. "I hope I'm not disturbing you. Were you in full flow at the typewriter?"

"Like a river in spate," I said, certain for no particular reason that he'd listened at the door before knocking.

"I mustn't bother you then," he said with a good deal of optical activity. Such bright glances! I said nothing, stood at the door without asking him in. He *was* bothering me. "But I thought," he said, "perhaps you might be persuaded to abandon your muse briefly for a sherry with me. Dreadful, really, we've been neighbours all these years and yet we scarcely know each other."

"I don't think it's dreadful at all," I said. "A friendly presence scarcely known can be quite nice." I hadn't meant that to be encouraging but it encouraged him.

"Then you'll come," he said, his eyes absolutely darting rays of light.

"Thank you," I said, "but I can't. I'm expecting someone in a little while."

"Pity," he said, lowering his sparkle. "Another time perhaps. How're the snails?"

"Cleaning up," I said, moving back a little with my hand on the door.

"Actually they have tiny wireless transmitters in them," he said with an evil smile. "So I get to know everything that goes on in your flat."

"I'm afraid it must be terribly dull listening for you," I said. "You must excuse me now."

"Till soon," he said as I closed the door.

I quickly took the snails out of the tank, put them in a peanut-butter jar full of water and left the jar outside his door.

What could have worked him up to that awful pitch? He'd seen me often enough without getting all excited. But until he fed Madame Beetle he hadn't seen my flat which perhaps looked as if a good deal of work was being done and a comfortable living being made. Maybe he was tired of young men and old ladies and wanted to settle down. Dreadful of me to think it but I thought it.

"There's a jar of snails outside your neighbour's door," said George when he arrived.

"I know," I said. "They were in Madame Beetle's tank for a while but I didn't like the way they looked at me."

"There'll be more," he said, and showed me little patches of eggs on the sides of the tank.

"That's all right," I said. "I'll get them before they get me."

He walked about the flat looking at things. I'd only seen him in shirt-sleeves before. He was wearing an old tweed jacket with leather patches on the elbows, no tie.

"You look different tonight," he said.

"How?" I said.

"Jolly. Full of smiles."

"That's how I feel," I said. We both drank gin neat, it was bright and velvety. We smiled at each other over our glasses, time seemed full and easy, available in unlimited amounts. George seemed to carry a clear space about with him that made all things plain and simple where he was. The room lost its tired complexity, became comradely and cheerful. Without going to the window I knew that the evening view of the lamplit square would be as round and juicy as a ripe plum.

We went to the Bistingo on the King's Road and had steak and drank red wine. The evening seemed very bright. We walked up the Embankment to Westminster afterwards, then over the bridge to the South Bank. We walked about on the different levels up and down the steps and by the river. The plaza by the Royal Festival Hall was like a gigantic stage-set, the night was full of quiet excitement, the river was shining, the music-boats had gemmed windows, the trains across the Hungerford Bridge were freighted with promise.

We had coffee at the National Film Theatre clubroom, then walked back to my place slowly and by devious routes. At two o'clock in the morning we came past the Albert Bridge. Five or six taxis always park there for the night by a little hut that must be a dispatcher's office. In the first taxi in the rank the driver was sitting in the back seat in the dark playing a muted trumpet. Dixieland. The music floated quietly through the open window, small and lively.

"What is it?" I said.

"*Muskrat Ramble*," said George.

At home we lay in bed smoking, watched the shapes of light on the ceiling, pale abstractions from the street lamps.

Before I fell asleep I saw green water, the white shark-glimmer. I looked at my watch. Half past three. I hope William's all right, I thought.

49

William G.

Sundays come round so quickly, sometimes there scarcely seems a day between them let alone a week. My mother had at least had the Methodist Church to go to and to stop going to, either way it was a positive action. I had nothing except a strong feeling of dread. Perhaps my mother had had that as well. I remembered it from earliest childhood, the awful Sunday daylight through the coloured glass of the front door, the quiet outside.

Sunday is the day when there you are with the people you live with and that's it. Or there you are alone. There'd been Sundays when I'd methodically picked up girls at the Victoria & Albert or the British Museum, Sundays drove strangers into each other's arms. But I simply hadn't that much enterprise now. I thought of Port Liberty but didn't fancy the trip to Greenwich. I decided to have a lazy day, maybe Sunday would just take care of itself and not bother me.

Sandor invariably went out on Sundays looking just like the rest of the week except no tie. He even carried his briefcase and I suppose he went somewhere where everybody spoke five languages and read many newspapers and argued about politics all day.

Miss Neap either solved or compounded the weekend problem at least once a month by visiting her mother in Leeds. At other times she maintained a full Sunday cultural schedule and working as she did at a ticket agency was never without something to do. She was an avid museum-goer in the afternoons and favoured music in the evenings, overdressing smartly and appropriately for each part of the day.

Mrs. Inchcliff was out scavenging as usual. I believe Sunday was her building-site day, she tended to bring home new-looking timber and sometimes clean bricks, all to be hoarded in the lumber-room, perhaps against the advent of a new friend handy with tools.

So I had the place to myself, and from my window looked out across the common where the trains clattered by and the shining rails maintained their perspective vanishing towards Putney. On the common people smiled and strolled on the paths and on the grass stepping round and over the dogshit while other people smiled and strolled as their dogs shitted on the paths and on the grass. The paddling pool was full of children. The sandbox, the roundabout, the swings, the rocking-horses and mums and dads were active on the playground. The washers of cars on our street were at it looking at the same time virtuous and given over to sensuality. The Greyhound Widow passed, her phantom husband dragging a silent foot. The trees had not so many leaves now, one day soon a heavy rain would leave them bare and winter would be here. "Ah," I said aloud standing at the window.

The Sunday papers were too many for me, they'd not get read today, I wasn't up to any intellectual activity. The turtles would be swimming, swimming and it occurred to me for the first time that for me they'd always be swimming. I'd never know whether they'd got to where they were going. At first I'd been obsessed with setting them free. Then it had become a heavy task I was committed to. Then we did it and afterwards it seemed a blank and empty thing. Now it felt a good thing again. The turtles were swimming to where they wanted to be. But that was *their* swimming, they couldn't do mine.

What was my swimming then? To go on working at the bookshop or somewhere else? To live alone or with someone? To stop smoking or not? To go on getting up in the morning or perhaps not? If I walked round the corner K257 would say "I believe." Believe what? I picked up the stone from Antibes. Look, Dad, here's a good one. Gone, gone, everything gone. Don't cry, Willy. I didn't. On the other hand, *do* cry, why not. I did.

I went downstairs. Miss Neap's *News of the World* was still lying in the hall by the front door, perhaps she'd decided to sleep in and let Sunday look after itself for once. I went over to the paddling pool. The children and the noise suddenly moved into close-up focus. A little boy punched a smaller one and seemed satisfied. Two little girls pranced splashing by, all flashing legs and flying hair. I dropped the stone from Antibes into the shallow water. It lay on the bottom looking up at me until the water glazed with light and I couldn't see the stone any more.

In the sunlight I went for a little walk down the New King's Road towards Putney Bridge. They'd been resurfacing the road. Here and there were little huddles of air-compressors, asphalt-spreaders and rollers, red wooden tripods, yellow blinker lamps drawn up and bivouacked until Monday. At a zebra-crossing all the Belisha beacons were bagged in black plastic. I felt that one was never really alone while there was someone to bag the Belisha beacons in black plastic.

I went back to my room. Evening was gathering in. The day hadn't been at all bad and this was the easy part, the downhill run. I didn't turn the lights on, let the room fill up with twilight and silence.

Mrs. Inchcliff came back, unloaded her plunder and put it in the lumber-room, rattled about in the downstairs kitchen. I went out for fish and chips, brought it back to my room, ate by the light of the street lamps, had a beer.

There was a knock at the door. Mrs. Inchcliff. "Have you seen Miss Neap today?" she said.

"No," I said, "I haven't seen her since yesterday evening."

"Neither have I," she said. "And I always do see her sometime on Sunday, either when she picks up her paper or when she goes out."

"Perhaps she's gone to Leeds," I said.

"I don't think so," said Mrs. Inchcliff. "She was here last night when I went to bed, I saw her coming out of the bathroom. And if she'd left this morning she'd have taken the paper with her. I've just gone up to her room with it and knocked on the door but there was no answer. The door's on the latch but I didn't open it."

We went down to Miss Neap's room on the first floor at the end of the hall. Mr. Sandor coming in just then saw us and paused at the foot of the stairs. I opened the door, turned on the light.

Miss Neap had hanged herself. The window in her room was a tall one and at the top of it behind the pelmet there was a stout old iron hook screwed into the window-frame. It had been put there a long time ago for a curtain rod and drapes much heavier than the present ones. She'd stood on a chair and used several bright-coloured silk scarves knotted together. The chair lay on the floor where she'd kicked it over. She was dressed for the street in her tightly-belted leopard-skin coat and her newest purple suede boots. Her pince-nez had fallen off her nose and dangled from its ribbon. She must have been hanging there for some time, her face had gone quite dark and her powder and rouge and shiny blue eye-makeup looked ghastly. When the police doctor came he said the time of death had been between three and four on Sunday morning.

The room was in good order. She'd been there ten years, had done the place over and bought new furniture just as I'd done. The wallpaper and the drapes had a floral pattern. The bed was made up smartly into a green couch, colourful pillows carefully arranged on it and a large cloth Snoopy dog. Some paperback thrillers, some P. G. Wodehouse. A paperback *Four Quartets*. A copy of *The Book of Common Prayer* open at *At the Burial of the Dead at Sea*.

On the dresser were her Postal Savings book, a funeral directors' card and a receipt showing payment of £130. A note told us that arrangements had been made for cremation, that she wanted no funeral service of any kind whatsoever and that it was her wish that the cremation be completely unattended. Her mother in Leeds was not to be notified until after the cremation and her savings were then to be sent to her. The book showed a balance of £936.27. Next to it was a framed photograph of her mother and father and Miss Neap as a girl. No more than nine or ten years old but you could recognize the face as being the same one.

50

Neaera H.

I didn't know how lonely I'd been until the loneliness stopped. Now when I looked at my flat it seemed to have been cleared of invisible wires criss-crossed in patterns of pain that had been there for years. I saw myself in days past, years past, stepping carefully and trying to keep my balance. There were the kitchen, the bathroom, the sitting-room, the bedroom, the spare room. There were the books, the drawing-table, the typewriter, Madame Beetle, the clutter, all the spaces and places where I stood or sat or lay down, all the things that I touched and used in my daily effort to piece together an eggshell life from broken fragments.

George had given me so much that even if there came a time without George I could bear it now and not step carefully nor build my broken eggshell with mad patience. He hadn't done anything special, it was simply his way of being. Like him I found that I no longer minded being alive. And the turtles were swimming, there was always that to fall back on.

It was extraordinary, the whole turtle affair. Nothing was ever said about it in the press, there was no furore at the Zoological Society, George wasn't sacked. He let it be known that he'd set the large turtles free and would be replacing them with smaller specimens and that he would do the same again when the two remaining turtles were larger. That was all there was to it, he wasn't even reprimanded.

The two turtles in the tank looked different to me now, seemed less dozy and more as if they had something to look forward to:

> And every one said, "If we only live,
> We too will go to sea in a Sieve, —
> To the hills of the Chankly Bore!"

I went to the British Museum again with my envelope full of blank paper. I felt friendly towards the coaches, cars and motorcycles in the forecourt, the people and the pigeons. I sat on the porch with the paper in my lap, sunlight again on my closed eyes.

I was waiting for something now and the waiting was pleasant. I was waiting for the self inside me to come forward to the boundaries from which it had long ago withdrawn. Life would be less quiet and more dangerous, life is risky on the borders. Gillian Vole and Delia Swallow live in safe places.

Come, I said to the self inside me. Come out and take your chance. After staring at the blank paper for a very long time I wrote:

> The fountain in the square
> Isn't there.

Well, I thought, it's not much but it's a beginning.

51

William G.

The Coroner's Court was a tall tight box with the lid always on it. Whatever was said in that room would not expand much laterally, would not move forward or back. It would stand and grow tall until its head touched the ceiling in the clear grey light.

The room seemed fully as tall as it was long. The dark green ceiling must have been at least twenty-five feet from the floor, deeply bevelled, with handsome white beams and braces. The walls were pale lemony green, there were tall windows, proper courtroom furniture: witness box, judge's bench, jury box. Just below the bench were red leather settees and a table with a red leather top for PRESS. Another such table for COUNSEL. A little plain narrow writing-stand for POLICE at the front of the spectators' pews. Ten Bibles in the jury box, two more by the witness box. There was a poor box by the door.

Three knocks. "Rise, please, to Her Majesty's Coroner," said the Coroner's Officer. We rose as the Coroner came in. "Oyez, oyez, oyez," said the Coroner's Officer as the Coroner passed to the bench, "all manner of persons who have anything to do at this court before the Queen's Coroner touching upon the death of Flora Angelica Neap draw near and give your attendance. Pray be seated."

We sat down. Behind the Coroner the royal arms said *DIEU ET MON DROIT*. I counted the people in the room: the Coroner, the Coroner's Officer, the Police Pathologist and the constable who'd come to the house, a lady from the ticket agency where Miss Neap had worked, a lady from the funeral directors, Mrs. Inchcliff, Mr. Sandor and me. Nine altogether. I wondered how long it had been since Miss Neap had had nine people pay attention to her all at once.

A frightening thought had been growing in me. I'd always assumed that I was the central character in my own story but now it occurred to me that I might in fact be only a minor character in someone else's. Miss Neap's perhaps. And I didn't even know the story. Draw near and give your attendance. Yes, we were doing that now. No one had done it when she was alive.

The constable testified that he had come to the house at a quarter to eight on Sunday evening and found the deceased lying on the couch where we'd put her. The pathologist testified that death had been from asphyxia due to hanging and had occurred between three and four that morning.

The lady from the ticket agency testified that Miss Neap had seemed in good spirits when she last saw her on Saturday and that she'd said she might go home at the weekend, she wasn't sure.

The lady from the funeral directors testified that Miss Neap had been last month to pay for her cremation, had said that she lived alone and it was something she wanted to take care of. Lived alone. I think Mrs. Inchcliff, Mr. Sandor and I all felt our faces go red at that.

Mrs. Inchcliff, Mr. Sandor and I swore in turn that we would speak the truth, the whole truth, and nothing but the truth but there was little more to be said than that Miss Neap had lodged at the house for ten years, that we had last seen her alive on Saturday evening looking much as usual and had found her dead on Sunday evening with the note, the Postal Savings book, the receipt and the funeral directors' card. Those were shown in evidence. The empty jury box seemed to fill up with blank-faced phantoms shaking their heads: Not the whole truth. But it was all we knew and all we could say. It stood there like a blind dumb thing and grew tall until its head touched the ceiling. The Coroner returned a verdict that Miss Neap had taken her own life and the court was adjourned.

The funeral directors were only a few minutes' walk down the street from the Coroner's Court. I wonder if Miss Neap had at some time taken the same walk. The lady who'd been at the inquest was a Mrs. Mortimer. She was a handsome brownhaired woman who looked more like a theatrical wardrobe-mistress than a funeral director, she looked jolly and as if she ought to be in and out of actresses' dressing-rooms with pins in her mouth. Here was the place, a few urns and vases in the window. Inside was a plain little reception room.

"Everything's in order," said Mrs. Mortimer. "She's having the *"Ely,"* which is a standard cremation coffin with good class fittings. It'll be covered in purple dommett with a pink lining and she'll be wearing a pink robe. Plate of inscription on the lid with her name, age, date of death. It isn't right to send her off without a service, poor lady, and alone."

"It's what she wanted," I said. Sandor nodded emphatically.

"Do it how she wanted," he said.

"That at least," said Mrs. Inchcliff.

"There's just one more thing," said Mrs. Mortimer. "I hate to mention it but our prices went up last week. The *"Ely"* is now £121.50 instead of £109.50. The rest of it's the same: £7.00 for sanitizing and robing, £13.00 for the crematorium which includes the minister but I don't think I can get a rebate even if there's no service, 50p gratuity for the chappie at the crem. That comes to £142.00 instead of £130.00, so there's £12.00 owing."

I wrote a cheque for the additional £12.00 for the *"Ely."* So many things have names: wedding-cakes, babies' prams, cars and coffins.

"Thank you," said Mrs. Mortimer. "We'll have the body brought over from the mortuary. Cremation will be on Tuesday and she'll be here at the chapel of rest until then. In her instructions she said no viewing and no flowers please."

No viewing, no flowers, no funeral service and no one at the cremation. Well, funerals are for the living. For good or ill one sees the dead removed from the scene and the departure is final. Miss Neap having been cheated of companionship while living wished to remain an undeparted presence when dead. Fair enough.

Miss Neap had died on Sunday, this was Thursday. That made four days running Sandor'd left the bath and cooker clean.

52

Neaera H.

It used to be that I stayed up till all hours and still felt time-starved, none of the day seemed to be metabolized into living. Now the minutes make me strong.

Frost this morning. Sharp it was, the air rang with it. I got up early and walked down the New King's Road to Parsons Green. Near where William lives there was a dead cat by a bus stop, pretty well flattened out. He looked as if he'd been run over by a lorry. A grey stripey tom he was with a head like a Roman senator, one eye open, one eye shut. His whole corpse seemed expressive of the WHAM! when his life met his death. He looked as if he'd been one hundred percent alive until the lorry closed his account in the flower of his tomcathood and his mortal remains were cheerful rather than depressing. To live with a yowl and die with a WHAM! Thinking about him whilst walking back I stopped and wrote:

> Stiff but not formal
> A dead cat says hello
> This winter morning.

Later I'd be having lunch with George at the Aquarium: sandwiches by the salt-water tanks, the poshest spot in town. Between now and then were all kinds of minutes, all of them good. Who knew what might happen at the typewriter?

Before going up to the flat I went into the square, played hopscotch in it just as it was, with no fountain.

53

William G.

Autumn kept going with fewer and fewer brown and yellow leaves until a big rain came just as it always does. Wham! Bare trees, winter, black mornings, people walking fast.

This morning near the bus stop by a tree a dead cat said hello to me. There he was, he too had gone into winter with a wham. He looked as if he'd been flying high until he was brought down. I've never seen such a lively-looking dead cat.

The morning had nothing special to recommend it, the shop was full of people wanting biros and greeting cards, neither of which we sell. But I felt good.

At lunch-time I bought a bottle of Moët-Chandon and went up to the Zoo. In the tube I thought about Miss Neap and Mr. Sandor and Mrs. Inchcliff. With no funeral to go to we'd found ourselves drawn together somehow and remembering her but not altogether mournfully. In fact we all got drunk and Sandor sang gypsy songs. Rather well too. Odd but not really. If Flora Angelica Neap was going to be an undeparted presence she'd have to share the good times as well as the bad. And I could imagine good times, why I don't know. Nothing was different or better and I didn't think I was either but I didn't mind being alive at the moment. After all who knew what might happen?

Camden Town is the windiest tube station I know. Coming up on the escalator with my hair flying I felt as if I was coming out of a dark place and into the light, then I laughed because that's what I was actually doing.

At the Aquarium I said hello to the two turtles, then opened various PRIVATE doors until I found George Fairbairn. Neaera was with him and they were eating sandwiches by the salt-water tanks. I gave George the champagne.

"I was just passing by," I said, "and I thought I'd drop this off."

"Lovely," said George. "Cheers! What's the occasion?"

"Just that I was passing by," I said.

They wanted me to stay and drink it with them but I couldn't stop. I took a taxi back to the shop, it was that kind of day.

PILGERMANN

I

Pilgermann here. I call myself Pilgermann, it's a convenience. What my name was when I was walking around in the shape of a man I don't know, I simply can't remember. What I am now is waves and particles, I don't need to walk around, I just go. When I want to appear I turn up as an owl. When I see myself in my mind I see myself flying silently across the face of a full moon that is wreathed in luminous clouds; heath and swamp and wood below me, silvered rooftops, sleeping chimneys glide. Pilgermann the owl. The owl has always been big in my mind. Once as a boy I was in a ruin of some kind, old fire-blackened stones and burnt and rotted timbers. Twilight it was, the dying day shivering a little and huddling itself up in its cloak. Suddenly there came flying towards me with a mouse dangling from its beak an owl, what is called a veiled owl, with a limp mouse dangling from its cryptic heart-shaped face. "Hear, O Israel!" I cried: "the Lord our God, the Lord is One!"

Ah! the flickering in the darkness, the passage of what is called time! I don't know what I am now. A whispering out of the dust. Dried blood on a sword and the sword has crumbled into rust and the wind has blown the rust away but still I am, still I am of the world, still I have something to say, how could it be otherwise, nothing comes to an end, the action never stops, it only changes, the ringing of the steel is sung in the stillness of the stone.

I speak from where I am; I speak from between the pieces; I speak from where Abram heard the voice of God:

> And it came to pass, that,
> when the sun went down, and
> there was thick darkness,
> behold a smoking furnace,
> and a flaming torch that
> passed between these pieces.
> In that day the LORD made
> a covenant with Abram . . .

A covenant with God is made from between the pieces of oneself; it's the only place where a covenant can happen, no covenant is possible until one has divided the heifer, the she-goat, the ram of oneself. The turtle-dove and the young pigeon being the heart and soul one of course does not divide them. When Abram sacrificed the animals of himself as instructed by God a deep sleep fell upon him, and the dread and the great darkness from which God spoke. Then came the thick darkness after the sun went down, and in that darkness were the smoking furnace and the flaming torch that passed between the pieces. So here already was shown the main theme of the people of Abraham: the furnace and the torch; the consuming fire and the onward flame.

If you measure with what is called time it's a long way from here back to Abram's pieces. But still there is the division of the animals of us, still the thick darkness, the smoking furnace, the flaming torch. And still there are covenants to be made between the pieces, between one fire and another. I am only the waves and particles of such as I was but I have a covenant with the Lord, the terms of it are simple: everything is required of me, for ever.

PILGERMANN

2

So. From wherever and from whatever I am now in what is called the present moment my being goes back to the year 1096 in the Christian calendar which was the year 4856 in the Jewish calendar. My being goes back to a particular morning in that year, the morning of the thirty-first of July which was for Jews the Ninth of Av, Tisha b'Av, the morning of that day when Jews who have already been fasting since the evening before sit on low stools or on the floor of the synagogue and mourn the destruction of the First and Second Temples; they mourn other disasters as well, among them that day when the twelve spies returned from Canaan and Joshua and Caleb rent their clothes because the children of Israel listened only to the evil report and turned aside from the land of milk and honey.

I no longer have a mouth with which to smile wryly but I think that the waves and particles of me must be arranged in something like a wry smile as I remember that land of milk and honey from which I did not turn aside on the Eve of the Ninth of Av, that land of milk and honey from which I was returning in the freshness of the summer dawn.

I was on my way home from the house of the tax-collector. I say tax-collector, it sounds right, but in fact I'm not certain what he was; he may well have been, may still be, something else. I know that he was an official of some kind, something of authority, a man of exactions, of that certain sort of neck, not actually fat, that in a more modern time bulges over the stiff uniform collar. The smell of such a man's freshly shaven face is oppressive across the centuries. It is a law of nature that such a man will have a wife of exquisite gentility and superb figure. A woman of regal buttocks and nervous, equine grace. A face of mercy and sweet goodness. That this man should have the management of such a woman is absolutely scientific in its manifestation of that asymmetry without which there would be no motion in the universe. Yes, such a coupling imparts spin to the cosmos, it creates action, it utterly negates stasis.

Such a man as that Herr Steuerjäger or Gerichtsvollzieher or whatever, such a man as that cannot live without a Jew to be other than. If there were no Jews he would invent them, he would dress up as a Jew and flog himself. He is like that act one sees in cabaret in which a woman is half-costumed as a gorilla with whom she dances and to whose advances she ultimately yields. What was it that he did, did he impose a candle tax on Jews because they were reading too much? Or was it that he required all circumcision knives to be inspected by his brother-in-law the butchery inspector, with an exorbitant fee to be paid for the stamp of approval? Or was it simply that he started the tale that Jews kept little live toads in their phylacteries for sorcery? It doesn't matter, if it wasn't one thing it was another.

Myself, I think I may have been a tailor or a surgeon or something of that sort. Whatever I was, my services had so far never been required by that man or his household; least of all that service I longed to render upon the body of that incomparable and to me unapproachable woman. Her name is Sophia: Wisdom. There's allegory for you, the vision of naked Wisdom and the Jew lusting after her. And such nakedness! It continues in my eye, splendouring. It will always be there, an image of such power as to confer unending Now upon the mind that holds it. Always now the great dark house in the Keinjudenstrasse late at night. Always now I, the solitary late-night Jew walking where he is not wanted. In the nights of the days before Tisha b'Av I walk there. I see late at night the dark house. Suddenly in an upper window I see a triangle of dim golden light, becoming a narrow oblong of dim golden light in which bulks the dark shape of a man in a nightshirt. The man moves away and there stands revealed, farther back within the room, the woman naked with her back to the window. Her shoulders are shaking, she has her hands up to her face. How I love her!

Never again! Always and for ever again and again. In my mind I see the night sky, I see three stars burning between the Virgin and the Lion, they are like a gesture, a Jewish gesture, the hand flung up, fingers spread: Well, then! What are your intentions, will you block the road for ever?

There she is, glorious and pathetic in that dim golden light. The splendid form of her contains her name as a candle contains its wick, her name still unknown to me, when I know it it will flame for me. Gone! the great dark house all black again.

Sophia! name unknown to me! Name that will burn in my mind like a candle flame burning straight up in still air above its translucent column of white wax.

Jews are known to be clever but I did nothing clever; I simply hung about the Keinjudenstrasse day and night with no thought for anything else until that bulging-necked man climbed heavily on to his horse and rode away. I bribed no servants, I asked no one how long he would be gone, I felt honour bound to take my naked chance. I came as one who seeks a miracle; caution seemed sacrilegious.

Nightfall, and he had not come back. I hear the hooting of an owl, I hear the wind sighing, the summer wind in the trees of the garden. Outside the forbidden garden of the great dark house I wait. This is perhaps the centre of time for me, this waiting in expectation of a miracle, this waiting in a state of transcendental desire, in a state of sin made holy by its purity.

The hours pass, the first-quarter moon appears in the sky like a password, I go into the garden. There is of course a ladder there; for the Jew desirous of Wisdom there is always a ladder. The house is all dark, there is no light showing anywhere. I have no plan, I lean the ladder up against the house and I climb up.

The shutters are open, the casement is open, I feel on my face the warm breath of the dark window, there is a scent of oranges, of bitter aloes, of lions, of tawniness, there is a scent of the nakedness of the unseen woman within. Suddenly she is there, glimmering in her nakedness like a glimmering fish in the river of night. I feel as if I am falling, falling backward with a silent scream into the garden. Has she pushed away the ladder? She has not pushed away the ladder, I am not falling, her two hands grip my wrists, she is pulling me into the window, she is whispering, "Thou Jew! My Jew!"

"Thou Jew! My Jew!" The miracle has happened, no explanations are necessary. With a miracle one is immediately *thou* and the rest follows, the rest has already been going on before one arrived, the moment is prepared and ready.

The centre of time is, as I have said, the waiting. This is now off the centre, this is the motion of the everything, the action of the universe, the destined world-line of the soul, the living heart of the mystery.

There are few words between us. I say, over and over again, "Thou beautiful, thou beautiful!" She says, "Thou Jew! My Jew!" Only one other thing does she say, her name when I ask it: her name is Sophia. Then I say, again and again in that wondrous warm breathy darkness, her name. Sophia, Sophia, Sophia.

3

See me, the Jew fresh from the attainment of Wisdom, the Jew returning
with the dawn of the Ninth of Av. See me as a bird might see me, as might
that stork that slowly flaps its way over the huddled roofs and chimneys,
over the narrow twisting streets of morning. What might this stork see
looking down? Here the Jew comes, turning this way, turning that way,
threading his homeward path and drawing closer, closer to those others
hurrying towards him, turning this way, turning that way as if by careful
prearrangement, these others with billhooks and pitchforks following a
sow who wears a scarlet cross. The sow has her snout uplifted and is
grunting loudly. "A Jew! A Jew!" shouts the man who holds her rope,
"She smells a Jew!" Here they come running towards me, reeking of cow
dung, sweat, beer, pigs, shouting, "A Jew! A Jew!"

They hurl themselves upon me, they throw me to the cobblestones,
some of them sit on my chest, some of them hold my arms and legs. My
tunic is pulled up, my hose are pulled down. O God! I feel the cool air of
dawn on my nakedness. O God! I know what they are going to do and I
cannot move a limb to help myself.

"The covenant!" cries some lout. "The mark of the covenant!"

"Cut it off and make a Christian of him," says the man with the sow.

"Look at that thing," says someone else. "You can be sure he's had Christian women with it, filthy brute."

"He won't have them any more," says the man with the sow.

O God! I pray in my mind. O God! Don't let this happen! I feel the knife on me. I think of Rabbi Hananiah ben Teradyon martyred in the Hadrianic persecutions, wrapped in the Scroll of the Law and burned at the stake. As he died he said that he saw the parchments burning but the letters of the Torah flying up out of the fire. I too now see the black letters shimmering and twisting as they rise on the heated air, soaring above the flames like birds of holy speech to the blue sky. I see the black letters writhing round the holy nakedness of Sophia going up, up, out of sight into the blue morning.

How can I be brave, strong, a real man, a hero? All I can do is not give them a screaming Jew to laugh at. "God wills it!" they cry with stinking breath as they cut off my manhood. I vomit but I do not scream.

"Finish him off," says someone.

"Let him live," says another sort of voice. It is the tax-collector on his horse at the head of the town militia.

"God wills it!" shouts the man with the sow.

"This also," says the officer of the watch, and he prods the sow with his pike. She squeals and runs off with the peasant soldiers of Christ followed by the town militia. The tax-collector, high above me on his horse that snorts and prances and paws the cobbles, looks down at me with a pale face then looks back over his shoulder. I hear voices approaching: "Jews, Jews! Give us more Jews!"

"Pray for me," says the tax-collector. "This way!" he shouts to the approaching peasants. With a scraping of hooves horse and rider plunge away, leading the peasants away from where I am, leading them towards the town gate.

Pray for him! Did he actually say that, did I hear him right? *"Betet für mich."* What else could it have been? *"Tretet mich"*? "Kick me"? Ridiculous; that man could not possibly have asked me either to pray for him or to kick him. I have a sudden hysterical vision of the two cherubim leaning towards each other over the Ark of the Covenant, the one saying, "Pray for me" and the other, "Kick me." I don't know what to make of it: this man, this husband of Sophia, this man whom I have just cuckolded, has saved my life, such as it now is.

PILGERMANN

I am lying on my back alone on the cobblestones, my tunic stuffed into my wound. It is broad day, above me arches the blue sky. High overhead, so very, very, high in the sky, circle a drift of storks, a meditation of storks, circling like those intersecting circles of tiny writing sometimes done by copyists with texts of the Holy Scriptures. They are so high, those storks, that one couldn't say what they are unless one knows, as I do, that every year faithfully come these great dignified black-and-white birds to nest on our rooftops and to circle high in the sky over our town, returning each year in their season.

I smell burning, there is smoke drifting between me and the sky; that will be from the synagogue. Here I must say that I had never been a devout Jew. I owned a skullcap and a prayer shawl and phylacteries; I always turned up at the synagogue for the High Holy Days and I had never before missed Tisha b'Av but my observances were mostly for the sake of appearances; in between I went my own way. God was to me as a parent to whom I had given little obedience and from whom I expected no inheritance.

Now, lying on the cobblestones looking up at the blue sky and smelling the burning I cry out to God in my agony: "O God!" I say, "Why is this? What's the use of it? What good is it to anybody?"

God says nothing to me.

"Hear, O Israel," I cry: "the Lord our God, the Lord is One. Magnified and sanctified be his great name in the world which he hath created according to his will. What are we? What is our life? What is our piety? What is our righteousness? What our helpfulness? What our strength? What our might? What shall we say before thee, O Lord our God and God of our fathers? Are not all the mighty men as nought before thee, the men of renown as though they had not been, the wise as if without knowledge, and the men of understanding as if without discernment? For most of their works are void, and the days of their lives are vanity before thee, and the pre-eminence of man over the beast is nought, for all is vanity."

Still no word from God. The blue sky is perfectly blank, the smoke of the burning synagogue drifts in the still morning air; it's going to be a hot day.

"God!" I cry, "Whatever you are and whatever I am, speak to me! O Lord, do it for thy name's sake. Do it for the sake of thy truth; do it for the sake of thy covenant; do it for the sake of Abraham, Isaac and Jacob;

do it for the sake of Moses and Aaron; do it for the sake of David and Solomon. Do it for the sake of Jerusalem, thy holy city; do it for the sake of Zion, the tabernacle of thy glory, do it for the sake of thy Temple's desolation; do it for the sake of the destruction of thy altar; do it for the sake of those slain for thy holy name; do it for the sake of those slaughtered for thy Unity; do it for the sake of those who went through fire and water for the sanctification of thy name. Do it for the sake of sucklings who have not sinned; do it for the sake of weanlings who have not transgressed; do it for the sake of the school-children.

"Answer us, O Lord, answer us; answer us, O our God, answer us; answer us, O our Father, answer us . . . "

It was then that the air began to shimmer and Christ appeared to me. He was tall, lean, and sinewy. One of those fair Jews with his hair further lightened by the bleaching of the sun. Very light blue eyes, perfectly intrepid eyes drooping a little towards the outside of the face, the eyes of a fighter, the eyes of a lion. He was wearing a patched robe, his sandals were worn, his feet looked hard and hard-travelled. He stood there with a silence flung down in front of him. He was no one in whom I had any belief but there he was and there was no mistaking who he was.

I looked at him and listened to his silence for a while. When I was able to speak I said, "You're not the one I was calling."

He said, "I'm the one who came through. I'm the one you'll talk to from now on."

I saw his lips move but his voice came from inside my head. It made me feel very strange, being on the outside of his voice. I knew that if I were capable of running and were to run away to a distance where I could no longer see his lips move I should still hear his voice inside my head. A woodwind sort of voice with something of the timbre of a modern oboe, it seemed to have in it a capability of vibration that would move the plates of the earth apart; it was a voice that made a great space happen all round it, and all that space was inside my head. Feeling vast and hollow, hearing only a silence all round me and my own voice far, far away inside my head, I said, trying to synchronize my lips with my words, "Until now I've dealt with your father."

He said, "Until now you've dealt with no one and no one's dealt with you."

I said, "Is this the Day of Reckoning then?"

He said, "Every day is the Day of Reckoning." The way his voice filled all the great echoing vastness inside my head was frightening; I wanted to get away from him but I was afraid to try even to stand up because of the bleeding. I looked all round me; my member and testicles were nowhere in sight. I thought of them thrown away like offal, I thought of them eaten by the Jew-finding sow, I vomited again.

I said, "I want to talk to your father," then I held my head and waited for his answer to echo inside me.

He said, "Humankind is a baby, it always wants a face bending over the cradle."

I said, "God's our father, isn't he?"

He said, "God isn't a he, it's an it."

I said, "Where is it, his strong right arm that was stretched out over us?"

He said, "It's gone."

I said, "Have I got to be my own father now?"

He said, "Be what you like but remember that after me it's the straight action and no more dressing up."

Neither of us said anything for a little while. I didn't want him to go away but I didn't want to hear his voice inside my head.

"Will there be a Last Judgment?" I said.

He said, "The straight action *is* the last judgment; there's no face on the front of it, it has no front or back."

We are walking, I am leaning on Jesus; with his right arm round me he keeps me from falling. I feel the strength in him rising like a column. In the morning sunlight rises the smoke from the synagogue. The fire crackles, the flames are pale in the bright morning. Suddenly there is so much space between the Jewish quarter and the rest of the town! Suddenly the Christian roofs are sharp and distant, they are looking away. In the great space all round the synagogue the bodies of the dead are vivid, the blood fresh and dark on the cobbles that seem to have put themselves into patterns I have not noticed before: there are twisting serpents, shifting pyramids, I see the face of a lion that comes and goes. There are many Jews flattened to the earth, limbs all asprawl, mouths open. The children are just as dead as the grown-ups, it seems precocious. It is a very informal gathering, there have been scenes of intimacy with no attempt at privacy.

Here among a scattering of random guests and witnesses is an impromptu bride of the soldiers of Christ. White thighs, black hose, skirt flung over her face. Did they call her *thou?*

"Thou Jew," I say to Jesus, "tell me about this conversion of the Jews."

"What conversion?" says Jesus.

"From life to death," I say. "Why does it keep happening? Why is it God's will?"

Jesus turns his face to me and opens wide his eyes. There come upon me such a shuddering and a blackness, such an expanding pleroma, such an intolerable fullness that I am filled to bursting with it. I open, open, open but cannot contain it, I explode in all directions to infinity, I contract to a point, I explode again from the point, I come back together and return shuddering and full of terror.

"Forgive me, Lord," I say.

There come into my mind thunders and lightnings and a thick cloud on the mountain and the voice of a trumpet exceeding loud. There comes into my mind the sanctified mountain that might not be touched, neither by beast nor man. There comes into my mind a voice saying in Greek:

> For not ye have approached to a mountain being felt and having been ignited with fire and to darkness and to deep gloom and to whirlwind and of trumpet to a sound and to a voice of words, which the ones hearing entreated not to be added to them a word; not they bore for the thing being charged: If even a beast touches the mountain, it shall be stoned; and, so fearful was the thing appearing, Moses said: Terrified I am and trembling . . .

Jesus says, "Can you contain even the expectation of the full reply of me to you? Can you contain even the silence before my answer to you?"

I say, "No, Lord, I cannot contain it."

Jesus says, "Can you contain even the thought of knowing the will of God? I speak not of the knowing; I speak only of the very thought of knowing."

I say, "No, Lord, I cannot even contain that thought."

Jesus says, "If it be God's incomprehensible will that the universe shall flower to the end of all things and from that end of all things seed itself anew, will you question the slaughter of Jews? You see on the cobbles the dead who were alive, who sprang from the leap of the lightning that cleaves the dark that waits for the leap after the stillness, the stillness after the leap. You see the dead: backward into their life and forward into their death extends the black-body spectrum of their being; their diffraction is as yours. Will you offer an opinion?"

I say, "I have no opinion, Lord."

Jesus incorporates me in his glance and I begin to see him in more than one way. Jesus is the great dead Lion of the World and in his mouth is the live black body of Christ Radiant. The great dead lion is walking the rocks and desert, walking the mountains and the high ground, looking down on deep gorges where rivers serpentine, and in his mouth the live black body of him the one radiant, him the Christ flickering his black-body spectrum, flames all dancing on the live black body of him in the mouth of the great dead lion of himself. The black body opens, it is a sky of lightning, a sea of fire, mountains of ice. The sky grows tiny, contracts to one black dot, absorbs the sea of fire, the mountains of ice. The black dot opens out into the great live Lion of the World. In his mouth the tiny dead golden body of Christ. In the mouth of the tiny dead golden body of Christ is the world, the sun, the moon, the stars, the wheeling heavens of night. Far and far the thunder of his silence rolls, the lion roars, the stars shake, flicker, burn to paleness and morning.

Silence. The lion is a great paper kite, blue and yellow, the paper fluttering in the morning wind. Far, far down goes the string to Jesus winding in the kite. The lion-kite bursts into flame, the flame runs down the string, Jesus is on fire.

All round the three hundred and sixty degrees of the horizon dance the avatars of Burning Jesus, Christ as fire in perfect silence dancing. One for every degree of the circle, three hundred and sixty avatars of Burning Jesus dancing the colour of Jew, dancing the full black-body spectrum of Jew. One by one the emissions cease, one by one the colours disband, the burning avatars rejoin each one the next and all go back to one, the live black body of Christ Radiant in the centre of the great circle of fire, the burning world-circle. The motion of the dance continues, it is bursting the skin of the sky. The colour of Jew is rent with a great ripping down the centre of the sky.

Leaning on Jesus and held up by him, suddenly I rage at him. Feeble, unmanned, weak from loss of blood I rage at him the Christ, him the anointed one. "Who are you to put these pictures in my eyes!" I say to him. "Thou Jew! Hear, O Israel! the Lord our God, the Lord is One! The Lord is not three and you are not the One. What kind of a Jew are you to turn the world against your people? Images are worshipped in your name! In your name Jews are slaughtered!"

"Whatever I am," says Jesus, "I'm the one you talk to from now on."

I think: O God, what if he's right? What if God's gone and I never really had a chance to talk to him. Forgotten prayers crowd my head, I look away from Jesus, I look up to the sky. "Answer us, O Lord!" I cry, "answer us on the Fast day of our Affliction, for we are in great trouble; turn not to our wickedness, and hide not thy presence from us, nor conceal thyself from our supplication; be near, we pray, to our cry, let thy kindness we beg, comfort us; answer us, even before we call unto thee, according to that which is said: 'And it shall come to pass that, before they call, I will answer; while they are speaking, I will hear!' For thou, O Lord, art the one that answerest in time of trouble, redeemest and deliverest in all times of trouble and distress! Blessed art thou, O Lord (Blessed be he and blessed be his name!) who answerest in time of trouble. (Amen!)"

There was a long silence after my prayer, then Jesus said, "Did you feel that prayer going anywhere or did it just go out of you?"

"It just went out of me," I said.

"You're shaking an empty tree," said Jesus. "You're letting down your bucket in a dry well. There was no answer when the knife was on your flesh and there'll be no answer now. And for what do you pray now? The thing has already been done and you are cut off from your generations."

"Thou Christ!" I say, remembering suddenly whom I'm talking to, "Thou Christ who fed the hungry, cast out demons, healed the sick and raised the dead! Surely thou wilt restore me to my manhood!"

Jesus shook his head. "The fig tree stayed barren," he said, "and you will stay a eunuch; it is what you wished."

I wasn't sure I'd heard him right, I couldn't believe what he was saying. When he said this we were not walking, I was in my bed, dispersed in two-dimensional sunlit patterns like an infinitely extending oriental carpet. I seemed to have been there for some time. "What did you say?" I said.

Jesus said, "I said it is what you wished."

I said, "Can you have seen Sophia and say that? I am young, the blood in me runs hot, I lust but I am unmanned. I lust, I long, I yearn, I hunger, I hum like a tuning fork, I flutter like a torn banner in the wind. That which I was I can never be again, that which I am is intolerable, that which I shall be I cannot imagine. I glimmer like a distant candle, I mottle like the sunlight on the carpet, like the shadows of leaves. I am something, I am nothing, I am here, I am gone."

"It is what you wished," said Jesus. "Only now do you hum, flutter, glimmer, mottle, be something, be nothing, be here, be gone with me. Only now are you tuned to me."

"Never did I wish to be a eunuch," I said, "and never did I wish to be tuned to you."

Jesus said, "And there are eunuchs who made themselves eunuchs on account of the kingdom of the heavens. The one being able to grasp it let him grasp."

I said, "I never made myself a eunuch."

Jesus said, "Life moves by exchanges; loss is the price of gain. Some pay with one thing, some with another; whatever is most dear, that is my price."

I said, "Why is that your price?"

Jesus said, "What is dear is what is held dear, and there can be no holding by those who go my road; there can be no holding by those who will be here with me and gone with me."

I said, "Never did I ask to go that road, never did I wish to be here with you, gone with you."

Jesus said, "Always you wished it, and most of all when you put hand and foot to that ladder of love and pleasure. In your soul you called to me, you longed for me when you climbed that ladder. With eager hands you reached for pleasure and held it fast but whoever holds on wishes to let go because attachment is not wholeness: the only wholeness is in being with everything and attached to nothing; the only wholeness is in letting go, and I am the letting go."

I said, "I know nothing of all this."

"You will know," said Jesus, "and your knowing in time to come will make you know it now."

"What is between us, you and me?" I said.

"Everything," said Jesus.

"Why me?" I said.

"Why not you?" said Jesus.

I, Pilgermann, poor bare tuned fork, humming with the foreverness of the Word that is always Now. Unbearing the Unbearable, intolerating the Intolerable, being not enough for the Too-Muchness. I, poor harp of a Jew twanging incessantly in the mouth of Jesus, in the lion-mouth of Christ Pandamator, Christ All-Subduer. There is a point where pattern becomes motion; the pattern has found me and I must move, must be aware of moving, must be a motion, an action of the Word. Poor bare tuned fork.

"Blessed are they that are tuned to me," said Jesus.

"Why?" I said.

"Because they shall move," said Jesus. "They shall go, they shall have action."

While he was saying that I was thinking: I, poor eunuch of my Lord, neither sheep nor goat, neither of the left hand nor of the right, subject always to Christ the redeemer, the ransom, the sacrifice, victim, torturer, murderer, bringer of death. Iesous Christous Thanatophoros. Kyrios.

Jesus said, "I am the light of day. Do you believe?"

"I believe," I said.

Jesus said, "I am the energy that will not be still. I am a movement and a rest but at the same time I am all movement and no rest and you will have no rest but in the constant motion of me. Do you believe?"

"I believe," I said.

"Why do you believe?" said Jesus.

"No belief is necessary," I said. "It manifests itself."

Jesus said, "Why in your mind do you call me bringer of death? Why in your mind am I Iesous Christous Thanatophoros?"

I said, "How can I not think of you as Thanatophoros? Whoever wants to kill a Jew does it in your name. In your name they kill the seed that gave you life."

Jesus said, "From me came the seed that gave me life."

4

There arises the question of the tax-collector. Drifting in my oriental-carpet patterns I see him high above me, sitting on his horse and looking down at me the bloody and castrated Jew, the mutilated and unmanned thing that has cuckolded him and entered the golden Jerusalem of his wife. Although he has never taken any notice of me he has seen me often enough in the town, he has me on his records, he knows me for a Jew. Famous as he is for his hatred and loathing of Jews, why has he saved my life? It is true that it is my *castrated* life that he has saved. Can there be some meaning, some message in this? Can he possibly know what has happened between his wife and me? Impossible. It happened only a few hours before he saw me, at a time when he was somewhere else altogether, there was no time for him to be told of it. But is it possible that he never left the town, that he became suspicious of the lurking Jew, pretended to go away but circled back unseen to see what happened? Possible. Or might he simply have instructed a servant to observe carefully and report to him in whatever place he has gone to? Even more possible. Well, which is it then—does he know or doesn't he know? I have no idea. No, I don't believe that he knows, I don't think that he has been suspicious, I don't think that it would ever occur to him as a possibility that a Jew should enter where he has entered.

But wait, maybe he dreams of such a thing constantly; maybe he is utterly consumed by the thought of a Jew by night creeping in through the window to enjoy his wife, maybe it burns in him like a constant lamp, maybe it is the one thing wanting for his happiness and peace. He sees me hanging about, sees the possibility, absents himself in hope. The wife opens the Jerusalem of her body to the lusting Jew, then as an unexpected treat the Jew is caught by the peasant soldiers of Christ, he is flung to the cobbles, stripped, castrated, he lies there shuddering in his blood and vomit while his penis and testicles are eaten by a sow. His fading lust renewed, the husband returns as a giant refreshed to the guilty and submissive wife whose only thought is to anticipate and satisfy his every demand. Is that how it is? God knows.

Can there be, there must be, some reasonable explanation, but what can it be? Here is a Jew, one of the people this man hates, lying bloody on the cobblestones, his death only a moment away. Why should the tax-collector have any interest whatever in saving the life of this man? And why should he say either "Pray for me" or "Kick me"?

When I become exhausted with thinking about the tax-collector my mind, like an automaton that cannot be stopped, returns again and again to the castration itself: if only I had taken another way home, if only I had turned and run, if only I had fought harder. Those faces above me in that dawn, I have seen such faces centuries later in the paintings of Hieronymus Bosch. Ah, the tax-collector again! I have seen his face, his particular face, in a particular painting by Bosch, a painting of Christ being crowned with thorns. The tax-collector is that man wearing the spiked red leather collar and a black astrakhan hat on which there is a sprig of oak leaves with an acorn. In his left hand he holds a staff, his right hand is on Christ's right shoulder; almost comforting and consoling that hand seems: "Bear up, old fellow; be brave; it'll all be over soon" might be the message of that hand. Maybe that man with the tax-collector's face is Pontius Pilate and he's saying, "I find no fault in you but this is how it must be; I wish it could be otherwise." A troubled man, Pontius Pilate; he died by his own hand some years later—that same hand, probably, that rests on Christ's shoulder in the painting. There it was on the end of his arm year after year: feeding him, writing letters, caressing his wife, holding whatever there was in life for him to hold. Suddenly it lets go of everything and jumps up and kills him. For how many years did that thought lurk in the hand? Always, perhaps. In this way are human hands made by God; they carry in them always a last mortal judgment. Perhaps it was to protect himself from that hand that Pilate wore such a spiked collar. Is this then a clue to the tax-collector's strange behaviour towards me? Did some time, perhaps in the dead of night, his hand leap up and take him by the throat and say, "Jews also must live!" Perhaps his hand said this on the very same night that my hand took hold of his naked wife! Only now, as these thoughts move among the waves and particles of me, do I perceive that every hand is the hand of God: hands doing good and hands doing evil, are not they all His (Its) work? Think of the constant action of all the hands of all the world, gathering and scattering, building and destroying and praying, holding on and letting go.

So. And what of my hand, also a hand of God? Did my hand perhaps carry in it a judgment? Did my right hand and its fellow cover my ears and my eyes so that I should be in ignorance of what was happening in the world at the time I climbed that ladder? They did not; I knew that the Pope's appeal had inspired peasants as well as knights to shed the blood of Jews and I knew that we in our town might at any time find ourselves in the path of trouble. Was I then vigilant on behalf of my fellow Jews and myself? Did I keep watch early and late, did I arm myself to defend the Scroll of the Law and God's children in the land of their exile? No. The only weapon I took in hand was the one with which I forgot thee, O Jerusalem, and entered the strange Jerusalem of the tax-collector's wife. Having done what I did in the great house in the Keinjudenstrasse did I then take myself in hand with prudence and with caution to make my way home? I did not; one hand pushed me from behind while the other pointed like a signpost to strange and unlucky streets where I would not have walked the day before; one hand showed the conquering hero the world that lay before him while the other patted him on the back in congratulation. And here I am: the waves and particles of a eunuch.

I talk and I talk and words come out of me in an unending stream but I cannot say the plain truth: I have done wrong, O God. Forgive me for climbing that ladder. For God's sake, Pilgermann, say it straight out: Forgive me, O God, for lusting after Sophia, for loving her, for consummating that love and lust. Forgive me that I have sinned, and forgive me that if I had the cock and balls to do it with I'd do it again this minute. O God! Why cannot I speak with a pure heart? I have done wrong and I know it, but how could you put Sophia into the world and expect me not to do wrong? It would be an insult to your creation not to climb ladders for that woman. Now I see why there must be a tree of knowledge in the garden of Eden: it bears that fruit which cannot possibly be resisted; God did not make it resistible, it must be eaten so that a mystery will be perpetuated, the mystery of the gaining of loss. Before we eat of the fruit we have no knowledge of loss, we don't know that there is anything to lose, nothing has any value; only when we are driven out into the world and the cherubim and the bright blade of a revolving sword stand between us and the forbidden garden, only then are we rich in loss, only then have we salt for the meat of life. Life has no value, means nothing until we have paid for it with the sin of disobedience; only after that original sin does one's proper life begin. What if Adam and Eve hadn't eaten of the fruit of the tree, what then? No Holy Scriptures, no story to tell. Who'd have wanted to know about them? They'd have stayed in their garden obedient and ignorant, bored to death with life and each other and tiresome in the sight of God, they'd have been like a picture that is hung on the wall and after a time not looked at any more. God *made* us such that we would eat of that fruit, God would have been ashamed of us if we hadn't done it. God would never have bothered to make a man and a woman to live out their days dreaming in a garden.

And yet, and yet! I have done wrong, O God, I know it. I made that tax-collector poorer when I enjoyed his wife, I know that. Maybe only on her glorious body could he pray, maybe only with her could he be with you, and I came between him and his prayer. But he was holding on then, wasn't he, being so attached to her, and Jesus said that holding on was no good. No, it's no use, no matter how I try to squirm out of it I've done wrong and reparation must be made. Because I violated that man's privacy, because I burst in upon his quietness. Not that he was all that good a man, certainly I never knew anyone to have a good word to say for him. Maybe his first good action was saving my life that day, maybe that was the first time he'd ever looked kindly upon a Jew, and it only happened after I'd had his wife. Ah! what's the use of twisting and turning, there's something required of me: what? What should I do, where should I go? "Jerusalem! Thou pilgrim Jew!" I did not speak those words, it was a voice that spoke within me: not so much a voice as the daughter of a voice, what is called in Hebrew a Bath Kol. There was about it the scent of Sophia's voice but I knew that it was expressing God's intention. "Jerusalem! Thou pilgrim Jew!"

I, a pilgrim! To Jerusalem! This thought entered me, I could already feel the road under my feet. A name, a word, has substance; the word Jerusalem colours the air. Yerushalayim! I say it, and I that have no face, I feel where there used to be a face, I feel that sharp sensation in the nasal passages, the ache in the throat as the tears start into the eyes of that face I no longer have. Yerushalayim! Flesh made word, soul made word, world made word. Yerushalayim! What longings come to a point in that name! Spin, world; be born, people, and die whoring after false gods, shrinking from the one true one. Speak, prophets, and be stoned by the unhearing. Yerushalayim, spinning domes of gold in the sea of the one mind that is God. Ineffable.

Knights in mail, peasants with billhooks were going to Jerusalem. What were the pictures, what were the words in their minds? I could feel the pull as one who stands at the water's edge feels the sea pulling at his feet. The figure of Christ loomed gigantic in my mind, a figure of gold at the heart of a black mountain. The word, the name of Jerusalem revolving in my mind sent out its glints of gold, and my mind revolving with it found a thread of gold spun out into my road away that beckoned me.

Now I knew what Jesus had meant when he said, "After me it's the straight action and no more dressing up." God was already gone from us. How much longer would Jesus be with us? If others had done as I had done the time might not be long. There came to me the thought that the world is full of mysterious, unseen, fragile temples; it was in these many temples that God used to dwell among us; they are easily destroyed, these temples, as I had destroyed the temple of the tax-collector's privacy in his wife. How many of them still remained? How many temples between us and Christ's last day, between us and the eternal faceless action of God as It? Quickly, quickly must something be done before all the temples were gone. Now I understood why everyone was rushing to Jerusalem, now I knew why this was a time unique in history: this was the time when people everywhere had all at once had the same thought that I had just had. Perhaps even the Bath Kol had spoken to each of them as it had spoken to me, and all of us were now hurrying to Jerusalem to make with the gathered power of our hearts' desire a church of all souls craving Jesus, a place of rebirth in the place of holy sepulchre and resurrection. True, it was a pope who had first called for this great going of multitudes to Jerusalem but no pope could have moved so many people had not God truly willed it. I determined to begin my pilgrimage as soon as I was strong enough, and when my wound had healed sufficiently I began to walk a little every day to get my strength back.

When I came out once more into the streets I saw everything very small, very sharp. How impossibly small was the blackened stump of the synagogue! How could even one whole Jew have fitted into it! Sometimes all the spaces where I walked seemed empty and I felt left behind, like horse dung on the cobbles. Many of the shops in the Jewish quarter had shut down; the butcher had become a vegetarian, the bookseller had been burnt to the ground. There were not many Jews to be seen; those who remained looked at one another with faces full of shame as if they had been caught in the practice of an unspeakable vice. Everyone wondered what was coming next, or rather when and in what manner would come that same thing that always came.

It was at this time that the Jewish population of the town were astonished—astonished is too weak a word, they were absolutely knocked over—by the appearance in the Jewish quarter of the tax-collector in a long coarse tunic, a scrip hanging from his shoulder and a staff in his hand. Nobody could believe it: the Jews were not called to assemble at the Town Hall to hear his words; he came alone and on foot and humbly asked the Rabbi (the son-in-law of our old Rabbi who had been killed by the sow-led peasants) whether we would be kind enough to come with him to the ruin of the synagogue where, under the open sky and in the plain sight of God, he had a few words he wished to say to us.

To me it was like something in a dream or like something seen in another life. His face as he spoke was no longer closed to us and hard, it was open and trusting. For the first time he looked at us as one looks at other human beings. As he spoke his hand kept straying to his throat. "Townspeople," he said, "friends, if I may call you that although until now I have never been a friend to you, I am here to say that I am truly sorry for any harm that I have done you. The candle tax is hereby abolished and the inspection and stamp of approval for circumcision knives will no longer be required. Any words of mine that may have injured you I take back with my whole heart and I ask God's forgiveness and yours; I have already retracted those words publicly at the Town Hall. I am leaving you now to go on a penitential pilgrimage to Jerusalem. I will pray for you and I hope that you can find it in your hearts to pray for me. Goodbye and fare you well, may God be with you and keep you from all harm."

Having said those words the pilgrim tax-collector departed as he had arrived, humbly and on foot. All of us were deeply moved and deeply grateful, and yet even while the figure of our new friend was receding humbly in the distance there appeared almost visible question marks in the air over our heads; and in front of the question marks there were questions: What? Why? How? What had brought about this sudden change of heart in a man who had until now been solidly convinced of the rightness of oppressing Jews? Why did he suddenly feel guilty for what he had done over the years? Or was there something new for him to feel guilty about? I saw again his pale face looking down at me as I lay on the cobblestones. He had come so close on the heels of those peasants with the sow; if only he had arrived a little sooner! Perhaps when he saw what they had done . . . but with that thought still unfinished there came another thought: what if he had brought them to our town? Those had not been peasants anyone had seen before on market days nor had there been any word, in the days before their arrival, of armed peasants moving towards us.

Yes, that was undoubtedly what had happened: the tax-collector had brought the peasants to our town and then, seeing what they had done, was overcome with remorse. And I had been reproaching myself for destroying the temple of that man's privacy with his wife! Ah! if only I could do it again and again and again! My guilt leapt from my shoulders, there surged up in me the virtue, the power, the innocence of the injured party.

But wait. Our God, the God of the Jews, works in strange ways. What if God, looking down at his world in the days before my castration, has noticed Pilgermann. Maybe Satan also, going to and fro in the world and up and down in it, has noticed Pilgermann lusting after the forbidden Gentile woman, has seen him moving through the darkness towards the forbidden garden. "Well," says Satan to God, "there's one of your chosen down there. What do you think he'll do? Perhaps you'd like to make a little bet?"

"Of course he'll climb the ladder," says God. "That's nothing to bet on; any man with balls would climb that ladder, I make them that way to keep the race going. The thing is, will he climb the ladder if God tells him not to?"

"That's nothing to bet on either," says Satan. "Of course if he hears your voice he'll do as you say, nobody is going to say no to YHWH if he hears your proper voice."

"Maybe a Bath Kol," says God.

"Same thing," says Satan. "No bet."

"A thought," says God.

"No visions," says Satan, "just a thought."

"A thought is all it takes," says God. "To a Jew a thought from God is as a thousand brazen trumpets. The thought of God is as the voice of God, and the voice of God will be obeyed."

"So what are you betting?" says Satan.

"Anything you like," says God.

"If you'll excuse my saying so," says Satan, "you could well be leaning on a reed."

"If he's a Jewish reed he'll hear, and if he'll hear he'll obey," says God.

"Will you bet half of the congregation of his town on it?" says Satan.

"Done!" says God.

It sounds like a joke when I tell it that way but it could well be how all those Jews in my town ended up dead that morning. Some may ask how God in his omniscience could be such a fool as to bet on Pilgermann. And how is it that God who is no longer even manifesting himself as He can have a conversation with Satan? Obviously God in his omnipotence can be absent as a world manifestation while being present in the individual or the collective mind as he chooses. As to his foolishness, it is just by this very willingness to lean on a reed that he shows his divinity, his difference from his mortal children: God does not learn from experience, he has never become cynical, he is innocent as only God can be. He approaches every mortal testing with a clean slate, always expecting from each of us the right action that is in us along with the evil impulse. So. God asked for right, I gave him wrong, and the guilt is back on me again.

I am not alone in my guilt, and it is perhaps at this point that I should begin to widen my narrative by bringing in figures from the great world beyond the gates of my town. Now, while the surviving Jews of the town are active with prayer shawls and with phylacteries in which there are no toads and before my onward road unrolling before me bears me away, I must tell of the Pope's dream. The pope I speak of is of course the very famous one who called for soldiers of Christ to save Jerusalem and the Holy Sepulchre from the Turks. His name is Urgent III or Umbral V, it's just on the tip of what used to be my tongue. Unguent, that's it. Unguent VII. How strange must be the life of such a man who happens to stand at a juncture of virtualities, an impending of immensities: perhaps this man is thinking that he would like to have a little more sky over his garden, and he is thinking this thought at a time when the sky is just getting ready to fall; he pulls at a little corner of the sky, the whole thing comes down, and he is known thereafter as the one who called for a skyfall.

Unguent had his practical side; he undoubtedly had political reasons for calling for the rescue of eastern Christendom, but once the thing had got itself moving his feelings went somewhat deeper: Unguent had a dream. I know about the dream because the waves and particles of me drifted into it. Not at the time when he first dreamt it but much later, quite recently. This dream goes on continuously, and in one corner of it, kneeling with clasped hands and looking upward, is Unguent, very small, like a donor in a painting.

This is the dream: in it are Unguent, a sparrow, and the great golden dome of the Church of the World. This dome is seen only in dreams, it is not to be found in ordinary daily life. The sparrow is sitting like a weathercock on a perch at the top of the dome and like a weathercock it is turning in the wind. It is the only sparrow in the world and Unguent knows it. A great golden voice resounds from the dome, it says, "Are not two sparrows sold for a farthing?" Unguent has a sling in one hand and a pebble in the other. He puts the pebble in the sling, he whirls the sling knowing that he cannot possibly hit the sparrow, that nobody can be that accurate with a sling at that distance; at the same time he is weeping because he knows that he is going to hit the sparrow. He looses the pebble, sees it hit the sparrow, sees the sparrow topple from its perch, strike the golden dome, slide down the great golden curve of it and disappear. Unguent is flooded with an inexpressible surge of black eternal grief. This black grief is so vast that all of what we call time is included in it; this black grief is what we call space. Unguent has become a great round universe enclosing all the black space. At this moment it comes to him that it was not a pebble that he slung at the sparrow, it was his gold seal-ring on which was engraved Saint Peter in a boat fishing.

For me the centre of this dream is Unguent whirling the sling and weeping. There I find it impossible not to feel for him.

5

Sometimes I don't know anything at all for large spaces; sometimes I know many things all in the same place. My perceptions are uneven, my understanding patchy but I have action; I go. I can't tell this as a story because it isn't a story; a story is what remains when you leave out most of the action; a story is a coherent sequence of picture cards: *One*: Samson in the vineyards of Timnah; *Two*: the lion comes roaring at Samson; *Three*: Samson tears the lion apart. That's a story but actually the main part of the action may have been that there was a butterfly in Samson's field of vision the whole time. The picture cards don't show the butterfly because if they did they would have to explain it. But you can't explain the butterfly.

See in Unguent's dream the great golden dome of the Church of the World. Hear the golden voice resounding, hear Unguent weeping and the swish of the whirling sling, hear the little thump as the body of the sparrow strikes the golden dome. Now while that's still going on—and it always is going on—hear the crackle of the flames: the Temple is burning, the Temple of Yerushalayim burning on the Ninth of Av, A.D. 70. Flames, flames for the Temple of the Jews. From the starved and defeated Jews goes up a cry like a sheet of flame. Titus runs to the Holy of Holies, with his sword he slashes the curtain, he must see for himself whether there are images or not. Hold the two together: Unguent weeping with the sling; Titus peering into that empty room. Empty for him. And the sword that was dry before he slashed the curtain has blood on it.

> I am the resurrection and the life,
> saith the Lord: he that believeth
> in me, though he were dead, yet shall
> he live: and whosoever liveth and
> believeth in me shall never die.

Well of course the action never stops. Look at me, not famous or anything yet here I am. Is this, then resurrection and life? I suppose so. Although my action continues I don't actually know who I am. By now I am only the energy of an idea; whoever is writing this down puts the name of Pilgermann to the idea, says, "What if?" and hypothesizes virtualities into actualities.

On some plane of virtuality the Temple stands, the Jews of A.D. 70 sing and dance while the scholars among them ponder God's choices. God is a scientist. He knows everything and, having all the time there is, he demonstrates everything including his actual non-presence. Names colour actualities; forget the names Jew and Christian, call them X and Y. Let X be those who said, "The blood of him on us and on the children of us." Let Y be those who sometimes call that to mind when killing X. What is being demonstrated? X is being demonstrated as victim, Y as avenger. X's action as victim shows us something of X's character; Y's action as avenger shows us something of Y's character. Will Y, red of hand with the blood of X through the centuries, ever say, "The blood of them on us and on the children of us"? It's a matter provocative of thought.

A matter provocative of thought, and new approaches continually offer themselves. For example: God being omnipresent is therefore everywhere at once in what is called time; all slaughter of X is therefore in his awareness simultaneously with the birth of him whose death the slaughter avenges. Might it even be possible that God, in his Hebrew aspect writing from right to left, writes first the slaughter of X and later the crucifixion for which they are slaughtered? If we look at it in that way we might see the slaughter as cause and the crucifixion as effect: the sin of the slaughter being heavy on the sinners, there comes the redeemer to offer his innocence for their guilt, the one for the many. As Pontius Pilate washes his hands X is heard to say (by an evangelist writing some four decades later), "The blood of him on us and on the children of us," quite accurately predicting that they, X, will be held accountable for the death of that one who gave his life in expiation of the sins committed and yet to be committed against them, X. The purist may argue that God, being everywhere in time at once, would not have written one thing "before" and another "after" but that argument is well answered when we point out that the Creator characteristically employs a sequential mode of presentation, even going so far as to work six days one after the other and rest on the seventh.

One seeks, as far as possible, reasonable explanations, but here, speaking as waves and particles freely ranging through what is called time, speaking as a witness to what has been done to six million or so X not so very far from here in what is called time, I must say, though lightning strike me as I speak, that there are moments when I begin to wonder whether God really is omniscient; I begin to think that it may be with him even as with some lowly mortal novelist who, having written a tremendous later scene, must perforce go back to insert an earlier one to account for it. Here of course I'm being arrogant, and maybe that's why God keeps writing slaughter scenes: the character gets out of hand; X, having been called the chosen, presumes too much, grows excessively familiar, requires too much of God, becomes like the relative who turns up uninvited on the doorstep to stay for a month. Maybe it's that simple—God is omnipresent but not omnipatient. He sometimes needs to make a little space around himself and Pfft! there go a few hundred or a few million X. Ah! to be an X, even to be the drifting waves and particles of an X long defunct, is to be not only arrogant but more than half mad. No matter.

> I am the resurrection and the life,
> saith the Lord . . .

So presumably there will always be action of one kind or another, some of us moving in flesh and blood, some of us in waves and particles.

I return now to my flesh-and-blood days. Being now strong enough to travel I prepare to go. I sell all my possessions except my books; my books I give away, I keep only my Holy Scriptures. How shall I dress for my pilgrimage? Not as a Jew, certainly. For the first time in my life I can travel incognito, nobody can prove that I'm a Jew. A wildness comes over me, a giddy sense of freedom. At the same time I think: What have I to live for? It's as if I am at once walking on very thin ice and drowning in the black water beneath. The Bath Kol then speaks to me for the second time. The same words: "Thou pilgrim Jew!" These words I accept as an answer. Ah! the scent of Sophia in that daughter of a voice!

I dress as did the tax-collector: I put on a long coarse woollen tunic, woollen hose, stout boots. I have an ash staff shod and tipped with iron; a dagger with a Damascus blade; a good thick woollen cloak with my spare underclothes and surgical instruments in a satchel slung on my back; in my scrip bread and cheese and apples; sausages too, I don't intend to be a kosher pilgrim; fifty gold besants in my purse, three hundred more sewn into a special compartment in my satchel; the same amount in diamonds sewn into the hem of my cloak.

I have no debts to pay; I make my farewells. And Sophia? Our hello and our goodbye will be for all time together in that one time we have been together; such as I am I will not climb that ladder again; I will not intrude upon that altar where I cannot offer. The Shechinah was present in our holy sinning, I know that; nothing can be added to it, nothing can be taken from it. All the same, when I leave the town that night I take my way past the great dark house in the Keinjudenstrasse. I look up at that grouping of the lower stars of the Virgin and those three stars between the Virgin and the Lion, that gesture like a hand flung up: What! will you block the road for ever?

I move on.

6

So. Wherefore is this night distinguished from all other nights? It isn't. The barking of a dog, the cry of an owl, the distant burning of the stars, these are of every night. The departure? Also every night. Every night the departure softly closes the door of the house behind it and puts its foot to the dark road; there is a continual walking into the dark on the road away. Other nights I have lain in my bed; tonight I hear my footsteps on the road, tonight I put my feet into my footsteps and I go.

Night, night, night. The owl is the Jew-bird, I have been told. Because we are called the children of darkness. Why children of darkness? Because we clung to the so-called night of our old belief, we turned away in A.D. 30 from the new dawn of Jesus Christ. And who should know better than I that A.D. 30 is, along with everything else, the present moment. It's all here and now, you can choose whatever line you like to follow through the space that is called time. Virtualities and actualities both. Look, here's a virtual time-line entangled with the others. What does it say on it? ROMANS. Very good, I'll follow it a little way, see where it goes. It looks quite interesting, things are altogether turned round: Rome is governed by Jews, Rome is an outpost of the far-flung Jewish Empire.

Rome with a Jewish governor! Maybe it's Jairus, the father of that

Eleazar who on another time-line commanded the Sicarii against the Romans at Masada. But on this time-line Masada won't be happening, and in A.D. 30 Jairus is Governor of Rome. So they bring before him this fellow Jesus, he's a wandering preacher from Arezzo or some place up in the hills. He's been getting the people all stirred up with his teaching and his miracles, he's been worrying senators and priests and officialdom in general, they don't know what he might bring down on their heads and they think it would be much better for everybody if he could simply be got out of the way. Mind you, he's no Jew, this Jesus; he's an uncircumcised Italian, he's one of theirs but they want no part of him, he's too dangerous. When Jairus says to them, "What then may I do to Jesus called Christ?" the assembled senators, officials, priests, and hangers-on all say, "Let him be crucified." Jairus is willing to let the Romans sort things out in their own way. He washes his hands before the crowd, he says, "Innocent am I from the blood of this man; ye will see to it." And the assembled Romans say, "On his own head let the blood of him be." I listen and I listen but no one says, "The blood of him on us and on the children of us."

The Jewish legionaries scourge this Italian Jesus and they nail him to a cross on the Capitoline Hill. After his death I mingle with the crowd, I listen to what they are saying.

"Lousy Christ-killers!" says the man next to me.

"Who?" I say.

"Who?" says the man. "Those murdering Jews! Who else?"

"I thought perhaps you meant the Romans who told the Jews to do it," I say.

"Never mind that," he says. "Who's governing Rome? Who put Jesus on the cross, eh? Who drove in the nails? It was those lousy Christ-killers, it was those murdering Jews."

I turn to others in the crowd. "Those lousy Jews!" is what they all say. "Those Christ-killers!"

Here I leave the Italian Jesus; I don't know whether or not he rose up and made further appearances.

Night, night, night. Perhaps the only realities are night and departure. Everything else is illusion. Staying anywhere in the light of day is illusion. If there were no Jews they would have to be invented.

Yes, I am a child of the night, a child of departures. The barking of dogs is my signpost, the voices of owls mark my road into the darkness.

Inside my head I have stopped talking, I am quiet. I give myself to the old, old night that waits within me, the old, old night in the old, old wood. In this night the charcoal-burners crouch listening by their hearths while the trees pray, the wind speaks, the leaves rustle like souls departing with the upward-flying sparks. Quiet, quiet, the mist is rising from the river, the bats are writing the names of darkness, the owl is teaching the mice: "Hear, O Israel: the Lord our God, the Lord is one."

I listen for my Bath Kol but I hear only the thumping of my heart and the sound of my footfalls. Why am I on this road through the dark wood? I am afraid. What have I to sustain me? Jesus has appeared to me but what have I to do with Jesus? I think of the tax-collector, perhaps he too has passed through this wood wondering what would sustain him. "Thou Jew!" whispers the Bath Kol suddenly, whispers the Bath Kol in my ear in the dark wood. "My Jew!" whispers the Bath Kol.

In fear I go forward. The quietness of the Bath Kol draws itself together in the dark, becomes a point of silence from which a hugeness grows. In the hugeness I perceive this wood, this rising ground to be the Mount of Venus between the opened thighs of the mother-space that is time. The wood is clamorous with the silence of birds and demons and great wordless mouths full of sharp teeth. When I close my eyes I see the colour of the dark: it is a strong purple-blue, very luminous and vibrating like a crystal. In those crystalline vibrations I seem to see a pale green phosphorescence in the shape of a man hanging head downward by one leg. He is hung by one ankle, his other leg is bent, the bent leg crossing the straight to make an upside-down figure four. His arms are bent to make a triangle on each side, his hands are behind him. He fades with the purple-blue and I hear the low voice of a bell that nods to the walking of an animal. "Thou also," says the rough and broken voice of the bell, so I know it to be the bell hung from the neck of Death's pale horse. I see Death on his horse, all luminous bones that look as if they would clatter but they move in perfect silence. Death beckons and I follow through the dark wood in which he moves like a lantern.

There is a stench of rotting flesh. I am standing in front of a tree; it is an oak tree. In the crystalline vibrations of the purple-blue I see the shapes of oak leaves trembling and I see the man hanging by one leg. He is naked. He has no head, his head has been cut off. Much of the flesh has been eaten off the bones by animals; what remains of the corpse is bloated and writhing with maggots. The swollen male member sticks out stiffly, uncircumcised and tumescent with rot. Death says to me in a low voice, "This is that man who saved your life when they cut off your manhood."

I begin to cry with great wracking sobs that shake my whole body. In this stinking maggoty corpse I see light like a candle in a tabernacle, within the stench I smell a sweetness. Inside the corpse I see Jesus Christ crucified, broken and twisted on his cross that is right-side up in the upside-down body. "No, no!" I cry, "It mustn't be like that! Stop it, thou Jew, stop being crucified! Come down off that cross!" I claw at the rotting corpse, trying to pull the crucified Jesus out of the dead flesh so that I can get him off his cross. Jesus smiles and begins to fade. O God! what will there be now? Only the black spin of the universe, only eternal motion without face or voice when Jesus is gone. "Jesus!" I cry, "Don't go away!"

"Hurry!" whispers the Bath Kol, "Hurry to Jerusalem!"

Hearing that urgent whisper I become terribly, terribly afraid that I shall not be able to get to Jerusalem quickly enough, that no one will get to Jerusalem quickly enough to keep Christ from going away. How do I yearn for the haunting dread and joy of his voice in the echoing dark of the world inside me, the comfort and terror of his presence. How do I long for him the virtuality without limit, him the quickener, him the mystery. Remembering no prayer I howl in my fear and I begin to kick the maggoty corpse. "Jesus!" I cry, "Come thou out of there! Thou Jew! Be with me!" But there is only darkness and rottenness in the corpse, the light that was within it has gone and the sweetness. The corpse is too high for me to kick properly; kicking it I fall down. Lying there in the wet grass under the corpse I feel maggots under my fingers and among them a gold ring, I feel the goldenness of it in the darkness, it must have fallen from the headless man's gullet when I kicked him.

It is of course the tax-collector's wedding ring, the circlet of gold that proclaims his union with Sophia. There has been a day in the life of this headless carcass when it knelt beside that splendid woman, exchanged vows with her, put a ring on her finger, received this ring on its own finger that is now bloated and glistening. I feel in this dead man's headless memory the touch of her hand, the scent of her breath, the softness of her mouth in the marriage kiss. In the memory of this rotting stump of flesh I hear the rustling of silk that slides away to reveal the dazzle of her naked flesh, the imperious and delicate scroll of her law. This golden circlet has dropped with the maggots out of the dead gullet because the pilgrim tax-collector before his death has swallowed his wedding ring, has renewed his covenant with his wife before being murdered and robbed. What am I to do with this ring from the finger of this maggot feast that was the lawful husband of my wife of one night?

Here I must speak of a particular phenomenon and to do so I must refer again to Hieronymus Bosch, that marvel among painters who never fails to notice the butterfly in Samson's field of vision. Bosch is above all the master of what is seen out of the corner of the mind, the essential reality behind the agreed-on appearance of things. Sometimes I manifest myself as an owl painted by Bosch and in this way I fly through the skies of his paintings and observe what is happening. My owl-by-Bosch manifestation is not a superficial one, it follows virtual lines back to his pencil and charcoal sketches and forward from underpainting to varnishing.

A very good example of the accuracy of Bosch's observation of the real behind the apparent is the upper left-hand side of the central panel of the "Temptation of Saint Anthony" triptych. It is not necessary to have seen this painting to recognize immediately what I am about to describe; I refer to it only as a convenient example.

The upper right-hand side of the central panel shows a daytime sky; extraordinary things are to be seen in it but none the less it is an ordinary daytime sky; the left-hand side of the central panel shows the night that is always waiting within the day and the fire that is always waiting within the night. It is in this night within the day, this fire within the night, that what I am going to talk about is to be seen. Bosch gives us burning farms and churches, falling steeples and gibbets, winged creatures (one of them with a ladder) flying through the air, companies of horsemen, sundry peasants and animals, and a woman washing clothes in the river by the light of the burning. One sees at once that this fire has not spread gradually from a small beginning; no, it has from its waiting state exploded into being, has burst the skin of night and time that could no longer contain it. On the right-hand edge of this night with the fire in it, in the space between the night on the left and the day on the right, the illumination is like that of a twentieth-century sports stadium in which a night game is being played; only there does one see light of such preternatural brilliance as that through which the creature (is it an angel or a devil?) with the ladder flies. Bosch could have seen such light and shadow only in a flash of lightning. But the light in this picture, this light between the night on the left and the day on the right, is not the flash that is gone in a fraction of a moment, it is lightning sustained and steady. This shows Bosch's virtuality as well as his virtuosity; I have flown beside that creature with the ladder (always uncertain as to its allegiance; it has a tail but I cannot be sure it's a devil) and I can testify that Bosch experienced that sky by quantum-jumping to the strange brilliance of total Now.

This condition of total Now manifests itself in a number of ways and one of them is that extraordinary lucence that I have just described, that epiphany of light immanent in our being and experienced in certain heightened states as the light-as-bright-as-day within the night, the light as bright as lightning. Now as I lie in the darkness on the wet and maggoty grass under the headless naked body of the tax-collector it is not darkness that I see but the crystalline vibrations of the purple-blue. These vibrations I recognize as being of the spectrum of total Now, that moment without beginning or end in which all other moments are contained.

I have spoken before this of the Now of Sophia's nakedness in my mind but it is not with Sophia nor with Jesus that I have seen the light of total Now. No, the headless naked body of the tax-collector has been the first thing that I have seen in this unearthly light. Now lying on the ground under his hanging body I hear in the purple-blue the multitudinous leaves whispering Now in the rising wind.

The purple-blue withdraws, the sky goes black; the thunder rolls, the lightning crashes and the jagged black doors of the sky jump apart to reveal the purple-blue multiplied, intensified to unbearable brilliance. Now I see that the life of humankind, the life of the world even, fits easily into the space of that lightning-flash. And how many lightning-flashes have there been, will there be. It is with the dead tax-collector that I have seen this and I begin to pray for him. The words come into my mind:

What is man that thou art mindful of him . . .

But no more words come; I don't know to whom or to what I pray. I perceive that what is receiving my prayers is nothing with whom one speaks in words, nothing of whom one asks anything, nothing to whom one tells anything.

PILGERMANN

The thunder crashes where I am, the lightning cleaves the tree to its roots, the stinking maggoty corpse falls on me. I jump up and run through the dark wood, and as I run I hear the bell that had been nodding slowly now ringing fast, I hear the clatter of bones, the neighing of the pale horse, the low chuckle of Gevatter Tod, Goodman Death himself. The Bath Kol hisses wordlessly in my ear; I stop running and walk forward slowly, feeling with my hand in the darkness before me. My hand finds a wire, a man-snare.

I draw my dagger and go on. In the air on my face I feel the approach of something, I step to the right, a blade rips through my left sleeve, someone grunts as with my left arm I get him in a neck-grip and with my right hand I strike with the dagger. "O my God!" cries a man's voice. Again and again I strike, there is gurgling, gasping, coughing, he falls to the ground and is silent. I move back off the path into the trees and wait to see if anyone else is coming. I am not afraid and this surprises me; I think: When I had balls I didn't have this much balls.

While I lean against a tree, panting in the dark of that dire wood and listening to the hooting of an owl, the world is full of domes: golden domes and leaden ones; domes with crosses, domes with crescents, great domes and small ones; broken domes and whole ones; domes in Jerusalem, domes in Constantinople. The biggest dome of course is that of the heavens, one can't in this world have a bigger one than that; but there is a human urge to enclose domes of air as large as possible, to shape lesser heavens in domes of human manufacture. So many domes!

It must be borne in mind that one is part of a vast picture the whole of which can never be seen; in this picture, as in Bosch's "Temptation of Saint Anthony," night and day are side by side—I have seen this myself. The world is two domes put together, the night curves round it, fading into day. Somewhere, while I lean against this tree in the dark, it is already broad day. This little wood of night with its tiny figures, its owls and mice, its rotting corpse, its luminous Death on his pale horse with its nodding bell, its river running beside it humming in the starshine, is a background detail; in the foreground of the central panel flash the gold, the domes, and among them none greater than that one enclosing its vasty heaven of silvery lucence, blue and golden dimness in Constantinople, decked with jewels and hung with lamps and lustres, starred with glimmering suspended candles burning in the air that is smoky with incense: the Church of the Holy Wisdom, Hagia Sophia. This dome that I have never seen has because of its name and the mystery of itself incorporated itself with Sophia in my mind.

Now, however, in my little wood in this little night part of the background, I see nothing of domes, I see only the darkness, hear only the owl, listen for Death, listen for my Bath Kol. I hear nothing for a long time but when I move away from the tree I do hear something; I throw myself to the side, hear a knife smack into the tree. Before I can make a move with my dagger a powerful female voice bellows, "Don't hurt me! I'm only a poor widow woman, I meant no harm!"

I grab her arm; even as she begs for mercy she is pulling with all her might to get the knife out of the tree for another try. "Meant no harm!" I say. "You tried to kill me!"

"Where's the harm in that?" she says, gripping my wrist with her free hand. "You're a gentleman, aren't you? I wasn't doing anything but sending you early to Heaven."

"How do you know you'd be sending me to Heaven?" I say. As I say it she twists suddenly and, still gripping my wrist, bends smoothly and throws me over her shoulder to the ground.

I land heavily on my back but I bring her down with me and in the struggle that follows I end up sitting on top of her. She's a well-built woman and I think longingly of times that will never come again. "Why are we fighting?" she says. "We're all God's children, aren't we? We're all brothers and sisters in Christ."

"Not me," I say. "I'm a Jew."

"So was Christ," she says. "It makes nothing. Are you just going to sit there, aren't you going to have me?"

"I can't," I say. "I'm a eunuch."

"Yet God be thanked!" she says.

"For what?" I say.

"That they didn't cut out your tongue as well!" she says.

Thus, in our little dark wood in our tiny bit of background on the night side of the picture.

The night is far gone when she takes me to a little hut deep in the wood and well off the travelled path. Hanging from a tripod over the embers of a fire is the head of the tax-collector, somewhat shrivelled and smoke-darkened. "God in Heaven!" I say.

"Pontius Pilate," she says. "He's not quite done but he'll certainly fetch twenty pieces of gold when he's ready. You won't get a Pilate like that anywhere for less than fifty; a Pilate like that will make any church rich, it's really unusual."

"Why Pilate?" I say.

"I don't know," she says. "That's just how it is. When I saw him I said, 'Pontius Pilate.'"

"Yes," I say, "but why would a church want the head of Pontius Pilate?"

"How could they not want him?" she says. "What kind of relics have they got? They've got Christ's foreskin and Mary's afterbirth and three hairs from Joseph's arse but what about the man who made Christianity possible? What if Pilate hadn't washed his hands? What if he'd turned Jesus loose and let him go on preaching, what then, hey?"

I ponder this.

"Why were you coming through this wood?" she says.

"I'm going to Jerusalem," I say, suddenly remembering that I'm in a hurry.

"What for?" she says.

"To keep Jesus from going away," I say.

"He's already gone," she says. "If Jesus had stayed buried in Jerusalem he'd have been divided up amongst all the churches in Christendom by now. You must know he was resurrected even if you are a Jew."

"I know," I say. "I've seen him."

"Did you get any relics of him?" she says.

"I'm not joking," I say. "I really saw him."

"How?" she says. "Had you a vision?"

"I don't know," I say. "I wasn't quite myself at the time. I was leaning on him, he was holding me up."

"Did he have a smell?" she says.

I put my mind back to when I was with Jesus. "He smells of stone and sweat and fire," I say.

"Then Jesus he wasn't," she says. "Jesus wouldn't have a smell, that's how you'd know him."

"Everybody has some kind of a smell," I say.

"Well I know it," she says. "That's just why Jesus would be different; he's the Son of God, isn't he? Do you think things came out of him like out of ordinary people when he was on earth? Do you think he made turds?"

I say, "Well, he ate and he drank and he bled so I suppose he must have done the rest of it as well the same as anyone else."

"There you show your heathen ignorance, thou child of darkness," she says. "If Jesus had made turds they'd never have corrupted like ordinary ones and they'd be in little golden jewelled caskets in churches."

This also I ponder.

"Maybe I should come with you," she says. "It isn't safe to travel alone these days."

I look at her. She's not at all a bad-looking woman, she's certainly strong enough to be a helpful companion on the road and she's good company as well. It's true that she's a murderess but in these times that's perfectly acceptable to me as long as she's murdering for me and not against me.

"You owe me something, you know," she says. "After all, it was you that widowed me."

"And it was you that almost made me a relic," I say. I want her to come with me but it would be a kind of holding on; my pilgrimage requires to be a solitary journey; it is a private matter between Jesus and me and the tax-collector. "I can't take you with me," I say, "I've made a vow."

"Of what?" she says. "Chastity?"

"A vow to go alone," I say. "You won't be without a man long, a woman like you. You can find yourself a real man instead of a eunuch."

"Give me that ring on your finger then," she says. "For remembrance."

I look at my hand. There it is, the tax-collector's wedding ring. I put it on her finger.

"If you had your proper parts you'd have taken me," she says. "You wouldn't have been able to do without me once you'd had me."

When she says that it comes to me suddenly that if I had my proper parts I'd not be in this wood, I'd not be on this pilgrimage. If I'd been more careful about what streets I walked in I might still be climbing that ladder while the tax-collector completed his metamorphosis into Pontius Pilate. It occurs to me then that it might have been my castration as much as anything else that started him on his penitential pilgrimage.

The poor maggoty stump of his corpse is still lying on the ground by the lightning-blasted tree while his head hangs from the tripod in the hut. That the head is either assuming or reassuming the identity of Pontius Pilate seems to me a destiny that is not for me to interfere with. To the body, however, I surely owe a burial.

"Why was he hung up like that?" I say.

"I don't know," says the woman. "Udo did that, the one you killed. He didn't like the look of him."

The woman has of course a shovel among the tools and implements of her trade and with it I dig the grave. We put the body into the grave and I hear the words of the Kaddish coming out of my mouth, I see the black Hebrew letters rising in the morning air: *"Yisgaddal v'yiskadash sh'may rabbo* . . . Magnified and sanctified be his great name . . . "

Hearing the words, seeing the black letters rising in the air, I find myself paying attention to what I am saying, paying attention to the first words of the prayer:

> Magnified and sanctified be his great name in the world which he hath created according to his will.

As I say these words I am looking at a spider's web pearled with the morning dew; the morning sunlight shining through it illuminates every droplet and every strand of the web; the spider, like an initial letter, witnesses the prayer and the fresh morning darkness of the oak leaves above it. My partnership with the tax-collector makes continual astonishment in me: it seems to me that never before have I noticed how much detail there is in the world which he hath created according to his will. That this headless stump with the absent face of Pontius Pilate should lie writhing with maggots under the freshly turned earth while each perfectly-formed drop of dew shines on the purposeful strands of the spider's web and the spider itself is a percipient witness and the oak leaves tremble in awareness of the morning air—all this is as the hand of God upon my eyes even though I know that God will never again limit its manifestation to any such thing as might have a hand to lay upon my eyes.

In the mounded earth of the tax-collector's grave I plant his pilgrim staff and to the staff I tie a sprig of oak leaves. I find myself wondering about the boundaries, the limits of the tax-collector. I find myself wondering whether his face might appear on more than one person. I go to the body of the man I killed, Udo. He is lying on his face where he fell. I turn him over and have a good look. It is not the face of the tax-collector.

"You want to remember him?" says the woman.

"I want to remember everything," I say.

"You want to remember me also?" she says.

"You also," I say.

"Here," she says, giving me her knife and taking Udo's knife for herself. "It'll bring you luck."

We stand looking down at Udo. "What about him?" I say. "John the Baptist maybe? The prophet Elijah?"

She shakes her head. "He never was any good for anything but being Udo," she says.

We bury him and I go. As I'm walking away into the morning I turn and look at her. A big strong murdering woman, but alone.

"What's your name?" I say.

"Sophia," she says.

7

In a red and smoky dream of Hell full of cranes and scaffolding and ladders, in a dream of Hell where demons and sinners labour constantly to build their flaming towers, Unguent VII, carrying a hod of bricks, climbs a shaky ladder made of bloody bones torn out of live Jews. Once on his scaffolding of stiff Jewish corpses he picks up his trowel, a Jewish shoulder-blade, and lays yet another course to make the wall of his circular tower one brick higher.

Within the circle of his wall rises the circumcised member of Christ Erect. With bricks and mortar made of the clay of Jews, made of the straw, lime, sand, water, and blood of Jews Unguent is trying to build the tower high enough so that he can put a foreskin made of flayed Jews on the member of Christ. As the tower rises so does the member but Unguent toils faster and faster.

Just as he is about to put the foreskin on and tie it down with a rope made of Jewish entrails the bricks dissolve into a sea of Jewish blood in which Unguent swims for thousands of years until he sees under that everlasting red and smoky night the lighthouse of Christ Lucent. It is an iron lighthouse, it is white-hot and the sea boils round it but Unguent must needs cling to it or drown.

Unguent clings and drowns, clings and drowns in the boiling sea of blood for thousands of years more until the sea recedes to reveal the endless empty desert in which rises the pillar of the Salt Christ. Not until Unguent licks the salt pillar down to the ground will the rain fall to slake his thirst. When the rain falls it is the blood of Jews. That is as far as Unguent has got in this dream in all the times he has dreamt it. Like the dream of Unguent related earlier this one goes on all the time and Unguent the donor, modestly small, kneels praying in a corner of it.

The fabric of the world being made as much of dreams and visions as it is of earth and stone, these virtual dreams of Unguent and these actual visions of Bosch centuries after my time are as real as anything else in my pilgrimage: they are as real as the castle on the mountain, as real as the gibbet at the crossroads where the crows flap cawing from the hanged men as I pass, as real as the wolves of the forest that drift like grey ghosts among the trees; the village dogs that guard the dust of the street and bark as I pass; the women at the well; the men outside the inn; the pigeons circling the pantiled roofs; the peasants in the fields; the signpost under a grey sky on the heath. By this same signpost will pass Bosch's gaunt wayfarer of the "Haywagon" triptych, will pass Schubert's heartbroken young winter traveller; there is only one road for all.

Like the crows flapping up from the hanged men my thoughts scatter and like the crows they return to what they were feeding on. This is a good comparison because for the crows there is life to be got from death and for me there is the life of my present state arising from the death of my past one. If I had my proper parts I'd not be on this road; that's a simple truth, not to be argued with. Had I my proper parts I'd still be prescribing for my patients or sitting cross-legged with my cloth and my needle, plying my trade and in my free hours finding what pleasure I could in life. Climbing that ladder is what I'd be doing as often as I had the chance. But how long could that have continued, my garden of Eden? Even God had to put Adam and Eve on the road before he could get on with the story. Thinking, thinking, and I can't think how I could have gone on living without coming on this pilgrimage, without being as I am being now. When I had my proper parts I must have been blind and deaf, the world had not come alive for me, I had never talked with Christ, had never put my feet into the footsteps of my road away, had never, alone in a dark wood, seen the light of Now. So, Pilgermann, let your heart have balls, and on to Jerusalem.

Under the sun, under the rain I trudged on. On the bank of the river I saw a man hanging a bear from a tree. Not bear meat but a whole live bear. He was hanging it with a rope passed over a branch and a hangman's noose on the end of it the same as if he were hanging a man. A big brown bear and it was coughing and moaning as its own weight slowly strangled it. The man was lean and ragged, his beard was full of twigs and leaves and rubbish, it looked as if it might have birds nesting in it. As he braced himself with his feet against the trunk of the tree and pulled on the rope he cried, "My God, my God, why hast thou forsaken me!"

Before I could think what I was doing I had cut the rope with the knife given me by the second Sophia. The bear crashed to the ground and lay there without moving. The man turned on me in a fury. "You murdering fool!" he screamed, "You've killed God!"

I said, "I didn't mean to kill him."

"But you *have* killed him!" he said. "God was everything to me, he was big and strong and shaggy, he was like a bear."

"He *was* a bear," I said.

"Of course he was," said the man. "God can be whatever he likes, completely and divinely; he always used to find me honey trees. And you've killed him, you've killed God." There were a bow and arrows and a hunter's pouch lying on the ground; he picked up the bow and fitted an arrow to the string, aiming it at me. At this moment the bear stood up on his hind legs. He began to low and grunt, making gestures with his paws like a man making a speech.

"Lies!" shouted the man. "Lies, lies, all lies!" He aimed his arrow at the bear.

The bear made a few more remarks; he put one paw over his heart and shook his head sadly, then he made a gesture clearly expressing that everything was over between him and the man. What a wonderful bear that was! How I wished that I could have him for a friend, what a travelling companion he would be—he clearly had a profound understanding and was one of those people who know when to talk and when to be quiet. While I was thinking this he dropped on to all fours and hurried off towards the trees. The man swung round to loose his arrow, I threw out my hand to knock him off his aim but there fell across my arm something as hard and heavy as an iron bar, a blackness came in front of my eyes and I fell down.

When I came to myself the bear, shot full of arrows, was lying dead and the man was sitting on the ground throwing dirt on his own head and crying, "O my God, my God, why hast thou forsaken me!"

I said, "Don't be such a fool, he hasn't forsaken you—you've killed him."

He said, "I killed him because he forsook me."

I said, "How did he forsake you?"

He said, "He wouldn't show me any more honey trees." He sat there rocking to and fro in his grief. It was that sort of a hot still day when one seems particularly to hear the buzzing of flies. I left him to his lamentations and went on my way.

I was thinking about the bear, how good it would have been to have him with me, how I should have heard the padding of his feet and seen out of the corner of my eye his shaggy brown back rocking along beside me through the long miles. Big and strong he was too, a match for half a dozen men in a fight; one would feel easy anywhere with such a friend. Perhaps he might even have danced a little now and then for our supper and a night's lodging. Pilgermann and his bear would have become famous on the pilgrim road.

There was a low chuckle in my ear and a hard hand clapped me on the shoulder in great good fellowship. It was that bony personage who had been riding his horse in the wood where the headless body of the tax-collector was hanging from the tree. This time he was on foot; he was dressed as a monk and like me he carried a pilgrim's staff. It was very shadowy under his hood, one couldn't properly say that there were eyes in the eye-holes of his skull-face but there was definitely a look fixed upon me; it was that peculiarly attentive sidelong look seen in self-portraits.

"Am I a mirror in which you see yourself?" I said.

"Everybody is," he said. "I am so infinitely varied that I never tire of myself. Mortals looking in a mirror see only me but I see all the faces that ever were and I love myself in all of them."

"You think well of yourself!" I said.

He hugged himself in a transport of self-delight. "When I say, 'Sleep with me!' nobody says no," he said. "Kings and queens, I have them all, no inch of them is forbidden to me; nuns and popes, ah! There's good loving! I am the world's great lover, that's a simple fact though I say it myself. Well, there's no need for me to blow my own trumpet—you'll see when you sleep with me."

He kept turning his face to me as he spoke, and his breath did not reek of corruption as one might suppose: it was like the morning wind by the sea. "Call me Bruder Pförtner," he said, "it's a name I fancy: Brother Gatekeeper. It has a kind of monastic humility but at the same time it goes with a swing."

"Bruder Pförtner," I said. I thought about the gates he kept.

"You've no idea," he said. "No idea at all." He made a graceful gesture and there opened upon my vision the brilliant lucent purple-blue of the crystalline vibrations of Now. His arm swept back, the gate was closed, the day seemed dark. We went on a little way in silence. His face was looking straight ahead and I saw only his cowl moving companionably beside me. "You know why I was chuckling when I first appeared to you?" he said.

"Why?" I said.

"I was chuckling at your bear thoughts," he said. "Really, you're no better than that other fellow, you know. Had the bear been your friend you'd not have been content to let him be, you'd have had him dancing for your supper, and you with all that money on you. That's how people are: they're trade-minded, they can't let anything be simply what it is. It was I that knocked your arm down when you tried to stop that fellow from shooting the bear."

"Why?" I said.

"That bear was finished," he said. "He had nothing left to live with. Did you understand what he was saying when he made his little speech?"

"No," I said.

"This is what he said to that man," said Bruder Pförtner: " 'I never wanted to be anything but a friend to you. The only use I wanted to make of you was to be with you sometimes; nothing more than that, and I didn't want any use to be made of me more than that. The first time I gave you honey it was just because honey was there, so we both had some of it, sharing like friends. But then you had to boast to everyone that you had a bear who found honey for you and I had to boast to everyone that I had a man who followed me to where the honey was. Then I showed you where the silence was and you thought I was God and I let you think it. We corrupted each other and so there had to be an end to it. Now I don't think I can even find the silence for myself, I don't think I even know how to be simply myself any more, and I want to go away and not be with anybody.' That's what the bear said just before the man shot him."

"Poor fellow," I said.

"People can't let anything be," said Bruder Pförtner. "They can't even let me be."

"What do you mean?" I said.

"This very moment while we're talking," he said, "you're feeling more and more friendly towards me. Very soon you'll be wanting to call me *thou*; next thing you'll be wanting me to dance for your supper. Have no fear, I'll dance for you; but not yet, not yet a little while. You mustn't presume on this slight acquaintance just because I said you were going to sleep with me, you mustn't become too familiar. Friendly, yes; but not too familiar." With that he disappeared.

I thought about Bruder Pförtner a little. I thought him visible again, trudging beside me companionably. "Why am I here?" he said.

"I just want you to know how things stand between us," I said. "I have no control over your actions but I am master of your appearances to me; my perception is the substance of your apparition, so you too must mind your manners if you want to go on being seen by me."

Bruder Pförtner chuckled. Quite a remarkable sound, his chuckle: bony and brutish. "Anything you like," he said, and disappeared again. The manner of his chuckling made me unsure that I was master of his appearances to me; I thought him visible again but he did not appear, only his bony chuckle returned to jog along with me.

Ahead of me I heard the thin and straggling voices of children singing:

> Christ Jesus sweet,
> Guide thou our feet,
> Our light in darkness be;
> Make straight the way
> By night, by day
> That brings us, Lord, to thee.

The day, as I have said, was hot and still. Behind me in that heat and stillness were the dead bear and the crying man; farther back in the little dark wood in a shallow grave rotted the maggoty headless corpse of the tax-collector while the second Sophia prepared his head for the role of Pontius Pilate; in another grave lay the relic-gatherer whose life I had gathered up; and ahead of me the children sang with silvery voices in the dust of the dry road.

The humps and hollows of the landscape tend always towards the human: on this day the horizontal head of Christ was clearly visible in woods and fields and rocky outcrops. It was the head of the dead Christ brought down from the cross, his eyes closed, his passion complete. I sensed that it was important not to tilt my own head to the horizontal the better to see his face; while I had no wish to make with the vertical of my head and the horizontal of his a cross, neither could I in good conscience avoid it.

> Nor mountains steep
> Nor waters deep
> Turn back the faithful soul;
> Nor fire nor sword,
> Christ Jesus Lord,
> Jerusalem our goal.

So feeble, so wan those voices, like a candle flame in the sunlight. The dry and dusty road was ascending the brow of the horizontal head of Christ; the children would not be in sight until I reached the top of the hill. Long and long I toiled up the brow of Christ in the heat and the stillness of the day. When I reached the top I saw the children. They were moving very slowly in the glimmering heat and in the dust that rose up from their going. Peasant boys and girls they were, between twenty and thirty of them, the oldest of them twelve or thirteen but most of them younger, all of them thin and ragged, carrying their pitiful little bundles and singing thinly as they walked in the dry and dusty road.

As I watched them I heard again that bony and brutish chuckle: not only Bruder Pförtner but a whole company of him, a bony mob of him came trotting past me throwing off their monks' robes and showing the tattered parchment of their skins stretched taut over their bones. All of them had great long bony members wagging erect before them so that it was difficult for them to run; all of them were giggling and chuckling as they stretched out their bony hands towards the children. When they reached the children they pushed them down on to their hands and knees in the dusty road, mounted them like dogs and coupled with them, grunting in their ardour, screaming in their orgasms. The children crept forward slowly on their hands and knees, singing as they were violated:

> Christ Jesus mild,
> Sweet Mary's child
> That hung upon the tree,
> Thy cross we bear,
> Thy death we share,
> To rise again with thee.

When the skeletons had sated their lust they fell away from the children and lay sighing and snoring in the road with limbs outflung. The children, their hands and knees bloody, stood up again and trudged on.

> Of the Rock that begot thee thou art unmindful,
> and hast forgotten God that formed thee.

This has come into my mind as I ascend the stone brow, the horizontal broken rock of Christ who is of the broken Rock of God, the Rock that was shattered by the unfaith of its people, the Rock that was drained of its strength by the lust for the seen and by the whoring after no-gods. I remember how our old Rabbi has said that only once in the Holy Scriptures is the unpronounceable tetragrammation of God written with a small *yod*, and it is here in Deuteronomy that it is written so to show God's loss of strength from Yeshurun's disrespect:

> But Yeshurun grew fat, and kicked:
> thou art grown fat, thou art become thick,
> thou art covered with fatness;
> then he forsook God who made him,
> and lightly esteemed the Rock of his salvation.
> They provoked him to jealousy with strange gods,
> with abominations they provoked him to anger.
> They sacrificed to powerless spirits;
> to gods whom they knew not,
> to new gods that came newly up,
> whom your fathers feared not.

PILGERMANN

Of the Rock that begot thee thou art unmindful,
and hast forgotten God that formed thee.

What is called time passes and yet all time is present; one has only to
turn one's head to see the happening of all things: there I am going up the
ladder while Satan smiles and God perhaps weeps. God being omnipotent
has the power, even while apparently absent, to manifest the idea of a
weeping God. But God as It, God without personification—can it truly be
that this God can be lessened and made weak by any human action, by
my disrespect, by my adultery? I don't know, I am full of doubt and worry
as I ascend the broken rock of the horizontal brow of Christ.

When one is a child, when one is young, when one has not yet reached
the age of recognition, one thinks that the world is strong, that the
strength of God is endless and unchanging. But after the thing has happened—whatever that thing might be—that brings recognition, then one
knows irrevocably how very fragile is the world, how very, very fragile; it
is like one of those ideas that one has in dreams: so clear and so self-ex-
plaining are they that we make no special effort to remember. Then of
course they vanish as we wake and there is nothing there but the awareness that something very clear has altogether vanished.

And God, we think that because he is all-powerful the amount of
available power is always the same; but it changes, it wavers, it shifts from
the kinetic to the potential, varying with the action of the universe, the
action of the world, the action of the individual. Earlier I have had the
thought of many mysterious unseen fragile temples in which God used to
dwell among us; now I perceive that these temples are each of us however
unreliable, each of us for good or ill, each of us as the total of our actions
and our being. It is because of such as I that God is absent and Christ
horizontal; it is because of such as I that these children are raped by skeletons on the road to Jerusalem.

I hurry to catch up with the children, I kick snoring skeletons out of
my way, I trample their mouldy bones and filthy parchment skins, I tread
on their great phalli and their ponderous testicles. They don't care, they
grunt and sigh and roll over in their sleep.

The children with bloody hands and knees trudge on. They are so
very thin, their arms and legs are like sticks, their cheeks are hollow, their
eyes sunken, truly they seem Death's own children as they sing:

Our faith our shield,
Thy word we wield
Of love and Christian pity.
The seas will part
That pure in heart
May reach Thy golden city.

"Brother pilgrim!" cry the children when they see me, "Brother pilgrim! Have you anything to eat?" I give them all the food I have, sausage and bread; it isn't very much for so many. A boy who seems to be the leader thanks me and divides it with great precision. There is no more than a mouthful for everyone, they chew it slowly and with great care.

"Have you nothing more?" says the boy. "You can have, you know, any one of us you like."

"Look at your bloody hands, your bloody knees!" I cry. "Look where your clothes are torn! You've just now been had by skeletons!"

The boy looks at his hands, his knees. "It's a rough road," he says. "One stumbles."

"Selling yourselves for food," I say, "is that how you've been making your way to Jerusalem?"

"We beg, we steal, we sell what we have to sell," says the boy. "God wills it."

"How can God will such a thing as that?" I say.

"If God wills that we should be on the road to Jerusalem then He wills the rest of it as well," says the boy. "Dead people can't walk to Jerusalem, and one must eat to live."

"Do you know where Jerusalem is?" I say to him. "Do you know how far it is to Jerusalem?"

The boy turns his face towards me and looks at me for a moment without saying anything. Looking at me out of his eyes I see the lion-eyes of Christ, and I am frightened. I hold my head because I know that when he speaks his voice will be a woodwind voice that comes from inside my head and resonates there. "Jerusalem will be wherever we are when we come to the end."

I look away, ashamed. I look down at the tawny dusty road. I feel as I did when as a child I was ill and did not go to my lessons. Lying in my bed I heard the voices of the other children as they passed my window. Over those voices I now hear the singing of these Christian children:

> Christ Jesus sweet,
> Guide thou our feet,
> Our light in darkness be.
> Make straight the way
> By night, by day,
> That brings us, Lord, to thee.

I walk on quickly, the children are left behind, the voices fade away. The road continues on high ground; below me I see peasants making hay, their voices float up to me singing and talking. Beyond them is a wood, a hamlet, houses, a church, a village green, a craggy height, the river winding in the distance. Men and women pass me with baskets of fruit and vegetables on their heads. For them this road does not go to Jerusalem, it goes to farm and cottage, to ease at the day's end, the evening meal and a good night's sleep, nothing required the next day but the next day's work in the same sure place. See the man on top of the haywain: for him at this moment the world is soft and fragrant. Perhaps not. Perhaps in his soul he walks barefoot on sharp stones.

"Rubbish," says Bruder Pförtner at my elbow. "Do you see that woman with the rake, the one that's bending over? In his soul he's lifting her skirt and he's giving it to her, Uh! Uh! Uh! Uh!" Pförtner is grunting and he's thrusting with his great bony pimmel as he thinks about what he thinks the peasant is thinking about.

"That's not in his soul," I say. "That's in his mind."

"Don't talk nonsense," he says, "that man hasn't got a mind, he's perfectly healthy; minds are a sickness. All he's got is a soul and his soul is in his scrotum."

"Filthy brute," I say. "Is that all you think of?"

"It's my whole purpose in life," he says. "I like to do it with thin girls best, you can get closer to them. Ah! I'm getting excited thinking about it!" His monstrous member is stiff again, he strokes it lovingly.

"Those children you've just done it with, they'll die now, won't they?" I say.

"My seed is in them," he says. "They'll give birth when the death in them comes full term." He begins to sing and dance, stamping his bony feet and raising the dust on the dry road:

> "Golden, golden, ring the bell,
> Go to Heaven, go to Hell,
> Go on land and go on sea,
> Go with Jesus, come with me."

"You're so full of jokes and fun," I say. "What happened to your more dignified manifestation as Goodman Death riding slowly on your pale horse with the slowly ringing bell?"

"That's for strangers," he says. "You're not a stranger now. I'll see you at the inn." And he's gone again.

Through the long day I walk my road to Jerusalem while the world on both sides of me makes hay, drinks beer, mends thatch, shoes horses, draws water, carries burdens, crows from its dunghill, grunts in its sty, grazes on its hillside. With evening I arrive at an inn, The Black Boar. In the inn yard are horses, carts, wagons, sledges, billhooks, scythes, rakes, pitchforks, dogs, peasants, pilgrims, and a sow wearing a red cross.

The sow is looking at me from under her blonde eyelashes. She turns her snout towards me and begins to grunt urgently, perhaps ecstatically. I say ecstatically because I note that she has been mounted by the ever-potent Bruder Pförtner who is himself grunting ardently as he makes love to her. "Uh! Uh! Uh! Uh!" grunts Bruder Pförtner. "Hoogh! Hoogh! Hoogh! Hoogh!" grunts the sow. The sow is on one end of a rope; on the other end is that peasant who said, "Cut it off and make a Christian of him." He is looking at me narrowly as if trying to remember where he has seen me before.

I kneel beside the sow listening attentively to her grunts. "Quick!" I say to the peasant, "Get a basin!"

"What for?" he says.

"To catch the blood," I say as I cut the sow's throat. Her blood spurts out and in the same moment with her dying squeal I hear Bruder Pförtner screaming as he comes. The peasant grabs a billhook but before he can take a step towards me Bruder Pförtner, his great bony pimmel still erect, has leapt upon him and is enjoying him. The peasant utters a choked cry, gives birth to his death immediately, and falls on his face on the ground.

I am left standing there with the knife of the second Sophia in my hand and in my mind the thought: Jerusalem is wherever I am when the end comes. The other peasants are looking from the dead man to me and back again. They make the sign one makes against the evil eye. The pilgrims as well are looking at the dead man and looking at me.

I look at them from one to the next. I look at them all. In the air in front of me I draw the two mingled triangles of a six-pointed star. I don't know why I do this, it simply comes to me to do it. They look at what I have drawn in the air, I wait for them to take up their knives, billhooks, scythes, rakes, pitchforks and staves and kill me. No one moves, no one says a word.

"You saw me listening to the sow," I say. "She was confessing to me, she was telling me her last will and testament. She was telling me of her many sins, how she repented of them; she had no wish to go on living. She leaves her corporeal being, her bacon, her ribs, her chops, her crackling, all of her sweet flesh and nourishing juices to you her countrymen and to you her fellow pilgrims on the road to Jerusalem, that golden city that is at the same time in the Holy Land far away and in the heart of each of us. May Jesus Christ how savoury be with you and keep you from all harm."

I let my eyes pass over all of them. I do not expect to leave this place alive. No one moves, no one says a word. Stepping very carefully, as if I am walking on crystal goblets, I go out of the inn yard and back to the road.

8

"Jesus Christ how savoury"! Almost I said, "Jesus Christ our Saviour," almost those words leapt out of my mouth. Strange, how eager those words are to be said, and stranger still how busy is the idea of being saved. As a boy I was told that there is a big book in which every deed is recorded; on the Day of Judgment one is shown this record, must examine it carefully and sign it. I was told that the righteous go to Gan Eden and the wicked to Gehinnom but even as a child I never believed it; even as a child I sensed that the arrangement of one place for the good souls and another place for the bad ones was simply not such a thing as would happen in a universe of sun and moon and stars, of night and day and the wheel of the seasons. God said a great many things in the time when it was manifesting itself as YHWH; some of them may well have been misunderstood or written down wrong. Or it may be that he put things in a very simple and vivid way so as not to require too much of the general understanding. Space and time have in them no Gan Eden and Gehinnom, no Heaven and Hell as what could be called places, and I cannot believe that anyone can now take seriously the idea of a soul that is simply righteous or wicked. Even the souls of such creatures as Torquemada and Hitler are not simply wicked although the weight of their actions is mostly in the gehinnom of things—I use the word as one might say right or left, up or down, plus or minus. It is in the rotation of eden and gehinnom that we feel the cosmic dance that is the motion of the universe, and in the play of these energies come punishment and reward. My punishment is that such evil as I have done has tuned me to the gehinnom frequency where I vibrate to the memories of all who have done evil; I share their being as well as their memories, and what I remember I remember as a doer re-members. My reward for being no worse than I am is that I remember no more than I do.

And what is this *I* that speaks now? Only a fiction, a name of conven-ience, a *poste restante* for whatever addresses itself to the persistence of memory and the force of idea: there is no Pilgermann distinct from any-thing else; why should there be? It is difficult for me now to understand why anyone should want a continuance of identity in a life after death. All those ancient mouldering kings entombed with their murdered wives, with their servants and soldiers and horses, with their weapons and chariots, their stone bread, their stony dregs of long-departed wine! Imagine the burial of a mouse with weapons, an ant with concubines! The arrogance, the greed of it! Even now the space all round me is thick with the fat glob-ules of undissolved souls blinking and bleeping their greed for more! more! until the signals fade to silence and the lights go dark. More indeed! Not only human souls—the dying Earth itself moans like a stunned ox; the deeps of space are clamorous with its panting, its unwillingness to be absorbed into the allness from which it came. I have lost my humanity, I have been waves and particles too long to feel what humans feel. And yet, and yet . . . I remember with something like a pang how I wanted God to come back, how I wanted Jesus not to go away.

I am on the road again. Life is so strange! It is nothing I have ever been able to take for granted, just simply being alive with the world in front of my eyes and looking out through those eyes at the world. And when the eyes are closed, the colours, the patterns, the flashes and flickers; pictures even. How can it be that pictures can be seen with the eyes closed? Dreams! Maybe there were dreams before there was anything else; maybe there were dreams before there were people to dream them. Maybe dream life is the real living and our waking life is just the necessary exercising of our bodily functions in the time between dreams.

I am on the road again, trying to remember the last thing Jesus said to me. "From me came the seed that gave me life," he said.

He may be right. Look at what he does with stone, it sets time at naught completely; give him any stone and any stonecarver whatever and he can make it happen, he can make his living and his dying be Now, for ever this very moment. He has no need of flesh and blood, he can live in stone as others live in flesh and blood. Partly I understand it: what one thinks of as the hardness of stone is actually its memory, its retention, its capability of holding images and thoughts. That's why Christ has always been so easy with stone, he comes to it so willingly because it goes with him so willingly; he likes to be long in stone, short in stone, likes to live out his story large and small in shapes of stone. Christ comes for any stonecarver who calls him with his chisel, calls him with his iron to the stone. He has no vanity, does not push himself forward, he takes his place modestly with the other figures, acting out his story as bidden. Because of this the stone is eager to please him, it's always thinking of new little touches that will put something more into the story. In my drift through what is called time I have my favourites here and there, and as often as not they are after my own time. What an odd thing to say: my own time! That time during which I lived is what I mean, and that sounds equally odd because I have always been somewhere in one form or another; precision with words is impossible.

But I wanted to say something about a particular stone Christ-story, the one in Naumburg Cathedral in the west rood-loft. I believe that it was done in the twelfth or thirteenth century, I don't know who the sculptor was. There are seven scenes in it: the first is the Last Supper, perhaps it is that moment when Christ is saying, in the Gospel of Mark, "Take ye; this is the body of me." As Christ speaks these stone words—they are not cut into the stone but they are there in the air of that stone scene—he puts into the mouth of Judas a piece of bread while Judas still dips with his own hand in the dish. The stone and the carver are good with this scene as they are throughout: as Christ with his right hand puts the bread into the mouth of Judas he draws back with his left hand his right sleeve to keep it out of the gravy and in this way the eye is led from the bread to the hand, wrist, and arm of Christ that extend the bread, showing the oneness of the bread with the self of him who gives it. Or it may be—and I rather believe it is—that the moment shown is that one in the Gospel of

PILGERMANN

John when Jesus, having been asked who will be the betrayer, answers, "That one it is to whom I shall dip the morsel and shall give him." And John goes on to say, "And after the morsel then entered into that one Satan." Yes, that for me is what is happening in that stone moment. Because all eucharists are double—this is what I know now, this is why I am easy now between the grinding of eden and gehinnom in the mill of the universe. When God was a he he never told us everything; where is it written that he told us all there was to tell? Nowhere. Nor did Jesus tell us everything. He never told—did he, is it written somewhere? I think not—that all eucharists are double; but they are. "Take ye; this is the body of me." "And after the morsel then entered into that one Satan."

What chance has Judas? He eats the bread of Christ as would a dog given a crust by his master, and with the bread comes Satan. There sits Christ, stolid and stocky in the Naumburg stone, solid as the stone itself. There is no fault to be found in him, he will betray no one. Ay! Judas, Adam and Eve, the Jews—what was to be expected of them? What did God as He, God as Logos, God as Christ, want of any or all of them? How were Adam and Eve to resist the fruit that God had created irresistible? How were the Jews to be other than imperfect and deviant from the will of that same God who created them imperfect and deviant from his will? How were they not to make a golden calf in the shadow of that holy, that terrifying and untouchable mountain of the Law? How was Judas not to betray Jesus after Satan had entered him in that double eucharist? Jesus was the one who could withstand Satan, he was the strong one; he required of Judas that betrayal that Judas, powerless to do otherwise, already a dead man and Satan-entered, enacted as his necessary part of the story.

What are we but creatures of the God who made us as we are? Either God is omnipotent, omniscient, and omnipresent or he isn't. If he isn't then he must take his chance with the rest of us and not demand special treatment; if he *is* all-powerful, all-knowing, and everywhere-present then he has nothing to complain of except that the universe would come to a halt without the dynamic asymmetry of Adam and Eve's original sin, of the Jews' whoring after false gods, of Judas's betrayal of Jesus, of Pilgermann's adultery and every other act of wrongdoing since the human race first took upon itself the task of maintaining universal spin and motion according to the will of God. Try to conceive of things as other than they are—it can't be done. While humankind exists there can only be the rotation of God's impossible requirements and humankind's repeated failures. Indeed, what *is* God but an impossible requirement? Any possible requirement would not be God.

So. Stone Judas, fed by his stone master, eats his stone bread while dipping his hand into the stone meats of the last supper. The stone, friend and brother to Christ and stonecarver and all of us alike, remembers this because the iron has told it to remember and it obeys.

In the next scene of the Naumburg stone story Judas gets his thirty pieces of silver from the high priest. Here we see the full power of that stone memory, that stone retention. This stone knows what it knows: Judas, his face that of a stunned brute, is not his own master, and this is not forgotten by the stone. But if Judas is thus sold even as he sells Jesus, what of this high priest through whose listless fingers slide the clinking silver coins into the fold of the cloak Judas holds out to catch them. Is this Caiaphas? It must be he. And what is in his face, this face that seems of all of them to be the most thoughtfully observed? Does Caiaphas choose to be Caiaphas? Why does he look out at us like this from the stone? Such a tired face. "There is left to me only this!" says that face.

Why? Why only this? What words of Caiaphas does John give us, what has Caiaphas to say of Jesus? "If we leave him thus, all men will believe in him, and will come the Romans and will take away both the place and the nation." What else does Caiaphas say to the council of the chief priests and the Pharisees? "Ye know not anything, nor reckon that it is expedient for us that one man should die for the people and not all the nation perish." And this, John tells us, Caiaphas "from himself he said not, but being high priest of that year he prophesied that Jesus was about to die for the nation, and not for the nation only, but that the children of God having been scattered he might gather into one. From that day therefore they took counsel that they might kill him."

So. Judas is entered by Satan, Caiaphas is doomed by reason and prophecy. How much freedom of choice has Caiaphas? He, like the rest of us, is free within the limits of his understanding. As I have said before, a story is what remains when you leave out most of the action. Vulgar tradition, like a painter who does not know how to render shadows, has filled in the sparseness of the Gospels with a sugary muck that makes the empty spaces dark and sticky. In the coloured picture cards in which Jesus now lives he and his twelve disciples move softly in their marzipan robes but the Jesus I saw was not a soft mover, and Caiaphas's concern indicates that Jesus's following was such as could well have moved Rome to take away both place and nation from the Jews.

Thus Caiaphas, acting for the good of his people, ensures their everlasting infamy. God as He, God as It has done this, has shown in this the never-to-be-understood mystery of his action in which Judas must betray Jesus and Caiaphas his people. All we can know is that there must be betrayal. Is not life betrayed by death? Is not up betrayed by down? Is not space-time betrayed by that recurrent contraction to the singularity from which it must burst anew? The Jesusness of Jesus cannot live without the Judasness of Judas, the Caiaphasness of Caiaphas, the Pilateness of Pilate. Ponderous wheel!

In the next scene Judas kisses Jesus while Peter with a sword cuts off the ear of the high priest's servant. Christ stares out in perpetual innocence from the stone while the guilty betrayer, submissive to the forces moving him, presses close like a dog to his master. In the Gospel of Matthew Jesus says to Judas, "Comrade, do that on what thou art here." In Mark he says nothing. In Luke he says, "Judas, with a kiss the Son of man betrayest thou?" In John again he says nothing. There it is: the Gospels say what they say and the stone remembers what it is told. Very good. Who is this Pilgermann, this drifting wave-and-particle vestige of a castrated Jew, who is this Pilgermann to have an opinion on the matter? From where I am now I see the universe isotropically receding in all directions. I am, equally with all other waves and particles, its centre. From that centre I speak as I find, and I find that I have questions for which neither the Gospels nor the Holy Scriptures offer answers. Theologians and fathers of the Church cannot confound me, they have no firmer ground on which to stand than I. So. Here is Christ, the one who makes the blind see, makes the crippled walk; here is Christ, the one who raises the dead, walks on the water, feeds the thousands with his loaves and fishes. Christ the Word made flesh, Christ the Son of God. And what says he to this mortal lump, this uncorrected sinner, this strayed sheep and Satan-entered? What says Christ, the Good Shepherd? "Judas, with a kiss the Son of man betrayest thou? Comrade, do that on what thou art here." Because Christ will have, must have his betrayal. "Comrade, do that on what thou art here." Do it that the cosmos may uncoil its onward energy, that the wheel may go on turning: night and day, plus and minus, eden and gehinnom, matter and anti-matter, Jesus and Judas.

Now I wonder, yes I wonder, on whom is it to forgive whom? Who is the sacrifice, the one for the many, the ransom, the redeemer? Who is to represent us all? Is it Jesus the betrayed, the crucified, or is it Judas the betrayer and his own hangman? Or is it the binary entity of Jesus/Judas alternating and inseparable? How the thunder rolls when certain words are put together! When certain mysteries are named! Not to be understood, not to be attempted even! Roll, thou eden and gehinnom of the rolling universe! Hurry on, thou road to Jerusalem, thou road returning! A rushing and a plodding, a palimpsest of footsteps rising from the ground under my feet up into the air high over my head so that I feel myself to be drowning in the going and the ghosts of going of those footsteps, footsteps upon footsteps and ghosts upon ghosts, a madness of going that moves both ways on this road. This road is the treadmill on which we walk day into night and night into day, eden into gehinnom into eden, Jesus into Judas into Jesus.

Jesus does not tell us everything but he has much to show us. In the next scene of the Naumburg stone story we see Peter on the left-hand slant of the roof of the porch of the rood-screen doorway. He is turning away from the high priest's maidservant who questions him; he is making one of the three denials he will make before the cock crows. Ah! the genius of that Naumburg stone, that Naumburg master! Look at the face of that maidservant, the eternal directness of the soul behind the stone eyes that are turned away from Peter as she looks towards what is not carved in the stone, towards Jesus brought before the high priest, chief priests, elders and scribes. She looks away from Peter but she stretches out her left hand, it is almost touching Peter's shoulder as she says, "And thou with the Nazarene wast — Jesus." Peter says, "Neither I know nor understand what thou sayest." What is meant by this triple denial of Christ? Is not each part of the Holy Trinity being denied once in it? As if Christ is telling us: "Look at this mortal lump, this thrice-denier; yet will he be my rock." Because mortal lumps are all humanity can offer, and if rocks are needed these must suffice. Having only mortal lumps to choose from, Christ will use this one for a betrayer, that one for a rock. Just as his father before him used this one to receive the tablets of the Law, that one to make a golden calf. Matter and anti-matter, yes and no of the treadmill that walks the rolling earth from night to day. Here stands in the stone Peter the rock in baffled recognition of what he is and what he is not in the numbers of eden and gehinnom. That the stone and the carver could produce these two faces, the maidservant and Peter, that is certainly in the eden side of the balance for all of us. Such a brutal innocence, that maidservant! An innocence not possible for Jesus, the innocence of the pure lump of mortality with no connexions in high places. And Peter! that face of his! The light of understanding that floods the stone of him!

Peter and the maidservant are on one side of the roof of the porch of the rood-screen doorway; on the other side are two soldiers of the watch. Underneath them in the rood-screen doorway and twice as large as they is Christ crucified, Mary on one side of him and John on the other.

After the maidservant and Peter and the soldiers of the watch here is Jesus before Pilate. Oh! that meekness of Jesus, that stone meekness. It is the meekness of plutonium. He is so very docile, like some absent-minded celebrity asked to pose in a group photograph. "Here? Is this all right, is this where you want me to stand?" Waiting patiently for the time when he will explode himself upon the world. Pilate holds out his left hand while a servant pours water over it into a basin. Pilate is thunderstruck and so is the servant; to both of them at once has come the realization that this moment is what it is for ever—it has never been before, it will never be again; it is Now and they are living it, never in life, never in death to escape from it. Pilate's mouth is open wide, it is as if a great thick invisible vine is growing out of it; or a snake. "Innocent I am from the blood of this man," he says; "ye will see to it." Of the two faces that of the servant shows the deeper feeling; Pilate's perception of this moment is confused by his official identity but the servant can take it in just as it is and he knows that never in the history of the human race will there be any going back from this moment. Here is the hump of the story, here is the last of the uphill part; after this it rolls like a monstrous and implacable wheel through the ages, crushing everything in its path and preparing the way of the Lord, the gone, the never-again-coming.

Christ is scourged then, and in the next and last scene of the rood-loft reliefs he goes off dragging his cross. These last two scenes, like the Crucifixion below, are not from the hand of the master who carved the first five scenes; it was the destiny of the original stone of the last two scenes not to endure with those other faces and gestures that are fixed for us upon the mirror of time. These last two scenes and the Crucifixion, all of them in wood and by a centuries-later hand, have not the power of the original stone. As I have said, Christ has a special way of being with stone and the Naumburg master knew how to let that special way of being happen.

I am on the road, this road through time and space to Jerusalem, but I am no longer alone: the sow I killed and her peasant master now walk with me; they are my new colleagues, and not only they: the bear who was slain by his worshipper also walks with me; Udo the relic-gatherer whom I killed in the wood is here, and the tax-collector. Yes, the tax-collector—how not?

The sow is walking upright, she minces on her trotters like a heavy woman in tiny shoes, her flesh shaking and wobbling erotically, her flesh that is naked among us; there is a scarlet necklace of beaded drops round her throat and a thin trickle of blood from her mouth. She is confused by her present condition and shakes her head as she walks. "Little love!" she says to her peasant master. "O my treasure!" she says, pressing close to him, "What gives it here?"

"He killed you, this one," says the peasant. "Smell him. Is he a Jew?"

"I don't know," she says. "I don't think I can tell the difference any more." She turns to me. "Ay!" she says, "how the life rushed out of me on to your blade, it was like an orgasm. Such a knifeman are you, such a thruster!"

"Such a sow are you," I say. "Such a Jew-finder, such a leaver-behind of dead bodies."

"How sweet she is!" This is Bruder Pförtner, he too is with us. "How I love her!" He throws himself upon the dead sow, forcing her down on all fours and entering her zestfully.

"Ah!" cries the sow to Pförtner, "you were always the best, you were always the most man of them all!"

"Get off her," says the peasant to Pförtner. "She's mine."

"There's enough of her for everybody," says Pförtner contentedly. "She's inexhaustible. You must be patient and wait your turn." He reaches orgasm quickly, screams with joy as the sow squeals under him, then falls off her and lies snoring in the road behind us as we go on.

"Tell me about yourself," I say to the sow. "Tell me your story."

"Ah!" she says. "There's so much to tell! There's more to tell than even I myself know. You know of course that I'm descended from the Moon Goddess, from Diana herself; yes, everyone knows that. That's why, you see, I'm so eternally desirable—I have that quality of virginity. Every time a man takes me it feels to him as if it's my very first time; it makes him feel so outrageous, so naughty, so triumphantly and impeccably male. Why don't you have me, you'll see what I mean."

"Not just now," I said. "I want to hear more about you." Wondering at the same time whether a penis and testicles might have such a thing as a ghost, and whether a live eunuch might couple with a dead sow by means of the ghost of a penis. Never in my life had there been so many sexual invitations as now when I was castrated.

"My sowhood," said the sow, "has not been like that of other sows. I am fecund, I am fertile, but I have never farrowed. I have not multiplied, have not increased myself; my essential virtue is intact, I have not gone beyond the original limits of myself. Only men have known me, I have never felt upon me the rough and bristly weight of a boar."

"How was that?" I said, remembering suddenly that it was probably she who had eaten the lost parts of me. There she was mincing beside me on her little trotters, looking at me sidelong from under her blonde eyelashes. The trickle of blood from her mouth and the red line round her throat made her seem a creature enslaved by lust.

"I seen to that," said the peasant. He was a big man, dirty, tattered, patched, and unshaven. In his face was a darkness other than the dirt and beard. The darkness of his eye sockets was such that his eyes could not be distinctly seen. I thought of all the years of his life in which he had looked at the world from out of that darkness. "I seen to that," he said. "I kept her safe. I made for her a harness with spikes on it. I knowed early on I weren't never going to have no wife, I knowed I'd have to provide for myself the best I could. I seen her when she were only a little thing and I fancied her."

"Fancy!" said the sow with a snort. "It was more than fancy, it was love; it was the same as what the high-born folk make songs about and play on lutes. Say it right out: it was love. Ah! what a little enchantress I was in those first days!"

"But you became a huntress," I said. "You became a smeller-out of Jews."

"How that happened," said the peasant, "it were like this: it were three or four year back the spring crop failed and the autumn as well. We run out of grain and beans, we run out of everything. Bodwild here, I had to keep her hid or she'd have been ate sure. There been a little girl went missing from the next village and folk were saying one thing and another, most of them thought that girl been ate. Such things been heard of before and it were always Jews done it. Sacrifices, you see. They drunk them children's blood for their rituals. A dog in our village dug up some bones, they was from a human child."

"There were folk in our village looking at my little Konrad and muttering this and that," said Bodwild. "He'd always lived alone and kept to himself. They knew we were in love and they begrudged us our happiness."

"Like I said," said Konrad, "I had to keep Bodwild hid or she'd have been turning on someone's spit. I found a hole in amongst some big rocks it were in the wood by the common. I put some straw in there for her, I done my best to keep her comfortable. Mind you, I weren't too comfortable myself what with people pointing the finger at me like they was because of them bones and some said they seen me burning that little girl's clothes. There's always people will try to take away your good name but they couldn't prove nothing."

"How well I remember that time!" said Bodwild. "How well I remember a particular November evening: it was dusk, it was raining; I remember the smell of the rain on the dead leaves, I remember the smell of the damp straw. Suddenly there came a fresh smell: it was strong, it was sharp, it excited me, it made me want to nip and cuddle, it made me quiver with lust. There crept into the hole with me a man, such white skin he had, such black hair, such red cheeks!"

"He were a clipcock," said Konrad. "He were some kind of Jew magician, he had papers on him with that kind of secret writing they do. He weren't from our part of the country; some of them in our village they seen him sneaking through the wood and they begun to chase him."

"It was his fear I smelt," said Bodwild. "So strong and sharp it was, almost like doppelkorn, almost like schnapps. It made me wild with desire. I kissed him and called him sweet names, I pressed close to him and offered myself, my pinkness and the sugar of me, I was like marzipan; who could refuse me?"

"They won't get near pork," said Konrad, "them children of darkness, them Jewish devils. They call up Asmodeus, they drink the blood of Christian children, they say the Lord's Prayer backwards, them Christ-killers. He pushed her away."

"Me!" said Bodwild. "He pushed *me* away. Men have paid good money to sleep with me, but he pushed me away."

"They haven't paid money but they'd give me a sausage or maybe a chicken or some doppelkorn," said Konrad.

"I was outraged," said Bodwild. "I had never been insulted like that, I wept bitterly."

"She were squealing her head off," said Konrad. "I heard her half a mile away and I come running. We burnt the Jew that night, there were human child bones found in his pouch."

"Clever little Konrad!" said Bodwild. "It all worked out so well, everyone was satisfied. How he writhed and crackled in the flames, his bones cracked and the marrow boiled out. I remembered the smell of his fear as I saw him twisting in the flames, it was almost better than making love. Watching him burn I came again and again."

"I had you under my cloak and I was playing with you," said Konrad. "I could feel how you loved it, how hot you were."

"Did you smell the Jew's fear when he was burning?" I asked Bodwild.

"No," she said, "I had to remember it from before to call up my excitement. He was singing but that did nothing for me."

"He were trying to save his self with his Jew magic what they call up devils with," said Konrad. "There's a spell they sing, it's called 'Schemmah Yisrowail'; I've heard it often when I've caught Jews. They sing it when they're burning but it never puts out the fire."

"Do you remember when you smelled me out?" I said to Bodwild. "Do you remember when you told the others to castrate me?" I said to Konrad.

"I *thought* it were you!" said Konrad. "I *thought* I remembered your ugly Jew face looking up at me when we had you spread out on the ground. Well, you won't be making no more little Jew brats, will you."

Bodwild came close to me, nuzzling and sniffing me. At her touch I felt the ghost of an erection spring up, I felt myself rocking like a chip on the torrent of lust that flowed through the first Sophia, the second Sophia, and this sow with her scarlet necklace of blood. Even now as I have these words in my mind I am confused by the presence among them of my lost

God, my remembered Christ. How I am flooded with the humming and the roaring of great waters, with the music of the great currents in which rock and dance the Great Mother, the Father, the Son, the Virgin and the Lion! Unseen! Chosen I am, chosen are my people to be the thrall of the multitudinous, of the humming and roaring unseen manyness that whirled the Jews like a bull-roarer round the head of its manifestation as YHWH, made of them a sounding of the unseeable, the unknowable, the utterly ungraspable. How it raged, that idea, when it was YHWH and the Jews whored after stocks and stones and golden calves! How it would not tolerate any limitation of form, of image, of substance! How the every-thingness of it commands every flash and glimmer of the mind, how all thoughts that ever were or ever will be run beneath its hand like sheep beneath the hand of the shepherd! Lion-sheep, star-sheep, ocean-sheep! "*Now* I remember you!" murmured Bodwild with her snout brushing my ear. "Now I remember the smell of your fear, it was dark and full, it was like music and strong drink to me. I didn't smell it when I saw you in the inn yard just before you killed me; you had no fear then, I smelled nothing."

"So it was the fear you smelled when you hunted Jews," I said, "it wasn't the Jewishness."

"It's all the same," said Konrad. "When you're hunting Jews and you smell fear that'll be a Jew sure enough."

"If they don't know you're hunting them they won't be afraid," I said.

"They know that a time will come when they will be hunted," said Bodwild; "that was what I could always smell."

"It doesn't seem to bother you any more that I'm a Jew," I said.

"Everything seems different now that I'm dead," she said. "I feel as if I'm letting go of things. And I've told you I wanted to make love with that first Jew; I've wanted to make love with all of them but I've had to content myself with their dying. I'm just like anyone else, I take my pleasure where I can."

"Here we're talking like old friends," I said, "and yet you must be full of rage because I killed you."

"Why should I be full of rage more than you?" she said. "I sniffed you out, they castrated you and I ate your male parts. So you killed me, that's reasonable. A little time one way or the other, it seems a big thing when you're alive but when you're dead you wonder what all the fuss was about. When I was alive we hunted you down; now we're dead and you're alive and already we're friends. Very soon you'll be dead also and you too will wonder why it ever mattered so much who was what and who did what."

"And you?" I said to Konrad. "You were the master of this sow, it was you who used her to sniff out the Jews that you tortured and killed. What have you to say for yourself?"

"What have I to say for myself?" said Konrad. "You lousy Jew eunuch with your soft white hands, in your whole life you probably never done nothing heavier than count your money. You're all usurers, the whole filthy lot of you, trying to get the whole world in your pocket. Knights going to Jerusalem, they have to pawn their castles to you. Many's the Christian lady you've crept into bed with, I'll bet, and her lawful husband gone to fight the heathen. Not that it don't serve them right, they're nothing but thieves and murderers and their foot on the neck of the poor from the time we're born till the time we die. Look at my hands next to yours, eh? Mine are more like hooves, ain't they. They're that hard. Here I am dead from your Jew magic and how much did I ever have in these hands. Tools to work another man's land with mostly. Heavy soil and a heavy plough and a six-ox team, you probably wouldn't have the strength in them white hands of yours to turn a plough like that. How much Christian blood have you drunk?"

"I wonder what makes Christians think that anybody would want to drink their blood," I said.

"If you don't drink it you do other things with it," said Konrad. "Everybody knows about Jew magic."

"You're a Christian, are you?" I said.

"What else would I be, you Jew Antichrist-worshipper," he said, "I been baptized, haven't I."

"And died with your sins heavy on you," I said. "Died all unshriven."

"What difference does that make," he said. "I ain't burning in Hell nor nothing like that, am I."

"Maybe your Hell will be to walk to Jerusalem with the Jew you castrated," I said.

"Whatever I have to do," he said, "I'll do it like a man, I've nothing to fear. It's yourself you'd better be worrying about; the Last Days are coming and then you'll see what burning is. There's been signs in the sky, you know—great flaming clouds in the shape of Christ with a sword in his hand fighting the Jewish Antichrist with three heads and seven horns."

"Who won?" I said.

"You'll see soon enough, clipcock," he said. "I forgot, you ain't even that no more, you're a no-cock clipcock."

"I'm so sorry you're dead," I said. "It's a great loss to me that you could only die once; it would be such a pleasure to kill you." Thinking, as I said it, that these dead ones were already like a family to me.

"It means nothing at all," said the bear, "whatever you see in the sky." The arrows that had killed him were still in him, they nodded as he walked upright with the others. "There's been a Great Bear in the sky all these years and even a Lesser Bear as well and nothing's come of it, nothing at all."

"Did you think anything would come of it?" I said.

"Of course not," he said. "Why should I. You can see anything you like in the sky, anything at all. And what it means is anything at all."

"That man who killed you," I said. "What do you think he's doing now?"

"He's looking for another bear," said the bear. "He's hopeless, he's incapable of learning."

"You think you're quite the thing, don't you," said Udo the relic-gatherer to the bear. "You think you're better than us. I seen you slipping through the woods now and again when you been alive. You wouldn't say nothing to us then, you wouldn't stop and pass the time of day, you were too good for us."

"If I'd stopped you'd have shot me full of arrows," said the bear.

"Yes I would," said Udo. "Yes I would just *because* you wouldn't stop and talk. If you'd talked with me we could have been friends, you could have showed me where the honey trees were."

"Another one," said the bear.

"Don't take that tone with me," said Udo. "How much honey have you had in your life and how much have I had in mine?"

"Whatever I've had I've found for myself," said the bear.

"Oh yes," said Udo. "Naturally. The wood is your village, isn't it. So you know where to find things the same as I did in my village. If you'd come to my village looking for the well or the inn or whatever I'd have shown you where to find it, I'd have had time to stop and talk, wouldn't I. But when I come to your wood a runaway and a stranger trying to stay uncaught for my year and a day it's not a word from you I get, is it. It's nothing, nothing, nothing I get from everybody. The lord and his lot they treat you like an animal till you run off and you think at least if the animals will treat you like an animal that's not so bad, you'll be a brother to them. But they won't, they turn their backs on you. Die, serf! Die, slave! Into the ground with you and give the maggots what they're waiting for."

"Excuse me," said the headless tax-collector. A thrill ran through me when I heard his voice, the voice of my brother in Sophia, the voice of my brother pilgrim whose temple I had destroyed, whose world I had blackened and made empty. These new colleagues of mine, these dead men and animals, all of them appeared to me as I had last seen them. So the tax-collector was of course naked and headless and writhing with the terrible swift energy of the maggots that continually consumed him but never diminished his dreadful corpse. I couldn't bear to look at him but my eyes were again and again magnetically drawn to the horror of him while in my mouth I tasted writhing maggots.

"Excuse me," said the tax-collector to Udo. "I don't want to offend a respectable murderer but when you talk of giving the maggots what they're waiting for, then I really must say something, I really must put in a word, must mention that you were eager enough to give me to the maggots. You seem to feel very sorry for yourself but you didn't feel sorry for me when you caught me with your wire and took my head off with your sword."

"That were business," said Udo. "I never wished you nothing ill. Anyhow what's one pilgrim more or less; you've died on the road but here's Herr Keinpimmel will go to Jerusalem for you; he'll make the journey for you and say however many prayers you like. So there's nothing lost, you've give the world up for Jesus and I say well done and Amen."

"Ah, yes," said the tax-collector. "My good friend Herr Keinpimmel, the illustrious Jew adulterer. The one takes my wife and the other takes my life. And my head will bear the name of that one who washed his hands and said that he was innocent of the blood of Christ. What more could I ask for? I am happy, I am content to dance with the maggots until . . . "

"Judgment Day?" I said. I couldn't keep silence, I had to speak to his absent face, I had to look at where his face would have been if he had had a head.

"Ah!" he said, "At last! The first words spoken by you to me! And it is the Day of Judgment about which you speak to me. It is with this thought, this question, that you break your silence. You cannot look me in the eye because my head is elsewhere but I think that even if my head were here you might not be able to look me in the eye, isn't that so?"

"Yes," I said, "that's true enough. But might not you also find it difficult to look me in the eye? Me and a few other Jews who lost their lives to the soldiers of Christ."

"I have already begged your forgiveness, have I not," said the tax-collector. "In front of your synagogue under the open sky in the sight of God have I humbled myself to the Jews."

"We were under the open sky because there was no roof to stand under," I said. "The synagogue had been burnt to the ground, and there were many Jews who could not attend because they were busy dancing with the maggots."

"Forgive me," he said. "Please, please forgive me. I would do it again if I had the chance."

"Do what?" I said.

"What I did," he said.

"Ah!" I said, "Do you now tell me that you brought those peasants to our town?"

"Naturally I did," he said. "How was I not to do it?"

"It was because of you that there were all those dead Jews on the cobblestones!" I said, listening with dread and with fascination for the words that I knew must come next.

"Indeed," he said. "Because of me and because of you."

Hearing this I found that my throat was affected in such a way that I could not swallow. My mouth was so dry, my tongue so thick that I could scarcely speak. "Because of what I did," I said.

"Yes," he said. "You are that Jew who finished me off. You are the last in a long succession of Jews who took away my life. Do you shake your head? No, you don't, you know what I'm talking about. I was already dead some little while before this lout here took my head off, dead and Jew-killed. I saw you hanging about in the Keinjudenstrasse, I knew what was in your mind, I knew what would happen when I rode away. I made my arrangements, and once you were on that ladder death was on its way to the Jews of our town."

"Why the others?" I said. "Why didn't you just kill me?"

"Killing you alone wouldn't have been enough," he said. "Did you think you were the only one? There were always Jews, they were like owls that one hears calling in the dark: one close by, one farther away; you never see them but they know where you are. They smelt out Sophia the way Bodwild smelt you out, they smelt her lust and her appetite for the other, for the circumcised, for the lurking Jew. Could you possibly have thought you were the first one?"

Looking at that headless mass of maggots I felt the stare of his absent eyes, I began to see in the empty air the eyes of the dead man, his desperate eyes looking into my desperate eyes. "Yes," I said, "I thought that I was the first one."

"You weren't," he said. "I could smell them always, smell them on her skin and on the silk she wore next to her skin, I could smell them in the bedclothes and in the folds of curtains, I could smell them in the passages of my house. They required no words, she and they, they made their wants known without language, like animals that go on all fours. Only a look, only a smell and they followed, like dogs running to mount a bitch in heat. A bitch in heat or a wild ass:

> "A wild ass used to the wilderness,
> That snuffeth up the wind in her desire;
> Her lust, who can hinder it?
> All they that seek her will not weary themselves;
> In her month they shall find her."

That desperate man with no head had found the right words, the words that with a rush made Sophia freshly real in my mind, the desert animalness of her in the hidden flesh, the covered nakedness. Gone from me for ever, I knew that I was never to see her again. For a moment the loss of her closed in upon me so crushingly that I thought I might kill myself on the spot; it seemed all at once that there was no space, no time for me to live in. Yet here before me was her husband: he too had lost her and death had given him no rest; the memory of her was a wheel on which he was broken again and again. When was there an end of pain, I wondered. Never. The cup was golden and it would not pass from me. While I was alive I should have to drink it empty and when I was dead it would be there to drink afresh. And still I drink it now, newly bitter after all the centuries. But the pain is the life, the pain is what separates the animate from the inanimate, the human from the stone. What is human may long for the stone of its innocence, the stone of its ease, of no pain; but the pain is the life. Even after death the pain is the life. This pain is not a simple one, it is complex.

Was there pain before there was a world? Was the world brought forth in pain? Yes, I am sure of this, I am convinced that it is so. What knowledge can there be of this? As these words come on to the paper by way of what goes by the name of Pilgermann I note that theoretical science has worked its way back deductively to the very first moments of the universe and the bursting forth of everything from the time-space singularity which had contained it just before that moment. All of this is imprinted on the waves and particles of me, it is in the mystical black letters that rise above all flames, it is the Word that is at once the birth-scream and the death-cry of the cosmic animal that is God, the It that is both creator and created. How should there not be pain? One has only to listen to music run backwards to sense the reversing cycles of consummation and creation, the continual ordering and re-ordering of the disturbance that is the endless idea that continually thinks itself into and out of the manyness of its being.

It is not from the loss of Sophia, the loss of Christ and the loss of God as He that the pain comes, no. It is from the pain that God comes, that Christ with his lion-eyes comes, that Sophia in all her beauty, her splendour, and her passion comes. It is from the cosmic intolerable of the nothing-in-everything alternating with the everything-in-nothing that all things come. This great pain, this ur-pain, swims its monstrous bulk in deeps far down, down, down below that agony of loss in which I grind my teeth remembering the golden bell of Sophia's nakedness and the sharpness of the knife of joy.

Knife of joy. At this thought almost do the waves and particles of me laugh. Perhaps this almost-laugh is seen somewhere as the shaking of a leaf in the evening wind, the shaking of a leaf seen in the light of a street lamp under a humpbacked moon in a modern place where the few trees speak to the dry stone. "Knife of joy," I said, and immediately there came to mind the knife of unjoy, the knife that drew the line for me. Now of course I know what I did not know then: I know that the pain waits in the joy as the dragonfly waits in the nymph. Almost I sense that the joy, as the nymph to the dragonfly, is a necessary stage in the development of the pain.

With my dead colleagues I was on the road to Jerusalem: with the sow Bodwild and her peasant master Konrad; with the bear shot full of arrows by his worshipper; with Udo the relic-gatherer; with the tax-collector the husband of Sophia, and with us was Bruder Pförtner in his appearances and his disappearances. And now I became aware of perhaps someone else, it was only the faintest light and shadow as it were sketched on the air, a ghostly chiaroscuro walking familiarly with the rest of us as if by right. This sketchy figure was in truth familiar, uncertain of feature as it was: it was immediately recognizable to me as an early state of my death. I felt drawn to it as a father to a son. This simulacrum was in no way childlike, it was a fully-grown duplicate of me but not yet fully defined, not yet fully realized, and therefore it was to me as a child to be looked after.

Child! Looking at my immature death, feeling protective towards it as if it were my son, I found myself thinking: What if Sophia and I have made a child! What if in her womb is growing new life from our sin, our adultery, our triumph! I laughed aloud as this thought leapt up in me. I looked sidewise at the tax-collector, my brother in Sophia. "In her month they shall find her," I said.

Strange, talking to a headless dead man. No face to look at, but from somewhere he was staring at me hard. "Judgment Day," he said. "You spoke of it just a little while ago. You must know in your heart, as I knew in my heart while I was alive, that the Day of Judgment is the only day there is. In our mortal life we play at dividing this one everlasting day into many tiny days and we say, 'Tomorrow I shall perhaps do better.' But there is only this one day in which we live our whole lives and from which we fade as consciousness fades. It is where I am now but in a little while I shall fade out of it and be gone while you for as long as you live must remain in it."

"Is that why you told those peasants to let me live?" I said. "So that I could suffer it continually?"

"I told them to let you live because I felt myself judged in that moment when I looked down at you lying in your blood and vomit," he said.

We said nothing more. Bruder Pförtner was with us again, he was walking close beside my young death and fondling it from time to time.

Walking the road to Jerusalem I find myself weeping. This is because my mind has shown me a connexion that it was just beginning to perceive when I was leaning against the tree in the little dark wood after I killed Udo the relic-gatherer. It was then that there came into my mind the great dome that I had never seen, the dome of Hagia Sophia in Constantinople. Ah! now as I walk I know that there is no separateness in the world, I know that the souls of things and the souls of people are inextricably commingled; I know that the dome and the woman both are manifestations of something elemental that is both beauty and wisdom and it is for ever in danger, for ever being lost, torn out of our hands, violated. It is impossible to keep it safe. That heaven shapen by human hands, that blue dome hung with lights and lustres, starred with flames and dim with incense, that spirit-bowl, that God-mother and Mother Goddess, that Wisdom of stone and gold, how should it not be violated, how should rough hands not be laid upon it, how should the holy silence not be broken by the thudding of hooves, how should war horses not be ridden up to that altar, how should the altar not be smashed? Altars are made for smashing. That thing in us that waits to jump up and smash, it stands looking over our shoulder as we build the altar. It rages, it smiles, it laughs deep in its belly, it dances on cloven hooves at the consecration of the altar, it looks ahead to the time of the smashing. More, more is there in this: that of which the dome is a visible aspect, the great Wisdom, golden Wisdom itself, is the mother of both the altar and the thing that smashes the altar. The Wisdom in its wisdom thus provides that beauty and wisdom shall never be within our grasp, shall only be a light upon our eyes and passing.

Passing, passing! *Echah*! O how! O how is the beauty passing, how is it departed, gone, gone! It is gone because the Wisdom in its wisdom has ordained that beauty is that which passes, it is that which will not stay; beauty is a continual departing, a continual going away. Sophia is one with the dome in my mind that arches over me like the Egyptian sky goddess arching over her earth-god brother who penetrates her and must be separated from her.

In the making of Sophia's beauty was the violation of it by separation, by departure, by shouts of impiety under the great dome of it, by the castration of its consort and the beheading of its protector. The great dome echoes with the clatter and the clamour of the horsemen, with the smashing of the altar, the tearing of the silken hangings. Listen, listen to the trampling of impious feet on sacred books, listen to this trampling that is the most constant road in history, the trampling of murderous feet on sacred books. In the writing, in the copying, in the binding of the books, in the very ink and paper, in the blood and bones of the original writer and in the blood and bones of every copyist thereafter lives coevally the trampler and the burner of the books of God and the God of books, lives the trampler and the burner of books and people, of beauty and domes.

I am on the road to Jerusalem with my dead colleagues, with Bruder Pförtner, with my death that is not yet ripened to term. The year is 1096 in the Christian calendar, *Anno Mundi* 4857, two thousand, four hundred and eight years since Moses brought down from the mountain the second tablets on the tenth day of Tishri. It will not be until A.D. 1204 that violent men mouthing Christ will sail from Venice to sack Constantinople. In the adzes and hammers of Venetian shipwrights not yet born, in their blood and bones, in the blood and bones of their mothers who will bear them waits to be born the sack of Constantinople and the fall of an emperor unborn, and all of this is under the dome of that Sophia who is or is not carrying my child, that Sophia who revealed her nakedness to me, gave it splendidly and lavishly to me, that Sophia, that nakedness that I shall no more see. *Echah!*

The above is my *kina*, my dirge, my lament that is suddenly in my mind as I recall walking with my colleagues on the road to Jerusalem. In my mind at the end of my lament on the inseparability of Sophia and Hagia Sophia is another thought: the enemy matters nothing; truly it is not the apparent enemy that sacks Constantinople, it is that which crouches always at the feet of beauty and in its season leaps up to destroy. It is the impulse that leaps up, and it gathers to itself whoever comes to hand whether it be Christians or Muslims; it clothes itself with whatever costume it finds. The fall of Constantinople that begins in 1204 with the French and the Flemings is consummated by the Turks in 1453; what is required is not that a particular enemy shall attack the dome, only that by sword and fire beauty shall be brought low, only that the holy books shall be trampled. *Echah!*

9

Now must I begin to speak of war, now must I make ready for dust and blood, for the smoke and flame of siege and battle, for the ringing of dinted iron, the quivering of severed limbs. Now must I see in my mind the secret colours of entrails sliding from the opened bellies of warriors while their eyes look down in disbelief. Now must I see Bruder Pförtner and his ready companions making sport while swords clang and arrows hiss all round them; now must I hear them screaming in their pleasure as they have the tumbling of heroes Christian and Muslim both.

What a ponderous labour is war, what preparations must be made years and years before the first blow is struck! Decades before the first battle must the first engines of war be brought into play: the first engines of war are men and women, they are the hammer and the anvil that in the heat of their action make soldiers. In order that the dead may be heaped on the walls and roofs and in the streets and houses of Jerusalem in 1099 there must be heavy coupling from about 1060 onwards among Christians and Muslims both. For the making of each soldier must a man and a woman labour in their lust, for the making of each soldier must an egg and a sperm conjoin to write their word of flesh, must a woman carry that word for nine months until her great-grown belly fulfils its term and is delivered of a manchild. Then must the boy be given suck, must he be kept alive to grow strong and active, must he be led safely past the ills of infancy and the perils of childhood to the day when he can take in his hands the weapons of war and go out to the place of killing.

Fields of grain and vegetables, herds of cattle must be grown to feed these ripening warriors. Wool of sheep, thread of flax, fur of fox and rabbit, hide of cattle must be grown to clothe and shoe the soldiers of Christ and Muhammad, and for this the sheep, the foxes and the rabbits, and the cattle must also couple tirelessly while the earth grows the sown seed in its belly. What chance would Mars have without the help of Venus? What hard breathing, what amorous sighing, what grunts of ardour and cries of joy sound in the gathered darkness of those soldier-making, soldier-feeding, soldier-clothing, soldier-shoeing nights!

And the arming of them! While these boys ripen like peaches on the tree of war there are heard, first here, then there, then everywhere the clink of hammers and the windy breath of bellows. All through the Christian world and all through Islam rise and fall the brawny arms of smiths beating out the passing moments into days and weeks and years of swords, spearheads and arrowheads, lances, pikes, maces, axes, mail shirts and iron helmets, spurs, stirrups, bits, and horseshoes. Hammers and anvils of flesh, hammers and anvils of iron striking the years! Fires of war in forges east and west, their red coals purring! Red-hot iron, red-hot steel and a leaping up of golden sparks under the hammer blows! Hungry iron, hungry steel, hungering for flesh!

And I too, Pilgermann! I too, with prayer-shawl, with fringes and phylacteries, with books and surgical instruments, I too have been ripening on this tree of war. But I am wrong to say "tree of war"; if one speaks of trees then there is only one tree: of war and peace and everything else; not only do soldiers ripen on it but all who live in this world; it is a wondrous tree and it bears different fruits in different seasons to be shaken down by the winds of necessity, plucked by the hand of circumstance. The dead Jews on the cobblestones before the synagogue, the dead girl with her skirt over her face, they too have grown on this same tree with the soldier-fruits. And my Sophias first and second. And these dead who walk with me. And my own young death as well. How difficult it is to speak of any single thing—one takes notice of a stone at the foot of a mountain, steps back to look at the mountain, walks far enough away to see the top of it, climbs another mountain to see the plain beyond the first one, and little by little widening the view sees from a very long way off our little cloud-wreathed planet swimming in the sea of space, and it is only one thing after all.

Stones! When the hammers are heard on the anvils of war the stones will not be found unready; they will come to hand equally for those who besiege and those who defend. Built up into strong walls they await the rumble of the seige tower, the shock of the ram, the crash of the stone that comes whistling from the mangonel. War sets one stone against another, calls this one a missile, that one a stronghold. But the freemasonry of the stones is stronger than the temporary loyalties imposed on them; they do what is required of them but in their hardness they retain their one essential fact: they know that they are all one thing. What do the stones say? "We have no enemy." This I have not read in a book, this I have heard them say and I know it to be true. Muslims build them up and Christians knock them down or Christians build them up and Muslims knock them down; war and peace and the passage of what is called time shake and throw them like dice and in the throws read winning and losing. But the stones of Jerusalem laughed when the Temple was destroyed. "Full quittance!" they shouted. "Full quittance for the sins of the Jews!"

And what were the sins of the Jews? The graven images, the idols, the high places, the Baalim and the Ashtaroth, the adulteries of spirit and of flesh. And why did God rage so because of these acts, why were they not to be tolerated by Him? Because the insult was too monstrous to be borne. Because He had chosen the Jews for His vessel, He had chosen them to be the ark of the idea of Him and of It, the idea of the Unseen, the Ungraspable, the Unknowable, the idea never to be contained by the mind that is contained by it. He had chosen them to be mind-heroes, to open their minds to the idea that could not be held by any mind, and what did they do? They fouled themselves, they rolled in the dung and the degradation of the seeable, the knowable, the ordinary. They said to stocks and stones, "Be thou our God."

I do not forget thee, O Jerusalem. But what is Jerusalem but the seeable and the knowable? What is Jerusalem but the stones that have no enemy? The stones on which Christ walked, the stones over which he dragged his cross, the stones of that Western Wall that alone remain of the Second Temple, are they to be held sacred, are they to fill the eye with the seen? It is the Jerusalem of the heart that must not be forgotten because in the Jerusalem of the heart is the heart of the mystery where lives the idea of the Unknowable that is God.

I say that now when I have been dead for centuries, I say it now that I am more or less full-grown. But in this time that I have been speaking of, in this time called A.D. 1096 when I trudged my road to Jerusalem I was going to a Jerusalem that lived in my mind as coarsely painted and as vividly coloured as an inn sign, a Jerusalem of blazing eastern sun and buzzing flies, of awninged blue-shadowed bazaars in the narrow streets walled in by tawny stone far, far away at the end of many days, many nights of perilous roads and long dusty approaches. When I thought of the gates of Jerusalem I thought of sunlight dazzling in its white brilliance, I thought of blue and purple shadows among which had moved the shadow of the very hand of God, a *seen* shadow. And it was a seen Christ that I was travelling towards, a Christ who had already appeared to me and had spoken to me.

Now help me, Memory! Let me find again that road of youth and pain, let me hear again the tramp of thousands to Jerusalem:

Thy dead shall live, my dead bodies shall arise—
Awake and sing, ye that dwell in the dust—
For Thy dew is as the dew of light,
And the earth shall bring to life the shades.

Marzipan. Manticore. Mazery. Manzikert. Manzikert, yes. And the name of that pope isn't Unguent VII, it's Urban II. But I was saying Manzikert. Nobody can deny that after the Battle of Manzikert in 1071 Byzantium was no longer what it had been. The Emperor Romanus, taken prisoner at Manzikert, was blinded; and it was a Jew who was forced to perform this office. I hear the voices of Romanus and his Jewish executioner mingled in a constant faint murmur barely audible among the stronger transmissions in the hum and crackle, the roar and whine and whistle of the cosmos; it's astonishing how many individual voices can be distinguished in what one would think of as a general uproar.

Any sequence of events is interesting because of its positive and negative shapes. Take a pair of scissors and cut something out. Anything. Why not a devil with horns and a tail and cloven hooves. So. There is your paper with a devil-shaped hole in it. Two devil-shapes, one positive, one negative, and both of them made at the very same moment. Was the Battle of Manzikert the shape of the paper or the shape of the hole? It's as I've said before: there is always a twoness in the oneness, and for this reason it's almost impossible to know what is happening in the space-time configuration. Not only that: as soon as an effort is made to look at any particular thing the aspect of that thing becomes other than what it was—that event that happened in full view when unlooked-at covers itself when observed, spins around itself one of those wonderful encrusted eggs with a peephole in one end of it; I the observer, receding reactively from the gaze that proceeds from my eyes, find myself shot into the distance thousands of miles away from the peephole. Inch by inch I think my way back; closer, closer, closer I come and here it is all tiny—the tiny, tiny Battle of Manzikert. Closer still and I am in the dust and the trampling of it, hearing the grunts and the shouts of the living and the sighs of the dying.

How nothing is simply one thing! There comes to mind unaccountably an order of the day from Jenghis Khan to his horsemen at some distance from 1071, a century or two perhaps. In this order he commands his men to leave their horses unbridled on the march—they are to have their mouths free, they are not to be galloped on the march.

Where was I when the Battle of Manzikert was fought in 1071, *Anno Mundi* 4831 in the Jewish calendar? That was the year of my birth; on some frequency still sounds my birth-cry in the hum and crackle, the roar and whine and whistle where lives the mingled murmur of Romanus and his Jewish executioner. Questions arise continually, everything must be kept in mind at once—at least one must try, must do one's best. Because everything is with us. Even now the fading heat of the universe's explosion into being warms the deeps of space, still it fades there, the echo of that first blind bursting shout of beginning. I note that everything that has ever happened is imprinted on me. I can feel it even though I cannot by my own volition recall most of it. With the bursting of the original explosion in me I am again in the year 1096, moving with the many, moving with the thousands towards the fall of Jerusalem, that golden city that I never lived to see. The fall of Jerusalem is at the centre of its space-time; the centre of anything is the centre of everything; how may it be looked at? Could the siege of Jerusalem have been painted by Vermeer? Can such a thing be looked at in such a way? Can the sunlight on mail shirts and blood and severed limbs be looked at as one looks at the daylight from a neat Dutch window in which a quiet woman weighs gold? A better painting to think of is the "Head of a Young Girl": the look that looks out from the face of that young beauty, such asking is there in that look! "Are you love? Are you death? Are you the beginning of everything, are you the end?" Not only does this young girl with her look see all of these but all of these look out at us from her face.

And the look with which Vermeer looked upon her face, that is the look with which everything must be seen; yes, even the severed limbs. Everything that is, everything that happens must be seen with the eye that is in love with seeing. All must be seen with a willing look. From the face of Vermeer's young girl looks out at us the heart of the mystery, the moving stillness in which again and again explodes, in which even now at this very moment explodes the beginning of all things. From her eyes the unseen looks out at us, and through our eyes looking back into hers also looks the unseen.

This unseen that sometimes we call God, has it a purpose or a destiny? What is its present work? Elephants, whales, mice, cockroaches, humans—from a single cell of any of them can be made the whole creature complete; there is in the cell that reservoir of potentiality. With what we call time the potentiality is unlimited: each moment has in it the matrix of all moments, the possibility of all action. Is it God's destiny to turn the wheel until every potentiality has become an actuality? For this has God come to hate the world? For this does God weep and curse continually as the wheel turns and there approach him over and over again popes, Jews, warriors, idiots, kings, queens, beggars, lepers, lions, dogs, and monkeys, each busy with its tiny mortal history and each tiny mortal history different from all the others. Even if each one were to try to live out that history exactly the same as the one before it can't be done; variations and permutations will always come into it.

Will there ever be an end to it all, is the end one of the possibilities? God doesn't know. God created all the possibilities of variation and permutation but he cannot calculate them. How can this be? Is not God omniscient and omnipotent? Yes, and being so he was able to conceive and create possibilities beyond his understanding and beyond his capability to deal with as agent, as doer. If he were not able to do this he would be less than all-powerful. There is of course a paradox here: if God has not the power to understand everything he is not omniscient, and equally if he has not the power to create something beyond his understanding he is not omnipotent. It is my belief that God is of an artistic temperament and has therefore chosen to let his own work be beyond his understanding; I think this may well be why he has abandoned the He identity and has moved into the It where he is both subject and object, the doer and the done. God is no longer available to receive or transmit personal messages; he has been absorbed into process and toils ignorantly at the wheel with the rest of us.

In this general process some potential actions are actualized, some not. In the channel of action where I moved with the thousands towards Jerusalem there moved also the unlived action of earlier popes who were unsuccessful in their attempts at what is now called a Crusade, *Kreuzzug* in German. The most direct translation of this word is Cross-pull, and indeed the Cross did exert a pull. Pope Sergius IV in 1011, Leo IX in 1053, Gregory VII in 1074 had tried but had not been able to set these thousands moving towards Jerusalem. Time after time had violent men sharpened the cross into a sword and made their silken vestments into banners; time after time had they spat out the wafer and the wine and shouted for real blood and real bodies. Again and again had this moment tried to come into being; blown out each time like a candle its light sprang up again whenever any flame approached the smoking wick.

Looking at it all from where I am now, looking at faraway events from this great distance I see them as if jumbled together or dancing in a ring, unseparated by time: Crusades, plagues, massacres of Jews, dancing madness, peasant revolts — a dance of life and a dance of death. A dance of life that spins itself into death like gold being spun into straw. Life cannot tolerate itself, life wants to become death. Almost one might say that the function of life is to manifest death. Perhaps death is the gold, life the straw. Death is the natural expression of life. See the swift and fluent dance of maggots in a dead mouse, such a relief, as when a smoking log bursts into flame. And of course it was in my country that the Dancing Madness arose, following hot on the heels of the Black Death which followed on the Crusades.

Because of what happened, because of what was done in the name of Christ, Jerusalem ceased to exist. What remained was not Jerusalem, it was an image fixed on a dead retina. An image retained on the dead retina of an idea. An idea is an eye given by God for the seeing of God. Some of these eyes we cannot bear to look out of, we blind them as quickly as possible.

I must be more precise: Jerusalem has not ceased to exist any more than bread has ceased to exist; the bread that has been eaten is gone, now there is more bread. The Jerusalem that was is gone, now there is more Jerusalem, other Jerusalem. One assumes that the world simply is and is and is but it isn't, it is like music that we hear a moment at a time and put together in our heads. But this music, unlike other music, cannot be performed again.

With the ear of the mind I hear the army of the Franks on the march, I hear the massed clinking of their tread, I hear the horses snort and whinny, the rattling of leaves of iron. With the eye of the mind I see spokes of sunlight revolving through marching figures, I see the night gleam of armour, I see the Orontes River. As I recall life now I sometimes think of it as a sort of raisin-cake with vast distances between the raisins. As I send the idea of my being questing back it is from raisin to raisin that it makes its way, like the line connecting the dots that make the constellations of the Virgin and the Lion on the star charts. Or the route of the Franks across plains and mountains as they headed, with the harmless migrant storks high above them, for the water-crossing at the Bosporus. The line seeks the image, it smells out the image-making dots as a salmon returning from the sea smells out the river of its birth, swims upstream, spawns and dies. So with the line: it swims upstream, spawns a dot, and dies. The action of the spawning and the death make a dot; what was smelled was the place wanting the dot. Why did the place want a dot, how could a place want a dot, what was the need of the place, whose need? The line's? The place's? God's?

No. We assume always too much, we assume what cannot be assumed. We see dots so we connect them with lines and we claim to know what the lines and dots signify. There is a marching, there is a galloping, there is a hissing of arrows, a clashing of swords; or it may be that there is simply a stretching forth of the neck to the sword, there is a wrapping in the Torah scroll, there is a burning alive and we assume (always the assumptions) that these things are happening to different people. We assume that the Frank is distinct from the Jew who is distinct from the Turk but I cannot now think of it as being like that. It seems to me now that that busy line, that motion in the circuitry, did not leap from one dot to another: from the leap of its original impulse its being continued on its way to flash into Christian, Jew, Muslim, fortresses, rivers, dawns, full moons, battles, crows, the wind in the trees, anything you like. Mountains in the dawn; the shock of Thing-in-Itself, the enormity of Now. So it is that although my being is in one way or another continuous I cannot present to you Pilgermann as continuous, only flashes here and there.

How there are vortices in the space-time! My mind keeps spinning down to Manzikert where in actuality I as Pilgermann never have been. It was one of the big dots, one of the juicier raisins. The dust! So much dust stirred up by those hooves, by those feet that trampled out, that trod the grapes of mortality into the wine of history for the Byzantine Empire. Wine! Wine and dust at the same time, at the same time the hot and dry and the cold and wet.

No. Not Manzikert. I mean to tell of Antioch. Yes, where the walls undulated like a serpent on the mountains, where the four hundred towers waited for the line to flash into a dot. Four hundred towers!

Before Antioch there were the Anti-Taurus Mountains. Perhaps I was not a Jew then, because I remember the heat and the weight of the mail shirt that rusted the skin and chafed the body bloody, I remember the donkeys plunging over the edge roped one to the other, the black letters of their braying frozen in the silence of their deaths.

"Now help me, Memory!" Only a little space from here have I heard myself speak these words. But as the words and pictures of my thoughts go out on those few millimetres of waveband assigned to me I begin to understand that I myself am a tiny particle of Memory. I am a microscopic chip in that vast circuitry in which are recorded all of the variations and permutations thus far. Not all of my experience is available for recall by my Pilgermann identity, only that in which the energy of the input was above a certain level. Thus it is that I can at any time call up that veiled owl to whom I said, "Hear, O Israel!" but most of my education is lost to me.

Like any parent I wanted the best for my death, I remember that well. Walking beside me he was scarcely more visible than breath on glass but the manifestation of him was continually more detailed and refined although his face was obscure. He was not as yet ready to speak, perhaps he never would speak, but he looked at me with a look that said plainly, "I know that I can trust you to do the right thing." I nodded with a false heartiness, trying to look reliable. When the time came I did the best I could. I don't know where he is now, I don't know what's become of him. One does what one can; the rest is a matter of luck and chance.

PILGERMANN

My recall is offering me Antioch but the last dot was still in Germany. How did I get to Antioch? Pirates. I was on a ship from Genoa bound for Jaffa when they appeared. Even now I must smile when I see with the eye of the mind the hungry triangle of that red sail cleaving the white dazzle of the sunlight on the dark blue sea. Larger, larger and more and more urgent it becomes and I smile because there is no surprise in it, perhaps even I am not unwilling that this should happen.

When I came down to Genoa out of the north there was the sea dividing with its horizon the picture in my eyes. Everything on this side of the horizon was in the world of HERE, everything beyond it was THERE. Here was a fresh and salty breeze from the sea, here were the clustered masts nodding in the harbour and the gulls soaring, circling, crying, crying, "Where are you going, Herr Keinpimmel? What is Jerusalem, that you should go from HERE to THERE?" This of course was the voice of the Mittelteufel, the halfway devil; I came to know it later but at that time I had not yet learned to recognize it. I was suddenly cowed by the overwhelming and undeniable reality of the sea, I was reduced to nothing by the objectivity of the gulls, I could not think why I wanted to go anywhere or do anything. In that particular Now that comes just before one embarks only the sea seemed real; not Christ; not God; not sin. I looked round for Bodwild and Konrad, for the bear, for Udo, for the tax-collector and my young death and Bruder Pförtner. There was no one, I was utterly alone.

In front of me stood a fat brown-faced shipmaster with a gold circlet in one ear, a look of contempt on his face, and his palm outstretched. He looked as if he might, after taking their money, chop one lot of pilgrims into pieces and salt them away in barrels for the feeding of the next lot. Behind him were the sea and the circling gulls and his ship tied up at the quay. The ship was a wallowing-shaped thing with its brown sail furled on the yard and its deck all a-clutter with wineskins, bales and bundles, chickens, pigs, and goats. I looked to see what the name of it was: *Balena*, *Whale*. "If this ship is a whale," I said to the master in Italian (I had studied medicine in Salerno), "I hope that doesn't make me . . ."

The master laid his finger across his lips. "Don't say it," he said. "Bad luck."

I paid him fifty ducats and abandoned all hope. That is, I thought that I had abandoned all hope until I went below decks and smelled the smell there; then I found that there was yet more hope to abandon. I paid five more ducats to be allowed to sleep on deck with the chickens and the pigs and the goats.

When it was time to sail the seamen all lurched aboard fit for nothing but vomiting and sleeping. Some did one, some did both. When woken up to raise the sail and haul up the anchor they all began to sing. Their singing had that peculiar falseness sometimes heard in the choruses of provincial opera companies; it made one lose all confidence in any kind of human effort whatever; it made one doubt that the ship, the anchor, the ocean or indeed the world was real. The ocean proved to be real enough and the ship wallowed in it in a way that was sickening as only reality can be.

So it was that when that red sail appeared three days out I nodded with a sense of the fitness of things. Clearly such a ship as that *Balena*, such a master as that one, and such a crew as that crew had never been meant, in the general design of things, to move a load of pilgrims from an unholy to a Holy Land. There were about fifty pilgrims on board, and when some of the more experienced ones said that they thought the fast-moving red sail might be pirates we all asked the master for weapons with which to defend ourselves and the ship. "Softly, softly, good sirs," he said. "Be tranquil, there's no use pissing into the wind." The crew then produced swords, pikes, and clubs and herded us into the after part of the ship where we watched the red sail growing ever larger until the pirates closed with us, lines were thrown from them to us, and the two ships linked arms like strolling sweethearts.

The pirate captain then came aboard without much ostentation but it was clear that he was accustomed to being treated with respect. He was a tall lean Muslim and as he stood facing the short fat Christian master of our vessel he seemed to embody some necessary complementarity; together they were obviously spin-maintainers. The two of them exchanged greetings with great civility and then began to haggle spiritedly in Arabic. We pilgrims naturally watched and listened with some interest, and it seemed to us that the master of the *Balena* was saying that we were very valuable while the pirate captain thought perhaps that we were not so very valuable. The negotiations concluded, money changed hands and we pilgrims changed ships. As we stepped over into the pirate vessel the pilgrim just ahead of me turned to me and said, "What's the name of this ship, did you notice?"

"*Nineveh*," I said, pleased with my own joke; I had noticed the name but could not read the Arabic characters. But later I asked a Greek-speaking pirate what the name was.

"*Nineveh*," he said.

To be sold for a slave is a startling experience. The rest of the world knows so little about one and yet it is they who set the price. We were all stripped and examined and relieved of our luggage and whatever was in our pockets or sewn into our clothes. The pirate captain was delighted to find that I was a eunuch in good condition; he made that gesture of kissing the fingers made by all vendors who reckon that they have something especially fine to sell. In the slave market in Tripoli, standing in the cool and coloured shade of awnings, smelling the smoke of water pipes and a variety of Middle Eastern cooking that invited one to abandon introspection and embrace such pleasures of the senses as now offered, hearing Arabic, Syriac, Armenian, Turkish, and Greek spoken all round me I was not so distressed as one might think; it had never before happened to me that I was valued, and highly valued, for my visible qualities alone. It occurred to me that I might be bought for harem duty and I felt a little stir of pleasure; orchards are pleasant even if one can't climb the trees.

A succession of prospective buyers stood before me and tilted their heads to one side, trying, I suppose, to imagine me in their houses as one imagines a table or a chair or a wall hanging. Would I go with the rest of it. A variety of people-buying faces looked at me from under turbans, fezzes, and kaffiyas. The pirate captain found many things to say about me, none of which I understood because he spoke in Arabic. He was at pains to show interested viewers that I had good teeth and he seemed particularly pleased by the arch of my foot, drawing attention to it frequently. In my mind I saw myself standing hour after hour outside the closed doors of a harem listening to laughter and low murmurings while little by little my feet grew flat.

There was standing before me a tall and noble-looking Turk with heroic moustaches, a red fez, a scarlet and purple jacket worked with gold. I judged him to be sixty or so. He put a large hand on my shoulder and drew me a few steps away from the others. He looked at me in such a way that I knew he was going to say something that would make me his friend. He said to me in Greek, "What if I say to you that the universe is a three-legged horse, eh? What then? What will you say to me?"

I said to him, "It is because the universe is a three-legged horse that the journey to the red heifer is so slow."

"Ah!" he said, "You're a Jew then."

"How does that follow?" I said.

"A Jew will consider anything," he said. "Are you or aren't you?"

"I am," I said.

"I need you," he said. "Do you need me?"

"Yes," I said.

"Done!" he said. My price was twenty-five dinars but he counted out fifty gold dinars and gave them to the pirate captain.

"This is twice as much as I have asked," said the pirate captain in Greek to the Turk. This pirate's name, by the way, was Prodigality. He had formerly been a slave named Thrift who had in trading for his merchant master put by enough money to buy his freedom, and having done so he changed his name and went into piracy. "Why are you doing this?" he said to the Turk.

"I am afraid not to," said my new owner. "I want Allah to take notice that I am taking notice of my good fortune."

"If Allah's taking notice I don't want to look bad," said Prodigality, and counting out twenty-five dinars he put them into my hand.

Both men looked at me with expectation.

"Can I buy myself back?" I said to my new owner.

"Just as you like," he said. Prodigality wrote out a bill of sale to him and he wrote out a bill of sale to me. I then gave him the gold that Prodigality had given me.

"Now you're a free man," said my former owner. "What will you do?"

"I'll come with you freely," I said, "as we need each other."

"Thus does the will of Allah manifest itself in human transactions," said my new friend.

"Wait!" said Prodigality as we turned to go, and taking my hand he put into it the remaining twenty-five dinars of the double payment.

"What's this?" I said.

"Allah wills what Allah wills," said Prodigality. "Let it be altogether circular."

"I am obedient to the will of Allah," I said, and put the gold back into the hand from which it had originally come.

"Let it be noticed by all who have eyes to see," said my new friend as he received the gold, "that Allah *has* taken notice."

"It's a pleasure doing business with you," said Prodigality. "It's spiritually refreshing. It's only a pity I can't afford this sort of thing more often."

With many expressions of mutual esteem we parted, and as I walked away with my former owner and new friend I marvelled at how Prodigality had been able to rise above the practical considerations of commerce. Certainly with my gold and diamonds and the plunder from the other pilgrims in his coffers he could afford to be generous but even so it seemed remarkable to me that gold and silver and gems could produce in him that degree of moral sensitivity that enabled him to behave so handsomely.

My new friend's name was Bembel Rudzuk; he was a wealthy merchant who lived in Antioch. I went with him to the khan where he and his party were staying, and the next morning we departed for Suwaydiyya on one of his dhows. "How strange that was yesterday!" I said to him. "How extraordinary!"

"Now more than other things," said Bembel Rudzuk. "To me everything is extraordinary and nothing is. Aeschylus was killed when he was hit on the head by a tortoise dropped by an eagle but that's not extraordinary when you consider that he was sitting directly below the eagle when it dropped the tortoise from a considerable height. On the other hand, that there *was* Aeschylus, *that* to me is extraordinary: that the world appeared in his eyes, that the world lived in him like the light in a lantern, that there are continually new lanterns for the world to live in, that you and I are two of them, yes, that to me is extraordinary."

"That the universe should be a three-legged horse," I said, "is that extraordinary, do you think?"

"I don't know what to think about that," said Bembel Rudzuk. "Although I said those words and know them to be true I have no idea what they signify. They came into my head when I first saw you yesterday. Perhaps they signify that for us our meeting is the fourth leg. What colour is the horse for you?"

"Red," I said, "like the heifer."

"For me also it is red," he said.

"Why do you need a Jew?" I said.

"Do you know that story of Abraham that is not to be found in the Holy Scriptures?" he said. "How Nimrod put him into the fiery furnace and God took him out?"

"Yes," I said, "I know that story."

"Do you perceive," he said, "that there is alchemy in this story?"

"Ah!" I said. "He was put into the furnace, he was taken out again."

"He will go in again," said Bembel Rudzuk.

"I believe you," I said. "And when will his base metal be transmuted to gold, how long will that take?"

"Ah!" he said. "It's the metal of those who put him into the fire that must be transmuted."

"Are there years enough for that?" I said.

"Whether there are or there aren't," he said, "that's nothing I can do anything about. But I'm curious about Abraham. Have you heard of the sulphur-mercury process?"

"I think I've seen diagrams of two triangles point to point," I said.

"That's right," he said. "In the diagrams one sees them point to point—the sulphur triangle with its hotness and dryness, the mercury triangle with its coldness and wetness. Look!" He flung out his arm towards the sea where the sun-points danced. "The hot and dry is dancing on the cold and wet; in everything can we see these combinations working. These two triangles that we see in the diagrams, they want to mingle their natures as they did in that veiled story in which the cold and wet of Abraham's water-nature was activated to neutralize the hot and dry of his fire-nature. Abraham, you know, is claimed by Jews and Arabs both. I myself believe that in this story he personifies the elemental complementarity that moves the universe. It is in the Holy Scriptures of your people that Abraham is first written of, and for this reason I want to avail myself of the action of your mind."

"How?" I said.

"There is a work that I have been thinking about for some time," he said. "I don't want to talk about it quite yet."

"Are you an alchemist?" I said.

"You mean with pots and furnaces?" he said.

"Yes," I said.

"No," he said. "That to me is greedy, it is a sweating after something to hold in the hand and look at, it is not a true giving, it is not an honest offering of the self to the Unity from which all multiplicity comes."

"But your two triangles," I said, "your sulphur-mercury process?"

"Look!" he said again. The crew were wearing the vessel round before the wind. The helmsman put the tiller over to bring the wind aft, the great triangle of the mainsail was let fly, the old windward shrouds were eased off and the new windward shrouds set up as we came about; the mainsail was sheeted home again and we filled away on the new tack. "Wind alchemy," said Bembel Rudzuk. "The triangle of the sail fills first on one side then on the other to drive us forward. Two triangles. My alchemy seeks no yellow metal; it is a continual offering to the Unity at the heart of the multiplicity. It makes no distinction between what is called something and what is called nothing, it knows such words to be without meaning." The sail swelled as if with the breath of God, the dhow pitched forward and reared back as if nodding in agreement with the words of Bembel Rudzuk, the sun-points danced on the water, the dark crew, some in white and some in faded colours, ranged themselves along the windward rail. I felt such a Nowness in the light of the day that Christ leapt into my mind like the visual echo of his unheard voice. "Ah!" I said, "This, this, this!" He was gone, there were only the sun-points on the water, the breath of God in the sail.

"Yes," said Bembel Rudzuk, "you see!"

We made our way up the coast in short stages, calling at Tortosa, Marquiya, Baniyas, and Ladhiqiyya to discharge and take on a variety of cargoes. Each port in the changing lights of the day would grow smoothly and mysteriously larger and more detailed in the eye as we approached: first the massed groupings of light and shadow of the moored vessels, the low waterside buildings, the domes and minarets of the town behind; then the slow shifting of the grouped lights and shadows into separate and varied lights and shadows growing larger, more clear, becoming individually defined masts and sails and rigging, painted boats rocking at their moorings, figures aboard them standing and moving, faces looking across the green and sheltered, the shining and the shadowed water above which drifted the smells of cooking, the smoke of charcoal fires against a background of warehouse roofs and windows and open doors, cordage and tackle, bales, barrels, carts and wagons of the waterside. And always in front of this the motion of vessels arriving, vessels departing, and aboard these vessels faces passing, passing, locked in unknownness, growing smaller, becoming unseen.

Although our business in Ladhiqiyya was finished early in the evening we did not leave until much later; Suwaydiyya was only three or four hours away and Bembel Rudzuk wanted to arrive with th⸍ dawn rather than in the middle of the night. "Dawn is the best time foɪ ⸜ɔming into port," he said, "and I always allow myself this pleasure when coming home."

The feeble lamp-glimmers of the coast shifted subtly in our passing and were swallowed in obscurity. I looked up at the sky but the Virgin and the Lion were not to be seen, there were no stars, the night was opaque; this was already November and the rainy season. "Would the Virgin and the Lion be visible if the sky were clear?" I asked Bembel Rudzuk.

"No," he said, "they are below the horizon now."

Towards morning it began to rain, and it was in the grey rainlight that Suwaydiyya offered to us the shapes of dawn all dark and huddled, the low waterside buildings curtained with rain, the water of the harbour leaping up in points to meet the downpour, the dawn boats rocking to the morning slap of the water on their sides, furled sails wet with dawn and rain and still heavy with night, crews sheltering under awnings, the smoke of their breakfast fires ghostly in the rain. And as always all of it, the whole picture in the eyes, had without seeming to come closer grown smoothly bigger in that particular way in which things reveal themselves when approached by sea, opening to the approacher more and more detail, more and more imminence of what is to come. And always, thus approaching, one feels the new day, the new place, coming forward to read the face of the approacher. Always the held breath, the questioning look of the grey morning, the seclusion of the rain.

On boarding Bembel Rudzuk's dhow I had noticed the name painted on the bows in Arabic characters but I had not asked what that name was; I didn't want to know. Having already been transferred from the *Balena* to *Nineveh* and having so far proclaimed nothing whatever on behalf of the Lord I preferred not to be aware of any further names of significance for a time; I wished if possible to be reabsorbed into the ordinary. But no sooner had we stepped ashore than I noticed again the Arabic characters painted on the bows, my mouth opened and was already asking Bembel Rudzuk what the name was before I could stop it.

"Sophia," he said.

Horses were brought and we rode to Antioch, a dozen or so miles up the Orontes. The rain lessened into a dull brightness, that particular dull brightness that is always a little frightening in its blank revelation: one perceives that there is nowhere anything ordinary; there is only the extraordinary. It was from miles away that I first saw Mount Silpius and the many-towered walls ascending from the plain where stood the houses, domes, and minarets of Antioch on the River Orontes. Bigger and bigger in my eyes grew the mountain and the towered walls, the tawny towered walls and high up on the mountain the tawny citadel with its green-and-gold banner hanging motionless in the dull brightness. The mountain itself was browny purple, then blue-green tawny. Everything in that land was tawny either over or under whatever colour else it had. A lion-coloured land.

The mountain! Even a small mountain is always a surprise, it is always so much itself. The first sight of any mountain is the actuality of its strangeness. Let Mount Silpius stand for all strange mountains as it manifests itself in the grey light of morning, as it shows its purple shadows and its tawny dust darkened by the rain, as it shows its strangeness and its dread. That Moses was given the Tables of the Law on a mountain is significant: every mountain is the dreadful mountain of the Law, there move over it the thunder and the lightnings, there move on it the smoke and fire, there sounds from it the trumpet of the dreadful summons. The dread is that now is Now, that here is Here, that everything that is actually is, and everything is irrevocably moving.

With the mountain continually in my eyes I entered that city quick with life, with sound and motion and colour; that city quick with wealth, quick with thought. I understood immediately what it was: it was what in one form or another comes between the pilgrim and Jerusalem. One says, " 'If I forget thee, O Jerusalem!' " and then one forgets Jerusalem and life for a time is sweet in Antioch. I wanted to embrace everything—domes and minarets and the shadows of awnings, even the cynical camels with their swaying loads of the goods of this world. In my heart I embraced the Mittelteufel, I said, "Perhaps there is no Jerusalem, perhaps nothing is required of me. Perhaps there is only Antioch."

Bembel Rudzuk said, "There *is* Jerusalem, and whatever is required of you is required; but in this present moment is Antioch and you are here to do what will be done by you here." The air in the courtyard of Bembel Rudzuk's house was misted by a fountain, passing, passing, not for ever. "We are brothers," said Bembel Rudzuk, and embraced me.

"What am I?" I said. "I am a eunuch, I am cut off from my generations, I am not a man, I am nothing." I wept by the silvery plashing of the fountain.

Bembel Rudzuk said, "What say your Holy Scriptures? 'Let not the eunuch say, I am a dry tree.'"

"But I *am* a dry tree," I said.

"Listen!" said Bembel Rudzuk. He had got a Greek Bible and was reading to me:

> "Thus saith the Lord to the eunuchs,
> as many as shall keep my sabbaths,
> and choose the things which I take pleasure in,
> and take hold of my covenant; I will give to them
> in my house and within my walls an honourable place,
> better than sons and daughters: I will give them an ever-
> lasting name, and it shall not fail."

"In the Hebrew it doesn't say 'fail,'" I said. "In the Hebrew it says 'be cut off'":

> "Even unto them will I give in my house
> and within my walls a monument and a memorial
> better than sons and daughters;
> I will give them an everlasting memorial,
> that shall not be cut off.

"Tell me if you can, what everlasting memorial is there better than sons and daughters? And how shall it not be cut off?"

"Better than sons and daughters is to be with the stillness that is always becoming motion," said Bembel Rudzuk. "And in being with this stillness-into-motion there is a continuity that is not cut off."

The words rattled on my head like pebbles on a roof. "Where am I?" I said.

"What do you mean?" said Bembel Rudzuk.

"In the dark wood with murderers, with the headless corpse of the tax-collector and the maggots I knew where I was," I said. "I had a whereness to be in. Now I don't know where I am, I don't have where to be."

"Let me show you something," he said. Taking me into the house he pointed to a geometric pattern of tiles ornamenting the front of a dais. "Look," he said.

I looked. The pattern went its way as such patterns do.

"This pattern is contiguous with infinity," said Bembel Rudzuk. "Once the mode of repetition is established the thing goes on for ever. It is apparently stopped by its border but in actuality it never stops."

I said, "You mean in potentiality, don't you? Potentially it could continue although actually it stops."

"Tell me," he said, "where does one draw the line between potentiality and actuality? It isn't as if we're looking at a rain cloud and we say, 'Potentially it could rain but actually it isn't raining.' This is something else: with patterns when you say what can be, you're describing what already is. Patterns cannot be originated, they can only be taken notice of. When a pattern shows itself in tiles or on paper or in your mind and says, 'This is the mode of my repetition; in this manner can I extend myself to infinity,' it has already done so, it has already been infinite from the very first moment of its being; the potentiality and the actuality are one thing. If two and two can be four then they already *are* four, you can only perceive it, you have no part in making it happen by writing it down in numbers or telling it out in pebbles. When we draw on paper or lay out in tiles a pattern that we have not seen before we are only recording something that has always been happening; the air all around us, the earth we stand on, the very particles of our being are continually active with an unimaginable multiplicity of patterns, all of them contiguous with infinity."

"That's no help to me," I said.

"Yes it is," he said. "It's a great help to everyone."

"How?" I said.

"For one thing it gives you a whereness to be in," he said. "The patterns traversing one place intersect the patterns traversing another place, and by this webbing of pattern all places are connected. Wherever you are at this moment you are connected with all places where you have ever been, all places where you will ever be, and all places where you never have been and never will be."

I held out my hand in front of me and looked at it. I thought of the patterns of veins and arteries, of muscles and bones beneath the skin. I thought of the patterns within the bone and muscle, I thought of the patterns contained in the sperm and the egg and the pattern of their combination, the thought of God, the word of flesh.

"People also are connected," said Bembel Rudzuk, "all people of every time and every place."

I thought of Sophia, I thought of the way in which we could never again be connected. "You and I," I said, "how are we connected?"

"We are brothers," he said.

"Yes," I said, "but how was it that we became brothers? You've said that you want to avail yourself of the action of my mind for a work you've had in your mind. Can you now tell me what this work is?"

"I want you to devise a pattern," he said.

"What kind of a pattern?" I said.

"With tiles," he said.

"A pattern with tiles," I said. "For this have you come to the slave market in Tripoli to find yourself a castrated Jew."

"That's not how it was," said Bembel Rudzuk. "I was there on my ordinary business, receiving a cargo and trading in the markets. Having done my business I came to the slave market as one does, strolling here and there. Prodigality was shouting, 'Jerusalem pilgrims! Jerusalem pilgrims! Very lucky! Don't miss this chance!'

"I said to him, 'How are Jerusalem pilgrims lucky?'

"He said, 'They'll bring luck.'

"I said, 'How?'

"He said, 'Who am I to know such things?'

"I said, 'Why, then? Why do you say they'll bring luck?'

"He said, 'Only think! Possessed by their Christ, driven by a mystical force, they swim rivers, they climb mountains, they strive with brigands who would take their lives, all to travel to Jerusalem! Buy a Jerusalem pilgrim and all this mystical force can be yours!'

"I said, 'Won't it rather bring ill luck, to come like this between a pilgrim and his goal?'

" 'Not at all,' said Prodigality. 'Obviously the Christ of these pilgrims has willed that they should become the slaves of the believers of the one true faith.'

"Walking slowly and pondering these things," said Bembel Rudzuk,

"I found myself standing before you. It was then that there came to me the words that I spoke to you."

I said, "But why do you want me to make a pattern with tiles?"

He said, "This idea came into my mind. An idea is an eye given by God for the seeing of God."

"Is that really so?" I said. "The idea of murdering someone comes into the mind of the murderer; is this also an eye given by God for the seeing of God?"

"The murderer too sees God," said Bembel Rudzuk, "and perhaps more than others. In any case this idea cannot possibly harm anyone as far as I can see. Can you see any harm in it?"

"No," I said, "I cannot."

This conversation was taking place at the close of day, after the sunset prayer. Behind Bembel Rudzuk's words I heard the falling water of the fountain, the cooing of doves. There came into my mind the twilight at Manzikert on the day of the battle in 1071, the year of my birth. This twilight I knew in my soul, I knew it to be Bruder Pförtner's courtyard, the quiet place where plashes the fountain of his reverie. At the close of that August day at Manzikert the Byzantine Emperor Romanus IV Diogenes must have felt what he had become as the day waned: no longer a man but a line on a map, the ebbing tide-line of Byzantium, ebbing from the sharp edge of the present like blood from a knife. Andronicus and the rear line gone and the Turks all round like murderous stinging bees. Romanus must have smelt Bruder Pförtner's breath, fresh and salty like the wind from the sea, he must have felt himself at that turning centre of all things where stillness revolves into motion and motion into stillness. Aiyee! must have cried the life in him as his blinding and his death moved towards him in that twilight at Manzikert. As Byzantium receded with him towards the allness of everything.

I found myself weeping for Romanus Diogenes and for that Jew who was made to be his executioner. In that twilight in the courtyard of Bembel Rudzuk in Antioch I thought also of Alexius Comnenus, now in 1096 Emperor of Byzantium. The reality of his empire presented itself to me all at once like a naked idiot: he was emperor of the passing of Byzantium, his empire was becoming moment by moment the illusion of, the non-reality of, the unpotentiality of Byzantium. At some point the naked idiot of this actuality became the naked truth of it and I saw, or perhaps I am only just

[443]

now seeing, or perhaps I have not yet seen and I am at some time going to see that the names of things, of times, of places, of events, are useful for reference and they have some subjective meaning but as often as not they obscure the actuality of the thing they attempt to describe. Now as I think about it I see that we don't always know what it is that we are putting a name to. We are, for example, clever enough to know that a year is a measure of passage, not permanence; we call the seasons spring, summer, autumn, and winter, knowing that they are continually passing one into the other. We are not surprised at this but when we give to seasons of another sort the names Rome, Byzantium, Islam, or Mongol Empire we are astonished to see that each one refuses to remain what it is.

"Why are you weeping?" said Bembel Rudzuk.

"I am suffering from an attack of history," I said.

"It will pass," said Bembel Rudzuk.

"Where is this tile pattern to be done?" I said.

"I have bought a piece of land just inside the wall at the foot of Mount Silpius not far from the Tower of the Two Sisters," he said.

"And you're having a house built on it?" I said.

"No," he said, "I have had it prepared as a plane for tiling. I have had the ground cleared and paved with stone so that it's perfectly flat. It's one hundred and twenty feet by one hundred and twenty feet."

"That's fourteen thousand four hundred square feet of pattern," I said. "Why does it have to be so big?"

"Ask rather why it's no bigger," he said. "And the answer to that is that this was the biggest piece of land available within the wall. Ideally the plane would extend to the horizon on all sides."

"Why is that?" I said.

"Because in this case the ideal is the maximum effort possible," he said, "and the horizon is the outer limit of how much of the pattern can be taken in by the eye."

"It wouldn't do to draw it on a piece of paper to hold in the hand?" I said.

"No," he said, "As you must know in your heart, it is not only the apparent quantity of a thing that changes with the degree of effort, the manifest character of it changes also as Thing-in-Itself reveals more of itself."

"Is that what the pattern is for?" I said: "To show Thing-in-Itself?"

"You know as well as I do," he said, "that Thing-in-Itself is not to be seen nor is it to be sought directly. My desires are modest; there are simply one or two things I should like to observe, one or two things I should like to think about."

"Can you tell me what they are?" I said.

"Motion is one of them," he said. "There is transitive motion and there is intransitive motion: the motion of a galloping horse is transitive, it passes through our field of vision and continues on to wherever it is going; the motion in a tile pattern is intransitive, it does not pass; it moves but it stays in our field of vision. It arises from stillness, and I should like to think about the point at which stillness becomes motion. Another thing I should like to think about is the point at which pattern becomes consciousness."

"Does it?" I said. "Can this be proved?"

"I know in my innermost being that it does," he said, "and I know that we ourselves are the proof of it, but whether this proof can be demonstrated I don't know. It may well be that the proof is being demonstrated constantly but in our ignorance we cannot recognize it."

"This design that you want me to make," I said, "how should it look?"

"That will come from you," he said. "It will come from your hand at the moment when you begin to draw. Try not to think about it beforehand, don't let your mind become busy with it."

"My mind is already busy with it," I said. "How could it not be?"

"In that case you should do it now," he said, "and we must go to the place where it is to be done." From a cabinet he took a straight-edge and a large wooden compass fitted with a piece of chalk and we left the house.

Through the darkening murmurous evening, past the lamps of evening and the smells of cooking we made our way to the paved space at the foot of Mount Silpius near the Tower of the Two Sisters. The town was still murmurous but all the voices of the day that had been close were now distant. Before us Mount Silpius gathered itself into night. The lamplight in the windows of the towers made the stone around them bulk darker against the sky. Someone was playing an oud, someone was singing; it was a woman's voice rising and failing in a pattern of repetition contiguous with infinity. Warm and sad the voice, a woman of flesh and bone, contiguous with infinity! On Bembel Rudzuk's paved square some boys were kicking a blown-up bladder that rasped with a skittering rush across the stone, each thump of the kicking like the unsequent beat of a disembodied heart; the voices of the boys appeared at sudden places in the gathering night, now near, now far; their feet scuffled mysteriously on the stone.

That evening Bembel Rudzuk and I felt ourselves to be inside the walls of Antioch, how could we not? There were the walls of stone all strong and thick and guarded by soldiers, there were the towers with their lamplit windows girdling the city in the encircling night. Yet even then, so contiguous was my mind, is my mind, with infinity that my thoughts found themselves here in this present space in which only broken remnants of those strong walls stand and the inside is seen to be one with the outside. My consciousness that evening in 1096 came forward to the present and the toothless broken stones of now, and my present consciousness goes back to the great thick towered walls forty feet high and paced by weaponed men.

Strong walls, always have strong walls been walked by weaponed men. And those who came and took Antioch, such stones they captured in their strong places up and down the land, such stones they put together in their Latin Kingdom, those strong men and those who came after them! As Pilgermann the owl I fly on silent wings above them looking down. Lion-stones, warrior stones, now they have peace. How they sing in their silence, how they are easy, the great strong stones, the lion-stones, the tawny. Even they, the strong stones of the great Jew-killers, even they have longed for ruin and the stillness, for the wind sighing over them, for the grass growing on roofless walls and alone-standing arches. Even when the arrows hissed from the loopholes the stones were singing the stillness to come, the clopping of cows' hooves up and down the stone steps where those iron-ringing men walked in their time. Now the stones have arrived at the strong life of the stillness of them, their strong song, their stillness dancing in the sun.

Warrior lords, those great and fierce men, recruiters of stone, of walls and towers on high ground, of strongholds commanding borders, river crossings, approaches. They said to the stones, as other warrior lords before them had said to the stones of Antioch, "Be thou firm against the enemy." And what did the stones say? The stones said, "We have no enemy." Lying in the sun they sing the stillness; toppling and rolling they shout, "God is motion!"

So. Bembel Rudzuk and I in the deepening night in Antioch. Bats fretting the darkness into little points and the woman's voice rising and falling in her song as we stood on the stone paving that was waiting for my design.

The centre of the square was marked by a wooden rod standing upright in the stone. It seemed to me that I could feel the power of the centre there, feel the radii going out from it and coming into it. There was no moon, there were no stars but we could see well enough for our purpose. We had brought no lantern nor did I want one; it seemed right that the design should come out of obscurity, and I wanted to be unobserved, I wanted the shelter of the dark.

Bembel Rudzuk was saying very quietly in Arabic:

"Labbaika, Allahumma, labbaika."

Then he said to me in Greek, "What I said was: 'At Thy service, O Lord, at Thy service.' These words are to be spoken only on pilgrimage to Mecca but I could not refrain from saying them." He took the rod out of its socket, inserted a wooden plug that he had brought with him, and stepped back.

I opened the legs of the compass, stuck the point of the centre leg into the plug and swept the outer leg round to make my first circle. It went just like that; I had no hesitation in deciding on the length of the radius; one action followed another, and as the compass leg swept round there followed it obediently through the darkness a white chalk line that closed itself into a circle as if the impulse had been already there waiting in the stone until, now summoned by the compass, it rose up to the surface.

Keeping the same radius I made the overlapping circles that divided the circumference of my first circle into six parts and produced a flower of six petals luminous in the white chalk. Connecting the points of the petals made a hexagon. From the six points of the hexagon came the two interlocking triangles of the six-pointed star within the hexagon. Connecting the points of intersection divided the two interlocking triangles into twelve small triangles. Extending the lines of the hexagon made the two large interlocking triangles of a second six-pointed star that contained the hexagon containing the first six-pointed star. Lines balanced on the points of the outer star gave an outer hexagon in which eighteen equilateral triangles enclosed the inner hexagon. This completed the unit that would repeat itself in my tile pattern.

"What is the name of this design?" said Bembel Rudzuk.

"I don't know," I said.

"Think on it," he said. "It will come to you."

We went back to Bembel Rudzuk's house. He gave me paper and coloured inks and drawing instruments and I made a drawing in which I repeated the unit twelve times in the pattern in which the tiles would be arranged. Then I coloured it, making the large and small triangles of the large and small six-pointed stars alternately red and black. The triangles contiguous with the right-hand sides of the star-points (which, going round like the blades of a waterwheel, became left-hand sides then right-hand sides again) were coloured red or black in contrast to the star-points. All other triangles were tawny-coloured.

My pattern was certainly a simple one, primitive even; I was surprised therefore to see how much action there was in it and how many different kinds of action there were: there were twisting serpents, there were shadowed pyramids, and when I tilted my head at the necessary angle the twelve small triangles of the inner stars became the deeply shadowed face of a red lion. When I tilted my head back to the vertical the triangles went blank, an empty mask looked at me instead of a lion. However one looked at the pattern there could be no doubt that the stillness had become motion but I hadn't noticed at what point it had happened. Sometimes the larger triangles revolved around the inner stars, sometimes they took angular courses, pausing occasionally to group themselves in pyramids before continuing on their way. The pattern was altogether regular and predictable but from time to time there came to the eye enclaves of apparent disorder that in a moment disappeared; this had to do with the alternation of the red and the black; the periodicity of the colours was not synchronized with that of the shapes.

"Can you tell me now what the name of this design is?" said Bembel Rudzuk.

I tilted my head, the shadowed lion looked at me; I tilted my head back, the triangles went blank. "The name of this design is Hidden Lion," I said. There leapt up in me a wild surge of terror and joy as virtuality, correctly named, leapt into actuality.

II

One wakes up in the morning and puts on oneself. Everyone has experienced this: the self must be put on before any garment, and there is inevitably a pause as it were a caesura in the going forward of things before the self is put on. Why is this? It is because our mortal identity is not the primary one, not the profound, not the deep one. No, what wakes up from sleep is not Tiglath-Pileser or Peter Schlemiel or Pilgermann; it is simply raw undifferentiated being, brute being with nothing driving it but the forward motion imparted to it by the original explosion into being of the universe. For a fraction of a moment it is itself only; then must it with joy or terror put on that identity taken on with mortal birth, that identity that each morning is the cumulative total of its mortal days and nights, that self old or young, sick or well, brave or cowardly, beautiful or ugly, whole or mutilated, that is one's lot.

Every morning when I woke up I had perforce to put on the identity of Eunuch. I had to make to myself a little oration that always began with, "Yes, but . . . ." As the raw being of me drew back from the identity that was offered I would say, "Yes, but still there are things to be done, still there is life and world, still there is action required of me." On the morning after drawing Hidden Lion on the stone and on the paper I woke up and said, "Yes, but there is Hidden Lion," and just at that moment there came moving upon the morning air the call of the mu'addhin. It seemed to me that his voice, contiguous with infinity, was tracing on the air the pattern I had drawn upon the stone and upon the paper, and I moved forward eagerly into the day.

The hum of the day arose from the city, the work of the day began: the beating of hammers, the baking of bread, the voices of buying and selling. Through these streets of the action of every day we walked to our paved square of stillness that was waiting to become what it would become. The morning sun slanted its light across the paving-stones, the wooden rod in the centre with its morning shadow told the time. The chalk lines drawn by me in darkness were shocking in the light of morning, strange and surprising in their actuality, like a mountain.

"Does it seem to you," said Bembel Rudzuk, "that this design was already waiting in the stone for the time when it would become visible?"

"Yes," I said. "I think that all possible patterns were in these stones even before they were cut and dressed and made into paving-stones."

We both stood looking at the chalk lines on the tawny stone. Having spoken the words we had just spoken we now found in our minds the next thought: the actions that would take place on those tiles that were not yet made, were those actions also waiting in the paving-stones that would then be under the tiles?

Bembel Rudzuk measured the three different triangles that in their multiples made up Hidden Lion and wrote down his measurements on a sheet of paper which he put into his document case.

"When can we start?" I said.

As I spoke the shadow of the wooden rod faded into the tawniness of the stone. We both looked up at the grey sky.

"In the spring," said Bembel Rudzuk, "when the rains are over."

I felt like a child deprived of a treat. I wanted something to happen immediately, I felt that such manhood as now remained to me could only live so long as there was action to nourish it. I stretched out my arms towards the corners of the stone square, trying to pull into myself the power that radiated from the centre and passed beyond the outer limits of the paving to infinity.

A small boy walked on to the stone at a corner of the square. He looked sharp and hungry, like a fox. Like a fox, wary and watchful, he came slowly step by step from the corner towards the centre, walking as one walks on thin ice; perhaps he was counting. At a certain point he stopped, knelt on the stone, and began to draw on it, first with a bit of charcoal then with red ochre. What he drew was a triangle with a short base and long sides; it was irregularly divided into pointed red and black shapes, some triangular, some diamond-shaped, unevenly massed and drawn all skewed and crooked, like scales on a deformed serpent; from base to apex there ran up the middle, like spines, a line of black diamond shapes. Near the triangle he drew a lopsided circle made up of other black and red shapes, masses of black, slivers of red; it suggested the giant eye of an unimagined insect. From this eye emanated red and black arrows.

I walked over to the boy. I had learned to say in Arabic, "What is this called?" and now I pointed to his design and said this to him.

He looked up at me attentively and shook his head.

I said in Greek, "What is this called? What is it meant to be?"

Again he shook his head, still looking at me attentively.

"Did you understand me?" I said.

He nodded.

"Are you able to speak?" I said.

He shook his head. Had his speech been castrated? Had his tongue been cut out? I didn't want to ask why he was unable to speak. Had he made a vow of silence?

Still looking at me with that same serious attention he held out his left hand with the fingers outspread and curved as if holding a sphere, then he slowly rotated his wrist. Having done this he stood up and walked back as he had come: first to the corner of the paved square then away into the town.

Then the grey sky opened and down came the rain. As it poured down and drenched me to the skin my heart leapt up to meet it, I didn't know why. That rain, the prospect of which had only a moment before filled me with despair, was now bringing me ease and refreshment.

Under that drenching rain we went to the brickyard. There was little to be seen but an expanse of mud leaping up in points, a little square mud-brick building with a dome, and two or three little square ziggurats that I took to be kilns. In the doorway of the mud-brick building lounged a little moon-faced man of fifty or so; his face was contemplative and serene.

"This brickmaster," said Bembel Rudzuk, "this lord of the bricks, his name is Bab el-Burj, Tower Gate. He used to be a slave and his name was Efficiency."

"Why is his name now Tower Gate?" I said. "I prefer to avoid people and boats with symbolic names if I can."

"There's no symbolism in it that I know of," said Bembel Rudzuk; "he simply liked the wordplay of Bab el-Tower, that's all."

"No bricks," said Tower Gate when we stood before him. "As you see, I have no bricks whatever, I have only the emptiness left behind by a great many bricks. I am contemplating this emptiness."

"May we contemplate it as well?" said Bembel Rudzuk.

"I don't think there's enough for the three of us," said Tower Gate. "Let me offer you rather some refreshment."

The interior of the little mud-brick building was sumptuously carpeted and adorned with gorgeous hangings and cushions. Bembel Rudzuk and I sat down while a puddle formed around us and Tower Gate gave us a drink made with dates and honey. He had no servant with him nor were there any workmen to be seen.

"Strange, is it not," said Tower Gate, "that in the Quran there is no chapter called 'The Kiln' or 'The Oven'? It's such a good metaphor, it lends itself so well to metaphysics."

"There's the Jonas chapter," said Bembel Rudzuk: "he went into the whale and came out of the whale as a brick goes into and comes out of the kiln."

"Jonas was half-baked," said Tower Gate; "he was still unfinished and without wisdom when the whale vomited him up. No, as a metaphor Jonas is not in a class with bricks." Tower Gate was given to making what might be called "Aha!" and "Oho!" gestures with his hands, and so he gestured now. "Neither is bread," he said ("Oho!" said his hands): "bread is baked and eaten and becomes excrement. Brick, which is bread of earth, bread of our origins, is also baked—like Abraham it is put into the fire and like him it emerges hard and enduring, ready to shelter the humble and the mighty both." ("Aha!" said his hands.) "It is eaten by time but only slowly, slowly through the alternating dawns and darks of this continuous demonstration that we call the world. No excrement."

"You have given me so much to think about that I cannot remember what I came to see you about," said Bembel Rudzuk.

PILGERMANN

"Bricks?" said Tower Gate.

"Ah!" said Bembel Rudzuk. "You read my mind." He took out of his document case the drawing in which I had repeated the Hidden Lion pattern and showed it to Tower Gate.

"Oho!" said Tower Gate with his voice and his hands both. "The Willing Virgin!"

"What willing virgin?" said Bembel Rudzuk.

"This pattern that you show me," said Tower Gate, "it's called 'The Willing Virgin.'"

"Why?" I said.

"Because the next time you look there's something different about it," he said. "Of course that's true of many patterns but this is the one with that name. Had you another name for it?"

"Hidden Lion," I said. I wasn't able not to say it although I had wanted the name to be known only to Bembel Rudzuk and me.

"Aha!" said Tower Gate. "Very good indeed! The lion is hidden in the willing virgin; after all who can say no to a lion?"

All of us pondered this for several moments.

"How big are the big triangles?" said Tower Gate.

"Nine and a half inches to a side," said Bembel Rudzuk.

Tower Gate took my right hand, spread it out, and measured the span with an ivory ruler. "Aha!" he said. "Nine and a half inches! Had you noticed that?"

"No," I said.

"Your design?" he said to me.

"Yes," I said.

"You're going to put this pattern on that empty square of yours?" said Tower Gate to Bembel Rudzuk.

"Yes," said Bembel Rudzuk.

"It's good that you come to me now," said Tower Gate. "I can think about it over the winter and I'll tell you in the spring."

"Tell us what?" I said.

"Whether I want to have anything to do with it," he said.

"Why does it need so much thinking?" I said.

Tower Gate looked at me as if he thought that talking to me might be a waste of time. "You're dealing with infinity," he said. "I suppose you know that?"

"Yes," I said.

"This pattern," said Tower Gate to Bembel Rudzuk, "this square of yours, it's not to be the floor of a building or the courtyard of a khan or anything like that, is it?"

"No," said Bembel Rudzuk, "it's just to be itself, it's not a part of something else."

Tower Gate tilted his head to one side and made with his mouth a sound expressive of doubt, misgiving, and deprecation. "That's it, you see," he said. "That's what gives me pause, that's what's putting the wind up me. Any other pattern I've seen has been ornamenting something, it's been *part* of something, it has not in itself been something. Do you see what I mean? To incorporate a pattern of infinity in a house is not immodest, one's eyes are in a sense averted from the nakedness of Thing-in-Itself. But here you're doing something else altogether: you're making this pattern with no other purpose than to look at Thing-in-Itself. This to me seems unlucky."

"On the other hand," said Bembel Rudzuk, "who has put this idea into my head if not Allah? And who has guided the hand of my friend if not Allah?"

"What a question!" said Tower Gate. "Do we not read in the Quran that whatever good happens to thee is from Allah but whatever evil happens to thee is from thy own soul?"

"And from where does my soul come if not from Allah?" said Bembel Rudzuk.

"What do we know? Who are we to say?" said Tower Gate's hands. With his voice he said nothing.

As we walked home through the rain Bembel Rudzuk seemed to be carrying on an interior conversation with himself. Sometimes he shook his head, sometimes he nodded, sometimes he shrugged.

"What is it?" I said.

"This matter of the tiles," he said, "there's nothing simple about it— one can so easily go about it the wrong way. At first I had in mind to make them of sun-dried mud; I wanted nothing too permanent, I wanted clay from the river bank that would endure only its little season as artifact before it returned to itself. Then there came to me a dream: I was standing on Hidden Lion near the centre of it. The pattern was complete. At the centre of it stood a little tower and at the top of the tower stood a hooded figure who pointed with his finger to the tiles. They were fired and glazed. This hooded personage said nothing but in my mind were the words: 'They have lasted this long because they have passed through the fire.'"

How strange it was to me, that rainy season through which passed the year 1096 into the year 1097. It was strange in the way in which it associated itself with a name and an image. Through the winter rains there echoed cavernously under the main street of Antioch a great rolling rush of waters in which could be heard the heavy sliding of earth and sand and gravel. This was the winter torrent that little by little was carrying Mount Silpius away into the river and the sea. Down through the cleft in Silpius ran the torrent, through the Bab el-Hadid, the Iron Gate, then under the city it rumbled through its vaulted channel to the Orontes. Onopniktes was the name of this torrent: Onopniktes, the Donkey-Drowner. When I first heard that name a thrill of recognition ran through me, there appeared in my mind the dark and echoing caverns of that churning flood in which rolled over and over dead donkeys in the wild foam. Because of its name, because of the idea of those dead donkeys rolling in the racing flood, because of the idea of the mountain rushing particle by particle under the city to the river and the sea, Onopniktes became in my mind one with the rush of history and the rising of a darkness in the name of Christ.

    While that greater Onopniktes that coursed its wild way under the cities of the world brought the Franks upon its flood to Antioch, Bembel Rudzuk carried on his business from day to day but ranged less widely than he used to, both in his shipments and in his travels; he was wealthy enough to be as busy or as unbusy as he chose, and for the present he confined his trading to the stretch of coast from Suwaydiyya south to Ghaza. Professionally well-informed by his correspondents, he noted that pirates were active more than usual; he also had news of the departures of the various armies of Christ on their way to our part of the world. Bembel Rudzuk traded mostly in silk and he found the rise and fall of the price of a standard bale a reliable index to the Mediterranean state of mind. "To-day the market is like a firm and well-shaped pair of buttocks," he said, "but tomorrow it could be like burnt stubble. Risk is salt to the meat of commerce but I don't like the smell of the world just now; it has the smell of disorder, it has the smell of a leaking ship in which sea water has got

[457]

into the silk and the crew have opened the wineskins and are looting the cargo; it has the smell of mildew and rotting oranges."

Strolling in his warehouse, snuffing up the scents of commerce from the corded canvas bales, Bembel Rudzuk clinked in his hand a sealed purse of gold dinars. "This purse is sealed," he said: "I cannot see what is in it but I believe the number and the weight of the coins written on it; I know that these coins are not made of glass or iron or brass because I know that I can trust the assayer who tested and weighed them and sealed them and the merchant who sent them and the slave who delivered them. Trust is what commerce is founded on; we merchants put our trust in God and in one another. We have no idea what God will do with his winds and weather, his storms and seas, we can't know whether he wills profit or loss until we have either profited or lost. We are in his hand, knowing nothing. When anyone tells me that God wills this or that, whether he be Christian or Muslim I grow uneasy."

Onopniktes the Donkey-Drowner bellowed like a minotaur in its caverns. Franks put their feet into their footsteps moving towards an Antioch and a Jerusalem full of corpses not yet ripe for the glory of Christ, corpses still green and walking about. December came and Chanukah to Antioch in Syria that had once been the kingdom of that Antiochus Epiphanes against whom fought and prevailed the Maccabees. The Jews of the Antioch of 1096, dyers and glass-blowers mostly, lit their daily candles, gave Chanukah money to their children; the children spun their dreidels on which the letters Nun, Gimel, Hey, and Shin stood for the words NAIS GADOL HAYAH SHOM: A GREAT MIRACLE WAS PERFORMED THERE. On the rain-glistening tawny stones of Antioch they spun their dreidels, the spinning contiguous with the rain and infinity.

Because non-Muslims were required to register and to pay the djizya or poll-tax, my Jewish presence had been known to the Nagid, the leader of the Jewish community, to the Rabbi of the congregation, and to every other Jew in Antioch almost as soon as I had arrived. The Nagid and the Rabbi welcomed me to the Jewish community and the Rabbi wanted to welcome me to the congregation as well. I had perforce to tell him that I was not eligible for this privilege, citing Deuteronomy 23:2:

> He that is crushed or maimed in his privy parts
> shall not enter into the assembly of the Lord.

PILGERMANN

"Pardon me," said the Rabbi (his name was Akiba ben Eliezer; he was stocky, muscular, red-haired, quarrelsome-looking), "now I'm confused—am I the eunuch and you're the Rabbi or are you the eunuch and I'm the Rabbi?"

"I'm the eunuch," I said.

"Good," he said. "I'm glad we got that straight. This is interesting for me because this is the first time I've been instructed by a Jewish eunuch. You're sure you're not an Egyptian and maybe you've been asleep in some pharaoh's tomb all these years?"

"I'm sorry I spoke," I said.

"Please," he said, "no excuses. If one member can't wag then let it be another, who am I to say no."

"Thank you," I said, "for your forbearance. I don't mean to be taking up your time like this."

"I've got more time than I have eunuchs," he said; "so at the moment my demand exceeds your supply and you're precious."

"Not according to the Holy Scriptures," I said.

"Big scholar, are you?"he said. He had a thrusting sort of face with light blue eyes, and now he eyed me thrustingly.

"No scholar," I said.

"Lucky for me," he said. "I have enough big scholars already, I don't need more. Let me point out that this Deuteronomy business is not that simple. After all, if God thought that His word needed nothing more to be said about it He wouldn't have created rabbis, would He. No. So let me justify my existence."

"You don't have to," I said. "Live and be well."

"Don't try to push me away," he said. "Listen, do you know about Noah?"

"What about him?" I said.

"Noah ended up castrated," he said. "Did you know that?"

"No," I said. "Who did it?"

"Some say it was a lion, some say it was his own son, Ham," he said. "The important thing is that this Noah who built the ark, who also built the first altar, this big shipper and worshipper, he ended up like you but we don't hear anything about his being thrown out of the congregation. I myself think that the crux of the matter is whether you start out as a eunuch or only end up as one. Did you start out complete?"

"Yes," I said. "At least physically."

"Think," he said, buttoning me on to his hard blue eye as if I were a buttonhole, "think of this tradition of a castrated Noah. What do you think about it?"

"I'm not yet able to take it in," I said. I imagined thunder and lightning, the ark rolling in heavy seas, Noah naked with blood streaming from his castration, Noah shaking his fist at God. I wanted to put my hands on the Rabbi's throat and cut off the supply of wind with which he continually made words.

"Tradition," he said with his red hair standing out all round his face like Saint Elmo's fire, "puts things together like a good cook: a little of this and a little of that. Tradition is a balancer, a bookkeeper, an accountant. Debits and credits, yes?"

"Which?" I said.

"This is why Noah, who was given so much, has something taken away," said the Rabbi, and folded his arms across his chest as does a man who has utterly dried up his opponent in debate.

"And to what conclusion does this bring us?" I said.

"That is for you alone to know," said the Rabbi. "I cannot tell you because I don't know what the Lord has given you in exchange for what has been taken from you."

I opened my mouth to speak. What could I tell him? That God was no longer He and had become It? That from Jesus himself came the seed that gave life to Jesus? Could I tell him about the tiny dead golden body of Christ in the mouth of the Lion of the World? Could I tell him of the maggot-writhing headless tax-collector and the other companions of my road? Could I tell him of Sophia?

"You don't have to say it aloud," said the Rabbi; "I don't have to know; God already knows and if you also know then that's enough."

"So what do you want from me?" I said.

"I want you to come to the synagogue and pray with your fellow Jews," he said.

The Nagid had so far been maintaining a dignified silence as befitted someone who was not a seeker-out of others but the sought-out of many; none the less it was a bustling kind of silence. This Nagid, whom I think of as Worldly ben Worldly although he had a name that I ought to remember, was a tall, grand-looking man who seemed to embody the principle of making arrangements and the idea that the ponderous wheel of time and history might not roll too crushingly on if one knew the right people. Now he made with his hands that gesture of holding a large invisible melon or model world so characteristic of top arrangers everywhere—I have often thought that the idea of the roundness of the world first came to scientific observers from seeing this gesture, so suggestive of a Platonic ideal that the existence of a physically real counterpart could not seriously be doubted—and said, "We Jews are scattered over the face of the earth; let us at least be united in those places to which we have been scattered."

Both the Nagid and the Rabbi, being classified as dhimmis, beneficiaries of Muslim hospitality, wore yellow turbans and belts and were not allowed to ride horses or carry weapons. Perhaps because I was already castrated I found this further diminution galling. I had not so far flouted the law by carrying weapons or riding a horse but I had not put on a yellow belt and turban. In my mind I tried to, but could not, put into words my reasons for not wanting to be welcomed into a community of yellow turbans. Nor would I ever again be a member of any congregation other than that vast and erring one called the human race.

"Matters between God and me have gone beyond synagogues and congregations," I said to the Rabbi and the Nagid. "I have no prayers."

"It's not as if you can pass for a Muslim by denying us," said the Rabbi; "you will simply be known as the eunuch Jew who does not wear the yellow belt and turban."

"So be it," I said.

Soon after Chanukah came the First Muharram, the new Muslim year, the Hijra year 490. On the Tenth Muharram Bembel Rudzuk fasted. "Not everyone fasts on this day which is akin to your Day of Atonement," he said. "And of course there are those who on this day pitch black tents and mourn the death of Husain at Kerbela. I am not devout in the usual sense of the word but I find that fasting refreshes my attention; so I do it because my attention is always flagging and there are times when I fail to see the she-camel."

"Tell me about this she-camel," I said.

"In the Quran we read of a people called the Thamud," said Bembel Rudzuk. "They dwelt in rocky places, they had their dwellings in the rock. There came to them a prophet, his name was Salih. He told the Thamud that he was bringing to them the Word of God but they asked him for proof. Salih then called upon Allah and there appeared from out of the solid rock a she-camel, pregnant.

"This she-camel was an exemplary camel; she grazed and she found her way to water and in this way she showed that God's gifts are meant for all of God's creatures, that pasturage and water should not be held fast by the rich and kept from the poor, they should be freely shared."

"What happened with this camel?" I said.

"Those people of the rocks, those hard and stony people, Salih told them that the eye of God was upon them; he told them to be hospitable to the stranger-camel, to let it graze where it liked and not to withhold water from it. They laughed at him, the Thamud, and after the camel had given birth they hamstrung both the mother and the foal. They killed the camel and her child and they dared Salih to call down punishment upon them.

" 'Go to your houses,' he told them. 'You have three days in which to prepare yourselves.' After three days the earth shook, thunderbolts crashed down among those people, the ground opened up, the rocks melted and ran down into the abyss, the people were annihilated; the Thamud people were no more.

"Those foolish Thamud people are often referred to in the Quran and thus are we reminded that not only is every she-camel the she-camel of God, but every other animal and all of us as well, we are all creatures of God. In every configuration of time and circumstance there is the she-camel of the matter to be discerned by those whose attention is strong and constant. All of us dwell in the stone and when the stone brings forth a she-camel we must take notice of it and respond appropriately. But it is so easy to see only the stone and not the camel; I am always afraid that I shall fail to see that she-camel of God."

All through the rains there was no word from Tower Gate. "Is he going to make the tiles or not?" I said to Bembel Rudzuk.

"I think he's going to do it," said Bembel Rudzuk: "he hasn't said no."

Passover that year came at the end of March. The day before the Eve of Passover Jews were to be seen selling their leaven to Muslims, and this little act of accommodation touched me. See, I thought, everyone does not wish us dead! and my eyes filled with tears. I remembered the Gentiles buying the leaven of the Jews in my town, the town of my boyhood and my young manhood, the town where I had climbed the ladder to Sophia. So far away it was already in space and time!

On Passover Eve when Jews were reading the Haggadah at the Seder, when the door was left open and a cup of wine was poured for Elijah, I walked in the rain to Bembel Rudzuk's empty stone square. Freed from the traditional observance of the festival my mind widened into the rain, into the night, widened across the space of time to Pharaoh's Egypt, to the killing of the lamb without blemish, to the dipping of the hyssop in the blood, to the striking of the lintel and the sideposts with the blood, to the passing of dread wings in the night and the smiting of the first-born of Egypt, both man and beast. Ah, God! I thought, when will you learn! Why must your arm be stretched out against anyone? Why must you choose us to be yours and to be punished for ever by you and by the world? Then I remembered that God was no longer He. Perhaps as It he remembered nothing, perhaps like blind Samson he simply felt for the pillars and put forth his strength against them.

And then, thinking those heavy thoughts in the rainy night I found myself laughing because it suddenly came to me that it was not only Passover for the Jews but Easter for the Christians; Christ having been crucified at Passover the two moon-coupled festivals were for all time chained together. In Antioch that night the Christians would be reciting the eternal crime of the Jews and worshipping their tortured Jew on his cross while that same cross in cloth of scarlet was moving eastwards on the shoulders of the Franks. While the Jewish doors of Antioch stood open for Elijah. When God was He there was nobody like Him for jokes.

Spring came, the Franks arrived in Constantinople and the price of a bale of silk went up by three dinars in Tripoli. "As when the leaves of the olive trees show their undersides before the rain comes," said Bembel Rudzuk. "These Franks inspire uncertainty, everyone is wondering what will happen next. Some think that fewer ships and caravans will be arriving and everything will be in short supply."

The weather grew fine, the wooden rod at the centre of the square cast a strong young shadow. My original chalk drawing and the drawing made by the speechless boy had both been washed away by the winter rains; the empty stone presented itself to the eye as if for the first time and the sun shone down as if there would never again be cold and wet, there would only be hot and dry. With the passing of days there began to arrive don-key-loads and camel-loads of triangular tiles, as startling in their actuality as Silpius, red and black and tawny as I had seen them in my mind. With the tiles there arrived workmen who unloaded the camels and the don-keys, sorted the tiles according to size and colour, stacked them on the paving stones, and began to mix mortar.

In my hand was the wooden compass with which I had made my first drawing, and now I opened it once more to the radius that would sum-mon to the surface of the stone that same circle I had first drawn in the darkness.

I removed the rod, inserted the plug, placed the compass foot, and then it was as if the chalk line moved the outer compass leg before it as it closed itself into a circle. Again I developed the flower of six petals, and line by line out of it grew the hexagons and triangles of Hidden Lion.

It was then that there appeared a fully armed man walking across the paved square towards us. "This man," said Bembel Rudzuk, "is Firouz. He used to be a Christian, now he is a Muslim. He is an emir and he is close to our governor, Yaghi-Siyan. The Tower of the Two Sisters is under his command and two other towers as well."

I watched Firouz walking towards us and I found myself not liking the man. He had a way of half-turning as he walked: a half-turn this way, a half-turn that way. "He's a turning sort of man," I said to Bembel Rudzuk.

"He is indeed a turning sort of man," said Bembel Rudzuk, "and more likely to take a bad turn than a good one. Try not to let yourself be drawn into a quarrel with him."

Firouz walked to the centre of the paved square; his shadow fell across my circles, triangles, and hexagons. He touched the central six-pointed star with his foot. "This is the star of the Jews, is it not?" he said to Bembel Rudzuk. (By this time I had sufficient Arabic to follow the conversation.)

"You have seen this star in Islamic patterns without number," said Bembel Rudzuk. "You have seen it in mosques and palaces and in houses everywhere; even is it stamped by some of our Muslim merchants on the canvas coverings of bales."

"That may well be," said Firouz, "but at the same time it is a device used by the Jews, is it not?"

"It is one of many devices used by many people," said Bembel Rudzuk.

"Was it drawn by you?" said Firouz.

"Yes," said Bembel Rudzuk, "it was."

Firouz's demeanour was such that I knew it could only be a moment or two until he asked me if I was a Jew. I think that he already knew that I was but did not want to appear to have taken the trouble to inform himself of such a trifling event as my Jewish arrival in Antioch; he preferred rather to go through this play-acting in which he pretended only now to have his curiosity aroused by the six-pointed star.

Such an interesting moment, that moment before someone who is not a Jew asks you if you are a Jew! The world being as it is, any live Jew is a survivor in that there will always be other Jews within living memory who are dead only because they were Jews. So whoever asks, "Are you a Jew?" is saying at the same time, "Are you one of those who has not so far been slaughtered?" To answer yes to this question has at one time and another assured the death of the answerer. At that moment in Antioch Jews were not being slaughtered but nevertheless the question would not be a neutral one, it would not be such a question as: "What do you think of our summer weather?" No, it would be a question with an under-question: "Are you a Jew who dies without fighting or a Jew who makes trouble?"

"As you say," said Firouz, still addressing his remarks to Bembel Rudzuk and affecting to take no notice of me, "it's a star one sees everywhere. And yet this particular version of it, with all those triangles appearing at the same time to move inward and outward—there's something one might almost call one-eyed about it, wouldn't you say? Wouldn't you say that the inward tends to be swallowed up by the outward in this design?"

"One of the virtues of this simple but at the same time complex design," said Bembel Rudzuk, "this design in which we see the continually reciprocating action of unity and multiplicity, is that it suits its apparent action to the mind of the viewer: those who look outward see the outward preeminent; those who look inward see the inward."

"Are you a Jew?" said Firouz to me suddenly.

"Hear, O Israel!" I said in Hebrew, "The Lord our God, the Lord is One!"

"I bear witness that there is no god but God and that Muhammad is the messenger of God," said Firouz. For a moment he stared at me wildly as if I had struck him in the face, then he turned to Bembel Rudzuk. "Has your Israelite friend registered for the tax payable by those non-Muslims who sojourn among us?" he said.

"Yes," said Bembel Rudzuk, "he has been paying the tax since he first came to Antioch."

"See to it also," said Firouz, "that he dresses in accordance with his station and that he does not ride a horse or carry weapons." He turned on his heel, walked back across the square to where an attendant was holding his horse, mounted, and rode off towards the Tower of the Two Sisters, turning once in the saddle to look back.

"This too will pass," said Bembel Rudzuk. "Firouz is a man of moods and many of them are unpleasant. As we can do nothing about him we might as well get on with our work."

There came then to the centre of the square Tower Gate's foreman. "You might as well fetch the bricks for the tower now," he said to some of the workmen: "that'll be the next thing after we do this hexagon."

"What tower?" said Bembel Rudzuk.

"The tower at the centre," said the foreman.

"Ah!" said Bembel Rudzuk.

"Did you commission this tower?" I said to Bembel Rudzuk when the foreman had moved away from us.

"No," he said, "but it will give us a platform from which to observe the action of the pattern, and as it will be built at the very beginning we shall thus better see the development of the pattern as it is assembled. I myself had been thinking of erecting a tower when the pattern was complete but it's better really to have it now."

The central unit, the hexagon from which would overlappingly radiate all the other hexagons and the stars they contained, measured six feet four inches at its greatest width, and it was on this hexagon that the hexagonal tower was to be built. On the underside of each of the thirty-six tiles of this central hexagon Bembel Rudzuk wrote one of the various names of Allah: The Beneficent on one, The Merciful on another, and so on. "You too must write on these tiles," he said to me.

"I cannot," I said. "God for me is beyond naming, nor have I any other words to write." As I said this I noticed two figures poised attentively at the edge of the stone square: one was the Imam, the leader of the local Muslim congregation; the other was Rabbi Akiba ben Eliezer. The Imam was tall and lean, the Rabbi short and stocky; the Imam had black eyes and a white beard, the Rabbi had blue eyes and a red beard; but their differences disappeared in the unanimity of their disapproval: their paired gaze was like four long iron rods, the two from the Imam pinioning Bembel Rudzuk and the two from the Rabbi pinioning me. Having declined the Rabbi's invitation to join the congregation I always felt defensive when I saw him. Bembel Rudzuk, while a perfectly respectable member of the Muslim community, was known to be a strongly individual thinker. I hoped that the Imam and the Rabbi would be content to leave us to our work as we left them to theirs; but of course we were their work so I resigned myself to that iron optical embrace.

The thirty-six central tiles having been duly inscribed were now ready to be set in mortar. The lines where paving stones met indicated the axes of the square, and guided by these the foreman and his helper stretched their strings, trowelled in the mortar, and caused the tiles to appear to their proper places. Their activity seemed nothing so gross as common tile-laying: rather the tiles leapt into their hands, there was written on the air a fleeting calligraphy of dark limbs and white garments and Aha! the tiles manifested the central hexagon. The foreman and his helper seemed (they did it so quietly that I couldn't be certain) to be hissing and humming some little song frequently punctuated by tiny explosive exhalations of breath: "Dzah!" and "Dzee!" and "Dzim!" To this almost silent sibilance moved the white garments, the dark limbs, the red and black and tawny triangles into Hidden Lion.

As Bembel Rudzuk and I stood looking at the design we both noticed at the same moment that it was as it had been with the drawing that I had made on paper that night in November when Hidden Lion first appeared to me: "The motion is already there," said Bembel Rudzuk.

"Did you notice when it first became apparent?" I said.

"No," he said, "I was intent on the placing of the tiles. Did you?"

"No," I said, "I simply forgot all about it."

"Our first lesson," said Bembel Rudzuk: "the heart of the mystery is meant to remain a mystery."

Hidden Lion! (For me that would always be the name of precedence; the Willing Virgin was the name for an aspect of the pattern that had not been made apparent to me by the pattern itself.) To see that central hexagon in its full-scale alternation of large and small red and black and tawny triangles, its solid and tangible actuality of fired and glazed tiles, was

quite astonishing, there was so much action in it. I have before this described my drawing of the twelvefold repetition and my surprise at the
quantity and variety of the action in it. But here there was as yet no repetition, there was only this hexagon made up of large and small triangles:
the eighteen large outer ones; the twelve small inner ones; the six shallow

ones between the inner and the outer. It was immediately apparent that the large interlocking red and black and tawny triangles of the outer hexagon were predisposed to turn, to revolve, to remind themselves that they were born of a circle. To this central hexagon at Bembel Rudzuk's request I gave a name: David's Wheel.

Firouz came to us again that day and stood looking at David's Wheel, magnetically drawn, it seemed, by the pattern. This time he seemed to be without animosity, seemed to look on us with respect, as when a little boy watches his father string a bow that he himself will not be able to bend until he is grown a man. He spread out his fingers as if gripping a small wheel, he rotated his outspread, hooked fingers. "It turns," he said, "there is a turning in it: the turning of the sun and the moon and the stars; the turning of the wheels of fate and fortune. Thus do we see that at the centre of the universe there is a turning, there is a turning at the heart of the mystery. This turning pattern that you have made with these tiles, has it a name?"

"David's Wheel," I said, and then I was sorry that I had said it; I didn't want him to know the name of anything that meant anything to me.

"David's Wheel," he said. "David slew Goliath and became a great king. And yet he turned, did he not. He turned from what was right, he turned to the wrong, he lusted after Bathsheba, he told Joab to put Uriah her husband in the forefront of the hottest battle. Then when Uriah was dead he joyed himself, did he not, with Bathsheba the juicy widow, the fruit of his wrongdoing."

"He was only a man," I said. "He made music, he sang and danced before the Lord."

"Only a man!" said Firouz. "Only a man!" He turned on his heel, always he left with that heel-turn, never did he simply walk away as others did.

Tower Gate now made his appearance, drawing near in a manner that commanded attention by the power of his attention; he came as if mystically summoned by David's Wheel, and he so focused his approaching presence on that hexagon that it seemed to be a winch that was winding him in with an invisible rope.

When he arrived at David's Wheel he looked down into it with a look that made me feel utterly left out and excluded from any understanding whatever of the thing that I had summoned with my compass and my straight-edge; one sees that always with specialists: a bowman picks up a bow in a way that leaves the non-bowman feeling poor; a silk merchant reads the silk with his fingers and almost there rise up from his touch phantom ships and camels, distant mountains, distant seas. Tower Gate looked down into David's Wheel and in his face I tried without success to read whether he looked into crystalline depths or into an abyss of smoke and flame.

"What do you see?" I blurted out.

He looked at me as if I had farted during prayers, looked away graciously, then looked back with a face that showed willingness to put the incident behind us. "Let me show you the plan and elevations for the tower," he said to Bembel Rudzuk, and opened a roll of drawings which he handed to his foreman, who laid them on David's Wheel and put loose tiles on the corners to hold them flat.

"This tower wants to be very plain," said Tower Gate; "it wants to be nothing immodest, nothing too commanding. It is a little hexagonal tower with its stairs going round the outside of it. This is not a seashell that grows itself round its own spiral and remembers in its windings the sound of the sea; this tower remembers nothing and its unsheltered spiral is open to the sky.

"To what is the height of this tower related? To the triangles on which it stands. These triangles offer us an angle of thirty degrees, an angle of sixty degrees, and an angle of one hundred and twenty degrees. The obtuse angle not being usable we try the other two: projecting a sixty-degree angle from the edge of your square to a point above the centre gives us a tower more than a hundred feet high, a real God-challenger and not to be thought of even if it were practically possible on a base only six feet four inches across; projecting a thirty-degree angle gives us a tower about thirty-five feet high which is still a little pretentious. What then remains to us? In reverence and in modesty (if indeed we can apply such words to a project so thoroughly dubious) we halve that angle and arrive at this tower just over sixteen feet high, taller than a man on a camel but not so high in the air as the mu'addhin; it is a height for broadening one's view a little but not for feeling too far above the world."

"I am powerfully impressed by the care you have taken in this matter," said Bembel Rudzuk, "and I am profoundly grateful for the discretion you have shown; one can so easily do the wrong thing."

"We may well have done the wrong thing in any case," said Tower Gate, "but life is after all a matter of making choices and one is bound to choose wrong in one or two of those matters that really matter."

So the tower was built. It had no ornamentation, no red and black triangles; it was made of plain tawny bricks. The platform at the top was built out a foot wider all round than the base; it was enclosed by a parapet three feet high and left open to the sky.

The tower being complete the pattern began to spread outward from it. I felt a pang of regret: once begun, a project can only be completed or abandoned; actuality is gained as potentiality is lost. There was no stopping the growth of Hidden Lion; the serpents twisted through the stars, the pyramids shifted and regrouped, the lions appeared and disappeared, the illusory enclaves of disorder were suddenly there, suddenly not there. And under each tile a name of God.

To visualize a pattern, whether in a drawing or in tiles or even to see it with the eye of the mind only, is to make visible the power in the pattern. Because of the scale of Hidden Lion the power was very clearly to be seen from the top of the tower; it was like the power that surges beneath the skin of a strong river.

"This motion that we see is the motion of the Unseen," said Bembel Rudzuk. "This power that we see is the power of the Unseen, and it is both conscious power and the power of consciousness. Here already are two of my questions answered: motion is in the pattern from the very beginning because the motion is there before the pattern, the pattern is only a mode of appearance assumed by the motion; consciousness also is in the pattern from the very beginning because the consciousness is there before the pattern, the pattern is only a kind of window for the consciousness to look out of. Although serpents, pyramids, and lions seem to appear in the pattern, that is only because the human mind will make images out of anything; the pattern is in actuality abstract, it represents nothing and asserts no images. It offers itself modestly and reverently to the Unseen and the Unseen takes pleasure in it."

I said, "May it be that there is no necessity to study this pattern or observe it methodically? May it not even be inadvisable to do so? May it not be that the best way of conducting oneself with this pattern is simply to take it in without any thought and to enjoy in it the presence of the Unseen?"

"I think you're right," said Bembel Rudzuk.

So. Bembel Rudzuk went on writing the names of Allah on the undersides of the tiles and the workmen went on dancingly fitting them into the pattern. And what was my work at this time? I was a witness. I was there to see every tile fitted, I was there to see Hidden Lion grow triangle by triangle. I wrote down no observations, kept no record of its progress from day to day; I drained off none of the virtue of it; I gave my mind to it and there it lived and went its way.

All the time that the work of putting together Hidden Lion was going on we were watched daily by children, by idlers and street sages, by all manner of people pausing on the way from one place to another. The children soon began to walk on the pattern in special ways and to dance on it, sometimes stepping only on the red triangles, sometimes only on the black. Seeing them always out of the corner of my eye I found in my mind new and unwritten names of God: The Tiptoeing; The Sidewise-Jumping; The Hopping; The Leaping; The Dancing; The Whirling.

One morning the baker who had a shop near Hidden Lion came and stood respectfully before Bembel Rudzuk. "My lord," he said, "I have heard that this design came to you in a dream, that you were commanded by Allah to cover this square with this pattern, and that on the underside of each tile is written a name of Allah in all the tongues of mankind. Is this true?"

"The design came to me in the mind of this pilgrim," said Bembel Rudzuk, indicating me. "Certainly it is by the will of Allah that we do this work, and it is true that there is written on the underside of each tile a name of Allah, but in Arabic only."

"This is virtuous action," said the baker, "and therefore one is not surprised that there is virtue in it. My son comes here to play in the evening, he does no harm, he only walks on the tiles. For three months he has had an infection of the right eye. Yesterday evening he walked from star to star on one line of stars for as far as the tiles went. Walking towards Mecca he trod only on the small red triangles and looked at them fixedly; walking back he trod only on the small black triangles and looked at them fixedly. This morning the eye infection is completely gone. I have no wish to intrude upon your good work but I ask in all humility that you take this small offering which is nothing really, it is only that something should pass from my hand to your hand in the name of Allah The Responsive, The Restorer." He put some money into the hand of Bembel Rudzuk.

"Will you not rather give this money to the poor?" said Bembel Rudzuk.

"I give to the poor as well," said the baker. "This is something else, this is in praise of Allah whose attributes are infinite, Allah who has caused this idea to move you; it is only to show that I in my insignificant way am grateful."

"So be it," said Bembel Rudzuk. "The pattern is abstract; let the money also be used abstractly. I shall put it into one of the tiles of the pattern where it will be united with the design on the pattern and with the names of Allah in celebration of your gratitude to Him The Responsive, Him The Restorer."

Bembel Rudzuk instructed a workman to chip out of the two-inch thickness of one of the tiles a shallow recess in the bottom; the money was mortared into the tile and the tile, inscribed with the desired names of Allah, was put into Hidden Lion.

On the next day came the potter whose shop was in the same street as that of the baker. "In the five years of our marriage," he said to Bembel Rudzuk, "my wife had not been able to conceive. At the end of the first day's work after the building of the tower she came here and stepped on every tile that was in the pattern, saying while she did so the names of Allah. For seven evenings she came here and did this. Now is her womb quickened with life. I beg that this wholly inadequate offering be incorporated in one of your tiles dedicated to Allah, The Generous One."

Bembel Rudzuk sighed. "Having accepted the money of the baker I cannot refuse yours," he said. "I shall do with it as you request."

"Wonderful are the ways of Allah!" said Bembel Rudzuk after the potter had gone. "For such a little time was Hidden Lion permitted to go its uncorrupted way! Yesterday I did a foolish thing and today I am forced to continue in my foolishness. Already is the integrity of the work marred physically and spiritually. Two of the tiles have been mutilated for this primitive good-luck commerce and now there will be no end to it. Yesterday the Imam scowled at me; today he will laugh: I have become a vendor of good-luck charms."

"Then don't let them give you any more money," I said.

"Too late," said Bembel Rudzuk. "I must go on as I have begun. Striving too hard after wisdom has made me a fool."

The visits of the baker and the potter made us aware that Hidden Lion had a life of its own in those evening hours when we were not there.

The pregnancy of the potter's wife reminded me that it had not been days but weeks since the tiles had begun to cover the square. People had been walking on the tiles, dancing on them, kissing them, counting them, contemplating them, acting in various special ways upon them, doing whatever they were moved by the place, the pattern, and the desire of their hearts to do. In the days that followed it was not single visitors who came but several at once, then more and more who waited patiently to tell Bembel Rudzuk how their wishes had been gratified and to give him their offering large or small for the work.

The Imam and the Rabbi were often to be seen observing what was going on. Bembel Rudzuk was right: the Imam, although not actually laughing, was smiling broadly. The Rabbi had on his face a particularly Jewish look: the pensive look of a man who while smiling almost fondly at people who are being childish is at the same time well aware that these childish people may at any moment require his life of him.

Firouz, a few days after his instructions as to dress, horses, and weapons, was reminded by the Rabbi's yellow turban and belt that I was not similarly distinguishable. He questioned me about this with some severity and I told him that as a eunuch I could not count myself a member of the Jewish congregation. He then asked the Rabbi if that was so. The Rabbi, buttoning me with his eye, said that it was so. I expected Firouz to say that exclusion from the congregation did not cancel my Jewish status in dhimma matters but he did not say that; he looked thoughtful and he never broached the subject again.

At this time the pattern was still expanding, it had not yet covered the whole square. Children, I noticed, were particularly fond of walking and dancing the shape of the unfinished edges. It became evident to me that the forward edge of a pattern's visible expansion is attractive, it excites in people and in things a desire to shape themselves to it, to meet it and move with its advance. I speak of the forward edge of the pattern's *visible* expansion because I had become more and more strongly aware that the visual manifestation of a pattern comes only after the pattern is already in existence and already infinite: the visible expansion is only a finite tracing of what, being infinite, cannot further expand.

It was at this time also that I noticed that Hidden Lion in its abstractness was capable of activating in my vision more than the serpents, pyramids, lions, and enclaves of apparent disorder that I have described: there rose up from the motion and consciousness of the pattern an apparition of Jerusalem, a phantom of place unseen. It was that Jerusalem of my ignorance, that inn-sign Jerusalem of coarse and vivid colour, the solid geometry of its forms tawny-stoned, golden-domed, purple-shadowed, the aerial geometry of its light and shade rising with the forms transparently upon the air over Hidden Lion. Sometimes it was there, sometimes not. I was uncertain of the meaning of this apparition; sometimes I thought one thing, sometimes another. Sometimes I tried to move my mind away from it.

Firouz of course remained attentive to our activities. Seeing people give money to Bembel Rudzuk and seeing the money then mortared into the tiles he said to Bembel Rudzuk, "What is this commerce that you do with your geomancy? What do you give for this money that you take?"

Bembel Rudzuk said, "It is not a commerce of my choosing but I don't know how to stop it; to refuse this money that is offered gratefully to Allah would be to deny the giver a part in the pattern."

"Will you accept money from me as well?" said Firouz.

"For what?" said Bembel Rudzuk. "What have you had from this pattern?" He didn't say the pattern's name, we only used that between us. To everyone else it was simply "the pattern."

"One night I stood at the top of your tower," said Firouz, "and there came to me a thought of great profundity."

I didn't like to think of Firouz at the top of our tower, I didn't like to think of any thought that might have come to him there. Clearly Bembel Rudzuk didn't want to take the money, he didn't want to accept Firouz into the membership of Hidden Lion but he didn't feel easy about saying no. "Your profound thought," he said to Firouz, "surely it would have come to you anywhere."

"Indeed not," said Firouz; "it came to me while I was contemplating the inwardness and outwardness of this particular pattern; I am convinced that it could not have come to me anywhere else. You have taken money from anyone who has offered it to you, I have seen you do it. Am I alone to be excluded from this multiplicity of people who have become unified with your pattern?"

"No," said Bembel Rudzuk miserably, "I have no wish to exclude you."

Firouz took Bembel Rudzuk's hand and pressed a piece of gold into it. "You see how I value this," he said. "To have my own tile in this great pattern! Tell me, what is the name of it?"

"The name of what?" said Bembel Rudzuk.

"The name of this pattern," said Firouz. "This design that is so mystical in the simplicity of its complexity, surely it has a name?"

"Ah!" said Bembel Rudzuk, "who am I to put a name to a pattern? Let each person who looks at it think of it with or without a name as Allah wills."

"Your humility is overwhelming," said Firouz. "It flattens me utterly. And yet, modest as you are, probably when you think of this pattern you think of it with a name."

Bembel Rudzuk shrugged. "Mostly I don't think of it, I simply become absorbed in it thoughtlessly."

"Ah!" said Firouz. "Thoughtless absorption! Yes, yes, I understand that absolutely: one simply becomes one with the everything, one is free for a time from the burden of one's self. What bliss! And yet, and yet—returning to the world and its burdens one puts names to things. So it is that I have lost myself in this pattern, but returning to the world I look at this abstraction with which I have merged; I turn my head this way and that way, I see twisting serpents, moving pyramids; suddenly there leaps forward the face of a lion, then it is gone again. 'Ah!' say I, 'I have been with Hidden Lion!'" With that he did his regular heel-turn and walked turningly away, but stopped after only a few steps and turned back towards us. "I was forgetting to ask," he said, "what name of Allah you'll be writing on the underside of my tile."

"The Watchful," said Bembel Rudzuk, "He who observes all creatures, and every action is under His control."

"Why that one?" said Firouz. "Why that particular one for me?"

"It came into my mind when you asked, so I assume that it was put there by Allah," said Bembel Rudzuk.

"'Every action is under His control,'" said Firouz. "How can that be, really? Think of the dreadful things that are done in this world every day."

"The child is under the control of the parents, is it not," said Bembel Rudzuk; "yet must the child creep on its hands and knees before it can walk, and when it first walks it can go only a step or two before it falls."

"True, true," said Firouz. "That's all we are: little children creeping on our hands and knees. The parent, however, doesn't punish the child for falling, while Allah The Watchful will surely punish the sinner, will he not?"

"The child who falls when learning to walk has not the choice," said Bembel Rudzuk, "but the sinner has."

"That what was the use of bringing the child into it at all?" said Firouz. "It's a useless analogy, it's no help whatever."

"It's a perfectly useful analogy," said Bembel Rudzuk: "the consequence of not being able to walk is to fall and the consequence of not being able to maintain moral balance is also to fall. How could it be otherwise?"

"To be in a fallen state," said Firouz, "that isn't so dreadful; all sorts of fallen people ride about on good horses wearing fine clothes and who can tell the difference? I'm thinking about later, I'm thinking about the Fire where one burns and burns and is given molten brass to drink. Do you think that's really how it is?"

"I think that the Fire is in the soul of each of us," said Bembel Rudzuk: "those of us consigned to the Fire burn every day and every night."

"You don't burn though, do you?" said Firouz. "You're cool and easy, your soul dwells in the Garden of its self-delight."

"Where my soul dwells is between Allah and me, not between you and me," said Bembel Rudzuk.

"You're so comfortable!" said Firouz. "You're so easy, you're like a cat that purrs before a dish of the milk of your own wisdom that is so delicious to you."

"I am as Allah made me," said Bembel Rudzuk, "and certainly I never asked you to drink from that dish."

"Always a clever answer," said Firouz. He turned to me. "And you," he said, "what name of Allah would you write on the tile?"

"God for me is nameless," I said.

"Ah!" said Firouz. "Profundity! How could I have expected otherwise!" Again he executed his heel-turn and I thought that we had perhaps seen the last of him for that day but no, here he was turning yet again to speak to us once more.

"How many tiles will there be in Hidden Lion when it is complete?" he said.

"I don't know," said Bembel Rudzuk. "We haven't calculated that."

"How many tiles are there in it so far?" said Firouz.

"We have not counted," said Bembel Rudzuk. "Allah is The Reckoner."

"Of course," said Firouz. "This is part of the milk of your wisdom, is it not. And yet if the Governor should impose a tax on paving-tiles then you with all your piety would have to do some reckoning."

The workmen were just then unloading a camel and two of them now approached the advancing edge of the pattern with a four-handled basket full of tiles. Firouz walked turningly towards them with his features composed in an official expression as if he were going to confiscate the tiles. The workmen stopped in their tracks and looked at him with fear and uncertainty.

It was at that moment that the Governor Yaghi-Siyan appeared, riding a horse and flanked by six of his bodyguard. At the edge of the stone square he dismounted and approached us. When he came to the outermost edge of Hidden Lion he ostentatiously took off his shoes and walked barefoot across the tiles to us. Bembel Rudzuk and I took off our shoes as well and made him a little bow. Firouz whirled round to face the Governor and seeing us all barefoot hurried to take off his shoes. He flung out a hand to steady himself against the basket that the two workmen were still holding between them; perhaps he leant on it too heavily or perhaps the workmen, already nervous and fearful of him, were startled by his sudden movement and let go of the basket—in any case it fell with its heavy load of tiles and there was a howl of pain from Firouz who had somehow contrived to have his foot under it.

The terrified workmen lifted the basket clear and while Firouz composed himself heroically I examined his foot and ascertained that the metatarsal bone was broken. A man was sent for bandages while I set the bone and bound it temporarily with my kaffiya. As I was doing this Firouz said to me, "I know that this design has come from your hand and not that of Bembel Rudzuk. It is your Hidden Lion, Jew."

"This Hidden Lion belongs to no one person more than to any other," I said. "It is simply the lion that remains hidden until it reveals itself."

Yaghi-Siyan seemed unmoved by Firouz's suffering. He looked down at him and said, "Tell me, Firouz, what have you done to this load of tiles that it should fall upon you like this, eh? Did it attack you or was it acting in self-defence? Were you perhaps threatening it? Or were you attempting to extort money from it?"

Firouz drew back his lips from his teeth in a ghastly smile. "This was a didactic load of tiles," he said. "It was teaching us that what is clay can fall."

"Also," said Yaghi-Siyan, "it was teaching you to step carefully." He looked steadily at Firouz until Firouz looked away; no more was said between them.

When I had properly bandaged Firouz's foot I had the thought of further immobilizing the broken bone by stiffening the bandage with clay from the riverbank to enclose the foot in a mud-brick shell. This being done Firouz was set aside to dry in the sun.

"Will you now write a name of Allah upon me?" said Firouz to Bembel Rudzuk. "Will you fit me into your design?"

"The tiles in this pattern," said Bembel Rudzuk, "have not only been dried in the sun; they have also passed through the fire."

"Ah!" said Firouz, but he said no more than that.

Yaghi-Siyan was standing before Bembel Rudzuk with a kind of aggressive humility, impatient for him to leave off paying attention to Firouz. "I am told," he said, "that this tiling is done for its own sake alone."

"Your Excellency," said Bembel Rudzuk, "this that we do here is only a kind of foolishness, a kind of vanity. It is done to be looked at."

"I don't think it is foolishness," said Yaghi-Siyan. "I sense here the presence of Allah."

"That may well be due to your own virtue rather than to anything in the work itself," said Bembel Rudzuk.

"I think not," said Yaghi-Siyan. "I think that this is something out of the usual run, something extraordinary, even inspired. Most things are a kind of commerce, even most piety: one gives something, one gets something. But this is original, this is abstract; it simply becomes itself, asking nothing."

"To hear your Excellency say this of course gives me great pleasure," said Bembel Rudzuk.

"You're being polite," said Yaghi-Siyan; "you're being careful, you're being closed. Say something careless to me, something open, something abstract."

"This is my abstraction," said Bembel Rudzuk indicating Hidden Lion with a sweep of his arm. "This is my openness, my carelessness, my impoliteness."

"May I climb your tower?" said Yaghi-Siyan.

"This tower is of course yours, Excellency," said Bembel Rudzuk. "It is my privilege to invite you to make use of it."

Yaghi-Siyan went to the tower and now I was able to see the profundity of Tower Gate's design: towers are naturally dramatic structures that intensify the image of any figure that is to be seen looking down from them. Particularly do they do this when the figure disappears into a doorway at the bottom and then reappears looking over a parapet at the top. But here the stairs round the outside of the tower kept the figure unremarkable by making visible the effort of going from the bottom to the top; at the top the low parapet continued this objectivity. There were to be seen only a little tower, only an ordinary man.

From this nameless tower did Yaghi-Siyan look down on Hidden Lion. Not a breath of air stirred his white burnous, the blue sky was utterly without a sign of anything. At just such an unheralded moment, I thought, might marvels appear to a watcher on a tower: the earth opening up; the kraken rising to the surface of the sea; the mountain lifting itself into the air over the city. It occurred to me that the Unseen might at any moment make use of any pair of eyes to see everything in an altogether different way, a way never thought of before. I felt the earth leap like a fish beneath me. An immeasurable time passed, perhaps it was only a moment, perhaps it is still continuing: the dark face of Yaghi-Siyan; the white burnous; the blue sky; the leaping earth.

When Yaghi-Siyan came down from the tower he looked up to where he had stood, then he looked down at the tiles he was standing on. "From there I saw the motion," he said; "from here I see the stillness. What is it, what is it that moves us? We were the wild horsemen out of the east, Byzantium drew back before us. Now I stand here in this city with a wall around it but the inside is continually rushing to join the outside. Almost I am dizzy with it." He began to weep; weeping he bowed his head to the tiles. Then he stood up, walked back to his shoes, put them on, mounted his horse, and rode back to the Governor's Palace.

12

Time, it seems, has passed. The triangular tiles of Hidden Lion have covered all of Bembel Rudzuk's stone square, but the pattern has in its turn been so covered by people, by stalls, by booths and tents and awnings that the surge of its action is obscured by the action of every day; the twisting serpents, the shifting pyramids, the appearing and disappearing lions are mostly hidden.

It happened by degrees. I have already told how men, women, and children walked on Hidden Lion in special ways, how they danced on it with particular things in mind, how they gave money which was put into the tiles. Without anyone's being told the name became known; people used it in giving directions. Hidden Lion became a meeting-place, and in due course a vendor asked permission to sell refreshments in the noon shadow of the tower at the centre. Permission granted, sweet drinks and little cakes became part of the pattern. Other applicants were quick to follow, and stallholders appeared selling cooked food, melons and oranges, pots and pans, carpets, caged birds, jewelry and weapons. They occupied their spaces rent-free; since the completion of the tiling Bembel Rudzuk had accepted no more money.

Hidden Lion became not only the liveliest of bazaars but also a good-luck place almost sacred to those who had experienced its power. There were lovers who had sworn to each other on a particular tile and by the appropriate names of Allah; there were children at whose birth money had been put into tiles inscribed with the names of Allah The Guide, The Preventer, The Enricher. Bargains were struck, partnerships founded, parents honoured and the dead remembered in the tiles of Hidden Lion.

Every day has a dawn, every day a midnight: sometimes we mark by the one, sometimes by the other. Came the month of July and its days marched like a procession of penitents towards the Ninth of Av; then did I count the days by the nights. When there came the first anniversary of my night with Sophia I paced the roof of Bembel Rudzuk's house feeling as if I were wrapped in the burning scroll of my love, my lust, my sin, my wisdom, my transcendent mortality. God was poor, I thought, to be immortal.

Towards the middle of August came Ramadhan. The city was like an oven. The sounds of the street withdrew into the silence of exhaustion and the continual growling murmur of the Quran. From that time before dawn when a white thread could be distinguished from a black one the Muslims fasted until sunset, when the call of the mu'addhin like the darkness eased the city into night, prayer, food, and more reciting of the Quran.

The twenty-seventh of Ramadhan, the Lailat al-Qadr, the Night of Power on which Muhammad received his first revelation, was to Bembel Rudzuk an especially important night. "The Quran tells us that this Night of Power is better than a thousand months," he said: "it is all time, it is no time, it is beyond the bounds of reckoning and measurement. It may be that even the idea of it puts the mind into a special state: always on this night I have a dream that is not like the dreams of other nights; always on this night comes a strong way-showing dream." His face looked young, it was so full of eagerness and excitement.

As on many nights that summer we were sleeping on the roof. We stayed up late talking, and I looked for but could not find the Virgin and the Lion among the stars. "Only part of the Lion can be seen now," said Bembel Rudzuk. He tried to show me where it was but I could only recognize the Lion when together with the Virgin it made that gesture that had so imprinted itself on my mind.

Towards dawn I was awakened by a thumping on the roof: it was Bembel Rudzuk dancing in his nightdress. His eyes were closed; he was dancing in his sleep. It was a shuffling, stamping dance in which there were many formal turnings of the body, many hieratic movements of the arms close to the body. It was an earthy dance, nothing of it moved up into the air; it was as if earth had formed itself into a man and the man was dancing himself back into the earth. Bembel Rudzuk danced more and more slowly and more and more deeply until the body that I saw before me stood motionless like the nymphal shell left behind by a dragonfly. But Bembel Rudzuk, unlike the dragonfly, seemed not to have flown away into the air but to have danced himself out of his body into the earth.

The shell of Bembel Rudzuk opened its eyes and Bembel Rudzuk looked out of them.

"Was this your dream?" I said. "Were you dancing your dream?"

"Earth," he said. "I was dancing earth."

"Are you awake?" I said.

"Which is the dream?" he said.

After the Lailat al-Qadr I began to think of preparing myself a little for the days that were coming. Now when I say that I see in my mind those stubborn Frankish tents before the walls of Antioch, I see the arrogance of the Franks in the way they walk, in the way they sit their horses. At that time I had seen nothing of them, I only sensed their approach, and this awareness of them moving towards us mingled with the picture that was always in my mind of the sprawled bodies of the dead Jews of our town, most of whom had never in their lives held a sword in their hands. I did not care for that style of dying, and accordingly I asked Bembel Rudzuk to instruct me in horsemanship and the use of weapons.

The prohibition of the riding of horses and the carrying of weapons by non-Muslims was not consistently enforced in Antioch; the rigour varied with the times and with the moods of the Governor and his officers. At that time Yaghi-Siyan had not yet become as uneasy about the loyalty of Christians and Jews as he was to be a few months later—it was Firouz that I had to be mindful of; as he had already taken notice of my non-wearing of a yellow turban and belt it seemed wise not to attract his attention again. Bembel Rudzuk and a servant used to ride out of the city leading a third horse and I would follow them on foot to the hills east of the Orontes where I then mounted and rode on with them. So I had the use of a horse and weapons as often as I liked, and Firouz, who of course knew about it, seemed content that his authority was recognized within the walls; in any case he made no trouble.

Bembel Rudzuk was an excellent teacher. His youth had been active and adventurous and his strength and vigour seemed little diminished at his present age; he was a dashing horseman and he was expert with bow and sword. Our rides continued even after the siege began—it was months before the blockade was complete—and after not too long a time I rode well enough for Bembel Rudzuk to say that I might have made a horseman if I had come to it earlier in life; eventually I shot well enough with the Turkish bow to bring down game; our swordplay continued in Bembel Rudzuk's courtyard long after the rides had stopped, and with the curved Turkish sword and the straight blade both I progressed to where Bembel Rudzuk was at least as eager as I for a rest at the end of our practice. Sometimes as I swung my blunted sword I seemed to see behind Bembel Rudzuk the shadowy and as yet faceless form of actuality to come.

One day followed another through months that bore different names, numbered themselves by the sun or the moon, and began and ended on different days in the Muslim, Jewish, and Christian calendars. Strange, to live again one's life and death in three calendars! Soon after the Lailat al-Qadr of the Hijra year 490 in the month of September of the Christian year 1097 came the Jewish High Holy Days, the Days of Awe: Rosh Hashanah, the New Year's Day of 4858, and ten days later Yom Kippur, the Day of Atonement. Ah! then I felt my eunuchhood, my separateness from any congregation! It was no use to tell myself that God was no longer He and that accounts were no longer being kept—centuries of moral reckoning leapt up in me. It was in me; I was in it: it was like a giant wave, an impulse racing across vast expanses of time, living its motion through successive particles of mortality.

This would now be the second Rosh Hashanah and Yom Kippur since I had left my town. The last time these Days of Awe had come I had been on the road alone, there had been no congregation to be cut off from when the shofar was blown, when the Kol Nidrei was sung at the beginning of the fast and when the Ne'ilah Service was recited, the book and the gates closed, and the Shema, the "Hear, O Israel!" heard at the end. Here in Antioch however there was a congregation and I had with words out of my own mouth cut myself off from it; I didn't want to be part of anybody else's traffic with God. But I wanted something; I thought perhaps that I wanted to hear the sound of the ram's horn, the shofar. The urgent maleness of that trumpeting always lifted me and quickened my blood: it was so much a call to action, it was so utterly not the murmur of praying, swaying, weaponless victims—was it not itself the weapon of the ram that had borne it? And did it not also recall that ram that had appeared when the Lord stayed the hand of Abraham as Isaac lay bound and waiting for the knife? And more: this trumpeting of the ram's horn was for me the summons from the dreadful mountain of the Law, a summons that could not be ignored or denied. And I see, now that my mind is no longer limited by my mortal identity, that this Law is nothing that could be limited to those commandments on the two stones: no, this Law that is so imperious is simply the law of the allness of the everything of which each of us is a particle. Quick! Now! Rise up from your sleep, from your unbeing! Be! Do! Respond!

Be! Do! What? Before Rosh Hashanah, as the end of the month of Elul and the beginning of Tishri approached, I went by night to the synagogue. It was huddled away among the houses of the Jewish quarter, it stood among the smells of various dyes, even those reds and purples flaunted by those knightly wearers of the Cross who were now approaching us. This not very large domed building, said by some to have been built on the ruin of a Roman smithy, had been chosen because of its thick walls through which the warlike sound of the shofar could not be heard. It stood among the houses and the rainbowed smells like an honest workman who, finished with the toil of the week, has cleansed himself and put on fresh clothes for the Sabbath. There were no windows facing the street, there was no light to be seen except what came through the open door from the inner court.

I put my hand on the wall that separated me from the space where the shofar had sounded that day as it had all through the month of Elul. The heat of the day had gone out of the wall, it was cool. As I stood there a man named Mordechai Salzedo, a merchant friend of Bembel Rudzuk, came to me and said, "From the roof of the synagogue we have seen the new moon; now the new year can begin."

"Good luck to it," I said.

At this irreverence he raised his eyebrows and tilted his head to favour, I suppose, the analytical side of his brain while he looked at me carefully. Having done this he put one hand on my shoulder and lifted the index finger of the other. "'Where he is,' eh?" he said. "'Where he is.'"

What a remarkable Salzedo this was! When he said those words it was as if there came through the cool thick wall of the synagogue, through my hand and arm and into my heart the New Year's Days of time past when our Rabbi had read those very words from Chapter 21 of Genesis, where it tells of Hagar and Ishmael in the wilderness, Hagar weeping because she thinks that her son will die:

> And God heard the voice of the lad; and the angel of God called to Hagar out of heaven, and said unto her: "What aileth thee, Hagar? fear not; for God hath heard the voice of the lad where he is. Arise, lift up the lad, and hold him fast by thy hand; for I will make him a great nation." And God opened her eyes, and she saw a well of water; and she went, and filled the bottle with water, and gave the lad drink.

Our Rabbi had always been fond of citing the Midrash Rabbah on these verses:

> WHERE HE IS connotes for his own sake, for a sick person's prayers on his own behalf are more efficacious than those of anyone else.
>
> WHERE HE IS. R. Simon said: The ministering angels hastened to indict him, exclaiming, "Sovereign of the Universe! Wilt Thou bring up a well for one who will one day slay Thy children with thirst?" "What is he now?" He demanded. "Righteous," was the answer. "I judge man only as he is at the moment," said He.

Wonderful. So WHERE WAS I? Could it be said of me that at this moment I was righteous? I couldn't think of any harm that I was doing just then. What about my pilgrimage, my road to Jerusalem that went on now without me? At this distance I believe that I am telling the truth when I say that it was not the Mittelteufel that kept me in Antioch. I had begun my pilgrimage wanting to save the many mysterious, unseen, fragile temples of the world so that Christ would not leave us as God had done when he ceased to be He. Now as I thought about it I found that Christ as a limited identity had already departed from my perception and been absorbed into the manifold idea of himself. And what for me had been Jerusalem was equally to be found wherever I joined the motion of the hidden lion. I remembered those poor hungry death-ridden children whom I had met on the road and I heard again in my mind the voice of that boy who had said, "Jerusalem will be wherever we are when we come to the end."

Salzedo was no longer standing before me, I was alone. The door through which the light had come was closed. In the darkness my hand was still touching the wall of the synagogue but now when I thought of the sound of the shofar it seemed to jar on the silence.

One day has followed another with the beating of hammers, the baking of bread, the cry of the mu'addhin. It is the winter of 1097. The walls of Antioch, those great mountain-ascending walls with their four hundred towers, those strong stones left from Justinian's strong time, those stones that have no enemy, now they look down on the tents of the Franks. Antioch has been under siege since October but it is the besiegers who are starving. How strange they are, these scarecrow conquerors, these soldiers of Christ who refuse to learn how to fight the Turks, who at Dorylaeum won the day by their very stupidity when the half of their divided host with whom they had lost contact came out of nowhere like miraculous saviours to astonish and defeat Qilij-Arslan's mounted bowmen. They walk, starving as they are, like victors; they walk as if they shake the ground, believing themselves to be invincible, believing that God wills it that they should win. The arrogance of those coloured tents of the Frankish knights! Through successive dawns they stand more frightening in their presumption than shouts and battlecries and the thundering of hooves, these tents in which these unturning men dare to sleep before the enemy walls, dare to sleep in their unclever and unshakable courage and the expectation of victory.

Soldiers of Christ! The marvel, the continual surprise of Christ is that he includes everything that attributes itself to the idea of him. Because I have seen Christ, have talked with him, have heard the strange woodwind of his voice inside my head, have looked into his lion eyes, I know that there looks out of his eyes, as out of the eyes of Vermeer's young girl with the pearl earring, the intolerable bursting of the beginning of all things.

From that unimaginable violence which is God as It has come all that there is: all the world, all the universe. I know this in many ways but I need to know it in more ways, I need to put myself where the Idea of It is, I need to move at the same speed as It, become altogether one with It so that there is no jump to be made, this jump that we so much fear at the time of death. I must become as advanced as possible in this because I sense that my time is fast approaching, that time when my young death will be full-grown and ready to go out into the world, leaving me, the fond and used-up parent, behind.

I know that my death will be ready soon because now in this winter of 1097 I have seen the tax-collector again for the first time since I came to this part of the world. Suddenly one morning he was there, his naked headless body still writhing with maggots, his member tumescent with bloat, his naked feet moving over the triangles of Hidden Lion. He was gesturing with his hand as if making a speech or admonishing someone or possibly counting, possibly reckoning up something. I tried to make myself not hear his voice while at the same time I strained to hear it. I *did* hear it, I heard his voice and I heard the words he was saying with utter clarity but even as I heard I forgot; it was like waking up from a dream with everything still in the mind but as you sit up in bed it is gone.

After that he was always there, always walking through the sounds and smells, the colour and motion of the Hidden Lion bazaar like someone with a fixed idea, like a madman who talks to himself; always did he gesture with his hand in that particular way; always did I forget what he was saying as soon as I heard it but one thing became inescapable: it was I that he was talking about, it was my account that he was reckoning up.

None of the others had turned up yet: not Udo the relic-gatherer, not the bear shot full of arrows, not Bodwild and Konrad, not Bruder Pförtner, not my young death. I understood that the tax-collector had come to give me notice that my life would soon be required of me but I did not think that the final stage of things would begin until I saw my young death once more. When last I saw him he had looked at me, as I have said, trustingly. It was my constant fear that I should fall short of his expectations—I wanted so much to do my best for him, I wanted so much to do my uttermost possible. More and more it was not the face of Sophia and her naked body that my mind offered me in its pictures: it was the obscure face of my young death; it was the shadowy form of actuality to come. I persevered with my martial exercises.

So. Now I walk a little differently from the way I used to, and I stand on the wall and look down at the enemy as one who will not die without making trouble.

These Franks encamped before our walls, they have come as the seasons come or as old age and death come; in their time they are there, they are not to be avoided. Antioch stands between them and Jerusalem; it cannot get out of their way nor can they afford to bypass it and leave a fortified enemy in their rear.

We have heard of the coming of the Franks; we have heard of them at Constantinople, we have heard how one of them sat himself down on the throne of Alexius Comnenus and told the Emperor that in his own country he had waited in vain at the crossroads for anyone to answer his challenge to single combat.

I have told how the price of a bale of silk went up by three dinars in Tripoli when the Franks arrived in Constantinople. When they besieged Nicaea and Nicaea surrendered to the troops of Alexius the price of silk went up by one more dinar. "Last time it was uncertainty of supply that sent the price up," said Bembel Rudzuk; "this time the sheep are not so frightened of the wolf as they were; some of the sheep are saying that this is not a devouring wolf, it is a buying wolf."

From Dorylaeum, from Heraclea, from Marash the wave of their coming ran ahead of the Franks. We heard of Baldwin in Edessa, how he became co-regent with Prince Thoros of Edessa and how Thoros ended up with his head on a pole. After Dorylaeum the price of silk went back to where it had been before the Franks arrived in Constantinople; it paused there, then dropped by one dinar. "Perhaps this is after all that end-of-the-world wolf of whom one has heard," said Bembel Rudzuk. "Perhaps this is the wolf who will swallow the sun. The market has become a swamp, a mire, a bog, a place with no firm ground whatever. The beggars are tying up their bundles and the great houses are closing the shutters."

It was the victory at Dorylaeum that made everyone begin to wonder whether the battle cry of the Franks, "God wills it!," might be a true statement of how things were. Perhaps God *did* will it. Or perhaps they were simply lucky. But what was luck if not the will of God? There were those in Antioch who dedicated themselves unsparingly to the pondering of that question, and if the smoking of water pipes and the drinking of sweet drinks could have repelled the Franks the city would never have been in danger.

It was pondered that at Dorylaeum the Franks had behaved so stupidly that almost it seemed the paradigm of a mystery not to be understood by the unfavoured. To divide their host into two columns not in communication with each other! To separate the foot-soldiers from the cavalry as they had done! To fall back upon the tents in panic and to be saved at the last moment by the arrival of the other half of the army! Did the two columns symbolize Jesus the son and God the father? Body and soul? Adam and Eve? Sulphur and Mercury? There were as many opinions as there were ponderers.

Yaghi-Siyan, uncertain of God's will, sent for help to Rudwan of Aleppo, to Duqaq of Damascus, to Karbuqa of Mosul. Rudwan said no; Duqaq said yes, as did his atabeg Tughtagin and Janah Ad-Dawla of Homs; Karbuqa also said yes. Yaghi-Siyan, hoping for quick relief, then organized his defences, laid in supplies, and made ready to become history.

It is to be assumed that the soldiers of Christ all thought of God as He, and to them it soon became evident that He did not will that Antioch should fall too quickly. I too out of habit still thought of him sometimes as He but mostly I recognized him as It, the raw motive power of the universe; and I was able to see in the systole and diastole of the siege of Antioch the reciprocal action of that asymmetry without which there would be only stillness and silence.

The four-hundred-towered walls built by Justinian and kept in good repair by the Byzantines were the pivot of the action; they were the fixed point at the centre of that particular dance; they would not give way, they would go on yet awhile defining an inside and an outside. Yaghi-Siyan on the inside still had enough food but not enough men; he could neither defend his walls at every point nor could he go out and defeat the Franks in one decisive battle.

The Franks could take up positions only on three sides of Antioch; they were prevented on the fourth side by Mount Silpius which kept a back door open for the besieged. As the Franks ran out of food some of them, like sparrows, picked through manure for the grain in it; some died of starvation; some deserted. They were always foraging through a countryside more and more empty of everything except Turks in ambush and they had of course to beat off such armies as came to relieve Antioch. Yaghi-Siyan made sorties when circumstances favoured; there were many engagements major and minor; history was daily sown like a crop to be harvested in its season.

Having thought of history as a crop that was sown I am left with the image of sowing but the picture in my mind is not one of seeds flung from the hand of the husbandman; it is of heads flung from the missile-throwing machines on both sides. Heads! Human heads that have spoken, kissed, whistled, eaten, drunk, done all those things that only heads can do! Heads as missiles! The heads slung into Antioch by the Franks were the heads of Turks killed in battle but the heads slung out of Antioch by the Turks were not those of Franks; they were the heads of Syrian and Armenian Christians of Antioch.

Those Syrian and Armenian Christians of Antioch and the country roundabout, I know not quite how to think of them, how to hold them in my mind. Until 1085 Antioch had been part of Byzantium, but as the tide of Byzantium ebbed they found themselves stranded on a beach that belonged to Qilij-Arslan. Sometimes I think of them as being like those little shore birds that run on long legs, crying as they glean the tideline. They were never static, never inactive, those Christians of that place and that time, they filled in whatever unoccupied spaces of action they found. They were constantly going backwards and forwards between the Franks and the Turks: sometimes they spied on the Franks for the Turks; sometimes they spied on the Turks for the Franks. When the Franks were starving those busy Christians in the country around Antioch sold them provisions at what might be called Last Judgment prices which effectively sorted out those who could afford to live from those who could only afford to die. Those same Christians, when they found Turks in flight from an engagement with the understandably testy Franks, ambushed the Turks and so struck a rough balance in their dealings with both sides. They had no peace, those Christians, they had no rest, they were continually gleaning that shimmering tideline against a background of towering breakers. The churning of the times they lived in had imparted to them a motion they could not resist, they were compelled by forces beyond them to keep moving in all directions and to be incessantly busy in many ways.

There came a particular day that winter when the Franks ambushed the Turks who were planning to ambush them. We were told that seven hundred Turks died that day while the Franks had no losses whatever. It was a cold grey day, the tents and awnings of the Hidden Lion bazaar were snapping in the wind; it was one of those grey days, it was one of those winds when no matter how many people gather together each one of them looks utterly alone and too small under a sky that is far, far too big. Little leaning pitiful figures. The tax-collector that day was pacing with ostentatious self-importance, like a man who knows that people breathlessly await his words.

There came to Hidden Lion then Yaghi-Siyan riding on his horse, his bodyguard with him as always. They were followed by a mule-cart covered with a tent-cloth. Yaghi-Siyan rode clip-clopping on to the tiles with the bodyguard clip-clopping after him and the mule-cart rumbling behind. He wore a helmet and a mail shirt with a gold-worked green robe over it. One couldn't tell whether he had been in the battle or not; he looked fresh and clean. He had a bow slung on his shoulder; I had never seen him carry a bow before; he looked as if at any moment he expected to have to fight or fly for his life. His face was wild with rage and (I thought) with despair. He looked all around him while his horse danced and tossed its head. (How strange, I thought, to be a horse; one might be carrying on one's back anything at all to anything at all: chaos to order; betrayal to trust; defeat to victory; death to life.)

Everyone became silent, and in the silence there came on the wind snatches of singing from the Franks encamped by the Gate of the Dog. They were singing in Latin and the only words that came clearly in the gusting of the wind were: *"Deus trinus et unus,"* "God three together and one."

"Do you know what tongue they sing in?" Yaghi-Siyan said to me.

"Yes," I said. "They are singing in Latin."

"Scholarly Jew!" said Yaghi-Siyan. "And what do they sing?"

" 'God three together and one,' " I said. "Those were the only words I could make out."

"'Three together and one'!" said Yaghi-Siyan. "Which is it? Is it three or is it one?"

"It is both three and one," I said. "The three are together in the one."

"How many gods do you worship, Jew?" he said.

"One," I said.

"I also," he said. Still looking at me he said over his shoulder, "Bring Firouz here." One of the bodyguard rode off at a trot towards the Tower of the Two Sisters.

Everyone waited in silence. There had been no command for silence nor was Yaghi-Siyan, Governor though he was, a commanding presence. It was clear to everyone, however, that something of great power was commanding him. The faces that were turned towards him were looking at what was commanding him. The awnings flapped and fluttered, the green-and-gold banner carried by one of the bodyguard snapped in the wind. Mount Silpius, continually surprising in its mountainness, seemed itself surprised to find itself where it was, surprised to find that the present moment had indeed arrived. I cannot say less than I must but I dare not say more than is permitted; for the first time in this narrative it comes to me that words are images, and what is sacred cannot be imaged. Still there is the obligation of the witness: though the world should pass away, what has been seen has been seen; the voice that does not speak is denying God.

Yaghi-Siyan himself seemed to be snapping in the wind like the banner as he sat there on his horse in silence. The horse arched its neck, pawed with its hooves, dunged upon the tiles that at another time Yaghi-Siyan had taken off his shoes to walk upon.

The guard returned, Firouz riding beside him. Yaghi-Siyan said to Firouz, "Get down off your horse, please."

Firouz dismounted, stood upon the tiles of Hidden Lion. The guard who had brought him took hold of the bridle of Firouz's horse.

"Firouz," said Yaghi-Siyan, "you have been a Christian, have you not?"

"I bear witness that there is no god but God and that Muhammad is the messenger of God," said Firouz.

"Yes, yes, we know that," said Yaghi-Siyan. "Now you are a Muslim. But you must tell me about the Christian god, the Three in One."

"What must I tell you?" said Firouz.

"You must tell me," said Yaghi-Siyan, "what this Three in One is. Is One the head and Two the body and Three the legs? What is this Three in One?"

"One is the Father, Two is the Son, Three is the Holy Spirit," said Firouz.

"Very good," said Yaghi-Siyan. "Here we are, you and I, upon Hidden Lion with its twisting serpents, contiguous with infinity: you are an Armenian, you have been a Christian and now you are a Muslim; I am only a simple Turk, I lack your experience in religious matters; I have always been a Muslim the same as I am now, I don't know anything else. But you, having been a Christian, must know all about Christians—probably you can immediately recognize them when you see them. How is it with them, have they got lines upon their bodies dividing them into Spirit, Son, and Holy Father?"

"Christians wear blue turbans," said Firouz.

"Ah, yes!" said Yaghi-Siyan. "Probably the blue signifies the Heaven that is waiting for those of them who are virtuous. In any case you will have no difficulty in knowing them on sight. And of course now that you have been living among Turkish Muslims you know very well what they look like, don't you?"

"I don't know," said Firouz.

"Show him a Turk," said Yaghi-Siyan to the cavalryman on the mule-cart.

The cavalryman lifted a corner of the cloth, put his hands into the cart, and lifted out a man's head. He did not lift it up by the hair, he held it respectfully with both hands. The nose was smashed, the open eyes were covered with dirt, the face was broken and smeared with blood. I looked from the face to the mountain, from the mountain to the face.

"This is the head of a Turk," said Yaghi-Siyan. "His name is Jhamil Muqtin. He was one of our bravest fighters, he was like magic with a horse, like magic with a bow. His body is not here, his body has been roasted and eaten by the Franks. They have slung his head over the wall with a stone-slinger. His wife, his two sons and his daughter have waited for his return from battle. His old mother has waited also. There are a hundred heads in this cart and there are hundreds more of our men dead. They are dead from treachery, they are dead because the Franks knew of our plans, they were lying in wait for us. We were betrayed by the Christians who live among us, Armenian and Syrian Christians. Now you must bring three hundred Christians to me here upon these twisting serpents. You will know the men by their blue turbans and the women by their blue headcloths. If you find Christians naked you will know the men by their uncircumcised members and you will know the women because they will be with the men. You will know the children because they will cry when you take the parents. I need these three hundred Christians urgently, I must send their heads over the wall to the Franks. They have sent me a hundred heads but as their god is three for one I must send them back three hundred."

Bembel Rudzuk spoke and his voice seemed to come from a very small quiet place far away, as from a cleft in the rock of a distant mountain. "Your Excellency," he said, "as you speak those words you are standing on tiles inscribed with the names of Allah The Compassionate, Allah The Merciful."

"Yes," said Yaghi-Siyan, "and that is why I shall overlook what you have just now said. A second time you won't be so lucky."

Bembel Rudzuk came forward and knelt before Yaghi-Siyan. He took off his kaffiya, bared his neck, bowed his head. "Let my Muslim head then be the first of the three hundred," he said. "I cannot turn away, and it is better that I do not look upon what you are going to do."

Having no sword with me I went up to Firouz who was standing as if in a daze and I drew his sword from its sheath. With it in my hand I stood over Bembel Rudzuk. "I prefer not to look upon the death of Bembel Rudzuk," I said. "Who kills him will have to kill me first."

"Devoted Jew!" said Yaghi-Siyan. "No one is going to kill either of you. I give you this gift because of what you have shown me with your Hidden Lion. But you shall not be allowed to interfere with what is going to happen here on your pattern that is contiguous with infinity. That is why it is being done here, that the beheading of these three hundred traitors may also be contiguous with infinity, may go on for ever and ever until time will have an end." From Firouz's girdle he removed the sheath of the sword and slid it over the blade as I held the weapon in my hand. "Keep this sword and remember me in time to come," he said. "Go now in peace, go up to the top of your tower and bear witness that this is also part of the pattern."

Soldiers of the bodyguard came and led Bembel Rudzuk and me to the tower that stood on David's Wheel. We climbed to the top, and when I looked down at the pattern it seemed for the moment not to have in it that motion that was always there; it seemed to be the frozen shards and fragments of a Law that was created unyieldingly hard and rigid and for ever broken. The red, the black, the tawny triangles were swarming with figures watching, figures waiting, staring eyes in staring faces. From the place above his shoulders where his head would have been I felt the tax-collector's eyes on me. Tower Gate's round face appeared in the crowd like the moon seen for a moment through the cloud-race of an angry sky. The Imam, the Nagid, and the Rabbi seemed to pass like sorrowing dark angels through that same sky. Ah! I thought, this would have been a good time to die; I ought to have killed Yaghi-Siyan when I stood before him with Firouz's sword in my hand but I had not done it.

Neither Bembel Rudzuk nor I sought death again that day. I knew that my time was coming soon, I knew that I must be alert to recognize the time and the place so that my death might be the best possible, the most useful possible. But even as that thought moved through my mind it was hurried on its way by another thought coming behind it. This second thought asked whether it might not be only vanity and a striving after wind to want so much for one's death; whether it might not be better to require nothing whatever of it or for it but simply to welcome it whenever and however it might come, to welcome it as one welcomes the stranger to whom one must always show hospitality.

As soon as I had taken in this second thought a wave of ease spread through me, a strong feeling that I had found the right way to be. With that feeling came an understanding that from then on every moment would be—indeed always had been—as the last moment. This wants to be made perfectly clear, it may be the only thing I have to say that matters; this idea has for me both the brilliance of the heart of the diamond of the universe and the inverse brilliance of the heart of the blackness in which that diamond lives: this moment that is every moment is always the last moment and it came into being with the first moment; it is that moment of creation in which there comes into being the possibility of all things and the end of all things; it is the blossoming jewel at the heart of the explosion, the calm quiet dawn at the centre of the bursting. This moment that is every moment—to see it whole is to synchronize one's being with the whole of time, to be everywhere in it at the same time. It is to be with everything by letting go of everything. It is through this awareness that my present state of being has come about. It is associated with that purple-blue of indescribable luminosity of which I have spoken before.

There are not three hundred Christians gathered here on Hidden Lion; there are one hundred; Yaghi-Siyan has said that he will balance justice with mercy, he will do to these Christians only what those Christians outside the walls have done to the Turks whose heads are in the mule-cart. That a human being should in this fashion show mercy is to me an equal horror with the rest of what is happening. Once only I look at the faces of the Christians as they are herded on to the tiles, then I look away, I look at their feet.

Now at this moment and then at that moment, in this same moment that will continue for the duration of the universe, in this same luminosity of purple-blue, in this same heart of the diamond, I see the gathering of the Christians on Hidden Lion. The presentness of it, the nowness and for everness of it, is intolerable, and for this that is happening I curse God as Him, I curse God as It, that he made us, whether as He or as It. That he made us what we are, to sling heads over a wall from the outside to the inside and from the inside to the outside. This is what He has done with His omnipotence: this feeble masturbation in a dark and ill-smelling place.

And yet, so are we made and such is the action of the everything in this one moment that is every moment, that another thought flickers over and under my first thought: what style God has! What a truly godlike extravagance, to burst out all at once with a universe in which everything is going at once and humankind is let run with nothing to stop it from doing anything at all. And to make this running-loose creature with a mind that knows what it is doing and a soul in which Hell burns always and Heaven is grasped so rarely and so briefly that it lives in us as a continual yearning for what can never be held on to, for what must always be lost—what invention!

The sacred is not to be imaged, there is no image to put to what God is nor is there any reason to want an image of such a thing. The evil that he has created is also in its inexplicable way sacred and not to be described beyond a certain point. Suddenly are these long-legged shore birds, these gleaners of the tideline, netted. Suddenly, with their dark faces, their speechless mouths, their uncircumcised members, their frozenness into such time as there will be until the end of time.

That is as far as I shall go with these words and the images they bring. What happened, happened.

Afterwards the bodies are taken away in wagons. There remains of course the blood on the tiles, on the red and black and tawny triangles of Hidden Lion. It is darker than the tawny, darker than the red, lighter than the black. The same people who stood looking on while the Christians were being beheaded now stand looking at the blood. The butcher and his helper from the shop near by bring a bucket of sand, two buckets of water, a scrubbing brush.

"No," says Bembel Rudzuk. "This blood is not to be washed away. It is now part of the pattern and it is obviously the will of Allah that it should be so."

"Perhaps you don't remember," says the butcher, "but one of the tiles with blood on it is mine. My money is mortared into it and it is inscribed with the name of Allah The Truth, He whose existence has no change."

"I remember," says Bembel Rudzuk, "but this blood is not going to be washed away." He stands there with his arms folded on his chest. The butcher and the butcher's helper look at him attentively, then walk away with their bucket of sand, their two buckets of water, and their scrubbing brush.

In twos and threes the people drift away. Still Bembel Rudzuk stands there like a man of stone. He and I have read the Holy Scriptures together, and I know that those verses of Ezekiel that are now in my mind must be in his mind as well:

> Wherefore thus saith the Lord GOD:
> Woe to the bloody city, to the pot
> whose filth is therein, and whose filth
> is not gone out of it! bring it out
> piece by piece; no lot is fallen upon it.
> For her blood is in the midst of her;
> she set it upon the bare rock;
> she poured it not upon the ground,
> to cover it with dust; that it might

cause fury to come up, that vengeance
might be taken, I have set her blood
upon the bare rock, that it should not
be covered. Therefore thus saith the Lord GOD:
Woe to the bloody city!

After a time Bembel Rudzuk ceases to stand like a stone man, he begins
to walk the boundaries of the square, then moves in a little, walking in
progressively smaller squares, moving a little closer to the centre each
time, walking slowly in concentric squares as if threading a labyrinth.
When he reaches the tower he walks hexagonally around it, then walks
from there outwards in concentric squares again to the outer limits of
Hidden Lion. The tax-collector with his eyes that are elsewhere stands
watching quietly with me. The sky is growing pale. Bembel Rudzuk and
I go home; the tax-collector remains on Hidden Lion.

Bembel Rudzuk and I went up to the roof of his house and waited
there for the day to come. It was unseasonably warm, the air was close
and heavy, the morning seemed to hold its breath in the dull grey before-
dawn light. In this light was something of that grey and rainy dawn in
which I first had come to Suwaydiyya with Bembel Rudzuk. The port with
its topography of morning, its long shadows, its low buildings, its boats
rocking to the morning slap of the water on their sides, furled sails still
heavy with night, crews moving slowly on their decks, the smell of cooking-fires — all this had without seeming to move grown smoothly bigger in
my eyes in that particular way in which things reveal themselves when
approached by sea, opening to the approacher more and more detail,
more and more imminence of what is to come. And always, thus approaching, one feels the new day, the new place, coming forward to read
the face of the approacher. Always the held breath, the questioning look
of the grey morning.

"I no longer have any questions that require answers," said Bembel
Rudzuk. "It is not in our power to know very much nor to understand very
much. Perhaps the most we can hope for is to learn to encounter what
comes without pissing ourselves." He said nothing for a while, then he
said, "The heads of the Christians were slung over the wall but not the
bodies. Do you know why?"

I knew why. Sometimes when the wind was blowing from the Franks to us I had smelled the smoke of their cooking. I listened to the twittering of sparrows, the crowing of cocks, I saw in my mind the blood on the tiles of Hidden Lion.

" 'And all as a garment will become old,' " said Bembel Rudzuk, " 'and as a mantle thou wilt roll up them, as a garment also they will be changed . . . ' This is the earth and the heavens being spoken of, the work of God's hands, they will grow old and be folded up like a garment. You and I have read this together in the Epistle of Paul to the Hebrews in the New Testament of the Christians, but for me it is no longer a matter of words; I can feel it in the air, I can feel the fabric of the world and its time collapsing upon itself like the folds of a tired garment." Bembel Rudzuk stood there solidly in the grey light with his arms folded, his moustaches as heroic as ever, his bearing as upright; but he looked like a deserted village.

"In the Quran also one reads of this folding up," he said. "This too we have read together, in Sura 81, *Takwir*, The Folding Up:

> "*In the name of Allah, Most Gracious, Most Merciful*
> 1. When the sun
>   (With its spacious light)
>   Is folded up;
> 2. When the stars
>   Fall, losing their lustre;
> 3. When the mountains vanish
>   (Like a mirage);
> 4. When the she-camels
>   Ten months with young,
>   Are left untended;

("And you must know," said Bembel Rudzuk, "that the camel being the jewel of the Arab's eye and his special pet, the she-camel almost come to her time is most especially precious; so when we speak of a time when such animals will be neglected we are speaking of the collapse of all things, the true and actual final folding up.)

> 5. When the wild beasts
>   Are herded together
>   (In human habitations);

("In this extremity," said Bembel Rudzuk, "the animals will no longer be afraid of humans, the animals and the humans will be folded up together at the end of all things.)

> "6. When the oceans
>   Boil over with a swell;
> 7. When the souls
>   Are sorted out
>   (Being joined, like with like);

("I no longer know what to think about this matter of the sorting of souls," said Bembel Rudzuk. "Is there more than one kind of soul, do you think? Is the soul of Yaghi-Siyan different from your soul and my soul? Wait, hear more before we talk.)

> "8. When the female (infant)
>   Buried alive, is questioned—
> 9. For what crime
>   she was killed;

("There have been," said Bembel Rudzuk, "Arabs who buried their baby daughters alive; they didn't want to have to provide for them or be burdened with protecting their honour. These are only words and one can speak them but if one thinks of the actuality then one must look at what is intolerable to look at. I am thinking now of your Abraham and Isaac who are Ibrahim and Isma'il in Muslim tradition. Never before have I dared to say aloud these words that I am going to say now: the fundamental flaw in God is that He will say that He requires the sacrifice of Isaac/Isma'il; the fundamental flaw in man is that he takes his knife in hand to do God's bidding. This story of God's testing of Abraham has become an easy thing to read, an easy thing to say in words, an easy point of reference; but if you let it become real in your mind then you have to look at a boy tied hand and foot by his father whose knife is at his throat. Think of it! There lies the boy trussed like an animal, he lies on the firewood that he has borne on his own back to the place where the fire will consume him when he has been murdered by his father whom he has trusted all his life. Murder in the name of God! And Abraham has no hesitation! He is completely willing to murder his son because a voice in his head has made him mad. If I had ever in my life come upon such a scene, if I had ever come upon such a madman with his knife upraised over a child I should have killed that man before God had a chance to speak again. Wouldn't you? See it in your mind! Be that father and look down into the eyes of your son while you raise the knife. What are you at this moment that is one moment away from murder, from human sacrifice? Will you call yourself the hand of God? Why should Yaghi-Siyan not call himself the hand of God a hundred times over? Word of God! If God is everywhere then every word is the Word of God, Yaghi-Siyan's word as well as Muhammad's. Wait, listen to more of this Sura of the folding-up:)

"10. When the Scrolls
      Are laid open;
  11. When the World on High
      Is unveiled:
  12. When the Blazing Fire
      Is kindled to fierce heat;
  13. And when the Garden
      Is brought near;—
  14. (Then) shall each soul know
      What it has put forward.

"Here I have been quoting verses of the Holy Quran and I cannot even properly call myself a Muslim," said Bembel Rudzuk: "I don't believe in a Last Day that will be different from any other day; I believe that the Last Day is every day; I believe that the Garden and the Fire are in each of us every day of our lives and we are in one or the other or somewhere between the two depending on our actions. I believe that every soul knows very well from one moment to another what it has put forward—do I not know what I have put forward with this Hidden Lion that I have called up? Do I not know how far I have overstepped the bounds of what is permitted in one's approach to the Unseen?"

"Why do you keep saying 'I'?" I said. "Whatever has been done with Hidden Lion has been done by the two of us; was it not I who drew the first unit of the pattern on the stone?"

PILGERMANN

"Ah!" said Bembel Rudzuk, "You see! You are trying to share the burden of blame because you know that there *is* a burden of blame!"

I thought of Hidden Lion, of its tawny triangles, its red and its black but as soon as the triangles came into my mind they were covered first by blood then by the terrified feet of the hundred chosen for death by Firouz. What should I have done in his place? Useless to ask such a question—he did what he did that day, I did what I did, each of us in our own place. It is so very, very easy to live one day longer than one ought.

"You don't deny what I have just said," said Bembel Rudzuk, "you don't deny that we have overstepped the bounds."

"No," I said, "I don't deny it. Everywhere there are patterns of tiles to be seen, most of them far more ambitious in their complexity and finish than Hidden Lion, but I think one may say that they were done in innocence."

"They were done without presumption," said Bembel Rudzuk; "they were done modestly and with no other purpose than that of ornamentation. They were done without intent to observe the Unseen, without intent to violate its privacy; they harmlessly adorn building, walls, floors; they were not made for the sole purpose of seeing the Unseeable. We have done that which ought not to be done although you are not to blame; it was I who asked you to make the design, I with my stupid ideas of sulphur and mercury and triangles, I with my greed for the Unseen. And yesterday the Unseen said, 'Do you still pursue me with your tiles? I have shown you, have I not, twisting serpents, moving pyramids, disappearing lions; I have shown you the surge of Me that is like a river of power, and still you crave more; very well then, I will show you more.'"

"Can you really believe that?" I said. "Can you really believe that Hidden Lion has called down this terrible thing upon itself?"

"Think," said Bembel Rudzuk, "what we have done. We have made a provocation and an insult. We have used the names of God and the habitation of the Unseen and we have made a good-luck charm with our tiles. We have made an idolatry for ignorant people to whom prayer is only a kind of begging, we have put the rubbish of the seeable and the touchable between them and Allah, we have sped them on their way from any hope of the Garden, we have pointed them towards the Fire."

"Have we truly done so much evil?" I said.

"Only consider," said Bembel Rudzuk: "if the pattern of Hidden Lion is contiguous with infinity (and there can be no doubt of this, in our very souls we know it to be so) then everything about it is contiguous with infinity. If our action in making it was wrong (and we both know now that it was) then that wrong action is contiguous with infinity; its connexions extend to things and places we know not of, we cannot imagine the vastness of the web to which Hidden Lion is an entrance and a passageway."

"All things being contiguous," I said, "Hidden Lion can as well be an effect as a cause; it cannot be proved to be the beginning of a chain of evil."

"Sophistry cannot help us," said Bembel Rudzuk; "every action has its consequences and the consequences of the action of making Hidden Lion cannot be without evil."

At that moment from the minaret there came the call of the mu'addhin. Bembel Rudzuk began his prayers and I drew a little apart from him and stood looking out over the city that I seemed to be approaching by sea in the grey dawn. Again I saw in my mind the terrified feet of the Syrian and Armenian Christians on the tawny, the red, and the black triangles and I wondered in what way any of what was happening could possibly have been willed by God in any of His or Its aspects. How far back would one have to go to find the cause from which this effect had arisen? All things being contiguous, one was driven back to the original bursting into being of the universe: immediately from that moment existed the possibility of everything that could possibly happen on this earth. From that moment two and two made four, and all else that could be until the end of time already was; on one or another, on a few or on many of the planes of virtuality and actuality that might at some time intersect, everything that could be already was. The choices that would have to be made by people who would not be born for thousands of millions of years were already forming with the galaxies and the nebulae, with the Virgin and the Lion. As far as I could see, the will of God was simply that everything possible would indeed be possible. Within that limitation the choice was ours, the reckoning His. And He was in us, one couldn't get away from Him, that was the Fire of it, that was the Garden of it, at the centre of every soul and contiguous with infinity. The possibilities of choice were beyond all calculation and the probability of wrong choice so high as to be almost a certainty. Only God could think of such a game, and only humans would bother to play it.

Refreshed and desperate from my meditation I turned and saw another figure on the roof with us. My heart leapt in me; it was my young death. This was the very first time he had appeared to me since I had crossed the sea to come here. He was naked and he was standing by the parapet with his back to me but I recognized him at once. He was full-grown but there was that about the way he was standing that made me think of a child who cannot sleep or has had perhaps a bad dream and comes to be comforted. How my heart went out to him!

He turned to me, his face somehow obscure, not to be held in the eye. I looked to see if he had all his parts. He had, he was a complete man. He looked at me for a moment only, then he walked slowly to the stairs and was gone, his face still obscure in my mind, not to be recalled.

13

Soon must I tell of the fall of Antioch but not yet. Mortal life is a difficult proposition because hardly anything can be experienced as what it actually is; everything is time-distorted. In childhood we wait for things that seem too long in coming, we wait for treats, for presents, for festivals and holidays, we wait for growing up. There is so much waiting that suddenly childhood itself is gone with all that was being waited for. As grown-ups we find ourselves pitched headlong down a steep and slippery slide with everything hurtling towards us at great speed; some things smash us full in the face, others streak past half-glimpsed or unseen; everything has happened before we were ready for it. Only after the hurly-burly of mortal life is over can one have a really good look at what has happened; unburdened by choice and unthreatened by consequences one is able to sort through the half-glimpses of a lifetime and find perhaps one or two workable fragments of recognition.

So it is that only now in this little space of centuries since my death have I been able not so much to understand anything as simply to look carefully at everything to see if this fragment and that fragment which do not fit together may yet both belong to a shape which might be recognizable if seen entire.

I have in mind the deeds of the Franks and the Turks, such as I was able to see or hear about; I have in mind how men would sometimes rush forward, sometimes back, some on horseback, some on foot. I have in mind one particular night of the winter rains of 1097, it was soon after Christmas. At that time I was often on the walls of Antioch in the small hours of the night; I was in a state in which I could feel the passage of time as if I were an hourglass through which the sand was running more and more swiftly. It was well towards morning on this night that I am speaking of; it had been raining steadily but the rain had stopped, and now in the dim cloudlight I saw what seemed to be thousands of Frankish horsemen moving out of their encampment and heading up the valley of the Orontes.

Bembel Rudzuk came and stood with me. We were on that part of the wall by the Aleppo Gate that overlooked the sector of Bohemond of Taranto. On the hill behind his encampment the Franks had built a tower that we called Evil Eye; now we saw lanterns moving on the top of it while between us and it the dark horsemen slowly rode away into the fading darkness. Stubbornly stood the sodden and threadbare tents they left behind; in some of them glimmered the dim light of candles. We had no idea how many had gone but from other watchers we heard that more than half of the Franks remained to keep the siege. Many of them were starving and by now were regularly drinking the blood of their horses; we guessed that this moving-out of the thousands was a foraging expedition and the size of it indicated to us that they intended to move deep into hostile territory.

The next night there was again no rain nor was there a moon; the darkness of the sky was opaque. "This night will bring out Yaghi-Siyan," said Bembel Rudzuk. We went up on to the wall over the bridge gate and waited there for hours, equally expecting Turks to go out or Franks to come in. Even from what little we knew of the Franks there was nothing that they could have done that would have surprised us; starving as they were and faced with impregnable walls they might yet at any moment storm those walls. In moments of quiet like this it seemed to us that any sortie by the Turks could well provoke a counterattack that would bring the Franks raging into the city.

Bembel Rudzuk and I had no doubt whatever that a night would come when the Franks, whatever the odds against them, would take Antioch; it seemed to us that it was simply in the nature of things. And of course when that night came it would bring certain death to the Muslims and the Jews of Antioch.

It would have been easy enough to leave the city—Mount Silpius, as I have said, kept a back door open—so that we might live yet awhile and do our dying elsewhere but neither of us wanted to. It was in Antioch that a readiness to die had come upon us and now we felt committed to that place; to take our dying elsewhere would have seemed frivolous and disloyal. Both of us admitted to a certain vanity about dying: we preferred to do it as handsomely as possible; but we agreed to be guided by the circumstances and not, when the proper moment came, to refuse a lesser death in the hope of winning a greater one some other time.

My original idea of attaining Jerusalem before it was too late, before Jesus withdrew from any further possibility of manifestation and the world was left with the bleakness of what he had called "the straight action and no more dressing up" now seemed like those fond hopes of childhood that even a child recognizes as being made of that kind of mental sugar-candy that melts in the hard sunlight of reality.

The siege as the months passed had developed, as does everything, its own particular rhythm and mode of being. When the Franks had first appeared outside the walls of Antioch Yaghi-Siyan had at every moment expected a major assault. He quadrupled the watch on the walls; he kept the citadel on constant alert; and he mobilized every male young and old who was capable of lifting so much as a stick or a stone against the enemy. All civilians were organized into a militia who in the event of an attack would respond to a trumpet call and would be under the command of an officer of the garrison. The months had passed; the attack had not come. This condition of no-attack became more and more a condition of no-attack, like a very thin-shelled egg that grew bigger and bigger, older and older until, enormous and rotten, it now hung suspended above us.

This night that I am speaking of, this winter night without rain and without a moon—I have called its darkness opaque but I was not being accurate: there was some light in the sky, it was not utterly black. It was a night of obscurity, yes, obscurity is the word I want; it is this that makes that night such a paradigm of the rushing forward, the rushing back, that so much of history is made of.

In this obscurity we stood and into it we looked across the river towards the encampment of the Franks. Some of the tents with candles burning in them were like dim and feeble lanterns. Between those few dim lanterns and us ran with a strong rushing, with a heavy running, the river heavy with the rains, darkly rushing, gurgling, like a giant animal that drinks blood. Mingling with the rush of the river was the subterranean echoing rumbling grinding rolling roar of Onopniktes. These strong rushing-water sounds made the dim and feeble lantern-tents seem even dimmer and feebler and farther away. In the quietness of the Frankish camp a man began to sing. His voice rose and fell sadly, there was no word that I could understand except the oft-repeated name of Jesus, *Jesu*. There was no accompanying instrument but the manner of the song was suggestive of a lute. After a time someone shouted, the singing stopped, there was only the running of the river, the roar of Onopniktes.

We could hear then behind us, on the road between Yaghi-Siyan's palace and the bridge, a trotting of horsemen coming and going and we could hear many shouts, now here, now there, of the sort that are heard when cavalrymen gird themselves for something of importance. The shouts, the clopping of hooves increased, horses whinnied, there was much shuffling, snuffling, snorting, stamping, jingling, clinking, slapping, and grunting as all of the sounds formed themselves into a concerted picture of dark colours, dark gleamings, dark horsemen girding.

The sound-picture gathered itself into a forward movement, came towards us, passed beneath us, appeared in front of us on the bridge in the dark images of itself, the dark gleamings of iron and leather, the forested lances nodding, the shaking of reins and bridles as the horses tossed their heads. The clop of hooves, the clinking and the jingling passed into the darkness across the river, quickened unseen to a trot, a canter; for the first time then the kettledrums were heard, they pounded out the headlong gallop of the charge as voices whooped in war cries, voices called on Allah. There came then Frankish cries to Jesus, cries to God, cries of "Saint-Gilles!"

Suddenly the clamour of the drums is heard again—a different beat, the choppy rhythm of unluck and about-turn. Here now the Turks are coming back in thunderous flight across the bridge. "To the gate!" they cry. "Back to the gate!" cries Yaghi-Siyan at the head of the rout. "*Deus le volt!*" cry the Franks, "Saint-Gilles!" "The gate!" cry the Turks. With these shouts we hear the clash of weapons, the screams of the wounded and the dying, the screams of horses and of men, the groans and curses, the grunts and trampling and scuffling of men fighting for their lives, and the splashing of men and horses into the river. "Saint-Gilles!" goes up the shout, it seems very close, almost beneath us. "*Jesu!*"

Back across the bridge ebb the voices of the Franks. "There is no god but God!" shouts Yaghi-Siyan, and once more the Turks gallop across the bridge and into the darkness beyond it. Now from across the river we hear again, but indistinctly and mingled with the running of the river and the subterranean roar of Onopniktes, the clash of weapons, the shouts and cries, the screams of horses and of men. Below us on the bridge the dead in their obscurity lie still, the wounded and the dying writhe and groan, both men and horses; the horses lift their long necks, their noble heads, and fall back; they can no longer gallop to the battle or away from it.

Now with others Bembel Rudzuk and I go down to the bridge to bring in the wounded and the dead. The crippled horses are killed with a sword stroke to the neck, the blood spurts out on to the stones of the bridge. I think of how this blood would be better than wine to the starving Franks. The horses that can walk are brought back inside the walls with the wounded men. With their eyes the horses acknowledge that they are slaves; if they were owned by scholars they might have led quiet lives but as they are ridden by fighting men they must suffer these wounds, they can expect nothing else. In the fluttering light of torches the wounded men look at me with eyes like the eyes of ikons or statues or like the eyes made of white and black tesserae in mosaics. The heads from which the eyes look out have been vertical only a little while ago; now they are horizontal, and these men, like the horses, acknowledge with their eyes that they are the slaves of that in them which has used them up in this rushing forward and back in the darkness; having used them up it will find others for its purpose.

These bodies that I try to repair, already have they been violated once by cold iron; now again I violate them, I intrude upon their privacy to stuff entrails back into the places where they belong, to sew up flesh that has been violently parted. How startling are the secret colours that in time of peace are hidden beneath the skin. We slaughter sheep and cattle and chickens as a matter of course; we are the vertical ones with the knives so we assume this as a right: we slit the throat, the heart pumps out its last bursts of blood into a basin, we open up their bodies and lay hands upon their varicoloured mysteries of red and purple, blue and yellow inner

parts. But in time of war each man is a cattle to his enemy and they struggle to see which one will be the slaughterer. The stranger, the unknown to
whom one must always offer hospitality, that sacred stranger has now become a murderer whom we must murder first. How strange that this is not
strange.

Certainly we are the slaves of that which looks out through our eyes,
and it is nothing simple, that outlooker; does it want to live, does it want
to die? As with my arms red up to the elbows I sew up the wounded I crave
to be where the shouting is, the cries and groans, the clash of weapons. I
am afraid to be there but what looks out through my eyes wants to put
me there, it doesn't want to be left out of anything, it wants to be everywhere at once, it wants to be included in all matters of life and death,
wants to be at the same time here in the shuddering light of the torches
and there across the river in the obscurity of battle and the night.

From the wounded we hear something of the fighting: when the Turks
had first attacked the Frankish camp one of the Frankish leaders, Raymond Saint-Gilles, had immediately got together some of his knights and
led a charge into the dark. Those Franks! You could wake them up out of
a sound sleep in the middle of the night and they would open their eyes
fighting. It was Raymond's charge that had driven Yaghi-Siyan back
across the bridge and had very nearly carried the Franks through the
bridge gate and into Antioch. But when they were more than halfway
across the bridge there had come galloping wildly back towards them in
the darkness a riderless horse and the Franks faltered and fled, pursued
by the newly confident Turks.

The Franks put to rout by a riderless horse! Surely here is a sign for
those who know how to read it! Surely here is an action parable! Now
Yaghi-Siyan and his cavalrymen, blood-spattered riders on blood-spattered horses, return. They are many fewer than they were when they rode
into the obscurity on the other side of the bridge. They are tired but their
eyes are bright; for the moment they are the slaughterers and not the cattle. The green-and-gold banner droops proudly on its staff like a male
member that has done a good night's work.

The morning comes again, every time is like a first time, every time
the morning happens it seems surprised at its actuality but it offers no
opinions, it only reckons up what has happened in the night. "Here there
are so many dead horses, so many dead men," says the morning. "See how

they are dead. These men will not do anything more. They have no more to say. The horses will not walk, trot, canter, gallop. They will do nothing. Here there is only so much dead meat."

Now in the first light of this grey and impassive morning this dead meat becomes newly active and inspires new activity in both the Franks and the Turks. While the Frankish bowmen shoot up at us and we on the walls shoot down at them, some of the Franks, protecting themselves as well as they can with their shields, gather up their dead from the river bank and the bridge. Some of the dead they sling over their backs to be newly killed by our arrows, some they drag away, some they carry off on litters. The arrows glance off their helmets, stick in their shields, stick in the rings of their mail shirts; at this close range some of the arrows pierce the mail and some find a naked throat. One of the Franks falls and lies shuddering with an arrow in his back, then is still, requiring now the labour of his comrades. There are some dead horses beyond the far end of the bridge; all the closer ones were dragged (by teams of horses that shied and danced sidewise and showed the whites of their eyes) into Antioch last night. These dead horses on the other side of the river, each of them may well have carried a man to his death last night; now each will give life to many men for several days. The shocking thought arises: how much better off everybody would be if the Franks would go away somewhere and butcher their horses and live quietly on the meat.

There are dead Turks beyond the far end of the bridge, and there are now seen among them other Franks who are not like the Franks that I have just been speaking of. These men move with perhaps something of a birdlike hop in their walk; one can imagine that a moment ago they have flapped down from the grey sky on black wings and turned into men. Some of the dead Turks they drag away by their legs, others they tie by their arms and legs to poles to be carried off by two men. The air is blackened with our arrows but at that distance they are only like bee-stings. Later we smell the smoke of the cooking-fires of these Franks.

Seeing all this in this grey dawn that is surprised to be here but is not surprised at anything else I have in my eyes what I see but I have also that riderless horse that I did not see, it is an image of green fire in the obscurity of last night that is still in my eyes.

There is in the light of this grey morning something that moves with a sickening motion behind the curtain of grey light. It is not like the riderless horse that galloped across the bridge, it is like those horses of last night that lifted up their heads and fell back again, lifted and fell back. This morning is seen as if in a flawed mirror. The curtain of air shakes and sways, one feels drunk, the ground beneath one's feet will not maintain its proper plane, its proper steady stillness. The earth seems to be retching, shuddering.

Bembel Rudzuk and I fling ourselves to the ground, others do the same. Perhaps the earth itself is a riderless horse, showing the whites of its eyes and galloping to its death. Lying prone on the top of the wall I feel the stones beneath me shift, I see cracks where there were none before. Hidden Lion cannot be seen from where we are but with the eye of the mind I see the tower on David's Wheel tottering, shaking, bricks are jumping off it; I see the tiles of Hidden Lion lifting, moving, leaping out of the pattern, breaking, crumbling. The thought comes to me that the earth is sick of humankind, it is trying to vomit itself up to be rid of us.

The curtain of grey light is still shaking, the world still looks out at us from a flawed mirror. Several horses have broken loose and are galloping through the streets as if in a dream; from the Frankish camp we hear singing and praying; in its caverns underneath the city Onopniktes shouts in the darkness, ecstatic like a prophet as stones topple from the four hundred towers, from Justinian's wall, from the bridge across the Orontes. I see in my mind the river, roiled and muddy, strangely heaving, shuddering as it runs with its surface pocked and dimpled by the trembling beneath the river bed. There is a gabble of voices all around us and a continual sobbing and praying. With my cheek against the stones and my vision at an unaccustomed angle I see the spire of the minaret of the central mosque slowly sway and fall.

In the gabble of voices on the wall and rising from the streets below we hear in Turkish, in Syriac, in Arabic, and in Greek the words "punishment" and "judgment." Some think the punishment is for one thing, some think it is for another; the Christians beheaded on Hidden Lion are spoken of by many. There is also some lamentation for the destruction of a shrine of Nemesis and the pulling down of a statue of Tyche, the Goddess of Fortune. ("All that happened centuries ago," says Bembel Rudzuk, "but still they talk about it when the earth shakes, all these good Muslims lamenting the departed goddesses of Rome.") Many think that the Christian Patriarch John, who is in prison, ought to be freed. It is thought by some that if he is freed he will pray for the safety of Antioch; others think that he is more likely to pray if he is kept in prison. All this time there is a wild neighing of unseen horses. Soon a wagon rattles past, it is pulled by men, the horses are too unmanageable to be put in harness. In the wagon is an iron cage and in the cage, desperately clinging to the bars, his face white, his beard flying, is the Patriarch. Later we hear that the cage has been hung by chains from the wall and that he has prayed constantly for God's mercy.

The shaking of the earth stops, the grey light of the day is once more steady. There are cracks in the walls, cracks in streets and houses, fallen bricks and stones here and there but no serious damage and no one killed as far as we know. Bembel Rudzuk and I go to Hidden Lion. The tower stands intact and unmarred and the pattern has suffered no damage whatever although there are cracks in the streets all around and in the nearby shops and houses. "Its time is not yet come," says Bembel Rudzuk.

When we look at Hidden Lion now it is difficult to recall the feelings we had when the pattern was first assembled. Now Bembel Rudzuk's idea of observing "that point at which stillness becomes motion" and that other point "at which pattern becomes consciousness" seems altogether ill-conceived and the words with which he described his intention make me shudder. When I call to mind those early days of Hidden Lion when the tiles were arriving from Tower Gate's brickyard and his foreman and workmen were with their swift and dancing movements putting the pattern together, when I remember how we walked about and viewed the expansion of those tawny and red and black triangles with a commanding eye as if we were in charge of the thing, I cannot help making a face of embarrassment.

As we stand there looking at Hidden Lion I find myself shaking my head; I no longer know how to approach this place in my mind, I no longer know what to think of it. Up until the time when the Syrian and Armenian Christians were beheaded it was everybody's good-luck place; afterwards I expected it to become a bad-luck place but I was wrong. Until the next rain the bloodstains remained to mark the tiles, and to those tiles during those few days came many people who stood and looked at them and pointed them out to other people who then stood and looked at them. All of these people who came and looked were Muslims. One day I saw a man squat and rub his hand over one of the tawny bloodstained tiles, then he put his hand inside his robe and rubbed his chest. After that many others did the same, and children began to walk in special ways on those tiles and to dance on them.

The tiles being glazed, the blood had not permeated the clay; when the rain came it washed them clean. The tiles that had been stained with blood did not, however, become unknown: by some general understanding amongst themselves those who took an interest in the tiles had noted their positions relative to the tower, and by counting carefully they found their way to them again. This was a source of great amusement to the headless and maggoty tax-collector, who now appointed himself a guide and would stand where the blood had been, stamping his foot and pointing with his finger to the tiles. I could of course not see his smile but I could hear his laughter and there was no mistaking the mockery in the way he stamped his foot and pointed with his finger.

One day a boy of eight or nine came and prostrated himself on some of the tiles that had been stained with blood. He was dressed the same as any other child, he was not wearing a blue turban. I recognized him as the same boy who had come to the paved square and drawn on the stone the morning after I made my first chalk drawing for Hidden Lion. After a few moments he stood up and looked all around at everyone, then walked away. The next day there appeared on those tiles an earthenware pot which filled up with money. The butcher volunteered to divide it among Christian orphans. This was done, and each day after that the pot was filled up and emptied in the same manner.

Now on this day of the shaking of the earth the shaking has stopped and people are returning to their ordinary activities; the stallholders are again at their places on Hidden Lion. Trade here has of course diminished with the progress of the siege; the caravans have left off coming to Antioch, the road from Suwaydiyya is dangerous, and goods are scarce. Vendors, having little to sell, have lately been reduced to trading among themselves; their collective scanty stock distributes itself anew every day: the copper pot with the hole in it that used to be at the stall of A makes its appearance at the stall of B, while the haftless dagger that was a veteran non-seller with B now tries its luck with A. Eventually, perhaps with P or Q, the pot and the dagger assume with the new venue a new aspect that gets them sold, proving yet again to those who knew it already that action creates action.

Today, however, the merchants sit or stand listlessly by their wares as if all buying and selling are gone out of the world. Most of them pack up and go home early. The man selling refreshments by the tower puts his syrups, his pots and cups into their wooden box, picks up the box by its leather strap, slings it from his shoulder, takes his brazier, says, "This place is finished," and turns to go.

"Why is it finished?" I ask him.

"Look," he says, pointing to the pattern with his foot, "there's not so much as a single tile cracked, it isn't natural."

"What do you think it means?" I say.

"It means that this place is being saved for something worse," he says, "and I don't want any part of it." He recedes into the distance, never looking back.

The butcher comes, takes the pot of money for the Christian orphans, spits on the tiles, and walks away.

"Wait," I say to him. "Why did you spit on the tiles, why do you look that way?"

Without saying a word the butcher makes with his index and little finger the sign against the evil eye and off he goes.

This day that has begun with the shaking of the earth moves on and there are more wonders to be seen: the dreadful grey curtain of the day becomes the darker curtain of night and there are seen moving behind it strange red lights in the sky that shift and slide from one shape to another. More praying and singing from the Franks and many voices lifted to God on our side of the walls as well. The Patriarch, who was taken out of his hanging cage and put back in prison when the earth stopped shaking, is brought out again to offer an opinion on the strange lights. He sees very plainly in the sky the sign of the Cross and is put back in prison. Bembel Rudzuk and I look up at the sky but we say nothing to each other of what we see—there is perhaps too much motion becoming stillness, too much consciousness becoming pattern for us to respond with anything but silence.

The sky stays grey the next day and rain comes pelting down like hopelessness turned into water; the earth becomes a soggy boggy mire; the river swallows up its banks, it is no longer to be trifled with, soon it must run over the bridge instead of under it, soon it must lose patience with this city, must rush it brick by brick and stone by stone away into the sea that drowns Muslims, Christians, and Jews impartially and says nothing about God, nothing about justice or mercy. Dismally falls the rain on Silpius, and slides of mud and stones go down the mountainside to join the ponderous rolling rush of Onopniktes that bellows and echoes under Antioch as if fulfilling a prophecy, as if it has been foretold centuries ago that when the mountain will have passed under the city a monstrous thing will happen, perhaps the end of all things will come; or worse, some great beast taller than the mountain will appear and say at the same time and with one voice in all the languages of humankind that there will be no end to anything, that everything will go on and on for ever.

Those thousands of Franks who rode off in the night come squelching back now under the grey sky and the rain. These thousands, we hear, have been led by Bohemond of Taranto and Robert of Flanders. Moving up the Orontes valley they have run into the armies of Duqaq, Tughtagin, and Janah al-Dawla coming from Damascus to relieve Antioch. We are told that Bohemond has learned how to fight Turks now, that he kept his cavalry in the rear to prevent the encirclement of Robert's men and then charged in at the right moment. So they have driven back the Turks, Bohemond and Robert and their thousands; they have won a battle but they have lost men, they have worn themselves out, and they have come back empty-handed to their rotting and sodden tents in the mud and such treats as horses' heads without the tongues for three solidi and goats' intestines for five.

Here they are then, the conquerors of Antioch held back from the conquering of it; it is like holding back the bull from the cow: he paws the earth, he rolls his eyes, his breath steams on the air. All that makes him a bull is hot and ready. But the cow is a cow of stone.

What is the nature of things? The nature of things is that what can happen will happen, often it has already happened before it is recognized. The walls of Antioch were built during the reign of Justinian, a time of strong stonemasonry; those walls are not be knocked down or undermined, and any attacker who scales them will only find himself on a short stretch of rampart between the massive towers with a bitter rain of arrows hissing down and the strong doors of the towers barred against him. How then can the Franks breach the unbreachable, pass the impassable? How can Antioch be taken? It can be taken if someone on the wall will turn away from his duty, it can be taken if someone will open the strong tower doors and let the soldiers of Christ in quietly. And will someone be found to do this? What a question! Such a question can only be asked by an atheist; anyone who recognizes the existence of God (whether as He or as It) and the intersections of virtuality and actuality is well aware of how easily such crossings on the plane of possibility can be sucked up into a point of happening. After the event one looks at all the many lines converging on the point and marvels because it seems that people were born, nations assembled, geography organized, roads laid out and bridges built expressly so that this event could happen. So rise now to a point of happening the turningness of Firouz and the unturningness of Bohemond, the one on what is called the inside and the other on what is called the outside of the walls of the four hundred towers, those stones that have no enemy.

At this time that I am telling of I have so far seen Bohemond only at a considerable distance. There is of course no mistaking him, he is so astonishingly tall, taller than most men by half an arm's length. When I see Bohemond, when I think of Bohemond, I know that I am seeing and thinking of more than Bohemond: as the arrow streaks to its target the point of the arrow is driven by the shaft behind it, the feathers that make the shaft fly true, and the bow that has loosed the energy of its bending into the flight of the arrow; so comes Bohemond from the loins of his father Robert Guiscard and the womb of his mother Alberada of Buonalbergo. But Bohemond's lineage is more than human, it includes generations of horses; the line of Bohemond goes back to *Eohippus*, the dawn horse, the very beginning of all chivalry. And yet the most prepotent of Bohemond's ancestors was neither a human nor an animal but an artifact: Bohemond is descended mainly from the stirrup. Bohemond is grown out of an aristocracy of warriors on horseback rising from the cavalry of Charles Martel; this aristocracy comes to the point of the present in the armoured man on the heavy horse with his feet firm in the stirrups that give power to the drive of his lance, the swing of his sword; the armoured man strong in the saddle, bred to fight and trained from boyhood to be unturning in attack; the armoured man superior in wealth, in breeding, in physique and in confidence to the man on foot.

Bohemond's ancestors of the fifth century who fought under Chlodovech, they fought without armour and on foot, they hurled axes and barbed javelins, God knows what stocks and stones they offered to. What did they know of Jerusalem? How in the world has Bohemond come to be a soldier of Christ? How has Bohemond become the Bohemond who cut up his scarlet cloak into crosses? This is not to be known by me, I shall die without knowing it.

Bohemond is always in my mind but I have no chance of understanding him. When he was first pointed out to me I was high up on the wall looking down at his distant figure but in my thoughts he at once took his place high up as if striding on ramparts built for him alone. He is everything that I am not, this quintessential warrior prince. I am told that he can, fully armed, leap from the ground to his horse's back; that no other man can wield with two hands the sword he wields with one; that he requires three women nightly to keep him tranquil; that he is a serpent in cunning, a thunderbolt in attack, he is simply not to be withstood. Red-haired and blue-eyed, he does what he wants and he gets what he wants. How should I not be obsessed with Bohemond? But his thoughts are beyond my imagination. In my drift through this space called time I have reported two dreams of Pope Urban II and I know that, whether virtually or actually, they are true. They are there, I have experienced them. But of Bohemond I can offer nothing sure, only intimations, only things half-sensed, half guessed-at. As the animals of the forest scent the questing hound I scent him, questing through the death of Christ and God's departure, questing on the track of gold and fame and power, questing for the tangible, the visible, questing for that which cannot be mistaken, that which can be held in the strong hand, that which can be gripped between strong thighs as a horse is gripped.

So. Bohemond is encamped before the walls of Antioch and now we are in the year 1098. Bohemond, greedy and lusting for the seen, cannot yet have what he craves; that time is not yet come. As I say this there comes into my mind an image of Bohemond opposed by Bembel Rudzuk; it is a night image, the background of it is darkness; against the darkness the two figures are luminous, they leap out of the dark, stopped in mid-motion as if by lightning—Bohemond with the gleam of his helmet, the glitter of his mail, the flash of his great sword, the scarlet cross on his surcoat, the iron nasal and the straight brow-line of his helmet simplifying his face, the face of the death-angel haloed by the rainbow arc of the great sword. Bohemond the death-angel, Bohemond the questing death-hound circling in the night beyond the circle of Christ's little wander-fire. Bohemond the tall, lit by the lightning as he leaps with his death-bringing, with his blood-drinking sword. And leaping at him with a flash of the gold brocade on his elegant scarlet jacket, with his Turkish sword heroic against the death-hound, with his moustaches heroic, Bembel Rudzuk the dauntless, Bembel Rudzuk who is at the same time like a lion of innocence, like an angel of folly, like a butterfly transfixed by the pin of actuality, Bembel Rudzuk the friend true unto death.

That is the image, held motionless against the dark as if by lightning, that comes into my mind as I think of the never-to-be-known, never-to-be-understood Bohemond. Simple greed, simple ambition, simple unlimited courage do not suffice to explain this man. Nothing I have so far said explains Bohemond. As one who is not a mathematical genius cannot understand one who is, so I cannot understand this genius of maleness and action; even simply counting up his attributes and his actions one arrives at something that cannot be accounted for: the total of the seen becomes the unseen, becomes a mystery. Bohemond has in the mystery of him such force as to make him a kind of un-Christ; in the greatness of his courage and his greed he looms gigantic; almost Death stands aside at the sound of his name and his great bones stand up shouting. His tomb in Apulia is domed, it has Romanesque arches, it has bronze doors. Sometimes as Pilgermann the owl I sit on the dome of Bohemond's tomb in the twilight when it is still warm from the last sun of the day.

But it is the year 1098 that I tell of now; the bones of Bohemond are still in active partnership with his flesh and I have not yet achieved owlhood. It is February, a Turkish army is again on its way to the relief of Antioch, and this time Rudwan of Aleppo is with them. The Frankish cavalry is much diminished now; they must have less than a thousand horses fit for war. I cannot help thinking of those battles in the Holy Scriptures in which God would diminish the armies of the children of Israel the better to show his power; I have come to believe that God, having departed, now wills that nothing should stand between the Franks and Jerusalem.

Bohemond does not wait for the Turks to come to Antioch; he leaves the foot-soldiers and the horseless cavalry to defend the camp against further sorties and with that cavalry numberless in arrogance but many times outnumbered by the enemy he moves out to take up a position between the Orontes and the Lake of Antioch where he cannot be encircled. Needs must when the devil drives, and he has learned by now that the harrying, stinging, in-and-out, encircling tactics of the Turks must be met with equal cunning if he is to beat them. And of course he does. On first sight of the Turks the Franks charge before the Turkish archers can be effectively disposed, then they withdraw, luring the Turks into that space between the lake and the river, that space chosen for the battle. Here the Frankish cavalry do again what they do better than anyone else, the straight charge with lance in rest. So again the relieving army is put to flight by Bohemond, by that unturning battle-greed of his. So ardent is he in his pursuit of the enemy that the points of his crimson banner, we hear, fly over the heads of the rearmost Turks.

Here at Antioch the absence of Bohemond reliably brings Yaghi-Siyan out through the bridge gate for yet another sortie on the Frankish encampment where there are only men on foot to oppose him. Things are going badly for the horseless Franks, the time must seem long to them until Bohemond returns in the afternoon like the sun and Yaghi-Siyan, like a wooden foul-weather figure, goes back inside. The soldiers of Christ put Turkish heads on poles outside their camp to stare with dead eyes at the walls of Antioch until the flesh rots away and they are no longer heads but skulls.

The Franks have so far held off two attempts to relieve the city but they have not yet been able to close it off completely from the world. The Suwaydiyya road, though no longer travelled by caravans, is still used by enterprising traders at unlikely hours and for high profits. Supplies are also moving through the Ladhiquiyya Gate at carefully chosen times.

At the beginning of March we hear of ships at Suwaydiyya and we hear that they bring to the Franks fighting men and horses, siege technicians from Constantinople, timber and every kind of tackle for the building of siege towers and giant war machines, also apparatus capable of shooting Greek fire from the far side of the Orontes into the centre of Antioch. There is little doubt that Antioch will soon be in Frankish hands unless the siege materials are intercepted.

It is Bohemond and Raymond who one night lead their men to Suwaydiyya to bring in the materials and the reinforcements. About an hour after their departure we hear the horsemen trotting to and from Yaghi-Siyan's palace, hear the shouting of commands, the slap and jingle, the shuffling and snuffling and whinnying as cavalrymen ready their horses and themselves. They ride out on the Suwaydiyya road and we of the civilian militia together with soldiers of the garrison man the walls to watch the Frankish camp and wait.

It is while I stand on this wall built by a Roman emperor and keep watch on the Franks with a Turkish bow in my hand that I find myself reflecting on where I am and what I am doing. It isn't that I haven't taken notice of the separate parts of it but somehow I haven't taken notice of how the parts look when they're all put together. I am carrying weapons that I was taught to use by a Muslim (we non-Muslims of the militia are now permitted to go armed) and I am keeping watch on the walls of this city that is being held by Muslims against Christians who call themselves soldiers of Christ. Bohemond himself may at any time come climbing over this wall with his sword that only he can wield with one hand, Bohemond the battle-greedy, the death-hound.

To this has my late-night walking in the Keinjudenstrasse brought me. And yet each step of the way had nothing surprising in it. There was the garden, there was the ladder; up I climbed to that naked and incomparable Sophia and here I am.

This castration that I have suffered, has it a use, has it a value? What was I before I was castrated? I was already castrated, was I not, by mortality? All of us are castrated by mortality, we are unmanned, unwomanned, we are made nothing because all we have is this so little space of time with a blackness before and after it (that I speak out of this blackness as Pilgermann is only a borrowing; it is to unself and the namelessness of potential being that I must return when I have said what I have to say). How to live then in this little space in which we have a self and a name, this little space in which we are allowed to accumulate our tiny history of tiny days, this moment that is at once the first moment and the last moment, this moment that contains our universe and such space/time as is unwound in the working of it?

We don't want to know about our mortal castration. We throw ourselves into the work of each day, the beating of hammers, the baking of bread; we find ourselves a spouse, we gather children around us to keep out the dark, we keep the Sabbath, pray to God, hope that all will be well. Ah, but there is more! Not for this alone was there smoke and fire and a quaking on the mountain while the voice of the horn sounded louder and louder. No, there is a mystery that even God cannot fathom, nor can he give the law of it on two stone tablets. He cannot speak what there are no words for; he needs divers to dive into it, he needs wrestlers to wrestle with it, singers to sing it, lovers to love it. He cannot deal with it alone, he must find helpers, and for this does he blind some and maim others. "Look," God has said to me, "what must I do to make you play the man? I have already castrated you with mortality but you pay no attention to it. So now let it be done with a knife, then let's see what happens. Let's see if you'll grow yourself some new balls and jump into the mystery with me."

"But what's it all about?" I cry.

"If I could tell you that it wouldn't be a mystery," says God. "Let it be enough that I ask for your help." (God has of course not actually been speaking here because he is no longer manifesting himself as He; but God as It has put these words into my mind.)

This is then the value and the use of my castration; with this must I be content. If even God in his omniscience doesn't know the answer then each of us must help however possible. And think how it would be if God *could* give the answer, if God could say, "All right, here it is: the answer is this and this and this and this; now you know the answer." Who would then have any respect for God, who would even have any interest in Him? "What!" we should say, "Is this the best you can do? Is there to be no mystery then? Feh!"

"I know what you mean," says the man in front of me in Turkish with an Italian accent. While thinking the thoughts that I have just been telling of I have been pacing my stretch of wall and I have come face to face with this remarkable Mordechai Salzedo of whom I have spoken once before: it was he who cited from Genesis the words, "Where he is" when we met in the street by the synagogue before Rosh Hashanah.

This Salzedo has come to Antioch by a route even less direct than mine. He was born in Barbastro in Spain and as a child of seven he escaped from the town when it was sacked by the French in 1064. Those Christian armies dealt with the Muslims and Jews of Barbastro in the traditional way, and when his mother lay dead with her skirt over her head and his father with his guts wound round a post young Salzedo crept away quietly to try his luck elsewhere. He fell in with a company of wine merchants, Italian Jews who were on their way to Barcelona, went with them when they sailed back to La Spezia, was taken into the family of one of the partners, grew up to marry one of the daughters, became a partner in the house, lost his wife when their ship bound from Cagliari in Sardinia to Bizerta in Tunisia sank in a storm, clung to a wineskin and drifted for three days, was picked up by a Neapolitan business associate, decided to go into textiles, came to Antioch to sell wine and buy silks and cottons, fell into conversation with Bembel Rudzuk, was unable to disengage himself, and so set up in business and settled here.

"What do you mean, you know what I mean?" I say.

"I noticed how you were shaking your head," he says, "and I said to myself: this man has in his mind the same thought that I have in mine."

"And what is that thought?" I say.

"That to be a Jew is to find yourself doing all kinds of things in all kinds of places," he says. "Here we are keeping watch against the Franks on a wall built by a Roman emperor around a city now held by Turks."

"If I'd kept watch from the wall of my town I might still have a pimmel," I say. It comes to me that if I hold my mind right a tremendous thought will illuminate it. This thought is a real treasure too. It is so cunningly and commodiously formed that it contains all other thoughts in a beautiful instantaneous order of total comprehension. I am trying so hard to hold my mind right that I get a crick in my neck. Come, wonderful thought, come! The ladder was presented, yes . . . Sophia was given, yes . . . my pimmel and my balls were taken away, yes . . . Bohemond is given . . . What? How? Ah! it's gone, the wonderful thought is gone.

"What's going to happen?" says Salzedo. He has maintained a respectful silence for what seems a very long time while I have been trying to hold my mind right.

"The Franks will take Antioch," I say.

"Yes," he says. "It's the kind of thing that happens. Everyone says that Karbuqa of Mosul will be here soon to relieve us but I doubt that he'll get here soon enough."

"You can still leave Antioch," I say. "They haven't got everything completely closed off yet."

"I don't think I'll bother," says Salzedo. "I've already had quite a bit of extra time, and if God needs dead Jews as badly as he seems to I'm ready to go. And you?"

I think of the tax-collector, I think of my young death whom I have seen in the dawning on the roof of Bembel Rudzuk's house. I think also of Bruder Pförtner and the others whom I've not yet seen here in Antioch. I think suddenly of Sophia (she is always in my mind like a continuo above which rise each day's new thoughts of her) and for the first time there comes to me the question: is she alive or dead? Why should she be dead? She is not a Jewess, no one will rape her and kill her on the cobblestones of our town; she is safe there. But is she there? Until now I have never thought of her as being anywhere else, she has been in my mind a world that continues inviolate while I disappear into chaos; in my mind she has been as static as that other Sophia in Constantinople. Now the curtain of my sight sways before me, the earth seems to move sickeningly beneath me, and in a suddenly clear sky the stars wheel as if the world is spinning like a top. I look up and see, perhaps in the sky, perhaps in my mind, those three stars between the Virgin and the Lion, that Jewish gesture of the upflung hand: What, will you block the road for ever? The whole world is moving, it is walking, it is riding on horses, it is sailing in ships to Jerusalem. Why should she be still, be safe?

"And you?" Salzedo is saying.

"I was going to Jerusalem," I say.

"And will you still go to Jerusalem?" he says.

"Jerusalem will be wherever I am when the end comes," I say.

"That could be soon," he says. "It could happen by Passover; Shavuoth at the latest. Yes, Shavuoth is probably when it'll be, it's a better time because Shavuoth celebrates the giving of the Torah to Israel at Sinai, the giving of the Law; yes, that's why it'll be Shavuoth: from Passover to Shavuoth is a development, it's the coming to maturity of the children of Israel. At Passover they left their bondage in Egypt, they began their wandering; when they came to the mountain of God they were given the Law. Also Shavuoth is a harvest holiday, and this that is coming is certainly some kind of harvest."

"Of whose sowing?" I say.

"It doesn't matter who does the sowing," he says. "Life is sown and Death comes to reap the harvest; when has it been otherwise? Have you ever seen this mountain where the children of Israel were given the Law?"

"No," I say.

"It isn't the biggest mountain in the world," he says, "but you know it when you see it: it looks only like itself, like a lion of stone, this mountain whose name is Horeb; the Arabs call it Djebel Musa, the mountain of Moses. It is called Sinai because of the thornbush, *seneh*. This thornbush from which God first spoke to Moses was on that same mountain whereon God later gave Moses the tablets of the Law. Perhaps you already knew this?"

"I didn't remember that about the thornbush," I say.

"Not everyone does," he says. "But it's a good thing to keep in mind because God is such a thorny business and we shouldn't expect him to be otherwise. But I'll tell you one good thing about being a Jew—whenever your time comes you don't have to worry that the day will be unmarked and forgotten because you can be sure that some really famous Jew has died on the same day, maybe even thousands of them. Akiba died around this time of year, it was sometime during the seven weeks of the Counting of the Omer. The Romans flayed him."

"His last words," I say, "were: 'Hear, O Israel, the Lord our God, the Lord is One.'"

Salzedo is content to let Akiba have the last word, and we resume our separate pacing. There comes to me then something that is both image and not-image. It has to do with a striking, a vast and not to be held in the mind striking of side-posts and a lintel beyond imagination, the striking of them with the hyssop that is the tree of the world, spattering the blood of all the world on the side-posts, on the lintel of the universe. And there must none of us go out of the house until morning, but will morning ever come? At such times as the not-image phases into image I see the right arm and shoulder and back of this striking. The spattering drops of blood fan slowly, slowly out, out, out, the drops of blood become the stars. Far and frozen the luminous drops of burning blood, far and frozen, drifting ever wider, wider, wider.

And there must none of us, none of us pass under the lintel, pass between the side-posts until morning comes, none of us beneath the spattered blood of the lamb without blemish, the word of blood to be read by the LORD in His aspect of Justice, the LORD in His aspect of Mercy passing in the night, passing with the destroyer.

I have described this that is both image and not-image as it comes to me and as it compels me to describe it. I describe what I do not understand because I am lived by it. Yes, that's what it is, why I have no choice, why I am compelled. This that I have described is not an idea that I have had or a vision or a dream, it is not a means of expression for me as poetry might be. No, I am a means of expression for it, God as He or God as It knows why. That is why I have not the privilege and the pleasure of telling stories, of showing brightly coloured pictures of Samson and the lion. Not only is storytelling denied me but history also—I may well be reporting nothing more than spiritual mirages and metaphysical illusions. I can only tell what, as far as I know, happened or seemed to happen to what I recognize as myself with such recognition as has been borrowed from the darkness.

Very well then, I return to the walls of Antioch. I am there now and I smell these old strong stones that have no enemy. I smell their tawniness, their sweat of years, I smell the slow clinging of the lichens and the mosses on them. I smell the blood as well, the blood that has been and the blood that is coming. I smell the hotness and the dryness baked into the stones by centuries of summer sun, I smell the coldness and the wetness of the winter rains; the stones forget nothing.

I feel in this wall of stone something else that is happening; the idea of sorting comes into my mind. Walls by their nature do sort: by defining an inside and an outside they sort the insiders from the outsiders, they sort what is happening inside from what is happening outside. More than that: on this wall that girdles Antioch in the year 1098 I pick up a bit of broken stone and as I hold it in my hand I feel the sorting that goes on continually inside it: this way, that way, this way, that way, Christ in every stone with arms outspread, not raging as he judges between the elect on his right hand and the damned on his left; he has put himself into a state of perfect balance, he does not weigh with a scale, measure with a rule: he himself, abandoning all self, is the rule and the scale, the pointer that wavers on the beam. He is entranced, he makes no judgments although he is the judge: he is a necessary, an essential instrument in the sorting process and it is the process that has brought the instrument into being. I have seen this necessary instrument, this Christ-as-balance, carved in stone in the century after mine by Gislebertus on the tympanum of Autun Cathedral in Burgundy, that same Burgundy from where came some of those soldiers who sacked Barbastro and orphaned Salzedo in 1064. The sorting being necessary, the instrument appears.

I have understood so little in my lifetime! Now in the centuries of my deathtime I am just beginning to understand a little more but my consciousness is not continuous, I am only a mode of perception irregularly used by strangers. Perhaps there will never be the possibility for me to understand what Christ is. I understand that he was born from the idea of him—that he told me himself: "From me came the seed that gave me life." That he is essentially a sorter I also understand; the sorting of course follows on that disparity without which the universe could not maintain spin; I think that I knew that even before I read Plato's *Timaeus* in which he says: "Motion never exists in what is uniform. For to conceive that anything can be moved without a mover is hard or indeed impossible, and equally impossible to conceive that there can be a mover unless there is something which can be moved—motion cannot exist where either of these is wanting, and for these to be uniform is impossible; wherefore we must assign rest to uniformity and motion to the want of uniformity."

That good and evil should be sorted along with right and left, up and down, light and darkness and all other complementarities is clearly in the nature of things, and that Christ should be a medium of this sorting is also clearly in the nature of things; but the rest of what he is continually moves on ahead of my comprehension like a great whale cleaving cosmic seas; I try to grasp the essence of him but I grasp only the fading wake of his passage.

Where was I? The walls of Antioch, and we are waiting for news of the Turkish cavalry who took the Suwaydiyya road after the Franks. The question arises whether apparent consistency of manifestation is to be accepted as reality. May it not simply be the persistence of image in the eye of the mind? This Turkish cavalry, for example, this whole numerous appearance of horses, men, and weapons—does it in actuality remain the same from one moment to the next? May it not suddenly and without any noticeable change be a black dog, not numerous at all, just one single black dog trotting inseparable from its little black noon shadow, even in the twilight trotting with that same little noon shadow which is also the shadow of a small stone both moving and still? Or trees, not many, just a clump of trees in the stillness of the dawn. The roundness and solidity of the shadowed trunks like circling dancers under the tented leaves. Wine of shadows, shadow music fading, fading to the shout of day.

Those other horsemen, the Frankish horsemen, or whatever it is that has offered to the eye this appearance of Frankish horsemen, may they or it not be a broken cathedral, inexplicable in a distant desert, the spire no longer in unity aspiring to heaven but toppled in pieces, pointing only to the sand? Broken stones, broken stones singing broken songs, broken verses chopped abruptly off, odd words leaping suddenly into silence? From these broken stones, these hewn and carven broken stones, there puts itself together a broken stone angel of death towering over the dawn trees, bigger than the cathedral ever was, the stones of it continually toppling as it strides but bounding up again to move as arms or legs or as a head that turns this way and that, turning in its looking but unturning in its questing. Questing is the name of this death angel made of broken stones, Bohemond is the name of this Questing.

Now at last Bohemond has become altogether real to me, not to be understood—nothing can be understood, I see now—but to be seen with the same solidity and shadow-casting reality as the port that is approached by crossing the water at dawn so that it grows larger, larger in the eye, so that at last it is arrived at. So have I at last arrived at Bohemond in his aspect of the death angel named Questing, the many-horsed, many-hoofed many-faced striding of the broken stones, the broken cathedral that crosses seas and deserts and mountains, questing on the death-track of the mystery that is Christ.

14

Night passes, morning comes, surprised as always to find itself here. This morning is full of urgent motion, of horsemen trotting to and from Yaghi-Siyan's palace, of shouted commands, of the slap and jingle of harness and the shuffling and snuffling and whinnying of horses as cavalrymen prepare for action. Action impends but does not come until the afternoon when a Turkish galloper clatters over the bridge, through the gate, and into the city with the news that the cavalry who rode out last night have ambushed the Franks returning from Suwaydiyya. The Turks have put the Franks to flight, have captured the wagons with the siege materials and are now on their way back with them.

Only a few minutes after the arrival of the Turkish galloper we on the wall see scattered horsemen coming from the direction of Suwaydiyya and making for the Frankish camp. These we guess to be Franks who have fled the ambush. Now the Frankish camp is in motion, they will be riding out to help their comrades. In Antioch the kettledrums are pounding; Yaghi-Siyan's cavalry come pouring out through the bridge gate, thundering across the bridge to engage the Franks and keep them from reinforcing the others.

The Turks are able to hold the Franks for a time but suddenly here are Bohemond and Raymond with their forces regathered and their lances levelled. As always I see him at a distance, and I recognize Bohemond by the gathering of galloping warriors into a point; I know that only he can be that point, only he can be that ardent forwardness with his name cleaving the air before him. Surely by now his name is like the roar of the lion: it is more than a sound, it is that which makes the knees shake. The Turks cannot now move forward against the man and the name, they must wheel their horses round towards the bridge and the gate, must turn themselves in the saddle to loose their arrows at the baneful man, the baneful name that overwhelms them.

As it lives again in the eye of my mind it seems all in one moment that Yaghi-Siyan's cavalry are galloping for their lives over the bridge while there rises stone by stone the tower of the Franks that will command the bridge and further tighten the blockade of Antioch. But before this can be done the Franks must recapture the building materials from the Turks, and for this must many Turks be killed.

On the far side of the river there is a Muslim cemetery, and this night the Turks come out of Antioch to bury their dead there. In the morning the Franks dig up the bodies, there is gold and silver to be taken from them. They use stones from the tombs in the building of their tower and this becomes a part of the picture in my mind, almost it seems to me that the tower is being built of dug-up Turkish corpses while yet the Turkish cavalry gallop for their lives across the bridge into Antioch. And in this same moment rises the other Tower, Tancred's tower that will command the Ladhiqiyya Gate.

Still the back ways of Mount Silpius and the postern doors in the walls are there for those who want to leave Antioch and for the more determined of the foragers and profiteers but from now on there will be no more sorties from Antioch nor will there be more than a trickle of provisions coming in. In the five months of the siege the Franks have been able to do nothing much with their mangonels and other missile-throwing machines, and the river has kept them from moving siege towers up against the walls. The rumours of advanced Greek-fire techniques have proved unfounded; but now the striding stones of the broken cathedral have walled in the unbroken stones of the walls of Antioch.

Now ships from Genoa are bringing provisions to the Franks and the Suwaydiyya road is under their control; now do their fortunes improve while those of Antioch decline. Well do we know that in each of us lives a skeleton that waits for the flesh to die, there is an absence waiting for the presence to depart—but a great city! A city like Antioch! As Pilgermann the owl I fly over it now and it looks like nothing really, it has retreated from its medieval boundaries, it has shrunk and dwindled, it has huddled itself together, has drawn back from the vaunt of its greatness and the largeness of its history, it is like a swimmer who has struggled barely alive out of a raging torrent and does not enter the water again. No, I think as I look down on this place that is so small, so diminished, so unspecial, this is not Antioch: Antioch was days and nights of vivid action, Antioch was a paradigm of history in which at one time and another every kind of thinker and doer, every kind of greatness and smallness jostled together and shouldered and elbowed their way through all the lights and reso-nances and colours, all the smells and flavours and motion of endless variations of circumstance and event in a large and crowded arena. In a particular time people fought and lived and died for particular things; now it is small, now it is quiet. An old woman in black walks a path with a basket on her head; a man leads a donkey loaded with firewood; perhaps they say to themselves that God wills it. And of course God wills every-thing: the beating of hammers; the baking of bread; the rise and fall of nations; the quiet clopping of the hooves of one small donkey.

Raymond's tower, the one commanding the bridge and the bridge gate, was built in March of 1098, and from that time Antioch moved forward faster and faster towards its fall. That tower was completed and Ray-mond's banner was run up on the top of it on the Eve of Passover.

Before that, while the tower was being built, while Passover was ap-proaching, there began to be in my mind the idea of Elijah and the antici-pation of that moment in the Seder when the door is opened for him. I be-gan to see that another idea was coming to me, it was the idea of Bohemond as Elijah, Elijah as enemy, enemy as messenger of God. Yes, the enemy as messenger of God, the enemy as teacher. Sophia was the beginning of my Holy Wisdom and Bohemond would be the end of it.

> Behold, he cometh,
> Saith the LORD of hosts.

But who may abide the day of his coming?
And who shall stand when he appeareth?
For he is like a refiner's fire,
And like fullers' soap;

Elijah sensed that everything was on him, the whole burden of a world of trouble. He said:

I have been very jealous for the LORD, the God of hosts; for the children of Israel have forsaken Thy covenant, thrown down Thine altars, and slain Thy prophets with the sword; and I, even I only, am left; and they seek my life, to take it away.

Is this perhaps God's gift and mystery, that he puts the world in and on each one of us as if there is no one else? And perhaps Bohemond, with the whole world in him and on him in a way that I can have no idea of, is without even knowing it jealous for the LORD; perhaps he has been appointed by God to call our attention to something, to the fragility of the temples that we daily destroy perhaps.

I sensed that it was important for me to understand, of the many things in my mind, at least one thing well in order to die properly, to let go of life in the right way. I craved to know what at least one of the important persons in my life was to me: Sophia or the tax-collector or Bohemond, the one in my mind called Questing, the angel of death and messenger of God.

Different people look ahead to different things. There were Jews in Antioch who had no doubt whatever that the Messiah was coming. This brute faith seemed a kind of madness to me; their faces seemed coarse with it, their eyes like stones. "What?" I said to them, "What will be when the Messiah comes?"

"The Temple rebuilt!" they cried, their stone eyes shining, "The glory of Israel restored!"

"The Temple rebuilt!" I said to them. Suddenly the absurdity of such a fast day as Tisha b'Av became overwhelming to me. To lament year after year, generation after generation, the toppling of stones! Stones that have no enemy, stones in whom God dances impartially for anyone or for no one, dances under whatever name is given, dances whether there is anyone to know of God's existence or not! What is the toppling of stones to

God? Is God overturned with the stones? My people! "If you want the Temple rebuilt then go and rebuild it!" I said. "One doesn't need a Messiah for that, one only needs carpenters and stonemasons and bricklayers."

"Don't be such a fool," they said. "You know very well that it isn't just the sticks and stones and bricks of it we're talking about. Don't you want the glory of Israel restored?"

"The glory of Israel has never been lost," I said. "When you say, 'Hear, O Israel, the Lord our God, the Lord is One,' then with those words and with that thought you speak the glory of Israel. To that perception of Oneness nothing can be added and from it nothing can be taken away."

"The ancient glory of the Kingdom of David!" they said.

"What kind of glory is that?" I said. "Saul slew his hundreds, David slew his thousands, Bohemond the same. Wait, you'll see glory when Bohemond comes over the wall."

Their stone eyes glared into mine. Hearing the words that came out of my mouth I realized that I was not of their world, I was no longer even of my own world, I was well on my way to where I am now.

This Elijah who now presented himself to me as enemy and teacher and messenger of God, this Elijah had long lived in my mind as forerunner; I had always pictured him running ahead as he ran ahead of Ahab's chariot, an athlete strong in his engoddedness, running like an animal and with his running prophesying the God in him; the beauty of his running makes a shout in the desert, a lightning in the sunlight. Elijah the forerunner of the Messiah, Elijah the warden of the covenant, Elijah for whom a chair is placed at circumcisions, Elijah for whom a place is set at the Seder, for whom a glass of wine is poured, for whom the door is left open, Ay! Elijah! Elijah feeling himself alone the covenant-keeper, Elijah with a silence all around him and a still small voice inside him. Elijah who bows himself to the earth and puts his face between his knees and waits for the rain, Elijah who runs away and throws himself aside until the angel of God calls him to action. Elijah fed by angels, fed by ravens, Elijah the magical, the one of us. His guises are many, one doesn't always know who he is, one doesn't always recognize him. One must make connexions, must find the combination that he is a part of. By learning to recognize Elijah one learns to recognize Messiah. Here in Antioch the evening of the fourteenth of Nisan in the Jewish year 4858 which is the nineteenth of March in the Christian year 1098 is the Eve of Passover. A place is set, a glass of wine is poured, the door is opened for Elijah. And I know that in this part of the space called time Bohemond is Elijah and for me the taking of Antioch will be the Messiah and Jerusalem both.

Passover has come and gone and the Franks have not come over the walls. The tower we call Evil Eye and Raymond's tower and Tancred's tower stare at us through days and nights as if by observation could be known the time when Antioch must fall to these soldiers of Christ who cannot breach the walls of Justinian.

The towers stare, the Franks await God's will while Karbuqa masses his armies and the reports of his imminent advance come every day with fresh detail and greater numbers. In Antioch the feeling is that of a very long night almost over and daylight almost here. The walls have not been breached, the Franks for all their engines of war and their will of God have not been able to bring the outside into the inside. Some of the people who have crept away from the city now return to take up life and business where they left off. There are many difficulties, many hardships, there are not enough goods to do much business with, but the people of Antioch wait patiently for the city to outlast its besiegers.

April passes and May. Salzedo was wrong: Shavuoth has come and gone and Antioch has not fallen. Here is the beginning of June in the Christian calendar, the end of Sivan in the Jewish one. The new moon of Tammuz will soon be seen, and some of the more old-fashioned Jews of Antioch will address it in the old-fashioned way:

> As I dance towards thee, but cannot touch thee,
> So shall none of my evil-inclined enemies
>   be able to reach me.

It is the night of the last of Sivan. I am asleep and I know that I am asleep. I feel like an instrument, like a compass needle quivering to the pull of the north or like a weathercock—yes, that's how I feel, like a weathercock high, high up on a steeple in a strong wind, my limbs rigidly extended north, south, east, and west but not fixed and still like the directionals of a weathercock; no, I am spinning, spinning through the space called time, over the miles, over the days, weeks, months to the fall of Jerusalem a year from now. My hands and feet burn as if they are on fire, spinning so high in a purple-blue sky, spinning down to the domes of Jerusalem the golden, down to Yerushalayim in the Christian summer of 1099, down to Yerushalayim with a pall of smoke hanging over it and a stench of fire and blood and death.

It is only a little while since the city has been taken, fires are still burning; the streets are slippery with blood and entrails; bodies of men, women, and children, severed limbs and heads are heaped everywhere. The colours of the clothes on the bodies cannot be distinguished, so steeped in blood are they. Some of the bodies still move a little, and groans can be heard.

Many of the Franks are busy with the dead and the near-dead; they cut them open and pull out the entrails, in this way some of them find gold coins. Screams are heard as well as groans, some of the Franks are active with women whom they have not yet killed while others take their pleasure with the dead.

Over the city circle the vultures while crows, bolder and more nimble, hop and flutter with red beaks and feet, picking and choosing. Dogs go cringing with their ears laid back, they seem stricken with guilt and terror at seeing so many masters slain at once; some are in an ecstasy of blood-frenzy, they snarl and growl and tear at the dead flesh, the corpses flop and jerk as they are pulled this way and that.

Here are the Western Wall and the Temple mound with the Dome of the Rock and the al-Aqsa Mosque. I have never seen these places before but I know them from maps and pictures, from dreams and from the phantom Jerusalem I have seen on Hidden Lion. Blood runs down the stones of the Western Wall and in the heat of the day the air quivers and sways above the dead who are heaped between the Dome of the Rock and the al-Aqsa Mosque. These are mostly Muslims; I can see no Jews here but I can smell their death in the smoke that rises from the synagogue to which they fled and in which they have been burnt alive. I am not walking, I am moving on the air in this waking sleep-travel, this night journey to a day that is coming; if I had to walk I should find little space on the red and slippery stones, I should have to walk on corpses.

Now I see among the blood-soaked bodies one that is like a naked ivory goddess in this butchery-place of the soldiers of Christ. The back of her head is crushed; her flawless limbs are sprawled in dishonour—but I am wrong to say that: her beauty of self and person cannot be dishonoured; she has been violated and murdered but such as she cannot be dishonoured; those who have done this have dishonoured only themselves. Here she lies, my dead and naked pilgrim, her Arab gown torn from her; flinging it over her head was not enough, they had to see all of her. I cannot cover her nor can I more modestly dispose her limbs, I have no corporeal existence in this place to which I have spun with burning hands and feet.

Here is a strange thing: in Sophia's left hand is a little shoe, a little scarlet slipper worked with gold. A child's shoe. Now do I seek and search, powerless to move so much as a dead finger of the numberless dead who lie here bearing witness.

I seek, I search; crows flap their black wings and cry their carrion-lust, dogs growl at my strange presence as I look everywhere to see if there will be a live two-year-old child with one foot bare. Have I been brought here to see the end of Sophia and that alone?

The sun goes down; the crows depart; the dogs are bolder now, the smacking and slavering and crunching of their feasting is loud in the twilight. There! Something moves! Fouled with the blood of the corpses he has sheltered under, there crawls out of this midden-heap of history a boy of perhaps two years and a few months. On his left foot is the mate of the slipper in Sophia's left hand. A fine boy, big for his age and strong-looking, with a face like Sophia's. It is growing dark, there is no moon to be seen. The little boy is not crying, his eyes are open wide and all his senses are alert as he walks slowly and quietly among the silent dead and the snarling dogs.

I cannot follow. My burning hands and feet, my north and south, east and west are spinning me up into the night and away from Jerusalem. "My son!" I cry, "My little son!" Never shall I know his name. His face was not only like Sophia's, there was something of me in it as well, also in the way he held his head.

I am in my bed. The last of the darkness is paling towards the dawn. My hands and feet still burn. I am naked. I look away from my mutilation and cover myself. At the foot of my bed stands my young death, naked but complete. For the first time his face is not obscure, and I see that it is like Sophia's face and yet it is my face too, the face of my child's soul grown into a better man than I ever was. Still I can't be such a bad fellow to have a death like this. He points to my hands and feet and I see there, written on the palms of my hands and on the soles of my naked feet, the four characters of the unutterable name of God.

He has done this for me, my young death: by writing on my hands and feet the sacred name he has sent me through the space called time to the taking of Jerusalem and the death of Sophia to show me our son walking alive out of the slaughter. Perhaps he will live only one day more, perhaps only one hour more, but he will begin his journey and will have in his eyes for however little time the same world that burned in the vision of his mother and his father. My son! Never to know his name! As I look at my hands and feet the letters fade with the paling of the sky. My night journey is done.

Now the cool dim tones of light that every morning build afresh the world are building it again this morning; the houses and the domes and minarets, Justinian's walls and towers all stand up in readiness for their dayward passage. Now appear before me, consubstantial with the light, the dead fellow-travellers of my pilgrimage in the order of their deaths: the tax-collector, headless and naked and writhing with maggots; Udo the relic-gatherer whom I killed in the little wood; the bear shot full of arrows by the man who called him God; Bodwild the sow and Konrad her master; the pilgrim children raped by Bruder Pförtner and his fellows—they must have perished at sea, they are bloated and eyeless, their hair is matted and tangled. My young death, respectful and attentive, stands a little to one side. His lips are moving, they shape the word, "Tonight."

I nod. "Tonight!" I say. I am ready, even eager. As comradely as I am with Bembel Rudzuk, as close as our friendship is, yet am I closer to these dead. As a pilgrim acquires merit by making the journey to Jerusalem, so have these acquired not only merit but magical power by completing the journey to the end of themselves, to the fullness of their action. In death they are intensified, they are more than themselves, they are more than philosophies; they are geographies, histories, they are sciences and guides for a soul sore troubled and perplexed. Where they are, where Sophia is, there would I be.

But Sophia is not standing before me with the other dead. Suddenly I recall that she is not dead. Jerusalem has not yet fallen to the Franks, this is not yet the year 1099, it is still 1098. Sophia is alive! Our little son is not alone among dogs and corpses. There is the delicate crescent of the new moon of Tammuz still in the morning sky. The evil decree is not yet upon us.

"Tonight" is the word shaped by the lips of my young death. This is the last day of my life! Only a moment ago I was eager to join the dead but now everything is different, I am not a dry tree, I have a son, I am needed by my child and the mother of my child, I must find them. Life is calling me now, not death.

I look at my young death, I shake my head and with my mouth I shape the words, "Not yet."

"Tonight!" Again the word appears on his lips. I look away, I don't want to see him now. The tax-collector and the others have gone, I am alone with my young death.

I am on my feet, I pick up my curved Turkish sword, Firouz's sword that Yaghi-Siyan has given me. My young death looks at me sadly; in his face I see the face of my little son alone among the dogs, among the dead. I raise the sword to strike but it is as if an iron bar has dropped across my arm. This has happened to me once before when I tried to save the life of the bear, and now as then it is the bony arm of Bruder Pförtner that has stopped me.

"You don't mean to do that," he says, breathing upon me with his breath that is like the fresh salt wind by the sea. "It simply isn't done."

"You don't understand," I say. "For myself I don't care, I'm quite ready to die. It's my son, you see—he's only a very little fellow and he needs me badly, and his mother, if I can find her perhaps she needn't die in Jerusalem."

"Yes," says Bruder Pförtner, "I *do* understand, you've no idea how often I hear this sort of thing. So many people are urgently needed elsewhere when the time comes. And what about me, eh? Have you perhaps a little thought for me? I am like a diligent housewife who cleans the house and cooks the meal and lays the table, all is in readiness but the expected guest suddenly can't be bothered to come. Only in this case I've cleaned the house and cooked the meal and laid the table of history, and one can't take liberties with history; it isn't possible, the complexity of the energy exchanges is absolutely staggering."

"History!" I say, "I'm talking about human lives!"

"And I'm talking about human deaths," says Bruder Pförtner. "Tonight is the fall of Antioch and I need all the Jews and Muslims I can lay my hands on. You have no more time for rushing about, this must be the whole world for you in the time you have left." With that he disappears. When I turn back to my young death he also is gone.

I dress and go to Bembel Rudzuk's room but he isn't there. I go to the roof: not there. Should I run to Yaghi-Siyan and tell him that I have been told by Bruder Pförtner that Antioch will fall to the Franks tonight? I think that he will believe me but he may well have my head cut off as his first act of preparation for the attack. Should I tell Firouz? Ever since Yaghi-Siyan gave me his sword he looks at me as if he wishes me dead; he would probably accuse me and Bruder Pförtner of being spies. To whom can I give this news? To whom can I say that Death has told me that Antioch will fall tonight? Meanwhile Sophia and our son are either on their way to Jerusalem or are already there. I must find them, I must get out of Antioch.

Seeking Bembel Rudzuk I go to Hidden Lion. It is desolate in the summer dawn. Here are gathered Bruder Pförtner and his fellows. No more do they present themselves as loutish creatures of lust; now they are serious, respectable, they wear breastplates, helmets, cloaks. They are grouped like generals around a huge map that Pförtner has spread out on the tiles. With a baton he points here and there, the others nod. People and movement flow around Hidden Lion as water flows around an island, no one takes any notice. These bony generals stand out with startling clarity in the foreground of the picture in my eyes, they are sharply defined by the space between them and the houses, domes, and minarets and by the particles of colour on the morning air that in the eye combine to form Mount Silpius tawny and empurpled. The mu'addhin has long since sounded the call to prayer and the prayers have risen in the dawnlight, in the freshness of those cool dim tones with which the world is first sketched-in each day. As the sun ascends the morning shadow of the eastern slopes of Silpius withdraws from the city like a transparent purple robe trailed across a floor.

There on the mountain climb Justinian's walls of the four hundred towers, each correctly casting its morning shadow; there on the mountain is the citadel with its tawny stone catching the light of the sun, its green-

and-gold banner rippling in the morning breeze; there in the cleft of Silpius is the Bab el-Hadid, the Iron Gate where in the winter runs Onopniktes the donkey-drowner, roaring, bellowing, grinding its stones in its caverns under the city.

This, under the inescapable reality of Mount Silpius, is the first of Tammuz, the month named for the Babylonian god who is also the Sumerian Dumuzi. Down, down under the earth into the nether world goes he in the winter for he is the corn god. For him does the Goddess Inanna make her famous descent, anointing her eyes with the ointment "Let him come, let him come":

> From the "great above" she set her mind toward the
> "great below,"
> The goddess, from the "great above" she set her mind
> toward the "great below."

The new moon of the risen Tammuz hangs in the morning sky but I feel intimations of the great descent, the dark and chill of winter in the light and heat of summer. Inside the earth the waiting darkness trembles. Standing on the barren tiles of Hidden Lion and looking at that always surprising mountain, that simple mountain that so shockingly asserts the actuality of its strangeness, that mountain that now for me is truly and finally the dreadful mountain of the Law, I curse the infirmity of purpose that has kept me here in Antioch. Turning and turning in my mind my thoughts of what to do next I turn physically, making myself dizzy on this repetition of twisting serpents, shifting pyramids, and occulting lions. There burns in my mind that vision more real than Mount Silpius, more real than anything else in the world, of the violated ivory nakedness of dead Sophia and the animal watchfulness of our little son making his way alone through the dogs, through the dead. I have spent my time playing with patterns and it has come to this. There leaps up in me hatred for Bembel Rudzuk.

I looked up at the tower and saw him standing at the top of it, a solitary dark figure against the morning sky. I looked away. How could I hate Bembel Rudzuk? Overcome by love and shame I went to him.

"You look dreadful," he said.

"This is the last day of my life," I said.

"All the more reason for looking your best," he said. "This is the last day of my life as well. How do I look?"

"Dreadful," I said. We embraced each other sadly.

"Before we talk of other matters," he said, "I must tell you how it is that I am called Bembel Rudzuk."

"I don't think I can take the time to listen to that now," I said, "I must go to Jerusalem."

"Don't you believe Bruder Pförtner when he tells you there's no longer anywhere for you to go?" he said.

"How do you know he told me that?" I said.

"He spoke to me as well," he said.

"As Bruder Pförtner or in some other manifestation?" I said.

"As Bruder Pförtner," he said. "I suppose he didn't bother to change because we're friends. Are you offended?"

"No," I said but of course I was. I was ashamed to have such stupid feelings at such a time but there they were.

"Pförtner likes to affect a playful manner," said Bembel Rudzuk, "but he means what he says. I don't think he'll let you leave Antioch, and if you try I think it will only make our last day more difficult."

Our last day! I had come to Hidden Lion seeking Bembel Rudzuk's counsel for *my* last day, mine alone. I didn't want to have to think about anyone else's last day, not even that of my dearest friend; and that his last day should now be the same day as mine seemed tactless of him, inconsiderate, even pushing. I no longer wanted to talk to Bembel Rudzuk but I wanted him to know how things stood with me. "Everything's different now," I said: "I have travelled through space and time to the fall of Jerusalem. I have seen Sophia dead and violated, I have seen our son wandering alone among the dead and the dogs. All this has not yet happened and it must not happen, I must do something to prevent it."

"I too have seen them," said Bembel Rudzuk.

"You too have made a night journey to the fall of Jerusalem?" I said. "You too have seen" (I was going to say "my wife") "Sophia and our son?"

"Yes," he said.

"How can this be?" I said.

"How can what be?" he said.

"That you have seen them in the sack of Jerusalem," I said.

"Why not?" he said. "If they were there to be raped and killed and orphaned then why not to be seen?"

I was so choked with rage that I could hardly find a voice to speak with. "What is this?" I said. "Are you trying to teach me some kind of lesson?"

"How could I?" he said. "I am no wiser than you and I have nothing to teach. And being thus without wisdom I can't help wondering why it is that all this time you have felt no need for action and now suddenly you want to change history."

I thought I should go mad. Silpius continued to offer itself in its unaccountable simplicity to the eye; Bruder Pförtner and his generals continued to confer. Their pretensions disgusted me; I had seen them being themselves with those pilgrim children on the road. History! I felt myself impaled on history, my own and the world's. The horror, the horror of cause and effect! The horror of the pitiless and implacable chain of one thing following another from the beginning of the world to the end of it with never a pause, never a year of Jubilee, never a clearing of the record! O God! to come so far and to end with so little. Now it was like that torture in which the victim, his belly opened up and one end of his entrails tied to a post, is made to walk round and round the post unwinding his guts. So walked my mind round its post while the images in it unwound, from the naked Sophia seen in the window to the naked Sophia dead and our son alone in the sack of Jerusalem. I wanted to smash every one of the tiles of Hidden Lion, every one of the bricks of the tower, I wanted Antioch and Onopniktes and Mount Silpius to disappear from my experience, to become unknown to me. I wanted to wind my time back into me, I wanted to be once more at the Eve of the Ninth of Av in the Christian year of 1096. I would sin again but I would be fierce and strong in my sin, I would go armed and wary in my sin, I would kill for it, would claim Sophia against all odds, I would die fighting if necessary but I would die complete, not a eunuch. What a fool I had been, neither a sheep nor a goat, suffering the loss of goodness without the rewards of badness, Aiyee! But what if Sophia hadn't wanted to be claimed by me? What if she wanted her Jew for one night only?

Bembel Rudzuk had been watching my face attentively. "Is this perhaps the moment," he said, "when I can tell you how I come to be called Bembel Rudzuk?"

"If you must," I said.

"This that I tell happened forty years ago," he said, "when I was trading for a big house in Tripoli—not as a partner, I was what we call a 'boy.' We'd come from Tabriz to Aleppo with a three-hundred camel caravan but coming out of Aleppo there were only nine of us—five merchants and four camel-drivers—with twelve camels. We were a day out of Aleppo when there appeared on an empty stretch of road six robbers who put their horses straight at us, three of them passing on either side and shooting arrows as they galloped past; it happened so fast that one simply couldn't believe it. And their accuracy, shooting at full gallop! A moment before there had been nine of us and now as they wheeled their horses for the second pass six of our party already lay dead.

"By then the other three of us had put arrow to string and we got two of them on their next rush. Then it was four against three; they were wild with rage, they couldn't believe that merchants would stand up to them. Of the first six they had killed four were mounted merchants and two were camel-drivers on foot. The two surviving camel-drivers leapt on to horses and tried to get away but they were quickly brought down by arrows. My horse was killed under me and I was nearly ridden down by the robber who did it. There was no time to think, I leapt at him and in the next moment he was rolling on the ground and I was bent over his horse's neck and galloping for my life.

"I was heading for some high ground and big rocks and I was already among the rocks when Tssss, thwock! Off I came with an arrow in my left shoulder, but as soon as I hit the ground I was in behind the rocks and climbing, they couldn't get a shot at me and they had to get off their horses to follow me.

"Up I went; I found a little opening between two big tall rocks and I squeezed through. It wasn't a cave; the rocks were about twenty feet high and there was a space between them open to the sky. I didn't know whether I was better or worse off than before. I had my sword and my dagger but I had dropped my bow when I leapt at the robber and in any case my quiver was empty. My wound was burning like fire; the arrow had gone right through my shoulder and the head was sticking out in front so that I was able to break it off and pull out the shaft.

"I had no time to do more than that before there appeared a robber between me and the sky in the opening at the top of the rocks. He laughed and was just reaching for an arrow from his quiver when I threw a stone and caught him full in the face with it. That's when I knew I was lucky because he lost his balance and fell, not backwards but forwards; he toppled from his perch, landed with a thump beside me and got my dagger in him for his pains.

"So then I had a bow and arrows: three arrows there were in the quiver, and when the next robber showed himself in the opening above me he got one of the arrows in his throat. That left me with two arrows and two more robbers if the one I'd pulled off his horse had taken up the chase; I assumed that he had, so I looked alternately up at the opening above me and down at the one I had squeezed through and waited for what would come next. This was in the spring, I could hear a bird saying, 'Plink, plink!' like drops of water falling into a basin. Above me the sky was blue, there was a fresh breeze blowing.

"I could hear some movement on the rocks and a voice said, 'You go in after him, I'll be right behind you.' Of course I knew that was meant for my ears so I was waiting for them to come at me at the same time from above and below. I knew by then that whoever climbed to the opening above was unable to do it with an arrow on the string, he would have to pause for a moment at the top to reach for an arrow. And if he was going to time his attack with that of the other robber he would probably make a sound. So I aimed an arrow at the space I had squeezed through, I thought that was where I'd first see movement.

"You know how it is at even the most desperate moments, even in matters of life and death—part of your mind is busy with its own affairs, perhaps making pictures, perhaps making words or singing a song while the rest of your mind takes care of the business at hand. Part of my mind was singing a little song, it hadn't much tune, it was just something the mind had made up by itself, there were no proper words, it just went:

> "Tsitsa tsitsa bem, tsitsa tsitsa bem,
> Tsitsa tsitsa bembel bembel bembel bembel bem.

"Like that over and over again. When I saw movement in the space I'd squeezed through I loosed my arrow and I heard a grunt. There was a little sound from above as if in reply and when the last robber appeared against the sky my last arrow found him and that finished the business of the day.

"So that was that. For a little while I just sat there leaning against a rock, looking up at the sky, listening to the bird, feeling the breeze on my face—just being alive and not dead. My mind was still busy with its song, now it was singing:

"Rukh, rukh, rudz, rudzl, rudzl, rudzuk.

"I was thinking what a lot of bems and rudzes there are in the universe, what an altogether bembelish and rudzukal thing it is, to say nothing of the tsitsas. I was glad for me that I was alive and sorry for the robbers that they were dead—it was such a good day to be alive in. I recognized that it could just as easily have been the robbers alive and I dead and that would have been fair enough, one mustn't be greedy, one can't always win the prize, the action goes on for ever but the actors come and go.

"It was then that I noticed sitting beside me and leaning back against the same rock our bony friend, all got up for the occasion like a true son of the desert with quite a princely robe and kaffiya and jewelled daggers. 'You're a good boy,' he said, putting a hand on my shoulder. 'I like you; you move well and you don't hang back when things warm up a little. You'll be lucky, you'll have a good life and years enough of it. One thing though you must never forget: you must never forget whose child you are, and when I say it's time for bed you must come promptly and cheerfully; you might as well do it with a good grace because in any case you'll have to come—no one can say no to me.'

"With that he whistled and there came not a black horse and not a white one but a dappled grey stallion. Such a horse, a horse of dreams, that one! Almost I wanted to go with Death at that very moment just to feel that horse under me. With a whoop he leapt to the stallion's back and galloped away like a thunderbolt, what a man! It struck me suddenly, there's no one more alive than Death; how could there be, he'll outlive us all!

"From that moment I called myself Bembel Rudzuk so that I should never forget the bembelish and rudzukal nature of the universe and whose child I was.

"When I came down from the rocks I found the robbers' horses tied to a thornbush and with them was the one I had ridden to the rocks. She was one of those clever little mares that can go all day and never miss her footing anywhere, I had her for years after that, she always reminded me of that ride. What a day that was!

"I found the camels all grazing where the robbers had attacked us and grazing with them were the other horses, both the robbers' and ours. Two of the horses had been killed but that still left me with four horses more than we had started the day with, and of course the six robber horses were all first-class, much better than ours; robbers can't afford to ride rubbish.

"Even better than the horses was what I found in the robbers' saddle-bags: two thousand and forty-two dinars! I couldn't believe it—all that gold and still they went on trying for more! I suppose they were for ever unsatisfied and that's why they had to be robbers.

"I rode back to the rocks and collected the four dead robbers there then I loaded all six robbers and my dead colleagues and the camel-drivers on to the horses and continued on my way to Tripoli with the carpets we had bought in Tabriz. On my return all the dead were buried with the proper observances. We did well in the market and altogether my employers were well pleased with me. As I had been travelling for them when I acquired the robbers' treasure I offered to share it equally with them but they refused to take so much as a single dinar. They wanted to make me a partner but I preferred to set up in business for myself under my new name and I came to Antioch to do it. I had always liked the look of the place, particularly the look of Mount Silpius in the dawn, and I had heard that long ago there was a statue of the Goddess of Luck here. I've never found the place where the statue used to be but I've always been as lucky as I needed to be.

"I have had a good life, I have spent my time as I wanted to spend it, and although I have never grown wise I have through trial and error come closer and closer to Thing-in-Itself, so that when my time comes I expect I shan't have too much of a jump to make from this state to the next one. I can understand your present bitterness and your regret that you have stayed so long in Antioch but for me what we have done with Hidden Lion was time as well spent as time ever is. To me it seems that the best we can hope for in life is honesty of error; more than that is not to be expected.

Sometimes we can see what is wrong action but that doesn't make everything other than that right action. I have said enough; I have lived enough. I do not forget whose child I am and I am ready to go when called."

"You say that Bruder Pförtner has spoken to you," I said. "Have you also seen your young death?"

"I have seen only Pförtner," said Bembel Rudzuk, "on his dappled stallion: that for me is the sign. I have seen him and spoken with him many times since that first time forty years ago but never until this morning has he ridden that particular horse again; it has been understood between us that the horse would be the sign."

"I wonder how it is that you also have travelled to the fall of Jerusalem and seen Sophia and my son," I said.

"You have a woman and a child to love," said Bembel Rudzuk. "I have only you and I have been eating the scraps from your table."

"Ah!" I said. "Whenever I think that I have seen the boundaries of my stupidity there suddenly open up new territories before me."

We both looked across the tiles to where Bruder Pförtner and his generals were. He was now strutting back and forth and making some kind of oration. The sky had become dull and grey. Silpius was intensified in the greyness, became the mountain wholly strange and never to be known, the mountain showing the traveller from afar how far he had come to find that nothing whatever could be known about anything at all. The nakedness of dead Sophia was as if printed on my eyes; I looked through it at the mountain as one looks through a transparent figured curtain. The watchful face of our son was as big as the world.

"We must do what we can," said Bembel Rudzuk. We looked at each other and the images printed on my eyes seemed to double in intensity.

"Are they in your eyes also, Sophia and my son?" I said.

"Yes," he said. "I'm sorry, I don't mean to intrude, I can't help it."

"We'll try together then to leave Antioch?" I said.

"Yes," he said, "we must at least try."

"Ought we to warn anyone before we go?" I said.

He shook his head. "Those who had in mind to leave have already gone and I don't think that the others will be moved to act on what we have seen in our night journey. What is more likely is that we shall be taken for spies."

We went back to the house and armed and provisioned ourselves. We were going to make the attempt on foot—in the present circumstances it was our best chance of going unseen and unheard and acting as the moment required. With a bag and a bow slung on my shoulder, with a quiver of arrows on one side and Firouz's sword on the other I paused to look at the fountain in the courtyard and to listen to the plashing of the silvery water, thirsting for it with my eyes.

When we came out into the street the very air seemed strange, apocalyptic. I doubted my own reality, I was surprised to hear footfalls and voices around me, surprised to smell the hot and pungent smells of every day. I waited for the earth to shake but it did not, I expected everyone to stare open-mouthed at us but they did not, then I thought that perhaps we might be invisible to them and I wanted to shout but I did not.

The walls were manned as fully as possible now night and day and there were always sentries at all of the gates. We dared not wait for the darkness and the chance of going over the wall with a rope—not only were there our own sentries to avoid but we both had no doubt whatever that the Franks would also be waiting for the darkness of this night to come over those same walls into Antioch. We had no plan beyond getting out of Antioch; if we were able to do that we should consider what to do next.

We headed for the Iron Gate east of the Citadel where in the winter Onopniktes entered its channel. It was by way of that cleft in the mountain that many people now went to forage and we hoped not to be noticed there. This day, however, was not like other days: on this day Firouz was at the Iron Gate with the soldiers of the guard.

Only a few moments ago I had felt as if we might be invisible but now suddenly it was as if all the crowded space around us became blank and empty and in the whole world only we were to be seen. Firouz was pacing back and forth with his turning walk. The sky had gone grey and the shadow that turned and twisted with him was dull and blurred. He had seen us approaching, and for us to turn away now would invite more trouble than to continue towards the gate.

There swept over me a wave of irritation: I was annoyed with everything and everybody, even with Sophia and my little son that they had come thus at the eleventh hour to interfere with the smooth and orderly winding-up of my affairs. My being was grating on this day as the teeth grate on a stone in the bread. In my heart and soul I knew it to be my last day; I knew that the stones of my little history and the world's great one were fitted together so precisely by cause and held in place so firmly by effect that the feeble knifeblade of my too-late good intention could not even find a crack between them let alone pry them apart. And it was in this state of mind that I stood before Firouz on the morning of the first of Tammuz in the Christian year of 1098.

Firouz looked at us with satisfaction. "Where are you going?" he said.

I wanted to say, "To find Sophia and my son." I didn't want to have to take Firouz into account sufficiently to have to lie to him.

"We're going to have a look around Suwaydiyya," said Bembel Rudzuk. "I think some of the merchants there may have provisions they've hidden away from the Franks."

"Very daring," said Firouz, "with so many Franks between here and Suwaydiyya. Very daring indeed." He was looking at the sword I was wearing that used to be his.

"I know the back ways," said Bembel Rudzuk.

"I don't doubt it," said Firouz. He took the bag that was slung from my shoulder and looked into it. "You won't starve while you're out looking for provisions, will you," he said. "You're got enough food here for a week. Will you be back in time to stand guard on the wall tonight?"

"Yes," I said. "We don't go on until midnight."

"Good," said Firouz. "I think it's probably best if I lock you up until then; that way you won't wear yourselves out walking all those weary miles and you'll be alert and well-rested for tonight."

"We haven't done anything to be locked up for," said Bembel Rudzuk.

"Not yet," said Firouz. "But you inspire doubt and mistrust in me, and as I'm in command of this part of the wall I'm taking it on myself to keep you out of trouble."

"No!" I cried out. "You mustn't do that!"

"Why not?" said Firouz.

"Because tonight may be the night the Franks take Antioch!" I blurted out.

Firouz jumped back as if I had thrust a viper into his face. "Who told you that?" he said.

"It came to me in a dream, a vision, a night journey," I said.

"Have you told this to anyone else?" said Firouz.

"No," I said.

Firouz motioned to two of the guards. "Lock these two up in the tower," he said.

I began to laugh, I couldn't help it.

"What are you laughing at?" said Firouz.

"Life and death," I said. "It's so hard to make a good job of either."

Firouz began to laugh too. "You're right," he said. "Truly it doesn't give me pleasure to lock you up, it's just that all of us have different things to do and this is what I have to do."

"It doesn't really matter," I said. "It's only life and death."

"It's strange," said Firouz: "people buy and sell, they go here and there, they make plans for this year and the next year as if there will be no end to life, as if there will always be a next day and a next year; but sometime there must come an end to the days and the years; it must be like walking into a wall where one has always found a door." While he said this reflectively and in a companionable manner as if we were dining together Bembel Rudzuk and I stood before him with a guard on either side of us. When he had completed this observation the guards took away our bows and arrows, our swords and daggers and our bags. "Your weapons and your other possessions will be given back to you later," said Firouz as the guards took us away to the tower.

Later than what? I thought. With the two guards behind us we climbed the stone stairs to that part of Firouz's tower that rose above the wall. There we were taken up more stairs to the top of the tower and put into a little room in which there was nothing but an overwhelming stench of urine and excrement and a bucket that had not been emptied for a very long time. A little dimness was provided by a high-up window that was too small to squeeze through.

I beat on the door to ask for the bucket to be emptied. There was no response of any kind. "This is to be our end then," I said, "in a little dim room with a bucket of old shit."

"Be glad we're in the room and not in the bucket," said Bembel Rudzuk.

We sat on the floor and looked up and down and all around the little room. It was so dreadfully *finite*. There was no possibility whatever of there being any more to it than we could see.

"What Firouz said about buying and selling, do you think he meant anything by it, do you think he wanted to be bribed?" I said.

"I think he's already been bought by the Franks," said Bembel Rudzuk.

The bucket stood there stinking in a corner in a buzzing of flies in the dimness of the little locked stone room. I thought: Is this a metaphor? Then a nearby bird said, "Plink, plink, plink." Ah! I thought, explanations are unnecessary. So I felt a little better until the naked headless tax-collector appeared, writhing with maggots as always. Never mind, I thought, this is only illusion.

From wherever the tax-collector's voice lived came a long sigh, "Ahhhhhhh!" He assumed the necessary position over the bucket and emptied his bowels with a torrent like Onopniktes, I half expected dead donkeys to come out of him turning over and over in that disgusting flood. This is metaphorical illusion, I told myself, dismiss it from your mind; have other illusions, better ones; see Sophia. But Sophia would not come, even Bodwild would not come. My young death, I thought, surely *he* will come, I am like a father to him, I *am* his father—let us at least have a proper leavetaking before he goes out into the world to seek his fortune, let there be a fond embrace, a manly clasping of hands, a tear or two would be nothing to be ashamed of. But no, he would not come. Comfortless I sat on the floor with my elbows on my knees and my head in my hands.

"Ahhhhhh!" sighed the tax-collector again. He must have left the bucket because now he was returning to it to relieve himself once more with the same torrential rush and with a noise that was like the bursting of the Unseen into the seen, which of course in its own way it was. Surely, I thought, this is no proper epiphany; surely if God is gone I shall at least see Christ one more time, I deserve at least that much.

Pffffffttttt! went the tax-collector. The stench was no longer within the limits of what could be called a smell, it had become something in the nature of a metaphysical premise. The grotesquerie of the tax-collector's appearing without a head while thus emptying himself of the waste of a lifetime, perhaps of more than one lifetime! Really, I thought, how much can be expected of my forbearance, my civility? After all, if this is illusion I must have something to say about it. "If you're going to keep doing that at least you must accept responsibility for it!" I shouted. "At least you can show your face!"

"What did you say?" said Bembel Rudzuk.

"Say!" I said. "Who can say anything with this constant noise, this unbearable stench!"

"I don't hear anything," said Bembel Rudzuk, "and I haven't been noticing the smell for a while."

"Everything's all right with you then, is it?" I said. "With you there's nothing to complain of?"

"I've already told you," he said, "that I've had a good life and I've had enough of it and I'm ready to go. Why should I have any complaints?"

"This smell," I said, "this smell isn't illusion, it's a real stink, it's a stench of actuality."

"Where I am there's not that much of a stench," he said.

"There's no need to be insulting," I said.

"Don't be ridiculous," he said. "Here we have an opportunity for preparation, we have a little quiet time in which there is nothing for us to do, nothing is required of us; it is like a silent desert in which we are not far from the track that will take us to that farthest lote-tree that is shrouded in unutterable mystery. All we need is a little patience, a little quietness of mind as we look for the track in the silent desert."

"You!" I said. "You are attached to nothing, you care for no one."

"The one doesn't necessarily follow from the other," he said. "I am attached to nothing but I care for you and I have cared for others in my time."

"Always you make me ashamed," I said.

"Stop disquieting yourself and stop being ashamed," he said. "Use this time to find the track in the desert."

"Ahhhhhhhh!" said the tax-collector returning to the bucket.

It seems now to be much later although I don't know how much time has passed, I don't know whether I've been asleep or not. The little stone room is full of darkness, but it seems to me that beyond the stench of the bucket I can smell the dawn that is coming. There enters my mind the thought that the bucket in the corner has been put there for Elijah. I don't want Elijah to come here and relieve himself in that bucket, I want to see Elijah running ahead of Ahab's chariot, running beautifully under a black sky in the rain and the wind, running in the thought of God to Jezreel.

Something is happening below us on the wall, there are footsteps and voices, there are armed men running, men shouting, "*Deus le volt!*" The Franks are in Antioch and we are locked up in this little room of stone.

Bembel Rudzuk, whose silent stillness in the darkness suggests not sleep but contemplation, now says, "If you stand on my shoulders you can empty that bucket out of the window."

This bucket-emptying is not a simple thing; there is no chair or table that I can use as a mounting platform, and one hand is of course required for the bucket. But Bembel Rudzuk at sixty-two is still a strong man. Facing the wall he kneels on one knee below the window. I step on to his broad shoulders and with one hand touching the wall I maintain my balance as he rises to his feet.

Bembel Rudzuk bracing himself with his hands against the wall is as steady as a rock. I am just high enough so that I can see the little crescent of the new moon of Tammuz and feel the freshness of the night on my eyes. From the sounds I hear I judge that our window overlooks the walkway on the top of the wall, and it is from this walkway that the shouts of the Franks are coming. There are cries and groans from the Turks; someone exclaims, clearly and distinctly as if required by history to bear audible witness, "We are betrayed!"

"Bohemond!" goes up the shout, "Bohemond! Bohemond! Bohemond!"

With my right hand under the bucket I slide it very slowly, very carefully up the wall to the window, keeping my balance with my face against the wall while I bring my left hand over to grasp the handle. There is in my mind an ardent prayer as I bring the bucket up over the window sill.

"*Deus le volt!*" I shout as I empty the bucket and hurl it after its contents. From below there comes a wild cry of rage as startling and primitive as the roar of a lion.

"Allah The Finder," says Bembel Rudzuk.

At that moment the door opens and in the candlelight from a sconce on the stairs we see Firouz. He lays our bags and weapons on the floor. "Forgive me if you can," he says. In the doorway is my young death also, his face shining with love as he points to my sword that used to belong to Firouz. Bembel Rudzuk and I as one man stretch out our hands for our swords, we have no need of anything else now.

Pell-mell down the stairs we go to the walkway on the wall; there are dead Turks there, we step over them, we hurry down the next stairs to the ground.

"Hidden Lion!" says Bembel Rudzuk. Yes, yes, I know what is in his mind as we run. The little crescent hangs in the sky so delicate and slender, shouts and screams run through the darkness like fire through stubble; the mu'addhin will not sound the call to prayer in the new morning, there will be a great silence where there used to be the prayer of many. Stronger grows the smell of the dawn that is coming, that alchemy by which substance of darkness becomes substance of light in which are bodied forth all forms moving and still; the disquietude of the invaded houses, domes, and minarets, the continual surprise of Silpius that waits to manifest itself tawny and empurpled, unsurprised at the heaped bodies of the dead, surprised only that there should be world at all and itself in the world.

Dawn has not yet come but everything is Now and the actuality of it illuminates the night in my eyes so that I seem to see whatever is before me in the purple-blue crystalline vibrations in which I first saw the upside-down body of the tax-collector in the little wood of night.

Dim and yellow against the vibrations of the purple-blue shudders the faltering light of a lantern that stands on the tiles of Hidden Lion. And here is Questing the death-hound, here is Elijah for whom Firouz has opened the door, here is Messiah following on Elijah, here is the giant Bohemond foul and stinking with excrement that stains his scarlet cross as he stands on Hidden Lion lifting his sword vertically with both hands and plunging it down again and again like a man breaking ground for a post-hole. All around him are broken tiles and among them are heaped the gold and silver coins that were mortared into the tiles.

Now I see what I have seen before in the darkness and the brightness in my mind, I see leaping and still like a butterfly transfixed by lightning the elegance of Bembel Rudzuk as he attacks Bohemond; I see the great Frankish sword that has been going up and down like a post-hole digger suddenly leap like a live thing as Bohemond shifts his grip and now a track of brightness horizontally cleaves the darkness, cleaves the purple-blue, cleaves with its savage arc the body of Bembel Rudzuk; now in two pieces falls the body of Bembel Rudzuk to the broken tiles of Hidden Lion.

Here now before me is Bohemond. This is the great moment when I shall see the face of this man who has become my world and my Jerusalem. His fouled and stinking mail shirt glitters in the purple-blue luminosity of Now, his helmet flashes as if wreathed in lightnings; the iron nasal of his helmet makes other than human this face that I strain to see but I cannot, I shall never see it, I see instead the face of that veiled owl of my childhood.

I raise my arm, I strike with my sword, I see it shatter like shards of ice as the great sword of Bohemond makes a rainbow in the night, in the dawn that is coming. I stare into the brilliance, I see the Virgin and the Lion wheeling in the darkness, in the light. I see the sun-points dazzling on the sea, the alchemy of the triangular sail changing from the hot and dry to the cold and wet; I smell the salt breath of Bruder Pförtner.

But I cannot see Bohemond in this night and dawn of brilliance, of purple-blue luminosity. No, as the great sword makes another rainbow in the pale dawn where hangs the new moon of Tammuz, the last thing that I see with my mortal eyes, very, very high in the sky and circling in the overlapping patterns of the Law, is that drifting meditation of storks that I have known from my childhood, each year returning in their season to their wonted place.

QUOTES AND REFERENCES

All Old Testament quotes except those on pp. 392, 393 and 440 are from *The Holy Scriptures*, Jewish Publication Society of America, 1955. The quotes on pp. 61 and 62 are from *The Jerusalem Bible*, Koren Publishers, Jerusalem, 1977. The quote on p. 440 is from *The Septuagint Version of the Old Testament* in Greek and English, translated by Sir Launcelot Lee Brenton, Samuel Bagster and Sons, London.

All New Testament quotes are from *The Interlinear Greek-English New Testament* translated by Reverend Dr Alfred Marshall, Samuel Bagster and Sons, London, 1958.

All Quran quotes are from *The Holy Quran*, translated and with commentary by A. Yusuf Ali, Sh. Muhammad Ashraf, Kashmiri Bazar, Lahore, Pakistan, 1977.

Page 343. Deuteronomy 6:4
   344. Genesis 15:17, 18
   351. Deuteronomy 6:4
         Mourner's Kaddish, p. 80, *The Authorised Daily Prayer Book of the United Hebrew Congregations of the British Common-*

wealth of Nations, translated by Rev. S. Singer, Eyre and Spottiswoode, London, 1962

Morning Service, ibid. p. 9.

351, 352. Selichot for the First Day, pp. 18, 19, *Selichot, Authorised Hebrew and English Edition for the Whole Year,* translated and annotated by Rabbi Abraham Rosenfeld, The Judaica Press, New York, 1979.

354. Hebrews 12:18–21

356. Morning Service for the Ninth of Av, pp. 77, 78, *Kinot, Authorised for the Ninth of Av,* translated and annotated by Rabbi Abraham Rosenfeld, The Judaica Press, New York, 1979.

356. The fig tree: see Matthew 21:19, Mark 11:13

Matthew 19:12

367. Matthew 10:29

370. John 11:25, 26

Matthew 27:25

371. John 11:25

372. The Shechinah: "The Divine manifestation through which God's presence is felt by man," *Gateway to Judaism,* Volume One, p. 300, by Albert M. Shulman, Thomas Yoseloff, 1972

374. Matthew 27:22, 24, 25

378. Psalm 8:4

383. Mourner's Kaddish, p. 80, *The Authorised Daily Prayer Book,* op. cit.

392. Deuteronomy 32:18

392, 393. Deuteronomy 32:15–18

400. Mark 14:22

John 13:26, 27

Mark 14:22

402. John 11:48, 50–3

403. Matthew 26:50

Luke 22:48

404. Matthew 26:50

Mark 14:67, 68

405. Matthew 27:24

415. Jeremiah 2:24

423. Full quittance: see Ruth, p. 15, Volume Four, *The Midrash Rabbah*, edited by Rabbi Dr H. Freedman and Maurice Simon, The Soncino Press, London, 1977. This part is translated by Rabbi Dr L. Rabbinowitz.

424. Isaiah 26:19

434. The red heifer: see Numbers 19.

436. Abraham and the fiery furnace: see Genesis p. 311, Volume One, *The Midrash Rabbah*, op. cit.
The sulphur-mercury process: see pp. 89, 90, *Islamic Cosmological Doctrines* by Seyyed Hossein Nasr, Thames and Hudson, London, 1978.

440. Psalm 137:5
Esaias 56:3–5, *The Septuagint Version of the Old Testament*, op. cit.
Isaiah 56:5

441. Bembel Rudzuk's remark about the pattern going on for ever: this derives from Richard Ettinghausen's caption on p. 72 of his Chapter Two, "The Man-Made Setting," in *The World of Islam*, edited by Bernard Lewis, Thames and Hudson, London, 1976.

456. Tower Gate's reference to the Quran: see Sura 4:79, *The Holy Quran*, op. cit.

458. Deuteronomy 23:2

459, 460. The castration of Noah: See Genesis, pp. 291, 293, Volume One, *The Midrash Rabbah*, op. cit. The Genesis volume is translated by Rabbi Dr H. Freedman.

461, 462. The she-camel: see Suras VII, 73–9; XI 61–8; XXVI 141–59; XXVII 45–53, *The Holy Quran*, op. cit.

486. Genesis 21:17–18
Genesis, p. 473, Volume One, *The Midrash Rabbah*, op. cit.

498, 499. Ezekiel 24:6–9

500. Hebrews 1:11–12

500, 501. Sura 81:1–14, *The Holy Quran*, op. cit.; see notes 5973, 5974.

518. Bohemond and the stirrup: see Chapter I, *Medieval Technology and Social Change* by Lynn White Jr, Oxford University Press, 1962.

528. Timaeus, 57E, *Plato, the Collected Dialogues*, edited by Edith

Hamilton and Huntington Cairns, Bollingen Series LXXI, Princeton University Press, Princeton, New Jersey, 1961.

532, 533. Malachi 3:1–2
I Kings 19:10

535. The new-moon formula is from p. 310, Volume One, *Gateway to Judaism*, op. cit.

541. The lines from "Inanna's Descent" are from p. 159, *History Begins at Sumer* by Samuel Noah Kramer, Doubleday Anchor Books, New York, 1959.

553. The farthest lote-tree: see Sura LIII 14–18, and note 5093, *The Holy Quran*, op. cit: " . . . the farthest Lote-tree marked the bounds of heavenly knowledge as revealed to men, beyond which neither angels nor men could pass."

Wherever I have used a particular idea (as opposed to general information) from someone else I have acknowledged it in the above list. The idea network, however, is such that I sometimes think that emanations or idea pheromones may well reach out from unread pages to connect with the mind that wants to connect with them; for that reason I shall list here two books that I have only turned the pages of but I am well aware that even chapter headings and picture layout can move the mind one way or another; one is *A Study of Vermeer* by Edward A. Snow (University of California Press, Berkeley, 1979). The elegance of the production of this book, the quality and choice of reproductions, and the general layout are so finely tuned to the spirit of the painter that it cannot fail to sensitize and stimulate even the unreader. The other is *The Prophet Elijah in the Development of Judaism* by Aharon Wiener, in the Littman Library of Jewish Civilization series (Routledge & Kegan Paul, London, 1978). It seems to me that just glancing at random lines in Wiener's text made Elijah, all strange and wild and falling apart with the power that possessed him, leap newly vivid into my mind where a place had already been prepared for him not only by the Holy Scriptures but also by a song that I heard in a shortwave broadcast from Israel: *Eliyahu*, sung by Mordechai Ben David (the LP is "Moshiach is Coming Soon," Aderet Records). This Sabbath-night song was translated for me in Jerusalem the Golden, the shop in Golders Green where I bought the record, by Alan Cohen, a stranger whose help I sought; he did it with a spontaneous enthusiasm that seemed to arise from the very essence of Elijah, the quintessential, the engodded stranger.

R.H.

MR RINYO-CLACTON'S OFFER

I

Mr Rinyo-Clacton

He was in formal gear, black tie. A tall man and broad, rosy cheeks, spar-kling eyes, military moustache, black hair greying at the temples—early fifties was my guess. Looked posh, looked like a man who was used to the best of everything. My vision was a little unreliable but he was in sharp focus, coming up the stairs towards me with an interested expression on his face. This was in the tube station at Piccadilly Circus and I was sitting on the floor in the corner at the top of the stairs where you go down to the left for the eastbound platform and to the right for the westbound. The prevailing smell was of hamburgers and frying. With the sound of many footsteps the world went past me coming and going. In a poster on the wall a large black rugby player hurtled towards me at full speed. "IMAG-INE A TRAIN HURTLING TOWARDS YOU AT FULL SPEED," said the poster. "NOW DOUBLE IT."

Mr Best-of-Everything stopped in front of me. "No instrument," he said. Big voice and he talked like a BBC correspondent, Martin-Bell-in-Sarajevo sort of thing. "Nothing for coins to be dropped into, so you're not busking. Are you begging?"

"No." I wasn't sure why I was there. I'd been drinking a lot since

Serafina left and I sometimes found myself doing odd things in unexpected places.

"Thinking about the Big What-Is-It, are you?"

"What's the Big What-Is-It?"

"You tell me."

"I don't think I want to."

"Perhaps another time."

"Are you cruising or what? Do I look like a bit of rough to you?"

"You look like a bit of misery. If you fancy a chat we could meet this evening at the opera. They're doing *Pelléas* with Celestine Latour—best Mélisande since Mary Garden. Turn up around seven and an usher will show you to my box." He took a card out of a silver case and handed it to me.

"Why me?" I said. "What do you want?"

"Come to the opera and we'll talk about it."

"Which opera? Covent Garden or the ENO?"

He winced. "Please—the idea of *Pelléas* in English is abhorrent. Must go now. See you later. Or not, whichever." In the fresh breeze he made as he passed me I smelled money and something else, medicinal and disciplinary, that I thought of as bitter aloes. As far as I know I've never smelled bitter aloes but the name suggests the smell I have in mind. The card said, in an elegant little typeface:

T. Rinyo-Clacton

2

Serafina

Long black hair. Sometimes it fell across her face like a raven's wing. Even in repose she seemed to be standing on some bleak northern strand, howling at the grey waves with her hair whipping in the wind. There is a Scottish expression: "to dree one's weird." To undergo one's destiny is what it means and you could see that happening in the long beauty of her face that was sometimes softly rounded and sometimes like the blade of a knife. Her great dark eyes under the flare of their black brows seemed always to be looking into a darkness beyond the light; her elegant mouth seemed murmurous with spells, succulent with kisses, speechless with sadness. She bought her clothes at cancer and multiple-sclerosis charity shops—droopy jumpers and long swinging print skirts worn with steel-toed boots. She looked thin in her clothes but the nakedness of her long body offered surprising curves and pearly roundnesses, aloof and exciting. So beautiful and strange she was, my Serafina, so magical. How could I have hoped not to lose her!

3

At the Opera

"Sexiest voice in the business, that Latour," said Mr Rinyo-Clacton. "So mysterious, her Mélisande, so haunted and haunting, so full of death! First words out of her mouth are '*Ne me touchez pas!*' Don't touch me! But she's expecting to be touched, she's a kind of touchstone—people reveal themselves by what they do with her; she seems so vulnerable that she makes things happen. She's afraid that Golaud is going to tear her clothes off and have her right there by the pool in the wood; maybe in some way she even wants it, who knows? Why is she crying when we first see her? What was done to her before Golaud found her by the pool? What about that golden crown glimmering under the water, eh? Is that her lost virginity or what?"

Although I'd heard bits of *Pelléas et Mélisande* here and there I rarely went to the opera and I'd never seen it before or read anything about it. Seeing it now from Mr Rinyo-Clacton's box I found that the story, the music, and the staging took me to a place where I couldn't be sure of anything; all of it seemed to be speaking to me in a way that I didn't understand. The dark wood through which Golaud followed a trail of blood, the pool by which Mélisande huddled so pitifully—the look of them troubled me.

With the help of the surtitles I followed the action carefully. When Golaud asked her if anyone had hurt her Mélisande said, "Everyone," and I felt guilty; she looked like Serafina. What had they done to her? She didn't want to say. She said her golden crown had fallen into the water. Golaud said he could see it glimmering down there and it was very beautiful. Where had she got it? *He'd* given it to her, she said. Who? Her answer to that was that she didn't want it. Golaud noted that the pool wasn't very deep and he could easily reach in and retrieve it but Mélisande threatened to throw herself into the water if he did—not much of a threat really, if the water was that shallow.

Golaud kept trying to find out where she'd come from but he couldn't get a straight answer out of her. She said she'd run away, that she was cold, that she'd come from far away. She marvelled at his grey hair, she asked if he was a giant. Partly she acted as if she could be picked up but she also behaved like an animal wary of traps.

When Golaud suggested that she come with him she said she'd rather stay alone in the wood. When he asked her a second time she said, "Where to?" He said he didn't know, that he too was lost. Then she went with him. The music had murmured and surged like the sea, full of darkness and death.

"What do you think of it so far?" said Mr Rinyo-Clacton.

"Golaud isn't right for her," I said.

"That's why it isn't called *Golaud et Mélisande*," he said. Sparkling and rosy-cheeked Mr Rinyo-Clacton with his silver card-case, slurping oysters and sipping Cristal '71, a champagne so far beyond my means that I'd never even heard of it. And I, too, sipping Cristal '71 and slurping oysters that smelled of the sea in Mr Rinyo-Clacton's crimson and gilded box at the Royal Opera House, our refreshments catered by his minder with hands that looked capable of crushing a skull like a walnut. He also was in formal attire and almost invisible in his attendance. Except for the hands. I thought his name might be Igor but it was Desmond.

"I have an odd collection of books," I said. "One of them is an archaeological dictionary."

"Ah!" said Mr Rinyo-Clacton, squeezing lemon juice on to an oyster.

"You call yourself Rinyo-Clacton," I said. The Cristal '71 was like liquid velvet and my worods, my woordos, my words came out of my mouth in such a way that I felt entirely other than what I was used to. "Rinyo-

Clacton is the name given to a Late Neolithic pottery style found in Scotland and in southern England."

"What are we but clay," said Mr Rinyo-Clacton, "and infirm vessels all. One million pounds."

The long darkness of Serafina's hair! The raven's wing of it sweeping over my face! Gone! "One million pounds what?"

"Later," he said as the house lights dimmed, the audience murmured, coughed, and shifted from buttock to buttock; the conductor appeared, bathed briefly in his spotlight, bowed to us, then faced the orchestra and lifted his baton. The curtain went up, the music and the voices rose and fell like the sea, after a time becoming Mélisande's song as she combed her hair in the tower window. *"Mes longs cheveux descendent . . ."* she sang. "My long hair goes down to the door of the tower; my hair is waiting for you . . . " said the surtitles over the stage, and I began to cry as Mélisande, leaning from her tower window, let down her long, long hair to cover the face of Pelléas.

4

The Low and Delicious Word

Rising and falling like the sea, the powerful Mr Rinyo-Clacton, long and strong, managing me with a firm hand in the dark wood of his shadowy bedroom, on silken sheets among the glints and gleams of gold and silver, porcelain, bronze, ebony, tinted mirrors, coloured glass, and the smell that I thought of as bitter aloes. In the black marble fireplace the flames flickered and purred. "Say it!" he whispered in my ear as he rode me. "Say it, the low and delicious word death!"

My head was still going round. "Death!" I said. "Death, death, death, death!"

"Yes!" He came, and still holding me to him, quietly began to weep. " 'Whereto answering,' " he murmured brokenly, " 'the sea,

> Delaying not, hurrying not,
> Whisper'd me through the night, and very plainly
> before daybreak,
> Lisp'd to me the low and delicious word death,
> And again death, death, death, death . . . ' "

Serafina! I thought, remembering the taste of her on my tongue, the fragrance of her skin, the scent of her hair. The music of *Pelléas et Mélisande* was still with me, rising and falling, surging like the sea, death glimmering in moonlight on the water. Serafina! Far away, the land receding in the night to leave the horizon empty in the dawn.

"How was it for you, Jonny?" said Mr Rinyo-Clacton.

I shook my head. I'd never before had sex with another male. What did it mean? I hadn't been too drunk to know what I was doing. Was I losing my manhood?

"Nothing to say? Still the shy little virgin?" He slapped my thigh. "I hadn't planned this," he said, "but we might as well begin as we mean to go on . . ."

"I don't think I want to go on." I pulled away and turned to face him. The champagne had worn off somewhat. His skin was blotchy, his breath was bad. I felt sore and thought I might be bleeding. He hadn't used a condom. How many others had he done this with? Why had he been weeping?

"What I mean," he said, "is that I must be master—you understand?"

"You've just given a pretty good demonstration of that, I think."

"I'm not talking about sex now. When I saw you sitting on the floor in the tube station I thought I saw death looking out of your eyes. Was I right?"

I picked my clothes up off the floor and started to get dressed. I wondered if there was anyone buried under the floorboards, and yet that room with its glints and gleams, its flickering shadows and its smell of bitter aloes had an atmosphere that I felt rather at home in. Good God! Had I wanted this? The shadows were peopled by African figures, most of them with erect members. I was stood by a low black bookcase, on top of which was a primitive-looking clay pot, greyish-black and decorated with a simple geometric pattern of grooves. It was about nine inches high, eight inches wide at the top, tapering to six at the bottom. It was like the illustration in my *Dictionary of Archaeology*: Rinyo-Clacton, Late Neolithic. It was filled with black pebbles. I held some in my hand, heard them clicking in the tidewash, heard the sighing of the sea. "What you saw looking out of my eyes was most of a bottle of gin," I said.

"It seemed like more than gin to me." He was still naked, flaunting himself.

"That's your problem," I said, turning away.

"Why had you drunk so much gin that you sat down on the floor in Piccadilly Circus tube station?"

"Serafina's gone." I needed to hear myself saying her name to him; it was like chewing a razor blade. In our flat were plants that she watered faithfully; I never remembered the names of them except the cyclamen and the one that hung in front of the window, sunlight through its leaves: the Russian vine. The cyclamen seemed to me a secret self of Serafina, as if it might at some time speak in a tiny Serafina voice and explain everything to me.

"Ah!" said Mr Rinyo-Clacton, putting on a dressing-gown, "Serafina's gone and that's why you sat down on the floor in the tube station."

"Something like that."

"I understand perfectly: she was everything to you, yes?"

"Yes."

"So it was as if the world had been pulled out from under your feet and you had to sit down."

"Yes."

"Maybe you found yourself not caring very much whether you lived or died."

I shrugged.

"I have a sure instinct in these matters," he said, "and I say again that I saw death looking out of your eyes. And if the death in you wants to come out, as I think it does, I'll buy it for a million pounds and give you a year to enjoy the million."

"You want to buy my death for a million pounds!"

"That's what I said: one million pounds, cash."

"What kind of a weirdo are you?"

"The kind with lots of money." His lips, I noticed, were wet. He had ugly hands, hairy and with thick fingers. "Death fascinates me," he said, "how there's one in each of us, waiting for its time. There's one in me as I speak to you but it's in no hurry. Yours, on the other hand, seems eager to come out. I want to watch it as one watches a woman undressing in a window; I want to think about how I'm going to fondle it and taste it when the time comes. Your death will be a juicy thing for me; when I was in you I could feel it, shy but ardent, responding to me."

I remembered a dream: Serafina and I crossing a lion-coloured desert until there mysteriously appeared before us an oasis, the feathery palm trees real in a way that only palm trees in dreams are; there were wild asses drinking at a shining dark pool in which the palms were reflected. I said, "What would the actual arrangement be?"

"As I've said, I'll give you one million pounds cash and one year to live. During that time I'll naturally want to stay in touch, visit you now and then, generally cultivate your ripening death. It'll be exciting for both of us, I think."

"What happens at the end of the year?"

"Not necessarily precisely at the year's end but whenever I choose after that I'll harvest you. It will be quick and merciful; you'll cease upon the midnight with no pain and your troubles will be over. If there's any money left I'll see that it goes to a loved one or the charity of your choice."

"Would you do the harvesting yourself or would Desmond do it for you?"

"I'll do it."

"Have you ever killed anyone before?"

"Gentlemen don't tell."

"Well," I said, "I've never had a proposition like this before. It's a big step to take, isn't it."

"Next to being born I'd say it's about the biggest."

"May I think about your offer?" I heard myself say that and I couldn't believe it. What was going on in my mind?

"It's definitely not to be undertaken lightly. Consider it carefully, dream about it even. *Pelléas* again tomorrow night—I'll be in my box. Desmond will drive you home."

In the lift I looked away from the mirror in which Desmond and I were reflected. The fluorescent light was both dim and unsparing. When we came out of the building the air on my face was cold but not refreshing.

Even at midday Belgravia looks like a necropolis to me but at least one has a sense of life going on not too far away; at three o'clock on this October morning, however, Eaton Place with its long vistas of sepulchral white-pillared black-numbered porticos seemed a street of ghost dwellings on a dead planet; I wondered what might be listening to my footsteps. Maybe this is a dream, I thought—a desert dream instead of an oasis one.

Mr Rinyo-Clacton's motor, said Desmond when I asked him, was a 1931 King's Own Daimler. It was in more than mint condition, a grand and stately shining black machine upholstered in leopardskin and with a bit more under the bonnet than had been available in 1931. It had of course the usual amenities: bar and escritoire, TV, telephone, fax, tape and CD players and a sound system of upper-class fidelity. This car, a fit conveyance for emperors, kings, sultans, and heads of public utilities, smelled like a life I had no idea of and slipped through the late-night streets like a shining shadow in a silent dream. I thought of Mélisande's golden crown glimmering beneath the water. "Have you been with Mr Rinyo-Clacton long?" I asked the back of Desmond's head.

"Yes."

"Has he done this sort of thing before?"

"What sort of thing do you mean?"

"Offering to buy somebody's death."

Desmond's eyes in the rear-view mirror were hooded and alert. "Gentlemen's gentlemen don't tell," he said.

5

The Goneness of Serafina

I was back at my flat at about half-past three that morning. When I turned on the lights the place came out of the darkness like an animal caught in the headlamps of a car. All the plants whose names I'd forgotten reproached me silently; the Russian vine looked moribund. "Sorry," I said. I filled a jug and poured water into the vine's pot but the water ran through the dry soil and dripped on to the floor. "I'll get back to you," I said.

Poofter, whispered the cyclamen.

"I know that's how it looks," I said, "but that isn't actually how it is." I went round and watered everyone and topped up the Russian vine, then I poured myself a large whisky. I found it difficult to look my flat in the eye; I felt ashamed, confused, guilty. "What can I say?" I said. "Maybe a year from now I'll be dead and you'll forget me."

I spent a long time in the shower. It's one of those that comes off the bath taps and there's never quite enough pressure. I wanted to be sheathed in clean hot water but I could never get myself completely covered by it.

It was quarter to five by the time I'd ministered to my soreness and got to bed and it took me a long time to fall asleep. I kept thinking about the unsheathed Mr Rinyo-Clacton and seeing newspaper and magazine photographs of rock, ballet and film stars as they looked before they died. I saw also men in hospices keeping vigil by their dying lovers. Listen, I told myself, maybe he hasn't got anything and you didn't get anything from him; he's a millionaire and probably he's very careful. Oh yes, I answered myself, he was very careful with you, wasn't he. What if—O God!—what if he's one of those people who get infected and then they want to pass it on? Stop that, I said, and my mind, like a child clutching a teddy bear, went to Serafina.

Serafina was cook and baker at the Vegemania Restaurant in Earl's Court Road. Her body smelled of fear and desire; her voice was soft; her eyes implacable. Her brown loaves were like bread from a fairy tale; her potato pancakes sizzled with lust and tasted of fidelity. At home and when we dined out she went for red meat and she liked it rare. Serafina was unique; she was impressive. I've seen the Whitbread Brewery horses standing in the rain with steam coming up off their backs and people plying them with apples and lumps of sugar and speaking privately to them—they wanted to ingratiate themselves with something ancient and elemental in these great animals. That's how people responded to Serafina. There was nobody like her and that she loved me was a continual astonishment to me. Now she was gone because I'd been an idiot.

I was an Excelsior salesman. My job was to sit in a little office over the Long Trail Travel Agency and ring people up to sell them the Excelsior Self-Realisation Programme. "Hello, Mr Dimbulb," I'd say. "I'm with the Excelsior Corporation. Our database shows that eighty-three per cent of the people of your age and socio-economic bracket realise only forty to sixty per cent of their personal potential. Of that eighty-three per cent, some twelve per cent have what it takes to do better and go farther and these are the people Excelsior wants to work with. Our computer tells us that you, Mr Dimbulb, are in that twelve per cent and you qualify for a free evaluation and consultation." And so on. If the prospect turned out to be a live one the next step was a visit from me with brochures, questionnaires, videotapes, books, and a contract. The Excelsior Self-Realisation Programme Starter Kit sold for £125 but the contract obliged the self-realiser to buy at least six more videos at £25 each from the monthly catalogues.

The Excelsior logo showed a muscular naked man with a chisel and mallet emerging from the rock out of which he was carving himself.

"SHAPE YOUR OWN DESTINY" was the slogan under the chiselling man. There was no chiselling woman on the logo but many of our customers were women and more than twelve per cent of them were interesting, attractive, and available. They didn't just want casual sex, they wanted meaningful sex with word action: they wanted love. My consultation and evaluation sessions were full of temptation which I resisted only some of the time. I liked crossing that magic line from stranger to lover; I liked the rumpled sheets of strange beds in which new women moaned with pleasure and told me things they'd never told anyone else. They also wrote letters to me, some of which Serafina found in my pockets.

"I gave you everything I had," she said, "and you shat on it."

I said I was sorry. I said it many times and in many different ways but to no avail; pleas were useless. There was a whirlwind of things being flung into bags. "I'll come back for the rest of it," she said, and was gone. The orphaned Russian vine hung by the window unwatered and the cyclamen cursed me in a tiny Serafina voice.

How could I have forgotten what she was to me? From the first moment when she spoke to me in the Vegemania four years ago I knew she was my destiny-woman, my everything-woman. She was strange and mysterious, and although after a while I could predict what she'd say and do in many situations, I never altogether understood her. We liked much of the same music, from Monteverdi to Portishead, but her reading taste ran to thrillers which bored me and she was also keen on such things as the Australian TV soaps, *Neighbours* and *Home and Away*, which I had no time for. She kept up with them on the TV in the kitchen at the Vegemania while preparing the evening menu; she liked Oprah Winfrey too, and various sitcoms with canned laughter, but I reminded myself that nobody was perfect.

Like every couple we had rows sometimes but we didn't argue by the same rules and I often wasn't clear about the outcome until later, when her actions would give me a clue: if, for example, she brought me a cup of rose-hip tea on a camomile night I knew it for a reminder that we were still each other's destiny-people no matter what. I'd never thought of how it would be if Serafina left me, and when she did, the effect was such that Mr Rinyo-Clacton found me sitting on the floor in Piccadilly Circus tube station.

At home I found that some things were no longer possible; I put on one of our favourite Purcell tracks, "Musick for a while," sung by Michael Chance, and not only did it not all my cares beguile, it made me want to jump out of a window. Most of our music collection was now nothing I could listen to.

Post addressed to Jonathan Fitch came through my letter-box and that was who I was. I had a National Insurance number and an account at Lloyds; I had a shoe size and a blood type and a bunch of keys. I was twenty-eight years old and not too bad-looking; in the past, when things came to an end with a woman, I'd always been able to find someone new. But now that Serafina was gone I realised too late that I was possessed by her—I had no self to offer anyone else. The house of my self is built on a rock of panic. Now the house was gone and only the panic remained.

My mind sorted desperately through its souvenirs of Serafina: her voice; her body; her potato pancakes. The look of her as she stretched to water the Russian vine; the slanty smile she gave me with the sunlight through the leaves haloing her hair. Destiny! That was the word that kept repeating itself in my head, and I remembered our beginning.

6

Our Beginning

Four years ago I went into the Vegemania for the first time, through a little hallway where a bulletin board offered several kinds of yoga and meditation, International Healing Tao, Creative Movement and Dance Improvisation, shiatsu, acupuncture, full body massage, rooms to let, vans for sale, Urdu tuition, and recorder lessons.

The Vegemania Restaurant and Whole Food Shop was in Earl's Court Road between a *bureau de change* and a one-hour photographic service. The place was full of sunlight (particularly bleak that day), stripped pine, and blackboards with the menu written in a bold round hand. I sat down facing the window with a view of the street and passers by, all of whom seemed to be free of any fixed routine and with better places to go than I. Many of them were strapped and belted into great bulging rucksacks that they bore effortlessly and most of them carried plastic bottles of mineral water that sparkled in the sun as if they'd been filled at the Fountain of Youth.

Not that I was old—I was only twenty-four back then—it was just that the man in the Excelsior logo was so much further out of his rock than I was. The first video in the Excelsior Starter Kit began with Dr Gunther Rumpel, our consultant psychologist, fixing the viewer with a steely blue eye and saying, "Be honest. In the matter of realising your potential, how would you grade yourself on a scale from one to ten?" At that time I had no idea how to grade myself because I hadn't yet worked out what my potential was.

Since university I'd had two jobs before Excelsior and been sacked from both. At Harmattan Academic Press I'd made myself redundant by differing with Dr Auguste Birnaud on seventeen points in his *Hermetic Modes of Semiosis in the Poetry of Rainer Maria Rilke*; my next job was writing copy at Folsom & Deere Advertising which lasted until a client meeting with Big Boy candy bars in which I suggested the line, "Get your mouth around a Big Boy." Shortly after that I answered an ad with the headline "REALISE YOUR POTENTIAL" and I became part of Excelsior.

It was lunchtime and the Vegemania was filling up with hungry people and the healthy smells of whole-food cuisine. I was looking at a blackboard and trying to decide whether I wanted tofu-fried tortellini with carbonara sauce and a green salad or tagliolini with pesto and sun-dried tomatoes when I became aware of a new smell that made the others fade to nothing. This smell was in its crispy golden-brownness the ultimate expression of the art of frying; it was earthy and transcendental, seductive and spiritual. I had to swallow my saliva before I could speak. "What is that smell?" I asked the waitress.

"Sorry about that," she said. "The extractor fan's quit on us."

"Please don't be sorry, just tell me what it is."

"Potato pancakes." She pointed to the blackboard where they were listed, served with sour cream and apple sauce, for £3.50.

Potatoes! Growing in the earth, achieving self-realisation underground, waiting to be dug up. "That's what I'll have, please," I said.

In due course they appeared, three of them crispy and golden-brown on a white plate with a blue-and-gold border. Two little tubs as well, one with sour cream and one with apple sauce. The pancakes tasted more than good; they tasted of destiny: I knew that I had come to a time and a place that had been waiting for me. The sunlight seemed less bleak and my plate was empty.

As she cleared my place the waitress, a tall blonde all in black with a very short skirt, said, "How were they?"

"Great. Same again, please." I waited, feeling the thing build. This time I turned in my chair and saw a woman appear in the kitchen doorway. She had her black hair tucked up inside a scarf but a few wisps escaped. She was wearing a white apron over her jeans and jumper. She was only there for a moment, then her absence became the single event in the room—nothing else was happening. I tried to see her face again in my mind: a long face, beautiful and intense and concentrated as if trying to remember something. Three more potato pancakes appeared with sour cream and apple sauce, then once again my plate was empty.

"Had enough?" said the waitress.

I belched quietly behind my napkin. "Do it again, please," I said.

The third order of potato pancakes was brought to me by the cook herself. She gave me that concentrated look, smiled slantily, and said, "Nice juicy potatoes this time of year."

I smelled her sweat that had in it fear and desire and frying. "Today is the beginning," I said.

"Of what?"

"Everything."

And it was.

7

Herbert Sledge

Serafina and I usually woke up facing away from each other, and the first thing I always did on coming out of sleep was reach behind me to lay a hand on her hip. Then the day could begin.

But this was the morning after Mr Rinyo-Clacton; when I reached behind me there was no Serafina, the October sunlight was coming through the blinds and the desolation and dread that were always waiting rushed in on me. The events of last night insisted on being real and not a dream and I was no longer sure who or what I was—it was as if I was clinging to a tuft of grass on the face of a cliff and the grass was coming away in my hands. I'd sat on the floor in Piccadilly Circus tube station and now here I was, dangling over empty air.

I rang up Chelsea & Westminster Hospital. "Where do I go for an HIV test?" I asked.

"The John Hunter Clinic," said the man at the switchboard. "It's just next door to us." He gave me the number.

"I think I need an HIV test," I said when the John Hunter Clinic came on the line.

"What sort of risk factor are we talking about?" said the man at the other end.

For a moment I thought he wanted some kind of number, then the penny dropped. Despite my sore bum, I tried to be as refined as he was. "I might have been exposed last night," I said. "It was the first and only contact of that kind I've ever had."

"It's too soon for anything to show up in a test—" he said, "there's a three-month window."

"A three-month window!" I imagined the ledge of that window; looking down past my feet I saw the street far, far below, where tiny faces looked up expectantly. Some of them shouted, "What are you waiting for?"

"Three months! I've got to wait three months before I know anything?"

"That's right. We'll be happy to test you at any time before that but it won't be conclusive. We can test you for other sexually transmitted diseases such as gonorrhoea and herpes simplex and so on and we can give you counselling. Our walk-in clinic is open every day from eight-thirty to four-thirty except Wednesday when we open at eleven-thirty."

"Thank you," I said, and rang off. Counselling! That's what I should have had before I started shaping my destiny in strange beds. Three months! I had no appetite for breakfast but I forced myself to have my usual grapefruit juice, muesli, and coffee. The sky was grey, the day looked doubtful and unsure of its potential as I set out for the Excelsior office, only a few minutes from where I live in Nevern Place. On the way I stopped at the Vegemania: it wasn't open yet and nobody was visible through the window. Where was Serafina staying? She'd no place of her own any more. Was there already someone else waking up beside her?

I still wasn't ready for Excelsior but I didn't want to be alone so I crossed the road and went on to the tube station. With a sinking feeling in my stomach and a tingling at the back of my neck I moved through the human swarm that poured out into Earl's Court Road. Where were they going, that they were all in such a hurry? Not just the young with their rucksacks and mineral water but middle-aged and old people as well, all with places to go that they were eager to get to. A young man at the entrance gave me a handbill:

★★★★KATERINA★★★
MODERN PSYCHIC AND CLAIRVOYANT
No crystal ball, no bullshit. This is the real thing.
You pay nothing if I can't help you.
★★★★★★★★★★

There was no address but the telephone number was a local one. Who knows? I thought. Maybe this is part of my destiny too. I stuck the hand-bill in my pocket, turned back towards Benjy's, picked up a takeaway coffee and a Danish, walked back to the corner, turned left into Kenway Road, continued past Al-Rawshi Take Away Lebanese Cuisine, Launder-ama, Hi-Tide Fish & Chips, and other international enterprises, opened the hallway door at Long Trail Travel, slowly climbed the stairs to Excelsior, said good morning to my colleagues Phil and Gary, both of whom observed that I looked terrible. I checked the first name on my list, and dialled the number.

"Hello," said the voice at the other end.

"Hello," I said. "Am I speaking to Herbert Sledge?"

"Yes. Who is this?" He sounded young and short on patience.

"My name is Jonathan Fitch, Mr Sledge, and I'm with the Excelsior Corporation. We've got a list of people with potential and you're on it."

"Get to the point. What are you selling?"

"Our database shows that eighty-three per cent of the people in your age and socio-economic bracket realise only between forty and sixty per cent of their personal potential. Of that eighty-three per cent . . . "

"Stop," said Sledge. "You sound like an educated man, Mr Fitch. How old are you?"

"What's that got to do with anything?"

"You don't want to answer the question, do you."

"I'm twenty-eight."

"I'm twenty-four and I'm Head of Genetic Research at Omni Labo-ratories. Right now I'm investigating hierarchal language analogues in non-coding DNA. What are you doing besides peddling some bullshit self-improvement course?"

"We can't all be investigating non-coding DNA," I said, feeling an upsurge of gastric acid. "Some of us have to sell bullshit self-improvement courses."

Sanjay Prasad walked in just as I said that: my boss, owner of Excelsior Corporation, Long Trail Travel, Prasad Printing and Copying Services, and Kashmiri Garden Furnishings. Gold Rolex, blue and white striped shirt with a white collar, and some really awful aftershave. "That's quite an original sales approach," he said. "I hope you have a lot of luck with it at your next place of employment."

"I have to go now," I said to Herbert Sledge. "It's been great fun talking to you. Have a nice DNA."

"See Yasmin in Accounting downstairs," said Sanjay, looking at his watch. "She will settle up with you."

"Are you telling me this is goodbye? I've consistently scored more sign-ups than anyone else in this room."

"I know. This isn't business, it's personal—I just happen to hate your guts. You read Classics at university and you think what we do here is shit."

"Don't you?"

"No, I do not. Our files are full of letters from clients who tell us that their lives are better in every way because of the Excelsior Self-Realisation Programme. The difference between you and me is that you're slumming and you think in a slumming way whereas I am an honest man selling an honest service and I take pride in what I'm doing. Maybe you should sign up for the course; I'll even give you a discount although you're no longer an employee. I'm serious—I think it would help you."

"I'm deeply moved by your concern, Sanjay, but I'm not sure I want to realise any more of myself than I've already done. Maybe I'll try it in my next incarnation."

"Ah! Is this a racist remark I'm hearing?"

"Not at all; if I had any best friends I'm sure some of them would be reincarnations. Bye bye, Sanjay. Have a nice life."

"And you."

We didn't shake hands.

As of that morning I had £204.28 in my account at Lloyds and £732.74 at the Halifax. The rent for the flat, due in eight days, was £450.

8

Room 18

I needed a quiet place where things weren't happening too fast; I have often found tranquillity at the National Gallery so I went there now. There was a gentle rain coming down when I emerged from Charing Cross tube station; the streets were bright with reflections, the buses were intensely red. Trafalgar Square was crowded as always and on the National Gallery porch tourists heavy with lenses peeped through viewfinders at Nelson on his column, at the fountains jetting their white water into the grey rain, at the bronze lions, and at other tourists wet and gleaming.

I headed directly for Room 18, a tiny room containing only the black perspective box or peepshow by Samuel van Hoogstraten (1627–1678). I'd been hoping to have it to myself for a moment or two but a Japanese couple were occupying both peep-holes. As they left, a rush of schoolgirls filled the room with the smell of rain, their hot and feral fragrance, and their chatter; then they were gone like a flight of starlings and I was alone with the peepshow.

It's about as big as a medium-large fish tank and the peep-holes, one at each end, offer two apparently three-dimensional views of the interior of a seventeenth-century Dutch house: in it are a number of red side chairs with leather seats, on one of which is a letter with the signature of the artist; there are pictures on the walls; there are windows and there are doorways to other rooms. In one of those rooms a woman lies in a curtained bed. Is she ill, is she dying? No one knows. In another room a woman sits reading while a man outside the window looks in at her. Elsewhere a solitary broom, that frequent emblem of Dutch tidiness, leans against a wall. There is of course one of those patterned marble floors one sees so often in Vermeer and de Hooch; alternate black and white concentric squares encouraging belief in the idea of order in the universe. On the floor sits a black-and-white spaniel of some kind; from the look on that dog's face I've always assumed it to be male. I call him Hendryk.

One side of the box is fitted with clear glass; probably in the seventeenth century that side was covered with translucent paper and the box placed near a window or a candle for illumination; now it has its own special lamp. When you look through the glass it becomes clear that the apparent reality seen through the peep-holes is all illusion: things are not always in proper scale or relation one to the other: seats and backs of chairs go up walls, legs lie on the floor; the head of the woman in the bed is like a pancake.

Hendryk has his lower part flat on the floor and his upper part going up the wall but when you see him through the peep-hole he sits solidly on the floor with space all around him. There are no lenses in the peep-holes and no mirrors in the box; the illusion is achieved by distorting a two-dimensional painting and controlling the angle and field of view in such a way that an undistorted three-dimensional scene is made to appear through the peep-holes.

It would have been a great deal simpler and certainly no more time-consuming to build a three-dimensional model of this interior but no, the illusion is the thing; and to produce this illusion van Hoogstraten had to work out the most abstruse calculations in perspective before painstakingly painting the walls and floor of the box. And the custodian of this illusion, the one who steadfastly contemplates it and meditates on it, is Hendryk. Inside his painted head he has of course his own illusory thoughts; we've had many interesting conversations and as often as not I find him helpful. Today, however, Hendryk gave me nothing. "What," I said, "am I all alone then?"

"Never, dear boy!" said the voice of Mr Rinyo-Clacton. Yes, there he was, no more smartly dressed than I, wearing jeans and a blue anorak, his smell compounded and intensified by the wet Gore-Tex.

"Have you been following me?" I said.

"Not really. You just happened to be ahead of me as I was coming here. That dog is really something, eh? That dog is at the heart of the illusion of reality, wouldn't you say?"

"I'd prefer not to say just now if you don't mind."

"Mind? Why should I mind? I respect your intellectual privacy. Let's have lunch, shall we?"

"Thank you but I think I need to be alone for a while."

"Right you are, Jonathan. I'm off then, see you tonight at the opera."

I didn't say anything. I watched him go, then I tried Hendryk again and again he gave me nothing. I abandoned the peepshow and fell back to a secondary position, Room 16 and de Hooch's *The Courtyard of a House in Delft*. The clean-swept courtyard and its tutelary broom, the goodwife with her daughter, and seen through a red-brick archway, the shadowy figure of a second woman with her back to the observer, standing like a sentinel guarding that cloistered domesticity—everything in that picture invited me to rest awhile in its quiet world. But today there was no rest. I had a solitary lunch at The Brasserie, then I went out into the rain again.

9

Katerina

"Hello," said a woman's voice.

"Is this Katerina?" I said.

"Yes."

"I've got one of your handbills and I think I need a no-bullshit modern psychic. Can I make an appointment to see you?"

She didn't answer. After a few seconds I said, "Hello? Are you there?"

"Sorry, I was still listening to your voice." Her own voice was very shapely, with a slight German accent. "You want to see me?" She said it as if she meant the actual seeing, and there came to mind the Caspar David Friedrich painting of his wife, seen from behind, standing at a window and looking across the River Elbe at a row of distant poplars.

"Yes," I said. "You sound as if you're standing at a window looking across a river."

"Like the Friedrich painting? No, I'm standing in the kitchen looking at a dripping tap. What is your name, please?"

"Jonathan Fitch."

"Your voice troubles me, Mr Fitch. What do you think I can do for you?"

"I don't know, but talking to you seems to be the next thing for me to do. What do you charge?"

"Twenty-five pounds if I can do something, nothing if I cannot. It comes and goes—sometimes yes and sometimes no. I'm seeing blue eyes, fair hair. Am I right?"

"Yes. What else do you see?"

"Nothing. I'm hearing that you're afraid, yes?"

"Yes."

"Me too. This is not unnatural to the human condition. Even sometimes it is useful. Can you be here in a quarter of an hour or so?"

"Yes, I can."

"OK, you come, we talk—we see how it goes." She gave me her address. "I am Flat A; the name on the buzzer is Bechstein, like the piano."

She was in Earl's Court Road, a little way past the Waterstone's at the corner of Penywern Road, in one of those big white Victorian houses converted to flats. When I came up the steps I saw a silver-haired woman looking out of the front window. I buzzed the Bechstein button, said I was Jonathan Fitch, and she came to the door. In her sixties, I thought; hair in a Psyche knot. She would have been a beauty when young—quite tall, with the daring look of one who might have parachuted behind enemy lines. Wearing an old grey cardigan and a faded print dress. Black stockings and snakeskin shoes that must have been fifty years old. I wondered if she was seeing into my mind where my night with Mr Rinyo-Clacton was replaying itself more or less continuously.

"So," she said, shaking my hand, "here are you and it's very bad, that I already feel. Come in." From the next floor came the sound of *Pelléas et Mélisande*. Also the smell of something with a lot of garlic. "Mr Perez," she said, "in the flat above me, is a heavy Debussy-user."

"It's a small world."

"He wears two-tone shoes, carries a malacca cane, and has an extensive record collection that I have come to know very well. Being psychic I predict Ravel within the next hour." *Pelléas* and the smell receded as she closed the door of her flat behind us.

The high-ceilinged front room, the one I'd seen from the street, had nothing in it but a table and two chairs. There was an Art Nouveau lamp on the table making a little pool of light in the dusk that was gathering in the room. The white walls were bare except for a large framed print of Dürer's *Melencolia*.

I hadn't looked at that engraving for a long time, and seeing the darkly brooding winged woman or angel now I was struck by the energy of her brooding, the power in it; her thinking was not simply contemplative, it was going to make something happen: what with the dividers in her hand, the plane and saw, the hammer and tongs and other ironmongery, she seemed to be in the planning stages of some decisive action. The sandglass behind her right wing—surely that indicated that time was running out. And the bell nearby—for whom and for what would it ring? Or had it already rung? That sleeping dog, was she going to let it lie? And what about the polyhedron—was that not a reminder of the many sides of everything? Angel or woman, Melencolia with her wings could rise above the immediate problem for a longer view. The dog, such a very thin dog with its ribs sticking out, looked like a greyhound, a dog that hunts not by scent but by sight—it sees its prey and gives chase. On the wall behind the figure in the picture was a magic square in which all the numbers added up to thirty-four whether you did them vertically, horizontally, or on the diagonal.

Melencolia was not alone in the picture. Seated by a ladder and a pair of scales (Justice?), either close by or on the polyhedron (hard to make out which), was a surly winged infant, possibly asleep or perhaps just sulking. Was he the child of Melencolia? The picture seemed full of clues and portents, like a whole deck of Tarot cards. Undoubtedly Dürer, when he engraved *Melencolia* in 1514, had his own symbology in mind but now the picture was alone and independent of its maker; it could say what it liked, speak freely to any stranger and differently to each. I was troubled by that surly child; what would he grow up to be?

"You like melancholy?" said Katerina. "For you it's a normal state, yes?"

"It is now."

"Maybe before now also. It's a natural state, melancholy—like fear. Both belong to the human condition. Now I am going to tell you something that I'm wondering about: apart from this session we're going to have now I have a feeling that some kind of connection exists or is going to exist between you and me, a link of some sort, a *Verbindung*. Strange, yes? Do you feel that?"

"I don't know—when the handbill was given to me I felt as if I'd been waiting for it."

She moved behind me. "I'm just going to put my hand on the back of your neck," she said. Her touch was light, her hand cool and dry. "Now, come and sit down. We talk about this."

We sat at the table facing each other. She was wearing silver earrings, little owls. It was getting dark outside and the two of us in the lamplight were reflected in the window. The room behind us was lost in shadow. The glass bell-flower shade of the lamp was a delicate blue; the light through it seemed to come from a time when all kinds of questions had better answers than they do now. At the base of the lamp was a graceful little woman, bronze not spelter, whose figure was more revealed than concealed by the clinging drapery loosely belted at her hips. She had a quill pen in her right hand and her left held one end of a scroll that was balanced on her thigh. Her bare right foot was forward; her left rested lightly on a book. Her hair was loosely pinned up at the back and she wore a wreath in it—laurel, I thought. Her eyes were downcast, her sweet face pensive. I put my hand around her and ran my thumb over her belly and down her thigh. The room grew darker beyond the circle of the lamplight.

Katerina was looking towards the street and absently rubbing her left arm. The sleeve of the cardigan slid up and I saw numbers on her wrist. She offered me a cigarette; I shook my head. Did I mind if she smoked, she asked, and when I said no she lit up, took a deep drag, and coughed for a while. "I thought I am already dying from so many cigarettes," she said, "but no, still I am here. Many times I have foreseen my death and many times it has not happened. Some psychic I am. Give me your hands. May I call you Jonathan?"

"Please do."

"Jonathan, do you know why I put my hand on the back of your neck?"

"I think so."

"Shall I say what I am feeling? I think it will not be a big surprise for you."

"Yes, say it."

"Death is following you."

"I'm not sure whether it's following me or I'm following it."

"I can feel your uncertainty and I feel the closeness of death but I don't know what this is all about."

"I'd rather not explain just yet; first I'd like to know what you're getting from me because I don't quite know where I am with what's happening."

"OK—I try to feel what goes on in you where the words are not. Two, I get: death times two. Here I am confused with these two deaths." She let go of my hands and brought her own together on her chest with their knuckles touching. "One is real, it threatens from the outside; the other is in the mind and it threatens with the mind, yes?"

"I hope it's only in the mind. I've got three months ahead of me before I can be HIV-tested."

"You have been with a man?"

"Once only, last night."

"No protection?"

"No protection."

She was quiet for a few moments. Upstairs the murmurous sea-changes of *Pelléas*, still in Act One, stopped and the Ravel trio for piano, violin and cello, the one featured in the film *Un Cœur en Hiver*, began. Serafina and I had listened to that trio in my flat the first time we made love; I remembered her undressing for me, the poignancy of her body in the lamplight, the pearliness and the shadows.

"So," said Katerina, "you have played arsehole roulette and now you are afraid. I have several clients who have come to me like this. Sometimes, not always, I can see what other people cannot but I have never been able to see into the future and I can't say what will be three months from now."

She took my hands again. "In each of us lives the little animal of the self: nothing to do with the mind, it goes its own way; there is no talking to it. Sometimes it wants to live; sometimes it wants to die. Maybe you are in hospital for surgery, and while you are anaesthetised the little animal of the self makes up its mind. 'OK,' it says, 'this time I don't die.' Or it says, 'That's it—I have had enough and it's time to pack it in.' So now I listen for what the little animal of you is saying and it says yes and also it says no. It's a little confused, I think."

"So am I." Upstairs, Ravel was cut off halfway through the first movement and Berlioz came on with *Symphonie Fantastique*.

"What is it with this Mr Perez?" I said.

She shook her head. "His thoughts are sad; he has many regrets. Talk to me about yourself. Have you now become a convert to love between men?"

"No, it's just that I seem to have come unglued since Serafina left me." Then of course I had to tell her all about Serafina.

"Jonathan," said Katerina, "this that you have told me about you and Serafina is of course a big thing in your life but it is not—how shall I say it?—too much off the beaten track. Left to yourselves, the two of you would either find a way of getting past this together or going ahead separately. What I think is the big priority here is this death business. Something comes into my mind now and I say it; perhaps it is stupid but I say it anyhow. Have you ever read a book by the American writer John O'Hara, *Appointment in Samarra?*"

"No."

"In the front of it, for an epigraph, there is a tiny little story, only a paragraph it is, by Somerset Maugham: a merchant in Baghdad sends his servant to the market and there the servant is jostled by a woman whom he recognises as Death. She makes what he thinks is a threatening gesture so he hurries home and says to his master, 'Please lend me your horse. I saw Death in the market and she threatened me, so I want to ride to Samarra to get away from her.' The merchant lends him the horse and then he goes to the market and accosts Death. 'Why did you threaten my servant?' he says. 'That was not a threatening gesture,' says Death. 'It was one of surprise. I was startled to see that man in Baghdad today because I have an appointment with him this evening in Samarra.'" She blew out a big cloud of smoke. "Tell me your thoughts about this story."

"My first thought is that in this story Death is a woman. Until now, whenever I've read of Death as a person or seen it pictured it's been male. Somerset Maugham was homosexual; maybe for him Death was a woman. Of course there's a feminine element in every man."

"In you?"

"In every man."

"What do you think it wants, your feminine element?"

"Katerina, I thought you were a clairvoyant, not a shrink."

"Have you ever watched Oprah Winfrey? These days everybody is a shrink. Don't answer me if you don't want to."

"I don't know what my feminine element wants but I think my masculine element is tired and full of uncertainty."

Katerina held up her right index finger and made it go from side to side like a windscreen wiper. "So—which way is the needle pointing now?"

"You mean, towards male or female?"

"What you like—maybe life or death, I don't know."

"Death, I guess."

"Mr Rinyo-Clacton, what in your mind does he represent?"

"Death, I guess. But he's no one I'm attracted to."

"Don't worry about it, every kind of thing goes on in the mind all the time. Say more about the story."

"Well, if Death is out to get you there's no escaping, is there. It'll find you in Earl's Court or Piccadilly Circus or Belgravia or wherever. Maybe when it's time you put out signals without knowing it and Death homes in on them."

"Say more. Look at *Melencolia*. Look at her face, the polyhedron, the dog. What about that winged infant perched just behind her? A boy, do you think? Is he asleep? Sulking? Is he the child of Melencolia?" She held both my hands tightly. "Maybe—no, I don't want to put thoughts in your head. Is she sexy, Melencolia? She's well-built, not? Her eyes, how they burn, eh?"

We were quiet for a while. Upstairs Berlioz, like a musical Delacroix, moved on to the next part of his crowded canvas, the tenebrous waltz of the second movement—a cast of thousands, all of them shadows. I was thinking of Mr Rinyo-Clacton and my death that I had seen in his eyes. I remembered the sound of his weeping and tried to move my mind away from it. In the print on the wall the eyes of the winged woman burned with . . . what? What was she thinking of?

"Eros and Thanatos," said Katerina.

"What about them?"

"I don't know; my mind is a big confusion and words come out of my mouth. So rarely is anything separate from anything else. Nothing is simple. Sometimes we move towards what we think we move away from."

The white walls seemed to vibrate. Her hands felt full of the voices of the dead. I closed my eyes and tried to see Serafina but I couldn't. Katerina pulled her hands away and as I opened my eyes she was covering her face. "What is it?" I said.

She removed her hands; her eyes were very big. For a moment I saw her as a young woman, a woman to fall in love with. "I don't know," she said.

"Are you all right?"

"Yes, but I don't think I can do any more today. I don't know whether I've helped you at all."

"You have, in some way that I don't quite understand." She looked awfully tired. God knew what she had to deal with at twenty-five pounds a time. As I paid her I felt a surge of pity for her, that this woman who had worn, perhaps danced in, those snakeskin shoes, should have to do this for a living. "Can I come and see you again?" I said.

"Yes, but I don't want any more money from you—just come and talk to me when you feel like it, yes?"

"Yes, thank you." I kissed her hand.

"Such gallantry!" she said with a bewitching smile. "I see you out."

As we left the room I noticed a box of sheet music on the floor with something by Debussy on top. On the worn carpet were several places that looked less worn. "You play the piano?" I said.

She flushed. "I sold it. I like to play late at night and people bang on the door and shout." At the front door she took my hand in hers for a moment. "Be careful," she said. "Come safe to your house."

"Thank you," I said. "See you." As I left, Berlioz was into the fourth movement, and the muffled thunder of drums announced *March to the Scaffold*.

The Oasis

As I came down Katerina's front steps I saw Desmond in evening clothes but no Daimler. "Wait here," he said. "I'll bring the car around."

"How'd you know where to find me?"

"It's my job."

When the car pulled up and Desmond opened the door, I got into it. Right, I said to myself, it's only a matter of life and death—just go with the flow. As we moved smoothly eastwards I leant back against the leopardskin and closed my eyes and remembered the oasis dream.

October was, in one way or another, always a big month for Serafina and me: we met in October and she left me in our fourth October. The dream was a year ago, in our third October. For me the name of the month has in it a leaning forward, a striding, the sound of a stick rattling along iron railings, a hastening towards year's end and the dreeing of one's weird.

We were in Paris for a long weekend. The days were mostly bright, the weather mild. We went up and down the Seine on a *bateau mouche* while a relentless taped commentary in four languages told us what we were seeing on the Left Bank and the Right. "You'll get a stiff neck," said

Serafina as we passed under the Pont des Invalides and I admired the natural endowments of the pneumatic bronze river-nymphs on the bridge.

We went to Sacré-Coeur and rode a little fun-fair sort of train from Montmartre to Pigalle under a grey sky. In the Place Pigalle between a *Ciné video* and a *boulangerie* there was the vacant shell of what must have been a tavern or some kind of drinking-place. Its bulging face was shaped like a barrel, with indications of hoops and staves. Two deeply recessed barrel-shaped windows were its eyes; its clownish nose was the bottom of a barrel with the name Au Tonneau weathering into blankness on it; its mouth was a Gothic arch with its peak just below the nose. The eyes were shuttered and blind, the mouth sealed; the colour was the brownish-grey of forgottenness. From the pavement to just below the eyes Au Tonneau was palimpsested with tattered and fading posters heralding events long gone: Harry Belafonte! That empty barrel whose wine was long since spilt, its face kept looking at me.

We went to Nôtre Dame, climbed the spiral stone stairs of the North Tower and photographed each other with gargoyles; we went to the Musée Rodin and agreed that we liked Camille Claudel better. We dared to use the Métro and never once got lost. We did many tourist things, walked many miles with bottles of mineral water in our rucksacks, and chewed and swallowed many baguettes. But the dream—

On our last full day in Paris, the day of the Musée Rodin, we walked back by way of the Jardin du Luxembourg and the Boulevard Saint-Michel. Our hotel was in the Rue de la Bastille. We were footsore and weary but not in the mood for going indoors, so we headed for the Place des Vosges.

Having thoughtfully provided ourselves with two glasses, we bought a bottle of unchilled sauvignon on the way, tried to buy some ice at a café but were given it free of charge, went to the Place des Vosges, and found an empty bench. With the corkscrew on my Swiss Army knife I opened the bottle. I poured; we clinked glasses and drank the cold brightness of the wine that seemed to contain the whole mystery of our mingled selves. We drank the roundness of the day, the gold and the blue of it, the pang of October and Time's iron railings.

In the arcade over the road a little band of buskers were playing speeded-up jazz and standards but we heard them slowly: "Petite Fleur";

"Won't You Come Home, Bill Bailey?"; Thelonious Monk's "Well, You Needn't"; "Caravan"; "The Sheik of Araby"; and others. Ours was a back-to-back double bench; several shifts of couples came and went in various languages and friendly smiles.

The sun declined with Hesperidean tints; I went back and bought a second bottle and we put it away silkily and with heightened appreciation of the music and everything else. The day had become archival and permanent and we recognised the specialness of it. We looked at each other not only with love but with new liking for the kind of person each of us was. When we left we crossed the road to where the buskers were packing up and I gave them money. Harmoniously we wove our way back to the hotel, made love, and fell asleep.

That was when I had the dream: Serafina and I crossing a lion-coloured desert until the oasis mysteriously appeared, the feathery palm trees real in a way that only palm trees in dreams are; there were wild asses drinking at a shining dark pool in which the palms were reflected.

I woke up around eight o'clock in the evening and when I sat up Serafina woke too. "Such a strange dream I had," she said: "there were donkeys drinking at a pool . . ."

"Wild asses," I said.

"How can you tell the difference?"

"It's just one of those things you know in a dream. And there were palm trees."

"Yes, feathery palm trees—it was an oasis, and the desert all around us. You and I had crossed that desert."

The Daimler had stopped. Desmond opened the door for me. "Royal Opera House," he said.

The foyer was quiet and empty except for staff. I showed an usher Mr Rinyo-Clacton's card and made my way to his box.

II

Yes or No

"We're in Act Two now," whispered Mr Rinyo-Clacton with his mouth close to my ear. "Mélisande's not happy at the castle, she wants to go away, she thinks she might not live much longer. She's nothing but trouble, that girl."

"Why do you keep coming to this opera then?"

"I love it—there's so much death and mystery and darkness, so much uncertainty in the music. You never know for sure what's what in that story. It's like the sea: you never know what's coming up from that deep, deep chill beneath you."

I was surprised at how accurately he was describing my state of mind and my feelings about my own story. The music and the voices rose and fell like the sea as I tried to call up the oasis dream but my mind gave me the dead blind face of Au Tonneau, then the brooding Melencolia with her hammer and tongs and her greyhound. Other pictures also it offered but I looked away.

Act Two became Act Three, and again Mélisande let down her hair and Pelléas sent his kisses up it while I pitied the doomed lovers and tried to think about what I was going to do; I wanted to talk to Serafina to find out if there was any chance of getting back together before I went further down the road with Mr Rinyo-Clacton. And I wanted to ponder the many Samarras where Death appeared at the appointed time. A million pounds! There was applause, the curtain fell on Act Three, the house lights came up, and Desmond entered the box with champagne and caviare and toast. He poured and withdrew, his hands disappearing last, like the smile of the Cheshire Cat.

Mr Rinyo-Clacton extended his glass. "*Salud, pesetas, y amor, y tiempo para gustarlos,*" he said with a wink and a grin. I watched my glass go out to meet his and we clinked.

"Speaking of *salud* and *tiempo,*" I said, "I find myself wondering about last night."

"Mmmm!" He kissed his fingertips with a smacking sound. "For me it was special; you were absolutely wonderful with your virginal, some-what reluctant, submission to my desire and your own—as I think about it I'm getting excited all over again." He gripped my thigh with his very strong ugly hands, showed his very good teeth, and breathed his bad breath on me. "How was it for you?"

"Worrying. I'm going to ask you a straight question and I want a straight answer."

"Oh, dear, it's come to that, has it?"

"Just tell me, are you HIV positive?"

"Jonathan, please! Do I ask you questions like that? Our pleasure was the more exciting because it was edged with uncertainty and dread. Be a man, Jonny! Don't wimp out on me after such a promising start."

"The short answer, then, is that you're not going to tell me?"

"The short answer is, I have no idea. If I were the worrying sort I'd take precautions to begin with. As I'm not and I don't, you surely don't expect me to observe a three-month period of chastity and then go for an HIV test, do you?"

"Arsehole roulette," I said.

"If you like, and I think you do. In any case, such trifling worries are scarcely appropriate for a man who's considering the sort of offer I've made to you." He refilled our glasses and clinked his against mine again. "Tonight's the night, my boy."

"For what?"

"For you to say yes or no. We can't go on meeting like this indefi-

nitely—no such thing as a free lunch and all that. What's it going to be?"
His mouth was wet, possibly from the champagne.

"You're offering a million pounds," I said.

"And a year to enjoy it."

"Why would you want to do this—buy my death? If you want somebody's death, why can't you simply go out and kill somebody like an ordinary murderer?"

"It's sexier this way: if you agree to these terms it's the ultimate submission: mmmmmm, yes! Dark pleasure! Secret joy!"

"I think you must be crazy."

"Crazy? The word is meaningless, read the papers and tell me that we
live in a sane world. In any case, don't attempt to understand me—you'd
find yourself well beyond your depth. Just tell me whether you accept my
offer or not."

I tried to picture a million pounds. As far as I knew, the biggest bank-
note was a fifty. A million pounds would be twenty thousand of those. I
thought of films in which people opened attaché cases full of money neatly
stacked. Sometimes they got shot, stabbed, or blown up. I thought of *The
Treasure of the Sierra Madre*, the empty cloth bags and the gold dust
blowing in the wind down the mountain. Quite a few films with banknotes
blowing about too. I thought of Serafina humming to herself contentedly
in a custom-built kitchen. No yachts, no flash cars for me, only the power
to do as I liked, to carve the potential me out of the rock of nothingmuch.
Serafina and I could live a whole lifetime on a million pounds—if I had a
whole lifetime. She'd talked sometimes of how it might be to own her own
restaurant. I could see it vividly: The Omnivore. With potato pancakes on
the menu along with choice cuts and a dessert trolley with not too many
healthy things on it.

But! Would the million pounds really make any difference to Serafina?
It wouldn't cancel my infidelities. Or would it? I knew what life was like
without a million pounds but I had no idea what it might be like with.
Surely, I thought, it must make a difference in everything, in ways I couldn't
even imagine. The very way in which you opened your eyes in the morning
must be different; the way you walked and talked; the way you saw yourself in the morning mirror and the way others saw you—yes! If I saw myself differently, as I must, then Serafina would see me differently, yes? I
wasn't sure of that.

A year! If Mr Rinyo-Clacton kept his word. Would he? Hard to say—his idea of honour and truth might be idiosyncratic. Desmond appeared and filled my glass which I seemed to have emptied. How could I protect myself against the possibility of Mr Rinyo-Clacton's breaking his word? A document of some kind to be left with my solicitor and Mr Rinyo-Clacton to be informed of it:

> *Be it known that I, Jonathan Fitch, have entered into an agreement with the man known as T. Rinyo-Clacton who resides at such and such an address. For the sum of one million pounds Mr Rinyo-Clacton is entitled to take my life at any time after one year from this date. If I should meet with death before this date, the police are to be notified of this arrangement.*

I didn't actually have a solicitor and it seemed ridiculous to engage one expressly for the Rinyo-Clacton business; even if I did, telling Mr Rinyo-Clacton that such a document existed seemed unlikely to guarantee me the promised year. More and more I felt that he was a man who did whatever he liked whenever he liked and never got caught.

"I can hear the wheels in your head grinding," he said, "and I can assure you that anything you can think of has already occurred to me. I expect you'll want to protect yourself with some sort of document left with your solicitor and of course I'll do the same. Although my intention is to buy *your* death I am well aware that the conditions of the agreement will give you a powerful incentive for terminating *me*. Makes the whole thing more of a sporting proposition, I think—adds a little spice to both our lives."

I was certain then that he'd done this before. I found myself thinking of an old black-and-white film, *The Hounds of Zaroff*, in which Count Zaroff on his remote island lures yachts to their destruction with false beacons. Survivors who reach the shore are wined and dined, then given a day's start before he hunts them down and kills them for his sport. "You're not a very nice man, are you?" I said.

"Nice is boring; I like excitement. So do you, or you wouldn't be here. Now are you going to give me your answer or are you going to keep dithering while you drink my champagne?"

I opened my mouth and watched the worods, the woordos, the words walk out into the peaceful murmur of the Royal Opera House interval. "My answer is yes," said the worods and the woordos and the words. "You can buy my death for one million pounds and a year to enjoy the million."

Mr Rinyo-Clacton gripped my thigh. "I'll drink to that," he said, and chortled in his joy.

"How do we . . . ?"

"Consummate our bargain? Back at my flat after the opera."

"You've got a million pounds in cash back at your flat?"

"I always like to have a little cash on hand. But first we have Acts Four and Five before us, and Pelléas and Mélisande are finally going to pull their fingers out and declare their love. In real life they'd have been having it off days ago out in the woods or down at the boathouse but this is opera and they've got to sing their way around it for a while before he even gets to stick his tongue in her mouth. And his stupid brother, Golaud, maybe he's meant to symbolise something because dramatically he's unbeliev-able: Mélisande's had wet knickers for Pelléas all this time and Golaud's not taken any notice till now. Well, women are built for deception, aren't they?"

"What do you mean?"

"Think about it—when a man doesn't want to do it he's going to have difficulty rising to the occasion, but all a woman's got to do is spread her legs and fake an orgasm. Actually, Mélisande's pretty much of a pain in the arse altogether. In real life one or the other of the brothers would have straightened her out smartish. Maeterlinck could have done better with the text."

"How many times have you seen it this year?"

"This is only the fourth. With all its dramatic flaws it's still my favour-ite opera. People die right and left in other operas but this one is all about death from beginning to end; it's like a gorgeous poison flower. You simply have to move your mind out of the everyday reality frame to enjoy it."

Debussy's music, like the sea, delaying not, hurrying not, took us through the long-awaited kiss, the killing of Pelléas, and the later death of Mélisande. "*C'était un pauvre petit être mysterieux comme tout le monde*," sang Arkel, the grandfather of Golaud and Pelléas. "She was a poor little mysterious being like all of us," said the surtitle. I was reminded that *être*, the infinitive *to be*, was also the noun, *being*. Everyone who was, was a being, a poor little mysterious being. Serafina and I, that's what we were. And Mr Rinyo-Clacton, was he also a poor little mysterious being? I looked at his dark profile and saw him naked in his bedroom, felt him penetrate me. Stop that, I said to myself: think about Mélisande, how it was her destiny not to belong to the one she loved, how sad that was. But my mind persisted in going its own way, sorting through its pictures and wondering what was coming after the opera.

12

Now, Then

"Now, then," said Mr Rinyo-Clacton in his study. The background music for this scene was the Debussy String Quartet in G Minor, coming out of a state-of-the-art Meridian sound system nestling among many shelves of CDs. To me that music always suggested beaded lampshades, oriental carpets, glass-fronted bookcases, and the word *neurasthenia*.

There was a very imposing desk of lustrous and highly-polished wood and many subtle curves, joinings, pigeonholes, drawers and compartments. I don't know anything about furniture but this was the sort of thing one sees on the *Antiques Roadshow* and learns that it's worth fifty thousand pounds. The desk was presided over by a double lamp of gleaming brass and green glass shades.

The other object that caught my eye was a large illuminated globe, the kind that sits in a wooden ring on handsomely turned legs. There were ranks of box-files and numerous guides to various countries but no other books.

The only picture on the walls was a framed reproduction of a Piero di Cosimo that's in the National Gallery—a satyr bending over a dead or dying nymph with a wound in her throat. They are on the shore of a bay. A sad brown dog watches the two of them. Other dogs play on the beach;

there are herons and a pelican. In the blue distance ships ride at anchor; beyond them are the buildings of a port. The scene is magical, dreamlike, desolate; the nymph, covered only by a bit of drapery over her hips, her girlish breasts pathetically exposed, is so luminously beautiful—her death seems a dream-death. She and the satyr seem to have strayed into a dream of the death of innocence.

"Do you think they'll wake up?" I said.

Mr Rinyo-Clacton turned away from the desk to look, first at the picture, then at me. "They won't and you won't. This is it."

The Debussy quartet had ended and the Ravel quartet that follows it on the CD (I have the same recording, with the Pro Arte Quartet) began. "Ravel after Debussy is quite nice, I think," said Mr Rinyo-Clacton. "There's a good little edge to it. Do you like music? I never thought to ask."

"Yes, I like music."

"This, as they say, is the beginning of the rest of your life. It will be a life of one year, so the music you hear and everything else will be heightened for you. 'Look thy last on all things lovely, every hour,' eh?"

See Mr Rinyo-Clacton, his jacket off and his tie undone, bending over the desk, brilliantly caught in my vision like a scene in a film or a dream. A large half-full glass of brandy stood at the edge of the green blotter. There was another in my right hand. Mr Rinyo-Clacton opened a drawer and took out a crisp white document. "If you'll read this," he said, and handed it to me. It was a proper piece of calligraphy, written in Chancery hand:

> I, Jonathan Fitch, being of sound mind and with my faculties unimpaired, not under duress or the influence of any drug, hereby assign to T. Rinyo-Clacton, for the sum of one million pounds, to be paid on signature, the right to terminate my life at any time from midnight, the 24th October, 1995. This agreement is binding and I understand that it remains in effect even if I change my mind and return the money. The agreement cannot be cancelled except by T. Rinyo-Clacton's exercise of the right assigned above.

"What's the T for?" I said.

"Thanatophile."

"Nobody's called Thanatophile."

"You asked me what the T was for and I told you. Don't sign this unless you're serious about it because you may be quite sure that I am. You might think I'm crazy but don't allow yourself to think we're just fooling around here or it's some kind of a joke. Once you sign that paper this thing is going to go all the way."

"I'm serious," I said, "and I know that you are."

"Desmond," he said without raising his voice, "signature for you to witness." Desmond appeared, watched me sign, signed his name after mine, and withdrew.

Mr Rinyo-Clacton put the document back in the drawer and closed the drawer. "Now," he said, turning to me, "for my part of the bargain." He swung the Piero de Cosimo reproduction out from the wall to disclose a safe. He dialled the combination, opened the safe, and said, "Desmond," whereupon Desmond reappeared. "Get him something to put the money in," said Mr Rinyo-Clacton, "but not any of my luggage."

"There's only Carmen's shopping trolley," said Desmond.

"That'll do. She can buy another one tomorrow."

Desmond got the shopping trolley, a blue-and-red-and-yellow plaid number, brought it into the study, and was gone. Mr Rinyo-Clacton reached into the safe and brought out two thick stacks of fifty-pound notes, each sealed in clear plastic. "There's twelve thousand, five hundred in each bundle," he said, "so you get eighty of them. Count." He handed me bundles of notes and I counted and loaded the trolley. I managed to get sixty bundles into it and Desmond fetched carrier bags from the kitchen for the rest of the money.

"Well," I said, "that's it then. Off I go to live out my million-pound year."

The Ravel quartet had ended. Now Mr Rinyo-Clacton put on the same trio Mr Perez had started earlier that day, the first-time-with-Serafina-music. He gripped my shoulder. "One for the road?"

"No more brandy for me, thanks."

"I wasn't talking about brandy, Jonathan."

"Give me a break! That wasn't part of the deal."

"You're absolutely right; this isn't business, it's personal. I need to feel that death in you again."

"And I need you not to."

"Tell you what—I'll wrestle you for it. We'll both enjoy it more if you put up a fight. If you'll just step into my dojo . . . "

"You've got a dojo?"

"With mats on the floor, You'll find it quite comfortable."

He was about six inches taller than I and two stone heavier and I had reason to know that he was a whole lot fitter. As he turned to lead the way I grabbed the desk lamp and would have brained him with it—what a wonderful, wonderful feeling of rightness and release!—but it was taken away from me by the magically appearing Desmond, who then clamped my arms behind me with his left hand while applying a strangle-hold with his right arm. Thus restrained I was taken to the dojo where I was stripped to my underpants while Mr Rinyo-Clacton also took off his clothes. Then I was released, put up the best fight I could, and lost.

The rest of it took place in the dojo as well, with Mr Rinyo-Clacton synchronising his movements to those of the Ravel trio and the violin and cello sonata that followed it. He continued with Ravel and me through the violin and piano sonata that came next on the CD, finishing triumphantly as the last movement, *Perpetuum mobile*, reached its climax.

"Nice bit of fiddling, that, don't you think?" he said.

"I think I don't ever want to hear it again."

"Sure you do. Your problem is that you don't really know yourself, Jonny. You've got a lovely little death in you, a really charming little death—we're going to be good friends, it and I. But now it's time you were getting home. Thank you for the pleasure of your company; we'll be in touch." Still naked, he turned his back on me and walked out of the dojo, leaving his clothes where he'd dropped them while the CD concluded with the *Berceuse sur le nom de Gabriel Fauré*.

I got dressed and Desmond drove me and my million pounds home. I felt no resentment towards him; I recognised that although he clearly enjoyed his work he was only doing his job and I had no one but myself to blame for what had happened. As we slipped through the quiet streets I replayed that wonderful moment of rage when, if not prevented, I'd have killed Mr Rinyo-Clacton with no thought whatever for the consequences. If I'd been able to do it and get out of the flat I'd have happily left the million pounds behind and called it quits, which was of course not a viable fantasy because consequences would have followed thick and fast.

Here we were: my place. Desmond helped me out of the Daimler with the shopping trolley and carrier bags, said, "Good luck," and drove off with the engine purring like a well-fed big cat. I went up to my flat and turned on the lights. The whole place shrieked silently at me. "For Christ's sake, it's me!" I said but the place kept shrieking. I went to the bathroom and looked in the mirror to see if I was who I said I was. In the mirror I saw Death wearing my face.

"Sorry," I said, "I'm not having that—you can't wear my face."

It's not your face any more, sweetheart, said Death, it's mine. And it made disgusting kissing noises.

For the second time I had a shower that did not cover me with cleanness. Then I got dressed, turned out the lights, put the shopping trolley and the carrier bags in the kitchen, and looked at my watch: quarter to three. I had the feeling that Katerina was someone I could ring up in the middle of the night; maybe she was even expecting my call. I picked up the telephone and dialled her number. She answered after one ring. "Hello," she said, sounding wide awake.

"It's Jonathan," I said. "Did I wake you?"

"No, Jonathan—I was reading Schiller."

"Can I come over? I can be there in fifteen minutes."

"Yes, come. See you in fifteen minutes. Tschuss."

I opened one of the bundles of banknotes, counted out fifty fifties, thought about muggers, put the notes in an envelope, lowered my trousers, taped the envelope to my leg, hitched my trousers up again, and took my poor little mysterious being out into the small hours of the night.

13

Sayings of Confucius

It was a chilly night and it began to rain as I left my flat; by the time I got to Earl's Court Road the streets were shining and vivid with bright reflections. It was a Friday night/Saturday morning and the scene ought to have been a lively one but it wasn't; everything had a low-spirited look: a few people in twos and threes with long intervals of no people; minimal signs of life at the Star Kebab House and Perry's Bakery; a man in an apron sweeping out the Global Emporium; the Vegemania dark and silent, sending out waves of no-Serafina; modest traffic at the 24 Hour 7/Eleven; shelves being stacked at Gateway. At the closed tube station a man was leaning against the grille and vomiting. Two men were standing in the middle of the pavement and kissing. I closed my eyes and tried to see the oasis but it was Mr Rinyo-Clacton that I saw instead, his face blotchy and red and his breath bad while the Ravel played itself in my head. Then once more came the rage and the feeling of my hand closing on the heavy desk lamp.

What is the reality of me? I wondered, looking down at the wet pavement and my walking feet. I have moved out of my proper time and space into something else where anything at all can happen. Or maybe I'm not really me; maybe when I sat down in Piccadilly Circus tube station Death crawled up inside me and that's why it was looking out of my eyeholes in the mirror.

Calm down, I said to myself. This just happens to be a part of reality and a part of you that you haven't been to before, OK?

As I drew nearer to Katerina's corner I was full of excitement and anticipation, the way I used to feel when I was going to see Serafina. What's happening here? I asked myself but got no answer. The Waterstone's window was devoted to Dr Ernst von Luker and copies of his book on the latest theory of consciousness: *Mind—the Gap*. Bald, bearded and bespectacled Dr von Luker, staring out of a giant photograph, looked into my poor little mysterious mind and his lips moved. "Arsehole," he said.

As I went up Katerina's steps I saw her looking out of the window and she came to the front door to let me in. Her hair was down and she was wearing a blue kimono decorated with little birds on flowering branches. Her scent was light and fresh. Feeling crazed and utterly correct I held out my arms and she came into them and I kissed her. Gone, gone, gone. I closed my eyes and saw a full moon over the sea, white and lonely, felt the pull of the moon that couldn't be seen this rainy night and the rising and falling of the sea.

"Plum blossoms," she whispered, "on a dry tree."

"Plum blossoms?"

"On my kimono. The bird is the *uguisu*, the Japanese bush-warbler. '*Uguisu no, nakuya achimuki, kochira muki*':

> An uguisu is singing,
> Turning this way,
> Turning that way."

"You're not a dry tree," I said, "you're some kind of sorceress—the ordinary rules don't apply to you." We were still standing just inside the front door and I was afraid to move, afraid I might disappear at any moment.

She kissed me again and led me into her flat. There was faint music, Ravel of course, the first-time-with-Serafina-trio again. Well, Katerina was a psychic, wasn't she. I was going to ask her to switch it off when I changed my mind and tried to listen past Mr Rinyo-Clacton for what else was in the music, the voices and the colours of it.

We went through a book-lined hallway into a bedroom full of books. "Apart from the front room there's only this one," she said. Other than the shelves, the only pieces of furniture were an old brass bed and a bedside table with an Anglepoise lamp. As well as the books there were several shelves of LPs. The turntable stood on the floor with the amplifier and the speakers. Beyond the circle of lamplight the room was shadowy like the music.

Katerina's recording was a Deutsche Grammophon LP; the artists weren't the ones who'd performed on the CD that Mr Rinyo-Clacton and I both owned; this lot had had no part in his synchronised buggery. The strings and the piano seemed to be engaged in a meandering colloquy in which sometimes reason and sometimes emotion prevailed; the mood overall was one of melancholy.

In the second movement, designated *Pantoum* (I'd looked it up once: it was the name of a kind of Malayan verse quatrain) the musical protagonist seemed to be trying to break free of something. *Pantoum*, I said to myself, *Pantoum*, liking the strange sound and the mystery of the word.

Katerina kept her kimono on when she got into bed; her shapely feet looked younger than her years. I undressed, removed the envelope from my leg, slid in beside her, and took her in my arms. A woman of seventy-something, for God's sake! I thought I'd do no more than hold her but our kissing had moved on to something more serious than before and the music now seemed especially of this strange moment in which the ordinary rules were suspended. I didn't have a condom.

"It's all right without," she said softly. "I know you've been with him again but this is how I want you. I'm not going to catch anything from you."

"How do you know?"

"I'm psychic, remember?"

"Strange woman, magic woman."

"Remember that when you wake up in the morning and find yourself lying beside a bundle of ancient papyrus." She switched off the Anglepoise and there were only the faint light from the hall and the little red beacon of the amplifier and the music.

Afterwards she said, '*Nur die Fülle führt zur Klarheit / Und im Abgrund wohnt die Wahrheit.*' Only fullness leads to clarity / And in the abyss dwells the truth."

"Is that Schiller?"

"Yes, 'Sayings of Confucius.'"

"What makes you quote those lines now?"

"I don't know—you mustn't expect me to be rational all the time. One does something and perhaps has no idea what it was that was done. Then much later there comes suddenly the understanding—Aha! So *that's* what it was. This that just happened with us, maybe we think it was only with the two of us here and now but nothing is separate from anything else: not people, not places, not times. The present is the fin you see cutting the water, and under it swims the shark that is the past and the future." She gripped my hand. "Jonathan, I know that you are in some kind of a life-and-death thing. Will you tell me what it is?"

I told her and the pillow rustled as she shook her head. "Mr Rinyo-Clacton was right," she said. "That *was* Death looking out of your eyes when he saw you in the tube station. It's very strong in you now. Don't you want to live?"

"Sometimes I think yes and sometimes I think no. Sometimes I feel as if Samarra is everywhere and Death is looking at his watch and waiting for me."

"For you Death is a man."

"Definitely."

"What if you were to tell Mr Rinyo-Clacton you've changed your mind and you give back the money?"

"Surely a modern no-bullshit psychic and clairvoyant can guess the answer to that one, Katerina?"

"I know—he's full of death also. You must understand when we talk about this: I can feel some of the big things but I don't always get details. And even with the big things I'm not always clear; there are often cross-currents and contradictions in what comes to me."

"Well, one of the details is that even if I return the money he's still going to require my death in one year."

"Do you think he'll honour the agreement and give you the full year?"

"I'm not at all sure he can be trusted."

"Oh God, what a thing you have got yourself into, Jonathan."

"Maybe in some way I needed to make this happen."

"Why?"

"I don't know—I can't always join up the dots but I feel that if I'd been more of a man, if I'd liked myself better and liked women better, I wouldn't have needed to get so many of them into bed; I'd have been too full of Serafina and what she was to me and things wouldn't be as they are now."

"You've just been unfaithful to her again with this old woman lying next to you."

"This is different—she's left me and she's probably sleeping with someone else this very moment." I said that but I didn't believe it.

"Have you got anything he's touched, this Rinyo-Clacton?"

"Here I am—I'm something he's touched."

"You're too full of you; I need something with no output of its own."

I took the envelope from the bedside table and put the banknotes in her hand. "This money," I said, "although it was sealed in plastic when he touched it."

"Doesn't matter." She held it in both hands, pressed it to her chest, and shut her eyes. Then her face changed—her lips drew back from her teeth in a long shuddering breath; she looked suddenly ancient and sibylline and altogether frightening. For the first time it came to me that I might be involved in something beyond my understanding.

"What?" I said. "What's happening?"

Still with her eyes closed, she shook her head and put her finger to her lips for silence. After a time she opened her eyes and said, "It's not good, too many words—the energy of the mind goes like water down the plug-hole. Some things I see again and again, years apart, and each time it means something else and I must think about it." With the index finger and thumb of her left hand she massaged her temples as if she had a head-ache. I listened to the ticking of her little bedside clock and waited for her to speak. After a few minutes she said, "One thing I tell you, though: there's fear in him."

"Fear in *him*!"

"Yes, in him."

"Fear of what?"

"I don't know. Could he be afraid of you?"

"Of *me*!"

"Sometimes you know what someone is to you but you don't know what you are to them. The fear is definitely there."

She gave me back the money. "Anyhow, he probably doesn't come after you already tonight so maybe we can get a little sleep."

"It just occurred to me—would a photograph of him give you anything?" As I said that I thought, what, is she your minder now? What a hero.

"No," she said, "it only gets in the way. When the time is right, maybe his face comes to me."

The lovemaking and the talk had drained some of the disquiet out of me; I kissed Katerina and fell asleep and dreamed that I was approaching the oasis with Mr Rinyo-Clacton.

I woke up when I felt Katerina's absence. Hearing watery noises from the bathroom and expecting a few more minutes alone I found a scrap of paper in my pocket and wrote a note which I slipped under the pillow with fifty fifty-pound notes:

> Dear Katerina,
>   This money is for a digital piano. You can play it late at night with headphones so no one can hear it and they won't bang on the door. Don't give me an argument about this.
>
>   Love,
>   Jonathan

When Katerina made her next appearance she still looked troubled. We kissed and hugged and said nothing more than "Good morning."

I smelled bacon and eggs and coffee when I came out of the shower. Grapefruit juice, too, I saw when I went into the kitchen. "Do you ordinarily have bacon and eggs for breakfast?" I said.

"No, but I'm a no-bullshit modern psychic and clairvoyant, remember? I think this is what you like when you have time for it, yes?"

"Yes," I said, and thought of Serafina.

On the way out I went into the front room for another look at Melencolia. It was really very hard to tell whether she was smiling or scowling. Had some winged male abandoned her and the sulking child and left all his tools behind? Or had she thrown him out?

When I left, Katerina hadn't yet made the bed so I didn't think she'd seen the money and the note. I imagined her lifting the pillow and smiled to myself.

The morning was bright and cold. Considering that I had only a year to live I felt pretty lively. Crazy but lively. I noticed that I was singing to myself, to the tune of a Haydn symphony the number of which had slipped my mind:

> *Nur die Fülle führt zur Klarheit,*
> *Und im Abgrund wohnt die Wahrheit.*

About the money I gave Katerina—to be honest I have to say that it wasn't only that I wanted her to have a piano; I needed to break the lump of that million pounds to convince myself that there was no turning back. Weird, yes? I've already said I was feeling crazy.

I4

What If?

"One does something and perhaps has no idea what it was that was done. Then much later there comes suddenly the understanding—Aha! So *that's* what it was." Katerina had put it very well. I recognised that my night with her had been only incidentally a sexual matter; obviously she represented to me some kind of female power that I wanted on my side; I didn't know what I was to her and could only hope that her needs had in some way coincided with mine.

Trying not to think too much about my deficiencies I headed for the Vegemania, hoping for a sighting of Serafina. The shop opened at ten, the restaurant not till twelve; it was quarter to eleven now and she'd be getting ready for the lunchtime rush.

As I walked through the faces coming towards me and past me I noted again how many of them seemed eager to get to wherever they were going. This morning I too was eager to get to where I was going but not only because I expected to see Serafina; no, I was just eager to get to the next part of the first day of the rest of my life. Odd, how exciting and vivid and valuable my contractually short life seemed now. All of my senses were sharpened and crossing over from one to another—I tasted the October-ness of the day in my mouth, saw the colours of passing footsteps and the other sounds around me, heard in my vision the approach of November, smelled possibilities that swarmed like golden bees, held in my hands . . . what? Ah! I said to myself, be patient and you'll see.

Yes! She was there. Through the window I saw Rima, one of the waitresses, setting tables. Beyond her I had brief and partial glimpses of Serafina passing and repassing the kitchen doorway. She was in jeans and a mauve jumper with the sleeves pushed up, her black hair held back by a leopard-spotted scarf worn as a headband, her whole throwaway manner wildly erotic as always. The scarf was one we'd bought in the Boulevard Saint-Michel on the day we drank the sauvignon in the Place des Vosges.

With my heart pounding I went through the hallway with its bulletin board of mental, physical and spiritual opportunities, through the empty stripped-pine tables and chairs of the restaurant, and into the kitchen where the luncheon menu in various stages of readiness was deployed in pots and bowls and dishes and on boards and trays. Zoë, the other waitress, was chopping tofu. Patsy Cline was coming over the sound system with "Crazy":

> Crazy—I'm crazy for feelin' so lonely,
> I'm crazy, crazy for feelin' so blue.
> I knew you'd love me as long as you wanted,
> and then someday you'd leave me for somebody new.

Serafina, with her look of howling into the wind on a bleak northern strand, was peeling onions with tears running down her cheeks. I would have liked to kiss them away but knew better than to try. When she saw me she fired off a black-browed glance that warned me to keep my distance. "What?" she said.

"What a warm and friendly greeting!"

"You've had all the warm and friendly you're getting from me, mate. This is a small kitchen and we need your space."

"I don't know where you're living now." When I said that, Zoë glanced up from her tofu and I remembered that she'd been looking for a flatmate a few weeks ago.

"You don't need to know," said Serafina. "You can forward mail and messages to me here."

"Are you going to stay angry for ever?"

"When you say 'you' you're talking to the woman you used to live with. She's not around any more. This woman you're talking to now is somebody else who hasn't got time for your whingeing."

She was a proud person and I could feel how humiliating it must have been for her to find those letters. How would I have felt if she'd had such letters from another man? Why hadn't I thought of that before? I'd be full of the same rage and disgust that was coming from her in waves. Still, she was the woman I'd had the oasis dream with and we both knew nothing could change that. "I wonder," I said, "how you'd feel tomorrow if you were to hear that I was dead."

She'd done with the onions for the moment; she wiped her eyes, took a knife and slit open a plastic bag of peeled potatoes. Her hands were strong and shapely, with long nimble fingers; whatever she took hold of she held in a good-looking way and her cooking was pleasing to the eye at every stage: the peeled onions, the bag of flour, the pot of salt, the box of eggs, the chopping board, tablespoon and little black-handled knife were a choreographed still-life that changed from moment to moment. "I'd probably feel about the same as I do now—" she said, "cheated because I'd been giving all of me while you were giving only part of you and now my honest time would be gone with your lying time. If you were going to be a shit you should have let me know in advance."

"I didn't know I was going to be a shit."

"Then when you felt it coming on, you should have told me so I could leave while I still had good things to remember. That would have been simple enough; if you'd found out that you'd got AIDS from someone you knew before me you'd have had the decency to tell me. I'm the woman you dreamed the oasis dream with, the woman you said was your destiny woman, but that wasn't enough for you. Can you tell me why it wasn't enough? I really would like to know because that's a great big gap in my understanding. Tell me, Jonathan—speak."

I tried to think of something useful to say but I couldn't.

"Nothing to say, Jonathan? In one of those letters in your pocket one of your bits on the side said, 'What we have between us is something special, Jonny.' Well, now you can have a special thing with as many as you like without having to lie about it."

She started putting potatoes into the electric grater. Through her alchemy these humble things out of the earth, compounded with onions, eggs, flour and salt, would sizzle as golden-brown pancakes on the griddle of their transformation. They would smell of their ingredients but beyond that they would smell of fidelity, of being steadfast and true to what really mattered. I couldn't help salivating a little. And all the while her movements had been revealing the subtle roundnesses of her that one didn't notice at first glance. "Serafina," I said. "I never stopped loving you."

"I'm thrilled to hear that—it's very flattening to know that you had a little room in your heart for me. You must be a very big-hearted man."

Again I had no words. I wanted so much to take her in my arms!

"What?" she said. "The Excelsior star salesman speechless?"

"What if," I said, "you found that I had only a year to live?"

She tilted her head a little to one side and looked at me narrowly. "Are you going to tell me you *have* got AIDS?"

"No, Serafina, I haven't got AIDS."

"What is it, then?"

"Never mind. You're busy now, I'll go." I left the kitchen, went through the restaurant and out into the hall. The shop was at one end of it, the street at the other. I was halfway out into Earl's Court Road when I had an impulse to buy some rose-hip tea. I spun around and was almost in the shop when I heard Mr Rinyo-Clacton talking to Ron, the owner.

"Is it true," he was asking, "what they say about ginseng?"

15

The Lord Jim Hotel

Was it actually Mr Rinyo-Clacton? At first I didn't want to know, I just wanted to shut him out of my consciousness. Then I had to know; I turned around and went out into Earl's Court Road and stood looking into the Vegemania. In a few minutes I saw him stick his head into the restaurant from the hallway. Rima pointed to the clock and said they weren't open yet and he withdrew. I turned away quickly and walked down Earl's Court Road without looking back.

Why was he here? Was he going to turn up wherever I happened to be from now on? What did he want at the Vegemania? Serafina? Was he going to suck up my whole life like a vampire before he killed me? Serafina! I could see him having lunch at the Vegemania, complimenting her on her cooking, being charming, chatting her up and inviting her to the opera, the ballet, whatever. There's nothing you can do about it, I told myself—the shop and the restaurant are open to the public and you can't prevent Serafina from talking to him. Don't think about it now, put it out of your mind and get on with whatever you were going to do today.

Around me a sketchy surreality put itself together with sounds and colours, buildings, cars, faces, footsteps, and the smell of exhaust fumes and roasting chestnuts. Contracting to be dead in one year definitely made everything look different; gigantic soft watches draped over trees and a downpour of bowler-hatted men with umbrellas would not have surprised me.

Steady on, I said to myself. Right now we've got to decide what to do with the money. You've got nine hundred and ninety-seven thousand, five hundred pounds and a whole year to live, less one day. Right, I said. A tall rucksacked girl with her blonde hair in two plaits strode past me swinging her mineral water. What if I were to live more than a year? Nobody could be dead sure of anything in this life: Mr Rinyo-Clacton might choke on a pearl in one of his oysters and never get around to harvesting me at all.

I bought a copy of the *Financial Times* and ran my eye over the front page. Nash & Weapman saw the recession receding; Morgenstern was expecting a downturn in the upturn. Morgenstern seemed to me the brighter of the two so I went back to the flat, averted my eyes from the plants, and rang them up. I told the telephonist I needed some investment advice and she turned me over to a Mr Reilly.

"Jim Reilly here," he said. "How can I help you?" He had an Excelsior kind of voice.

"I've come into some money," I said, "and I need investment advice."

"Yes. And how did you hear of us, Mr Fitch?"

"I saw your firm quoted in the *Financial Times*."

"Right. I'm sure we can work something out for you, Jonathan. Just so I can begin to put a frame around this, may I ask what sort of amount you're thinking of investing?"

"Close to a million, give or take a few bundles."

"I see. That kind of money has considerable potential, Jonathan, and our job is not simply to realise that potential—what we're here for is to maximise it."

"That's what I want, Jim: maximisation of my potential."

"We're going to give it our best shot, Jonathan, and we've got a pretty good track record. This is going to require careful planning, and the best way to begin is for you and I to meet . . . "

"You and *me* to meet," I said. "Sorry to be pedantic."

"No problem. As I was saying, the best way to begin is for the two of us to meet here at our offices so we can look at your whole financial picture and assess your needs as fully as possible. Would that be convenient for you?"

"Fine. When can you see me?"

"I've got a cancellation at three o'clock this afternoon. How's that for you?"

"That's good. You're in Gray's Inn Road, nearest tube station Chancery Lane?"

"That's it. Coming up Gray's Inn Road from the tube station you'll see a modern building on the right. We're on the third floor."

There was still the matter of the shopping trolley and three carrier bags full of banknotes. I trundled the lot over to Lloyds, made out a deposit slip, and queued up at a window. An alert-looking young member of the staff approached and became interested in the trolley. I opened the flap and showed him the contents. "You think they're real?" I said.

"Not my problem. Do you want to deposit that in your account?"

"Yes."

"It'll have to be counted. Come with me, please." He recruited a teller named Brenda and we went to a room where my seventy-nine sealed packets and the one opened one were unpacked and laid out on a desk.

"Aren't there a lot of fake fifties about now?" I said to Brenda. "Won't you have to put them under ultra-violet light or something?"

"Not unless they feel funny." She sighed, tore open the sealed packets, and began to count the nineteen thousand, nine hundred and fifty fifty-pound notes. She was wearing a navy-blue woollen dress and a little string of pearls; her dark hair was cut in a Lulu-style bob. Her hands were graceful and articulate, her long fingers themselves seeming to count as she murmured hundreds into thousands and replaced the elastic band around each stack as she finished. While pondering the paperness of money, I thought of Serafina peeling onions and the way her hand took hold of a potato.

The silence around Brenda's quiet voice purred softly; my breathing seemed very loud. The young man—his name was Steve—stood by with canvas bags into which he put the banded stacks as she finished with them. It was a scene that was part of the surreality that was by now the usual thing for me—just another sequence of moments in the new life and death of Jonathan Fitch.

After a while the counting and bagging stopped, the three of us went back to the teller's window, the bags were sealed, and Brenda stamped my deposit slip. "That's the biggest I've had so far today," she said.

"How was it for you?" I said.

"Just numbers. In this job you've got to stop thinking of money as money or you'll go crazy."

As I was about to leave the bank with my empty trolley a man I took to be the manager came out of his office. "Mr Fitch," he said, taking me in with a practised smile. I was in non-business mode: Mr Scruffy. "I'm Henry Dargent, Branch Manager here. I don't believe we've actually met before."

"How do you do?" I said, and we shook hands.

"You know, Mr Fitch, the interest on your Classic Account scarcely offers an appropriate return on the sort of money you've just deposited. Our advisers are always available to help you with a financial programme."

"Thank you," I said, "I'm going to have to explore various possibilities." I was already feeling burdened by the money. I went back to the flat with the trolley but I couldn't bear to stay there. The place was filled with the goneness of Serafina but saying that doesn't begin to describe how it was. I was used to being there alone for hours on end while she was busy with dinners at the Vegemania but her presence was always there. I know I sound gross talking about food so much but the kitchen particularly was ghastly now that she hadn't been in it and wouldn't be in it, handling things in that good way of hers, maybe singing softly to herself while she cooked. Gone, gone, gone.

I put a few things in a weekend bag and walked down Earl's Court Road to Penywern. Some of the tall white Victorian houses with pillared and balconied fronts were hotels and I cruised slowly past them waiting for one of them to reach out and pull me in.

LORD JIM HOTEL, said the gilded letters on a green awning. Lord Jim! Conrad's flawed hero, Chief Mate of the *Patna*, who abandoned what he thought was a sinking ship and left hundreds of Mecca-bound pilgrims to their fate. Quite an august entrance with broad steps, two white urns filled with healthy-looking vines, and three sturdy white pillars. Through the glass doors I saw an Art-Deco chandelier, three tiers like an upside-down wedding cake and all pinky-orange and glittering like a beacon of tranquillity and elsewhereness.

There was a beautiful black-haired girl at the Reception window. "Are your people from Bombay?" I asked.

"Yes," she said, "but I was born here."

"Have you read *Lord Jim*?"

"Yes."

"How did the hotel come to have this name?"

"The original owners were Polish and they were big Conrad fans."

"Did they ever abandon ship?"

"I don't know."

A room with a shower and toilet was forty-five pounds. There was a ten-pound deposit for use of the telephone. "How long will you be staying?" she asked.

"I don't know. Can I tell you later?"

"All right. Checkout time is twelve noon." She gave me the key to Room Twenty-one on the second floor and I took the lift up to it. By now I had settled into my new mode of perception, an *ad hoc* kind of thing in which each sequence put itself together in its own way. I opened the door into the high-ceilinged room and breathed a little sigh.

This was a quiet place that had nothing in it that was personal to anyone; it was not the big blast of reality (and surreality) that waited outside; it was the limited reality of a small hotel room, like a simple melody played on a bamboo flute, cool as the plashing of water falling from level to level in the ferny-dappled sunlight of a garden. The soap dispenser over the sink charmed me. The upholstered headboard of the bed offered a muted view of distant mountains and winding rivers. The wallpaper gave me no backtalk, the bedspread and the carpet effaced themselves in pinks and greys. A print on the wall showed a foreground of something botanical, cow parsley for all I knew, with what might have been the South Downs in the distance.

The mirror on the door had no pretensions to deep insights and contented itself with a generalised and simplified me. I looked out of the window and saw two chestnut trees. "Yes!" I said, and took off my shoes and lay back on the bed. I notice that men in films often put their feet on a bedspread without taking off their shoes. Another thing they do in films in moments of stress or heavy portent is go to the sink and splash cold water over their faces and the backs of their necks. I don't do that either.

I had a half hour before I had to leave for my consultation with Jim

Reilly; I rang the desk and asked the beautiful black-haired girl to call me in thirty minutes, then on an impulse I checked the two drawers of the bedside table for a Gideon Bible. There was none. I closed my eyes and had a tiny kip in which I dreamed of a dark place where I saw, far away, the green glow of Mr Rinyo-Clacton's desk lamp.

16

Objectives?

I took the Edgware Road train to Notting Hill Gate and the Central Line from there to Chancery Lane. The afternoon reality was a low-budget sort of thing; I wasn't sure that everything I saw even had a back to it. None of the people in the underground had speaking parts and many of the faces were blank. The Gray's Inn Road scenery had been done without much detail—a shop that sold secondhand office furnishings and another that cut keys were fairly realistic but I doubted that the doors actually opened and closed. The Morgenstern building was a little more convincing—a pseudo-Bauhaus thing with practical glass doors.

The security man at the reception desk looked me over critically but I brazened it out, signed in, and took the lift to the third floor. "Jonathan Fitch to see Jim Reilly," I said to the smart young woman who greeted me. She asked me if I'd like a coffee, I said yes, and she showed me to a conference room filled with business-grade sunlight.

Jim Reilly appeared shortly; he looked and sounded pretty much like me. There are probably a lot of people in the potential-realising-and-maximising-business who look and sound like us—decent, clean-cut types with good teeth, firm handshakes, and clear eyes that don't blink too much. Jim had about two kilos of bumph under his arm which he laid on the dark and shining table. He took a sheet from the top and handed it to me. "I've put together a little agenda here," he said, "of the points I'd like to cover in this first meeting."

I looked at the agenda:

1 MORGENSTERN—WHO WE ARE AND WHAT WE OFFER
2 CLIENT HISTORY
3 CLIENT OBJECTIVES
4 INVESTMENT PHILOSOPHY—BUILDING THE PYRAMID
5 PORTFOLIO PRIORITIES—CAPITAL GROWTH OR INCOME?

And so on for a dozen or more points. My eyes travelled down the agenda but my mind had already fixed on Point 3: CLIENT OBJECTIVES! Did I have any, and what were they? The smart young woman brought in coffee and I drank it while Jim Reilly went on for quite a long time like a TV with the sound turned off. Every now and then he paused to remove some of the papers from the top of the two-kilo stack and place them before me while I nodded or tilted my head to one side appreciatively and made such verbal responses as my mouth could manage. Objectives!

Jim Reilly was looking at me expectantly; it seemed to be my turn to speak. "I think I'd like to invest some of the money in a business," I heard myself say.

"Have you a particular business in mind?"

"A restaurant."

"Right." He made a note. "Any idea of how much you'd want to set aside for that?"

"Not yet but I can find out. And I'd like the rest of the money to produce income for two people to live on."

"Marriage plans?"

"It's always a possibility." I told Jim I'd be in touch when I was further along with my restaurant thoughts and I left feeling very much a man of the world.

17

Two Minds, One Thought

I wonder if riding the Central Line east and west across London is more easeful than going north and south? Travelling from Chancery Lane to Notting Hill Gate I felt, I don't know—at home? Yes, that's the right way of putting it. I felt at home beneath the surface of things, out of the light of day, between here and there. Yes, the betweenness of it was good, nothing was final; everything was in suspension, not yet precipitated by the forces I felt in me and around me. I believe everything I read about ley lines and force-fields and the power of earth and stones. London clay must have some power as well. "What are we but clay, and infirm vessels all," Mr Rinyo-Clacton had said.

The rush hour hadn't begun yet, the faces and the spaces were of the afternoon calm. A man with an accordion came into the train at Tottenham Court Road, one of those terribly extrovert buskers with a weather-beaten face and a gravelly voice. The woman bottling for him had a similar face and eyes like an owl. "Ladies and gentleman!" said the accordion man in a peat-bog accent, "a little music for your entertainment between the hither and the farther shores of your journey!"

I always give money to buskers in the corridors of the underground but I hate it when these gravelly-voiced extroverts come into my carriage through the London clay beneath the surface of things. Naturally the first number he played was "Caravan" and with it came the Place des Vosges and the feathery palms and the dark and shining pool. O God! I thought, why didn't you make me a better man?

"God bless ya, love," said the woman with the owl-eyes as I dropped some coins into her cup and wiped away my tears. "It really gets to ya, doesn't it."

"Please," I said, "tell him not to play 'The Sheik of Araby' next."

But he did. The two of them got out at Bond Street while the music kept going on in my head.

"Are you all right?" asked a sixtyish woman with a National Gallery carrier bag and a copy of *The Family of Pascual Duarte*.

"He shot his dog," I said.

"Who?"

"Pascual Duarte. He had a setter bitch and she looked at him as if she was going to accuse him of something and he shot her."

"I haven't got to that part yet," she said. "Are you having a bad time?"

"Nothing special." I wanted to rest my head on her bosom but I thought I'd better not. "Thanks," I added with a grateful smile while the accordion and the Place des Vosges and the palm trees and the dark and shining pool continued.

At Notting Hill Gate the reality was very solid—everything three-dimensional and fully functioning. I went up the escalator and down the stairs to the District Line. Little clumps of dark figures moving about or standing, sitting and squatting against the wall under dim yellow lamps. The board said the Wimbledon train was next. I always go to the far end of the westbound platform where you can look up at the sky and a high brick wall on the other side of the cut. It's an interesting space, that: the curved glass-and-steel canopy of the station comes to an end; then this red brick wall rears up with street-level houses at the top of it under the open sky; at the end of that short open space the tunnel again shows its round black maw.

This red brick wall is faced with tall narrow arches, something like the arches one sees under aqueducts except that these are filled with brick instead of air. This wall always makes me think—I don't know why—of Florence in the time of the Borgias. It was evening now; beyond the feeble yellow lamps the sky was dark; the wall looked sinister, standing tall in bricks of shadow. Did Lucrezia Borgia actually poison people? I couldn't remember what the latest word was on that.

At Earl's Court I phoned Katerina. "Can I come round?" I said. Listen to me, I thought—always needing something from a woman.

"Twenty minutes," she said. "I've got someone with me now."

I went to the Waterstone's at her corner. From the giant photo in the window Dr Ernst von Luker fixed me with his piercing gaze. "Wimp," he said. He pronounced it "Vimp." The massed copies of *Mind—the Gap* sang their titles at me like a Eurovision entry.

"What gap?" I said. "Between the real and the ideal? Between then and now?"

"Between you and Jesus," said a bearded passer-by who passed by before I could think of anything clever to say.

I went into Waterstone's and in the Reference section I opened a copy of *Who's Who* but there was no Rinyo-Clacton listed. Browsing aimlessly to kill time I found a table stacked with *The Carnivore Cookbook* by Celestine Latour—the famous soprano's favourite meat dishes. From the jacket smiled the delicate carnivorous Mélisande who looked so much like Serafina. I turned a few pages idly and was looking at a photogragh of *osso bucco* when I felt a hand on my bottom.

I jabbed backward with my elbow into the iron-hard stomach of Mr Rinyo-Clacton. "You see?" he said, indicating the cookbook. "They're all carnivores, every one." He was wearing a black shell suit and black Reeboks and smelled as if he'd run all the way from Belgravia.

"You bastard," I said.

"Listen to this." He was holding a copy of *Mind—the Gap*. He opened it and read from the flap copy:

> " 'For too long, says Dr von Luker, author of *Illustrations of Reality*, the brain has huddled by the little fire of limited reality while the mind prowls like a hungry animal in the darkness beyond. In this new work he challenges the reader to make the vital hook-up between brain and mind.'

"That's where the real things happen, Jonny—in the darkness beyond the fires. This book is from me to you."

"Never mind that—I saw you at the Vegemania. You're out to ruin even the little bit of time I've got left, aren't you."

"You'll probably see me at the Vegemania often. Serafina's potato pancakes are absolutely magical. She's a beautiful girl, Jonny, and sexy like anything. I can see why you went all to pieces when you lost her."

I turned to go but he said, "Just let me pay for this and inscribe it and I'm off."

I was about to tell him what to do with the book when it occurred to me that Katerina might find his handwriting interesting. At the till he produced a gold card and a gold fountain pen from a black belly-pouch, paid, quickly wrote something on the flyleaf, gave me the open book, and made his exit with a thumbs-up sign.

I looked at his inscription:

FOR JONNY—
"The Bird of Time has but a little way
to flutter—and the Bird is on the Wing."

Thinking of you always,
T.

Black ink, and the writing was large and spiky, with many slants and angles and a lot of up-and-down to it. The Fitzgerald version of *The Rubaiyat of Omar Khayyam* was a favourite book of mine when I was sixteen and I still knew most of the quatrains by heart. When thinking of Serafina I often recalled:

The Moving Finger writes, and having writ,
Moves on: nor all thy Piety nor Wit
   Shall lure it back to cancel half a Line,
Nor all thy Tears wash out a Word of it.

The ink was still wet. With a finger between the cover and the flyleaf I left Waterstone's and went down the road to Katerina's place.

She kissed me hello. "Jonathan!" she said. "He was in Waterstone's just a moment ago."

"How do you know that?"

"I've seen him in my mind, felt who it was. Only from the back did I see him, a big man, tall and broad, a dark shape of malice standing in front of you, blotting you out."

"He hasn't blotted me out quite yet, Katerina."

"An unfortunate choice of words. Sorry. I am so much disturbed by him."

We went into the front room and sat down at the table where the little bronze woman waited under the blue-shaded lamp with her quill and her scroll while Melencolia brooded on the bare wall with her ironmongery, her dog, the surly winged-infant, and the magic square that totalled thirty-four in all directions. She noticed that I was watching her as she toyed with her dividers. What divides the men from the boys, she said, is that the men do something while the boys just talk.

Katerina took my hand. "Thank you for your note and the money," she said, "but I haven't ordered a piano. I know that spending some of the million is your way of locking yourself into your contract with Mr Rinyo-Clacton and I don't feel good about it. Tell me what is happening with him."

I handed her the book. "He gave me this just now in Waterstone's."

"Aha!" she said, holding it close to her chest with both hands. "Oh!" Again that change in her face—the ancient sibylline look with the lips drawn back from the teeth.

"That's the look I saw on your face when you held the money," I said.

As before, she shook her head, dismissed it with a gesture, then, clutching the book, said, "Here there is death, death, death, death! I'm talking about the death in *him*."

"What about it?"

"It's all tangled up, not clearly focused; partly it points out and partly it points in."

"What, murderous and suicidal both?"

"And fear, yes? This have I already said before, not?"

"Yes, when you handled the money he'd given me. What's he afraid of?"

"This I still don't know."

"Look at what he wrote on the flyleaf."

She looked. "This is a quotation, yes?"

"From the *Rubaiyat*."

"I know it only in a German translation—these lines about the Bird of Time I don't recognise."

"The full quatrain is:

> 'Come, fill the Cup, and in the fire of Spring
> Your Winter Garment of Repentance fling:
>   The Bird of Time has but a little way
> To flutter—and the Bird is on the Wing.' "

"So," said Katerina, "whose time is he talking about, do you think?"

"Mine, there's no doubt about that."

"His handwriting is almost like that of a child, a child big and strong but confused. He's right-handed, yes?"

"Yes."

"Look—slanting away from the writer it goes and slanting back towards him with its pointyness like spears and arrows, death pointing out and pointing in. Up it goes and down like the waves of the sea. What is sticking in him that could be the death of him? Oh God."

"We both know what it is, don't we, Katerina: that son of a bitch has got AIDS and now I've probably got it and given it to you."

Katerina's eyes were blue, quite a vivid blue, not the sort of eyes you expect an old woman to have. As she looked at me steadily I remembered the number tattooed on her arm. She took my hand. "That we don't know yet, Jonathan. Maybe he's got HIV but not yet AIDS and maybe you've caught nothing from him. I don't feel any sickness in you."

I thought back to the first time, in Mr Rinyo-Clacton's bedroom: I'd had a lot of champagne and I was in a strange state of mind and I . . . what? I wanted to get the burden of myself off my back. He said later he could feel the death in me responding to him. What a poetic image. And the second time he simply did it his way because he was strong enough to. When I went to meet him at the opera was I hoping to get AIDS? Was I that crazy? I saw myself sitting on the floor in Piccadilly Circus tube station. What a poor excuse for a man!

"Jonathan," said Katerina, "mostly I get the big things right, like the death in him—but whether this is your death by violence and his own from illness or only the death that lives always in the mind I can't be sure.

And even if illness, it could be anything, not only HIV or AIDS. With details I am not at all reliable. And as I've already told you once, maybe you have nothing from him. Now you must wait three months and then you get yourself HIV-tested and we know what's what."

"Three months of not knowing!"

"Ah, Jonathan! There's a saying in German: no matter which way you turn, your arse stays always behind."

"Thank you for your input, Katerina. God knows how long it might have taken me to work that out for myself."

"Now you're angry."

"I'm sorry—it's not you I'm angry at. Now I'm thinking something that I don't want to say out loud. Can you read my thought?"

"Yes, but there's something else I want to talk about: have I only thought it or have you said to me that Serafina is your destiny-woman?"

"I don't remember, but that's what she is—or was. I'm not sure that she thinks of herself that way any more."

"Tell me, please, what is a destiny-woman."

"For me a destiny-woman is the one that your whole life has brought you to—whatever you've done or not done, whatever roads you've kept to and whatever turns you've taken and when you find her your two life-lines are joined from then on."

"What do you mean when you say 'life-line'?"

"I'm not sure it's definable. Sometimes I think I can feel how things are moving and where they're going."

"Is it a predestined line, do you think?"

"Not exactly but I think there are probabilities: if you see a pig and a chicken in a farmyard you might predict bacon and eggs in their life-lines."

"What do you predict in yours?"

"Well, you know the contract I've signed with Mr Rinyo-Clacton."

"I'm not sure that's an accurate prediction. Life-lines are strange things—what you've done and haven't done, the roads you've kept to and the turns you've taken. My own life is incomprehensible to me; I can feel it following some unknown line like a dog on a scent but I don't know what it is. Your life too is following a line unknown to you. That thought you were thinking—I advise you not to act on it just yet. Wait and see how things go. Do you understand me?"

"Yes."

"This is a heavy time for you, Jonathan. If you want to stay here tonight you know you are welcome."

"Thank you, but tonight I think I have to be alone with whatever's going to be looking out of the mirror at me."

She kissed me. "Come safe to your house."

"I'll try."

18

Where's Ruggiero?

I found myself thinking of *Orlando Furioso*. It was years since I'd read it and I'd forgotten most of it but not the part in Canto X where the beautiful Angelica, chained naked to a rock on the Isle of Tears, is about to be devoured by the sea-monster, Orca. Ruggiero, flying over the outer Hebrides on the hippogriff, sees her plight and speeds to her rescue. He wounds Orca, unchains Angelica, and off they go, Angelica on the pillion seat and Ruggiero lusting for his reward. He lands on the shore in expectation of heroic delights but while he's struggling out of his armour Angelica puts a magic ring in her mouth, becomes invisible, exits with her virginity intact, and leaves Ruggiero to his own devices.

It struck me, as I walked to the Lord Jim, that the Angelica/Ruggiero/Orca pattern is a paradigm of the human condition: in every situation large and small there is an Angelica, a Ruggiero, and an Orca. Take a simple everyday thing like the shopping: the near-empty larder, Angelica, needs to be rescued from emptiness, Orca; the one who goes to the shops for food is Ruggiero. Or a big thing like a coronary bypass: the heart is Angelica; the thrombosis is Orca; the surgeon is Ruggiero. There is, of course, no frustration for either of these Ruggieros.

At the present time I seemed to be Angelica to Mr Rinyo-Clacton's Orca. What a position to be in! And within myself the Angelica of my essential identity was threatened by the Orca of my stupidity. Or my death-wish. Or something else? How well did I know myself? Where were my Ruggieros, internal and external?

19

Whichever Way You Turn

I was certain that Mr Rinyo-Clacton was HIV-positive at the very least. Because that's how things are—you open the door to a possibility and the next thing you know, an actuality has you by the throat. O God, I thought, if only I could turn back the clock to the other day when I hadn't yet met Mr Rinyo-Clacton. Actually I don't believe in a God that can be talked to, prayed to, haggled with, and so on. There might be something dreaming the universe or even consciously thinking it but I very much doubt that its eye is on the sparrow. Maybe it thinks in waves and particles and patterns, and one of the patterns is Mr Rinyo-Clacton.

Back at the Lord Jim I got a knife out of my bag—a French one with a four and three-quarter-inch blade that folds into the wooden handle. I'd never used it for anything but cutting baguettes and sausages but I kept it razor-sharp. I put it in my jacket pocket and went back to Earl's Court Road.

I thought I might have dinner at the Vegemania but when I got there I saw Mr Rinyo-Clacton at a table by the window. Zoë and Rima were busy at other tables and Serafina was serving him, yes, potato pancakes while he smiled up at her. My right hand fitted itself around the smooth and shapely handle of the knife in my pocket. Forget it, I said to myself—you're not cut out for this sort of thing.

As I stood there watching I could almost smell the whole scene, him and her and the potato pancakes—bitter aloes, fear and desire, and the crispy golden-brownness that was the ultimate expression of the art of frying. Everything I saw seemed more so: Serafina in jeans, grey jumper, and leopard-spotted scarf, blushing slightly as she looked down at him from under her long lashes, her face thoughtful; Mr Rinyo-Clacton elegant in a black suit, white shirt and what was probably a regimental tie; his black brows and moustache, his rosy cheeks and bright eyes as he smiled up at her; the warm lustre of the varnished pine tables; the soft glow of the bell-flower lamps; the gleam of the bentwood chairs; the pancakes on the blue-and-gold-rimmed plate with the little tubs of apple sauce and sour cream.

As if it were a scene in an opera I could see the Daimler pulling up later and Serafina getting into it while the music voiced its foreboding with strings and woodwinds. I could see Mr Rinyo-Clacton, delaying not, hurrying not, rising and falling like the sea as he took his pleasure on the long body of Serafina. On the leopardskin back seat, on the silken sheets of his bed, perhaps even standing up in his white-pillared doorway. Mr Rinyo-Clacton who had never been HIV-tested.

He'd probably leave the Vegemania after his second or third order of potato pancakes but he'd be back between ten-thirty and eleven when Serafina finished for the evening, and if I waited until the Daimler came round it would be too late to warn her. The whole-food shop was still open and there was access to the kitchen through it. I told Ron I needed a quick word with Serafina and went into the kitchen where more potato pancakes were sizzling on the griddle and sending out their pheromones. Serafina half-smiled when she saw me. "If you want some," she said, "you'll have to sit down at a table like the rest of the punters."

"Not this time, Fina. That man out there with the moustache, the one who looks like Lord Lucan—I know he had lunch here and I saw you talking to him before . . ."

The half-smile vanished. "Should I have asked your permission?" Zoë came in at that moment, gave me a less than friendly look, and became busy with tortellini.

"Please listen to me," I said to Serafina. "I know him and he's bad news. If he asks you to go out with him, don't do it. He's not to be trusted."

"What else is new?"

"Maybe we should talk about this privately."

"If you've got anything to say, say it now."

I paused while Zoë, shaking her head, exited with the tortellini. "He's not to be trusted," I said, "because one way or another he'll get you into bed and he won't use a condom and he might well be HIV-positive."

"What?" Serafina's eyes were suddenly very large. "How do you know that? Oh, no!" Smoke was rising from the griddle as the pancakes burned. "Shit!" she said, and with the spatula she lifted them up and dropped them into the bin.

"Fina!"

"What?" Her face was turned away from me.

"Look at me!"

When she turned towards me she was blushing. "Serafina, you've slept with him, haven't you?"

"Jonathan, tell me how you know so much about this man's sex life."

"Will you answer my question if I answer yours?"

"Yes."

"What I'm going to tell you—it isn't how it might sound; I'm still the same Jonathan, I haven't changed and become something else, I . . . "

"For God's sake, Jonathan, just say it."

"Goddam it, Fina, I don't think you know what it did to me when you left. I was depressed all the time and drunk a lot of the time and I was really at an all-time low when I met this guy and he invited me to his box at the opera . . . "

"Go on," she was looking at me as if everything that had been between us was suddenly wiped out and she didn't know who or what I was.

"Well, I had a lot of champagne and we went back to his place and he . . . "

"He what? I need to hear you say it."

"Well, he had me."

"He had you. Are you telling me that he buggered you?"

"Yes—it just sort of happened without my intending it."

"Without a condom?"

"Without a condom."

"How come? Why didn't you ask him to use one?"

"Jesus, Fina, don't make me give you a play-by-play description. We didn't talk about what was going to happen—it was a situation where he just took charge and there we were."

"And how was it for you, Jonathan?"

"Embarrassing."

She shook her head. "Whew! This is a side—or should I say a backside?—of you that I'd no idea of. When you were having all those affairs with the Excelsior ladies, were you doing it with the men as well?"

"Give me a break, Fina—nothing like that ever happened before."

"Well, I'm thankful for that. I mean, I'd like to think that *something* of what we had was real."

"You know it was, it *is*, real—all of it."

"You can say that but I don't know what I know any more."

"Yes, you do. But let's come back to my question—I've answered yours and now it's your turn to answer mine."

She was blushing furiously but she looked me in the eye with something like defiance. "The short answer is that he's had me too."

I shook my head as I tried not to see her and Mr Rinyo-Clacton naked on that bed. "When, for God's sake?"

"This afternoon."

I ground my teeth. I'd been thinking of him as dangerous only at night and I'd forgotten that Serafina was off between three and five. "I don't believe this. Have you ever seen him before today?"

"No."

"Was it rape?"

"No."

"My God, I'd no idea you were that easy, Serafina. How'd he manage it—'Come up to my place and look at my African sculptures'? What?"

"Don't," she said.

"Did he say anything about me?"

"Only that you were a friend of his and he'd heard about the Vegemania and my potato pancakes from you."

"My friend Mr Rinyo-Clacton! O God, who would have thought you and I would ever be having this conversation! Did he use a condom?"

"Goddam it, Jonathan, you're not in a position to play the outraged husband."

"All right, but did he?"

She shook her head. "No."

"O God, what if you get pregnant from him?"

"Wrong time of the month."

"But the other possibility! Why couldn't you have been more careful?"

"Like you, right? Somehow there isn't always the moment for careful; there wasn't for you and there wasn't for me. We'd been to a place in Sloane Square and I'd had a lot to drink and I was feeling low the same as you and I think I just wanted some consolation. He knew how to say the right things, he was very sweet and gentle and it just happened the way it happened."

"And how was it for *you*, Serafina?"

"Oh God, I don't think I've got the words for it. It was like an out-of-body experience where I was looking down at the two people on the bed and I knew that I was one of them but it was all so strange, so strange!" She covered her face with her hands.

"When I looked through the window and saw you serving him potato pancakes I didn't know whether you fancied him or what."

She took her hands away. "He wanted me to go out with him tonight. I said no. *Is* he HIV-positive? Are you sure about that?"

"I can't prove it but he told me he never takes precautions and he's never been tested and I'm pretty sure he's had a lot of partners. And if he's HIV-positive he probably gets a thrill out of spreading it around. And there he sits eating your potato pancakes, that son of a bitch."

Zoë came in with a tray of dirty dishes. "Table One wants to know what happened to his second order of potato pancakes," she said.

"Potato pancakes are off," said Serafina.

"I'll tell him," said Zoë, and was gone.

"I can't get over it," I said. "Two days ago I'd never set eyes on him and today here we are like this."

"Both of us maybe HIV-positive," she said, looking at me sadly. I wanted to hug her; I stretched out my arms to her but she backed away. "Damn you, Jonathan, none of this would have happened if you hadn't cheated on me." She was shaking her head despairingly. "I think maybe you've destroyed us, I think you've taken our lives away." She covered her face again, and again I tried to hug her but her arms were in the way. "You used to give me comfort when I needed it," she said, "but not any more—that's all over, all gone with all the rest of what we had: all gone, all gone."

What could I say? Zoë came in with more dirty dishes and a folded envelope which she stuck in the little wall-mounted box they used for notes and messages. "It was on the window sill between the rubber plant and the aspidistra by Table One."

"Is he still there?" I said.

"Gone." She picked up an order of tagliatelle and withdrew. Serafina grabbed the empty brown C5 envelope with a printed label addressed to T. Rinyo-Clacton, Esq; no indication of where it was from. It had been folded in half to make it pocket-size and the back was covered with Mr Rinyo-Clacton's handwriting. At the top was what looked like a telephone number. Below it we read:

> Space between—like moat to keep animals from getting out—jump over space between mind and brain
> MR RINYO-CLACTON'S OFFER
> Clay—infirm vessels all—leaky & easily broken—death in every one—return to earth. Millionaire Aquarius, bisexual, HIV-positive, afraid of dying, seeks companion in death. Offers to buy someone's death. No control over his own except suicide but controls death of other—offers £1m + year to live. Will other take £1m, try to kill R-C? Other's wife or girlfriend—will R-C sleep with her, spread his death around?

"Oh God," said Serafina. " 'Millionaire Aquarius, bisexual, HIV-positive.' "

HIV-positive. There goes my life, was my first thought. I might as well say now that when I signed that document in Mr Rinyo-Clacton's study I did it thinking I'd find some way for him to predecease me. It was a thought that came to me that first time he buggered me. I'd been hoping to enjoy a full life plus the million pounds but now I had no doubt that I'd been infected by him—this was the destiny I'd shaped for myself and Serafina. "Other's wife or girlfriend—will R-C sleep with her, spread his death around?" And he'd already done it!

"What's he playing at?" said Serafina.

Ron looked into the kitchen. "Please forgive my rudeness in interrupting your conversation," he said, "but this place is actually a restaurant. That is, people come here to pay money for food which we prepare and serve to them. Crazy idea, I know, but there it is."

"Sorry," I said, "I was just going." I stuck Mr Rinyo-Clacton's envelope in my pocket. "Can I come back for you when you're ready to go home?" I said to Serafina.

She nodded and I left.

20

At Zoë's Place

The telephone number on the back of the envelope was a central London one that might possibly have some connection with Mr Rinyo-Clacton's notes. I was used to his style by now: it was in his nature to flaunt rather than hide his intentions; his notes might even have been left for that very purpose. If the notes were for a book, then the number could be that of a publisher. A title page appeared in my mind: *The Carnivore Cookbook*, by Celestine Latour. I saw Mr Rinyo-Clacton grinning at me in Waterstone's, felt his hand on my bottom, saw Serafina being devoured by him, saw him smacking his lips as he tasted her sweet flesh. The title page had had a publisher's logo with a little angel: Derek Engel. That same logo was on the title page of *Mind—the Gap*. Was Derek Engel going to publish Mr Rinyo-Clacton? Would the seduction of Serafina be in it?

All the way back to the hotel my mind regaled me with a continuous showing of Serafina and Mr Rinyo-Clacton in action, with many close-ups and amplified location sound. The slow-motion sequence of my Serafina with her legs wrapped around him had an awfulness that was fascinating. Other and worse images offered themselves. Stop it, I said to my mind, but it wouldn't stop. Had Serafina had similar pictures in her mind when she discovered my infidelities? Nothing would ever be the same again.

Full of rage and regret I arrived at the Lord Jim and looked up Derek Engel Ltd in the telephone directory. The number was the one that Mr Rinyo-Clacton had written on the envelope. Too late to phone today — I'd have to wait until tomorrow. When I got to my room it no longer seemed a refuge but a place of dead air and inaction. The mirror on the door was full of darkness and foreboding. I began to pack my things and when I found *Mind — the Gap* in my hands I opened it at random and read:

> Human beings are not naturally lawful; one has only to watch children at play to confirm this. Adults acquire knowledge and understanding as they mature but essentially they remain children who have been trained (or not) to behave in socially acceptable ways. In films and novels passionate and violent men and women act out, for those of us so trained, what we dare not act out for ourselves. "The greatest pleasure," said Genghis Khan, "is to vanquish your enemies and chase them before you, to rob them of their wealth and see those dear to them bathed in tears, to ride their horses and clasp to your bosom their wives and daughters."
>
> Most of us are brought up to be rather less straightforward than Genghis Khan but the limbic system win always have seniority over the cerebral cortex. Try this simple test: here are some imaginary headlines; which story will you read first?
>
> PEACE TALKS STALLED
>
> FIVE NEW BODIES IN HOUSE OF HORROR
>
> NEW CURFEW IN KABUL
>
> NUDE ROYALS IN SEASIDE ROMP
>
> MORE CUTS IN NHS SERVICES
>
> GAY VICAR KILLED IN CLUB BRAWL
>
> FILM STAR RAPED ON YACHT
>
> Special interests apart, I doubt that the peace talks, the curfew, or the NHS cuts will be first choice. Sex is reliably interesting, as is death. The death of others is always life-affirming; who has not felt, on reading of a disaster in which hundreds have died, a little inner leap of "not me!" Life is energy, constantly in motion. The plains Indians believed that the taking of a life gave power to the taker; the natural psychology of the hunter is one of balance maintained through energy transfer from prey to predator.

Dr von Luker continued in this vein with the urgency of a would-be cult leader, his text heavily supported by quotations from Darwin, Nietzsche, Freud, Jung, Ouspensky, Gurdjieff, Krishnamurti, Canetti, Lévi-Strauss, L. Ron Hubbard, Obi-Wan Kenobi, and thirty or forty others.

I went back to the title page: Derek Engel, Bedford Square. "Tomorrow, Derek," I said. I looked at the author's photograph on the back of the dust jacket: bald and bearded. Was there something familiar about him? How would he look with a wig and a military moustache? Yes? No? Difficult to be certain.

It was time to leave this place of dead air; I packed my bag and made ready to climb back aboard my *Patna*. Without looking in the mirror I left the room, went down to Reception, and said to the beautiful black-haired girl, "This is goodbye."

"I still have to charge you for tonight," she said. I nodded, paid up, and left.

"Be nice," I said to the plants when I got back to my flat, "this is a tough time for me." I went to the bathroom and splashed cold water on my face—the moment seemed to require it.

At half-past ten I turned up at the Vegemania and found Serafina waiting outside while Zoë and Rima finished up. "Do you mind if we go to Zoë's place?" she said. "I've been staying with her and I'll feel more comfortable there than anywhere else right now. It's near Fulham Broadway, in Moore Park Road."

"Fine," I said. As we walked towards the tube station she took my arm, then realised what she was doing and removed it.

"Those notes on the envelope—" she said, "is he writing a factual account or is he plotting a novel and acting it out? What do you think he's doing?"

"The telephone number with the notes was for Derek Engel—he's a publisher who does a lot of offbeat stuff. Knowing Mr Rinyo-Clacton I'd guess he's planning a novel with real people and himself as the hero. Tomorrow I'll ring up Derek Engel and ask if they know him. Rinyo-Clacton is obviously a pseudonym; maybe he's got others. Maybe he hasn't even talked to them yet."

"But buying someone's death for a million pounds—do you think that's real?"

"I know it is," I said as we entered the station and went through the turnstiles.

"How do you know?"

"I know whose death he's buying."

Her eyes were on my face and she grabbed my arm as we went down the stairs to the westbound platform. "Whose is it?"

"I'll tell you in a moment, but first I want to know if he told you his first name or did you call him Mr when he was humping you?" She was still holding my arm; it felt like old times, almost, except that old times were never quite this weird. The station seemed bright and exciting, a good place to be, maybe there were other good places ahead. Maybe I could make the picture of the two of them in bed go away.

"He said his name was Tod," she said. "And what did you call him when he was doing you?"

"I didn't call him anything. He told me his first name was Thanato-phile."

"Death-lover!"

"That's his game and that's the name he wants me to know him by."

"OK, now tell me whose death this weirdo is buying."

"Mine."

"Yours!"

"That's what I said."

"You're the other in his notes?"

"That's right, Fina."

"You're joking."

"I'm serious."

"Are you telling me that he . . . " She lowered her voice. " . . . took you back to his place, buggered you, then offered you a million pounds for the privilege of killing you in a year's time, and you said yes? You agreed to that?"

"Yes."

She was squeezing my arm so that it was pressed against her; it felt good. "In God's name, why, Jonno?" She hadn't called me that since she moved out.

"I don't know, it seemed a good idea at the time."

"Tell me, for God's sake!"

"Fina, I've told you how I've been feeling since you left me. The night I met him I didn't really care all that much whether I lived or died and when he made his proposition I thought I could at least leave you a million pounds and you could buy your own restaurant and have quite a nice life."

"Oh, you stupid Jonno, you stupid, stupid Jonno!" She hugged me then. We stood there holding each other while Richmond and Ealing Broadway trains came and went; our side of the platform grew more crowded but the Wimbledon arrow on the board remained dark; Wimbledon trains are always in the minority at Earl's Court.

"Let me see that envelope again," she said, and I gave it to her. "*'Other's wife or girlfriend—will R-C sleep with her, spread his death around?'* she read. "That bastard! That man is *evil*. Has he given you the million?

"Oh, yes, he's done *his* part."

"My God! A million pounds! Cheque or cash?"

"Cash."

"You've held a million pounds in your hands?"

"That's right."

"Then he really intends to kill you?"

"It's a jungle out there, Fina."

"How can you be so nonchalant?"

"When you hug me I feel that nothing bad can happen to me, besides which I'm half out of my mind so it's easy to be nonchalant."

"What about this: *'Will other take £1m, try to kill R-C?'*"

I put my finger to my lips. "Let's not think about that just now. Please hug me again."

She did, but she turned her face away when I tried to kiss her. "I still can't," she said in a very small voice, "I don't know where I am with you any more."

Earl's Court station encloses many volumes of echoing space and many lights and shadows, all of which pressed in upon us now and intensified the distance between us even though our bodies were touching. "Strange," I said, "to be together and not together like this."

"Everything is strange now," she said, "there's nothing familiar any more."

Eventually a Wimbledon train arrived and we took ourselves and the distance between to Fulham Broadway. We came out into a lot of noise and people outside the pub next to the station, then crossed and went down Harwood and turned right into Moore Park Road. Walking down that road to a house where Serafina now lived apart from me I felt that my life had flown away in all directions and left me behind.

Zoë's flat was in a house at the Eel Brook Common end of the road. On the far side of the common an eastbound District Line train rumbled past with golden windows. In the dim pinky-yellow of the street lamps I looked at Serafina and saw tears running down her face. We went up the steps, she unlocked the front door, we climbed the stairs past the smells and sounds of unseen strangers and arrived at the top and Zoë's place.

Serafina didn't switch on the lights immediately. I smelled cat and in the darkness of the sitting-room I saw on the mantelpiece the glow of a lava lamp in which ghastly red shapes like frozen damned souls huddled in their violet night. "The cat switches it on," said Serafina. "It must have done it just a little while ago—those are its warming-up shapes."

She turned on the other lamps to reveal a large black tomcat who was sitting on the floor contemplating the lava lamp; the flex trailed across the carpet and there was a cat-operable switch on it. There were a couple of wicker chairs and a low table, a brownish depressed-looking couch with some colourful cushions, a wall of well-stocked plank bookshelves supported by bricks, a poster of Leon Trotsky, and another, for In Your Face, featuring the rear end of a baboon. A beaded curtain separated the room from the kitchen.

"What's the cat's name?" I said.

"Jim."

"I was expecting something with a little more political resonance."

"Jim has no politics, he's more into meditation."

"Neutered?"

"Yes."

"That'll make anybody meditative."

"Will Zoë be coming directly home from the Vegemania?"

"I think she'll be staying at Mtsoku's place tonight." She wasn't looking at me as she said it. We took off our coats as if we had nothing on under them. She lit the gas fire and it purred softly as it glowed into life.

"Would you like something to drink?" she said. "There's a bottle of red or I can make some tea."

"Tea, please."

"What kind?"

"Rose-hip, please."

She looked at me sadly and went through the beaded curtain into the kitchen.

For a moment I stayed where I was, watching the lava lamp as the damned souls unfroze and sank into the primordial red. Zoë, though absent, was a presence in the room. She's twenty-seven, a statuesque six feet tall, does her blonde hair in many little plaits interwoven with coloured yarn and (when she's not waiting tables) headphones, wears kohl, patchouli, a silver nostril stud, and black garments with a lot of leg. The last time I asked her about the music in the headphones it was *Mind the Rap*, the latest album from In Your Face. Her current carrying book was a biography of Frida Kahlo. She has a degree in Politics and Modern History from Manchester University, is a member of the Socialist Workers' Party, and frequently gets time off from the Vegemania to take part in protests and demonstrations. Her boyfriend, Mtsoku, is a black saxophonist from Kenya who performs with In Your Face. Zoë's absent presence seemed to be watching me with a certain amount of cynicism.

I went into the kitchen and leant against the cabinets watching Serafina while she filled the kettle. "Why don't you put on some music?" she said.

Looking through the CD collection I was surprised to find the same Purcell disc we had at home. I put it on at Track 4, "Musick for a while":

> Musick, musick for a while,
> Shall all your cares beguile;
> Shall all, all, all,
> Shall all, all, all,
> Shall all your cares beguile; . . .

"Is this Zoë's," I said, "or did you buy it?"

"I bought it," she said from the kitchen.

With Serafina there I could listen to that song that I hadn't been able to bear alone: the haunted and haunting melancholy of Purcell's music and Chance's counter-tenor, a male voice not coming from the usual male place but from a soul-place beyond that, where in a flickering shadow-world of flame and darkness the guilty were whipped by a fury whose head was wreathed in snakes:

> Till Alecto free the dead
> From their eternal bands,
> Till the snakes drop . . . from her head
> And the whip from out her hands.

The beaded curtain rattled as Serafina came into my arms and I kissed her and hugged her and we cried a little. The kettle whistled; she went back to prepare the tea, then she brought in the jug and two mugs on a tray and put it on the low table by the couch where I was sitting. She sat down not on the couch but in a wicker chair opposite and there we were then. Jim rubbed against Serafina's legs, then jumped into her lap and purred loudly.

There sat my Serafina in her old faded jeans and baggy grey jumper, my destiny-woman who wasn't mine any more. I looked at her and looked and looked, wondering if I had ever really seen her and trying very hard to see her now—her face that was at the same time sharp and softly rounded, her ripe mouth a little open as if for another kiss, her blue-green eyes as she leant forward, her long fingers caressing the self-satisfied cat. You can't step into the same river twice, I was thinking. Sometimes you can't even find the river.

"Fina," I said, "why are you sitting so far away?"

"Jonathan, a hug and a kiss can't take us back to where we were before."

"I'm not trying to get back to where we were, I'm trying to move for-ward to a new place." As I said the words I heard them coming out in soap-operaspeak.

"That's easy to say, but if you put in salt instead of sugar when you're making a cake and then you put in sugar to cancel out the salt, it doesn't— all you have is a ruined cake."

Purcell and Chance were now into "O Solitude" and the lava lamp was doing swaying red cobras and phallic shapes whose heads came off and rose to the top of the cylinder. "I'm not trying to cancel out the salt," I said, "but is there no such thing as forgiveness?"

"Forgiveness . . . " She lapsed into silence, then began to laugh.

"What?"

"I just had a vision of Humpty-Dumpty lying on the ground all in pieces, and he says to whatever made him fall, 'I forgive you.' But he's still lying there all in pieces."

"But you're not a broken egg."

"You don't know what I am, Jonathan. And I don't know what the act of forgiveness is. If I say, 'I forgive you,' what does that do? What happened doesn't go away. Maybe some of me goes away."

"Maybe what goes away can come back."

"Do you really think so? Zoë used to live with a man who cheated on her and she forgave him, whatever that is; but she said her anger didn't go away, it got worse as time went on and she changed in little ways, like she found that she couldn't stand the sight of the pubic hairs he left in the bath, and in bed if he touched her when she was asleep she'd give him the elbow without waking. She decided to end it before she started spitting in his tagliatelle."

"What can I say? For Zoë it's the politics of sex that matter."

"OK, let's come back to us. When we were together I was really with you—all of me. But you were living a whole other life separate from me. How were you able to do that? I don't think I really know who you are."

"Fina, I think most men want as much sex as they can get; some restrain the urge better than others and some are greedier than others. I never stopped loving you."

"Oh well, that makes everything all right then. Great. So what happened after I behaved so unreasonably and walked out? Then it seems you got greedy for men and you backed into our friend Rinyo-Clacton who got greedy for me and now maybe we'll both end up dying of AIDS. Is that the new place you want to move forward to? Is that the new bond between us?"

That stopped me for a while. The gas fire purred softly, the cat loudly; in the lava lamp red misshapen worlds rose and fell. Purcell and Chance carried on with:

> Lord, what is man, lost man,
> That thou shouldst be so mindful of him?

"And yet," I said, "you were in my arms and you kissed me only a few minutes ago. I don't think love can disappear just like that, I think you still love me."

"Maybe love doesn't disappear, maybe it just turns to stone, heavy inside you for the rest of your life. Kissing doesn't mean anything—it's a reflex that you can still trigger if I forget for a moment how things are. You look the same but you're so strange to me now! It's as if I'd been reading a book in English but the next time I opened it the whole thing was written in Transylvanian. So maybe I was out of my mind when I thought I could read it because now the pages are full of strange words that have no meaning for me." Her long fingers still caressing the cat as she spoke.

"That day when we got drunk in the Place des Vosges," she said, "all of me was with you and it felt so good. I'd never had that before, and you looked at me as if you were seeing the whole Serafina of me and I thought, Yes! this is really, really it. Then back at the hotel when we made love it felt as if all of you was with me, no part of you was anywhere else. Then the dream: my God, Jonathan, how many people ever have anything like that—the oasis that showed itself to both of us while we slept, the place of good water where the palm trees grow, and the desert all around. Lots of people wander in the desert all their lives, lots of people die in the desert but we'd crossed that desert and found the oasis in each other." She paused.

"Thrice happy lovers, . . . " sang Michael Chance. I stopped the CD player and switched it off. The naked silence rushed in upon us. Leon Trotsky looked down from the wall disdainfully. Little worlds of nothing rose and fell in the lava lamp.

"Mr Rinyo-Clacton is HIV-positive," she said, "and now where's our oasis? Maybe now all we've got is the death in each other." She covered her face with her hands and wept, then stopped after a few moments, noticed that the tea was ready, and poured it.

"You see what you just did?" I said. "After wiping me out completely with all that you've just said, you pour the rose-hip tea, my favourite kind that you made for the two of us, because life goes on. Look at Germany, look at Japan, for Christ's sake—after the horrible things they did in the last war and before that we're still doing business with them and hoping they'll build more cars and computers and TVs and everything else here because we need the jobs. Because life goes on, it has to. Forget forgiveness—there's only this imperfect world full of imperfect people to work with."

"Yes, Jonathan, but you're not the only man in the world, are you. And I've already quit the job."

"I'm the only one for you, Serafina."

"You *were*, Jonathan. But I wasn't the only one for *you* and that's what brought us to where we are now."

"Where we are now doesn't have to be the end of us, Fina: the thing is, do you want to realise our potential or do you want to give up and never know what might have been?" The words just came out that way before I could stop them.

She couldn't help laughing. "Are you going to sell me an Excelsior Couples Kit now?"

"Would you buy one?"

"I don't know, Jonno, I just don't know."

"You called me Jonno."

"It's hard not to."

"Should I take that as a yes?"

"Take it with a grain of salt."

"What does that mean exactly?"

"It means that I'm scared and confused and whatever I say is subject to change without notice."

"Maybe we should just drink our tea and be quiet for a while."

"That sounds like a practical suggestion."

Serafina went to the CD player, removed Purcell, and put on something that began with the chatter of a crowd, then slid into a smoky tango. "What's that?" I said.

"Astor Piazzolla—*Tango: Zero Hour*."

"It keeps trying to move forward while pulling itself back."

"Like life." She put the cat on the floor, switched off all the lights except the lava lamp, and came and sat beside me on the couch. She leant against me and I put my arm around her and sighed a deep sigh. "Grain of salt, Jonno," she said. "It looks to me as if we've got some heavy business ahead of us—you can help me make it through the night but all I'm taking is your time, OK? Nothing more than that."

I buried my face in her hair. "OK, Fina, whatever you say." So we made it through the night. Nothing more than that.

21

Maybe Loss

In a dream I was looking into a long, long dimness that stretched back to before the beginning of the world. Lost, lost, lost, I thought. There was something before this and now it's all lost. "Maybe," I said, and woke up as I heard myself saying it, "loss is where everything starts from."

"It's where it ends, too," said Serafina.

I rolled over and there we were, face to face in a strange bed, under the same duvet. I lifted it a bit: Serafina was in her knickers and a long Minnie Mouse T-shirt and I was wearing underpants and a T-shirt. Maybe all our troubles had never happened? "Have they?" I said.

"What?"

"Have all our troubles really happened?"

"Yes, and they're still happening. Go to sleep."

So we slept—uneasily.

22

So Many Are

"Hello," said a man's voice at the Derek Engel number. The word was spoken in a suave and leisurely drawl, with the first syllable stretched out and the second on a rising inflection. "Hehh-lo?"

"Is this Derek Engel?" I said.

"Speaking."

"Oh. You're Derek Engel himself?"

"So far."

"Sorry—I was expecting a telephonist."

"Would you like me to go away?"

"No, please—it's just that I didn't want to take up your time; I thought perhaps your publicity department could answer my query."

"Which is?"

"Have you got an author named Rinyo-Clacton?"

"Ah, what are we all but clay!"

"Odd that you should say that."

"Well, Mr . . . ?"

"Fitch, Jonathan Fitch."

"Mr Fitch. The only Rinyo-Clacton I know of is Late Neolithic pottery. You say there's an author by that name?"

"There's a *man* who uses that name. I thought he might be one of your authors."

"An interesting deductive leap. Has he written something you think we should publish?"

"I think he might be in the process of writing something now."

"So many are."

"Just one more question and I'll go away—do you think Dr von Luker might have any connection with Mr Rinyo-Clacton?"

"Why should he?"

"It's just another of my deductive leaps."

"Dr von Luker's here now; I'll ask him." He put down the phone. "Ernst," I heard him say, "know anyone by the name of Rinyo-Clacton?"

A second voice said, "No."

"He says, 'No,'" said Engel.

"Thank you. Well, I mustn't keep you."

"No, my authors do that, more or less. I shall be on the lookout for Mr Rinyo-Clacton's effort, Mr Fitch, and if it comes flying over the transom I'll make sure it gets read. Thank you for this advance notice."

"Thank *you*, Mr Engel."

"Goodbye."

"Goodbye."

As soon as I put down the phone I hurried to the tube station, took the Edgware train to Notting Hill Gate, changed to the Central line to Tottenham Court Road, and headed for Bedford Square. Turning into Great Russell Street I saw Dr von Luker's face advancing towards me. I had imagined him to be tall and broad, to be, in fact, Mr Rinyo-Clacton without a wig and with a beard but von Luker's head was on the shoulders of a man about as big as Toulouse-Lautrec.

I caught his eye. "Dr Lautrec!" I said. He favoured me with a cold stare. "I mean, Dr von Luker!"

This brought him to a halt. "What do you want?" he said, speaking as from a considerable height.

"I just wanted to tell you how much I'm enjoying your new book."

"Thank you," he said without an accent. He nodded and continued on his way. I went back to the corner, crossed Tottenham Court Road, mooched about in the Virgin Megastore for a while, then went home.

Thursday morning, this was, the day after the night when Serafina and I slept together apart.

23

Several Possibilities

Thursday afternoon. The men and women in the waiting room of the John Hunter Clinic, each frozen in single stillness, sat with eyes averted from one another. Although every one of us was in living colour we were like black-and-white portraits by one of those photographers who make everything look worse.

"IT'S YOUR CHOICE," said the sign over a display of condoms on a bulletin board in the corridor outside the counselling room. The unrolled sheaths dangled like the ghosts of passion under labels that identified them as SUPER STRONG, FETHERLITE, LOVE-FRAGRANCED, ALLERGY/HYPO-ALLER-GENIC, EXTRA-SAFE and so on. There was a diagram showing how to use them.

"Both of you with the same man," said Mrs Mavis Briggs with an air of scientific interest. Behind her was a colourful array of condom packets and a Van Gogh print of a sidewalk café in Arles at night. All of the tables in the foreground were empty. "I haven't come across that before."

"It never happened before," I said, "with us, I mean."

Mrs Briggs was a good-looking woman in her thirties in tight jeans and a black sweatshirt that said SHIT HAPPENS in white letters. She had black hair cut short, a husky voice, and the sort of face favoured by rock stars who sing of loves that end badly. Serafina was elsewhere in the clinic talking to another health adviser.

The room was bright and warm; I'd have liked to stay there for a long time. I thought fleetingly of Hendryk, the reality/illusion dog in Van Hoogstraten's peepshow. "There are several possibilities here," said Mrs Briggs: "maybe you'll both test negative when the time comes; on the other hand we can't rule out a result with both of you HIV-positive; or one of you positive and the other not. Have you thought of how you'd deal with either of those last two scenarios?"

"This is a strange time for us — we're not actually together right now."

SHIT HAPPENS said her T-shirt.

"I see," said Mrs Briggs. "That doesn't make things any easier, does it. The three months' wait before the test can be a pretty tough time to get through, and if there's any possibility of the two of you sorting out your problems this would be a good time to do it."

"What about it?" I asked Serafina later. We were over the road at The Stargazey drinking gin-and-tonics. Dusk outside. *Dusk* — the word has in it the sound of night impending, descending, owl-light in the city. The place seemed full of darkness. "Are we going to get through this together?" I said.

"In sickness and in health, eh? You and me together, right, Jonno?"

"Don't take cheap shots, Fina — it's too easy."

"I'm not strong enough for quality shots right now, OK? You want clever remarks, try somebody else in your wide circle of acquaintance."

Where was the Serafina with whom I'd made it through the night? "I can't believe that everything we had is gone," I said, recalling Piazzolla's *Tango: Zero Hour* that tried to move forward while pulling itself back.

"I don't understand you, Jonathan. First you piss all over what we had, then you get yourself buggered and bring this weirdo into both our lives, and now for all we know we're both HIV-positive; and you reckon this should bring us together?"

"Tell me what to do, Fina."

"Give me some time to get my head around this (pause), Jonno."

24

Hendryk Not Quite Himself

Thursday night I spent at my flat, alone. I got a fair amount of whisky down my neck to ease the pain of Serafina's absence and hoped that it would make me sleepy but it only sharpened the pain and made me wakeful; I found that there was no side of me that was the right side to fall asleep on. At first there was too much noise from the street—cars starting up or parking and people chattering loudly; then there came a silence that seethed in a sinister way; then a dream in which Hendryk kept trying to tell me something but I couldn't hear him. "What, Hendryk?" I kept saying until I heard myself and woke up and it was Friday.

In due course I stepped out into a harshly sunlit day, went to the tube station and headed for the National Gallery. As always, Trafalgar Square, the National Gallery steps, and the rooms inside were dense with tourists and clamorous with foreign tongues. With scarcely a glance at the masterworks of centuries, I went directly to Room 18. As if by special dispensation it was empty.

I looked through the peep-hole in the near end of van Hoogstraten's perspective box and there was the skeleton of Hendryk looking at me. "Jesus!" I said. I blinked, and when I looked again I saw nothing but blackness. "Give me a break!" I said. I kept my eye to the peep-hole but there was nothing to see and the room was full of people waiting to peep. "I have to go now, Hendryk," I said to the blackness. "I'll get back to you." The Japanese couple behind me looked at me quizzically and I realised I'd been speaking aloud.

In Trafalgar Square there was no rain to ease the sharpness of the day; the sunlight was coming down like splinters of glass on Nelson and the lions, on the fountains and the tourists and the pigeons, on the pavements choked with people and the cars that choked the road. I hurried to the darkness of the underground and went home.

25

A Useful Idea?

I went to the Vegemania at Serafina's quitting time, not knowing if I'd be welcome. She saw me through the window and came to the door. The evening was a brisk one, and she was wearing a long dark green home-spun-looking skirt, a black polo-neck, and a baggy grey pullover prob-ably knitted by an old woman who smoked a pipe and gathered wool from mountain bushes. She wore a tiger-striped scarf round her neck and her favourite steel-toed anti-rape boots to complete the effect. She had a big leopard-spotted bag slung from her shoulder. A great wave of desire swept over me at the sight of her. "Got your head around things a bit more?" I said.

"Not really. Let's walk." She took my arm (yes!) and we started down Earl's Court Road. "I won't say I'm sorry for being unpleasant yesterday," she said, "but I do see that it wasn't useful in any way." All around us people were eating, drinking, provisioning themselves at nocturnal green-grocers and supermarkets, laughing, cursing, arguing, embracing, and planning the rest of the evening or the decade while moving purposefully or weaving randomly towards whatever came next.

"I have a useful idea," I said.

"What?"

"Let's go to Paris for a couple of days, eat high-cholesterol things and get pissed in parks."

"What will that achieve, except to remind us of happier times?"

"It'll achieve not being here, and maybe if we put ourselves in a receptive state of mind we'll have some kind of epiphany."

"We've already had a couple of epiphanies, wouldn't you say? Right now I think I'm only about half an epiphany short of a nervous breakdown."

"Well, actually, there's something I want to see again."

"What?"

"Do you remember that place in Pigalle, Au Tonneau? Shaped like a barrel, looked as if it'd been shut down for a long time—Harry Belafonte posters on the doors?"

"Of course I remember it: the little train from Sacré-Coeur stopped there, the sky was very grey, the place looked haunted. There were sex shows and dirty cinemas all around there. Why do you want to see it again?"

"I don't know. Sometimes a thing that I've seen comes up in my memory and wants to talk to me—nothing I can explain, really."

Her arm was still linked in mine, her breast rubbing against me. "Can we go to the flat?" she said.

"Zoë's?"

"I said *the* flat."

"OK. The plants have missed you." We turned around and went back up Earl's Court Road to Nevern Place. When we reached the house I unlocked the front door after a few fumbles, stood aside to let Serafina in, and followed her up the stairs to the top floor, hearing in my mind the Ravel trio of our first night. She took out her own key and opened the door of the flat.

As the door swung inward all our nights and days, our sleepings and our wakings, all the everything of our four years together rushed out at us. Serafina covered her face with her hands and I took her in my arms but she kept her hands over her face. "Bear with me, Jonno," she said. "It isn't easy."

I switched on the lamps. "The plants don't look too happy," she said.

"I've been watering them but you have to remember that they were hooked on you and it's been cold turkey for them. What'll you have to drink?"

"Got any red?"

"Coming." I opened a bottle and watched the glasses filling as I poured. As soon as Serafina came into the flat everything looked more like itself; things reassumed their proper colour, texture and character; the lamplight had more warmth in it, the wine gurgled with surcease of sorrow. She went to the shelves where the CDs were and I wondered what music she'd put on. "Takemitsu!" I said, as it made its entrance like Bruce Lee coming over a wall and sneaking up on the bad guys.

"Right," she said: "*November Steps*, for orchestra with shakuhachi and biwa. It sounds the way I feel." By then Bruce Lee had abandoned the sneak-up and was banging on dustbin lids with a stick.

"As if you're in a dark and narrow place where something might jump out at you?"

"Something like that." We clinked glasses and sat down on the couch. She gave me one of her slanty smiles, somewhat careworn, took off the anti-rape shoes, and put her feet in my lap. "I think better this way," she said.

"What are you thinking about, Fina?"

"Just at this moment I'm thinking about Victor Noir."

"Who's Victor Noir?"

"He was a French journalist, only twenty-one when he was shot dead by Pierre Bonaparte in 1870."

"How come?"

"He and a colleague had been sent to challenge Bonaparte to a duel with a republican journalist named Grousset. Bonaparte claimed that Noir slapped his face and that was why he shot him."

"Why did Grousset want to fight Bonaparte?"

"Politics. The republicans were pissed off with Bonaparte because they thought he'd abandoned them when he became reconciled with Napoleon the Third."

"But why're you thinking about Noir?"

"I'm getting to it. On his tomb in Père Lachaise Cemetery there's a life-size bronze statue of him as he looked just after he was shot. He's flat on his back with his coat lying open and his shirt unbuttoned so you can see the bullet-hole in his chest. His trousers are partly undone to help him breathe as he died. He was shot on the 10th of January, only two days before he was due to be married."

"Not a good way to go."

"No, it wasn't. Now women visit his tomb and they kiss him and rub his crotch and his boots."

"As any right-thinking woman would, but why the boots?"

"I don't know, but he seems to have become a symbol of the virility and fertility of the republican ideal. He was originally buried at Neuilly but in 1891 he was moved to Père Lachaise and the tomb with the statue was paid for by National Subscription."

"National Subscription! Was he that big politically?"

"Evidently he started getting bigger as soon as he was dead, and Zoë says he's got a considerable following now. His bronze hat is lying upside-down beside him, and women hoping for a lover or a husband put flowers in it and kiss the statue on the lips. Those who want to get pregnant also give him a little rub. Some of them go a bit further . . . "

"How far?"

"All the way, actually, with a partner or just with Victor."

"Zoë told you all this?"

"Yes."

"Has she been to the tomb?"

"That's where she met Mtsoku."

"Was she there to do the business with Victor?"

"She'd been visiting Oscar Wilde nearby and was just browsing."

"And Mtsoku?"

"He'd been looking in on Marcel Proust but he'd heard about Noir's female following so he cruised over for a recce."

"But you still haven't said why you're thinking of Victor Noir."

"Who knows? Maybe if I leave some flowers in the hat and give Victor a rub I can find a faithful lover. I've rubbed your crotch often enough but that didn't seem to do it." She paused. "Or maybe if I ask very nicely he'll keep the HIV virus away from us." She began to cry, and made no protest when I gathered her up in my arms and kissed the top of her head. She said *us*, I was thinking, and the air seemed full of angel trumpets.

"Then you'll come to Paris with me?" I said.

She stopped crying, moved out of my arms, blew her nose, rearranged herself on the couch, drank some wine, and said, "Probably. But I need to talk a little more before I decide, and if I ask you to explain things I'm not attacking you—I just need to understand, OK?"

"OK, Fina." That one word, *us*, made me feel cosy and safe despite the fact that Death might well have me on its shortlist inside my body as well as outside my door. Takemitsu wasn't doing Bruce Lee any more, just sounding lonely. Au Tonneau showed itself to me: the empty barrel, wine all gone. Then the number on Katerina's wrist. Why do I do the things I do? I wondered.

Serafina drank her wine and pondered silently for a while, then she said, "What I'm wondering about is the difference between you and me—how you wanted other women besides me and I didn't want any other man. Maybe you didn't just want them, maybe you needed them. What kind of want was that, Jonno, what kind of need?"

"Fina, I've told you this before: I think most men—at least all the men I've ever known—just want as much as they can get."

"As much sex."

"Right. Men are programmed to spread their seed as widely as possible—scientists acknowledge that."

"But this wasn't just raw sex, was it? It wasn't so urgent that you did it standing up wherever the need took you—they wrote love-letters and so did you. You *courted* them, you had 'something special' with this one and that one."

"Jesus, Fina!" Her feet were on the floor; my lap felt empty.

"What?"

"Not everything can be explained."

"Try."

"Do you know the poem by Baudelaire 'To a Woman Passing by'?"

"No."

"He sees her in the street, in the deafening street that howls around him—a tall, slender woman in deep mourning, her hand lifting and swinging the hem of her skirt as she walks. She's agile and noble, with a statuesque leg. They look at each other, he says he drinks from her eyes. He knows he'll never see her again, and he ends the poem with, 'O you whom I could have loved, o you who knew it!'"

"Right—so he was deeply moved by a statuesque leg and I know that you are too. But he doesn't say he wooed this woman until he got her into the sack."

"Maybe she was too agile for him."

"Stick to the point—you brought up that poem because we were talking about romantic love as opposed to straight shagging. Apart from anything else, romance is time-consuming. How many can you handle at the same time?"

"I think that's a rhetorical question."

"Answer it anyhow, please."

"I don't think you're asking how many I can handle—what you want to know is why I did what I did."

"OK, tell me that."

"It's very hard to spell it out."

"Not everything can be easy, Jonno."

"I keep feeling as if I'm going to lose you for ever."

"Don't be so cowardly—whatever you tell me won't lose me more than you've done already."

"Then maybe I've already lost you for ever."

"Whatever happens, it's better to be honest with me and yourself, isn't it?"

"I'll try. The thing is, to me the sexual act was secondary—it was the *idea* that excited me: the idea of pulling a woman out of the unknown, someone you've never seen before but you sense a possibility and you want to get to that point where she lets you into her innermost privacy."

"And then what? Then you move on to the next one?"

I shrugged. "I never moved on from you, Fina."

"No, I was the home base—I can see that. But when you were having these affairs, didn't you think there might be consequences if I found out?"

"I didn't think you'd find out."

"But the deception itself has consequences—what you were doing had to make you different from the Jonathan I thought was with me. You must have compared me with the others: how I was in bed, how I looked, smelled, tasted, felt; the sounds I made, the things I said while I thought I was alone with the Jonathan I knew. So it was like a cloak of invisibility for you—you knew something that I didn't—we weren't both coming from the same place."

I found nothing to say.

"And there's the matter of the contract between us: it wasn't written down, it wasn't even spoken. But we did have an unspoken contract: you knew that you could trust me not to have anyone else on the side, and in accepting my fidelity and letting me believe in yours you made a contract with me. But you didn't honour it. Do you believe in such a thing as honour?"

"Yes."

"And does honour matter to you?"

"Of course it does, Fina."

"Can you explain how you can reconcile that belief with what you did?"

Takemitsu had stopped. There was only silence and the noises from outside. I heard the voices of other women in strange beds. Look at me, said Au Tonneau: empty. "You know I can't explain that," I said. "You say you're not attacking me but you've demolished me completely. My behaviour was dishonourable and I can't find any way of justifying it. All I can do is say I'm sorry and hope you'll give me a second chance."

"The thing is, Jonno, I wonder if you'll ever change. I think maybe you're afraid of women and that's why you have to keep knocking them over like tenpins. If you've needed to do that up to now, how are you going to stop?"

"I'll stop because I want you back and I don't want to lose you again."

"You say that now but can I ever trust you again? If I were to come back, could I ever believe anything you told me? In bed together, could I believe that it was just the two of us alone and private, with no one else getting between us?"

"We could try making love, see how it feels," I said stupidly.

" 'Making love.' There's a whole lot of making going on but there's not that much love about. Let's move on to the Rinyo-Clacton thing. What kills me is that I'd never have gone to bed with him if you hadn't been unfaithful. Your infidelities made me leave you and my leaving led to both of us ending up with Mr R-C and maybe HIV."

"You could have said no to him."

"Yes, and so could you. And here we are. I feel so tired—I can't talk any more tonight."

"Don't go back to Zoë's," I said. "Sleep here."

"But I want to sleep alone. Can I use the couch?"

"Take the bed. At least I'll have the smell of you when you've gone."

So once more we slept our separate sleeps. In the flat where we'd had so many sleeps together.

26

Insect Life

When I woke up on Saturday morning I felt more myself than I'd done for a long time; then I realised it was because I'd gone to sleep knowing that Serafina was sleeping in our bed, in the bed where she belonged. It was quarter past eight and there were comfortable sounds and the smell of coffee coming from the kitchen. My next thought was, O God, next year at this time—probably sooner—I'll be dead if I don't do something about Mr Rinyo-Clacton. And why do I always think of him as *Mr*?

Serafina was already dressed, bright-eyed and wide awake, ready for the day. "Good morning," she said as I came into the kitchen.

"Good morning. How was your night?"

"Wonderful. I still haven't got used to that futon at Zoë's place."

"You can sleep here every night, you know." I moved my mouth towards hers for a good-morning kiss. She turned so that I caught her on the cheek. "Right," I said. "Will you be around when I come out of the shower?"

"Yes, I don't have to leave for a while yet. Bacon and eggs?"

"Sounds good."

After breakfast I phoned Eurostar and booked us on the 08:23 from Waterloo on Monday. The telephone is a wall model that I never got round to fixing to the wall. The cord that connects the handset to the base is a thing of tightly coiled ringlets that often get entangled in each other and cause me to drop one or both parts of the telephone, which is what I did after booking the seats on Eurostar. The base fell to the floor and out of a recess in it rolled a small wad of tissue and a little high-tech bug—I'd seen enough thrillers to recognise such things. There'd been nothing to secure the device, no glue or tape or Blu-Tack, just that little wad of tissue that would allow it to fall out at the slightest jolt. I took the thing into the bathroom, lifted the lid of the cistern, and dropped it into the water so he could have a good listen whenever the toilet was flushed. Then I phoned Eurostar and changed the booking to Tuesday, after which I phoned Paris and booked the hotel.

"He's bugged the phone," I said to Serafina, "and he wanted me to find it." I told her what I'd done about it.

"Oh God, you mean to say he's been here in this flat?"

"With Desmond, probably. I'm pretty sure his skills go well beyond chauffeuring."

"But bugging's illegal, isn't it? And if he got in here without a key, that's breaking and entering, right? You *haven't* given him a key, have you?"

"No."

"Are you going to the police?"

"Oh sure, and the first thing they'll ask me is, 'Why would anybody want to break in and bug your flat?' and then I'll tell them I sold my death to some nut for a million pounds and they'll sort the whole thing out, yes?"

"So what are you going to do about it?"

"What I just did—drop the bug in the cistern."

"But if he wanted you to find that one, maybe there are others you won't find. If he's trying to freak us out, he's certainly succeeding with me."

"Well, I'm not going to turn the place upside-down looking for the others." I raised my voice and spoke to the plants, the lamps, the book-shelves, the coffee table. "Can you hear me, Mr Rinyo-Clacton? If this is how you get your jollies, be our guest."

"This isn't funny," said Serafina. "Maybe it doesn't bother you but I wonder if I'll ever feel safe here again. Are you going to change the locks?"

"What's the point? If these locks didn't stop him, new ones won't either."

"What about those fancy systems you see in New York flats in films, where these long steel bars slide into place?"

"He'll always find a way to get in, Fina. I refuse to panic about this."

"He could have been in the flat last night, watching us while we slept. What would you have done if you'd woken to find him standing over you?"

"If we caught him in the flat he probably could be had up for it. Unless he's had a key made, in which case he'd say I'd given it to him."

"Shit."

"You see what he's doing? He's making us spend more and more time thinking about him, trying to guess his next move. Please, let's not do this."

"I'll try not to."

But we didn't stop thinking about him.

27

Lumps of Time

Mr Rinyo-Clacton's presence, once I'd discovered that bug, filled the flat like a smog. We saw his invisible shadow huge upon the wall, smelled him in the air, tasted him in our food, heard him in the silence, felt his ugly hands all over us.

Serafina was now back at Zoë's and I was going to have to make it through the nights remaining between us and Paris alone. Time lay about in lumps and blobs, refusing to move. I went to the National Gallery to check out Hendryk again in Room 18. He was his normal self but gave me nothing. Why, I wondered for the first time, was there a woman in a bed glimpsed through a doorway. Perfectly respectable—just her head in a nightcap showing above the counterpane. Was she ill? Was she dying?

I went to the British Museum to look at two of my favourite things: the first was the little bronze head of a goddess, probably Aphrodite (Greek, second century BC), found near Mersin, Cilicia: not a solid head, just a shell of the face and the front of the hair, almost a mask. Hauntingly beautiful, her face: thoughtful and compelling. Her painted eyes, viewed from above, were seductive; from below, full of doubt. Now they seemed more full of doubt than usual. I'd visited her many times but only this time did it occur to me that Aphrodite knew all there was to know about love. On the other hand, maybe she was an ignorant goddess who made all kinds of love happen but knew nothing about any of them.

This whole thing, I said to her, is about me and women, isn't it?

No answer.

I went to the Assyrian Saloon and King Ashurbanipal's lion-hunt reliefs from Kuyunjik to visit a particular lion, the one who grasps and bites the chariot wheel that pulls him up to his death on the spears of the king and his huntsmen. I looked into the shadowed eyes under the lion's frown, fixed for ever in the tawny stone. There are two arrows in the lion and two spears; his stone rage and his stone dying have endured for more than twenty-five centuries.

This lion-hunt, apart from being a remarkable work of art, is interesting in that the king, with his carefully curled hair and beard, is only a generalised formal figure as are all the other humans; but the lions are individual tragic portraits. The lion grasping and biting the chariot wheel is undoubtedly the king of the lions, the one whose frown and shadowed eyes are fixed for ever on that mystery that he so violently embraces.

What do you think? I said to him.

His answer was his action; it was between him and the wheel—what else is there to hold on to?

It was an unusually warm day for October, and girls from everywhere were sitting on the museum steps. Life would go on, leaving me behind with the lion, the goddess, and the little dog Hendryk.

I went to see Katerina, feeling a little uncomfortable about it. My night with her now seemed a strange dream and I knew it wasn't going to happen again. When she'd held the banknotes, her face, with the lips drawn back from the teeth in that dreadful rictus, had seemed almost a gorgon-face, full of a terrible power. Well, even Ashurbanipal had the help of a powerful grandmother.

With a no-bullshit modern psychic and clairvoyant no explanations are necessary: this meeting was strictly business. "You feel it?" she said when we sat down at the table with the little bronze woman and the blue bellflower lamp.

"Feel what?" I said as Mr Perez favoured us with the overture to *La Forza del Destino*.

"How it all comes to a point now. Very soon the waiting is over and we see connections that we did not see before."

"Katerina, what do you know that I don't know?"

"I know nothing, Jonathan, but I can feel the shape of what's below the fin that cuts the water. He also, this Rinyo-Clacton—he wants it to be over soon."

I told her about our Paris plans. "Should we not go?" I said. "Is there something else I should be doing?"

"Don't change whatever plans you have—go to Paris with Serafina and be open to whatever comes to you there. Enjoy yourself, even. You don't have to jump whenever Mr Rinyo-Clacton rattles your cage."

Melencolia, on my way out, favoured me with a look of genial contempt.

That evening I hired *Bring Me The Head of Alfredo Garcia* at the video shop. That film pretty well covers everything; I'd already seen it four or five times, and as I sat down to watch Warren Oates as the doomed Bennie I was wondering if there was any point in the story where he could have stepped out of the train of events that was bringing him to his death. Even at the end, though, he needn't have died: he gave *El Jefe* the rotting head, *El Jefe* gave him the million dollars, and Bennie could have walked out of there with the money. But by then his woman had died in the quest for the head and the death in Bennie could no longer be held back: he killed *El Jefe* and his bodyguards and was himself shot dead in his car as he drove away. His death had been in him from the very beginning, only waiting its chance to come out.

I watched the film again and ended up feeling tough, fatalistic, and doomed. I could make it through three more nights alone; I could even water the plants.

28

The Tomb of Victor Noir

Racing through Kent, Eurostar was due at the Gare du Nord at 12:23. Really, I thought, why all this speed? Things are already coming at me much too fast. There were no vents through which thoughts could escape, and I was being suffocated by mine. Probably other people's thoughts were adding to the air pollution as well. Why couldn't they have a red circle on the window enclosing a brain with a diagonal red line through it?

"Have you read this?" said Serafina, showing me her book, *The Wonderful History of Peter Schlemihl*, by Adalbert von Chamisso.

"Yes." I'd have felt better if she'd brought something else for the trip.

"That's quite an idea," she said, "selling your shadow to the Devil for a purse that never runs out of gold."

"He was sorry for it later when he lost the woman he loved."

"Well, she wanted all of him, didn't she. What're you reading?"

"*Carmen*—not the opera but the Prosper Mérimée story."

"May I have a look? I want to see the ending." She found it and read aloud, "'She fell at the second thrust, without a cry. It seems to me that I can still see her great black eyes fixed on me; then they became dimmed and closed.'"

"She told him she couldn't love him any more, so he killed her," I said.

"That's one way of dealing with it. Do you think he's on this train?"

"Don José?"

"Don José Rinyo-C. Do you think changing the booking did any good?"

"Yes, I think he's probably on this train, so it follows that I don't think changing the booking did any good. But I don't think he's got rape and murder on his mind at the moment—he's just fondling my unripe death while mentally replaying his afternoon with you."

We ate sandwiches, drank tea, and were informed by a voice, first in English then in French, that we were entering the tunnel and would be out of it in twenty minutes. "What worries me," said Serafina as Eurostar plunged through the darkness beneath the English Channel, "is that maybe *everything* is connected by tunnels: you think *A* is separate from *B* but no, below the surface things are constantly sliding around and making connections."

Monstrous creepy-crawlies came to mind, wet and slimy. "The things below the surface, they're not all necessarily bad," I said.

"They're hidden though, aren't they. You've no idea what's there till it jumps out at you."

I thought it best to say nothing for a while. Through the tunnel and out into France we read or closed our eyes in meditation. We were going to be in Paris for one night only, returning tomorrow morning. "What I don't want," Serafina had said, "is some pathetic attempt to recapture what's gone. I'm full of pointy thoughts and sharp edges and all I'm looking for is clarity. You want to see Au Tonneau and I want to see Victor Noir and that's it, OK?"

Our passports were checked, and after a time the voice spoke again to say that the train had attained its maximum speed of one hundred and eighty-six miles an hour. Beside me Serafina was moving a little faster than that and leaving me behind. I wanted to taste her mouth, her body, I wanted her to be my Serafina again. I wanted never to have met Mr Rinyo-Clacton.

The voice told us that we were approaching the Gare du Nord. People were getting their bags down from the racks and standing in the aisle. The terminal appeared outside the windows and we stepped out of the train, looking anxiously to right and left but seeing no Mr Rinyo-Clacton. I think it was only then that the full weirdness of my situation hit me with the realisation that Death is always waiting for any door to open at any time.

Ahead of us was a modern clock with a black face and yellow hands. The dial had yellow hour markers but no numbers. Some distance beyond it was an older clock with a white face and Roman numerals. The time was 12:28. I was thinking that clocks in railway stations are more momentous than the ones in airports but it seemed an unlucky thing to say.

"Clocks in railway stations are more momentous than the ones in airports," said Serafina.

"Yes, and here we've got one with a black face and one with a white face."

"The black face is for tunnel travellers; the white face is from a long time ago."

I'd booked us into the Hotel Bastille Speria in the Rue de la Bastille where we'd stayed last time: one room, two beds, as specified by Serafina. We had no luggage but our rucksacks, so we took the Métro to Bastille and walked from there. The sky was grey and promising rain. We checked in, then took the Métro to Père Lachaise.

It was raining when we came out into the street, scattered herds of umbrellas moving slowly or swiftly over the glistening pavements. We had lunch at a brasserie on the corner, then went to the florist next door where Serafina bought three long-stemmed roses and I bought a map of the cemetery. Then we made our way under our umbrella down the Boulevard de Ménilmontant to the entrance of the necropolis.

Once inside we walked steadily uphill on rain-freshened cobblestones and wet brown leaves, tombs on either side of us compounding silence and slow time and the presences of absence. Deaths of all kinds watched us pass: deaths by age and illness and violence; by accident or intention; by one's own hand or someone else's; in bed, on the street, on the field of honour or against a wall. Here and there we saw other hooded and umbrellaed pilgrims with maps, heading for Jim Morrison, Maria Callas, Héloïse and Abélard, and others of the many celebrities gathered here. The grey rainlight was like a bell-jar of quiet over all. There was no sign of our friend. "It's so tranquil here," I said.

"Well, all their troubles are behind them, aren't they."

Onward and upward we went, past angels and obelisks and yew trees, past the Avenue de la Chapelle and Avenue Transversale No.1. Victor Noir was in Division 92, Avenue Transversale No.2. Rowan trees diminished goldenly to vanishing points in both directions. There was a little huddle of visitors at the tomb on which were plastic-wrapped bouquets of irises and chrysanthemums, a pot of cyclamen, and one gorgeous long-stemmed pink rose emerging from the hat and lying across Victor's burnished crotch. The huddle dispersed and we moved in for a closer view.

"I don't think I've ever seen a freshly killed statue before," said Serafina.

"It's a startler." Bronze Victor looked as if he'd been alive only a moment ago, his mouth still slightly open—handsome fellow with a moustache. How am I going to look when I'm dead? I wondered.

"Looks as if he might have been a good dancer," said Serafina.

"Aren't you going to give him the roses?"

"In a moment."

A slender black woman wearing a sky-blue turban hesitantly approached the tomb. Under her umbrella and the vivid blue her face looked out with a delicately melancholy air. She was carrying a bouquet of red and yellow chrysanthemums.

"I think she wants to be alone with Victor," said Serafina. We moved down the line a little way and she peeped round the corner of a tomb. "She's put the flowers between his legs and she's rubbing his boots," she reported. "Now she's leaving."

The woman's departing figure grew small in the rowan-lined Avenue Transversale No.2. The rain was coming down a little harder, and we moved to the tomb next to Victor Noir and sheltered under its portico. "What now?" I said. "Are you going to give Victor a rub and make a wish?"

"Maybe I am, and I'd rather you didn't watch me while I do it."

"Right. Here's the umbrella."

"No, thanks."

I guessed that she needed both hands free to get a grip on his boots which stuck up like handles and I hoped that Victor was as good against HIV as he was for pregnancy. I turned my back and waited two or three minutes until she tapped me on the shoulder. "He must be pretty efficacious," I said, "if women are still giving him flowers and a rub after all these years. I wonder how many husbands, lovers and babies he's delivered."

"You used to know when to keep quiet, Jonathan. It was one of the nice things about you."

"Sorry. Just tell me, are we finished here?"

"Yes."

She took my arm; her body rubbed against mine as we walked and the pattering of the rain on the umbrella was a cosy sound but there was nothing said between as we made our way back to the Boulevard de Ménilmontant. Our return route from Division 92 was slightly different from the one we'd taken going there. Père Lachaise offered view after view of the shadowy grey houses and monuments of the dead gracefully framed by foreground trees and backed by shapely dark and pale recessions of yew, larch, rowan and chestnut. Fallen chestnuts lay smashed on the shining cobbles. From one of the tombs two bronze arms, as if breaking through the stone, reached up, the hands grasping each other and a wilted iris. "DIEU NOUS A SÉPARÉS; DIEU NOUS RÉUNIRA," said the chiselled words.

"Where to now?" said Serafina. "Pigalle?"

"Right: Au Tonneau."

The Métro is one of my favourite Paris things; it's sleeker and shinier than the London Underground; the doors of the carriages open and shut in a snappier way; the whole system inspires confidence that things can be arrived at in an orderly manner.

Au Tonneau is just over the road from the Pigalle Métro station. I hadn't realised, the first time I saw it, that its emptiness had been taken over by the *Ciné Video* which has its entrance next door. The barrel-face was even more desolate than the last time, stripped of its Harry Belafonte posters and whatever else had been pasted there. The blind barrel-face with its gaping Gothic mouth seemed a paradigm of everything—all the problems of my life and my self reduced to one simple image: an empty vessel, the wine all gone. And in front of the boarded-up doorway Mr Rinyo-Clacton, debonair in a belted mac, smiling at us from under his umbrella.

"Look!" I said. "There he is."

"I see him," said Serafina. "What does he want, for Christ's sake?"

"He wants us to see him, he's teasing us. Wait here for me."

"What are you going to do?"

"Just give him the attention he craves. Maybe he'll leave us alone after that." I crossed the road to where he stood.

I had my knife in my pocket and I felt reasonably comfortable.

"*Bon jour*, Jonny," he said. "*Ca va?*"

"Can't complain. Are you enjoying Paris?"

"All the more for seeing you and the lovely Serafina. Are you sleeping together again or have I put her off lesser lovers?"

"If you're serious about being a great lover you should do something about your breath."

"You say that but you don't mean it; I know what you like. My breath didn't bother Serafina either. I tell you, that girl is really something—even in the heat of passion with her legs wrapped around you she's somewhere inside herself that's cool and far away. Inspired me to heroic efforts which were well and truly appreciated. Maybe we can make it a threesome to-night, eh?"

"Maybe you can make it a onesome."

"Your trouble is that you don't know how to loosen up and enjoy yourself. Actually, it's your uptightness that makes you so sexy—if you're not careful I'll have your trousers down right here."

"It could damage your health, Thanatophile."

"Why? Have you picked up something since the last time?" His mouth was laughing but his eyes were hard. "Jonny, Jonny, you'd like to kill me because you're afraid of me, and you're afraid because you recognise in me an aspect of yourself that scares you. You've surrendered your life to me but you're trying to keep a tight sphincter. And of course, now that you've had the million you can't help thinking how nice it would be to go on living."

"It's always a pleasure to talk to you," I said. "We'll be in touch. Bye bye."

He mouthed a kiss as I turned and went back to Serafina. "What were you two talking about?" she said.

"He likes to wind me up, that's all. He needs to be noticed."

"You shouldn't have given him the satisfaction."

"He'd have had more satisfaction if I'd tried to avoid him. Now that he's had his fix it's even possible that he won't turn up again until we're home."

We took the Métro to Bastille, bought two glasses and a corkscrew in the Rue St Antoine, acquired two bottles of Côtes de Beaune in the Rue de Turenne, and arrived shortly at the Place des Vosges which was only sparsely peopled now. I had a couple of carrier bags in my rucksack and I put them on the wet bench for us to sit on.

"I'm not trying to bring back the past," I said as I poured; what a pleasant gurgle. The wine looked full and red and juicy. "It's just that this is my favourite drinking spot. Here's looking at you, Fina."

"Cheers."

The wine tasted as good as it looked. How marvellous it is, I thought, when something is what you expect it to be. Of course sometimes it isn't marvellous. No oasis this October.

"I was just thinking," said Serafina, "of the Kris Kristofferson song where he says, 'I'd trade all my tomorrows for a single yesterday.' I can't believe anyone would really say that unless he was about to be stood up against a wall and shot. Would you trade all your tomorrows for a single yesterday?"

"No—I think we've still got good tomorrows up ahead, don't you?"

"I'll answer that after we've been HIV-tested."

I was looking past Serafina at one of the four fountains. The trees behind it were artfully massed as in a drawing by Claude Lorraine; against this golden backdrop the water cascaded from the rim of the upper bowl to fill the lower one, and from vents all round the lower bowl it spurted in silvery streams to the basin below. Like time, I thought—my minutes, hours, days and weeks falling, falling, but not recycled like the fountain water. Beyond the golden trees were dark ones, their trunks black in the grey light. Around the square the elegant houses stood and looked historic.

"The Place des Vosges dates back to the seventeenth century," said Serafina. "I looked it up in the guidebook. It's perfectly symmetrical."

"That's a relief." Our glasses were empty; I refilled them. "Did the visit to Victor Noir do what you wanted it to do?"

"I don't know that I can explain the Victor Noir thing—somebody tells you about something and you get a picture in your mind and a feeling. I'd never been to Père Lachaise and I thought of his tomb as being on a little hill away from the others. I was expecting something to come to me there—I don't know what. And then there he was, lying on top of his tomb in a long row of tombs as if he'd just been dumped there. I thought, Jesus! he's so dead! Somebody killed him and that was the end of him. It was strange that a statue should make death suddenly so real. It made *your* death terribly real, your death that you've sold to Mr Rinyo-Clacton. Just think—if only you'd never met him! If only you hadn't sat down on the floor in Piccadilly Circus tube station!"

"Nothing to be done about that now; 'the past is action without choice.'"

"That's deep. Who said it?"

"Krishnamurti; it's the one line I remember out of the ten pages I read." Our glasses were empty. I divided what remained in the first bottle, then opened the second and topped up the glasses.

"I'm glad we got two bottles," said Serafina. "This is not a one-bottle situation."

"I hope two are enough. Bottles seem smaller than they used to be."

"It's because the universe is expanding—it's a relative thing."

"Did anything come to you at Victor Noir's tomb other than the reality of his death and mine?"

"I don't know yet, maybe I'll know later. What about Au Tonneau?"

"It's empty." I refilled both glasses.

"We knew that before. What else?"

"It's full of absence."

"Go on."

"Like me."

"What absence is that, Jonno?"

"The absence of you and the absence in me that made you asbent. Absent."

"What absence is that, the absence in you that made me asbent? Absent, that made me absent, what?"

"I don't know if I have the worods for it. The woordos."

She moved closer to me and put her hand on my arm. "Find the worods and the woordos, Jonno. You were always good with worms. Words."

The sky was getting darker and there was a little chin in the air. Our glasses were empty and so was the second bottle. "What made you absent," I said, "was the absence in me of what would have made you stay."

"What was that? What was absent in you?"

"A real understanding of what was between us, Fina, and what there was to lose. You're my destiny-woman and I behaved as if you weren't. I wouldn't have wanted you to treat me the way I treated you."

"Took a lot of woordos to get there, Jonno." She squeezed my arm. The day was completely gone; the sky gave itself over to evening. The park attendant came out of his kiosk, blew his whistle several times and began his gate-closing round. *"Fermeture du soir!"* he said as he passed us.

We packed up the glasses and the corkscrew and dropped the empty bottles into the litter bin. Serafina took my arm and we found our way to Ma Bourgogne by the corner of the square, where after a short wait we were given a table in a corner. The place was crowded and noisy and the conviviality and good cheer around us made me feel suddenly alone and lost. All through dinner we were mostly silent; I knew that Serafina was thinking, as I was, of the coming night and morning and the rest of our lives.

29

Yes and No

We were lying in our separate beds wide awake in the dark. After a while Serafina said, "Can I come in with you?"

"Sure."

"I don't want to do anything except just be with you, OK?"

"OK, Fina."

When she crept in under the covers I hugged her and she hugged me back. "Jonno," she said, "I'm so scared."

"I know."

"Are you?"

"Yes and no. I'm worried about the HIV test but all we can do is wait. About the other—I'll think of something."

She evidently found that a workable answer, because she snuggled up to me and fell asleep.

30

Tombeau Les Regrets

We returned from Paris Wednesday morning, once more leaving the daylight behind us and speeding into the darkness of the tunnel. On yesterday's train to Paris, Serafina, though beside me, had not been really *with* me. On the way back she was with me but the weather between us seemed always on the point of changing from moment to moment; nothing could be taken for granted. What did you expect? I said to myself. At least she called me Jonno most of the time now.

On Wednesday afternoon an envelope was slipped through my letterbox. Inside were a note and a ticket for the Purcell Room that evening at 7.30: a concert of pieces for two viols by Sainte Colombe performed by Jordi Savall and Wieland Kuijken. The note said:

> *No, sex, Please! Cultural bonding only.*
> *Be there!*
> *T.*

Cultural bonding! That man certainly wanted value for money. And I felt that cultural bonding was actually what he meant: he was able to hold in his mind at the same time the idea of killing me and that of greater intimacy through music. It would be simple enough to stay away from the concert if I chose but I felt myself in some obscure way responding to the need that I sensed in his invitation, and of course there was the music. I'd first heard the compositions of Sainte Colombe and his pupil Marin Marais in the film *Tous les Matins du Monde*, and they had the sort of deep melancholy that I was very much in the mood for at present; I'd bought the soundtrack CD shortly after seeing the film and I was looking forward to hearing more of Sainte Colombe.

Serafina was at the Vegemania, due back at the flat tonight. I left a note for her and set out at six so as to have plenty of time for a leisurely coffee.

I came out of the underground at Embankment, made my way through the busy station, and mounted the stairs to the Hungerford Bridge. There are always homeless people at both ends, huddled in blankets or sleeping bags: gatekeepers between the glittering view and the hard realities of life. I gave money to the man at the near end, joined the many pedestrians coming and going, and paused at the viewing bay in the middle to take in the shining river and its boats, the distant dome of St Paul's, and the luminous sweep of London from the Festival Hall on my right to Charing Cross Station on my left.

The evening was cold, the air crisp and clear; the panoramic view was needle-sharp and bright with promise: this is where it's all happening, declared the domes and spires, the twinkling lights beyond, the boats showing green for starboard, red for port, and the trains behind me rumbling in and out. Charing Cross Station, all agleam with its swaggering arches, urged action. Live! it said. Go! Do!

I crossed the bridge, gave money to the woman at the far end and the recorder-player at the bottom of the stairs, and proceeded to Queen Elizabeth Hall where I found Mr Rinyo-Clacton sitting at a table with a cup of coffee and a chunky paperback. Early as it was, many of the tables were already in use by eaters, drinkers, readers and talkers. This was a far cry from the box at the Royal Opera House but Mr Rinyo-Clacton seemed comfortable enough among the common folk.

"What," I said, "no Cristal '71? No oysters, no Desmond? And they haven't got boxes here. How are you coping?"

"Every now and then I like to mix with the plebs, as you may have noticed."

"What are you reading?"

He held up the paperback: *Orlando Furioso*. "Noticed this in your bookshelves when we were bugging your flat," he said. "It's something I've always been meaning to read so I got a copy for myself, bought the Italian edition as well so I could hear the sound of the original.

I got myself a coffee, then sat down to hear what he had to say about Ariosto. "This part in Canto VIII," he said, "where naked Angelica's chained to a rock waiting to be devoured by Orca and Ruggiero comes to her rescue, you had a marker stuck there in your copy."

"Yes."

"Do you especially like that part?"

"Yes."

"Have you seen the Redon pastel, *Roger and Angelica*?"

"Only in reproduction—the original's at the Museum of Modern Art in New York."

"I've seen it there. They never get the colour right in reproductions; reducing it from the original doesn't help either. It's mostly murk, that picture, which is why it's so true to life: all those rich blues and purples and greens are full of paradises and delights you can't have because the murk is impenetrable."

"Still, despite the murk, you can see Angelica well enough and Ruggiero *did* manage to rescue her."

"Angelica! The nakedness of her! Here she is in Stanza 95 with her . . . (reading from the book)

> . . . lily whiteness and
> Her blushing roses, which ne'er fade nor die,
> But in December bloom as in July.

In Italian it's juicier." From a shoulder bag he produced that edition and read:

> *i bianchi gigli e le vermiglie rose,*
> *da non cader per luglio o per dicembre . . .*

"Mmm! You can taste the deliciousness of her! But please note the shape of the rock she's chained to. Almost like a head, yes? Almost like a face, and whose face is it? Redon's of course. And the Angelica chained to him is the Angelica in his mind, the unattainable object of desire, the unhavable fleshly paradise of Angelica who vanishes when you stretch out your hands for her; she becomes invisible with the magic ring that you yourself, Ruggiero, have given her. It's a no-win situation."

"And of course," I said, "oneself is sometimes . . . "

"Angelica! the one hoping for rescue, how right you are!"

Amazing, I thought, how comfortable I feel with him when we're talking like this.

"The first time I saw you," he continued, "I knew at once that you were Angelica and I was your Ruggiero, come to save you from the sea monster . . . "

"Who is . . . ?"

"Life, my boy! Life is the monster I'm saving you from: it's too much for you: full of teeth and rocks and hard places and drowning. Not everyone can be a hero—indeed the heroes would be out of work if there weren't always a good selection of little sweeties to be rescued. You are one of those in need of rescue, naked and defenceless in a murk of uncertainty and chained to the rock of your inadequacy. Really, you should see the Redon original; we could go and have a look at it if you fancy a short break in *La Grande Pomme*. With Concorde we could leave in the morning, come back in the evening; or next morning if you want to do it in a more leisurely way."

"You really are crazy, aren't you?"

"And you're not?"

"I've never offered to buy anyone's death."

"But you were willing to sell yours."

We stared at each other in silence while the five-minute bell sounded, then we went along to the Purcell Room and our seats. I'm always interested in the differences in South Bank audiences for the various events: seventeenth-century music attracts, in addition to non-addicted punters like me, many people who look as if they read the *Independent*, avoid meat, and are not averse to a bit of morris-dancing in the month of May.

"Do you know Sainte Colombe's music?" said Mr Rinyo-Clacton.

"Only what's on the soundtrack CD from the film."

"Like it?"

"Very much."

"Would you say it's life-affirming or death-affirming?"

"That's a strange question, because any death-affirming art comes from the vital perception of a live artist, so the affirmation of death is at the same time an affirmation of the life in the artist and life itself."

"Ah!" said Mr Rinyo-Clacton, and squeezed my arm as the lights dimmed. There was applause; the bearded perfo·mers came onstage, bowed, and took their places. Using binoculars, I ⌣amined the carved female heads on the scrolls of the viols. It was as if the instrument-maker had in this way accorded recognition to the voice of the instrument. The viols were placed between the legs like cellos but the bows were held with the palms turned up so that the action of bowing seemed more one of supplication than command.

The polished gleam of the viols, the light glancing off the gliding bows, and the golden sonorities of the music seemed to constitute a magical being that had its own existence, independent of artists and audience, that could be reached by any mind that put itself in the right place. There was definitely a Lethean flavour to it and a beckoning to a state of tranquillity and no desire, a state beyond all pain and sorrow. The piece being played was *Tombeau les Regrets*. " 'The low and delicious word death, . . .' " Mr Rinyo-Clacton whispered in my ear as he gripped my thigh. I elbowed him in the ribs and he let go.

In the interval he went out to stretch his legs while I stayed in my seat and wondered what my chances were of taking my leave of him at the end of the concert. What is it with you? I said to myself. Why did you come in the first place? Don't bother me, I replied, and went back to my going-home thoughts. If Desmond wasn't in attendance, was Mr Rinyo-Clacton driving himself? If this was a night for mingling with the hoi polloi he'd probably cross the bridge with me, then go with me by tube as far as Sloane Square and walk from there to Eaton Place.

An elderly gentleman on my right had also remained in his seat: bearded, bespectacled, no morris-dancing. He was reading a book from which he now looked up. "Apropos of death-affirming," he said, "there was a song a while back before you were born: 'Gloomy Sunday'; 'the Hungarian suicide song' it was called, or maybe it was Romanian—one of those places. People used to play it on the gramophone, then go and kill themselves. Young, too, many of them. What a thing, eh?"

"Takes all kinds."

He shook his head and returned to the book he'd been reading. "Hmmph," he said.

"What?"

"What what? I didn't say anything."

"You said, 'Hmmph.'"

"So? A person's not permitted to think aloud?"

"Sorry, I had the impression that you wanted me to take notice."

"Really, it's not for me to say."

"Say what?"

"Nothing."

"It's not for you to say nothing?"

"You got it. He's a friend of yours, that man?"

"Not exactly. Why do you ask?"

"I'm a pawnbroker. In my business you get into the habit of reading people—you get a feeling as soon as they walk in: how they carry themselves, the look in their eyes and so on. The shop is in the East End and I've been robbed four times. Now I'm allowed to keep a gun for protection, and sometimes a person walks in and my hand reaches for it. If not for this instinct of mine it would already be six robberies. I tell you this so you won't think I'm just some old nutter. This man you're with, when I saw him come in it was like a cold wind blew over my heart." He nodded and said, with more emphasis, "A cold wind." He was wearing a cardigan, and as he thoughtfully scratched his left wrist with his right hand I saw, as on Katerina's arm, a number tattooed there.

"This man," he said, "you know him a long time?"

I counted back. "A little over a week."

"I thought maybe he only picked you up tonight."

"Do I look as if I could be picked up?"

"Maybe it's that he looks like someone who picks people up. Look, I didn't mean to meddle so much in your business, OK? I'll go back to my book now."

"What are you reading?"

He showed me: Rainer Maria Rilke, *Ausgewahlte Gedichte*. "You read German?"

"No, I've only read Rilke in translation."

"Rilke you can't translate. Even in German it's not always easy to know what he's saying: '*Denn das Schöne ist nichts als des Schrecklichen*

Anfang . . . ' In English this is 'For beauty is nothing but the beginning of terror . . . ' But that hasn't got the same bite as *des Schrecklichen Anfang*, which simply grabs you by the throat. What I just gave you wasn't even the whole line and already there's enough to think about for a long time."

Mr Rinyo-Clacton returned to his seat, the lights dimmed, the musicians reappeared with their viols, and began the first movement of *Le Tendre*. I thought about Rilke's words during the second half of the concert while navigating the waters of Lethe with Sainte Colombe. Beauty is nothing but the beginning of terror, I said to myself but I couldn't get my head around it. The dark river of music, instead of bringing forgetfulness, reminded me of the Thames and the Hungerford Bridge. I saw Mr Rinyo-Clacton and me crossing the bridge, saw us stop in that viewing bay that projected over the water . . .

The idea of the dark river, the night river, stayed with me all through the music, and it began to seem to me that everything that was between Mr Rinyo-Clacton and me was about this dark river. I felt that it must be in his mind as well, and I wanted to hear what he would say about it.

The concert ended; there was bowing and applause. The musicians were gone; the audience dispersed. Like a letter from a distant sender, the music of Saint Colombe had been delivered to each of us, to be read and re-read later when alone.

There were no buskers about and the night was cold when we went up the stairs to the bridge. The woman who sat there wrapped in a blanket was not the same one who'd been there earlier. Mr Rinyo-Clacton gave her a twenty-pound note. "They don't live long, these people," he said.

"Life is pretty short for some of the rest of us too."

He shrugged. The footbridge was crowded with concert-leavers. We moved among their footsteps until we reached the viewing bay, where we stepped aside to look at the river. There was a little sickle moon in the sky.

"Look at the river—" he said, "the lights and the glitter and the shine of it. But underneath there's only the blackness, only the blackness. Like that music: shining golden goblets but the wine is black water; that's all there is now and for ever." He covered his face with his hands and his shoulders shook.

"Are you all right?" I said.

"Do you care?"

I couldn't find any words.

"Tell me what you're thinking, Jonathan."

I shook my head and closed my eyes and saw a figure falling, falling to the dark waters below.

"Come home with me, Jonny. Help me make it through the night."

"No," I said, "all you've bought is my death. Let's go." When we came off the bridge he hailed a cab and was gone.

31

Camomile Tea

After the concert I was more confused than ever. "I know it sounds weird," I said to Serafina, "but it's almost as if he wants to be my friend."

"With friends like that you don't need enemies."

"No, really. Obviously he's some kind of crazy but he could be entering a new phase of it, or even coming out of the current one."

"That's as may be but I don't think I'd buy a used car from him."

"Maybe he's got no intention of killing me. Maybe he's so rich he can amuse himself by seeing what happens when he picks up some loser and makes the offer he made me."

"Is that what you are, a loser?"

"That's how I felt and I expect that's how I looked when he found me in Piccadilly Circus tube station."

"Which brings us back to the question: if losing me made you a loser, why did you let it happen?"

"We've been through all that, Fina. It's like dehydrated shit and you keep adding water and stirring."

"I don't want to but it keeps not going away."

The phone rang. It was Mr Rinyo-Clacton. "Jonathan," he said, "I need to talk to you. Please." He sounded humble; it was shocking.

"What about?" I said in a dead voice.

"Everything. Can we meet?"

"I'm not sure."

"God! You sound so hostile!"

"Well, as you said, Thanatophile, I'm chained to the rock of my inadequacy."

"Look, this is a strange thing we've got ourselves into but we can still talk, can't we? You like talking to me sometimes, I can feel it."

"Which reminds me, you're probably recording this very conversation from one of those bugs I haven't found."

"Some people are voyeurs; I'm also an auditeur, I can't help it, and I like the sound of your voice."

"Well, you can get your jollies playing this back but I need not to be bothered by you for a while."

"Jonathan . . . "

"What?"

"This could be the last time."

"You mean you intend to harvest me already? All the more reason to stay away from you."

"I have no intention of harming you. I humbly ask you as a friend— and in some mysterious way we *are* friends—please give me an hour of your time tomorrow."

Somehow, the balance of power was changing; doomed as I was, I was becoming the stronger one. Perhaps I wasn't doomed? "All right, meet me in Earl's Court Road in front of the tube station tomorrow afternoon at half-past five. Come by underground, maybe you'll make new friends on the way."

"Five-thirty—I'll be there."

"What is it with you and him?" said Serafina. "I'm beginning to think that the buggery established a real bond between the two of you."

"There's certainly *something* between us and I can't say I understand it."

"Let me know if you ever do."

"You'll be the second to know."

Serafina made tea for us, camomile, then we went to bed with a space between us. It took me a long time to fall asleep. I kept hearing him say, "This could be the last time."

32

Tchaikovsky's Sixth

I'd told Mr Rinyo-Clacton to come to Earl's Court by underground because I wanted him to be down among non-millionaires in the rush hour, wanted him to be uninsulated by his wealth when he came to our meeting. He'd sounded so humble on the telephone! Until now, when I thought about him, it was mostly him in relation to me, not him in relation to himself and whatever made up that self. Now I found myself wondering what it was like to be Mr Rinyo-Clacton when he woke up in the morning and when he went to sleep at night. Katerina had said there was fear in him. Of what? Was it possible that he could be afraid of me? Had he ever actually killed anyone? I had no facts about him except those that were part of our brief history. He'd said he was serious about killing me but he'd also said, in his new humble mode, that people change, that he intended me no harm in this meeting that could be our last.

Serafina was out doing the shopping; the flat was full of dumbness and irresolution and I had a lot of time to get through before the meeting with Mr Rinyo-Clacton. I needed some music and I was cruising the CD shelves when I found myself humming the opening of the second movement of Tchaikovsky's Symphony No. 6, the *Pathétique*, to which my mind was singing:

Earl's Court at half-past five today—
what is it that he want to say?

"Give me a break," I said, but I did want to hear that music and I didn't have it on CD. There was a tape somewhere in the flat so I rummaged in boxes, behind books, through random stacks of this and that and *ad hoc* heaps of clutter for about an hour and a half while hot waves of aggravation flooded through me. Finally I gave up and went to the Music Discount Centre by South Ken tube station and bought the recording by Mikhail Pletnev and the Russian National Orchestra.

Funny, I thought as I left the shop and walked into the unblinking daylight, here I've got this poor bastard's heart and soul, his life and death really, all digitalised on a little disc and I can play it straight through or start it in the middle or repeat each track several times or jump up and down on it and throw it in the dustbin. Destroy this one and there are hundreds of thousands more, recorded by every orchestra that's internationally known and some that aren't. The man himself is dead and gone but his misery is alive and well and available worldwide. T-shirts too, undoubtedly.

When I got home I slid the disc into the player and heard first the low hum of the darkness where the soul of the thing lived, then the bassoon slowly dragging itself all unwilling into the light. Oh, what a sad bassoon!

"Kindred spirit?" said Serafina, back from the shops.

"He certainly knew what trouble was."

"Don't we all."

"Yes, but not many of us are advised by a so-called 'court of honour' to kill ourselves and then go ahead and do it."

"Look who's talking."

"I wasn't pressured into this thing I'm in."

"This thing *we're* in," she said over her shoulder as she put things in the fridge. "Poor old Pyotr Ilyich lived in the wrong time and place for being queer. If he were alive in London now he'd be knighted and completely at home in the world of the arts and he wouldn't need to compose a pathetic symphony."

"The word that Tchaikovsky used, according to my *Oxford Dictionary of Music*, was *patetichesky*, which means 'emotional' or 'passionate' rather than 'pathetic.'"

"Whatever. He was still a pathetic man."

"Fina, why do you sound so hostile?"

"Because sometimes I think that when you met your new friend you connected with the real you. Maybe there are still bugs in this place, so I'll say it loud and clear, CAN YOU HEAR ME, MR RINYO-CLACTON? SOMETIMES I THINK YOU AND JONATHAN ARE THE REAL ITEM AROUND HERE."

Speaking to me again, she said, "If we both come out of this alive I might eventually get over your womanising but this other thing could really finish us."

The music seemed to be begging forgiveness and looking for a way ahead. I put my arms around Serafina but she made herself rigid and turned her face away from me. "Maybe, Jonathan," she said, "you've got decisions to make."

"No, I don't—the only future I want is one with you. What happened with me and him wasn't primarily a sexual act for me."

"What was it then?"

"You were gone and I didn't think you'd ever come back and I felt so low and lonely . . . "

"Go on."

"I wanted to be relieved of the burden of myself, of my manhood—I wanted someone else to take charge of me.

"And what now? Are you expecting me to take charge of you?"

"No."

"Well, what have you got in mind? What are your plans for the future?"

Something made me hold back from talking about the future until after my meeting with Mr Rinyo-Clacton. "I haven't done that much planning."

"Now might be a good time to begin. I'm off to the Vegemania." As always when she went out, she left an absence behind her.

Tchaikovsky had apparently pulled himself together and was marching along purposefully with a snappy *allegro molto vivace* as if he was going in to win. I knew how it ended so I stopped the music, made myself a cup of tea, sat down at my desk, and began to write this.

33

Wimbledon Train

Early dark, November dark, November lamps and faces and shop windows and footsteps sharp and cold. People bursting from the silent-roaring ocean of the day and swimming upstream like salmon into the November evening. The finale of the *Pathétique*, the *adagio lamentoso* that I hadn't listened to at home, was playing in my head and it seemed to me the proper soundtrack for Pizza Huts and Taco Bells and big red 74 buses novembering down the Earl's Court Road. Fifty-three years old he was when he died, Pyotr Ilyich, nine days after conducting the première of the *Pathétique* in October 1893. Where was that court of honour now, that told him death would be a good career move?

I'm always early for every appointment, I can't help it; it was only twenty past five when I reached the tube station and stood there smelling roasted chestnuts and waiting for Mr Rinyo-Clacton. "This could be the last time," he kept saying in my mind. How? Was it possible that he was dying, that he had tried to shelter from his own death in mine and now was relenting? I saw myself visiting him in hospital, being his comrade in his last moments. But the awful things he had done—his calculated seduction of Serafina and his various intrusions into our lives! How could I be the comrade of such a man? Whatever was about to happen, I felt now that he was the weak one and I was the strong one, and I liked that feeling.

Suddenly here came Katerina looking like a storm-driven ship about to smash itself on rocks. "Katerina!" I said. She seemed not to hear me, but hurried into the station and down the stairs. I followed as she went through the turnstile with her travel permit; when I saw her go down to the westbound platform I bought a ticket to West Brompton and went down the stairs after her as a Wimbledon train pulled in.

Katerina made her way through the crowd, moving quickly past the refreshment kiosk, past the board that showed the incoming trains, past the Piccadilly Line stairs. She stopped by the next stairs as I caught up with her. The doors of the Wimbledon train stood open; passengers getting on pushed past those getting off as Mr Rinyo-Clacton stepped on to the platform and found himself face to face with Katerina.

"Kandis?" she said. She passed a hand over her eyes and shook her head in evident disbelief. "No, not possible—Theodor, is it you?"

Mr Rinyo-Clacton's eyes opened very wide, his mouth was a silent O. He stepped back, the doors of the carriage closed on his coat, and the train moved out, dragging him along the platform and into the tunnel as people shouted and pointed. "No!" I said. "Wait!" But he was gone, and never said a word.

34

Magic No

So here I am—Jonathan Fitch on Chapter 34 of my story. I'm very super-
stitious and superstition creates its own rules: I knew it would be wrong
to contrive to end this with a chapter total the same as that of Melencolia's
magic square but I thought it would be a good omen if it fell out that way.
That's not going to happen now: melancholy yes; magic no.

When I saw Mr Rinyo-Clacton step back and get caught in the carriage doors I said, "No! Wait!" A useless thing to say, I know, but I was
overwhelmed by a sense of this thing being cut off short, being stopped
unresolved. I was shocked by the taking-away of his death from me by
this weird *deus ex machina*. *Dea*, rather, this old woman who suddenly
finished off a man who'd become some kind of a cornerstone of my existence. There were so many things to be worked out before I could be the
hero of my story, and now the process would never be complete and I'd
never be that hero.

Platform 4 was taped off and the station closed. People streamed out
into Earl's Court Road, marvelling at the drama that had heightened their
reality. I told a London Transport policeman that I was a close friend and
he directed Katerina and me to Chelsea and Westminster Hospital.

"Kandis?" I said to Katerina, "Theodor Kandis, was that his name?"

"That was his name."

"Who was he?"

She stifled a sob and shook her head. We took a taxi, and all the way to the hospital she sat with her hands over her face, speechlessly rocking back and forth.

35

Smaller

Accident and emergency at Chelsea and Westminster Hospital: cloistered and quiet, full of quickness and slow time, close to but distant from the crawling traffic in the Fulham Road and the rain now making the streets shiny. Sister Melanie Quinn, large and well-built, reminded me of Melencolia, whose face, as I recalled it now, was quite a nice one, friendly even. She drew aside the curtain of the cubicle and there he was, completely submissive to Death.

"There was no damage to his face," she said, and lifted the sheet. His face looked much smaller than usual, softer and younger, not sulking at all. The eyes were closed.

"That's him," I said. "T. Rinyo-Clacton."

"That's him," said Katerina. "His face is just exactly the same as his father's."

"Are you next of kin?" said Sister Quinn.

"I'm his mother," said Katerina.

36

The Face of Dieter Kandis

"To know what is coming," said Katerina, "and to be able to do nothing about it is not good. When Hitler came to power in 1933 I was nine years old, but already when I was seven I was seeing in my dreams the railhead and the chimneys at the end of the journey. My father was a well-connected lawyer who thought of himself as more German than Jewish. He and my mother did not take my fears seriously, they thought I am a hysteric. When they finally realised what was happening it was already too late.

"About Auschwitz I tell you only what concerns us now. I was on the list for medical experiments but this did not happen. Dieter Kandis was one of Mengele's assistants. He helped with the experiments and he helped himself to any females he fancied. His name actually means "sugar-candy." This was in 1942. I was eighteen then and pretty, and after he raped me he took me off the experiment list and installed me in his quarters.

"He had a piano there and a good collection of music; he himself was not very advanced but when he found that I was he made me play for him every evening. He was particularly fond of Haydn sonatas. So I was a well-fed whore who played the piano while other women were tortured and starved and worked to death. And there was the smell from the crematoria. My parents by then were dead.

"In 1943 I became pregnant by Kandis and he told me I will go back on the experiment list if I try to abort it. So I didn't. The child, a son, was born on the fourth of November. Kandis named him Theodor, "gift of God," and handed him over to the eugenics people for research in what they called "cross-breeding." I didn't see him again and for these many years I didn't know if he is alive or dead. I don't think he ever knew who his mother was.

"Towards the end of 1944 I was again and again seeing Russian soldiers in my dreams. Kandis had me moved to the IG-Farben barracks where the forced-labour women lived. These workers did not get the famous Buna soup but were properly fed. He gave me some money and he said, "Thank you for the Haydn. *Tschuss.*" Then I didn't see him again.

"When the Russians came in January 1945 I walked out of there with the forced-labour women, mostly Poles." She rubbed her left wrist. "Since then I have tried not to meet anyone else who was at Auschwitz."

In the light of the blue bell-flower lamp her face was soft and dreamy. Her glass was empty and I filled it again. On her wall Melencolia also had a soft and dreamy look. A whole lot of woman, Melencolia: drawn by Dürer but promising opulence of the Rubens sort under her clothes. The child, perhaps I'd been too hard on him in the past; he was, after all, only a little fellow. Had he been crying? The dog was sleeping as before; the polyhedron flaunted its many facets. The sound of the rain and the drops running down the window panes curtained us in and made the room more cosy. I said to Katerina, "When I saw you hurrying to the tube station, did you know then . . . "

"That he was my son? I think I almost knew. In our very first session, when I suddenly pulled my hands away from yours it was because I saw the face of Dieter Kandis bending over me. I have seen his face often in dreams but this was a very strong apparition when I was fully awake. The second time it happened was when you put the bundle of money into my hands. It hit me like a bolt of lightning, I thought my heart would jump out of my body. It happened again when I held the book in my hands. Then, this afternoon, it was like a film in my head: this man with the face of Dieter Kandis on the Wimbledon train coming to Earl's Court. When I saw him get off the train and I spoke to him, he looked at me as if the name hit him also like a bolt of lightning from the past."

"Are you dead certain this was your son?"

"I have many doubts about many things, Jonathan, but when I know something I know it."

"And now he's dead."

"Now he's dead, yes. But the past doesn't die."

37

All There Is

I had met Mr Rinyo-Clacton on a Monday. On Thursday of the following week he was dead. Eleven days. That whole thing with him from beginning to end, that's all it was: eleven days. Well, no, actually. Because things don't end; they just accumulate. It was only three months ago that he died; it seems longer.

That Thursday evening after identifying the body Katerina and I bought a bottle of Glenfiddich, went to her flat and drank more than half of it. "What about the funeral?" I said. "The phone's ex-directory but maybe if I go round to the flat Desmond will tell me."

"Wait," she said.

On Friday the papers reported the death and said that the name was thought to be an alias but there was no mention of a funeral.

Saturday morning a motorbike messenger brought me a parcel wrapped in brown paper. For a weird moment I wondered if it might be Mr Rinyo-Clacton's head. When I'd undone the paper and the bubble-wrap I found the Rinyo-Clacton pot I'd seen in his bedroom. "What are we all but infirm vessels?" I said.

"Did you say something?" said Serafina from the kitchen.

"Not really." The pot had no lid but was covered with brown paper secured by masking tape. Taped to the paper was an envelope on which was written, in neat block letters, NO FUNERAL. In the envelope were the torn pieces of the document that began:

> *I, Jonathan Fitch, being of sound mind and with my faculties unimpaired, not under duress or the influence of any drugs, hereby assign to T. Rinyo-Clacton . . .*

I took the pot in both hands and shook it gently. The contents shifted with a soft and whispery sound. I removed the brown paper and saw, as I had expected, greyish-white ashes. Serafina came over to have a look. "Is that who I think it is?" she said.

"Probably."

"Give it to Katerina—she's his mother after all."

I rang up Katerina, and that evening while Serafina was at the Vegemania we went to the Hungerford Bridge. The weather was wet and blowy; we were both wearing anoraks, and the rain pattering on my hood made me feel roofed and indoors. To the man huddled in a blanket at the near end I gave a twenty-pound note. "Compliments of Mr Rinyo-Clacton," I said. He gave me a suspicious look but thanked me.

Traffic was heavy on the bridge: people full of Saturday night heading for their culture fix on the South Bank. Katerina and I walked through and around puddles to the bay where Mr Rinyo-Clacton and I had stood looking down at the dark river. "Shining golden goblets," he had said, "but the wine is black water; that's all there is, now and for ever."

The wind had died down; the air was calm and still; the view sparkled through the rain. To our right the Festival Hall beckoned, Come! To our left Charing Cross Station signalled, Go!

I looked at Katerina. "Do you want to say anything?"

She shook her head.

I held the pot out over the water. "That's all there is," I said, and turned it upside-down. Just then there was a sudden gust that blew some of the ashes back on to Katerina and me. I let go of the pot, watched it fall, had almost the sensation of falling with it, saw and heard the splash as it filled and sank. "Now and for ever," I said as I wiped the ashes off my face and anorak.

38

The Kakemono of Kwashin Koji

Now I'll never know what Mr Rinyo-Clacton wanted to talk about that Thursday. Had he had a change of heart? Was he going to call the whole thing off? Was he perhaps terminally ill and wanted to die with a clear conscience? Or had he in fact been writing a novel and had decided to abandon his researches and perhaps the writing as well? Had he meant this meeting to be our last conversation and he would then step out of my life or was it to be the last time for us to talk and our only meeting after that would be at the time of my death?

When I finally did go around to his flat there was a new occupant and no forwarding address for Desmond; he probably wouldn't have told me anything anyhow. And actually I don't need to know more of Mr Rinyo-Clacton's personal history than I do now.

My mind sometimes makes up little rhymes that it sings to itself; it's singing one now that seems to have reached the top of the mental charts:

> No more action
> with Rinyo-Claction.

Which is not strictly true; Mr Rinyo-Clacton has departed the scene but the action continues: everything that happened between us replays itself on a loop of memory but I'm not as tortured by it as I used to be; I know now how fragile are the walls that keep out chaos—there are many weak spots and there will always be something or someone waiting to break in. Maybe I can reinforce those weak spots with the rock I'm leaving behind as I carve myself out and shape my destiny.

Having written this, I found that I wanted it to go out into the world. I sent it to Derek Engel with a note recalling our telephone conversation and I was surprised to receive from him, after a two-month wait, an offer to publish. "Who knows?" he said. "You may well have backed into a new career." The advance was modest but so am I, and I'm hanging on to my day job yet awhile.

Katerina insisted on returning the money I'd given her; she simply wanted no part of it. "I have had enough," she said, "of the father and the son." So the million remained mostly intact, less the expenses of the trip to Paris and various incidentals.

Serafina and I both tested negative for HIV at the John Hunter Clinic and the future lay before us, more or less. All of a sudden, like a rug being pulled out from under us, the drama was gone from our lives and we've had to deal with the ordinary business of getting from one day to the next.

When I mentioned the restaurant idea again Serafina fixed me with her bleakest northern-strand stare. "Jonathan," she said, "do you mean to tell me that you expect to build some kind of a future on money from that man?"

"Well," I said, "a good thing *can* come out of a bad thing. Can't it?"

"Jonathan, as far as I am concerned, that money is the fruit of the poison tree, and if we're going to go on together it will have to be without that million."

"That's twice you've called me Jonathan instead of Jonno. Do you want to go on together?"

The phone rang. "Hello, Jonathan, this is Jim Reilly at Morgenstern. I hope you're well?"

"Yes, I'm all right, thanks. You?"

"Very well, thank you. I haven't heard from you for a while and I was wondering if we should meet so we can go on to the next stage of your financial planning and your restaurant thoughts."

Listening numbly to the worods, the woordos coming out of my mouth, I told Jim that my situation had changed and I was no longer in a position to go ahead with those plans. He said, well of course these things happened; he knew how it was and would be delighted to meet with me again whenever the time seemed right. I rang off, wondering, now that I was back in the real world, what Morgenstern's note of charges would be for my brief fling as a man with enough money to require financial advice. Serafina hadn't answered my question. I looked at her and said wordlessly, with my hands, "Well?"

"Oh, all right. You're rotten but I suppose most men are, and I've already put a substantial amount of time into you, so I guess we might as well stay together."

"With that kind of positive thinking we can't lose." We drank to that, one thing led to another, and we made the most of our HIV-negativity.

Nowadays I'm writing copy at Pottley & Trewe; I'm on HERO Men's Toiletries, doing print ads for *Mon Brave* aftershave. The latest has a black-and-white photo with that pearly, high-fashion nudity one sees so much of these days—a close-up of a young man in bed—mostly his bare upper torso and a bit of chin and smile, with a woman's arm thrown across his body. "THE SMELL OF SUCCESS" is the line and the product is shown with it. Everybody liked it but I find myself wondering about the words I wrote. The success, one assumes, is that, assisted by *Mon Brave*, he got a woman into bed. If he were alone would the line have to be "THE SMELL OF FAILURE"? Well, if his object was to find someone to help him make it through the night, sleeping alone *would* have to be a considered a non-result, wouldn't it. But of course if he were sleeping alone he wouldn't have been in the ad. Sometimes I wonder what the fictional people in our ads are doing when they're not in the photo or on the screen. Do they hang out with Hendryk in unseen rooms of Van Hoogstraten's peepshow?

I was hired by Gary Willoughby, the Copy Supervisor. He tends to brush against me in places where there's plenty of room to pass. Lots of interesting women go into advertising, and a fair number of them can be found at Pottley & Trewe and at the Serpent & Apple where the agency crowd gather at lunchtime and after work. Eye contacts; body language; a hand on your arm while talking; pheromones zinging back and forth— sometimes the certainty that something can be made to happen exerts pressure to *make* it happen but I've restrained myself.

I replaced the money I spent and gave the full one million pounds to the Terence Higgins Trust, which impressed me even more than it did them. Serafina and I have settled into a comfortable routine and life is pretty good. As good as it used to be?

Well, there comes to mind "The Story of Kwashin Koji," translated from the Japanese by Lafcadio Hearn. Kwashin Koji is an old man who earns his living by busking with a wonderful Buddhist scroll painting, a kakemono. There are several attempts to get this picture from him by foul means and fair, and after some astonishing twists and turns in the story he agrees to sell the painting to Lord Nobunaga, the ruler of the province, for one hundred ryo of gold. The scroll is then unrolled for its new owner but the picture, which had been magically vivid and full of life before, now looks a bit dim. Nobunaga wants to know why. Kwashin Koji explains that formerly the picture was beyond price, but since a price has been put on it, it has become just one hundred ryo's worth of painting.

What I have now is what I've bought with my actions. I think I love Serafina more than I did before; I'm now mindful of the value of what I almost lost for ever. She loves me too, I think, although she doesn't use the L-word any more and neither of us has mentioned the oasis dream since we've been back together. She kicks me a lot in her sleep but at least she doesn't do it when she's awake.

SHORT STORIES

The Man with the Dagger

There is a short story by Jorge Luis Borges called "The South." It is a story full of sharpness, having in it a lance, a sword, the edge of a door, two knives, the strangeness of life and the familiarity of death.

The protagonist of the story is Juan Dahlmann, secretary to a municipal library in Buenos Aires in 1939. His paternal grandfather, a German immigrant, was a minister in the Evangelical Church. His maternal grandfather was "that Francisco Flores, of the Second Line-Infantry Division, who had died on the frontier of Buenos Aires, run through with a lance by Indians from Catriel . . . " Dahlmann keeps the sword of Francisco Flores and his daguerreotype portrait, and has, "at the cost of numerous small privations . . . managed to save the empty shell of a ranch in the South which had belonged to the Flores family." He has never lived on this ranch; year after year it waits for him.

Hurrying up the library stairs one day, Dahlmann strikes his head against the edge of a freshly painted door and comes away with a bloody wound. The next morning "the savour of all things was atrociously poignant. Fever wasted him . . . " He nearly dies of septicaemia, and after a long stay in a sanatorium he leaves the city to go to his ranch for his convalescence.

On his arrival in the South he has a meal at a general store near the railway station. Three men are drinking at another table; one of them has a Chinese look. This man provokes Dahlmann by throwing breadcrumb spitballs at him, then challenges him to a knife fight. Dahlmann knows nothing of knifeplay and is unarmed but an old gaucho throws him a naked dagger which lands at his feet. "It was as if the South had resolved that Dahlmann should accept the duel. Dahlmann bent over to pick up the dagger and felt two things. The first, that this almost instinctive act bound him to fight. The second, that the weapon, in his torpid hand, was no defence at all, but would merely serve to justify his murder."

Dahlmann picks up the dagger and goes out into the plain to fight. "Without hope, he was also without fear . . . He felt that if he had been able to choose, then, or to dream his death, this would have been the death he would have chosen or dreamt."

With the dagger Dahlmann has seized the critical moment that defines . . . what? The right time to die? No use to attempt an analysis of Borges's intention—by the time Dahlmann picks up the dagger he is a fiction of his own making.

Now for as long as there will be print on paper, even longer—for as long as there will be one rememberer to pass this story on to another, even longer, even when all the rememberers are dead, Dahlmann, with his being vibrating between the strangeness of life and the familiarity of death, will live in this moment of unknown definition that he has seized. I wanted to talk to him.

The White Street

I thought the story would be the most likely place to look for Dahlmann, so I went there. I found it in a quiet street where the trees made little black shadows in a dazzling whiteness; it was an old rose-coloured house with iron grill windows, a brass knocker, and an arched door. Beside the door was a brass plaque; engraved on it in copperplate script: *The South*.

I knocked, and after a time I heard slow footsteps within and the thud of bolts being drawn back. The door opened slowly and in a very narrow aperture there appeared a vertical fraction of an old woman's face at the top of a blackness of clothing. Her one visible eye was black and difficult to meet.

"Good afternoon," I said (my watch had stopped but the street was white with heat and light and the sun seemed almost directly overhead). "Is Señor Dahlmann at home?"

"There's no one here," she said. "We're closed." The aperture and her face became narrower and disappeared with a click. There was the sound of bolts thudding home; her footsteps receded. Behind me the white street shimmered in the heat; far away a dog barked. I didn't want to turn around and see that white street again; I felt myself to be a prism through which the white light would reveal its full spectrum of terror.

I stood facing the centuries-darkened door until I felt myself flickering into black-and-white, then I turned back to the street. It too was flickering in black-and-white like an old film in which nothing had yet happened.

There was a boy flickering in front of me. His head was bent so that his straw sombrero concealed his face, his hands were behind his back. I didn't notice his feet.

"Where's Dahlmann?" I said.

"New in town?"

"Yes."

"Do they have discretion where you come from?"

"Some do."

"But not you."

"I'm a writer, I need to know things."

"What you need is not to be in too much of a hurry. I'll take you to the hotel."

His manner was that of one who has seen everything. "I bet the stories you could tell would make a hell of a book," I said, "if only you knew how to get them down on paper."

He shrugged. "Not everything needs to be written down."

We walked without speaking past many churches and past many squares with fountains. Everything continued black-and-white, the streets gradually filling with voices and footsteps and people. Eventually there appeared, not in the most expensive part of town, a small hotel with its name in unlit neon tubing: HOTEL DEATH. On its glass doors were the emblems of American Express, Diners' Club, and Visa. Opposite was a square with a fountain; on the far side of the square was a church.

"I'll see you later," said the boy, and wasn't there any more.

Hotel Death

"What can I do for you?" said the skeleton at the desk. He was wearing a garish print shirt outside his trousers, he had a bottle of whisky and a glass and he was smoking an inexpensive cigar. The black-and-white was holding steady. A slowly turning fan in the ceiling stirred the grey shadows and the drifting dust-motes in the lobby.

"Have you got a Señor Dahlmann registered here?" I said.

He blew out a big cloud of inexpensive-smelling smoke. It came out of his mouth in the usual way. "No."

"You haven't looked."

"I don't need to." He poured himself a whisky and lifted his glass. "Here's looking at you."

I looked into the hollows where his eyes would have been; the shadows were not unfriendly. The whisky didn't run out of the back of his jaw, it just disappeared. He noticed my staring.

"It didn't bother you that I can talk without a tongue but you draw the line at drinking without a throat, is that it?"

"Not at all," I lied.

"You want to check in?"

"No."

"You look pretty old. Why not do it now and beat the rush? We got TV in every room and if you get lonesome I can send somebody around."

"Skeleton whores?"

"Don't knock it till you've tried it."

"Later," I said. "I've still got things to do."

"Like what?"

"Like finding Dahlmann."

"Are you sure you want to?"

"That's what I came here for."

THE MAN WITH THE DAGGER

"Are you sure?"

"Look, let's not turn this into a philosophical exercise. I'll see you later."

"You know it."

I went outside and stood by the doors and stared at the flickering black-and-white of the church and the square and the fountain and the dusty street through which passed mules and ox-carts and dark people with sandalled feet and white cotton clothing. There was a smell of faeces and rotting fruit; there were the tolling of a bell and the buzzing of flies. From an upstairs window came the sound of a guitar.

There was a little whiff of lemony fragrance. "Hi," said a soft voice next to me. I turned and saw a really stunning skeleton with just the faintest touch of grey on her cheekbones; I recognised it as blusher. No eye shadow, her eyes were nothing but shadows. She was wearing a black poncho, a shiny black Rudolph Valentino hat with a flat top and a broad brim, and black boots. She was shapely in a way that made flesh seem vulgar.

"Why the blusher?" I said.

"I've seen things. Why are you looking for Dahlmann?"

"I think he may have something to tell me."

"Perhaps I too have something to tell you."

Together we walked off into the sunlight that would have made a blackness before my eyes if we had been in colour.

Noir's Room

I thought she would rattle but she didn't. What happened was that after the first few moments she stopped being a skeleton for me and simply became who she was, clean and elegant and more naked than I should have thought possible. With her lemony fragrance and that improbable blush on her cheekbones she was utterly girlish in my arms while there echoed in my mind an ancient scream of desolation and all sweetness gone, gone, gone with her clean white feet running and her black poncho flapping down endless corridors of neverness.

"What's your name?" I said.

"Noir."

"How much do I owe you, Noir?"

"Nothing, I'm not working now."

"Why aren't you working now?"

"Sometimes I make love for money and sometimes I do it for me. This one was for me."

"How come?"

"You ever do it with a skeleton before?"

"No."

"I wanted your skeleton cherry," she said, and kissed me. The room was a subtle composition of grey and black shadows with lines of brilliant white between the slats of the blinds. Through the front window came the sounds of a street market. On a table there were white lemons in a basket, there was a bottle of gin. I could feel colour impending but I held on to the black-and-white. Across the patio someone with a guitar was playing and singing a tango. The shadowy guitar and the quiet husky male voice made the gin seem miraculous.

"What do the words mean?" I asked her.

She listened for a moment, then she whispered in my ear:

> "Such a little, such a little, such a little
> difference, my heart—
> such a little difference between the one
> and the other."

"Is it really such a little difference?" I said.

"Listen," she said with her mouth still close to my ear, "I'll sing you a verse of my own:

> You were with me, with me, with me, my heart—
> you were naked in my arms, to you
> I gave my naked self, my onlyness.
> Was it less than you've had from others?"

I kissed her delicate ivory face. Her mouth was sweet.

"Don't go looking for Dahlmann," she said. "What can he tell you that I can't?"

"I don't know. I don't even know what I'm going to ask him." I got

THE MAN WITH THE DAGGER

out of bed and put my clothes on. I didn't look back at her as I opened the door and went out.

"It could have been good," she said.

Sidekick

Again I was hearing the buzzing of flies in a street that smelled of faeces and rotting fruit. Here also there were a square and a fountain and a church; the market stalls clustered under awnings along the near side of the square. The flickering seemed a little less steady than before.

There was a skeleton boy with his hat over his eyes, he was sitting on the ground leaning against the house I'd just come out of. He pushed the hat back and looked up at me as if expecting something.

"What is it?" I said.

"Don't you recognise me?"

"No."

"I'm the kid that took you to the hotel."

"Funny, I never noticed you were so bony. This place is full of regular people; why am I always talking to skeletons?"

"Maybe you speak our language."

"Why is that? Am I dead?"

"What a question! You don't ask questions like that around here, it isn't that kind of a place, there's nothing that simple."

"All right, then, I'll ask you something else: what's your interest in me? Why did you take me to that hotel and why have you been waiting for me here?"

"What's the matter with you? Don't you go to the movies? I'm the little clever street kid who helps you out; I'm your sidekick, I'm the only one on your side."

"What's your name?"

"Whitey."

"What about Noir? Isn't she on my side?"

"Shit. Women!"

"Well, is she or isn't she?"

"She's my sister but she hasn't got much sense and she gets mixed up with all kinds of people."

"Like me."

"And others."

"What others?"

"All kinds. You see that big guy in the rumpled white suit down at the end of the square?"

I looked. The man was over six and a half feet tall, weighed about three hundred pounds, and appeared to be the standard sort of henchman or subordinate villain one sees in films. He had nothing of a Chinese look about him and he was not entirely unfamiliar to me but I seemed not to remember who he was. "Who's he?" I said.

"Don't you know?"

"Why should I know?"

"Because this is that kind of a place, some of us are skeletons and some are extras but anybody else with any real action in the story is somebody you know."

"Maybe I'll know him later but I don't know him now. You say he's one of the people Noir's mixed up with?"

"I'm not sure."

"Never mind him for now. What about Dahlmann?"

"What?"

"Do you know where he is?"

"I don't exactly know where he is but I think I know when you can find him."

"When will that be?"

"Later. Have another look around the square."

I had another look. There was a second big man more or less the same as the first one. Now I seemed to be remembering these men from times when they were less big and I was much younger: the first one would be . . . John? John Something. Tum-tee-tum. DeGrassi? Bonanno? "We'll settle this after school down by the boathouse," he'd said. I'd preferred not to. Long, long ago. Some things you walk away from and they walk after you. I'd fought Joe Higgins and I'd lost but that had never bothered me. The second one, was he Sergeant Somebody from my army days whose offer to take off his stripes and step outside I'd declined? Matson? Mason?

" . . . around the square," said Whitey.

"What did you say?"

THE MAN WITH THE DAGGER

"Have another look around the square."

There was a third big man in a rumpled white suit. He was from no more than fifteen years ago, this one. I'd never known his name; he'd been a stranger in a bar, another of my backdowns. "What's happening?" I said. "Is this the day when all my cowardice falls due?"

"What can I tell you? Every day has in it all your days. The past is something that sticks to your shoes like cowshit. If Yesterday had kept his pants on Tomorrow wouldn't have a big belly. Run is a good dog but Fight is a better one."

"O God, skeleton aphorisms."

"When I first saw you, you were knocking at the door of *The South*. Why were you knocking at that door?"

"I wanted to ask Dahlmann what happened when he picked up the knife."

"Why?"

"It's something I've thought about for a long time."

"Why?"

"Various reasons."

"Maybe because there were so many knives you didn't pick up?"

"What are you, the skeleton of Sigmund Freud as a boy?"

"No, I'm your sidekick. I'm the clever little street kid who helps you and I'd like to know how many big guys in rumpled white suits we're talking about. How many are there altogether?"

"More than one would like, certainly."

"Then let's get out of here before more of them turn up. One thing . . . "

"What?"

"What you're doing now, keep it going as long as you can until you're ready for the other."

"You mean keep the black-and . . . "

"Discretion."

"And the other?"

"Is what you think it is."

It was night. Flickering steadily I moved the slats of the blind apart and looked down into a deserted black-and-white square with a ruined fountain. "I'm tired of running," I said.

"I love it when you talk discreet," said Whitey.

Night Run

We were in the deserted square. The streetlamps offered only a feeble and hopeless glimmer that seemed continually to be swallowed up in obscurity. Dim lights punctuated the darkness at odd intervals. Whitey and I stood listening to footsteps that never receded into the distance quite as they should have done.

"Let's get ourselves a car," he said. We crossed to the far side of the square and he slipped along silently trying doors until an infirm pickup truck opened for us. We climbed in, Whitey was busy with his hands under the dashboard, there were sparks, the motor started with a roar and we were off.

"Turn on the headlamps for Christ's sake," I said.

"It's better that you don't see too much, you'll lose your nerve." Rattling and roaring we disappeared into the obscurity that had swallowed up the feeble glimmer of the streetlamps.

John Kobassa & Co.

There was a van blocking the road. In the beams of its headlamps I saw Noir struggling in the grip of one of the big men in rumpled white suits. Whitey braked hard and we jolted to a stop in a cloud of dust. The other two big men were there as well.

"I knew this was going to happen," I said.

"What did you expect?" said Whitey. "Cucumber sandwiches?"

"I guess not. But really . . . "

"What?"

"What can they do to her? She's already a skeleton."

"What a gringo you are."

"What do you mean by that?"

"Honour is nothing to you, eh? Do you want to watch all three of them having my sister here in front of you? Is that the sort of thing you like?"

"No, I shouldn't like that at all."

" 'No, I shouldn't like that at all,' " he mocked. "What are you going to do about it? Have you got balls or are you a miserable capon?"

THE MAN WITH THE DAGGER

"Aren't you going to help? She's your sister."

"I'll do sidekick things, like stand on the bonnet and hit them with the starting handle if they get close enough."

I got out of the truck. Now I remembered them clearly: John Kobassa; Sergeant Moxon; Nameless Stranger.

"You remember us, do you?" said John. He was the one holding Noir.

"Don't worry about me," Noir said. "There's nothing they can do to me that hasn't been done before."

"They're not going to do anything to you," I said. "It's me they want. Let her go," I said to John. "Here I am."

"It's about time," said John.

"Hello, chicken," said Sergeant Moxon. "I've been waiting for you for forty-three years."

"I'm here now. How come all of you are so much bigger than I remember and nobody's old except me?"

"That's how it goes when you put things off too long," said Nameless Stranger. "Now if you're ready, we'll do what we didn't do that other time."

So we did it. When I came to, the pickup's headlamps were on, the three big men and the van had gone, and Noir was kissing me. I'd been very wise to keep it black-and-white; if it had been full colour they might well have finished me off altogether. As it was, I doubted that my injuries were any worse than if I'd been run over by a medium-sized car: seven or eight of my ribs were broken along with one or two limbs, my head, and my dentures; also there seemed to be a fair amount of bleeding both external and internal. All in all I thought it best not to try anything too active for a while so I stayed where I was and looked at Noir out of my one working eye.

"How are you?" she said.

"Terrific," I mumbled toothlessly. "If I'd known how good I was going to feel afterwards I'd have looked them up sooner." It was then that I noticed that the blusher on her cheekbones was pink and not grey and things weren't flickering any more. "Where's Whitey?" I said.

"Here I am." He was climbing down from the top of the pickup.

"Did you stand on the bonnet and hit them with the starting handle?"

"Nobody came close enough."

"Can we find Dahlmann now?"

"You don't have to find me," said a new voice. "I've found you."

"You're Dahlmann?"

"I'm Dahlmann."

Without ever having seen a photograph of Borges that indicated his height I'd always thought of him as a short man and I'd assumed that Dahlmann would be short as well, so I was surprised to see that he was a tall thin man of forty or so, wearing a rumpled white suit but nonetheless elegant and soldierly in his bearing. His face was long and narrow, with the watchful eyes and cultivated blankness of a man of action; his hair was very black and he had just such a daguerreotypical beard as Francisco Flores must have worn.

"Why were you looking for me?" he said in a perfectly flat and uninflected voice.

Had I expected friendliness? I couldn't remember. I tried to scramble to my feet but one of my legs gave way. Noir came to me and effortlessly lifted me up, then drew back and stood watching me intently. Before the unforeseen actuality of Dahlmann I tried to be as dignified as possible. I no longer wanted to speak the words that I had planned to say but I spoke them as if damned and preordained to do so: "I wanted to talk to you about what you did, I wanted to know what happened and how it was when you took the dagger in your hand and went out into the plain." What I said sounded wet and stupid and it was a lie: I no longer wanted to know what had happened and how it had been; I just wanted to go home. I looked at Noir and she blew me a kiss.

"You mean this dagger?" he said. He threw it into the air, the blade flashed in the light of the headlamps as it went end over end and the dagger returned haft-first to his hand. With his face still blank he said, "What do you think happened?"

"I think you were killed."

"That's your opinion, is it?"

"Yes."

"Would you care to back that opinion?"

"How do you mean?"

"Would you like to try me?"

Inwardly I sighed but I said nothing aloud. It was night, the darkness was full of the many and mysterious colours of black. In the light of the headlamps there seemed to be a genuine blush on Noir's painted cheek-bones; the shadowy hollows of her eyes sparkled with tenderness. It was night, it was dark, but in my mind a vast and tawny plain opened before me under the sun of the South as Whitey threw me a long knife that made a small hiss as it stuck into the ground at my feet.

My Night with Léonie

"What time do you get off work?" I said to her.

"Are you crazy?" she said. "I'm a sphinx." Her voice! Like the sea but also like honey—the wideness and the ancientness of it, the sweetness. I trembled all over.

"I can see that you're a sphinx. I asked you when you get off work."

"We have not been introduced." Her lips barely moved when she spoke. Her accent was enchanting; her English was perfect but it came out as if from a phrase book while she crouched immobile with naked breasts.

This was my first time in Paris. I'd have thought a French sphinx would be freer in her behaviour; her regard for convention excited and inflamed me. "How can one introduce what is already there," I said, "what is already known, what has been presented from antiquity, from before antiquity even? Always you have been who you are and I have been who I am. Always what is between us has been between us." I wanted to say simpler things, better things, but those were the words that came stilting out of my mouth.

"As you see," she said, "I am made of stone."

"You are made of yourself, you are made of the magical power of your sexuality and your wisdom that is before words, before thought. You are made of the desire and the longing that you have inspired in me."

"I'm a virgin," she said.

"One begins where one begins," I declared. Passers-by moved on discreetly without stopping to listen to our conversation. I believed her when she said that she was a virgin; she looked like a young person careful of her reputation. I had no idea when she might have been installed there on the south terrace of the Jardin des Tuileries at the corner of the Avenue du Général Lemonnier but I didn't suppose she was any more than two or three hundred years old. Her face was more modern than neo-classical: a plump little chin; a small, closed, unsmiling mouth; blank eyes staring straight ahead. Either a beauty mark or some birdshit high on her left cheek. Not a lovely face nor an inviting one but so erotic in its utter propriety. To see that mouth open for a kiss, to feel the bite of those presumably small and regular teeth! Her ears, behind which fell the stone stripes of her Egyptian headdress, were surprisingly large. Was it possible, I wondered, that she'd been listening all this time for someone to say what she wanted to hear. Her breasts were magnificent. Ordinarily I'm a bottom and leg man but her breasts were perfect and commanding, defiant of time and history in their ardour, their innocence, their authority. Each one was bigger than my head but these are technicalities; love conquers all. Her haunches seemed small and repressed but were provocative because of that. Her motionless tail seemed to twitch.

"I appreciate your sincerity and your conviction," she said. "Nothing like this has happened to me before but I am open to what life offers. If what you desire is possible then you will know when to come for me and what to say. Now you must go so that I can compose myself to be photographed by the seven Japanese gentlemen waiting patiently behind you."

I recognised the seven Japanese as guests at the hotel where I was staying. I had seen them at breakfast and I had seen them after breakfast busy with their cameras at Saint-Germain l'Auxerrois opposite. Their greedy lenses made me anxious: I was afraid they would suck out the souls of all the buildings and places and leave only emptiness for me. The seven nodded and smiled and I nodded and smiled back.

My mind was bursting with her words as I walked away: "If what you desire is actually possible then you will know when to come for me and what to say." Behind her lay the unseen desert, the hot and dry waiting for the cool and wet. I was certain that what I wanted was possible because I couldn't believe myself to be so out of touch with reality as to attempt the impossible. On the other hand I wasn't sure just what it was that I wanted. Or perhaps I should say that I knew what but not precisely what kind of what. The whatness of the what was what I was uncertain of.

Her face now came to me more clearly than when I'd been standing in front of her. It was the face of any self-respecting young person pressed into service as a sphinx: not the face of anyone special but the more special because of that, the more universal. "Yes," I said aloud as I passed three stout German women standing by a coach and consulting their maps, "you are the sphinx in every woman, that is your triumph and your specialness. I have slept with a number of women and I have lived with several but I have never found the right way to be with a woman, never found how to give what was in me to give. I know that to make love with you would be a kind of alchemy in which the dull and leaden self of me would be transmuted to the gold required by you."

"*Quatsch*," said one of the women.

"Not quatsch," I said. "Alchemy."

The stone of my lion-woman had been cool and grey but in my mind she now became hot and tawny in the wide desert of me where shimmering mirages mingled with the musky colours of eastern music and the clashing of ankle bells as I hastened back to my room. The Hôtel Le Relais du Louvre is opposite the south side of Saint-Germain l'Auxerrois and my third-floor window offered a near-level *vis-à-vis* with a gargoyle with whom I had struck up an acquaintance as soon as I arrived. This was a human gargoyle, not a chimerical one. He was wearing a long-eared jester's hood and he stuck out at right angles to the cornice just below the balustrade to the right of the south porch. He was the fourth gargoyle on the right and also the last one. Four being a hermetic number I felt lucky to have arrived at the window facing him. His mouth was wide open in a perfectly dry shout as there was no rain at the moment. His mouth was so urgently, so strenuously open that I knew that if his neck were not concealed by the hood I'd have seen the veins standing out on it. This jester's expression was that of a bearer of immense tidings: the sky is falling, the end of the world is at hand—something of that magnitude. Perhaps he had tried to shout a warning on that Saint Bartholomew's Eve when in this very church the bell named *La Marie* had summoned the deaths of eight thousand Huguenots. He was sitting on the shoulders of another figure which necessarily stuck out at the same perilous right angle so that both were parallel to the ground and about ten metres above it. This second figure, which had long since lost its head, was supported by a stone bracket; on the bracket, serving as a sort of hoddy-doddy caryatid, was a squat and squarish stone woman (well past the age of lactation, I should have thought) suckling a dog. These figures had obviously demanded of the sculptor that he carve them so as to make them visible to the general public. They seemed possessed of and by a powerful sapience and I was confident of getting practical advice from the jester who appeared to be the spokesman or shoutsman for the group. There he was, rigid with open-mouthed silence in the afternoon sunlight while two pigeons walked around on him. The sunlight was singing, as foreign sunlight always does:

> This, yes this, how strange it is that this
> is this, is this, is this, is this . . .

Although there was no rain I knew that the jester could speak if spoken to. Fixing him with my eye across the street-wide open air between us I told him what I had said to the sphinx and what she had said to me. "What do you think?" I said.

"Go for it," he shouted in his stone voice. He too spoke English, with a rough manner and what I took to be a medieval accent.

"Thank you for your encouragement but what I want is technical advice. When should I go back and what should I say?"

"She's by the Louvre?"

"Yes, she's at the corner of the Quai des Tuileries and the Avenue du Général Lemonnier."

"That's First Arrondissement. In what direction is she facing?"

"East."

"Tante Celestine," said the jester to the stone wet-nurse: "First Arrondissement sphinx facing east at the corner of Quai des Tuileries and Avenue du Général Lemonnier—when should our friend go back and what should he say to her?"

"He should go back when the full moon is shining on her face," said Tante Celestine without interrupting her nourishment of the dog. "He should say her name . . . "

"O God," I said, "I forgot to ask it."

"Tante," said the jester, "he doesn't know her name."

"Her name is Léonie," said Tante Celestine.

"Léonie," I murmured, "Léonie."

"And after he says her name," said the jester, "what then should he say?"

"Fifty francs, please."

"You want me to ask her for money?" I said.

"She means," said the jester, "that you should put fifty francs in the box in the church."

I went downstairs immediately and did so.

"All right, Tante," said the jester when I returned, "continue."

"When the full moon is shining on her face," said Tante Celestine, "he should stand in front of her and say, 'Léonie, I am here.'"

"'Léonie, I am here.' I think I can remember that," I said. "What then?"

"What then, Tante?" said the jester.

"Then he must watch carefully because the moment will flicker like a fish turning in the water and the stone sphinx of Léonie's public self will smile. Then the Léonie of hot blood and willing flesh will separate herself from the stone and leap to the ground. When that happens he must very quickly move in behind the flickering to the moment under the moment; he must climb over the gate and into the garden of his desire where he will find that Léonie who is the sphinx-woman of herself."

"Very quickly behind the flickering, I've got it. When's the next full moon?"

"Tonight," said the jester.

"There's a destiny in these things. What time does it rise?"

"Minutes and hours are nothing to me. Phone the Observatoire."

"OK, I'll do that. What's your name?"

"Gaspard."

"Many thanks, Gaspard and Tante Celestine. I'll let you know what happens."

"We'll be here," said Gaspard.

MY NIGHT WITH LÉONIE

I left another fifty francs in the box in the church and this time I lingered to look at the polychromed statue of Sainte-Marie L'Égyptienne holding the three loaves with which she went into the desert. When her clothes wore out she made do with her knee-length blonde hair. The statue was showing a lot of leg but the hair was keeping her decent and for added security the sculptor had provided a stone apron. The shapeliness of her thighs accentuated the somewhat sour piety of her face. I doubted that the sexual act had ever been one of alchemical transformation for her. According to my *Oxford Dictionary of Saints* this Marie had been a whore in Alexandria from the age of twelve. When she was twenty-nine she joined a pilgrimage to Jerusalem, paying her way by sleeping with the sailors. When she arrived she was prevented by an invisible force from entering the church. "Lifting her eyes to an ikon of the Blessed Virgin, she was told to go over the Jordan where she would find rest." That's when she bought the three loaves and went into the desert where she spent the rest of her life living on dates and berries and being "divinely instructed in the Christian faith." She met a monk called Zosimus from whom she hoped to receive communion the following Maundy Thursday but when he turned up he found her dead. A lion helped him bury her. This story depressed me. Sainte-Marie and I had no conversation: she had nothing to say to me and I had nothing to say to her. I wished that I hadn't allowed her into my field of vision, I didn't want her standing in front of Léonie in my mind.

I went back to the hotel, phoned the Observatoire, and was told that moonrise would be at 20:01 — more than five hours to get through. I didn't want to see Léonie before then and I didn't want to take in anything new but I was unwilling to wait passively in my room. I left the hotel and walked without taking much notice of where I was until I found myself in the Place des Vosges, boxed in by a four-sided frieze of stylised leaf-and-branch patterns printed on the air with a background of buildings. Figures on benches, like rocks in a Japanese garden, made islands in the clean gravel. There may have been a ringing of bells, perhaps not. The minutes roared and bellowed like minotaurs, the tides moved with the unseen moon, years passed, I grew old, and after a long time there was twilight with rain.

I walked back along Saint-Antoine and the Rue de Rivoli. The streets glistened with a constant susurration of colour and motion in which dark figures hurried through labyrinths and fireworks of traffic and the moment that was not yet. The sky offered no clarity, only rain. The moon did not exist, there had never been a moon, there never would be a moon, the idea of a moon was nothing to be taken seriously.

At 19:52 I manifested myself at the Rue de Rivoli end of the Avenue du Général Lemonnier. Léonie was at the other end of the avenue and could not be seen from where I was. I felt that it would be improper to show myself before the time dictated by Tante Celestine, and with the weather as it was there was no certainty that the moon would appear at all this night. There was nothing to do but maintain a state of readiness while awaiting further developments.

The rain was gentle but my jacket was not waterproof and although April was only one day away this evening seemed more like November. Colour and motion continued all around me; people with maps in their hands rushed past me to hurl themselves upon Paris; the Rue de Rivoli was euphoric with reflections and the sound of engines, the lights and the hiss of tyres disdained my silence, my stillness.

It was at this moment that the death of Général Lemonnier approached me. It was without form but it was as big as a church and while not making itself visible it made everything else go away so that there was nothing before me but it and nothing around us but silence. The story of this death appears on a bronze plaque on the end of the terrace wall on which Léonie crouches. The top of her head is about four metres above the ground and as you face her you see, reading from the top down, Léonie; plinth; plaque; street sign. The plaque says:

AU GÉNÉRAL EMILE LEMONNIER
Commandant la 3ème Brigade de la Division du Tonkin
LE DIX MARS 1945, CAPTURÉ À LANG-SON PAR L'ENNEMI,
À BOUT DE MUNITIONS, A REFUSÉ PAR DEUX FOIS
DE SIGNER UNE CAPITULATION TOTALE,
A PRÉFÉRÉ AVOIR LA TÊTE TRANCHÉE
PLUTÔT QUE DE FORFAIRE À L'HONNEUR,
DEMEURERA DANS L'HISTOIRE
COMME UN EXEMPLE SAISISSANT DE CE QUE SONT
LA VOLONTÉ ET LA CARACTÈRE FRANÇAIS
(Citation posthume—Extrait)

Below it is the street sign in white letters on a Prussian Blue ground:

MY NIGHT WITH LÉONIE

AVENUE
DU GÉNÉRAL
LEMONNIER
1893–1945

MORT IN INDOCHINE

The death of Général Lemonnier spoke not in the manner of Léonie
and Gaspard and Tante Celestine but inaudibly to the mind. Do you matter? it enquired.

Not at all, I said. And yet . . .

And yet what?

One does one's possible, yes?

The death of Général Lemonnier seemed to relax a little.

You and the sphinx, I said, you're not . . . ?

There is nothing between us, said the death of Général Lemonnier. She's
young, I'm old; I was old even at Thermopylae. She's modern, she . . .

What? I said. She what?

Nothing. You're in love with her?

Yes.

Good luck.

"Thank you," I said aloud as the world returned with lights and noise
and traffic. The time was 19:59 and the sky was dead, touched up with a
pinkish glow as by an embalmer. There had never been stars, there had
never been a moon.

I ran down the avenue—I didn't want to be early but I didn't want to
be late in case the sky should suddenly come to life and produce a moon.
I arrived in front of Léonie's terrace at 20:01 just as the seven Japanese
gentlemen came round the corner of the Quai des Tuileries.

They were all wearing black waterproof tracksuits and black plim-
solls and carrying various black cases of a technical nature; at first glance
one couldn't say whether they meant to shoot a film, transmit messages
by satellite, or rob a bank. When they saw me they gave only the briefest
of nods and the smallest of smiles. They didn't look at Léonie at all.

Ignoring the rain and working with military snap while they exchanged
short sharp words they set up what appeared to be a weather station—

at least I recognised the anemometer and the balloon that was inflated from a gas cylinder and sent aloft with an instrument packet and a radio transmitter. Next out of the cases was something possibly deriving from a sextant, an astrolabe and an infra-red sniperscope. This apparatus was mounted on a tripod and one of the Japanese took sights of the dense over-cast and called out his readings while another entered the data on a calculator. A wireless receiver was deployed as well as several laptop com-puters and all of the seven became very busy, those who were not operat-ing a scientific device or piece of communication equipment making notes in electronic notebooks or calculating with their calculators or computing with their computers, the dim red glow of the screens illuminating the intensity of their faces.

After about fifteen minutes they exchanged more short sharp words, packed up their gear, and disappeared round the corner whence they had come. What had they done? What did they know that I didn't? I had no idea but I was full of a fear that I didn't want to put into words.

I had avoided looking at Léonie while all this was going on and I didn't look at her now—it seemed unlucky to do so and I sensed that the stone of her was not in an interactive mode. There was still the possibility that the sky might clear so I leant against the wall of the terrace with my back to her and my face towards the south-eastern quarter of the sky in which I hoped there would eventually be a moon.

The rain continued and I fell into a reverie or possibly a delirium in which my wetness became a river that carried me to the sea where I swam with singing whales and silent turtles following their submarine destinies. Below us in tropical waters mantis shrimps with strange compound eyes looked at colours invisible to humans while the great-winged wandering albatross soared and swooped above the southern ocean or slept rocking on the waves. Under the rain and over the sea spread the shadow of Saint-Germain l'Auxerrois and the deaths in their thousands that answered its bell while a mermaid Sainte-Marie with her long hair streaming behind her swam with three loaves of coral in her hands.

I must have been asleep because I woke up to the sound of Léonie's name followed by something in Japanese. It was 22:45; the rain had stopped, the clouds had parted and the white moon floated serenely above the domes and spires and gargoyles of Paris. I stepped away from the ter-race and looked up; the moonlight was full on the face of the sphinx but the stone was empty—Léonie was elsewhere. From behind the locked gate of the Jardin des Tuileries came cries of pleasure, ululations of ecstasy, words in Japanese. Silence, then I saw one of the seven Japanese gentlemen leaving the garden. He climbed over the gate as lithe as a cat and dropped to the ground as another of the seven came round the corner of the Quai des Tuileries.

I looked up and saw that Léonie was once more present in the statue on the plinth; the stone was now responsive as the next man looked up and said, "Léonie . . . " and the rest in Japanese. The sphinx smiled voluptuously, I saw the moment flicker like a fish turning in the water, saw the stone go empty as the living lion-woman leapt down from her plinth, tearing off her formal Egyptian headdress to let her long red hair flame out behind her. O God, the tawniness of her long lion-body and the ivory of her woman-body, the savage flaunt of her breasts and haunches and lashing tail, the invitation of her red mouth and white teeth and wild green eyes. I had fallen in love with the statue and had imagined the stone become flesh but the reality of her put my imagination to shame. Her more than animal, more than human sexuality was so transcendently elemental, was such a startling and unwordable mystery that it utterly overwhelmed all reason and intellect. The brilliant strangeness of her printed itself on my eyes and I understood then how the idea of the sphinx had persisted century after century in successive minds and would persist as long as there was a single mind to contain it.

Only for a fraction of a second was Léonie-as-herself visible, then she disappeared into the garden while the empty statue kept watch on the plinth as the new man vaulted the fence like a champion. I turned away, went round the corner into the Quai des Tuileries, walked past the six Japanese who waited there (the first man had now joined the end of the queue), returned their nods and smiles, and made my way slowly back to the hotel. I drew the curtains, had a hot shower, and crept into bed around midnight without looking out of the window.

I woke up the next morning sneezing and sniffling and opened the curtains. There they were, Gaspard and his headless partner and Tante Celestine. "Good day," said Gaspard. "It goes?"

"You lousy pimp," I said. "Why didn't you tell me she was a whore?"

"Whore!" said Gaspard. "She's a saint, that Léonie. Have you any idea how much it costs to keep this church in repair, how inflation has raised the price of everything from candles to roof tiles? You think your night with her wasn't worth the piddling fifty francs you paid? You want your money back because she's not a virgin? You watch how you talk to me, arsehole—I can easily arrange for something to fall on you."

"Kill," said Tante Celestine. "Kill the son of a bitch, Gaspard. Drop your head on him and teach him a lesson."

I closed the window and turned away. At breakfast the Japanese and I smiled and nodded. Not one of them was sniffling or sneezing. After breakfast I walked to where Léonie crouched in her public mode. The sunlight, as always, sang its little song:

> This, yes this, how strange it is that this
> is this, is this, is this, is this . . .

This time she spoke first. "Hey, big shot," she said, "where were you last night? Lots of talk but no action, eh?"

"I seemed to have arrived a little late."

"And you didn't want to be the last in the queue? Life is like that, my old—so many wanting the same thing and so little time to serve them all."

"But you were so different when we spoke that first time, you even said . . . "

"I said what you wanted to hear. I sensed that you wanted to be my first, wanted to awaken the wildness in me, wanted me to open my little mouth to you. Listen, don't be cross—come back tonight and I'll be a virgin for you. I'll dress up as a nun, you'll like that. For fifty francs more I'll beat you with a little whip, yes? Come on, my gallant, be a sport."

"I'm leaving today. Adieu." I walked away.

"Don't say *adieu*, say *au revoir*," she called after me.

"Adieu," I said again. One may be a fool but one has one's standards, one draws the line, however faintly, somewhere.

When I got back to London I was going to change my French money but then I didn't. I like seeing the notes and the coins on my desk; sometimes I put my passport on top of them and the red-covered *Plan de Paris par Arrondissement* beside them. I like the way they look together, I like the way they feel in my hand.

MY NIGHT WITH LÉONIE

The Raven

One says "a black time," but actually the black of things is all kinds of colours. Sometimes it's the grey rainlight in an empty room; sometimes it's the sound of one's own footsteps under yellow streetlamps; sometimes it's an unaccompanied cello from a long time ago. It was difficult to understand the reality of my days, that this was now my life that would last until my death, that I had closed a door and gone, that there was no going back, that no one was there any more. No one was there because you don't just leave people, you leave a time. And the time wasn't there any more.

I wanted to talk to somebody about the black so I went down into the underground, came up out of it on the long and windy escalator at Camden Town, walked up Parkway to Regent's Park, followed a footpath through green distances and the autumnal shouts of football players, and turned into a road in which a squad of trotting men in red T-shirts and green shorts came towards me, their leader chanting words to which they responded. The words were indistinct, probably not:

> There was a man, his name was Jack,
> he tried to swim across the black.

The road took me to the Zoo entrance, where I entered, went past the apes and a little white clock tower and found the ravens. There were two of them perching on a sawed-off dead tree in their cage. When I took some grapes out of a bag one of the ravens opened its wings and the whole out-spread blackness of the bird suddenly appeared in front of me. Standing on well-worn and polished black feet, it folded its wings and stuck its bill through the chain-link mesh of the cage. It was a large black bill of cleri-cal aspect, the upper mandible hooked over the lower with a long curv-ing point that was like a fingernail that needed trimming. A little yellow sign on the cage showed the silhouette of a hand with a large piece bitten out, so I sidled away from the raven and dropped a grape through the wire mesh.

The raven picked up the grape neatly between its upper and lower mandibles, walked a little way off with an old-man walk, placed the grape on the concrete floor, tore it into three pieces, and ate them one at a time. Then it went to its bath, a circular concavity in the floor; it sipped some water, lifted its head and stretched out its neck as it swallowed, and came back to the wire-mesh. Its wet throat-feathers were like a beard, its purple-blue blackness was as precise as an engraving, its shining black eye when it blinked showed a clear bluish-white disc like a little round mirror of scepticism.

How's it going? I said to it, not speaking aloud but with my mind.

Well, you know, said the raven, also not speaking aloud, there's not a lot happening here.

The cage was small, with neighbours on both sides. I think there was some kind of vulture in the cage to the left, some exotic corvid to the right. From time to time the vulture flapped its wings and lifted itself off its branch, then settled down again. The October day was warm and humid, people carried their coats and jackets over their arms. Someone stood next to me and pointed to the raven and said to a child, "See how tame it is." I looked down at the child, a boy of three or four. His face was pale and sticky like a bun that had been standing in the sun. His expression was doubtful, his eyes wild. The sky was grey, dead leaves rattled on the pav-ing, in the distance something screamed.

THE RAVEN

How can you live without flying? I said to the raven. How do you get through the days? How do you not go crazy?

The raven looked at me for a while, the little round eye-mirror blinked like a camera shutter. Lots of people live without flying, it said.

But you used to have the whole sky to move around in.

Wait a minute, said the raven.

What?

How do I know I'm not talking to myself? Maybe I'm just imagining this conversation.

I've been thinking that very same thought, I said. Tell me what to do to show that I'm receiving you.

Hold out your arms and flap them up and down.

I held out my arms and flapped them up and down.

"What's that man doing?" said a passing child to its mother.

"Perhaps he's trying to get above himself," she said.

I've given you a sign, I said to the raven. How about you? Walk in a circle round your bath if it's really you speaking to me.

With its old-man walk the raven slowly walked around the bath. Then it came back to where I stood. You were saying, it said. Its voice in my mind had changed: it was all around me in vast and reverberant diapason, as if rebounding from the face of a black escarpment that ringed the horizon under a grey and primordial sky. It was a giant voice of supernatural power, and a thrill of fear went through me as the raven grew before my eyes. The cage and the zoo seemed to have faded away; the raven loomed over me like a black cliff walking towards me on well-worn and polished black feet in the grey October afternoon. How could I ever have been such a fool as to speak to it as if I were its equal?

The immense raven flashed its eye-mirror in which I saw only blankness. Its voice filled the sky. You were saying, it said.

How do you not go crazy? I whispered in my mind.

I have a lot to do, I'm busy all the time, chorused the massed echoes from the black escarpment.

What is it that you do?

I do the black.

Of course, the black. I'd come for the express purpose of talking to the raven about that very thing and I'd forgotten all about it. When you say "the black," I said, you mean . . . ?

Different things at different times.

And when you do the black, how do you do it?

I just go with it.

How do you do that, how do you just go with it?

All kinds of ways and very, very far sometimes.

How far? I was looking into the raven's left eye when I said that. Then the mirror flashed and I was in that eye looking out. Around me the vast blackness of the bird opened and lifted and the earth fell away below us, all the feeble constructions of humankind and the smoke of its engines blurring into dimness and distance as we rose above the grey sky and into the brilliant clarity of the blue dome in which the present curved endlessly upon itself to compass past and future.

Up we flew, high, high into the blue dome, then whistling down in a dizzying black-winged rush we shot the long, long curve past faces huge and tiny on the flickering screen of memory, faces in the shadows, in the light, lips shaping words remembered and forgotten in the moving gleams of time, the wavering of candlelight, the whispering of gold watches, the boom of tower clocks, the fading ink of letters tied with faded ribbons; faces wheeling with horsemen and battles and cannon, marching with armies, screaming in burning cities, drowning in shipwrecks and the thunder of the wild black ocean; palimpsested voices, distant figures and the changing colours of processions, plagues, migrations, ruins, standing stones, cave drawings, jungles, deserts, dust, meteorites, dinosaurs, giant ferns, volcanoes, floods, blue-green algae, silence, the grey rainlight in an empty room, the sound of my footsteps under yellow streetlamps, and an unaccompanied cello from a long time ago.

That's rather a long way to come for not very much, I said to the raven.

With this kind of thing it's always trial and error, said the raven. We can go a little further if you want to.

We might as well give it a try.

All right, then, here we go.

Down, down we arrowed blackly through the silence and the rainlight and the footsteps and the streetlamps and the unaccompanied cello to a dim and smoking red that seethed and cracked and bubbled and was veined with golden rivulets of lava. Down, down through that red to a dimmer red, a deeper silence, an older stillness.

Where are we? I said.

THE RAVEN

In the black.

This isn't black, it's red.

Sometimes the black is red. We have to walk from here.

I looked down at the raven's worn and polished black feet. They seemed far, far away. I imagined the raven sitting down on the edge of its bed and lacing them up every morning. Far below me in the dim, dim red the raven's left foot moved and then its right. Is it very far? I said.

It's where we are when we come to it.

The raven's old-man walk made its head lurch from side to side so that I swung like a pendulum in a black clock. We didn't talk, there wasn't anything to say. Sometimes the red was smooth, sometimes it was gritty underfoot. Some kind of music would have been suitable for the gait of the raven but there was no music. Do you come here often? I said.

It isn't always here when I come.

Well, yes, I could understand that. There were no landmarks at all and the densities and textures of the red were probably unreliable. Time and silence receded before us steadily until they became the same as they were before. We were in a cavern dimly lit by the red and flickering light of our mind, the raven's and mine.

Here, we said.

What?

Here, here, here. Our voice had become many voices, voices without number, tiny and great. The raven was no longer a raven, raven, raven, raven. Nor was I what I had been; we were without form, we were not yet alive: tiny, tiny dancing giants looming greatly in uncertain shapes and dwindling in the shadows; fast asleep and dancing in the dim red caverns of sleep.

Through agelong dimnesses of red we danced and sang incessantly the long song of our sorting: yes and no we sang in silence, grouping and dispersing and regrouping in the circles and the spirals of the sleep-dance. Many, many, sang the many of us, all of everything the same.

We danced the red until it became red-orange; then we danced red-orange in the sameness of our unbeing; in the caverns of sleep we danced orange and orange-yellow while the mountains cooled under the long rains and the deeps filled up with oceans. When the yellow came and the yellow-green it seemed that green and blue-green were only a matter of time.

Same, same, sang we tiny, tiny dancing giants through all the colours of the years: all of us the same.

What us? said some.

All of us, said others.

All of us what?

All of us the same.

Same what?

Same us.

What us?

All of us.

And so on through revolving repetitions over hundreds of thousands of millions of years. From time to time there were attempts to move the discussion on to new ground but always it reverted to the same revolving repetitions. Little by little we were losing energy, and although I had at that time no identity I was becoming more and more impatient with the apparent unwillingness of my fellow tiny, tiny dancing giants to pull themselves together so that we could make something of ourselves. My particles were beginning to scatter when, with a tremendous effort, I said, Un . . .

Un what? said the others.

Un the same, I said. Unsame.

Same, insisted many.

Unsame, said more and more. Over the next hundreds of thousands of millions of years this alternating challenge and response slowly developed in us a forward motion; we could feel ourselves moving out of unbeing into a new state. SAME, UNSAME, we chanted all together as we surged forward through shallow seas and primordial salts into the blue-green algae of our beginning.

Having begun, we pressed forward through floods, volcanoes, giant ferns, dinosaurs, meteorites, dust, deserts, jungles, cave drawings, standing stones, ruins, migrations, plagues, the changing colours of processions and distant figures, palimpsested voices, faces huge and tiny on the flickering screen of memory, faces drowning in shipwrecks and the thunder of the wild black ocean, screaming in burning cities, marching with armies, wheeling with horsemen and battles and cannon; faces in the shadows, in the light, lips shaping words remembered and forgotten in the moving gleams of time, the whispering of gold watches, the boom of tower clocks, the fading ink of letters tied with faded ribbons. Nothing stopped us, and in time we arrived at the grey rainlight in the empty room, the sound of my footsteps under yellow streetlamps, and the unaccompanied cello from long ago where the raven stood on its well-worn and polished black feet looking at me through the chain-link mesh of the cage.

I wanted, said the raven, speaking to me with its mind, to ask you about the black.

What can I tell you? I said. It's different things at different times but it's more or less the same.

I left the Zoo and walked back the way I'd come. When I turned into the road where the trotting men had chanted I saw them coming towards me again. Again their words were indistinct, probably not:

> There is a thing, it has no name,
> this thing is everywhere the same.
> THIS THING IS DEEP, THIS THING IS WIDE,
> IT HASN'T GOT A FARTHER SIDE.

I walked down Parkway, went down the long and windy escalator at Camden Town, came up out of the underground at my desk but didn't sit down at it. I lay down on the couch, fell asleep, dreamed that I was writing, and woke up unable to remember what I'd written.

Dream Woman

The dim light, the faceful shadows murmured, tinkled, gleamed. The steady flame of the candle on the table made a globe of stillness around the two of us, a warm bright globe of stillness in which she raised her glass and the luminous rosy wine made a smaller bright globe, a little world of the poised wine of this moment. She tilted the glass, the wine poured out, its brightness in the candlelight falling, falling. With an indescribable smile she looked at me and poured out the wine and never said a word, saying with her smile that she knew herself to be a dream and lost to me. That was how the first time ended.

The next time I saw her she said straightaway, "Why do you bother when you know I'm not real?"

"I don't know that. I refuse to know that."

"How am I real then? You know I'm only a dream."

"What is that? What does it mean when you say 'only a dream'?"

"I'm only in your mind," she said.

"What does that mean? The whole universe is only in the mind of God and nobody says the universe isn't real."

"Maybe your mind isn't as real as God's mind. In any case you'll have to go back, you can't stay here. Why should I begin something with a man who can't stay?"

"You're in the world that's in me," I said. "I'll find a way to stay."

"For me there's no future in this. I've seen it happen before with dream women and realies and it never works."

"Is that what they call us? 'Realies'?"

"Yes, and it never lasts. They see the man a few times and that's the end of it. Sometimes they're left with a child. It's hardest on the children I think — it's like growing up in a whorehouse."

"But you're not a whore. You're not here for anyone else, are you?"

" 'Not here for anyone else'! You amaze me. I've seen you once before and for all I know I'll never see you again and you want me to keep myself pure for you. You're not even young: in a few years you'll be dead and this world in your head will still be here in other heads and I'll still be in it. What am I to do then, wear black and live on memories?"

"You're saying you've been with other men," I said. "Other realies."

"You don't seem to have a very quick mind. How do you suppose I occupied myself until you turned up? With needlepoint? How would you like to live in this awful tatty place where nothing ever works properly? You go to the bathroom to wash your hair and maybe there's a sink and maybe it's the front half of a crocodile. Whole neighbourhoods disappear overnight without a trace, you're lucky if you can find the supermarket two days running. And in between times you sit around waiting like those whores in that painting by Toulouse-Lautrec. Sitting in that awful lounge in their depressing underwear and waiting for the punters."

"Don't let's quarrel. It's only our second time together and I don't even know your name."

"That's a typical realie remark. There aren't all that many names to be had for the asking around here, it isn't that pimple."

"Surely you mean simple," I said.

"Squeeze it how you like," she said, and wasn't there any more.

Between then and the next time it occurred to me that perhaps if I could die while I was with her we might stay together always, moving from head to head as necessary.

The third time was in the same restaurant where she and I had sat together the first time. She was with Phil Worril. At school we used to call him Worril the squirrel. Her back was to me and Worril sat facing me in that same warm bright globe of candlelit stillness that had enclosed her and me. As I stood outside and looked past the menu in the window I saw his lips move but I couldn't make out what he was saying. She lifted her glass, luminous and rosy, bright globe of the poised wine of this moment, then she poured out its brightness in the candlelight.

I haven't seen her since. Sometimes when I'm doing the shopping I remember how she couldn't always find the supermarket.

DREAM WOMAN

Dark Oliver

Oliver sometimes dreamed a face that was green like pale fire, black like earth and ashes. It was huge, this face, and it was all around him as if it were the inside of an endless tube that slowly turned as he fell endlessly through it. And a sadness, an ache in the throat, a loss. What name was there to call? Who was gone? Oliver was ten.

The playground at school was for Oliver a grey place of rage and boy-sweat and Geoffrey. Geoffrey was two years older and four inches taller and he twisted Oliver's arm and rubbed his head in painful ways. Oliver fought him and lost. Geoffrey called him "Olive Oil." Geoffrey sang:

> "Olive Oil had a boil
> right on the bottom of his bum."

At the end of the summer term Oliver and his mother and father flew to Corfu and there they boarded a boat for the island of Paxos where they'd rented a house. The name in Greek letters on the bows of the boat was PERSEPHONEIA.

The air was clear, the sun was hot, the engine droned, the sunlight danced in dazzling points on the blue sea. There were stone fortresses, the coast was mountainous, on the upper deck a man played a bouzouki. The boat was full of people eating, drinking, smoking, playing cards. Sun-glints moved slowly across the glasses and the bottles of beer and cloudy lemonade on the bar. On the lower deck were a lorry and two cars and a motorcycle; there were a goat and a donkey; there was a cockerel with bronzey and green and red feathers, it looked at the mountains and crowed. Oliver's father stood in the bow and looked down at the constant parting of the water that slid along the sides and joined the white wake marbling astern. His mother, her bare legs and sandalled feet already brown from after-noons at the Hurlingham Club, sat on a hatch cover, reading and smoking.

Oliver was listening past the drone of the engine, the slap of the bow wave, the jangling of the bouzouki: he was listening to the silvery flicker of olive trees in the sunlight, the olive trees of the island. It took so long to get there, hours and hours over the sea to the island.

When the boat dropped anchor in the harbour at Gaios and the chain rattled through the hawsepipe Oliver looked up at the hills and terraces beyond the red-tiled roofs of the town. "What kind of trees are those?" he said. "The silvery ones."

"Those are olive trees," said his mother.

"Persephoneia," whispered Oliver.

"What are you whispering?"

"Nothing."

The house looked as if it had been stained long ago with the juice of pome-granates. It had a red pantiled roof, it had a flagged courtyard. There was a table under a grape arbour; there were orange trees and a pomegranate tree. Oliver was astonished at the pomegranates, that this fruit he had read about in fairy tales should actually be growing on a tree where he was. He'd eaten pomegranate seeds at home but now as he held the fruit in his hand it was an orangey-red world of unknownness.

Oliver's father cut a pomegranate into thirds and offered one to Oliver's mother. She looked at him as she bit into it but said nothing. For a mo-ment the other two thirds lay on the white plate among drops of red juice. From a distance came the gigantic braying of a donkey, to Oliver it was the sound of something shut out and banished from happiness: it was a black sound that lay on the white plate with the two thirds of pomegran-ate and the drops of red juice.

DARK OLIVER

"Persephone," said Oliver, "ate seven pomegranate seeds in the realm of the dead and because of that she has to spend three months of every year down there with Hades and the earth is barren until she returns."

"How many seeds have you eaten?" said his father to his mother.

"Too many," she said.

Years later Oliver remembered some details and forgot others. He remembered tins of NOYNOY evaporated milk, they had a label with a picture of a pretty young Dutch woman breast-feeding a child, in the background a canal and windmills; he remembered bottles of gin with unknown labels, unremembered names; pistachio nuts; black wrinkled olives and goat cheese; mosquito-averting spirals of some green compressed substance that burned with the dark holiday smell of lost childhood.

He remembered a tiny dead scorpion on the floor of a cupboard. He remembered a polychaete sea-worm; magnified by the clear water, it was mythical-looking, pink and purple, its body fringed with undulating black bristles that moved it over the pale stones; the idea of it was huge.

There were three Swedish girls who wore no tops, their breasts were large and buoyant; they swam together like a sign of the zodiac.

One day a young woman in a black wet-suit speared an octopus. She slid it off the spear, took it by a couple of its arms and beat it to death on a flat rock, spattering Oliver with briny drops. Each time the octopus struck the rock it gripped it with its free arms, they came away with a sound like kisses.

Oliver and his mother went to the beach every day, his father less often. Oliver's mother swam, sun-bathed, smoked, wrote letters, read mysteries while his father sat at the table under the grape arbour, reading Marlowe's *Doctor Faustus* and making notes for his next book. In the evenings the two of them drank gin by candlelight.

Every day the sunshine was as flat as a postcard. Old women in black sat knitting outside the shops. At the harbour wall the old boatmen looked up from their boats as the near-naked summer women passed by.

Water for the house came from a cistern that was a little square edifice the same colour as the house, with steps going up to the low flat top of it. Rainwater supplied the cistern through a long pipe from the roof gutters of the house. Whenever a tap was turned on or the toilet flushed, the pump in the cistern gasped and panted as it laboured to bring water to where it was wanted.

Lying in his bed at night Oliver heard the crowing of a cock while the pump howled in the dark. He remembered the condemned voice of the donkey, the red juice of the pomegranate, the green and black face of his dream. At night this month of August was like a great animal of unknown shape and colour that turned and turned and turned away.

There were dry stone walls all over the island; they held the earthen terraces to the hillsides; sometimes they encircled single olive trees. Everywhere were stones and fragments of stone with flat surfaces that were good to draw on with a fibre-tip pen. Some were sand-coloured, some grey, some white. Some looked like curtains of stone, some like broken monuments. On the beach and in the water crouched great humped and hollowed ancient sea-worn shapes of stone. They had heard radios playing rock-and-roll and they had heard Orpheus. Lying half-submerged, Oliver held on to them while his body rose and fell with the rocking of the tide. Sometimes he spent hours on the beach bent over his shadow as he gathered hand-sized stones of various rounded shapes. Some of them fitted together in curious ways.

At first Oliver drew monsters and dragons on some of the stones; later he began to write on them. On some of the long-shaped rounded ones he wrote a single word in spirals round and round the stone: Down down down down down down . . . or Green green green green . . . He also wrote, in the Greek letters he had seen on the boat, the name Persephoneia.

The road that led from the hills down into the town passed between terraces of olive groves. There was rubbish scattered everywhere, people simply threw it down the hillsides. Blue plastic mineral-water bottles were scattered through the olive groves where thrown-away cookers lay rusting. Many of the trees had been planted long, long ago when there were no such things as plastic mineral-water bottles. They twisted their roots into the stony ground of their stone-walled terraces while in their silvery leaves the changing winds, the light of centuries whispered.

There was one particular olive tree that Oliver looked at whenever he passed it. Often there was a black donkey tied to it; sometimes there was a black-and-white goat nearby. The donkey was the one that Oliver had heard while eating the pomegranate under the grape arbour. When it opened wide its jaws and brayed it made a tremendous heehaw that was much too big a sound for an animal of that size; clearly the donkey was a medium for something else. This is my annunciation, said the voice that spoke through the donkey; this is my revelation of something so horrendous that there is no word for it and the voice with which I speak is taken no notice of.

The tree wasn't far from the house; Oliver went to it alone one afternoon. The donkey had wound its rope round and round the tree and now stood silent. The goat looked calmly at Oliver with its strange eyes that were like ochre-grey stones in which were set oblongs of black stone. A cock crowed among the blue plastic mineral-water bottles.

The tree was alive, there were silver leaves whispering in the sunlight, there were black olives growing on it. Yet the trunk was empty, it was only the shell of a tree with darkness inside the ancient twisted shape of it. The thick greenish-grey bark all ridged and wrinkled stood open as if two hands had parted it. The tree wasn't shaped like a woman and yet it was a woman-shaped tree, as if a woman had been wearing the tree and had stepped out of it.

Where is she now? thought Oliver. He looked at the ears of the donkey. What were they listening for? He looked at the eyes of the goat. What did they see that was different from what he saw? The cock crowed again.

"Here?" said Oliver.

The leaves whispered.

"Gone?" said Oliver.

The empty tree held open its darkness to him. The donkey sounded its tremendous heehaw, the goat looked at Oliver, the cock crowed a third time. Oliver stepped closer to the tree. He thought he heard music but he couldn't have said how it sounded. Perhaps it was only the idea of music in his mind.

Oliver was inside the tree, he didn't know how he'd got there. For a moment he saw the stone walls and the olive trees across the road, blue sky and silver leaves, green shade and golden sunlight and a yellow plastic meat grinder lying by the roadside; then everything blurred upward past him, he was falling, falling with a sick feeling in his stomach. There was a great sighing in him and around him; he remembered the eyes of the goat, the ears of the donkey.

Falling, falling, with the darkness leaping inside him like a black frog, Oliver began to cry but it wasn't from fright, he was crying from sadness. With a terrible ache in his throat he was crying for something lost to him, he didn't know what. And all the time he was falling and wondering when he'd be smashed like an egg dropped from the nest.

A name was roaring in him, bellowing in him: PERSEPHONEIA. He thought his skull would burst from it, he thought his bones would break from it. He was still falling, he was nowhere, there was nothing but blackness, and into the blackness there came the idea of the face that he sometimes saw in his dreams. Was he thinking it or was it thinking him? Inexplicably it was all around him as he fell. Bigger and bigger it grew, blotches of black on pale green, like a rubbing done on green paper. But the green was more like pale cold fire. Cold, yes, it was bitter cold, icy cold and a freezing wind blowing.

Oliver began to know that this was the face of Hades all around him; there was no end to it, the stony black and cold green fire of it turning, turning, a turning hollowness going straight down. Oliver fell and fell and kept on falling through it while the lips of Hades slowly moved, his mouth roared silently, PERSEPHONEIA.

Like the sea flooding a cave the idea of Hades and Persephone filled Oliver. It was in him that the green and golden summer of the world was winter for Hades, his black time, dead time, lost and broken time without Persephone. Persephone was everything beautiful and she was gone into the upper world of sunlight whispering in the olive groves. How could Hades know that she would ever come back to him? Why should she want to return to the sombre world of the dead as his dark queen? The king of the dead raged and wept in his terror, always turning, turning, slowly turning the face of his rage below the world.

Still Oliver was falling, and still that slowly turning face rushed upward from below all around him as he fell. The idea of it was too hard and heavy for him to hold in his mind, the pain of it was too much for him to bear. "I think I'm going to die of it," he said. But he didn't die.

The falling had stopped, the slowly turning face of Hades was gone. Oliver saw the eyes of the goat, he saw the donkey's ears turned back and

DARK OLIVER

listening. He heard the crowing of the cock, the whisper of the olive leaves. He was in the greenlit shade of the olive grove. The woman-shaped tree stood before him holding open its emptiness to him. Perhaps nothing had happened?

There was a stone in Oliver's hand that filled it comfortably and had a pleasing heaviness. It was a tawny broken stone with sharp edges and irregular facets that tapered to a triangular base; it looked like abstract sculpture of monumental size, it looked commemorative. There was a shallow concavity where his thumb fitted, and when he removed his thumb and held the stone at a certain angle to the light this hollow filled with the shadow of a great bird of the realm of the dead that stood with its back to him. He knew that it was a bird of power: it was a bird of loss, a winged sorrow for what was gone for ever. The thought of it was suddenly overwhelming and he cried.

Oliver thought of the stone as his Hades stone. He kept it in his pocket during the day and he kept it under his pillow at night. He didn't write on it or draw on it; with his thumb he felt the shape of the shadow-bird. He imagined it spreading its dark wings and he wondered about the unseen face of it.

When Oliver and his mother and father came back from Paxos the London streets looked mean and grey.

"Hades," whispered Oliver.

"'Hell hath no limits,'" said his father, "'nor is circumscribed in one self place; for where we are is hell, and where hell is there must we ever be.'"

"Speak for yourself," said Oliver's mother.

*

When Oliver went back to school he had the Hades stone in his pocket, fitting his fingers, fitting his thumb.

It was a cold September, the air was grey, the streets were grey, the tarmac of the playground was hard under Oliver's feet.

There was Geoffrey again. "Hello, Olive Oil," he said.

Oliver didn't say anything. He saw the olive tree holding open its dark emptiness; with his thumb he felt the shape of the shadow-bird whose face he had not yet seen.

"What's the matter?" said Geoffrey. "Cat got your tongue?"

Oliver took the stone out of his pocket. "Do you know where this is from?"

"No. Where's it from?"

"Perhaps you'll find out soon. Hell hasn't got any limits—did you know that? It's wherever we are."

"I think you've gone right round the twist, Olive Oil."

"Perhaps you'll go somewhere too." Oliver wanted to exact something from Geoffrey, wanted Geoffrey to feel the sorrow that he felt without knowing why. "There's a darkness inside the tree," he said.

"Sounds like there's a darkness inside your head."

"Nothing is for ever—summer comes, summer goes. Geoffrey comes . . ."

"But he's jolly well not going, Olive Oil."

Oliver moved back three steps. He tilted his head, listening to the great voice that spoke through the donkey. "The darkness is waiting; the donkey says go."

"You're the donkey and I think what you need is a good thumping."

Oliver moved three steps to the left. He made his eyes like ochre-grey stones with oblong black stones set in them. "The goat says go."

"Baaa," said Geoffrey. "Why don't you try to make me go?"

Oliver moved forward three steps. At the back of his throat he crowed silently. "The cock says go. Because it's time."

"It's past time, Olive Oil," said Geoffrey. He drew back his fist.

Oliver held the Hades stone so that the great shadowy bird appeared. He saw the bird rise high into the air, he saw its face that was black like earth and ashes, green like pale fire. "Time for you to go," he said to Geoffrey as the shadow bird stooped.

Oliver was all alone, falling endlessly while the slowly turning face of Hades rushed upward all around him. Not endlessly—he had stopped falling and it was the unturning face of the school nurse that he saw as he came awake gasping from the little bottle she held under his nose. The Hades stone was no longer in his hand.

"Are you with us again?" said the nurse.

"What happened?"

"It seems that you fainted after your exertions."

"What exertions?"

DARK OLIVER

"Geoffrey says you were showing him a judo throw."

"Where's Geoffrey now?"

"They've taken him to hospital for stitches on his head. The playground is not the place for judo practice. Someone might have been seriously hurt."

"We won't do it again."

"I should hope not."

"Here's your stone back," said Geoffrey later. "You know, it's a funny thing. When you bashed me with it I saw a great big face all around me, it was green and black and it kept turning."

"I've seen that face," said Oliver.

"Where? When?"

"On the island of Paxos last month."

"How come you saw it?"

"I can't talk about it."

"I'll swap you an Iron Maiden cassette for that stone."

"Sorry, but no."

"It's got my blood on it."

"I've got another good stone from Paxos, from the beach; I'll give you that one but you have to stop calling me Olive Oil."

"OK."

The autumn term went well for Oliver; the other boys seemed to look at him differently from the way they had before. There was a school play about King Arthur and he was given the part of Merlin.

The Ghost Horse of Genghis Khan

John was eight years old and he liked to be in his father's study. It was full of books and all kinds of things that his father needed for his writing. Sometimes after school John would lie on the oriental carpet and draw. Sometimes he would sit in the reading chair and read or look at videotapes that he listened to with headphones while his father worked.

There were shadowy places and lamplit places in the study. There were maps on the wall. There was a human skeleton that made gentle clacking sounds when you moved it. There were three pendulum clocks that struck the hours at different times when they were running. Now they were stopped at different times. There was a model of a Portuguese fishing boat, there was a stuffed barn owl. There were rocks and seashells from many places and a stone from a Crusader fort in Galilee with chisel marks on it. John ran his thumb over the chisel marks and thought of the hand that had held the chisel long ago. He held the left hand of the skeleton and moved its arm.

Among the clutter on the desk were some books with markers in them: *The Mongol Empire; The Mongols; The Devil's Horsemen; The Secret History of the Mongols*. John read bits here and there about Genghis Khan.

He looked at drawings of thirteenth-century Mongol horsemen twisting in the saddle to shoot arrows. He read how Mongol children learned to ride before they could walk, how the warriors slept on horseback, how they drank the milk of their mares or opened a vein in a horse's leg to drink the blood.

"Genghis Khan," he said aloud. He was alone in the lamplight and the shadows of the study. His father was in hospital, recovering from heart surgery. He slept wired to a cardiac monitor, his heartbeat regularly repeating its line of jagged peaks across the screen.

Genghis Khan, said John's mind. The mind was much older than the boy, it was as ancient as the stars, it remembered all sorts of things that John had never known. It was curious about everything and it was playful, it was obsessed with names and the sounds of words: Khwarizm; Khurasan; Karakorum; Genghis Khan. Genghis, Genghis, Genghis, it said, Genghis galloping, galloping. The thudding of unshod hooves is in the name; the bending of the bow is in the name, the bow of horn and sinew and lacquer. The rider twisting in the saddle draws the bowstring back and looses the arrow, the hiss of the hungry arrow cleaving time and darkness, cleaving forgetfulness so that the galloping of the ghost horse of Genghis Khan is fresh and strong in me.

The Mongols lived in tents, in yurts, thought John. My father and I have never slept in a tent. He sits at his desk writing except when he's napping or watching TV. He goes up and down the stairs slowly. I wonder what he was like when he was young. Did he ever gallop, did he ever have a bow and arrows?

In his father's typewriter was an unfinished page two. On the copy-holder beside the typewriter was page one. It was headed: THE GHOST HORSE OF GENGHIS KHAN. John read:

> Genghis Khan, the name lives its own life apart from the man who was whatever he was. Genghis, Genghis, Genghis Khan galloping, galloping in the long night. Hundreds of horses he must have ridden in his warrior lifetime and now he lies no one knows where and all the hundreds of horses have become one shape of galloping in the long night.
> What colour is this galloping?
> Red.
> Is there a particular red horse?

There is now: a red roan with a white nose.

Is there a story about him?

Yes, I see it happening.

What do you see?

Here is Genghis Khan before he was Genghis Khan, when he was young, when he was called Temujin. Here he is, galloping for his life on the red roan. A close-coupled leggy horse, a clever-looking horse, a steadfast one, galloping, galloping. Behind him on the tawny steppe drifts the dust cloud of his going and through the dust gallop three riders hot on his track. Temujin has an arrow in his right shoulder, he cannot use his bow, nothing can save him but his horse. He leans low over its neck, he sees its eye roll back as the red roan listens for his voice.

"O thou of two worlds," says Temujin. He doesn't know why he says this, he thinks of nothing, the words alone fill his mind, the surging gallop of the red roan is like a prayer wheel. On and on it gallops through the long afternoon, on and on until a long, long shudder . . .

There the unfinished page two ended. What do you think? said John's mind.

About what? said John.

About what's happening in the story, said his mind.

I'd rather not say, said John.

Three o'clock in the morning, said the three stopped clocks.

John looked at his watch. That isn't the time, he said. It's not even eight o'clock at night, it's not even my bedtime.

Not even your bedtime, said the clocks. Not all that much time though.

For what? said John.

It isn't for us to say, said the clocks.

John pushed the typewriter carriage return and the unfinished page moved up two spaces. That's not the end of the story, said his mind.

"Time to get ready for bed," said his mother, and John went upstairs. His mother kissed him good night and he fell asleep and his mind began to speak to him again.

What is the shape of the galloping of the ghost horse of Genghis Khan? it said. Not of the eye, not to be seen, shadow of a memory, hoofbeats on the plains of here and gone. Here and gone, thought John in his sleep. Two places. Is there a drum, said his mind, is there a rattle, is there a bone whistle? How does one call up the ghost horse of Genghis Khan? Out of

THE GHOST HORSE OF GENGHIS KHAN

the herds of the dead, out of the shadows and the dust and the silence, out of the white pages of scholars and the smell of ink how does one call up that moving shadow on the screen of memory?

If you call me I will come, said the ghost horse.

Where are you? said John.

In your mind, said the ghost horse. In the shadows and the long night and the herds of the dead.

I don't know your name, said John. How can I call you if I don't know your name?

My name is not a name, said the ghost horse. Call me how you can. Call me and I will come.

What is it to be alive? said the sleeping John. What is it to be dead?

Ideas never die, said the ghost horse. I am an idea.

John woke up and went into his father's study. He turned on the lamps so that the places of lamplight and shadow appeared in their proper order. Three o'clock in the morning, said the three stopped clocks.

John looked at his watch. That's not the time, he said. It's only a little past two. Only a little past two, said the clocks. John looked at them very hard. They were telling the right time. He wound them and started them going. Then he sat down at the typewriter.

The unfinished page seemed to move in its blank whiteness, seemed to dance in its blankness before him. In that dancing was the red roan galloping, galloping until a long, long shudder broke its rhythm. In everything, said his mind, there is the animal of itself, the animal beyond the moment, beyond all moments. In the horse and in the man and in the boy, the animal of itself galloping, galloping.

John felt the dancing in the paper move towards him as he moved towards it. I'm not as good at stories as my father is, he said.

It isn't a question of being good at stories, said his mind. It's a question of how far you'll go.

At three o'clock in the morning in the hospital ward the pattern on the cardiac monitor lost its regularity and jumbled into random peaks and valleys. The staff nurse flung the pillows off John's father's bed and began to massage his chest while a student nurse gave him mouth-to-mouth respiration. The night sister dialled 222, said, "Cardiac arrest!" and ran for the emergency trolley. "Crash!" said the bleepers as the student started a bicarbonate drip while the staff nurse put an airway into John's father's throat and attached a re-breather bag. When the crash team arrived the anaesthetist inserted an endotracheal tube, put John's father on oxygen, and took over the re-breather. The doctor at the defibrillator applied the electrode jelly and said, "Stand back." He pressed the paddles against John's father's chest and delivered a 400-joule shock; John's father arched convulsively but the random peaks and valleys continued on the monitor screen. "Stand back," said the doctor, and did it again.

What did you say? said John to his mind.

I said it's a question of how far you'll go.

John wasn't aware of answering but he must have said something, thought something. There was a horrendous rushing, ripping, rending sound, a searing blast of pain as all before and after tore away from him and all the clocks struck three.

He whirled through blackness, wheeled high up into clear blue air and scanned the tawny steppe below him, saw the dry dust drifting, saw the horses and their riders strung out on the lion-coloured plain. Their shadows raced in silence over pebbles, blades of grass, old hoofprints. In the distance stood the wrinkled silent mountains, intolerably real.

Then the ground swooped close and blurred back under him in utter silence, he was in the galloping, in the animal of it. On and on he galloped; an immense fatigue dragged at him and there came a long, long shudder but the animal of him left all else behind, the animal of him became its motion, became the never-tiring motion of itself as sounds rushed in upon him, the incessant rhythmic thudding of his galloping hooves. He felt the weight of his rider, felt his own unending strength become a long, long rocking like the sea and far away.

In the hospital his father opened his eyes. "O thou of two worlds," he said.

"How are you feeling?" said the night sister.

"I almost didn't get here."

"Tell me about it."

"I felt my horse sink underneath me, then . . ."

"Then what?"

John's father laughed. "It was a dream," he said.

THE GHOST HORSE OF GENGHIS KHAN

It was almost four o'clock in the morning when John's mother woke up and went into the study. She saw her son asleep at the desk with his head cradled on his arms. She read the page in the typewriter that had ended: " . . . on and on until a long, long shudder . . . " Now there was more. She read:

> . . . on and on until a long, long shudder passes through the horse but it doesn't stumble, it keeps on galloping. The pursuers have no more arrows and they stop chasing Temujin.
>
> It was getting dark when the red roan brought Temujin to his camp. His brother Khasar pulled out the arrow and bandaged the wound and got him a fresh horse. It was time to move camp, and they rode away. Temujin's wound hurt, he'd lost a lot of blood. He fell asleep in the saddle.
>
> When he woke up the moon was shining and they were up in the hills. The horses were put out to graze and he went to look for the red roan but he couldn't find it.
>
> "Where's the red roan?" he asked Khasar.
>
> "How should I know?" said Khasar.
>
> "But I rode into camp on it," said Temujin.
>
> "I found you lying on the ground at the edge of camp and there was no horse," said Khasar.
>
> "Were there any tracks?"
>
> "No tracks."
>
> Then Temujin knew that the red roan had galloped beyond death to save him.

In two weeks John's father came home. He sat down at his desk and looked at the page in his typewriter. "Someone's been typing on my page," he said.

"It was me," said John. "I woke up in the middle of the night and came in here and I sort of had a dream at your desk."

"Sleeptyping?" said his father.

"Something like that," said John.

"It's not bad," said his father. "Not bad at all."

ESSAYS

"I, that was a child,
my tongue's use sleeping . . . "

Written for the June 1984 Seminar of the Israel Association of American Studies in Tel Aviv. The theme of the seminar was "The American Dream."

Everyone lives a life that is seen and a life that is unseen. Our dreams are part of our unseen life. We often forget our own dreams and we have no idea whatever of the dreams of others: last night the person next to you in the underground may have ridden naked on a lion or travelled under the sea to the lost city of Atlantis. Along with the dream life there is the life of ideas and half-ideas, of glimmerings and flashes and indescribable atmospheres of the mind. What we actually do in what is called the real world depends largely on how we live this unseen life in our inner world of words and images, songs and bits of poems, names and numbers and memories and dreams remembered and unremembered. Whether the song in our heads is Michael Jackson or Franz Schubert it is fitting itself to and reinforcing something in us that comes forward to meet it. That's how art affects life; we use it to be more what we are and to become what is in us wanting us to become it. The world of the song or the poem is met by other worlds known to us or hidden in our dreams.

In dreams one often sees the house of one's childhood. Years and years have passed, one's own children have grown up and gone out into the world; but in dreams the house of childhood is fresh and strong, the smell of its closets, the creak of its floors, the light through its windows and the shadows of leaves—everything resonates in the sleeping mind. Perhaps tonight one will find the lost toy or see more clearly something only half-glimpsed long ago. And perhaps today if I begin with the house of my childhood I can find my way to that unseen part of my life that grows out of and into what is called The American Dream.

The house of my childhood was in Lansdale, Pennsylvania. My parents were Russian Jews from a town in the Ukraine called Ostrog. They're both dead now and my two sisters and I continue their outward journey from that town we've never seen. They were both young when they came to America. My father had been poor in Russia, he told me how once outside a bakery he had seen a boy with a freshly-bought cheese pastry take out the cheese and throw away the crust which he, my father, then picked up and ate. There was in our house a halting little oil painting he had done on a wooden panel: it was a platoon of Russian cavalry, horsemen with slung carbines and bed-rolls, just a little clump of figures on horses, seen from the back. Now I call to mind this picture that I haven't seen for almost fifty years and I have no idea what it was to him.

My mother came to America before my father, in 1911 I think, when she was seventeen. She came with her sisters and she worked as a seamstress to earn my father's passage. He became a newsboy in Philadelphia, he had a dog who sat on the back of his bicycle. He made friends with some of the staff of *The Jewish Daily Forward* who used to buy papers from him. He went to night classes and lectures; I am named after Dr Russell Conwell who gave a famous lecture called "Acres of Diamonds" in which a man travelled the world in search of wealth and then found it in his own backyard.

My father bought Dr Eliot's Five-Foot Shelf, the Harvard Classics; also E. Haldeman-Julius's Little Blue Books in one of which Dr Emil Coué said that every day in every way he was getting better and better; also Krafft-Ebing's *Psychopathia Sexualis* in which all the best parts were in Latin; also *Sunshine and Health Magazine* in which respectable ladies and gentlemen were shown in respectably drooping nakedness drinking tea and playing tennis.

My father gave me a book, *Fairy Tales for Workers' Children.* I was taught never to cross a picket line and always to eat the union label on loaves of rye and pumpernickel for good luck. My father had become Advertising Manager of *The Jewish Daily Forward* and Director of the Drama

Guild of the Labor Institute of the Workmen's Circle of Philadelphia. He directed Yiddish classics and contemporary American plays of social comment such as *Stevedore, 1931,* and *Can You Hear Their Voices?* Sometimes my sisters and I got onstage; in the play *1931* a jobless man begged a dime from a passer-by who tossed it so that it fell to the ground. I was a newsboy who grabbed the dime. I had one line to speak: "It's mine, I saw it first!"

My mother raised pigeons, two thousand of them. We had a hired man who helped with the pigeons and our one-acre truck patch. My father's younger brother, my uncle Jack, had a frequently broken-down roadster called Natasha and liked to play baseball. Sometimes I rode in Natasha's rumble seat. On the wall by my bed I had a chromolithographed cardboard display figure of King Kong on top of the Empire State Building with an aeroplane in one hand and Fay Wray in the other. Ethel Waters sang "Stormy Weather" on the radio and sad-faced men came to the back door and asked if they could do some chores for a meal. My mother fed them and I sat on the porch with them while they ate their share of the American Dream.

One speaks of the American Dream and the meaning varies with the speaker but always what is meant is a montage of heart-pictures, desire-pictures, richly coloured wishes and memories and expectations of what people variously want from America or associate with America. This montage may have in it the Declaration of Independence, John D. Rockefeller, the Ku Klux Klan, Daniel Boone and Joseph McCarthy, Shirley Temple and the mountain men and Charlie Parker; it may have Abe Lincoln and Billy the Kid and the Statue of Liberty lifting her lamp beside the golden door of the Land of Opportunity where the plough breaks the plains, the West is won, the Yanks are coming, the Wright brothers and the astronauts go up and the economy comes down, Henry David Thoreau plants beans at Walden Pond, the Okies roll out of the dustbowl in battered Fords and talking blues by Woody Guthrie, Frank Sinatra sings at Las Vegas, Thomas Wolfe burns in the night and Jack Dempsey, Marilyn Monroe, Diamond Jim Brady, P. T. Barnum and the *Enola Gay* gleam in the high sunlight over Hiroshima while Bartolomeo Vanzetti writes a letter to his son and survivalists in Texas stockpile provisions and machine guns. The American Dream is pretty much whatever montage of heart-pictures you like to look at.

In every montage of heart-pictures lives the house of childhood, the physical one that still stands and perhaps is lived in by strangers or has burnt down or been demolished or stands desolate with broken suitcases and old letters with blurred writing under rotting leaves and broken glass and the rain coming in through empty windows.

There is another house of childhood and this one is of the mind. In my house of childhood of the mind lives Vol. xvii of the Harvard Classics. Vol. xvii was the only book in the Five-Foot Shelf much handled; Locke and Hume and Darwin looked as new as the day they were unpacked but Vol. xvii was *Folklore and Fable*, Andersen and Aesop and the brothers Grimm, and it was in heavy use. Oscar Wilde's *House of Pomegranates* and *The Arabian Nights* live there also. As a child I did much of my reading in the room in our house called the library. It was lined with books in Russian, Yiddish, and English and had a massive oak table. No one else I knew had such a room. I had outdoor reading places as well, and of these my favourite was a big old wild cherry tree where in season I read *Robin Hood* and ate little sun-warmed black cherries.

This house that childhood builds in the mind is a learning place and a place where we test words and images and ideas to find out what rings true. Also it's like a safe house in a spy film: in it the secret agent that is the child's mind can stay hidden until ready to venture armed into the hostile city. It isn't the world that is hostile—the stone and the leaf and the door of the world beckon and welcome—it's the grey city of the world that threatens, the grey city of the failed children of the world, the dry thinkers, the juiceless minds, the poison skulls that dream in numbers and megadeaths. They run the world, these failed children; they speak in all languages and in all languages their speech is vile. In bemedalled uniforms, in costly business suits and ties they mouth pompous words printed out by grey machines. Each one thinks the other is the enemy while the real enemy, the monster they have called up together, sings to itself outside the window. The grey city is why the safe house of childhood of the mind is needed, and long after the child is grown this safe house is still needed in the shadows and the narrow alleys by the waterfront in the grey city of terror.

This house of childhood is not a foolish place, it is the true place where first recognitions happen all through life; it is the place where I heard for the first time what is in the Beethoven quartets and Bach's *Art of Fugue* and Schubert's *Die Winterreise;* it is where Oedipus made his tragedy belong to him and was no longer a victim, where Conrad's Jim jumped from the *Patna* into lostness, where Rubashov in *Darkness at Noon* accepted one by one the consequences of the ideas he had lived by; it is where I took in unknown pages that came alive years later like water in the desert, it is where T. S. Eliot said, in *Little Gidding:*

> We die with the dying:
> See, they depart, and we go with them.
> We are born with the dead:
> See, they return, and bring us with them.
> The moment of the rose and the moment
> of the yew-tree
> Are of equal duration.

Since 1969 I've lived in London. I'm a stranger at home under grey English skies and walking by European rivers but I still weapon and provision myself in the house of childhood that was built in America. Are there in that house recognitions that are peculiarly American? Yes, I think so. Here is one:

> Out of the cradle endlessly rocking,
> Out of the mocking-bird's throat, the musical shuttle,
> Out of the Ninth-month midnight,
> Over the sterile sands and the fields beyond, where the
> child leaving his bed wander'd alone, bareheaded,
> barefoot,
> Down from the shower'd halo,
> Up from the mystic play of shadows twining and
> twisting as if they were alive,
> Out from the patches of briers and blackberries,
> From the memories of the bird that chanted to me,
> From your memories sad brother, from the fitful
> risings and failings I heard,
> From under that yellow half-moon late-risen and
> swollen as if with tears . . .

In Walt Whitman's magical lyric the poet listens through the night to the "lone singer wonderful," the mocking-bird, the solitary he-bird who guards the nest and the eggs to which his mate never returns.

Demon or bird! (said the boy's soul),
Is it indeed toward your mate you sing? or is it really to me?
For I, that was a child, my tongue's use sleeping, now
    I have heard you,
Now in a moment I know what I am for, I awake,
And already a thousand singers, a thousand songs, clearer,
    louder and more sorrowful than yours,
A thousand warbling echoes have started to life within
    me, never to die.

In the last part of the poem he asks for a word from the sea:

Whereto answering, the sea,
Delaying not, hurrying not,
Whisper'd me through the night, and very plainly
    before day-break,
Lisp'd to me the low and delicious word death,
And again death, death, death, death,
Hissing melodious, neither like the bird nor like my
    arous'd child's heart,
But edging near as privately for me rustling at my feet,
Creeping thence steadily up to my ears and laving me
    softly all over,
Death, death, death, death, death.

Which I do not forget,
But fuse the song of my dusky demon and brother,
That he sang to me in the moonlight on Paumanok's
    gray beach,
With the thousand responsive songs at random,
My own songs awaked from that hour,
And with them the key, the word up from the waves,
The word of the sweetest song and all songs,
That strong and delicious word which, creeping to my
    feet,
(Or like some old crone rocking the cradle, swathed
    in sweet garments, bending aside,)
The sea whisper'd me.

This poem was first published in 1859, and at this distance Whitman
seems not so much a man as a manifestation, as if the nature of America

and its history generated this voice that must inevitably appear. He seems a kind of lesson, a paradigm, this Walt Whitman who read almost inaudibly to a baffled and not very responsive audience and then wrote the newspaper account of the same reading in which he described himself as filling the auditorium with his booming masculine voice and being interrupted continually by applause; Walt Whitman the non-boomer, the whisperer in the darkness at the heart of the American Dream, driven by his demon to step out from behind his laborious persona for this profound and shadowy rite of passage. Nations have national characteristics: I think that we Americans have both a propensity for bullshit and an inborn drive to cut through the bullshit. (I have to use this word, there isn't any other for what I mean—"bombast" won't do it.) The wonderfully American thing about this poem is that it took this bullshit artist of the open road and made him write it so that it could become itself. I love that.

"Out of the Cradle Endlessly Rocking" is a hermetic lyric; it is of the realm of Hermes, the whisperer in the darkness, the guide of souls and the god of thieves and roadways and journeys. On the day Hermes was born he invented the lyre and stole the cattle of Apollo. To make the sound-box of the lyre he scooped a living tortoise out of its shell, he killed something to make an emptiness for his music to come out of. Then after making music he was hungry for meat so he stole Apollo's cattle.

Hermes is not officially the god of artists and the arts but he is for me: in some way there is always the killing of something to make that necessary emptiness from which the art comes and in some way the artist is always stealing what he hungers for, stealing cattle that can never be owned, cattle of beauty, cattle of truth and pain, cattle of minutes and hours—as often as not simply stealing that part of himself that is somebody else's cattle, stealing it for a secret life of finding and losing and mystery.

However it came to be there, that emptiness in Whitman wherein he heard the sea and the word from the sea is an American emptiness—you can see it in the heartbreaking summer dusk over the pines and the illuminated globes on the gas pumps in an Edward Hopper painting; you can see it in the faded lettering that says PURINA CHOWS on the side of a deserted Pennsylvania barn. Hopper and Whitman both bring their music out of that emptiness and both of them stole the cattle of themselves out of the herd of not-belonging-to-self.

Hermes is the god of journeys, and that long road that passes Edward Hopper's Maine gas station is the one that America has travelled from its beginning: the spirit of America is a journeying one; everyone in America has always been on the way from one place to another, one condition to another. Our only original music comes from the descendants of slaves on their way from otherness into America's idea of itself. American blues and jazz have always in them the long road and the shining rails dwindling to a point ahead and behind; our characteristic music is always going somewhere, moving, travelling, on that train and gone with long-gone John from Bowling Green, gone with Easy Rider where the Southern meets the Yellow Dog, gone where that Midnight Special shines its light on you and me and the journeying and imprisoned soul of the Land of the Free.

How imprisoned? Like all individuals and like all nations America is a prisoner of its history, of what was done and what was not done. How many dead bodies and dead hopes has the American Dream left behind it in the domestic and foreign venues where it has played? And like all individuals and nations America is a prisoner of its own idea of itself. False legends and tall stories proliferate faster than the truth. Too often we have come blinking out of the cinema of our hopeful vanity and ridden off into the pollution tall in the saddle with John Wayne. What we truly are is a mystery to us; this mystery is continually in the process of finding a voice and for this it used Walt Whitman in his time; it used him to speak the darkness below all history and all legend, the darkness that is not only death but the womb of that mystery out of which comes new becoming.

In his chapter on Hermes in his book, *The Homeric Gods*, Walter F. Otto has this to say about the mother-darkness that is the realm of Hermes :

> A man who is awake in the open field at night or who wanders over silent paths experiences the world differently than by day. Nighness vanishes, and with it distance; everything is equally far and near, close by us and yet mysteriously remote. Space loses its measures. There are whispers and sounds, and we do not know where or what they are. Our feelings too are peculiarly ambiguous. There is a strangeness about what is intimate and dear, and a seductive charm about the frightening. There is no longer a distinction between the lifeless and the living, everything is animate and soulless, vigilant and asleep at once . . . Danger lurks everywhere . . . Who can protect him, guide him aright, give him good

counsel? The spirit of Night itself, the genius of its kindliness, its enchantment, its resourcefulness, and its profound wisdom. She is indeed the mother of all mystery.

And a word from the other great Hermes-friend, Karl Kerenyi:

> For the great mystery, which remains a mystery even after all our discussing and explaining, is this: the appearance of a speaking figure, the very embodiment as it were in a human-divine form of clear, articulated, play-related and therefore enchanting, language—its appearance in that deep primordial darkness where one expects only animal muteness, wordless silence, or cries of pleasure and pain. Hermes the "Whisperer" (*psithyristes*) inspirits the warmest animal darkness.

This also from Kerenyi:

> What he [Hermes] brings with him from the springs of creation is precisely the "innocence of becoming."

For me innocence of becoming is associated with the idea of the unfailed and unfailing child. This follows on my earlier thought of the grey city of failed children. Now I have to say a little more about the unfailed child. In order to do this I must go back in my thinking and my reading to the sources of this idea.

"The overall number of minds is just one," said Schrödinger. There's no way of proving this; one can only test it against one's own experience. Does consciousness feel like that, as if there's only one mind? To me it does. I feel inhabited by a consciousness that looks out through the eyeholes in my face and this consciousness doesn't seem to have originated with me. I feel like a receiver made for a transmission that was going on long before I arrived.

It feels to me as if the total experience of the universe and every image ever imagined or seen, every word ever written or spoken, every thought ever thought is in this one mind, ceaselessly active. And I believe that whatever is in the one mind is in each of us. That being so, the total experience, not only of humanity but of the universe, is in each one of us in this one mind that is always now.

We are the children of the mystery that inhabits us and I believe that it wants us to meet it with innocence of becoming; not to meet it is to be a failed child. Perhaps there haven't yet been any unfailed children but I think that all of us have unfailed moments. Whitman was unfailing that night on the beach; by tuning himself to the bird he entered innocence of becoming and met the mystery. And something of the American soul followed him and still follows him into the wondrous dark of it.

As if to demonstrate that they were two aspects of the same thing, Walt Whitman and Herman Melville were both born in the same year, 1819, and died in the same year, 1891. Whitman heard the song of the bird and the word from the sea on Long Island for which he used the Indian name Paumanok. Melville hunted his whale with a ship called the *Pequod*, the name of an extinct Indian tribe. It was as if each man wanted the ghosts of the original inhabitants at his back when the one invoked the savage mother and the other the white whale.

> "Hark ye yet again, — the little lower layer," says Ahab. "All visible objects, man, are but as pasteboard masks. But in each event — in the living act, the undoubted deed — there, some unknown but still reasoning thing puts forth the mouldings of its features from behind the unreasoning mask. If man will strike, strike through the mask! How can the prisoner reach outside except by thrusting through the wall? To me the white whale is that wall, shoved near to me. Sometimes I think there's naught beyond. But 'tis enough He tasks me; he heaps me; I see in him outrageous strength, with an inscrutable malice sinewing it. That inscrutable thing is chiefly what I hate; and be the white whale agent, or be the white whale principal, I will wreak that hate upon him."

"I have written a wicked book," said Melville in a letter to Hawthorne, "and feel spotless as the lamb." So far I've avoided reading any critical analyses of *Moby Dick* and I hope to continue doing so; still, I can't help wondering how much of Melville there was in Ahab and whether the Melville/Ahab balance changed after the last harpoon was thrown and the harpoon line that connected Ahab to the whale took him to his death.

The man who does battle with the unknown but reasoning thing behind the mask is dragged under by it and his mother-ship sunk. The innocent heathen Queequeg perishes with the others but his unChristian life-buoy coffin saves Ishmael:

Buoyed up by that coffin, for almost one whole day and night, I floated on a soft and dirge-like main. The unharming sharks, they glided by as if with padlocks on their mouths; the savage sea-hawks sailed with sheathed beaks.

The only survivor is neither the God-maddened Ahab nor the simple savage but the civilised mariner who seems to have attained innocence of becoming. I wonder whether Melville was by then more Ishmael than Ahab, whether through his tragic and absurd hero he had purged himself of rage and recognised that his hate was a kind of love and that the duality of which one element was the enemy was in fact a unity where there was no enemy.

Moby Dick was published in 1851; "Out of the Cradle Endlessly Rocking" wasn't until 1859; perhaps the American child had to shake its fist at the father before it could be soothed by the mother. Certainly it's a continually growing child and it seems not bound for failure, this child loving enough to beg the word of darkness from the sea and bold enough to steer for the monstrous malevolent jaw. A promising child, I think, personified in 1884 by one Huckleberry Finn who, having written the note that will tell Miss Watson the whereabouts of the runaway slave Jim, finds himself pondering the matter:

> I felt good and all washed clean of sin for the first time I had ever felt so in my life, and I knowed I could pray now. But I didn't do it straight off, but laid the paper down and set there thinking—thinking how good it was all this happened so, and how near I come to being lost and going to hell. And went on thinking. And got to thinking over our trip down the river; and I see Jim before me, all the time, in the day, and in the night-time, sometimes moonlight, sometimes storms, and we a floating along, talking, and singing, and laughing. But somehow I couldn't seem to strike no places to harden me against him; but only the other kind. I'd see him standing my watch on top of his'n, stead of calling me, so I could go on sleeping; and see him how glad he was when I come back out of the fog; and when I come to him again in the swamp, up there where the feud was; and such-like times; and would always call me honey, and pet me, and do everything he could think of for me, and how good he always was; and at last I struck the time I saved him by telling the men we had small-pox aboard, and he was so grateful, and said I was the best friend old Jim ever had in the world, and the *only* one he's

got now; and then I happened to look around, and see that paper.

It was a close place. I took it up, and held it in my hand. I was a trembling, because I'd got to decide, forever, betwixt two things, and I knowed it. I studied a minute, sort of holding my breath, and then says to myself:

"All right, then, I'll *go* to hell" — and tore it up.

Huck Finn, standing alone against the authority of the failed-child establishment and refusing to sell his dark brother down the river, is about as unfailed a child as you can find: a child eminently practical and resourceful, cunning enough to survive the grey city of the world, a child in touch with the mystery of being and always in a state of innocently becoming. An American Dream with him in it has a good chance of not being a nightmare.

I said at the outset that I was going to try to find my way to the unseen part of my life that grows into and out of the American Dream. I've done what I could with that. The seen part of my life is my writing and I was late getting started. It wasn't until 1963 that I, that was a child, my tongue's use sleeping, took typewriter in hand and began to put a novel together. Since then I've tried to keep moving on that wavering edgeline where the sea of the mystery meets the strand of the more or less known, leaving my American footprints in the sand where others have walked before me, listening to the word from the waves, sometimes seeing a ghostly spout far off, and hearing always the long and lonesome whistle of the Midnight Special.

1984

With a Choked Cry

"With a choked cry, the coxwain loosed his grasp upon the shrouds, and plunged head first into the water." That was the caption under one of the illustrations in the copy of *Treasure Island* I owned as a boy: Jim Hawkins, looking desperate, perched in the mizzen cross-trees of the *Hispaniola*, firing both his pistols as Israel Hands's dirk pins him to the mast. I haven't got the book now and I'm not sure of the name of the illustrator—I think it may have been Reade. I seem to remember a frontispiece in colour, Long John Silver with his parrot, but the rest of the illustrations were pen and ink. Reade (if indeed that was his name) drew with a Romanesquely reiterative line: if a form was worth going around once he went around it two or three times—not sketchily but insistently, like a dog with a bone—and each time the line went round it put a few pounds on whatever it delineated; his people, consequently, had somewhat haggard faces, a lot of wrinkles in their clothes, and they all walked with a heavy tread. When Hands hit the water he would have made a pretty big splash. I haven't seen those drawings for forty-eight years and I can't recall every one but the *look* of them is vivid in my mind and brings back the cosiness, the delight, the sheer well-being I felt when I first read that book, sitting in our wild cherry tree in the summer when I was ten.

Years later we lived in a building that had an incinerator chute on each floor. In the hall there was a metal flap in the wall that let out a current of warm air and the smell of burning when you opened it. In March 1943, just before I left for the army, I opened that flap and down the chute went *Treasure Island, Robin Hood, The Arabian Nights,* and some lesser favourites, all books that I loved and had read several times. I was eighteen and going off to the war, maybe I wasn't coming back; I was presiding over the death of my childhood so I burned those books and when I got to the induction centre I gave my civilian clothes to the Red Cross.

The books that underwent this enforced suttee were all illustrated ones and of course I've been looking for those same editions ever since I came back from the war and found that my early years and I were still alive. The only one that I was able to replace was *Robin Hood,* illustrated by Edwin John Prittie: twenty pictures, four in colour, looking as good as in my childhood, with the people in them, as before, a little better-looking and a little more elegant in gesture and action than one sees in real life. Pictured on the board cover is that first meeting on the narrow bridge when John Little (not yet Little John) knocks Robin into the stream with his quarter-staff. I hold the book in my hand and I can almost feel it hum with the hours of contentment I spent in the company of its departed brother.

My thrown-away *Arabian Nights* was a wonderful job of bookmaking of a much freer kind than *Treasure Island* or *Robin Hood.* The illustrations were all brush and ink by an unforgettably exuberant draughtsman whose name has vanished from my mind; wild they were, every one, and rumbustious with life—some were full-page, some were vignettes, some took up part of a page and the type ran around them. They were all over the book, as if they'd been waiting behind the printed words and had burst out when they couldn't hold themselves back any longer. The blacks of those black-and-white drawings were black like anything, the line was ragged and splotchy, the style was bold and loose and everything was well beyond the ordinary—when the people on those pages saw something that surprised them their eyes nearly jumped out of their heads; when they howled with rage you could hear it for miles; when Sinbad tied himself to the leg of the roc you could see by the terror in his face and the look of that leg (the rest of the bird was off the page) that he was in for a really scary ride. As I recall those drawings now they come with the shouts and background noise of oriental bazaars, the bass rumblings of genies loosed from jugs and lamps, the sweet voices of veiled women, the cries and curses of heroes and villains in strange and violent encounters, and all the sound effects required by the astonishing action of the stories. I've read somewhere of a Chinese or Japanese god of ink, and those drawings were certainly blessed by that god. The paper was coarse and thick, the ink lived in it with a strong life. That book was a treasure, my thrown-away *Arabian Nights*, gone for ever.

Ink on paper makes books; books make worlds. You don't need a printing press, you don't even need to be grown-up. Little children take pieces of paper, of different sizes as often as not; on them they print great gangling words with capitals and lower-case letters not always in the usual places; they draw pictures on the pieces of paper and they staple them together and the pages turn and it's a book with monsters and space-craft from beyond the galaxy. Or trees and flowers and there was a princess who lived in a castle.

Making books with pictures is a natural function of the human animal—we need them because the world in our eyes is not enough, it has to be imaged in other ways and other styles, it has to be brought into the what-iffery of the mind where everything is more so and where anything can happen. Illustrated books for children help to furnish the mind and improve the critical faculty; they help lookers become perceivers—most of all they simply give more world to the reader all through life.

One of the books I didn't throw away is the Lakeside Press edition of *Moby Dick* illustrated by Rockwell Kent whose drawings, together with the typography and layout, rank with Doré's *Don Quixote*. I lusted after that book and I finally got it for my fourteenth or fifteenth birthday. I knew from the first moment I held it in my hands that we were going to be friends for life. I haven't tried to put into words until now what Kent's austere and passionate evocations of Melville's metaphysics do: what those drawings do, what the best book illustration always does, is to take the mind to a special and peculiar place where mystery lives and words can't go, then return it to the word place sensitised, responsive, and newly perceptive of the world.

1991

POEMS

03.00 Abroad

Quietly, somewhere across the darkened town,
a clock struck three. It spoke
its hour in a friendly way, as if to say,
"Hello, I think we've met before." I
wasn't sure—the time seemed
different here, clothed in a distant
night and in a foreign place; I didn't
think I'd recognise its face until it
softly said, "Remember me?"
"Ah, yes," I said, "you're three."

Crystal Maze

"Think about it," Harry said: "infinite regress."
That's my brother Harry; he knew how to give me
stress.
Coloured lights around us, music, laughter, shrieks
and yells,
the roar and clatter of the rides, the fun-fair with
its smells
of mustard and of frying;
there were pitchmen shouting, babies crying,
punters winning great pink teddy bears
and so on—it was pretty much like other fairs
I'd been to other summer days
except I'd never seen a Crystal Maze.

"It's just a hall of mirrors," Harry said—
"it's no big deal unless you lose your head.
You want to try it? Want to have a go?"
"I'm not so sure about this, Harry, I don't know.
What is it with this infinite regress?

Is that when more and more gets less and less?"
"Of course," he said, "it's only an illusion.
The thing you must avoid, though, is confusion:
there are angles and reflections
which can take you in directions
that could bring you to a place that I won't mention:
we're talking danger here, you
can't let them disappear you,
or you'll end up well into the fourth dimension."

We bought our tickets then,
and I sort of shivered when
I saw a hundred of us or a thousand, maybe more.
"Don't look at those," said Harry—"keep your eyes
down on the floor;
then you'll see what isn't mirror
and with luck we'll find the way
that will get us home today."

So I kept on looking down
though I felt my head go round
and the hundreds and the thousands of me
sometimes pulled me, sometimes shoved me
into strange and spooky places
where I saw all kinds of faces
that were not my brother Harry and they
certainly weren't me.

But finally I was out
and I gave a happy shout:
I said, "Harry, we have done it,
we have beat it, we have won—it
was a scary thing to do
but we have made it, me and you."
But Harry didn't answer because Harry
wasn't there.

Well, I told the man outside and we went in
and we tried
to find my brother Harry but we never found a
clue.
So he scratched his head awhile and he smiled
a sorry smile,
and he gave our money back—it was the best that
he could do.
When I came home all alone
I heard both my parents groan—
first my dad and then my mother
said, "You've come home short one brother,
which is more than somewhat careless, it's a
silly thing to do;
we think you'd best be grounded for a week or
maybe two."

And when I cleaned my teeth that night
the mirror gave me quite a fright—
the face I saw was not my face
but in another time and space
my brother Harry in the glass
looked out at me but could not pass
from that place I will not mention
homeward through the fourth dimension.

We change the mirror every week;
we've called in mediums to seek
my brother on whatever plane
he is, to bring him back again
but nothing helps. I've tried and tried
to cross him over to this side
but there he stays—though bright they shine,
I'm brushing Harry's teeth, not mine.

The Owl-Woman

"Do you love me?" says the owl-woman,
long legs reaching for the ground as she lands,
yellow eyes burning into mine.
Snowy white and speckled brown she is, from the
North she comes to my dreams and says,
"Do you love me?" always the same, from
the North, where the ice bear
swims in the sea, miles from the land, never lost.
"Yes," I say, "I love you."
"Do you think I am beautiful?" says the owl-woman,
sunlight through her wings, turning and turning,
yellow eyes burning. "Say it," she says.
"Yes," I say, "you are beautiful."
"I know," she says. "Now you can sleep."

Turtle Prince?

Jim Frog sat on a lily pad;
he was feeling lonesome, feeling sad,
feeling more than somewhat fed-up
when a snapping-turtle stuck her head up
(caused a few ripples round the pond),
said, "Hello, sailor! Do not despond!
I fancy you, and I'll be quite frank—
although I'm of superior rank
(I'm a turtle princess, actually),
I'm asking you to marry me.
This offer is too good to miss;
now, how about a great big kiss?"

Jim knew the stories; he'd read the books.
He didn't really like her looks;
her forthright manner made him wince,
but still, he thought—a turtle prince!
So he kissed her. I haven't seen him since.

Fred to Samantha

I've read somewhere: on Chesil Beach,
the sea sorts pebbles, each from each,
from large to small,
and smooths them all
with grinding, rubbing, rolling, rounding,
in the clicking tidewash sounding
under the gull's cry
and the long, lone sigh
of the wind.

I wondered, in my thoughts of you,
just how the two of us might do:
though I am short and you are tall
I hoped you would return my call;
I hoped the telephone would ring
to make my heart triumphant sing.
I hoped, in every wind and weather
the two of us might rub together.

But no, long silence fills the day
and all my hopes have ebbed away.
I think perhaps some colder sea
sorts me from you and you from me.

POEMS

Dragon into
Dressing Gown

I know a dragon dark and green
(he's quite the handsomest I've seen)
who, sometimes less and sometimes more,
lives just behind my bedroom door.

And, sometimes less but often more,
that dragon just behind the door
rolls one eye up and one eye down
and turns into my dressing gown.

He doesn't do it in the night,
but in the early morning light
where dragon was, there on its hook
that dressing gown gives me a look.

I've asked the dragon if he'd stay
and be a dragon through the day,
but with a smile and with a frown
he turns into my dressing gown.

The Hippogriff

Long centuries have I soared above the Earth;
the mind of Ariosto gave me birth.
Sired by a griffon (he imagined) on a mare,
I course the currents of the upper air
(in his time unpolluted, crystalline, and pure
but now a mixture that I scarce endure
to breathe). My mighty pinions have grown tired;
I fly, no more by winged words inspired,
from habit only. What else can I do?
The times are out of joint, and heroes few.
No more do maidens chained to rocks
want rescue—now in tiny frocks
they seek out monsters more to be abhorred
than poor old Orca; all he hoped to do was eat
a juicy virgin for a little treat:
Angelica it was, Miss World of her time—
a real stunner; horrid was the crime
of sacrificing one so young in all her beauty,
but heroes then were sworn to do their duty;

and so Ruggiero sped to the attack
in heavy armour, mounted on my back.
I bore him swiftly to the fray;
he did the job and then we came away,
Angelica now riding in the pillion seat,
Ruggiero looking forward to his treat.
My youth is gone and shrivelled is my fame;
I'll end my days in some computer game
with characters whose lips move when they read
their circuits, myrmidons who need
no seas nor mountains, neither skies of blue.
How are the mighty fallen! My last hope is you.

What the Fairy Said
to the Bibliophile

The elderly hero of Anatole France's *The Crime of Sylvestre Bonnard* encounters, in a country library late one night, a beautiful fairy sitting on an old German leather-bound *Cosmography of Munster.*

• • •

He wasn't sure that he was seeing right:
there, sat before him in the candle's light,
a fairy woman with a queenly smile.
Her many charms were such as did beguile
that old man, made him feel quite young again,
made him uncertain where he was or when.
Her figure pleased him and her hair was blonde;
she held, quite properly, a hazel wand.
The time was well past midnight, I should think;
it might be that he'd had too much to drink —
at all events, he found it nothing shocking
to glimpse a shapely leg in a pink stocking:
gold-clocked it was, the height of Paris style;
perhaps there was flirtation in her smile?

POEMS

A handsome woman, although very little—
her wit was quick, her patience somewhat brittle.
Was she, he wondered, really there?
To this she answered with a haughty air:
"Nothing is real," she said, (and here's the twist)
"except what is imagined; therefore I exist."
Or words to that effect. Now neurologic
experts find,
what the eye sees is mainly in the mind.
Anatole France knew this some time ago
and I as well confirm that it is so:
I know she really is imaginary—
that's why she's real, that chic pink-stockinged
fairy.

The Dragon
underneath the Mat

The dragon underneath the mat,
he wore a shiny opera hat.
I always squashed it very flat
each time I trod upon the mat.

The dragon said that would not do,
the dragon said his wants were few:
a little peace; a little mat;
and no one flattening his hat.

I never thought how he might feel,
I trod him underneath my heel.
Yes, every day beneath that mat
his hat was squashed completely flat.

One day I found a little note
and this is what the dragon wrote:
"Goodbye, I'm leaving home. My hat
too often has been trodden flat."

I know that I was very wrong;
I think about it all day long;
I wish the hat had been more strong.
Sometimes I hum a dragon song.

CHILDREN'S WRITING

The Marzipan Pig

There was nothing to be done for the marzipan pig. He fell behind the sofa and that was that. No one had seen him fall and no one knew where he was. He shouted, "Help!" but no one heard him. Night came, and morning, and there he still was.

"One would think they'd miss me," he said after a day or two. "One would think they'd look for me."

Perhaps they missed him and perhaps they looked for him but he was never found. Days passed and he sweated as marzipan will. He grew swarthy with the dust that settled on the glistening pinkness of him.

By day he listened to footsteps and voices that never came near him. Through the nights the street lamp shone outside the window and he waited in the dark behind the sofa listening to the ticking of the clock and the striking of the hours and the hooting of the owl on the common.

"There is," he said, "such sweetness in me!" No one heard him. He heard the rain beyond the window and the hiss of tires on the street but no one came for him. Day after day he waited as the months went by. "I am growing hard," he said, "and bitter. What a waste of me!"

One night he heard a gnawing sound behind the skirting board. "Help is coming," said the pig. He listened and he listened. Every night the gnawing sound came closer.

"Friends unknown to me have heard of my disappearance and are coming to the rescue," said the pig. "No doubt there'll be a big celebration when they find me. Crackers and party hats and probably a cake with pink icing. Perhaps I'll be stood on top of the cake and asked to make a speech."

He began to think of the speech he would make. "Dear friends," he said, "having spent long months in solitude behind the sofa, I speak to you tonight of . . . "

"Sweetness," said a voice behind him.

"Who's that?" said the pig.

It was a mouse. She was nibbling at him. "You're sweet," she said.

"There was a time when I was sweet," said the pig, "but I have known such . . . "

"Sweetness, sweetness, sweetness," murmured the mouse, and she ate him up entirely.

After eating the pig the mouse dozed for a time behind the sofa. When the clock struck three she woke up. "I wonder what that pig was going to say?" she said. "I couldn't stop eating him but now I wish I'd listened." In her were a craving and a sadness she had never known before.

"I'm so alone," she said. "It's so quiet here." She listened and she listened to the ticking of the clock. She watched the moving glimmer of the pendulum in the dim light from the street lamp. "Speak to me," she said to the clock, "do."

"Night," said the clock. "Only, only, only night."

"Surely there's more?" said the mouse.

"Lonely night," the clock said. "Lonely, lonely, lonely night."

"Ah! The loneliness!" the mouse said. "That's what the pig was going to say, I'm sure of it."

"Minutes, hours, days and years," the clock said.

"You have a kind face," said the mouse. "Make me happy! Love me, do!"

"Half past three," said the clock, and went on ticking.

"You've more than that to say to me," said the mouse. She gnawed a little hole in the case of the clock and crept inside it so that she could be closer to the moving glimmer of the pendulum. She sat there listening to the ticking and the striking of the hours but the clock would tell her nothing but the time.

In the morning the mouse came out of the clock and went back behind the skirting board. But she came back that night and every night and sat inside the clock and waited for the clock to say it loved her. But the clock would tell her nothing but the time.

One night she didn't come back. The clock struck midnight and there was no mouse. Half past twelve and one o'clock and still no mouse. While the lamp shone outside the window he struck all the hours and half hours of the night but the mouse never came. The little warm place where she used to sit was cold and empty.

By day the clock could feel himself coiled tight inside and waiting for the night. By night he felt the empty place inside him as he waited for the day to come. The next time he was wound his spring broke and his ticking stopped and time went on without him.

The owl in the plane tree on the common was sitting where he always sat on Thursday nights, and it was raining. He was looking at the row of houses opposite the common when he saw a mouse come out from under the front door of No. 6.

The owl swooped down in silence through the rain and caught the mouse. He flew back up to the plane tree and ate the mouse, then he sat staring through the rain and he thought new thoughts.

"Love," said the owl. "Love, love, love!" he shouted to the rain. "I'm in love," he said more quietly. He looked down at the street and saw the violet glow of a taxi meter. Slowly the taxi puttered black and shining up the street, and in it was the meter violet-glowing in the dark.

"You!" said the owl. "I love you!"

On the taxi's roof the amber light lit up and said, "FOR HIRE."

"For ever!" said the owl. He swooped down on the taxi and landed on the bonnet with a thump. The bonnet was slippery with the rain, the owl slid on his tall till the windscreen stopped him.

When the driver saw the owl's feet staring at him he stopped the taxi and rolled down the window. The owl stood up and looked in at the meter. "I love you," he said.

"FOR HIRE," said the meter.

The taxi driver couldn't understand what the owl was saying. He thought the owl wanted to ride in the taxi. "I don't think you've got any money," he said.

"Who?" said the owl.

"You," said the driver. "Money. You know what money is?"

"Who?" said the owl.

"You," said the driver. "Money." He took a handful of coins from his pocket and showed them to the owl.

"Ooh," said the owl.

"That's money," said the driver. "No money, no ride." He started up the taxi and off he went. The owl flew up to the roof of the taxi and sat on top of the amber light.

The taxi driver drove to the cab stand by the Albert Bridge. The bridge was all lit up and shining in the rain. "Love!" said the owl. "Everything is bright for me!"

A lady came walking by. She was carrying a small handbag. The owl knew there was money in handbags. He swooped down and snatched it from her. He flew back to the taxi and dropped the bag on the bonnet. He looked in through the windscreen at the meter. "I love you," he said.

"FOR HIRE," said the meter.

"Stop, thief!" said the lady.

The driver gave the handbag back to the lady. He said to the owl, "You can't do that."

"Who?" said the owl.

"You," said the driver. "If you want a ride that badly, I'll give you one. But you'll have to pay me back some time, and not by stealing. Get in."

The driver opened the door and the owl perched on the back of the front seat by the meter. The driver started the meter and they drove off.

"I love you so much!" said the owl to the meter. "How much do you love me?"

"25p," said the meter.

"Love me more," said the owl.

"30p," said the meter.

"More and more!" said the owl.

"35p," said the meter. "40, 45."

"Yes," said the owl, "that's how it is. More and more and ever more. I am so happy with the lovely violet glow of you!"

"50p," said the meter as the cab pulled up at the cab stand by the bridge again. The driver stopped the taxi and turned off the lights. The meter went dark.

"Light up again," said the owl. "Tell me again how much you love me."

"That's it for tonight," said the driver. "Now it's time for trumpet practice."

"Who?" said the owl.

"Me," said the driver. He took a trumpet out of its case, climbed into the back seat, put his feet up on the back of the front seat, and began to play "When the Saints Come Marching In."

"Speak to me," said the owl to the taxi meter. "Glow violet and lovely again."

The meter stayed dark and the driver kept playing his trumpet.

"This isn't fair," said the owl to the meter. "What have I done?" He jumped out of the taxi and danced with rage on the pavement. Without noticing it, he began to dance in time to the music. "What have I done, what have I done, what have I done to make you dark?" he hooted in time with the trumpet.

A man walking by threw 10p on the pavement by the owl.

"I want to see you glowing violet, I want to see your light again!" hooted the owl, still in time with the trumpet.

Another 10p dropped on the pavement.

"Nobody ever threw money before," said the driver. "You've got talent."

"Who?" said the owl.

"You," said the driver. "Keep singing and dancing. When you've made 50p you can have another ride."

"I want to see her glowing violet!" hooted the owl.

"That's it," said the driver. "Just carry on like that." And he went on playing his trumpet.

When the owl had 50p the driver started the taxi and the meter lit up again.

"Love!" said the owl. "You've come back to me!" And off they drove in the rain.

Under the plane tree where the owl had eaten the mouse there grew up a little pink flower. A passing bee noticed the flower and buzzed over to it. The bee sipped a little of the nectar.

"Different," said the bee. "Interesting." It sipped a little more. "Marzipan," it said. It sipped some more, and grew a little dizzy. "I've been working too hard," said the bee. "That's what it is." It stopped buzzing and sat down to rest.

The day was warm, the breeze was mild, the District Line trains rumbled past on the far side of the common and the bee fell asleep.

When the bee woke up it was dark. The houses standing opposite the common and the trains that rumbled past it were all lit with golden windows. The street lamps showed their globes of bluish light; footsteps and shadowy figures passed on the pavement. There was a full moon over the trees; there was a smell of honeysuckle in the air.

The bee looked up at the moon. "No sun," said the bee. "I can't possibly find my way home without the sun to go by. I'll have to stay in town tonight."

The bee flew up over the street lamps and past the top-floor windows of the houses. At No. 6 a window was open, and the bee saw the face of a pinky-orange hibiscus looking round the edge of the window frame.

The bee flew into the room and saw that the hibiscus was growing out of a pot that stood on top of a bookshelf about a foot and a half to one side of the window. The stem of the plant leant to the window and curved up gracefully so that the flower could look out.

The bee flew round the flower and hovered in the darkness of the room, smelling the pinky-orange perfume of the hibiscus and looking at the light from the street lamp shining through her leaves and petals.

"Seen enough?" said the hibiscus.

"I'm sorry," said the bee. "I didn't mean to be rude." It flew round to the front where the flower could see it.

"You're not a gentleman, are you?" said the hibiscus.

"No," said the bee, "and I'm not a lady either. I'm just a worker."

"Never mind," said the hibiscus. "We can't all be posh."

"I might have been a Queen," said the bee.

"Oh yes," said the hibiscus, "and I might have been the Duchess of Gloucester but I'm not."

"You've gone to a lot of trouble to look out of that window," said the bee.

"That's not me, that's the plant," said the hibiscus. "The plant stays but the flowers come and go. Now I've had my turn. Tomorrow morning

I'll be lying on the floor all crumpled like a dress thrown down after a dance."

The bee didn't say anything.

"At least I've got a full moon for my last night," said the hibiscus. "That's something. I wish I could have music." She began to hum in a high tinkly voice. "They play records here sometimes but they're out tonight. It's getting colder, isn't it?" She drew her thin and pinky-orange petals in a little. "So cold," she said, and wrapped her petals closer round her.

"I can't even sing for you," said the bee. "I can do a honey-dance though. Shall I dance for you?"

"Oh yes!" said the hibiscus. "Dance for me, do! Do it on the window-sill so I can see you and the moon together."

"This is the dance that tells where the sweetest nectar is," the bee said. "It means, 'Sweet, sweet, so sweet! Sweet, sweet, this way!'"

"Sweet, sweet, so sweet!" murmured the hibiscus as the bee danced by the light of the street lamp and the trains rumbled past the common under the sinking moon. "Sweet, sweet, this way!"

As the bee danced it gave off the faintest scent of marzipan that mingled with the pinky-orange perfume of the hibiscus.

"Sweet, sweet!" whispered the hibiscus. She drew her petals tightly round her and drooped towards the sinking moon. "Fly away now for the honey," she said to the bee. "Fly so I can see you flying against the last of the yellow moon."

"I wish I could have been a gentleman for you," said the bee, and it flew off towards the golden passing windows of the District Line and the last of the yellow moon.

The upstairs mouse at No. 6 had watched the hibiscus plant in the front bedroom for a long time. She had seen the showy flowers one after another bloom and shrivel and fall to the floor. She used to sit behind the skirting board thinking how she would go about it if she were a hibiscus flower. Sometimes when there was no one in the bedroom she would run out onto the carpet and strike hibiscus poses in front of the full-length glass.

"Poor silly things," she used to say to herself. "They're pretty enough but they have no grasp. One after another they make the same mistake: they let go. The thing to do is, once you've bloomed, hold on. Just simply hold on and don't let go. There one is and there one stays. Yes," she said as she turned round and round in front of the glass, "and I've certainly got more of a figure than any of them, though I say it myself."

One morning the mouse came out of the hole in the skirting board and saw a hibiscus flower lying crumpled and closed on the floor. For a few moments the mouse paced back and forth, clasping and unclasping her paws. She stopped in front of the glass and looked at herself. "Today is the day," she said.

The mouse went to the sewing basket and got a needle and thread. She stripped the pinky-orange petals from the crumpled hibiscus flower and out of them she made herself a stylish little frock.

"Chic," she said, turning round and round in front of the glass. "Either one has it or one hasn't."

"Now, then," said the mouse. She looked up at the flowerpot on top of the bookshelf. The graceful curving stem of the plant leant out to the open window and its leaves all quivered in the autumn breeze.

The mouse climbed up the bookshelf and into the flowerpot. She carefully began to work her way up the long curving stem of the hibiscus plant so that she could take her place as a flower on the end of it.

"The thing to do is simply hold on," she said, but the stem drooped and swayed with her weight, the tight frock made her clumsy, she lost her grip and fell out of the window.

The postman was just coming to the steps of No. 6 when the mouse plummeted into his post bag. The postman already had the letters for No. 6 in his hand. He hadn't seen the mouse fall into the bag and he didn't put his hand into the bag until he was coming down the steps.

When the mouse saw the postman's great big hand coming at her she was very frightened. She bit his finger, and not knowing what else to do, she kept her teeth closed on the postman's finger and held on.

"Ow!" yelled the postman. He flung up his arm and the mouse shot up into the air like a rocket.

The mouse flew through the air into the plane tree on the edge of the common. It was a Monday morning, and the owl in the plane tree was dozing where he always dozed on Monday mornings.

The mouse thudded into the owl and knocked him off the branch he was sitting on. "Oof!" said the owl as he went off the branch with his eyes still shut and his wings folded.

"Oof!" said the owl again as he hit the next branch ten feet down.

"Love!" shouted the owl as he grabbed the branch and opened his eyes. "Love has hit me like a thud in the stomach! Love, love, where are you? Who, who, who is it?"

He looked up and saw the mouse looking down at him. Not knowing what else to do, she was holding on to the branch the owl had fallen from.

"Love!" shouted the owl. "The breakfast of your eyes!" He meant to say "brightness."

The owl flew up and the mouse ran down the tree trunk as fast as she could, across the street, up the steps, under the door, and into No. 6. Once inside the front door she stopped to catch her breath. "What a morning this has been," she said.

The mouse looked up at the letter basket on the door and saw among the letters a small brown-paper packet. She was very fond of brown-paper packets. "What harm can it do to look?" she said.

The mouse climbed up into the letter basket. "There's a corner of that packet just the least little bit torn open," she said. She sniffed the open corner and smelt something sweet. "It's not as if I opened it myself," she said, and began to nibble.

She nibbled her way into the packet and found a marzipan pig. "Lovely," said the mouse, and ate up the pig. The pig was fresh from the confectioner's and had no experience of life whatever. There was not a single thought in him, just marzipan. The mouse was tired from the morning's hurly-burly, and the sweetness made her drowsy. She fell asleep inside the brown-paper packet.

The little boy who lived at No. 6 came to the letter basket and saw the packet. That day was his birthday and the packet had his name on it. "Perhaps it's another marzipan pig from Aunt Constantia," he said. He saw the hole in one corner of the packet. "Perhaps someone's been here before me," he said.

He opened the packet. The tearing of the paper woke the mouse. She sprang out of the packet, leapt to the floor, and ran into the nearest hole in the skirting-board.

As the mouse sat there breathing hard, she heard the boy's mother call from the kitchen, "Any letters?"

"Three for you and one for Dad," said the boy, "and a mouse in a pink frock for me but she ran off."

"A mouse in a pink frock!" said his mother.

"Maybe she wanted to be a hibiscus," said the boy.

"Not any more," said the mouse as she sat behind the skirting-board. She did not take off her hibiscus-petal frock though. She went out that evening and did not get eaten by the owl. She was seen at three o'clock in the morning dancing on the Embankment by the Albert Bridge.

Manny Rat
A Fragment

When I finished *The Mouse and His Child* I was not surprised to find that there was nowhere for the clockwork father and son to go; they had already done their thing, and had got to where they were going. Not so with Manny Rat. There was more to him, I perceived, than simple villainy. He had gone through that and had got beyond it. He had given what was in him to what the world called evil and he had given it to what the world called good. In both cases the whole thing blew up in his face.

In a sequel, *The Return of Manny Rat*, that I never finished, a student revolt at The Last Visible Dog, where Manny Rat teaches "Tinkering 1" and "Salvage and Repair (Advanced)" forces him to reassess his life. It is borne in upon him that his apparent reformation and dedication to good may have had no better motivation than his toothlessness, and he acts swiftly. He leaves The Last Visible Dog and strikes out on his own again:

> He was walking through a little vale of drifting ash and cinders when suddenly he stopped, retraced his steps, and looked down at an object he had just passed by. His first glance had not identified it as anything of use, but curiosity drew him back to it.
>
> It was a human denture, a complete lower jawful of white teeth set in

pink plastic gums. Long he looked at it. He had seen humans, had noticed, in a professional way, their teeth. Now gradually from the part his active mind was able to project the whole, a fully dentate pair of jaws. He saw an upper plate clap shut against the lower with a satisfying chop. The implications overwhelmed him; he felt giddy, light, went hot and cold by turns. His imagination leaped from the extrapolated human jaws to his own bare, toothless gums; the future opened up before him with a blinding flash. He wept with joy, and murmured faintly, "Teef! New Teef!"

In order to make dentures for himself, Manny Rat selects a rat whose dental armament he fancies, ambushes him, and using a rock for an anaesthetic, extracts the teeth with which he hopes to start a new life:

> The work had been difficult, and the patient had had to be re-anaesthetized several times. But the thoughts of Manny Rat had metamorphosed into action: he carried now, wrapped in a piece of newspaper, the orphan, unfrocked, teeth of Reverend Immenso Joy.
>
> Now he needed time to re-equip himself, and a place where he could work in privacy to do it. He wanted space between him and the life that he had so recently left, and now in the freshening darkness he left the dump and made his way across the meadow to the church that stood there.
>
> He had no idea why he went there and not some other place. There was a choir practice that evening—perhaps the lighted windows and the music drew him; perhaps the freshness of the old white clapboard church against the starlit night, the fragrance of it on the eye, the soundness of it, staunch among the seasons, sisterly with time that sang around it on the winds of each new evening, each new dawn. The scent of coffee came to him, and fresh-baked brownies; a sense of cosiness enveloped him. The tall spire sharp against the sky, the warmth and brightness streaming through the leaded fanlights, the whole strong building standing firmly in its faith, each line of it expressive of the will to bear up steadily, and the clean length of the trimly painted rainspouts equally aspiring with the steeple—all beckoned to the old rat newly juvenescent and carrying his parcel of teeth. He circled once around the church, found a rathole that seemed little used, and stepped into the warm and spicy dark within the wall.
>
> Manny Rat followed an old tunnel through the rock-wool insulation between the lath and plaster of the interior wall and the outer pine

sheathing. The choir practice had just finished, and he heard the murmur of conversation as the singers came down the steps from the gallery and passed through the rear hallway to the parish house. The aroma of coffee and brownies grew stronger, and gave him a feeling of snugness and well-being as he moved forward, climbing the now ascending tunnel.

The musical director of the church had stayed at the organ when the choir left, and now he began to play Bach's *Passacaglia and Fugue in C Minor*. It was just then that Manny Rat, having come out of the rock wool, was in an uninsulated space within the wall that ran along the gallery where the organist sat. The sound of the organ came through the wall with complete clarity, and Manny Rat heard the eight-bar subject of the Passacaglia as the pedals alone introduced it.

The hoarse voice of that *basso ostinato*, halting, slow, remotely sighing, was in itself a sound of no great power. But nothing in Manny Rat's life had prepared him for what it was. He had heard recorded music in the shops of the town; had long known the cracked waltz of the rats' carousel, the freight train's single cry. But it had never occurred to him that the uttermost thingness of things should find a voice in the original blackness of creation, and having found it, speak.

Listening, he withdrew with it into the shadowed mazes of its variations, receded with it down dim passageways and windy maunderings of its selfness, flowed out with it to rise and fall upon the rocking of its ancient, cradling, sea. Below, in depths unspeakable, the bass theme rolled its dread, leviathanic bulk. Above, in strings and reeds and diapasons, the variations interweavingly descended to the darkness, spiralled to the light.

With the twentieth variation Manny Rat, alone among immensities, emerged into the channel of the fugue, bobbing in the foaming wake of giant traffic as the subject and the countersubjects relentlessly pursued their exposition. He had lost by then the wholeness of that first appalling recognition, but something he still held of it in terror and delight.

He knew then, as the fugue went surging to its end, that he had heard a monstrous and indifferent violence speak its tetragrammaton forbidden; had heard it name with infinite and orderly design the chaos at its core. As the music had gone beyond music, so the thing revealed within it had gone beyond good and beyond evil: it was what it was. And Manny Rat, perceiving that, sank down in a faint.

Later, newly toothed, Manny Rat encounters the instrument of his destiny:

"This," said Manny Rat. "Thus; these; them; that; those." The teeth were firmly set in the papier-mâché plates with epoxy glue, the plates were varnished so as not to go soggy, and his jaws were now once more complete. "Teeth," he said. "This tooth; that tooth; these teeth." He opened his mouth, closed it with a vicious chop, and laughed with pleasure. The flavor of his dentures left something to be desired, but his bite was as formidable as of old. Thus restored, he set out to explore the church.

Taking the tunnel that led upward from the kitchen, he followed it past the point where he had first entered the church, and found an exit that brought him out into the gallery above the sanctuary. The place being empty, Manny Rat wandered among the rows of gracefully armrested, brown-plushcushioned pews that were arranged in a long U on three sides of the building, snacked briefly on a hymnal, and arriving at the bottom of the U at that point in the gallery furthest from and opposite to the pulpit below, found himself standing before a large wooden machine of lustrous finish and unfamiliar design.

It was a great, tall box or chest of some kind. A bench apparently identified the operator's side of the thing, and at the base of that side a horizontal fanshaped wooden frame, its wide end attached to the machine, projected toward the bench. Within the frame he saw a radial arrangement of long and short wooden bars. Whatever was above the bench was for the moment out of his field of vision.

Manny Rat walked all around the thing, smelled it for a while—fruitwood of some kind it was under the varnish evidently—and found it pleasing. The long and short bars interested him, and he climbed over the frame and walked back and forth upon them, each smooth member with its rounded edges sinking with a soft thump underneath his weight and rising as he stepped on to the next. The wood was cool to his feet, and he paced dreamily, soothed by the rising-falling motion and the successive cryptic smoothnesses he walked on.

Next he climbed up to the seat of the bench and stood there facing the machine with his back to the distant pulpit. A hinged lid was folded back, and exposed to view before him were three broad steps, the risers of the same dark wood as the rest of the box, but the treads of ivory, divided regularly into what looked remarkably like teeth—many even, white oblong teeth, with secondary groups of short black teeth overlaid on them. Steps of teeth, thought Manny Rat. Strange! Between the steps were numbered white knobs, and on each side, angled out from the steps, was a panel on which were rows of long, white, ivory or plastic tabs. All of this he took in quickly, seeking some dominant feature having to do with the control and use of the apparatus facing him.

He found it at the bottom of the panel on the right-hand side: an authoritative pair of pushbuttons, one black, one red, labeled START and STOP. Manny Rat was well acquainted with various kinds of power switch, and did not hesitate. He climbed from the bench to the little triangular space between the steps and the panel, and pushed START.

From somewhere inside the steeple a large hum originated; wind whooshed through unseen passages from one place to another. Before him, between the steps and the panel, a red light labeled WIND, an amber light labeled CRESCENDO, and a green light labeled SFORZANDO, all winked on. Manny Rat was gratified, and felt that there were things to be done here. He liked the look of SFORZANDO especially, and all of the controls seemed promising in their complexity. Whether their manipulation would result in digging a hole or heaving out the front of the church or flying or some simpler form of locomotion he could not guess, but he was confident that the outcome would be both satisfying and large in scale.

The teeth-steps before him were related in design, he noted, to the wooden bars that he had walked upon. In his experience the movable members of any mechanism had always had some function, and he trusted that a careful examination would reveal the use of these to him. He walked slowly across the bottom step—its name was CHOIR, he noticed—and the teeth sank clicking beneath his feet, rising after him as the wooden bars had done: thirty-six white teeth; twenty-five black ones, but no effects of any kind. He climbed to the next level, named GREAT, and walked back. Thirty-six more white teeth; twenty-five more black ones. Nothing else. If that was greatness it was very unassuming, thought Manny Rat. He climbed up to the top step, identified slangily as SWELL, and paused awhile.

He was facing the right-hand panel again. GREAT, said the small white rectangular plate fixed above the rows of tabs. The machine obviously had strong pretensions. Manny Rat read the names imprinted in black letters on the first row of tabs:

DIAPASON	DOPPEL GEDECKT	DOLCAN	OCTAVE	FLUTE	TWELFTH	FIFTEENTH	KRUMMHORN
8′	8′	8′	4′	4′	2 2/3′	2′	8′

Here he thought that he had better be discreet. There had entered his mind the notion that this might easily be a dwelling and not a machine at all: those tabs might very well be knockers or doorbells, and who knew what sort of tenants might answer his summons? Foreigners, by the look of it, and all of them great. He would certainly take no chances with DOPPEL GEDECKT or KRUMMHORN. FLUTE might be a mild chap, he thought. But FIFTEENTH, although his name was long, must be, with his 2′ designation, the smallest of the group. Manny Rat drew a deep breath, pressed FIFTEENTH, and stepped back quickly.

Three high, descending, silvery notes sounded sweetly, and nothing threatened. Manny Rat stepped farther back, and went three more notes down the scale. Placing the sound, he climbed to the step, the teeth of which remained silent, and from there to a stack of large sheets of paper, curiously lined and marked, on the top of the machine.

As he stood on the papers he saw in front of him, no more than six feet away peaked ranks of upright metal pipes in an open space between two rooms that had mesh screens instead of ordinary walls. It was clear to Manny Rat that walking on the GREAT teeth had called up the silvery voice from somewhere in the neighborhood of those pipes. The sound had been pleasant enough—certainly not a cry of rage or pain; he seemed to have done no harm and to have offended no one so far. He looked down at the paper he stood on, read *Passacaglia and Fugue in C Minor* at the top of the page, scanned the unrecognizable symbols below that title, and climbed down again, having as yet no reason to associate the six notes of the single voice he had produced with those awful mysteries whose sound had stretched him senseless in the tunnel.

Now he was more resolute as he stood before the white tabs. He boldly pushed down all of the names in the top row, even DOPPEL GEDECKT and KRUMMHORN. The first two tabs in the second row were blanks, awaiting ranks of pipes as yet beyond the means of the congregation; those too he depressed. Next were two important-looking red-lettered tabs: GREAT TO GREAT 16′ and GREAT TO GREAT 4′. Ambitious as he was, Manny Rat felt in modesty bound to exclude himself from such august dialogue for the present. Then he read the last three labels in that row, also red-lettered: SWELL TO GREAT 16′; SWELL TO GREAT 8′; SWELL TO GREAT 4′. What was this if not the printed voice of fate? Swell to great! He would indeed. 4′, 8′, and 16′—one did the thing in stages here, it seemed. With a flourish he pushed down all three, expected thunder and lightning, and found the eight-voiced polyphony as he stepped down the scale very small beer indeed. His explorations were brought to an end by the janitor's footsteps on the back stairs. Manny Rat disappeared into the hole in the wall, and the janitor, arriving at the deserted organ bench, shook his head at the irreverence and speed of foot of the local children.

MANNY RAT: A FRAGMENT